D1338631

THE NEW WESSEX EDITION
OF THE STORIES OF THOMAS HARDY
VOLUME TWO

LIFE'S LITTLE IRONIES
and
A CHANGED MAN

THE NEW WESSEX EDITION

Life's Little Ironies

and

A Changed Man

THOMAS HARDY

EDITED BY

F. B. Pinion

THE NEW WESSEX EDITION OF THE STORIES OF THOMAS HARDY
VOLUME TWO

Thomas Hardy's text © Macmillan London Ltd

Editorial arrangement, introduction and notes
© Macmillan London Ltd 1977
Typography © Macmillan London Ltd 1977

ISBN: 0 333 19984 7

The New Wessex Edition first published 1977 by
MACMILLAN LONDON LTD
London and Basingstoke
Associated companies in New York Dublin
Melbourne Johannesburg & Delhi

Published in the United States by
ST MARTIN'S PRESS INC.
175 Fifth Avenue, New York

Printed in Great Britain by
WESTERN PRINTING SERVICES LTD
Bristol

Contents

The frontispiece is a pencil drawing of Thomas Hardy made in 1919
by William Strang, R.A.

LIFE'S LITTLE IRONIES

Prefatory Note
to
'Life's Little Ironies'

OF the following collection the first story, 'An Imaginative Woman', originally stood in *Wessex Tales*, but was brought into this volume as being more nearly its place, turning as it does upon a trick of Nature, so to speak, a physical possibility that may attach to a wife of vivid imaginings, as is well known to medical practitioners and other observers of such manifestations.

The two stories named 'A Tradition of Eighteen Hundred and Four' and 'The Melancholy Hussar of the German Legion', which were formerly printed in this series, were also transferred to *Wessex Tales*, where they more naturally belong.

The present narratives and sketches, though separately published at various antecedent dates, were first collected and issued in a volume in 1894.

May 1912   T.H.

An Imaginative Woman

WHEN William Marchmill had finished his inquiries for lodgings at the well-known watering-place of Solentsea in Upper Wessex, he returned to the hotel to find his wife. She, with the children, had rambled along the shore, and Marchmill followed in the direction indicated by the military-looking hall-porter.

'By Jove, how far you've gone! I am quite out of breath,' Marchmill said, rather impatiently, when he came up with his wife, who was reading as she walked, the three children being considerably further ahead with the nurse.

Mrs Marchmill started out of the reverie into which the book had thrown her. 'Yes,' she said, 'you've been such a long time. I was tired of staying in that dreary hotel. But I am sorry if you have wanted me, Will.'

'Well, I have had trouble to suit myself. When you see the airy and comfortable rooms heard of, you find they are stuffy and uncomfortable. Will you come and see if what I've fixed on will do? There is not much room, I am afraid; but I can light on nothing better. The town is rather full.'

The pair left the children and nurse to continue their ramble, and went back together.

In age well-balanced, in personal appearance fairly matched, and in domestic requirements conformable, in temper this couple differed, though even here they did not often clash, he being equable, if not lymphatic, and she decidedly nervous and sanguine. It was to their tastes and fancies, those smallest, greatest particulars, that no common denominator could be applied. Marchmill considered his wife's likes and inclinations somewhat silly; she considered his sordid and material. The husband's business was that of a gunmaker in a thriving city northwards, and his soul was in that business always; the lady was best characterized by that superannuated phrase of elegance 'a votary of the muse'. An impressionable, palpitating creature was Ella, shrinking humanely from detailed knowledge of her husband's trade whenever she reflected that everything he manufactured had for its purpose the destruction of life. She could only recover her equanimity by assuring herself that some, at least, of his weapons were sooner or later used for the extermination of horrid vermin and animals almost as cruel to their inferiors in species as human beings were to theirs.

She had never antecedently regarded this occupation of his as any objection to having him for a husband. Indeed, the necessity of getting life-leased at all cost, a cardinal virtue which all good mothers teach, kept her from thinking of it at all till she had closed with William, had passed the honeymoon, and reached the reflecting stage. Then, like a person who has stumbled upon some object in the dark, she wondered what she had got; mentally walked round it, estimated it; whether it were rare or common; contained gold, silver, or lead; were a clog or a pedestal, everything to her or nothing.

She came to some vague conclusions, and since then had kept her heart alive by pitying her proprietor's obtuseness and want of refinement, pitying herself, and letting off her delicate and ethereal emotions in imaginative occupations, day-dreams, and night-sighs, which perhaps would not much have disturbed William if he had known of them.

Her figure was small, elegant, and slight in build, tripping, or rather bounding, in movement. She was dark-eyed, and had that marvellously bright and liquid sparkle in each pupil which characterizes persons of Ella's cast of soul, and is too often a cause of heartache to the possessor's male friends, ultimately sometimes to herself. Her husband was a tall, long-featured man, with a brown beard; he had a pondering regard; and was, it must be added, usually kind and tolerant to her. He spoke in squarely shaped sentences, and was supremely satisfied with a condition of sublunary things which made weapons a necessity.

Husband and wife walked till they had reached the house they were in search of, which stood in a terrace facing the sea, and was fronted by a small garden of wind-proof and salt-proof evergreens, stone steps leading up to the porch. It had its number in the row, but, being rather larger than the rest, was in addition sedulously distinguished as Coburg House by its landlady, though everybody else called it 'Thirteen, New Parade'. The spot was bright and lively now; but in winter it became necessary to place sandbags against the door, and to stuff up the keyhole against the wind and rain, which had worn the paint so thin that the priming and knotting showed through.

The householder, who had been watching for the gentleman's return, met them in the passage, and showed the rooms. She informed them that she was a professional man's widow, left in needy circumstances by the rather sudden death of her husband, and she spoke anxiously of the conveniences of the establishment.

Mrs Marchmill said that she liked the situation and the house; but, it being small, there would not be accommodation enough, unless she could have all the rooms.

The landlady mused with an air of disappointment. She wanted the visitors to be her tenants very badly, she said, with obvious honesty. But unfortunately two of the rooms were occupied permanently by a bachelor gentleman. He did not pay season prices, it was true; but as he kept on his apartments all the year round, and was an extremely nice and interesting young man, who gave no trouble, she did not like to turn him out for a month's 'let', even at a high figure. 'Perhaps, however,' she added, 'he might offer to go for a time.'

They would not hear of this, and went back to the hotel, intending to proceed to the agent's to inquire further. Hardly had they sat down to tea when the landlady called. Her gentleman, she said, had been so obliging as to offer to give up his rooms for three or four weeks rather than drive the new-comers away.

'It is very kind, but we won't inconvenience him in that way,' said the Marchmills.

'O, it won't inconvenience him, I assure you!' said the landlady eloquently. 'You see, he's a different sort of young man from most – dreamy, solitary, rather melancholy – and he cares more to be here when the south-westerly gales are beating against the door, and the sea washes over the Parade, and there's not a soul in the place, than he does now in the season. He'd just as soon be where, in fact, he's going temporarily, to a little cottage on the Island opposite, for a change.' She hoped therefore that they would come.

The Marchmill family accordingly took possession of the house next day, and it seemed to suit them very well. After luncheon Mr Marchmill strolled out towards the pier, and Mrs Marchmill, having despatched the children to their outdoor amusements on the sands, settled herself in more completely, examining this and that article, and testing the reflecting powers of the mirror in the wardrobe door.

In the small back sitting-room, which had been the young bachelor's, she found furniture of a more personal nature than in the rest. Shabby books, of correct rather than rare editions, were piled up in a queerly reserved manner in corners, as if the previous occupant had not conceived the possibility that any incoming person of the season's bringing could care to look inside them. The landlady hovered on the threshold to rectify anything that Mrs Marchmill might not find to her satisfaction.

'I'll make this my own little room,' said the latter, 'because the books are here. By the way, the person who has left seems to have a good many. He won't mind my reading some of them, Mrs Hooper, I hope ?'

'O dear no, ma'am. Yes, he has a good many. You see, he is in the literary line himself somewhat. He is a poet – yes, really a poet – and he has a little income of his own, which is enough to write verses on, but not enough for cutting a figure, even if he cared to.'

'A poet! Oh, I did not know that.'

Mrs Marchmill opened one of the books, and saw the owner's name written on the title-page. 'Dear me!' she continued; 'I know his name very well – Robert Trewe – of course I do; and his writings! And it is *his* rooms we have taken, and *him* we have turned out of his home ?'

Ella Marchmill, sitting down alone a few minutes later, thought with interested surprise of Robert Trewe. Her own latter history will best explain that interest. Herself the only daughter of a struggling man of letters, she had during the last year or two taken to writing poems, in an endeavour to find a congenial channel in which to let flow her painfully embayed emotions, whose former limpidity and sparkle seemed departing in the stagnation caused by the routine of a practical household and the gloom of bearing children to a commonplace father. These poems, subscribed with a masculine pseudonym, had appeared in various obscure magazines, and in two cases in rather prominent ones. In the second of the latter the page which bore her effusion at the bottom, in smallish print, bore at the top, in large print, a few verses on the same subject by this very man, Robert Trewe. Both of them had, in fact, been struck by a tragic incident reported in the daily papers, and had used it simultaneously as an inspiration, the editor remarking in a note upon the coincidence, and that the excellence of both poems prompted him to give them together.

After that event Ella, otherwise 'John Ivy', had watched with much attention the appearance anywhere in print of verse bearing the signature of Robert Trewe, who, with a man's unsusceptibility on the question of sex, had never once thought of passing himself off as a woman. To be sure, Mrs Marchmill had satisfied herself with a sort of reason for doing the contrary in her case; since nobody might believe in her inspiration if they found that the sentiments came from a pushing tradesman's wife, from the mother of three children by a matter-of-fact small-arms manufacturer.

Trewe's verse contrasted with that of the rank and file of recent minor poets in being impassioned rather than ingenious, luxuriant rather than finished. Neither *symboliste* nor *décadent*, he was a pessimist in so far as that character applies to a man who looks at the worst contingencies as well as the best in the human condition. Being little attracted by excellences of form and rhythm apart from content, he sometimes, when feeling outran his artistic speed, perpetrated sonnets in the loosely rhymed Elizabethan fashion, which every right-minded reviewer said he ought not to have done.

With sad and hopeless envy Ella Marchmill had often and often scanned the rival poet's work, so much stronger as it always was than her own feeble lines. She had imitated him, and her inability to touch his level would send her into fits of despondency. Months passed away thus, till she observed from the publishers' list that Trewe had collected his fugitive pieces into a volume, which was duly issued, and was much or little praised according to chance, and had a sale quite sufficient to pay for the printing.

This step onward had suggested to 'John Ivy' the idea of collecting her pieces also, or at any rate of making up a book of her rhymes by adding many in manuscript to the few that had seen the light, for she had been able to get no great number into print. A ruinous charge was made for costs of publication; a few reviews noticed her poor little volume; but nobody talked of it, nobody bought it, and it fell dead in a fortnight – if it had ever been alive.

The author's thoughts were diverted to another groove just then by the discovery that she was going to have a third child, and the collapse of her poetical venture had perhaps less effect upon her mind than it might have done if she had been domestically unoccupied. Her husband had paid the publisher's bill with the doctor's, and there it all had ended for the time. But, though less than a poet of her century, Ella was more than a mere multiplier of her kind, and latterly she had begun to feel the old afflatus once more. And now by an odd conjunction she found herself in the rooms of Robert Trewe.

She thoughtfully rose from her chair and searched the apartment with
the interest of a fellow-tradesman. Yes, the volume of his own verse was
among the rest. Though quite familiar with its contents, she read it here
as if it spoke aloud to her, then called up Mrs Hooper, the landlady, for
some trivial service, and inquired again about the young man.

'Well, I'm sure you'd be interested in him, ma'am, if you could see
him, only he's so shy that I don't suppose you will.' Mrs Hooper seemed
nothing loth to minister to her tenant's curiosity about her predecessor.
'Lived here long? Yes, nearly two years. He keeps on his rooms even
when he's not here: the soft air of this place suits his chest, and he likes
to be able to come back at any time. He is mostly writing or reading, and
doesn't see many people, though, for the matter of that, he is such a
good, kind young fellow that folks would only be too glad to be friendly
with him if they knew him. You don't meet kind-hearted people every
day.'

'Ah, he's kind-hearted . . . and good.'

'Yes; he'll oblige me in anything if I ask him. "Mr Trewe," I say to
him sometimes, "you are rather out of spirits." "Well, I am, Mrs
Hooper," he'll say, "though I don't know how you should find it out."
"Why not take a little change?" I ask. Then in a day or two he'll say
that he will take a trip to Paris, or Norway, or somewhere; and I assure
you he comes back all the better for it.'

'Ah, indeed! His is a sensitive nature, no doubt.'

'Yes. Still he's odd in some things. Once when he had finished a poem
of his composition late at night he walked up and down the room re-
hearsing it; and the floors being so thin – jerry-built houses, you know,
though I say it myself – he kept me awake up above him till I wished
him further. . . . But we get on very well.'

This was but the beginning of a series of conversations about the
rising poet as the days went on. On one of these occasions Mrs Hooper
drew Ella's attention to what she had not noticed before: minute
scribblings in pencil on the wall-paper behind the curtains at the head
of the bed.

'O! let me look,' said Mrs Marchmill, unable to conceal a rush of
tender curiosity as she bent her pretty face close to the wall.

'These,' said Mrs Hooper, with the manner of a woman who knew
things, 'are the very beginnings and first thoughts of his verses. He has
tried to rub most of them out, but you can read them still. My belief is
that he wakes up in the night, you know, with some rhyme in his head,

and jots it down there on the wall lest he should forget it by the morning. Some of these very lines you see here I have seen afterwards in print in the magazines. Some are newer; indeed, I have not seen that one before. It must have been done only a few days ago.'

'O yes! . . .'

Ella Marchmill flushed without knowing why, and suddenly wished her companion would go away, now that the information was imparted. An indescribable consciousness of personal interest rather than literary made her anxious to read the inscription alone; and she accordingly waited till she could do so, with a sense that a great store of emotion would be enjoyed in the act.

Perhaps because the sea was choppy outside the Island, Ella's husband found it much pleasanter to go sailing and steaming about without his wife, who was a bad sailor, than with her. He did not disdain to go thus alone on board the steamboats of the cheap-trippers, where there was dancing by moonlight, and where the couples would come suddenly down with a lurch into each other's arms; for, as he blandly told her, the company was too mixed for him to take her amid such scenes. Thus, while this thriving manufacturer got a great deal of change and sea-air out of his sojourn here, the life, external at least, of Ella was monotonous enough, and mainly consisted in passing a certain number of hours each day in bathing and walking up and down a stretch of shore. But the poetic impulse having again waxed strong, she was possessed by an inner flame which left her hardly conscious of what was proceeding around her.

She had read till she knew by heart Trewe's last little volume of verses, and spent a great deal of time in vainly attempting to rival some of them, till, in her failure, she burst into tears. The personal element in the magnetic attraction exercised by this circumambient, un-approachable master of hers was so much stronger than the intellectual and abstract that she could not understand it. To be sure, she was surrounded noon and night by his customary environment, which literally whispered of him to her at every moment; but he was a man she had never seen, and that all that moved her was the instinct to specialize a waiting emotion on the first fit thing that came to hand did not, of course, suggest itself to Ella.

In the natural way of passion under the too practical conditions which civilization has devised for its fruition, her husband's love for her had not survived, except in the form of fitful friendship, any more than, or even so much as, her own for him; and, being a woman of very living ardours, that required sustenance of some sort, they were beginning to feed on this chancing material, which was, indeed, of a quality far better than chance usually offers.

One day the children had been playing hide-and-seek in a closet, whence, in their excitement, they pulled out some clothing. Mrs Hooper explained that it belonged to Mr Trewe, and hung it up in the closet again. Possessed of her fantasy, Ella went later in the afternoon, when nobody was in that part of the house, opened the closet, unhitched one of the articles, a mackintosh, and put it on, with the waterproof cap belonging to it.

'The mantle of Elijah!' she said. 'Would it might inspire me to rival him, glorious genius that he is!'

Her eyes always grew wet when she thought like that, and she turned to look at herself in the glass. *His* heart had beat inside that coat, and *his* brain had worked under that hat at levels of thought she would never reach. The consciousness of her weakness beside him made her feel quite sick. Before she had got the things off her the door opened, and her husband entered the room.

'What the devil—'

She blushed, and removed them.

'I found them in the closet here,' she said, 'and put them on in a freak. What have I else to do? You are always away!'

'Always away? Well. . . .'

That evening she had a further talk with the landlady, who might herself have nourished a half-tender regard for the poet, so ready was she to discourse ardently about him.

'You are interested in Mr Trewe, I know, ma'am,' she said; 'and he has just sent to say that he is going to call to-morrow afternoon to look up some books of his that he wants, if I'll be in, and he may select them from your room?'

'O yes!'

'You could very well meet Mr Trewe then, if you'd like to be in the way!'

She promised with secret delight, and went to bed musing of him.

Next morning her husband observed: 'I've been thinking of what you said, Ell: that I have gone about a good deal and left you without much to amuse you. Perhaps it's true. To-day, as there's not much sea, I'll take you with me on board the yacht.'

For the first time in her experience of such an offer Ella was not glad. But she accepted it for the moment. The time for setting out drew near, and she went to get ready. She stood reflecting. The longing to see the poet she was now distinctly in love with overpowered all other considerations.

'I don't want to go,' she said to herself. 'I can't bear to be away! And I won't go.'

She told her husband that she had changed her mind about wishing to sail. He was indifferent, and went his way.

For the rest of the day the house was quiet, the children having gone out upon the sands. The blinds waved in the sunshine to the soft, steady stroke of the sea beyond the wall; and the notes of the Green Silesian band, a troop of foreign gentlemen hired for the season, had drawn almost all the residents and promenaders away from the vicinity of Coburg House. A knock was audible at the door.

Mrs Marchmill did not hear any servant go to answer it, and she became impatient. The books were in the room where she sat; but nobody came up. She rang the bell.

'There is some person waiting at the door,' she said.

'O no, ma'am! He's gone long ago. I answered it,' the servant replied, and Mrs Hooper came in herself.

'So disappointing!' she said. 'Mr Trewe not coming after all!'

'But I heard him knock, I fancy!'

'No; that was somebody inquiring for lodgings who came to the wrong house. I forgot to tell you that Mr Trewe sent a note just before lunch to say I needn't get any tea for him, as he should not require the books, and wouldn't come to select them.'

Ella was miserable, and for a long time could not even re-read his mournful ballad on 'Severed Lives', so aching was her erratic little heart, and so tearful her eyes. When the children came in with wet stockings, and ran up to her to tell her of their adventures, she could not feel that she cared about them half as much as usual.

'Mrs Hooper, have you a photograph of – the gentleman who lived here?' She was getting to be curiously shy in mentioning his name.

'Why, yes. It's in the ornamental frame on the mantelpiece in your own bedroom, ma'am.'

'No; the Royal Duke and Duchess are in that.'

'Yes, so they are; but he's behind them. He belongs rightly to that frame, which I bought on purpose; but as he went away he said: "Cover me up from those strangers that are coming, for God's sake. I don't want them staring at me, and I am sure they won't want me staring at them." So I slipped in the Duke and Duchess temporarily in front of him, as they had no frame, and Royalties are more suitable for letting furnished than a private young man. If you take 'em out you'll see him under. Lord, ma'am, he wouldn't mind if he knew it! He didn't think the next tenant would be such an attractive lady as you, or he wouldn't have thought of hiding himself, perhaps.'

'Is he handsome?' she asked timidly.

'*I* call him so. Some, perhaps, wouldn't.'

'Should I?' she asked, with eagerness.

'I think you would, though some would say he's more striking than handsome; a large-eyed, thoughtful fellow, you know, with a very electric flash in his eye when he looks round quickly, such as you'd expect a poet to be who doesn't get his living by it.'

'How old is he?'

'Several years older than yourself, ma'am; about thirty-one or two, I think.'

Ella was, as a matter of fact, a few months over thirty herself; but she did not look nearly so much. Though so immature in nature, she was entering on that tract of life in which emotional women begin to suspect that last love may be stronger than first love; and she would soon, alas! enter on the still more melancholy tract when at least the vainer ones of her sex shrink from receiving a male visitor otherwise than with their backs to the window or the blinds half down. She reflected on Mrs Hooper's remark, and said no more about age.

Just then a telegram was brought up. It came from her husband, who had gone down the Channel as far as Budmouth with his friends in the yacht, and would not be able to get back till next day.

After her light dinner Ella idled about the shore with the children till dusk, thinking of the yet uncovered photograph in her room, with a serene sense of something ecstatic to come. For, with the subtle luxuriousness of fancy in which this young woman was an adept, on learning that her husband was to be absent that night she had refrained from incontinently rushing upstairs and opening the picture-frame, preferring to reserve the inspection till she could be alone, and a more romantic tinge be imparted to the occasion by silence, candles, solemn sea and stars outside, than was afforded by the garish afternoon sunlight.

The children had been sent to bed, and Ella soon followed, though it was not yet ten o'clock. To gratify her passionate curiosity she now made her preparations, first getting rid of superfluous garments and putting on her dressing-gown, then arranging a chair in front of the table and reading several pages of Trewe's tenderest utterances. Next she fetched the portrait-frame to the light, opened the back, took out the likeness, and set it up before her.

It was a striking countenance to look upon. The poet wore a luxuriant black moustache and imperial, and a slouched hat which shaded the forehead. The large dark eyes described by the landlady showed an unlimited capacity for misery; they looked out from beneath well-shaped brows as if they were reading the universe in the microcosm of the confronter's face, and were not altogether overjoyed at what the spectacle portended.

Ella murmured in her lowest, richest, tenderest tone: 'And it's *you* who've so cruelly eclipsed me these many times!'

As she gazed long at the portrait she fell into thought, till her eyes filled with tears, and she touched the cardboard with her lips. Then she laughed with a nervous lightness, and wiped her eyes.

She thought how wicked she was, a woman having a husband and three children, to let her mind stray to a stranger in this unconscionable manner. No, he was not a stranger! She knew his thoughts and feelings as well as she knew her own; they were, in fact, the self-same thoughts and feelings as hers, which her husband distinctly lacked; perhaps luckily for himself, considering that he had to provide for family expenses.

'He's nearer my real self, he's more intimate with the real me than Will is, after all, even though I've never seen him,' she said.

She laid his book and picture on the table at the bedside, and when she was reclining on the pillow she re-read those of Robert Trewe's verses which she had marked from time to time as most touching and true. Putting these aside she set up the photograph on its edge upon the coverlet, and contemplated it as she lay. Then she scanned again by the light of the candle the half-obliterated pencillings on the wall-paper beside her head. There they were – phrases, couplets, *bouts-rimés*, beginnings and middles of lines, ideas in the rough, like Shelley's scraps, and the least of them so intense, so sweet, so palpitating, that it seemed as if his very breath, warm and loving, fanned her cheeks from those walls, walls that had surrounded his head times and times as they surrounded her own now. He must often have put up his hand so – with the pencil in it. Yes, the writing was sideways, as it would be if executed by one who extended his arm thus.

These inscribed shapes of the poet's world,

> 'Forms more real than living man,
> Nurslings of immortality',

were, no doubt, the thoughts and spirit-strivings which had come to him in the dead of night, when he could let himself go and have no fear of the frost of criticism. No doubt they had often been written up hastily by the light of the moon, the rays of the lamp, in the blue-grey dawn, in full daylight perhaps never. And now her hair was dragging where his arm had lain when he secured the fugitive fancies; she was sleeping on a poet's lips, immersed in the very essence of him, permeated by his spirit as by an ether.

While she was dreaming the minutes away thus, a footstep came upon the stairs, and in a moment she heard her husband's heavy step on the landing immediately without.

'Ell, where are you?'

What possessed her she could not have described, but, with an instinctive objection to let her husband know what she had been doing, she slipped the photograph under the pillow just as he flung open the door with the air of a man who had dined not badly.

'O, I beg pardon,' said William Marchmill. 'Have you a headache? I am afraid I have disturbed you.'

'No, I've not got a headache,' said she. 'How is it you've come?'

'Well, we found we could get back in very good time after all, and I didn't want to make another day of it, because of going somewhere else to-morrow.'

'Shall I come down again?'

'O no. I'm as tired as a dog. I've had a good feed, and I shall turn in straight off. I want to get out at six o'clock to-morrow if I can. . . . I shan't disturb you by my getting up; it will be long before you are awake.' And he came forward into the room.

While her eyes followed his movements, Ella softly pushed the photograph further out of sight.

'Sure you're not ill?' he asked, bending over her.

'No, only wicked!'

'Never mind that.' And he stooped and kissed her. 'I wanted to be with you to-night.'

Next morning Marchmill was called at six o'clock; and in waking and yawning she heard him muttering to himself: 'What the deuce is this that's been crackling under me so?' Imagining her asleep he searched round him and withdrew something. Through her half-opened eyes she perceived it to be Mr Trewe.

'Well, I'm damned!' her husband exclaimed.

'What, dear?' said she.

'O, you are awake? Ha! ha!'

'What *do* you mean?'

'Some bloke's photograph – a friend of our landlady's, I suppose. I wonder how it came here; whisked off the mantelpiece by accident perhaps when they were making the bed.'

'I was looking at it yesterday, and it must have dropped in then.'

'O, he's a friend of yours? Bless his picturesque heart!'

Ella's loyalty to the object of her admiration could not endure to hear him ridiculed. 'He's a clever man!' she said, with a tremor in her gentle voice which she herself felt to be absurdly uncalled for. 'He is a rising poet – the gentleman who occupied two of these rooms before we came, though I've never seen him.'

'How do you know, if you've never seen him?'

'Mrs Hooper told me when she showed me the photograph.'

'O, well, I must up and be off. I shall be home rather early. Sorry I can't take you to-day, dear. Mind the children don't go getting drowned.'

That day Mrs Marchmill inquired if Mr Trewe were likely to call at any other time.

'Yes,' said Mrs Hooper. 'He's coming this day week to stay with a friend near here till you leave. He'll be sure to call.'

Marchmill did return quite early in the afternoon; and, opening some letters which had arrived in his absence, declared suddenly that he and his family would have to leave a week earlier than they had expected to do – in short, in three days.

'Surely we can stay a week longer?' she pleaded. 'I like it here.'

'I don't. It is getting rather slow.'

'Then you might leave me and the children!'

'How perverse you are, Ell! What's the use? And have to come to fetch you! No: we'll all return together; and we'll make out our time in

North Wales or Brighton a little later on. Besides, you've three days
longer yet.'

It seemed to be her doom not to meet the man for whose rival talent
she had a despairing admiration, and to whose person she was now
absolutely attached. Yet she determined to make a last effort; and having
gathered from her landlady that Trewe was living in a lonely spot not
far from the fashionable town on the Island opposite, she crossed over
in the packet from the neighbouring pier the following afternoon.

What a useless journey it was! Ella knew but vaguely where the house
stood, and when she fancied she had found it, and ventured to inquire
of a pedestrian if he lived there, the answer returned by the man was
that he did not know. And if he did live there, how could she call upon
him? Some women might have the assurance to do it, but she had not.
How crazy he would think her. She might have asked him to call upon
her, perhaps; but she had not the courage for that, either. She lingered
mournfully about the picturesque seaside eminence till it was time to
return to the town and enter the steamer for recrossing, reaching home
for dinner without having been greatly missed.

At the last moment, unexpectedly enough, her husband said that he
should have no objection to letting her and the children stay on till the
end of the week, since she wished to do so, if she felt herself able to get
home without him. She concealed the pleasure this extension of time
gave her; and Marchmill went off the next morning alone.

But the week passed, and Trewe did not call.

On Saturday morning the remaining members of the Marchmill
family departed from the place which had been productive of so much
fervour in her. The dreary, dreary train; the sun shining in moted
beams upon the hot cushions; the dusty permanent way; the mean rows
of wire – these things were her accompaniment: while out of the window
the deep blue sea-levels disappeared from her gaze, and with them her
poet's home. Heavy-hearted, she tried to read, and wept instead.

Mr Marchmill was in a thriving way of business, and he and his
family lived in a large new house, which stood in rather extensive
grounds a few miles outside the midland city wherein he carried on his
trade. Ella's life was lonely here, as the suburban life is apt to be,
particularly at certain seasons; and she had ample time to indulge her
taste for lyric and elegiac composition. She had hardly got back when
she encountered a piece by Robert Trewe in the new number of her
favourite magazine, which must have been written almost immediately

before her visit to Solentsea, for it contained the very couplet she had
seen pencilled on the wall-paper by the bed, and Mrs Hooper had
declared to be recent. Ella could resist no longer, but seizing a pen
impulsively, wrote to him as a brother-poet, using the name of John
Ivy, congratulating him in her letter on his triumphant executions in
metre and rhythm of thoughts that moved his soul, as compared with
her own browbeaten efforts in the same pathetic trade.

To this address there came a response in a few days, little as she had
dared to hope for it – a civil and brief note, in which the young poet
stated that, though he was not well acquainted with Mr Ivy's verse, he
recalled the name as being one he had seen attached to some very
promising pieces; that he was glad to gain Mr Ivy's acquaintance by
letter, and should certainly look with much interest for his productions
in the future.

There must have been something juvenile or timid in her own epistle,
as one ostensibly coming from a man, she declared to herself; for
Trewe quite adopted the tone of an elder and superior in this reply. But
what did it matter ? He had replied; he had written to her with his own
hand from that very room she knew so well, for he was now back again
in his quarters.

The correspondence thus begun was continued for two months or
more, Ella Marchmill sending him from time to time some that she
considered to be the best of her pieces, which he very kindly accepted,
though he did not say he sedulously read them, nor did he send her any
of his own in return. Ella would have been more hurt at this than she
was if she had not known that Trewe laboured under the impression
that she was one of his own sex.

Yet the situation was unsatisfactory. A flattering little voice told her
that, were he only to see her, matters would be otherwise. No doubt she
would have helped on this by making a frank confession of womanhood,
to begin with, if something had not happened, to her delight, to render
it unnecessary. A friend of her husband's, the editor of the most important newspaper in their city and county, who was dining with them
one day, observed during their conversation about the poet that his (the
editor's) brother the landscape-painter was a friend of Mr Trewe's, and
that the two men were at that very moment in Wales together.

Ella was slightly acquainted with the editor's brother. The next
morning down she sat and wrote, inviting him to stay at her house for a
short time on his way back, and requesting him to bring with him, if

practicable, his companion Mr Trewe, whose acquaintance she was anxious to make. The answer arrived after some few days. Her correspondent and his friend Trewe would have much satisfaction in accepting her invitation on their way southward, which would be on such and such a day in the following week.

Ella was blithe and buoyant. Her scheme had succeeded; her beloved though as yet unseen one was coming. 'Behold, he standeth behind our wall; he looked forth at the windows, showing himself through the lattice,' she thought ecstatically. 'And, lo, the winter is past, the rain is over and gone, the flowers appear on the earth, the time of the singing of birds is come, and the voice of the turtle is heard in our land.'

But it was necessary to consider the details of lodging and feeding him. This she did most solicitously, and awaited the pregnant day and hour.

It was about five in the afternoon when she heard a ring at the door and the editor's brother's voice in the hall. Poetess as she was, or as she thought herself, she had not been too sublime that day to dress with infinite trouble in a fashionable robe of rich material, having a faint resemblance to the *chiton* of the Greeks, a style just then in vogue among ladies of an artistic and romantic turn, which had been obtained by Ella of her Bond Street dressmaker when she was last in London. Her visitor entered the drawing-room. She looked towards his rear; nobody else came through the door. Where, in the name of the God of Love, was Robert Trewe?

'O, I'm sorry,' said the painter, after their introductory words had been spoken. 'Trewe is a curious fellow, you know, Mrs Marchmill. He said he'd come; then he said he couldn't. He's rather dusty. We've been doing a few miles with knapsacks, you know; and he wanted to get on home.'

'He – he's not coming?'

'He's not; and he asked me to make his apologies.'

'When did you p-p-part from him?' she asked, her nether lip starting off quivering so much that it was like a *tremolo*-stop opened in her speech. She longed to run away from this dreadful bore and cry her eyes out.

'Just now, in the turnpike road yonder there.'

'What! he has actually gone past my gates?'

'Yes. When we got to them – handsome gates they are, too, the finest bit of modern wrought-iron work I have seen – when we came to them we stopped, talking there a little while, and then he wished me good-bye and went on. The truth is, he's a little bit depressed just now, and doesn't want to see anybody. He's a very good fellow, and a warm friend, but a little uncertain and gloomy sometimes; he thinks too much of things. His poetry is rather too erotic and passionate, you know, for some tastes; and he has just come in for a terrible slating from the —— Review that was published yesterday; he saw a copy of it at the station by accident. Perhaps you've read it?'

'No.'

'So much the better. O, it is not worth thinking of; just one of those articles written to order, to please the narrow-minded set of subscribers upon whom the circulation depends. But he's upset by it. He says it is the misrepresentation that hurts him so; that, though he can stand a fair attack, he can't stand lies that he's powerless to refute and stop from spreading. That's just Trewe's weak point. He lives so much by himself that these things affect him much more than they would if he were in the bustle of fashionable or commercial life. So he wouldn't come here, making the excuse that it all looked so new and monied – if you'll pardon—'

'But – he must have known – there was sympathy here! Has he never said anything about getting letters from this address?'

'Yes, yes, he has, from John Ivy – perhaps a relative of yours, he thought, visiting here at the time?'

'Did he – like Ivy, did he say?'

'Well, I don't know that he took any great interest in Ivy.'

'Or in his poems?'

'Or in his poems – so far as I know, that is.'

Robert Trewe took no interest in her house, in her poems, or in their writer. As soon as she could get away she went into the nursery and tried to let off her emotion by unnecessarily kissing the children, till she had a sudden sense of disgust at being reminded how plain-looking they were, like their father.

The obtuse and single-minded landscape-painter never once perceived from her conversation that it was only Trewe she wanted, and not himself. He made the best of his visit, seeming to enjoy the society of Ella's husband, who also took a great fancy to him, and showed him everywhere about the neighbourhood, neither of them noticing Ella's mood.

The painter had been gone only a day or two when, while sitting upstairs alone one morning, she glanced over the London paper just arrived, and read the following paragraph: –

'SUICIDE OF A POET

'Mr Robert Trewe, who has been favourably known for some years as one of our rising lyrists, committed suicide at his lodgings at Solentsea on Saturday evening last by shooting himself in the right temple with a revolver. Readers hardly need to be reminded that Mr Trewe has recently attracted the attention of a much wider public than had hitherto known him, by his new volume of verse, mostly of an impassioned kind, entitled "Lyrics to a Woman Unknown", which has been already favourably noticed in these pages for the extraordinary gamut of feeling it traverses, and which has been made the subject of a severe, if not ferocious, criticism in the —— Review. It is supposed, though not certainly known, that the article may have partially conduced to the sad act, as a copy of the review in question was found on his writing-table; and he has been observed to be in a somewhat depressed state of mind since the critique appeared.'

Then came the report of the inquest, at which the following letter was read, it having been addressed to a friend at a distance: –

'DEAR ——, – Before these lines reach your hands I shall be delivered from the inconveniences of seeing, hearing, and knowing more of the things around me. I will not trouble you by giving my reasons for the step I have taken, though I can assure you they were sound and logical. Perhaps had I been blessed with a mother, or a sister, or a female friend of another sort tenderly devoted to me, I might have thought it worth while to continue my present existence. I have long dreamt of such an unattainable creature, as you know; and she, this undiscoverable, elusive one, inspired my last volume; the imaginary woman alone, for, in spite of what has been said in some quarters, there is no real woman behind the title. She has continued to the last unrevealed, unmet, unwon. I think it desirable to mention this in order that no blame may attach to any real woman as having been the cause of my decease by cruel or cavalier treatment of me. Tell my landlady that I am sorry to have caused her this unpleasantness; but my occupancy of the rooms will soon be forgotten. There are ample funds in my name at the bank to pay all expenses.

R. TREWE'

Ella sat for a while as if stunned, then rushed into the adjoining chamber and flung herself upon her face on the bed.

Her grief and distraction shook her to pieces; and she lay in this frenzy of sorrow for more than an hour. Broken words came every now and then from her quivering lips: 'O, if he had only known of me – known of me – me! . . . O, if I had only once met him – only once; and put my hand upon his hot forehead – kissed him – let him know how I loved him – that I would have suffered shame and scorn, would have lived and died, for him! Perhaps it would have saved his dear life! . . . But no – it was not allowed! God is a jealous God; and that happiness was not for him and me!'

All possibilities were over; the meeting was stultified. Yet it was almost visible to her in her fantasy even now, though it could never be substantiated –

> 'The hour which might have been, yet might not be,
> Which man's and woman's heart conceived and bore,
> Yet whereof life was barren.'

She wrote to the landlady at Solentsea in the third person, in as subdued a style as she could command, enclosing a postal order for a sovereign, and informing Mrs Hooper that Mrs Marchmill had seen in the papers the sad account of the poet's death, and having been, as Mrs Hooper was aware, much interested in Mr Trewe during her stay at Coburg House, she would be obliged if Mrs Hooper could obtain a small portion of his hair before his coffin was closed down, and send it her as a memorial of him, as also the photograph that was in the frame.

By the return-post a letter arrived containing what had been requested. Ella wept over the portrait and secured it in her private drawer; the lock of hair she tied with white ribbon and put in her bosom, whence she drew it and kissed it every now and then in some unobserved nook.

'What's the matter?' said her husband, looking up from his newspaper on one of these occasions. 'Crying over something? A lock of hair? Whose is it?'

'He's dead!' she murmured.

'Who?'

'I don't want to tell you, Will, just now, unless you insist!' she said, a sob hanging heavy in her voice.

'O, all right.'

'Do you mind my refusing? I will tell you some day.'

'It doesn't matter in the least, of course.'

He walked away whistling a few bars of no tune in particular; and when he had got down to his factory in the city the subject came into Marchmill's head again.

He, too, was aware that a suicide had taken place recently at the house they had occupied at Solentsea. Having seen the volume of poems in his wife's hand of late, and heard fragments of the landlady's conversation about Trewe when they were her tenants, he all at once said to himself, 'Why of course it's he! . . . How the devil did she get to know him? What sly animals women are!'

Then he placidly dismissed the matter, and went on with his daily affairs. By this time Ella at home had come to a determination. Mrs Hooper, in sending the hair and photograph, had informed her of the day of the funeral; and as the morning and noon wore on an overpowering wish to know where they were laying him took possession of the sympathetic woman. Caring very little now what her husband or anyone else might think of her eccentricities, she wrote Marchmill a brief note, stating that she was called away for the afternoon and evening, but would return on the following morning. This she left on his desk, and having given the same information to the servants, went out of the house on foot.

When Mr Marchmill reached home early in the afternoon the servants looked anxious. The nurse took him privately aside, and hinted that her mistress's sadness during the past few days had been such that she feared she had gone out to drown herself. Marchmill reflected. Upon the whole he thought that she had not done that. Without saying whither he was bound he also started off, telling them not to sit up for him. He drove to the railway-station, and took a ticket for Solentsea.

It was dark when he reached the place, though he had come by a fast train, and he knew that if his wife had preceded him thither it could only have been by a slower train, arriving not a great while before his own. The season at Solentsea was now past: the parade was gloomy, and the flys were few and cheap. He asked the way to the Cemetery, and soon reached it. The gate was locked, but the keeper let him in, declaring, however, that there was nobody within the precincts. Although it was not late, the autumnal darkness had now become intense; and he found some difficulty in keeping to the serpentine path which led to the quarter where, as the man had told him, the one or two interments for the day had taken place. He stepped upon the grass, and, stumbling over some pegs, stooped now and then to discern if possible a figure against the sky. He could see none; but lighting on a spot where the soil was

disclosure comes; and in the present case,
he head, at length revealed herself, she was
ople behind her had supposed, and ever
why.

mmonness of this complaint), she was less
d her to be. Yet attractive her face un-
at all sickly. The revelation of its detail
to talk to a boy of twelve or thirteen who
pe of whose hat and jacket implied that h
public school. The immediate bystander
: 'Mother'.

l was reached, and the audience withdrew
y out by passing at her elbow. Almost al
ull and near look at the interesting woman
he chair till the way should be clear enoug
thout obstruction. As if she expected thei
ratifying their curiosity, she met the eye
 lifting her own, showing these to be sof
a little plaintive in their regard.

he gardens, and passed along the pavemen
w, the schoolboy walking beside her. T
sons who watched her away, the answe
l wife of the incumbent of a neighbourin
She was generally believed to be a woma
e, but a story of some sort or other.

heir way home the boy who walked at he
father had not missed them.

ble these last few hours that I am sure
eplied.

e!' exclaimed the public-school boy, wi
hat was almost harsh. 'Surely you kno

d the correction, and did not resent h
might well have done, by bidding him
is, whose condition had been caused
piece of cake without taking it out of t
d. After this the pretty woman and t

bore upon her history, and she fell in

trodden, beheld a crouching object beside a newly-made grave. She heard him, and sprang up.

'Ell, how silly this is!' he said indignantly. 'Running away from home – I never heard such a thing! Of course I am not jealous of this unfortunate man; but it is too ridiculous that you, a married woman with three children and a fourth coming, should go losing your head like this over a dead lover! . . . Do you know you were locked in? You might not have been able to get out all night.'

She did not answer.

'I hope it didn't go far between you and him, for your own sake.'

'Don't insult me, Will.'

'Mind, I won't have any more of this sort of thing; do you hear?'

'Very well,' she said.

He drew her arm within his own, and conducted her out of the Cemetery. It was impossible to get back that night; and not wishing to be recognized in their present sorry condition he took her to a miserable little coffee-house close to the station, whence they departed early in the morning, travelling almost without speaking, under the sense that it was one of those dreary situations occurring in married life which words could not mend, and reaching their own door at noon.

The months passed, and neither of the twain ever ventured to start a conversation upon this episode. Ella seemed to be only too frequently in a sad and listless mood, which might almost have been called pining. The time was approaching when she would have to undergo the stress of childbirth for a fourth time, and that apparently did not tend to raise her spirits.

'I don't think I shall get over it this time!' she said one day.

'Pooh! what childish foreboding! Why shouldn't it be as well now as ever?'

She shook her head. 'I feel almost sure I am going to die; and I should be glad, if it were not for Nelly, and Frank, and Tiny.'

'And me!'

'You'll soon find somebody to fill my place,' she murmured, with a sad smile. 'And you'll have a perfect right to; I assure you of that.'

'Ell, you are not thinking still about that – poetical friend of yours?'

She neither admitted nor denied the charge. 'I am not going to get over my illness this time,' she reiterated. 'Something tells me I shan't.'

This view of things was rather a bad beginning, as it usually is; and, in fact, six weeks later, in the month of May, she was lying in her room, pulseless and bloodless, with hardly strength enough left to follow up one feeble breath with another, the infant for whose unnecessary life she was slowly parting with her own being fat and well. Just before her death she spoke to Marchmill softly: –

'Will, I want to confess to you the entire circumstances of that – about you know what – that time we visited Solentsea. I can't tell what possessed me – how I could forget you so, my husband! But I had got into a morbid state: I thought you had been unkind; that you had neglected me; that you weren't up to my intellectual level, while he was, and far above it. I wanted a fuller appreciator, perhaps, rather than another lover—'

She could get no further then for very exhaustion; and she went off in sudden collapse a few hours later, without having said anything more to her husband on the subject of her love for the poet. William Marchmill, in truth, like most husbands of several years' standing, was little disturbed by retrospective jealousies, and had not shown the least anxiety to press her for confessions concerning a man dead and gone beyond any power of inconveniencing him more.

But when she had been buried a couple of years it chanced one day that, in turning over some forgotten papers that he wished to destroy before his second wife entered the house, he lighted on a lock of hair in an envelope, with the photograph of the deceased poet, a date being written on the back in his late wife's hand. It was that of the time they spent at Solentsea.

Marchmill looked long and musingly at the hair and portrait, for something struck him. Fetching the little boy who had been the death of his mother, now a noisy toddler, he took him on his knee, held the lock of hair against the child's head, and set up the photograph on the table behind, so that he could closely compare the features each countenance presented. By a known but inexplicable trick of Nature there were undoubtedly strong traces of resemblance to the man Ella had never seen; the dreamy and peculiar expression of the poet's face sat, as the transmitted idea, upon the child's, and the hair was of the same hue.

'I'm damned if I didn't think so!' murmured Marchmill. 'Then she did play me false with that fellow at the lodgings! Let me see: the dates the second week in August . . . the third week in May. . . . Yes . . . yes. . . . Get away, you poor little brat! You are nothing to me!'

1893

disappointed as soon as the
when the lady, by a turn of
not so handsome as the p
hoped – they did not know

For one thing (alas! the
young than they had fanc
questionably was, and not
came each time she turned
stood beside her, and the sh
belonged to a well-known
could hear that he called he

When the end of the reci
many chose to find their w
turned their heads to take a
who remained stationary in
for her to be wheeled out w
glances, and did not mind
of several of her observers t
brown, and affectionate orb

She was conducted out of
till she disappeared from vi
inquiries made by some pe
came that she was the secon
parish, and that she was lam
with a story – an innocent o

In conversing with her on
elbow said that he hoped hi

'He have been so comfort
cannot have missed us,' she

'Has, dear mother – not ha
an impatient fastidiousness
that by this time!'

His mother hastily adopt
making it, or retaliate, as she
wipe that crumby mouth of
surreptitious attempts to eat
pocket wherein it lay concea
boy went onward in silence.

That question of gramma

reverie, of a somewhat sad kind to all appearance. It might have been assumed that she was wondering if she had done wisely in shaping her life as she had shaped it, to bring out such a result as this.

In a remote nook in North Wessex, forty miles from London, near the thriving county-town of Aldbrickham, there stood a pretty village with its church and parsonage, which she knew well enough, but her son had never seen. It was her native village, Gaymead, and the first event bearing upon her present situation had occurred at that place when she was only a girl of nineteen.

How well she remembered it, that first act in her little tragi-comedy, the death of her reverend husband's first wife. It happened on a spring evening, and she who now and for many years had filled that first wife's place was then parlour-maid in the parson's house.

When everything had been done that could be done, and the death was announced, she had gone out in the dusk to visit her parents, who were living in the same village, to tell them the sad news. As she opened the white swing-gate and looked towards the trees which rose westward, shutting out the pale light of the evening sky, she discerned, without much surprise, the figure of a man standing in the hedge, though she roguishly exclaimed as a matter of form, 'O, Sam, how you frightened me!'

He was a young gardener of her acquaintance. She told him the particulars of the late event, and they stood silent, these two young people, in that elevated, calmly philosophic mind which is engendered when a tragedy has happened close at hand, and has not happened to the philosophers themselves. But it had its bearing upon their relations.

'And will you stay on now at the Vicarage, just the same?' asked he.

She had hardly thought of that. 'O yes – I suppose!' she said. 'Everything will be just as usual, I imagine?'

He walked beside her towards her mother's. Presently his arm stole round her waist. She gently removed it; but he placed it there again, and she yielded the point. 'You see, dear Sophy, you don't know that you'll stay on; you may want a home, and I shall be ready to offer one some day, though I may not be ready just yet.'

'Why, Sam, how can you be so fast! I've never even said I liked 'ee; and it is all your own doing, coming after me!'

'Still, it is nonsense to say I am not to have a try at you like the rest.' He stooped to kiss her a farewell, for they had reached her mother's door.

'No, Sam; you shan't!' she cried, putting her hand over his mouth.
'You ought to be more serious on such a night as this.' And she bade
him adieu without allowing him to kiss her or to come indoors.

The vicar just left a widower was at this time a man about forty years
of age, of good family, and childless. He had led a secluded existence in
this college living, partly because there were no resident landowners;
and his loss now intensified his habit of withdrawal from outward
observation. He was seen still less than heretofore, kept himself still less
in time with the rhythm and racket of the movements called progress in
the world without. For many months after his wife's decease the
economy of his household remained as before; the cook, the housemaid,
the parlour-maid, and the man out-of-doors performed their duties or
left them undone, just as Nature prompted them – the vicar knew not
which. It was then represented to him that his servants seemed to have
nothing to do in his small family of one. He was struck with the truth
of this representation, and decided to cut down his establishment. But
he was forestalled by Sophy, the parlour-maid, who said one evening
that she wished to leave him.

'And why?' said the parson.

'Sam Hobson has asked me to marry him, sir.'

'Well – do you want to marry?'

'Not much. But it would be a home for me. And we have heard that
one of us will have to leave.'

A day or two after she said: 'I don't want to leave just yet, sir, if you
don't wish it. Sam and I have quarrelled.'

He looked up at her. He had hardly ever observed her before, though
he had been frequently conscious of her soft presence in the room. What
a kitten-like, flexuous, tender creature she was! She was the only one of
the servants with whom he came into immediate and continuous
relation. What should he do if Sophy were gone?

Sophy did not go, but one of the others did, and things went on
quietly again.

When Mr Twycott, the vicar, was ill, Sophy brought up his meals to
him, and she had no sooner left the room one day than he heard a noise
on the stairs. She had slipped down with the tray, and so twisted her
foot that she could not stand. The village surgeon was called in; the
vicar got better, but Sophy was incapacitated for a long time; and she
was informed that she must never again walk much or engage in any
occupation which required her to stand long on her feet. As soon as she

was comparatively well she spoke to him alone. Since she was forbidden
to walk and bustle about, and, indeed, could not do so, it became her
duty to leave. She could very well work at something sitting down,
and she had an aunt a seamstress.

The parson had been very greatly moved by what she had suffered on
his account, and he exclaimed, 'No, Sophy; lame or not lame, I cannot
let you go. You must never leave me again!'

He came close to her, and, though she could never exactly tell how it
happened, she became conscious of his lips upon her cheek. He then
asked her to marry him. Sophy did not exactly love him, but she had a
respect for him which almost amounted to veneration. Even if she had
wished to get away from him she hardly dared refuse a personage so
reverend and august in her eyes, and she assented forthwith to be his
wife.

Thus it happened that one fine morning, when the doors of the
church were naturally open for ventilation, and the singing birds
fluttered in and alighted on the tie-beams of the roof, there was a
marriage-service at the communion-rails, which hardly a soul knew of.
The parson and a neighbouring curate had entered at one door, and
Sophy at another, followed by two necessary persons, whereupon in a
short time there emerged a newly-made husband and wife.

Mr Twycott knew perfectly well that he had committed social suicide
by this step, despite Sophy's spotless character, and he had taken his
measures accordingly. An exchange of livings had been arranged with
an acquaintance who was incumbent of a church in the south of London,
and as soon as possible the couple removed thither, abandoning their
pretty country home, with trees and shrubs and glebe, for a narrow,
dusty house in a long, straight street, and their fine peal of bells for the
wretchedest one-tongued clangour that ever tortured mortal ears. It was
all on her account. They were, however, away from every one who had
known her former position; and also under less observation from without
than they would have had to put up with in any country parish.

Sophy the woman was as charming a partner as a man could possess,
though Sophy the lady had her deficiencies. She showed a natural
aptitude for little domestic refinements, so far as related to things and
manners; but in what is called culture she was less intuitive. She had
now been married more than fourteen years, and her husband had taken
much trouble with her education; but she still held confused ideas on
the use of 'was' and 'were', which did not beget a respect for her among

the few acquaintances she made. Her great grief in this relation was that
her only child, on whose education no expense had been and would be
spared, was now old enough to perceive these deficiencies in his mother,
and not only to see them but to feel irritated at their existence.

Thus she lived on in the city, and wasted hours in braiding her
beautiful hair, till her once apple cheeks waned to pink of the very
faintest. Her foot had never regained its natural strength after the
accident, and she was mostly obliged to avoid walking altogether. Her
husband had grown to like London for its freedom and its domestic
privacy; but he was twenty years his Sophy's senior, and had latterly
been seized with a serious illness. On this day, however, he had seemed
to be well enough to justify her accompanying her son Randolph to the
concert.

II

The next time we get a glimpse of her is when she appears in the
mournful attire of a widow.

Mr Twycott had never rallied, and now lay in a well-packed cemetery
to the south of the great city, where, if all the dead it contained had
stood erect and alive, not one would have known him or recognized his
name. The boy had dutifully followed him to the grave, and was now
again at school.

Throughout these changes Sophy had been treated like the child she
was in nature though not in years. She was left with no control over
anything that had been her husband's beyond her modest personal
income. In his anxiety lest her inexperience should be overreached he
had safe-guarded with trustees all he possibly could. The completion of
the boy's course at the public school, to be followed in due time by
Oxford and ordination, had been all previsioned and arranged, and she
really had nothing to occupy her in the world but to eat and drink, and
make a business of indolence, and go on weaving and coiling the nut-
brown hair, merely keeping a home open for the son whenever he came
to her during vacations.

Foreseeing his probable decease long years before her, her husband in
his lifetime had purchased for her use a semi-detached villa in the same
long, straight road whereon the church and parsonage faced, which was
to be hers as long as she chose to live in it. Here she now resided, looking
out upon the fragment of lawn in front, and through the railings at the

ever-flowing traffic; or, bending forward over the window-sill on the
first floor, stretching her eyes far up and down the vista of sooty trees,
hazy air, and drab house-façades, along which echoed the noises common
to a suburban main thoroughfare.

Somehow, her boy, with his aristocratic school-knowledge, his
grammars, and his aversions, was losing those wide infantine sympathies,
extending as far as to the sun and moon themselves, with which he, like
other children, had been born, and which his mother, a child of nature
herself, had loved in him; he was reducing their compass to a population
of a few thousand wealthy and titled people, the mere veneer of a
thousand million or so of others who did not interest him at all. He
drifted further and further away from her. Sophy's *milieu* being a
suburb of minor tradesmen and under-clerks, and her almost only
companions the two servants of her own house, it was not surprising
that after her husband's death she soon lost the little artificial tastes she
had acquired from him, and became – in her son's eyes – a mother whose
mistakes and origin it was his painful lot as a gentleman to blush for.
As yet he was far from being man enough – if he ever would be – to
rate these sins of hers at their true infinitesimal value beside the yearning
fondness that welled up and remained penned in her heart till it should
be more fully accepted by him, or by some other person or thing. If he
had lived at home with her he would have had all of it; but he seemed
to require so very little in present circumstances, and it remained stored.

Her life became insupportably dreary; she could not take walks, and
had no interest in going for drives, or, indeed, in travelling anywhere.
Nearly two years passed without an event, and still she looked on that
suburban road, thinking of the village in which she had been born, and
whither she would have gone back – O how gladly! – even to work in the
fields.

Taking no exercise she often could not sleep, and would rise in the
night or early morning to look out upon the then vacant thoroughfare,
where the lamps stood like sentinels waiting for some procession to go
by. An approximation to such a procession was indeed made early every
morning about one o'clock, when the country vehicles passed up with
loads of vegetables for Covent Garden market. She often saw them
creeping along at this silent and dusky hour – waggon after waggon,
bearing green bastions of cabbages nodding to their fall, yet never falling,
walls of baskets enclosing masses of beans and peas, pyramids of snow-
white turnips, swaying howdahs of mixed produce – creeping along

behind aged night-horses, who seemed ever patiently wondering between their hollow coughs why they had always to work at that still hour when all other sentient creatures were privileged to rest. Wrapped in a cloak it was soothing to watch and sympathize with them when depression and nervousness hindered sleep, and to see how the fresh green-stuff brightened to life as it came opposite the lamp, and how the sweating animals steamed and shone with their miles of travel.

They had an interest, almost a charm, for Sophy, these semi-rural people and vehicles moving in an urban atmosphere, leading a life quite distinct from that of the daytime toilers on the same road. One morning a man who accompanied a waggon-load of potatoes gazed rather hard at the house-fronts as he passed, and with a curious emotion she thought his form was familiar to her. She looked out for him again. His being an old-fashioned conveyance, with a yellow front, it was easily recognizable, and on the third night after she saw it a second time. The man alongside was, as she had fancied, Sam Hobson, formerly gardener at Gaymead, who would at one time have married her.

She had occasionally thought of him, and wondered if life in a cottage with him would not have been a happier lot than the life she had accepted. She had not thought of him passionately, but her now dismal situation lent an interest to his resurrection – a tender interest which it is impossible to exaggerate. She went back to bed, and began thinking. When did these market-gardeners, who travelled up to town so regularly at one or two in the morning, come back? She dimly recollected seeing their empty waggons, hardly noticeable amid the ordinary day-traffic, passing down at some hour before noon.

It was only April, but that morning, after breakfast, she had the window opened, and sat looking out, the feeble sun shining full upon her. She affected to sew, but her eyes never left the street. Between ten and eleven the desired waggon, now unladen, reappeared on its return journey. But Sam was not looking round him then, and drove on in a reverie.

'Sam!' cried she.

Turning with a start, his face lighted up. He called to him a little boy to hold the horse, alighted, and came and stood under the window.

'I can't come down easily, Sam, or I would!' she said. 'Did you know I lived here?'

'Well, Mrs Twycott, I knew you lived along here somewhere. I have often looked out for 'ee.'

He briefly explained his own presence on the scene. He had long since given up his gardening in the village near Aldbrickham, and was now manager at a market-gardener's on the south side of London, it being part of his duty to go up to Covent Garden with waggon-loads of produce two or three times a week. In answer to her curious inquiry, he admitted that he had come to this particular district because he had seen in the Aldbrickham paper, a year or two before, the announcement of the death in South London of the aforetime vicar of Gaymead, which had revived an interest in her dwelling-place that he could not extinguish, leading him to hover about the locality till his present post had been secured.

They spoke of their native village in dear old North Wessex, the spots in which they had played together as children. She tried to feel that she was a dignified personage now, that she must not be too confidential with Sam. But she could not keep it up, and the tears hanging in her eyes were indicated in her voice.

'You are not happy, Mrs Twycott, I'm afraid?' he said.

'O, of course not! I lost my husband only the year before last.'

'Ah! I meant in another way. You'd like to be home again?'

'This is my home – for life. The house belongs to me. But I understand—' She let it out then. 'Yes, Sam. I long for home – *our* home! I *should* like to be there, and never leave it, and die there.' But she remembered herself. 'That's only a momentary feeling. I have a son, you know, a dear boy. He's at school now.'

'Somewhere handy, I suppose? I see there's lots on 'em along this road.'

'O no! Not in one of these wretched holes! At a public school – one of the most distinguished in England.'

'Chok' it all! of course! I forget, ma'am, that you've been a lady for so many years.'

'No, I am not a lady,' she said sadly. 'I never shall be. But he's a gentleman, and that – makes it – O how difficult for me!'

III

The acquaintance thus oddly reopened proceeded apace. She often looked out to get a few words with him, by night or by day. Her sorrow was that she could not accompany her one old friend on foot a little way, and talk more freely than she could do while he paused before the house.

One night, at the beginning of June, when she was again on the watch after an absence of some days from the window, he entered the gate and said softly, 'Now, wouldn't some air do you good? I've only half a load this morning. Why not ride up to Covent Garden with me? There's a nice seat on the cabbages, where I've spread a sack. You can be home again in a cab before anybody is up.'

She refused at first, and then, trembling with excitement, hastily finished her dressing, and wrapped herself up in cloak and veil, afterwards sidling downstairs by the aid of the handrail, in a way she could adopt on an emergency. When she had opened the door she found Sam on the step, and he lifted her bodily on his strong arm across the little forecourt into his vehicle. Not a soul was visible or audible in the infinite length of the straight, flat highway, with its ever-waiting lamps converging to points in each direction. The air was fresh as country air at this hour, and the stars shone, except to the north-eastward, where there was a whitish light – the dawn. Sam carefully placed her in the seat and drove on.

They talked as they had talked in old days, Sam pulling himself up now and then, when he thought himself too familiar. More than once she said with misgiving that she wondered if she ought to have indulged in the freak. 'But I am so lonely in my house,' she added, 'and this makes me so happy!'

'You must come again, dear Mrs Twycott. There is no time o' day for taking the air like this.'

It grew lighter and lighter. The sparrows became busy in the streets, and the city waxed denser around them. When they approached the river it was day, and on the bridge they beheld the full blaze of morning sunlight in the direction of St Paul's, the river glistening towards it, and not a craft stirring.

Near Covent Garden he put her into a cab, and they parted, looking into each other's faces like the very old friends they were. She reached home without adventure, limped to the door, and let herself in with her latch-key unseen.

The air and Sam's presence had revived her: her cheeks were quite pink – almost beautiful. She had something to live for in addition to her son. A woman of pure instincts, she knew there had been nothing really wrong in the journey, but supposed it conventionally to be very wrong indeed.

Soon, however, she gave way to the temptation of going with him

again, and on this occasion their conversation was distinctly tender, and
Sam said he never should forget her, notwithstanding that she had
served him rather badly at one time. After much hesitation he told her
of a plan it was in his power to carry out, and one he should like to take
in hand, since he did not care for London work: it was to set up as a
master greengrocer down at Aldbrickham, the county-town of their
native place. He knew of an opening – a shop kept by aged people who
wished to retire.

'And why don't you do it, then, Sam?' she asked with a slight
heartsinking.

'Because I'm not sure if – you'd join me. I know you wouldn't –
couldn't! Such a lady as ye've been so long, you couldn't be a wife to a
man like me.'

'I hardly suppose I could!' she assented, also frightened at the idea.

'If you could,' he said eagerly, 'you'd on'y have to sit in the back
parlour and look through the glass partition when I was away sometimes – just to keep an eye on things. The lameness wouldn't hinder
that. . . . I'd keep you as genteel as ever I could, dear Sophy – if I might
think of it!' he pleaded.

'Sam, I'll be frank,' she said, putting her hand on his. 'If it were only
myself I would do it, and gladly, though everything I possess would be
lost to me by marrying again.'

'I don't mind that! It's more independent.'

'That's good of you, dear, dear Sam. But there's something else. I
have a son. . . . I almost fancy when I am miserable sometimes that he is
not really mine, but one I hold in trust for my late husband. He seems
to belong so little to me personally, so entirely to his dead father. He is
so much educated and I so little that I do not feel dignified enough to be
his mother. . . . Well, he would have to be told.'

'Yes. Unquestionably.' Sam saw her thought and her fear. 'Still, you
can do as you like, Sophy – Mrs Twycott,' he added. 'It is not you who
are the child, but he.'

'Ah, you don't know! Sam, if I could, I would marry you, some day.
But you must wait a while, and let me think.'

It was enough for him, and he was blithe at their parting. Not so she.
To tell Randolph seemed impossible. She could wait till he had gone up
to Oxford, when what she did would affect his life but little. But would
he ever tolerate the idea? And if not, could she defy him?

She had not told him a word when the yearly cricket-match came on at Lord's between the public schools, though Sam had already gone back to Aldbrickham. Mrs Twycott felt stronger than usual: she went to the match with Randolph, and was able to leave her chair and walk about occasionally. The bright idea occurred to her that she could casually broach the subject while moving round among the spectators, when the boy's spirits were high with interest in the game, and he would weigh domestic matters as feathers in the scale beside the day's victory. They promenaded under the lurid July sun, this pair, so wide apart, yet so near, and Sophy saw the large proportion of boys like her own, in their broad white collars and dwarf hats, and all around the rows of great coaches under which was jumbled the *débris* of luxurious luncheons: bones, pie-crusts, champagne-bottles, glasses, plates, napkins, and the family silver; while on the coaches sat the proud fathers and mothers; but never a poor mother like her. If Randolph had not appertained to these, had not centred all his interests in them, had not cared exclusively for the class they belonged to, how happy would things have been! A great huzza at some small performance with the bat burst from the multitude of relatives, and Randolph jumped wildly into the air to see what had happened. Sophy fetched up the sentence that had been already shaped; but she could not get it out. The occasion was, perhaps, an inopportune one. The contrast between her story and the display of fashion to which Randolph had grown to regard himself as akin would be fatal. She awaited a better time.

It was on an evening when they were alone in their plain suburban residence, where life was not blue but brown, that she ultimately broke silence, qualifying her announcement of a probable second marriage by assuring him that it would not take place for a long time to come, when he would be living quite independently of her.

The boy thought the idea a very reasonable one, and asked if she had chosen anybody. She hesitated; and he seemed to have a misgiving. He hoped his stepfather would be a gentleman, he said.

'Not what you call a gentleman,' she answered timidly. 'He'll be much as I was before I knew your father'; and by degrees she acquainted him with the whole. The youth's face remained fixed for a moment; then he flushed, leant on the table, and burst into passionate tears.

His mother went up to him, kissed all of his face that she could get at, and patted his back as if he were still the baby he once had been, crying herself the while. When he had somewhat recovered from his paroxysm he went hastily to his own room and fastened the door.

Parleyings were attempted through the keyhole, outside which she waited and listened. It was long before he would reply, and when he did it was to say sternly at her from within: 'I am ashamed of you! It will ruin me! A miserable boor! a churl! a clown! It will degrade me in the eyes of all the gentlemen of England!'

'Say no more – perhaps I am wrong! I will struggle against it!' she cried miserably.

Before Randolph left her that summer a letter arrived from Sam to inform her that he had been unexpectedly fortunate in obtaining the shop. He was in possession; it was the largest in the town, combining fruit with vegetables, and he thought it would form a home worthy even of her some day. Might he not run up to town to see her?

She met him by stealth, and said he must still wait for her final answer. The autumn dragged on, and when Randolph was home at Christmas for the holidays she broached the matter again. But the young gentleman was inexorable.

It was dropped for months; renewed again; abandoned under his repugnance; again attempted; and thus the gentle creature reasoned and pleaded till four or five long years had passed. Then the faithful Sam revived his suit with some peremptoriness. Sophy's son, now an undergraduate, was down from Oxford one Easter, when she again opened the subject. As soon as he was ordained, she argued, he would have a home of his own, wherein she, with her bad grammar and her ignorance, would be an encumbrance to him. Better obliterate her as much as possible.

He showed a more manly anger now, but would not agree. She on her side was more persistent, and he had doubts whether she could be trusted in his absence. But by indignation and contempt for her taste he completely maintained his ascendency; and finally taking her before a little cross and altar that he had erected in his bedroom for his private devotions, there bade her kneel, and swear that she would not wed Samuel Hobson without his consent. 'I owe this to my father!' he said.

The poor woman swore, thinking he would soften as soon as he was ordained and in full swing of clerical work. But he did not. His education had by this time sufficiently ousted his humanity to keep him quite firm; though his mother might have led an idyllic life with her faithful fruiterer and greengrocer, and nobody have been anything the worse in the world.

Her lameness became more confirmed as time went on, and she

seldom or never left the house in the long southern thoroughfare, where she seemed to be pining her heart away. 'Why mayn't I say to Sam that I'll marry him? Why mayn't I?' she would murmur plaintively to herself when nobody was near.

Some four years after this date a middle-aged man was standing at the door of the largest fruiterer's shop in Aldbrickham. He was the proprietor, but to-day, instead of his usual business attire, he wore a neat suit of black; and his window was partly shuttered. From the railway-station a funeral procession was seen approaching: it passed his door and went out of the town towards the village of Gaymead. The man, whose eyes were wet, held his hat in his hand as the vehicles moved by; while from the mourning-coach a young smooth-shaven priest in a high waistcoat looked black as a cloud at the shopkeeper standing there.

December 1891

For Conscience' Sake

WHETHER the utilitarian or the intuitive theory of the moral sense be upheld it is beyond question that there are a few subtle-souled persons with whom the absolute gratuitousness of an act of reparation is an inducement to perform it; while exhortation as to its necessity would breed excuses for leaving it undone. The case of Mr Millborne and Mrs Frankland particularly illustrated this, and perhaps something more.

There were few figures better known to the local crossing-sweeper than Mr Millborne's in his daily comings and goings along a familiar and quiet London street, where he lived inside the door marked eleven, though not as householder. In age he was fifty at least, and his habits were as regular as those of a person can be who has no occupation but the study of how to keep himself employed. He turned almost always to the right on getting to the end of the street, then he went onward down Bond Street to his club, whence he returned by precisely the same course about six o'clock, on foot; or, if he went to dine, later on in a cab. He was known to be a man of some means, though apparently not wealthy. Being a bachelor he seemed to prefer his present mode of living as a lodger in Mrs Towney's best rooms, with the use of furniture which he had bought ten times over in rent during his tenancy, to having a house of his own.

None among his acquaintance tried to know him well, for his manner and moods did not excite curiosity or deep friendship. He was not a man who seemed to have anything on his mind, anything to conceal, anything to impart. From his casual remarks it was generally understood that he was country-born, a native of some place in Wessex; that he had come to London as a young man in a banking-house, and had risen to a post of responsibility; when, by the death of his father, who had been fortunate in his investments, the son succeeded to an income which led him to retire from a business life somewhat early.

One evening, when he had been unwell for several days, Doctor Bindon came in, after dinner, from the adjoining medical quarter, and smoked with him over the fire. The patient's ailment was not such as to require much thought, and they talked together on indifferent subjects.

'I am a lonely man, Bindon – a lonely man,' Millborne took occasion to say, shaking his head gloomily. 'You don't know such loneliness as mine. . . . And the older I get the more I am dissatisfied with myself. And to-day I have been, through an accident, more than usually haunted by what, above all other events of my life, causes that dissatisfaction – the recollection of an unfulfilled promise made twenty years ago. In ordinary affairs I have always been considered a man of my word; and perhaps it is on that account that a particular vow I once made, and did not keep, comes back to me with a magnitude out of all proportion (I daresay) to its real gravity, especially at this time of day. You know the discomfort caused at night by the half-sleeping sense that a door or window has been left unfastened, or in the day by the remembrance of unanswered letters. So does that promise haunt me from time to time, and has done to-day particularly.'

There was a pause, and they smoked on. Millborne's eyes, though fixed on the fire, were really regarding attentively a town in the West of England.

'Yes,' he continued, 'I have never quite forgotten it, though during the busy years of my life it was shelved and buried under the pressure of my pursuits. And, as I say, to-day in particular, an incident in the law-report of a somewhat similar kind has brought it back again vividly. However, what it was I can tell you in a few words, though no doubt you, as a man of the world, will smile at the thinness of my skin when you hear it. . . . I came up to town at one-and-twenty, from Tone-borough, in Outer Wessex, where I was born, and where, before I left, I had won the heart of a young woman of my own age. I promised her marriage, took advantage of my promise, and – am a bachelor.'

'The old story.'

The other nodded.

'I left the place, and thought at the time I had done a very clever thing in getting so easily out of an entanglement. But I have lived long enough for that promise to return to bother me – to be honest, not altogether as a pricking of the conscience, but as a dissatisfaction with myself as a specimen of the heap of flesh called humanity. If I were to ask you to lend me fifty pounds, which I would repay you next midsummer, and I did not repay you, I should consider myself a shabby sort of fellow, especially if you wanted the money badly. Yet I promised that girl just as distinctly; and then coolly broke my word, as if doing so were rather smart conduct than a mean action, for which the poor victim herself, encumbered with a child, and not I, had really to pay the penalty, in spite of certain pecuniary aid that was given. . . . There, that's the retrospective trouble that I am always unearthing; and you may hardly believe that though so many years have elapsed, and it is all gone by and done with, and she must be getting on for an old woman now, as I am for an old man, it really often destroys my sense of self-respect still.'

'O, I can understand it. All depends upon the temperament. Thousands of men would have forgotten all about it; so would you, perhaps, if you had married and had a family. Did she ever marry?'

'I don't think so. O no – she never did. She left Toneborough, and later on appeared under another name at Exonbury, in the next county, where she was not known. It is very seldom that I go down into that part of the country, but in passing through Exonbury, on one occasion, I learnt that she was quite a settled resident there, as a teacher of music, or something of the kind. That much I casually heard when I was there two or three years ago. But I have never set eyes on her since our original acquaintance, and should not know her if I met her.'

'Did the child live?' asked the doctor.

'For several years, certainly,' replied his friend. 'I cannot say if she is living now. It was a little girl. She might be married by this time as far as years go.'

'And the mother – was she a decent, worthy young woman?'

'O yes; a sensible, quiet girl, neither attractive nor unattractive to the ordinary observer; simply commonplace. Her position at the time of our acquaintance was not so good as mine. My father was a solicitor, as I think I have told you. She was a young girl in a music-shop; and it was represented to me that it would be beneath my position to marry her. Hence the result.'

'Well, all I can say is that after twenty years it is probably too late to think of mending such a matter. It has doubtless by this time mended itself. You had better dismiss it from your mind as an evil past your control. Of course, if mother and daughter are alive, or either, you might settle something upon them, if you were inclined, and had it to spare.'

'Well, I haven't much to spare, and I have relations in narrow circumstances – perhaps narrower than theirs. But that is not the point. Were I ever so rich I feel I could not rectify the past by money. I did not promise to enrich her. On the contrary, I told her it would probably be dire poverty for both of us. But I did promise to make her my wife.'

'Then find her and do it,' said the doctor jocularly as he rose to leave.

'Ah, Bindon! That, of course, is the obvious jest. But I haven't the slightest desire for marriage; I am quite content to live as I have lived. I am a bachelor by nature, and instinct, and habit, and everything. Besides, though I respect her still (for she was not an atom to blame), I haven't any shadow of love for her. In my mind she exists as one of those women you think well of, but find uninteresting. It would be purely with the idea of putting wrong right that I should hunt her up, and propose to do it off-hand.'

'You don't think of it seriously?' said his surprised friend.

'I sometimes think that I would, if it were practicable; simply, as I say, to recover my sense of being a man of honour.'

'I wish you luck in the enterprise,' said Doctor Bindon. 'You'll soon be out of that chair, and then you can put your impulse to the test. But – after twenty years of silence – I should say, don't!'

II

The doctor's advice remained counterpoised, in Millborne's mind, by the aforesaid mood of seriousness and sense of principle, approximating often to religious sentiment, which had been evolving itself in his breast for months, and even years.

The feeling, however, had no immediate effect upon Mr Millborne's actions. He soon got over his trifling illness, and was vexed with himself for having, in a moment of impulse, confided such a case of conscience to anybody.

But the force which had prompted it, though latent, remained with him and ultimately grew stronger. The upshot was that about four months after the date of his illness and disclosure, Millborne found himself on a mild spring morning at Paddington Station, in a train that was starting for the west. His many intermittent thoughts on his broken promise from time to time, in those hours when loneliness brought him face to face with his own personality, had at last resulted in this course.

The decisive stimulus had been given when, a day or two earlier, on looking into a Post-Office Directory, he learnt that the woman he had not met for twenty years was still living on at Exonbury under the name she had assumed when, a year or two after her disappearance from her native town and his, she had returned from abroad as a young widow with a child, and taken up her residence at the former city. Her condition was apparently but little changed, and her daughter seemed to be with her, their names standing in the Directory as 'Mrs Leonora Frankland and Miss Frankland, Teachers of Music and Dancing'.

Mr Millborne reached Exonbury in the afternoon, and his first business, before even taking his luggage into the town, was to find the house occupied by the teachers. Standing in a central and open place it was not difficult to discover, a well-burnished brass door-plate bearing their names prominently. He hesitated to enter without further knowledge, and ultimately took lodgings over a toy-shop opposite, securing a sitting-room which faced a similar drawing- or sitting-room at the Franklands', where the dancing lessons were given. Installed here he was enabled to make indirectly, and without suspicion, inquiries and observations on the character of the ladies over the way, which he did with much deliberateness.

He learnt that the widow, Mrs Frankland, with her one daughter, Frances, was of cheerful and excellent repute, energetic and painstaking with her pupils, of whom she had a good many, and in whose tuition her daughter assisted her. She was quite a recognized townswoman, and though the dancing branch of her profession was perhaps a trifle worldly, she was really a serious-minded lady who, being obliged to live by what she knew how to teach, balanced matters by lending a hand at charitable bazaars, assisting at sacred concerts, and giving musical recitations in aid of funds for bewildering happy savages, and other such enthusiasms of this enlightened country. Her daughter was one of the foremost of the bevy of young women who decorated the churches at Easter and Christmas, was organist in one of those edifices, and had subscribed to the testimonial of a silver broth-basin that was presented to the Reverend Mr Walker as a token of gratitude for his faithful and arduous intonations of six months as sub-precentor in the Cathedral. Altogether mother and daughter appeared to be a typical and innocent pair among the genteel citizens of Exonbury.

As a natural and simple way of advertising their profession they allowed the windows of the music-room to be a little open, so that you

had the pleasure of hearing all along the street at any hour between
sunrise and sunset fragmentary gems of classical music as interpreted
by the young people of twelve or fourteen who took lessons there. But
it was said that Mrs Frankland made most of her income by letting out
pianos on hire, and by selling them as agent for the makers.

The report pleased Millborne; it was highly creditable, and far better
than he had hoped. He was curious to get a view of the two women who
led such blameless lives.

He had not long to wait to get a glimpse of Leonora. It was when she
was standing on her own doorstep, opening her parasol, on the morning
after his arrival. She was thin, though not gaunt, with greying hair; and
a good, well-wearing, thoughtful face had taken the place of the one
which had temporarily attracted him in the days of his nonage. She wore
black, and it became her in her character of widow. The daughter next
appeared; she was a smoothed and rounded copy of her mother, with
the same decision in her mien that Leonora had, and a bounding gait in
which he traced a faint resemblance to his own at her age.

For the first time he absolutely made up his mind to call on them.
But his antecedent step was to send Leonora a note the next morning,
stating his proposal to visit her, and suggesting the evening as the time,
because she seemed to be so greatly occupied in her professional capacity
during the day. He purposely worded his note in such a form as not to
require an answer from her which would be possibly awkward to
write.

No answer came. Naturally he should not have been surprised at this;
and yet he felt a little checked, even though she had only refrained from
volunteering a reply that was not demanded.

At eight, the hour fixed by himself, he crossed over and was passively
admitted by the servant. Mrs Frankland, as she called herself, received
him in the large music-and-dancing-room on the first-floor front, and
not in any private little parlour as he had expected. This cast a distress-
ingly business-like colour over their first meeting after so many years
of severance. The woman he had wronged stood before him, well
dressed, even to his metropolitan eyes, and her manner as she came up
to him was dignified even to hardness. She certainly was not glad to see
him. But what could he expect after a neglect of twenty years!

'How do you do, Mr Millborne?' she said cheerfully, as to any chance
caller. 'I am obliged to receive you here because my daughter has a
friend downstairs.'

'Your daughter – and mine.'

'Ah – yes, yes,' she replied hastily, as if the addition had escaped her memory. 'But perhaps the less said about that the better, in fairness to me. You will consider me a widow, please.'

'Certainly, Leonora. . . .' He could not get on, her manner was so cold and indifferent. The expected scene of sad reproach, subdued to delicacy by the run of years, was absent altogether. He was obliged to come to the point without preamble.

'You are quite free, Leonora – I mean as to marriage? There is nobody who has your promise, or—'

'O yes; quite free, Mr Millborne,' she said, somewhat surprised.

'Then I will tell you why I have come. Twenty years ago I promised to make you my wife; and I am here to fulfil that promise. Heaven forgive my tardiness!'

Her surprise was increased, but she was not agitated. She seemed to become gloomy, disapproving. 'I – fear I could not entertain such an idea at this time of life,' she said after a moment or two. 'It would complicate matters too greatly. I have a very fair income, and require no help of any sort. I have no wish to marry. . . . What could have induced you to come on such an errand now? It seems quite extraordinary, if I may say so!'

'It must – I daresay it does,' Millborne replied vaguely, 'and I must tell you that impulse – I mean in the sense of passion – has little to do with it. I wish to marry you, Leonora; I much desire to marry you. But it is an affair of conscience, a case of fulfilment. I promised you, and it was dishonourable of me to go away. I want to remove that sense of dishonour before I die. No doubt we might get to love each other as warmly as we did in old times?'

She dubiously shook her head. 'I appreciate your motives, Mr Millborne; but you must consider my position; and you will see that, short of the personal wish to marry, which I don't feel, there is no reason why I should change my state, even though by so doing I should ease your conscience. My position in this town is a respected one; I have built it up by my own hard labours, and, in short, I don't wish to alter it. My daughter, too, is just on the verge of an engagement to be married, to a young man who will make her an excellent husband. It will be in every way a desirable match for her. He is downstairs now.'

'Does she know – anything about me?'

'O no, no; God forbid! Her father is dead and buried to her. So that, you see, things are going on smoothly, and I don't want to disturb their progress.'

He nodded. 'Very well,' he said, and rose to go. At the door, however, he came back again.

'Still, Leonora,' he urged, 'I have come on purpose; and I don't see what disturbance would be caused. You would simply marry an old friend. Won't you reconsider? It is no more than right that we should be united, remembering the girl.'

She shook her head, and patted with her foot nervously.

'Well, I won't detain you,' he added. 'I shall not be leaving Exonbury yet. You will allow me to see you again?'

'Yes; I don't mind,' she said reluctantly.

The obstacles he had encountered, though they did not reanimate his dead passion for Leonora, did certainly make it appear indispensable to his peace of mind to overcome her coldness. He called frequently. The first meeting with the daughter was a trying ordeal, though he did not feel drawn towards her as he had expected to be; she did not excite his sympathies. Her mother confided to Frances the errand of 'her old friend', which was viewed by the daughter with strong disfavour. His desire being thus uncongenial to both, for a long time Millborne made not the least impression upon Mrs Frankland. His attentions pestered her rather than pleased her. He was surprised at her firmness, and it was only when he hinted at moral reasons for their union that she was ever shaken. 'Strictly speaking,' he would say, 'we ought, as honest persons, to marry; and that's the truth of it, Leonora.'

'I have looked at it in that light,' she said quickly. 'It struck me at the very first. But I don't see the force of the argument. I totally deny that after this interval of time I am bound to marry you for honour's sake. I would have married you, as you know well enough, at the proper time. But what is the use of remedies now?'

They were standing at the window. A scantly-whiskered young man, in clerical attire, called at the door below. Leonora flushed with interest.

'Who is he?' said Mr Millborne.

'My Frances's lover. I am so sorry – she is not at home! Ah! they have told him where she is, and he has gone to find her. . . . I hope that suit will prosper, at any rate!'

'Why shouldn't it?'

'Well, he cannot marry yet; and Frances sees but little of him now he has left Exonbury. He was formerly doing duty here, but now he is curate of St John's, Ivell, fifty miles up the line. There is a tacit agreement between them, but – there have been friends of his who object, because of our vocation. However, he sees the absurdity of such an objection as that, and is not influenced by it.'

'Your marriage with me would help the match, instead of hindering it, as you have said.'

'Do you think it would?'

'It certainly would, by taking you out of this business altogether.'

By chance he had found the way to move her somewhat, and he followed it up. This view was imparted to Mrs Frankland's daughter, and it led her to soften her opposition. Millborne, who had given up his lodging in Exonbury, journeyed to and fro regularly, till at last he overcame her negations, and she expressed a reluctant assent.

They were married at the nearest church; and the goodwill – whatever that was – of the music-and-dancing connection was sold to a successor only too ready to jump into the place, the Millbornes having decided to live in London.

III

Millborne was a householder in his old district, though not in his old street, and Mrs Millborne and their daughter had turned themselves into Londoners. Frances was well reconciled to the removal by her lover's satisfaction at the change. It suited him better to travel from Ivell a hundred miles to see her in London, where he frequently had other engagements, than fifty in the opposite direction where nothing but herself required his presence. So here they were, furnished up to the attics, in one of the small but popular streets of the West district, in a house whose front, till lately of the complexion of a chimney-sweep, had been scraped to show to the surprised wayfarer the bright yellow and red brick that had lain lurking beneath the soot of fifty years.

The social lift that the two women had derived from the alliance was considerable; but when the exhilaration which accompanies a first residence in London, the sensation of standing on a pivot of the world, had passed, their lives promised to be somewhat duller than when, at despised Exonbury, they had enjoyed a nodding acquaintance with three-fourths of the town. Mr Millborne did not criticize his wife; he could not. Whatever defects of hardness and acidity his original treatment and the lapse of years might have developed in her, his sense of a realized idea, of a re-established self-satisfaction, was always thrown into the scale on her side, and outweighed all objections.

It was about a month after their settlement in town that the household decided to spend a week at a watering-place in the Isle of Wight, and while there the Reverend Percival Cope (the young curate aforesaid) came to see them, Frances in particular. No formal engagement of the young pair had been announced as yet, but it was clear that their mutual understanding could not end in anything but marriage without grievous disappointment to one of the parties at least. Not that Frances was sentimental. She was rather of the imperious sort, indeed; and, to say all, the young girl had not fulfilled her father's expectations of her. But he hoped and worked for her welfare as sincerely as any father could do.

Mr Cope was introduced to the new head of the family, and stayed with them in the Island two or three days. On the last day of his visit they decided to venture on a two hours' sail in one of the small yachts which lay there for hire. The trip had not progressed far before all, except the curate, found that sailing in a breeze did not quite agree with them; but as he seemed to enjoy the experience, the other three bore their condition as well as they could without grimace or complaint, till the young man, observing their discomfort, gave immediate directions to tack about. On the way back to port they sat silent, facing each other.

Nausea in such circumstances, like midnight watching, fatigue, trouble, fright, has this marked effect upon the countenance, that it often brings out strongly the divergences of the individual from the norm of his race, accentuating superficial peculiarities to radical distinctions. Unexpected physiognomies will uncover themselves at these times in well-known faces; the aspect becomes invested with the spectral presence of entombed and forgotten ancestors; and family lineaments of special or exclusive cast, which in ordinary moments are masked by a stereotyped expression and mien, start up with crude insistence to the view.

Frances, sitting beside her mother's husband, with Mr Cope opposite, was naturally enough much regarded by the curate during the tedious sail home; at first with sympathetic smiles. Then, as the middle-aged father and his child grew each gray-faced, as the pretty blush of Frances disintegrated into spotty stains, and the soft rotundities of her features diverged from their familiar and reposeful beauty into elemental lines, Cope was gradually struck with the resemblance between a pair in their discomfort who in their ease presented nothing to the eye in common. Mr Millborne and Frances in their indisposition were strangely, startlingly alike.

The inexplicable fact absorbed Cope's attention quite. He forgot to smile at Frances, to hold her hand; and when they touched the shore he remained sitting for some moments like a man in a trance.

As they went homeward, and recovered their complexions and contours, the similarities one by one disappeared, and Frances and Mr Millborne were again masked by the commonplace differences of sex and age. It was as if, during the voyage, a mysterious veil had been lifted, temporarily revealing a strange pantomime of the past.

During the evening he said to her casually: 'Is your step-father a cousin of your mother, dear Frances ?'

'O no,' said she. 'There is no relationship. He was only an old friend of hers. Why did you suppose such a thing ?'

He did not explain, and the next morning started to resume his duties at Ivell.

Cope was an honest young fellow, and shrewd withal. At home in his quiet rooms in St Peter's Street, Ivell, he pondered long and unpleasantly on the revelations of the cruise. The tale it told was distinct enough, and for the first time his position was an uncomfortable one. He had met the Franklands at Exonbury as parishioners, had been attracted by Frances, and had floated thus far into an engagement which was indefinite only because of his inability to marry just yet. The Franklands' past had apparently contained mysteries, and it did not coincide with his judgment to marry into a family whose mystery was of the sort suggested. So he sat and sighed, between his reluctance to lose Frances and his natural dislike of forming a connection with people whose antecedents would not bear the strictest investigation.

A passionate lover of the old-fashioned sort might possibly never have halted to weigh these doubts; but though he was in the Church Cope's affections were fastidious – distinctly tempered with the alloys of the century's decadence. He delayed writing to Frances for some while, simply because he could not tune himself up to enthusiasm when worried by suspicions of such a kind.

Meanwhile the Millbornes had returned to London, and Frances was growing anxious. In talking to her mother of Cope she had innocently alluded to his curious inquiry if her mother and her step-father were connected by any tie of cousinship. Mrs Millborne made her repeat the words. Frances did so, and watched with inquisitive eyes their effect upon her elder, which was a distinct one.

'What is there so startling in his inquiry then?' Frances asked. 'Can it have anything to do with his not writing to me?'

Her mother flinched, but did not inform her, and Frances also was now drawn within the atmosphere of suspicion. That night when standing by chance outside the chamber of her parents she heard for the first time their voices engaged in a sharp altercation.

The apple of discord had, indeed, been dropped into the house of the Millbornes. The scene within the chamber-door was Mrs Millborne standing before her dressing-table, looking across to her husband in the dressing-room adjoining, where he was sitting down, his eyes fixed on the floor.

'Why did you come and disturb my life a second time?' she harshly asked. 'Why did you pester me with your conscience, till I was driven to accept you to get rid of your importunity? Frances and I were doing well: the one desire of my life was that she should marry that good young man. And now the match is broken off by your cruel interference! Why did you show yourself in my world again, and raise this scandal upon my hard-won respectability – won by such weary years of labour as none will ever know!' She bent her face upon the table and wept passionately.

There was no reply from Mr Millborne. Frances lay awake nearly all that night, and when at breakfast-time the next morning still no letter appeared from Mr Cope, she entreated her mother to go to Ivell and see if the young man were ill.

Mrs Millborne went, returning the same day. Frances, anxious and haggard, met her at the station.

Was all well? Her mother could not say it was; though he was not ill.

One thing she had found out, that it was a mistake to hunt up a man when his inclinations were to hold aloof. Returning with her mother in the cab Frances insisted upon knowing what the mystery was which plainly had alienated her lover. The precise words which had been spoken at the interview with him that day at Ivell Mrs Millborne could not be induced to repeat; but thus far she admitted, that the estrangement was fundamentally owing to Mr Millborne having sought her out and married her.

'And why did he seek you out – and why were you obliged to marry him?' asked the distressed girl. Then the evidences pieced themselves together in her acute mind, and, her colour gradually rising, she asked her mother if what they pointed to was indeed the fact. Her mother admitted that it was.

A flush of mortification succeeded to the flush of shame upon the young woman's face. How could a scrupulously correct clergyman and lover like Mr Cope ask her to be his wife after this discovery of her irregular birth? She covered her eyes with her hands in a silent despair.

In the presence of Mr Millborne they at first suppressed their anguish. But by and by their feelings got the better of them, and when he was asleep in his chair after dinner Mrs Millborne's irritation broke out. The embittered Frances joined her in reproaching the man who had come as the spectre to their intended feast of Hymen, and turned its promise to ghastly failure.

'Why were you so weak, mother, as to admit such an enemy to your house – one so obviously your evil genius – much less accept him as a husband, after so long? If you had only told me all, I could have advised you better! But I suppose I have no right to reproach him, bitter as I feel, and even though he has blighted my life for ever!'

'Frances, I did hold out; I saw it was a mistake to have any more to say to a man who had been such an unmitigated curse to me! But he would not listen; he kept on about his conscience and mine, till I was bewildered, and said Yes! ... Bringing us away from a quiet town where we were known and respected – what an ill-considered thing it was! O the content of those days! We had society there, people in our own position, who did not expect more of us than we expected of them. Here, where there is so much, there is nothing! He said London society was so bright and brilliant that it would be like a new world. It may be to those who are in it; but what is that to us two lonely women; we only see it flashing past! ... O the fool, the fool that I was!'

Now Millborne was not so soundly asleep as to prevent his hearing these animadversions that were almost execrations, and many more of the same sort. As there was no peace for him at home, he went again to his club, where, since his reunion with Leonora, he had seldom if ever been seen. But the shadow of the troubles in his household interfered with his comfort here also: he could not, as formerly, settle down into his favourite chair with the evening paper, reposeful in the celibate's sense that where he was his world's centre had its fixture. His world was now an ellipse, with a dual centrality, of which his own was not the major.

The young curate of Ivell still held aloof, tantalizing Frances by his elusiveness. Plainly he was waiting upon events. Millborne bore the reproaches of his wife and daughter almost in silence; but by degrees he grew meditative, as if revolving a new idea. The bitter cry about blighting their existence at length became so impassioned that one day Millborne calmly proposed to return again to the country; not necessarily to Exonbury, but, if they were willing, to a little old manor-house which he had found was to be let, standing a mile from Mr Cope's town of Ivell.

They were surprised, and, despite their view of him as the bringer of ill, were disposed to accede. 'Though I suppose,' said Mrs Millborne to him, 'it will end in Mr Cope's asking you flatly about the past, and your being compelled to tell him; which may dash all my hopes for Frances. She gets more and more like you every day, particularly when she is in a bad temper. People will see you together, and notice it; and I don't know what may come of it!'

'I don't think they will see us together,' he said; but he entered into no argument when she insisted otherwise. The removal was eventually resolved on; the town-house was disposed of, and again came the invasion by furniture-men and vans, till all the movables and servants were whisked away. He sent his wife and daughter to an hotel while this was going on, taking two or three journeys himself to Ivell to superintend the refixing, and the improvement of the grounds. When all was done he returned to them in town.

The house was ready for their reception, he told them, and there only remained the journey. He accompanied them and their personal luggage to the station only, having, he said, to remain in town a short time on business with his lawyer. They went, dubious and discontented; for the much-loved Cope had made no sign.

'If we were going down to live here alone,' said Mrs Millborne to her daughter in the train; 'and there was no intrusive tell-tale presence! . . . But let it be!'

The house was a lovely little place in a grove of elms, and they liked it much. The first person to call upon them as new residents was Mr Cope. He was delighted to find that they had come so near, and (though he did not say this) meant to live in such excellent style. He had not, however, resumed the manner of a lover.

'Your father spoils all!' murmured Mrs Millborne.

But three days later she received a letter from her husband, which caused her no small degree of astonishment. It was written from Boulogne.

It began with a long explanation of settlements of his property, in which he had been engaged since their departure. The chief feature in the business was that Mrs Millborne found herself the absolute mistress of a comfortable sum in personal estate, and Frances of a life-interest in a larger sum, the principal to be afterwards divided amongst her children if she had any. The remainder of his letter ran as hereunder: –

'I have learnt that there are some derelictions of duty which cannot be blotted out by tardy accomplishment. Our evil actions do not remain isolated in the past, waiting only to be reversed: like locomotive plants they spread and re-root, till to destroy the original stem has no material effect in killing them. I made a mistake in searching you out; I admit it; whatever the remedy may be in such cases it is not marriage, and the best thing for you and me is that you do not see me more. You had better not seek me, for you will not be likely to find me: you are well provided for, and we may do ourselves more harm than good by meeting again.

F.M.'

Millborne, in short, disappeared from that day forward. But a searching inquiry would have revealed that, soon after the Millbornes went to Ivell, an Englishman, who did not give the name of Millborne, took up his residence in Brussels; a man who might have been recognized by Mrs Millborne if she had met him. One afternoon in the ensuing summer, when this gentleman was looking over the English papers, he saw the announcement of Miss Frances Frankland's marriage. She had become the Reverend Mrs Cope.

'Thank God!' said the gentleman.

But his momentary satisfaction was far from being happiness. As he formerly had been weighted with a bad conscience, so now was he burdened with the heavy thought which oppressed Antigone, that by honourable observance of a rite he had obtained for himself the reward of dishonourable laxity. Occasionally he had to be helped to his lodgings by his servant from the *Cercle* he frequented, through having imbibed a little too much liquor to be able to take care of himself. But he was harmless, and even when he had been drinking said little.

March 1891

A Tragedy of Two Ambitions

I

THE shouts of the village-boys came in at the window, accompanied by broken laughter from loungers at the inn-door; but the brothers Halborough worked on.

They were sitting in a bedroom of the master-millwright's house, engaged in the untutored reading of Greek and Latin. It was no tale of Homeric blows and knocks, Argonautic voyaging, or Theban family woe that inflamed their imaginations and spurred them onward. They were plodding away at the Greek Testament, immersed in a chapter of the idiomatic and difficult Epistle to the Hebrews.

The Dog-day sun in its decline reached the low ceiling with slanting sides, and the shadows of the great goat's-willow swayed and interchanged upon the walls like a spectral army manœuvring. The open casement which admitted the remoter sounds now brought the voice of some one close at hand. It was their sister, a pretty girl of fourteen, who stood in the court below.

'I can see the tops of your heads! What's the use of staying up there? I like you not to go out with the street-boys; but do come and play with me!'

They treated her as an inadequate interlocutor, and put her off with some slight word. She went away disappointed. Presently there was a dull noise of heavy footsteps at the side of the house, and one of the brothers sat up. 'I fancy I hear him coming,' he murmured, his eyes on the window.

A man in the light drab clothes of an old-fashioned country tradesman approached from round the corner, reeling as he came. The elder son flushed with anger, rose from his books, and descended the stairs. The younger sat on, till, after the lapse of a few minutes, his brother re-entered the room.

'Did Rosa see him?'

'No.'

'Nor anybody?'

'No.'

'What have you done with him?'

'He's in the straw-shed. I got him in with some trouble, and he has fallen asleep. I thought this would be the explanation of his absence! No stones dressed for Miller Kench, the great wheel of the saw-mills waiting for new float-boards, even the poor folk not able to get their waggons wheeled.'

'What *is* the use of poring over this!' said the younger, shutting up Donnegan's *Lexicon* with a slap. 'O if we had only been able to keep mother's nine hundred pounds, what we could have done!'

'How well she had estimated the sum necessary! Four hundred and fifty each, she thought. And I have no doubt that we could have done it on that, with care.'

This loss of the nine hundred pounds was the sharp thorn of their crown. It was a sum which their mother had amassed with great exertion and self-denial, by adding to a chance legacy such other small amounts as she could lay hands on from time to time; and she had intended with the hoard to indulge the dear wish of her heart – that of sending her sons, Joshua and Cornelius, to one of the Universities, having been informed that from four hundred to four hundred and fifty each might carry them through their terms with such great economy as she knew she could trust them to practise. But she had died a year or two before this time, worn out by too keen a strain towards these ends; and the money, coming unreservedly into the hands of their father, had been nearly dissipated. With its exhaustion went all opportunity and hope of a university degree for the sons.

'It drives me mad when I think of it,' said Joshua, the elder. 'And here we work and work in our own bungling way, and the utmost we can hope for is a term of years as national schoolmasters, and possible admission to a Theological college, and ordination as despised licentiates.'

The anger of the elder was reflected as simple sadness in the face of the other. 'We can preach the Gospel as well without a hood on our surplices as with one,' he said with feeble consolation.

'Preach the Gospel – true,' said Joshua with a slight pursing of mouth. 'But we can't rise!'

'Let us make the best of it, and grind on.'

The other was silent, and they drearily bent over their books again.

The cause of all this gloom, the millwright Halborough, now snoring in the shed, had been a thriving master-machinist, notwithstanding his free and careless disposition, till a taste for a more than adequate quantity of strong liquor took hold of him; since when his habits had interfered with his business sadly. Already millers went elsewhere for their gear, and only one set of hands was now kept going, though there were formerly two. Already he found a difficulty in meeting his men at the week's end, and though they had been reduced in number there was barely enough work to do for those who remained.

The sun dropped lower and vanished, the shouts of the village children ceased to resound, darkness cloaked the students' bedroom, and all the scene outwardly breathed peace. None knew of the fevered youthful ambitions that throbbed in two breasts within the quiet creeper-covered walls of the millwright's house.

In a few months the brothers left the village of their birth to enter themselves as students in a training college for schoolmasters; first having placed their young sister Rosa under as efficient a tuition at a fashionable watering-place as the means at their disposal could command.

II

A man in semi-clerical dress was walking along the road which led from the railway-station into a provincial town. As he walked he read persistently, only looking up once now and then to see that he was keeping on the foot-track and to avoid other passengers. At those moments, whoever had known the former students at the millwright's would have perceived that one of them, Joshua Halborough, was the peripatetic reader here.

What had been simple force in the youth's face was energized judgment in the man's. His character was gradually writing itself out in his countenance. That he was watching his own career with deeper and deeper interest, that he continually 'heard his days before him', and cared to hear little else, might have been hazarded from what was seen there. His ambitions were, in truth, passionate, yet controlled; so that the germs of many more plans than ever blossomed to maturity had place in him; and forward visions were kept purposely in twilight, to avoid distraction.

Events so far had been encouraging. Shortly after assuming the mastership of his first school he had obtained an introduction to the Bishop of a diocese far from his native county, who had looked upon him as a promising young man and taken him in hand. He was now in the second year of his residence at the theological college of the cathedral-town, and would soon be presented for ordination.

He entered the town, turned into a back street, and then into a yard, keeping his book before him till he set foot under the arch of the latter place. Round the arch was written 'National School', and the stonework of the jambs was worn away as nothing but boys and the waves of ocean will wear it. He was soon amid the sing-song accents of the scholars.

His brother Cornelius, who was the schoolmaster here, laid down the pointer with which he was directing attention to the Capes of Europe, and came forward.

'That's his brother Jos!' whispered one of the sixth-standard boys. 'He's going to be a pa'son. He's now at college.'

'Corney is going to be one, too, when he's saved enough money,' said another.

After greeting his brother, whom he had not seen for several months, the junior began to explain his system of teaching geography.

But Halborough the elder took no interest in the subject. 'How about your own studies?' he asked. 'Did you get the books I sent?'

Cornelius had received them, and he related what he was doing.

'Mind you work in the morning. What time do you get up?'

The younger replied: 'Half-past five.'

'Half-past four is not a minute too soon this time of the year. There is no time like the morning for construing. I don't know why, but when I feel even too dreary to read a novel I can translate – there is something mechanical about it I suppose. Now, Cornelius, you are rather behind-hand, and have some heavy reading before you if you mean to get out of this next Christmas.'

'I am afraid I have.'

'We must soon sound the Bishop. I am sure you will get a title without difficulty when he has heard all. The sub-dean, the principal of my college, says that the best plan will be for you to come there when his lordship is present at an examination, and he'll get you a personal interview with him. Mind you make a good impression upon him. I found in my case that that was everything, and doctrine almost nothing. You'll do for a deacon, Corney, if not for a priest.'

The younger remained thoughtful. 'Have you heard from Rosa lately?' he asked; 'I had a letter this morning.'

'Yes. The little minx writes rather too often. She is homesick – though Brussels must be an attractive place enough. But she must make the most of her time over there. I thought a year would be enough for her, after that high-class school at Sandbourne, but I have decided to give her two, and make a good job of it, expensive as the establishment is.'

Their two rather harsh faces had softened directly they began to speak of their sister, whom they loved more ambitiously than they loved themselves.

'But where is the money to come from, Joshua?'

'I have already got it.' He looked round, and finding that some boys were near withdrew a few steps. 'I have borrowed it at five per cent from the farmer who used to occupy the farm next our field. You remember him.'

'But about paying him?'

'I shall pay him by degrees out of my stipend. No, Cornelius, it was no use to do the thing by halves. She promises to be a most attractive, not to say beautiful, girl. I have seen that for years; and if her face is not her fortune, her face and her brains together will be, if I observe and contrive aright. That she should be, every inch of her, an accomplished and refined woman, was indispensable for the fulfilment of her destiny, and for moving onwards and upwards with us; and she'll do it, you will see. I'd half starve myself rather than take her away from that school now.'

They looked round the school they were in. To Cornelius it was natural and familiar enough, but to Joshua, with his limited human sympathies, who had just dropped in from a superior sort of place, the sight jarred unpleasantly, as being that of something he had left behind. 'I shall be glad when you are out of this,' he said, 'and in your pulpit, and well through your first sermon.'

'You may as well say inducted into my fat living, while you are about it.'

'Ah, well – don't think lightly of the Church. There's a fine work for any man of energy in the Church, as you'll find,' he said fervidly. 'Torrents of infidelity to be stemmed, new views of old subjects to be expounded, truths in spirit to be substituted for truths in the letter....'

He lapsed into reverie with the vision of his career, persuading himself that it was ardour for Christianity which spurred him on, and not pride of place. He had shouldered a body of doctrine, and was prepared to defend it tooth and nail, solely for the honour and glory that warriors win.

'If the Church is elastic, and stretches to the shape of the time, she'll last, I suppose,' said Cornelius. 'If not— Only think, I bought a copy of Paley's *Evidences*, best edition, broad margins, excellent preservation, at a bookstall the other day for – ninepence; and I thought that at this rate Christianity must be in rather a bad way.'

'No, no!' said the other almost angrily. 'It only shows that such defences are no longer necessary. Men's eyes can see the truth without extraneous assistance. Besides, we are in for Christianity, and must stick to her whether or no. I am just now going right through Pusey's *Library of the Fathers*.'

'You'll be a bishop, Joshua, before you have done!'

'Ah!' said the other bitterly, shaking his head. 'Perhaps I might have been – I might have been! But where is my D.D. or LL.D.; and how be a bishop without that kind of appendage? Archbishop Tillotson was the son of a Sowerby clothier, but he was sent to Clare College. To hail Oxford or Cambridge as *alma mater* is not for me – for us! My God! when I think of what we should have been – what fair promise has been blighted by that cursed, worthless—'

'Hush, hush! . . . But I feel it, too, as much as you. I have seen it more forcibly lately. You would have obtained your degree long before this time – possibly fellowship – and I should have been on my way to mine.'

'Don't talk of it,' said the other. 'We must do the best we can.'

They looked out of the window sadly, through the dusty panes, so high up that only the sky was visible. By degrees the haunting trouble loomed again, and Cornelius broke the silence with a whisper: 'He has called on me!'

The living pulses died on Joshua's face, which grew arid as a clinker. 'When was that?' he asked quickly.

'Last week.'

'How did he get here – so many miles?'

'Came by railway. He came to ask for money.'

'Ah!'

'He says he will call on you.'

Joshua replied resignedly. The theme of their conversation spoilt his buoyancy for that afternoon. He returned in the evening, Cornelius accompanying him to the station; but he did not read in the train which took him back to the Fountall Theological College, as he had done on the way out. That ineradicable trouble still remained as a squalid spot in the expanse of his life. He sat with the other students in the cathedral choir next day; and the recollection of the trouble obscured the purple splendour thrown by the panes upon the floor.

It was afternoon. All was as still in the Close as a cathedral-green can be between the Sunday services, and the incessant cawing of the rooks was the only sound. Joshua Halborough had finished his ascetic lunch, and had gone into the library, where he stood for a few moments looking out of the large window facing the green. He saw walking slowly across it a man in a fustian coat and a battered white hat with a much-ruffled nap, having upon his arm a tall gipsy-woman wearing long brass ear-rings. The man was staring quizzically at the west front of the cathedral, and Halborough recognized in him the form and features of his father. Who the woman was he knew not. Almost as soon as Joshua became conscious of these things, the sub-dean, who was also the principal of the college, and of whom the young man stood in more awe than of the Bishop himself, emerged from the gate and entered a path across the Close. The pair met the dignitary, and to Joshua's horror his father turned and addressed the sub-dean.

What passed between them he could not tell. But as he stood in a cold sweat he saw his father place his hand familiarly on the sub-dean's shoulder; the shrinking response of the latter, and his quick withdrawal, told his feeling. The woman seemed to say nothing, but when the sub-dean had passed by they came on towards the college gate.

Halborough flew along the corridor and out at a side door, so as to intercept them before they could reach the front entrance, for which they were making. He caught them behind a clump of laurel.

'By Jerry, here's the very chap! Well, you're a fine fellow, Jos, never to send your father as much as a twist o' baccy on such an occasion, and to leave him to travel all these miles to find 'ee out!'

'First, who is this?' said Joshua Halborough with pale dignity, waving his hand towards the buxom woman with the great ear-rings.

'Dammy, the mis'ess! Your step-mother! Didn't you know I'd married? She helped me home from market one night, and we came to terms, and struck the bargain. Didn't we, Selinar?'

'Oi, by the great Lord an' we did!' simpered the lady.

'Well, what sort of a place is this you are living in?' asked the mill-wright. 'A kind of house-of-correction apparently?'

Joshua listened abstractedly, his features set to resignation. Sick at heart he was going to ask them if they were in want of any necessary, any meal, when his father cut him short by saying, 'Why, we've called to ask ye to come round and take pot-luck with us at the Cock-and-Bottle, where we've put up for the day, on our way to see mis'ess's friends at Binegar Fair, where they'll be lying under canvas for a night or two. As for the victuals at the Cock I can't testify to 'em at all; but for the drink, they've the rarest drop of Old Tom that I've tasted for many a year.'

'Thanks; but I am a teetotaller; and I have lunched,' said Joshua, who could fully believe his father's testimony to the gin, from the odour of his breath. 'You see we have to observe regular habits here; and I couldn't be seen at the Cock-and-Bottle just now.'

'O dammy, then don't come, your reverence. Perhaps you won't mind standing treat for those who can be seen there?'

'Not a penny,' said the younger firmly. 'You've had enough already.'

'Thank you for nothing. By the bye, who was that spindle-legged, shoe-buckled parson feller we met by now? He seemed to think we should poison him!'

Joshua remarked coldly that it was the principal of his college, guardedly inquiring, 'Did you tell him whom you were come to see?'

His father did not reply. He and his strapping gipsy wife – if she were his wife – stayed no longer, and disappeared in the direction of the High Street. Joshua Halborough went back to the library. Determined as was his nature, he wept hot tears upon the books, and was immeasurably more wretched that afternoon than the unwelcome millwright. In the evening he sat down and wrote a letter to his brother, in which, after stating what had happened, and expatiating upon this new disgrace in the gipsy wife, he propounded a plan for raising money sufficient to induce the couple to emigrate to Canada. 'It is our only chance,' he said. 'The case as it stands is maddening. For a successful painter, sculptor, musician, author, who takes society by storm, it is no drawback, it is sometimes even a romantic recommendation, to hail from outcasts and profligates. But for a clergyman of the Church of England! Cornelius, it is fatal! To succeed in the Church, people must believe in you, first of all, as a gentleman, secondly as a man of means, thirdly as a scholar, fourthly as a preacher, fifthly, perhaps, as a Christian – but always first as a gentleman, with all their heart and soul and strength. I would have faced the fact of being a small machinist's son, and have taken my chance, if he'd been in any sense respectable and decent. The essence of Christianity is humility, and by the help of God I would have brazened it out. But this terrible vagabondage and disreputable connection! If he does not accept my terms and leave the country, it will extinguish us and kill me. For how can we live, and relinquish our high aim, and bring down our dear sister Rosa to the level of a gipsy's step-daughter?'

III

There was excitement in the parish of Narrobourne one day. The congregation had just come out from morning service, and the whole conversation was of the new curate, Mr Halborough, who had officiated for the first time, in the absence of the rector.

Never before had the feeling of the villagers approached a level which could be called excitement on such a matter as this. The droning which had been the rule in that quiet old place for a century seemed ended at last. They repeated the text to each other as a refrain: 'O Lord, be Thou my helper!' Not within living memory till to-day had the subject of the sermon formed the topic of conversation from the church door to the churchyard gate, to the exclusion of personal remarks on those who had been present, and on the week's news in general.

The thrilling periods of the preacher hung about their minds all that day. The parish being steeped in indifferentism, it happened that when the youths and maidens, middle-aged and old people, who had attended church that morning, recurred as by a fascination to what Halborough had said, they did so more or less indirectly, and even with the subterfuge of a light laugh that was not real, so great was their shyness under the novelty of their sensations.

What was more curious than that these unconventional villagers should have been excited by a preacher of a new school after forty years of familiarity with the old hand who had had charge of their souls, was the effect of Halborough's address upon the occupants of the manorhouse pew, including the owner of the estate. These thought they knew how to discount the mere sensational sermon, how to minimize flash oratory to its bare proportions; but they had yielded like the rest of the assembly to the charm of the newcomer.

Mr Fellmer, the landowner, was a young widower, whose mother, still in the prime of life, had returned to her old position in the family mansion since the death of her son's wife in the year after her marriage, at the birth of a fragile little girl. From the date of his loss to the present time, Fellmer had led an inactive existence in the seclusion of the parish; a lack of motive seemed to leave him listless. He had gladly reinstated his mother in the gloomy house, and his main occupation now lay in stewarding his estate, which was not large. Mrs Fellmer, who had sat beside him under Halborough this morning, was a cheerful, straight-forward woman, who did her marketing and her alms-giving in person, was fond of old-fashioned flowers, and walked about the village on very wet days visiting the parishioners. These, the only two great ones of Narrobourne, were impressed by Joshua's eloquence as much as the cottagers.

Halborough had been briefly introduced to them on his arrival some days before, and, their interest being kindled, they waited a few moments till he came out of the vestry, to walk down the churchyard-path with him. Mrs Fellmer spoke warmly of the sermon, of the good fortune of the parish in his advent, and hoped he had found comfortable quarters.

Halborough, faintly flushing, said that he had obtained very fair lodgings in the roomy house of a farmer, whom he named.

She feared he would find it very lonely, especially in the evenings, and hoped they would see a good deal of him. When would he dine with them? Could he not come that day – it must be so dull for him the first Sunday evening in country lodgings?

Halborough replied that it would give him much pleasure, but that he feared he must decline. 'I am not altogether alone,' he said. 'My sister, who has just returned from Brussels, and who felt, as you do, that I should be rather dismal by myself, has accompanied me hither to stay a few days till she has put my rooms in order and set me going. She was too fatigued to come to church, and is waiting for me now at the farm.'

'O, but bring your sister – that will be still better! I shall be delighted to know her. How I wish I had been aware! Do tell her, please, that we had no idea of her presence.'

Halborough assured Mrs Fellmer that he would certainly bear the message; but as to her coming he was not so sure. The real truth was, however, that the matter would be decided by him, Rosa having an almost filial respect for his wishes. But he was uncertain as to the state of her wardrobe, and had determined that she should not enter the manor-house at a disadvantage that evening, when there would probably be plenty of opportunities in the future of her doing so becomingly.

He walked to the farm in long strides. This, then, was the outcome of his first morning's work as curate here. Things had gone fairly well with him. He had been ordained; he was in a comfortable parish, where he would exercise almost sole supervision, the rector being infirm. He had made a deep impression at starting, and the absence of a hood seemed to have done him no harm. Moreover, by considerable persuasion and payment, his father and the dark woman had been shipped off to Canada, where they were not likely to interfere greatly with his interests.

Rosa came out to meet him. 'Ah! you should have gone to church like a good girl,' he said.

'Yes – I wished I had afterwards. But I do so hate church as a rule that even your preaching was underestimated in my mind. It was too bad of me!'

The girl who spoke thus playfully was fair, tall, and sylph-like, in a muslin dress, and with just the coquettish *désinvolture* which an English girl brings home from abroad, and loses again after a few months of native life. Joshua was the reverse of playful; the world was too important a concern for him to indulge in light moods. He told her in decided, practical phraseology of the invitation.

'Now, Rosa, we must go – that's settled – if you've a dress that can be made fit to wear all on the hop like this. You didn't, of course, think of bringing an evening dress to such an out-of-the-way place ?'

But Rosa had come from the wrong city to be caught napping in those matters. 'Yes, I did,' said she. 'One never knows what may turn up.'

'Well done! Then off we go at seven.'

The evening drew on, and at dusk they started on foot, Rosa pulling up the edge of her skirt under her cloak out of the way of the dews, so that it formed a great windbag all round her, and carrying her satin shoes under her arm. Joshua would not let her wait till she got indoors before changing them, as she proposed, but insisted on her performing that operation under a tree, so that they might enter as if they had not walked. He was nervously formal about such trifles, while Rosa took the whole proceeding – walk, dressing, dinner, and all – as a pastime. To Joshua it was a serious step in life.

A more unexpected kind of person for a curate's sister was never presented at a dinner. The surprise of Mrs Fellmer was unconcealed. She had looked forward to a Dorcas, or Martha, or Rhoda at the outside, and a shade of misgiving crossed her face. It was possible that, had the young lady accompanied her brother to church, there would have been no dining at Narrobourne House that day.

Not so with the young widower, her son. He resembled a sleeper who had awaked in a summer noon expecting to find it only dawn. He could scarcely help stretching his arms and yawning in their faces, so strong was his sense of being suddenly aroused to an unforeseen thing. When they had sat down to table he at first talked to Rosa somewhat with the air of a ruler in the land; but the woman lurking in the acquaintance soon brought him to his level, and the girl from Brussels saw him looking at her mouth, her hands, her contour, as if he could not quite comprehend how they got created: then he dropped into the more satisfactory stage which discerns no particulars.

He talked but little; she said much. The homeliness of the Fellmers, to her view, though they were regarded with such awe down here, quite disembarrassed her. The squire had become so unpractised, had dropped so far into the shade during the last year or so of his life, that he had almost forgotten what the world contained till this evening reminded him. His mother, after her first moments of doubt, appeared to think that he must be left to his own guidance, and gave her attention to Joshua.

With all his foresight and doggedness of aim, the result of that dinner exceeded Halborough's expectations. In weaving his ambitions he had viewed his sister Rosa as a slight, bright thing to be helped into notice by his abilities; but it now began to dawn upon him that the physical gifts of Nature to her might do more for them both than Nature's intellectual gifts to himself. While he was patiently boring the tunnel Rosa seemed about to fly over the mountain.

He wrote the next day to his brother, now occupying his own old rooms in the theological college, telling him exultingly of the unanticipated *début* of Rosa at the manor-house. The next post brought him a reply of congratulation, dashed with the counteracting intelligence that his father did not like Canada – that his gipsy wife had deserted him, which made him feel so dreary that he thought of returning home.

In his recent satisfaction at his own successes Joshua Halborough had well-nigh forgotten his chronic trouble – latterly screened by distance. But it now returned upon him; he saw more in this brief announcement than his brother seemed to see. It was the cloud no bigger than a man's hand.

IV

The following December, a day or two before Christmas, Mrs Fellmer and her son were walking up and down the broad gravel path which bordered the east front of the house. Till within the last half-hour the morning had been a drizzling one, and they had just emerged for a short turn before luncheon.

'You see, dear mother,' the son was saying, 'it is the peculiarity of my position which makes her appear to me in such a desirable light. When you consider how I have been crippled at starting, how my life has been maimed; that I feel anything like publicity distasteful, that I have no political ambition, and that my chief aim and hope lie in the education of the little thing Annie has left me, you must see how desirable a wife like Miss Halborough would be, to prevent my becoming a mere vegetable.'

'If you adore her, I suppose you must have her!' replied his mother with dry indirectness. 'But you'll find that she will not be content to live on here as you do, giving her whole mind to a young child.'

'That's just where we differ. Her very disqualification, that of being a nobody, as you call it, is her recommendation in my eyes. Her lack of influential connections limits her ambition. From what I know of her, a life in this place is all that she would wish for. She would never care to go outside the park-gates if it were necessary to stay within.'

'Being in love with her, Albert, and meaning to marry her, you invent your practical reasons to make the case respectable. Well, do as you will; I have no authority over you, so why should you consult me? You mean to propose on this very occasion, no doubt. Don't you, now?'

'By no means. I am merely revolving the idea in my mind. If on further acquaintance she turns out to be as good as she has hitherto seemed – well, I shall see. Admit, now, that you like her.'

'I readily admit it. She is very captivating at first sight. But as a step-mother to your child! You seem mighty anxious, Albert, to get rid of me!'

'Not at all. And I am not so reckless as you think. I don't make up my mind in a hurry. But the thought having occurred to me, I mention it to you at once, mother. If you dislike it, say so.'

'I don't say anything. I will try to make the best of it if you are determined. When does she come?'

'To-morrow.'

All this time there were great preparations in train at the curate's, who was now a householder. Rosa, whose two or three weeks' stay on two occasions earlier in the year had so affected the squire, was coming again, and at the same time her younger brother Cornelius, to make up a family party. Rosa, who journeyed from the Midlands, could not arrive till late in the evening, but Cornelius was to get there in the afternoon, Joshua going out to meet him in his walk across the fields from the railway.

Everything being ready in Joshua's modest abode he started on his way, his heart buoyant and thankful, if ever it was in his life. He was of such good report himself that his brother's path into holy orders promised to be unexpectedly easy; and he longed to compare experiences with him, even though there was on hand a more exciting matter still. From his youth he had held that, in old-fashioned country places, the Church conferred social prestige up to a certain point at a cheaper price than any other profession or pursuit; and events seemed to be proving him right.

He had walked about half-an-hour when he saw Cornelius coming along the path; and in a few minutes the two brothers met. The experiences of Cornelius had been less immediately interesting than those of Joshua, but his personal position was satisfactory, and there was nothing to account for the singularly subdued manner that he exhibited, which at first Joshua set down to the fatigue of over-study; and he proceeded to the subject of Rosa's arrival in the evening, and the probable consequences of this her third visit. 'Before next Easter she'll be his wife, my boy,' said Joshua with grave exultation.

Cornelius shook his head. 'She comes too late!' he returned.

'What do you mean?'

'Look here.' He produced the Fountall paper, and placed his finger on a paragraph, which Joshua read. It appeared under the report of Petty Sessions, and was a commonplace case of disorderly conduct, in which a man was sent to prison for seven days for breaking windows in that town.

'Well?' said Joshua.

'It happened during an evening that I was in the street; and the offender is our father.'

'Not – how – I sent him more money on his promising to stay in Canada?'

'He is home, safe enough.' Cornelius in the same gloomy tone gave the remainder of his information. He had witnessed the scene, unobserved of his father, and had heard him say that he was on his way to see his daughter, who was going to marry a rich gentleman. The only good fortune attending the untoward incident was that the millwright's name had been printed as Joshua Alborough.

'Beaten! We are to be beaten on the eve of our expected victory!' said the elder brother. 'How did he guess that Rosa was likely to marry? Good Heaven! Cornelius, you seem doomed to bring bad news always, do you not?'

'I do,' said Cornelius. 'Poor Rosa!'

It was almost in tears, so great was their heart-sickness and shame, that the brothers walked the remainder of the way to Joshua's dwelling. In the evening they set out to meet Rosa, bringing her to the village in a fly; and when she had come into the house, and was sitting down with them, they almost forgot their secret anxiety in contemplating her, who knew nothing about it.

Next day the Fellmers came, and the two or three days after that were a lively time. That the squire was yielding to his impulses – making up his mind – there could be no doubt. On Sunday Cornelius read the service, and Joshua preached. Mrs Fellmer was quite maternal towards Rosa, and it appeared that she had decided to welcome the inevitable with a good grace. The pretty girl was to spend yet another afternoon with the elder lady, superintending some parish treat at the house in observance of Christmas, and afterwards to stay on to dinner, her brothers to fetch her in the evening. They were also invited to dine, but they could not accept owing to an engagement.

The engagement was of a sombre sort. They were going to meet their father, who would that day be released from Fountall Gaol, and try to persuade him to keep away from Narrobourne. Every exertion was to be made to get him back to Canada, to his old home in the Midlands – anywhere, so that he would not impinge disastrously upon their courses, and blast their sister's prospects of the auspicious marriage which was just then hanging in the balance.

As soon as Rosa had been fetched away by her friends at the manorhouse her brothers started on their expedition, without waiting for dinner or tea. Cornelius, to whom the millwright always addressed his letters when he wrote any, drew from his pocket and re-read as he walked the curt note which had led to this journey being undertaken; it was despatched by their father the night before, immediately upon his liberation, and stated that he was setting out for Narrobourne at the moment of writing; that having no money he would be obliged to walk all the way; that he calculated on passing through the intervening town of Ivell about six on the following day, where he should sup at the Castle Inn, and where he hoped they would meet him with a carriage-and-pair, or some other such conveyance, that he might not disgrace them by arriving like a tramp.

'That sounds as if he gave a thought to our position,' said Cornelius.

Joshua knew the satire that lurked in the paternal words, and said nothing. Silence prevailed during the greater part of their journey. The lamps were lighted in Ivell when they entered the streets, and Cornelius, who was quite unknown in this neighbourhood, and who, moreover, was not in clerical attire, decided that he should be the one to call at the Castle Inn. Here, in answer to his inquiry under the darkness of the archway, they told him that such a man as he had described left the house about a quarter of an hour earlier, after making a meal in the kitchen-settle. He was rather the worse for liquor.

'Then,' said Joshua, when Cornelius joined him outside with this intelligence, 'we must have met and passed him! And now that I think of it, we did meet some one who was unsteady in his gait, under the trees on the other side of Hendford Hill, where it was too dark to see him.'

They rapidly retraced their steps; but for a long stretch of the way home could discern nobody. When, however, they had gone about three-quarters of the distance, they became conscious of an irregular footfall in front of them, and could see a whitish figure in the gloom. They followed dubiously. The figure met another wayfarer – the single one that had been encountered upon this lonely road – and they distinctly heard him ask the way to Narrobourne. The stranger replied – what was quite true – that the nearest way was by turning in at the stile by the next bridge, and following the footpath which branched thence across the meadows.

When the brothers reached the stile they also entered the path, but did not overtake the subject of their worry till they had crossed two or three meads, and the lights from Narrobourne manor-house were visible before them through the trees. Their father was no longer walking; he was seated against the wet bank of an adjoining hedge. Observing their forms he shouted, 'I'm going to Narrobourne; who may you be?'

They went up to him, and revealed themselves, reminding him of the plan which he had himself proposed in his note, that they should meet him at Ivell.

'By Jerry, I'd forgot it!' he said. 'Well, what do you want me to do?' His tone was distinctly quarrelsome.

A long conversation followed, which became embittered at the first hint from them that he should not come to the village. The millwright drew a quart bottle from his pocket, and challenged them to drink if they meant friendly and called themselves men. Neither of the two had touched alcohol for years, but for once they thought it best to accept, so as not to needlessly provoke him.

'What's in it?' said Joshua.

'A drop of weak gin-and-water. It won't hurt 'ee. Drink from the bottle.' Joshua did so, and his father pushed up the bottom of the vessel so as to make him swallow a good deal in spite of himself. It went down into his stomach like molten lead.

'Ha, ha, that's right!' said old Halborough. 'But 'twas raw spirit – ha, ha!'

'Why should you take me in so?' said Joshua, losing his self-command, try as he would to keep calm.

'Because you took me in, my lad, in banishing me to that cursed country under pretence that it was for my good. You were a pair of hypocrites to say so. It was done to get rid of me – no more nor less. But, by Jerry, I'm a match for ye now! I'll spoil your souls for preaching. My daughter is going to be married to the squire here. I've heard the news – I saw it in a paper!'

'It is premature—'

'I know it is true; and I'm her father, and I shall give her away, or there'll be a hell of a row, I can assure 'ee! Is that where the gennleman lives?'

Joshua Halborough writhed in impotent despair. Fellmer had not yet positively declared himself, his mother was hardly won round; a scene with their father in the parish would demolish as fair a palace of hopes as was ever builded. The millwright rose. 'If that's where the squire lives I'm going to call. Just arrived from Canady with her fortune – ha, ha! I wish no harm to the gennleman, and the gennleman will wish no harm to me. But I like to take my place in the family, and stand upon my rights, and lower people's pride!'

'You've succeeded already! Where's that woman you took with you—'

'Woman! She was my wife as lawful as the Constitution – a sight more lawful than your mother was till some time after you were born!'

Joshua had for many years before heard whispers that his father had cajoled his mother in their early acquaintance, and had made somewhat tardy amends; but never from his father's lips till now. It was the last stroke, and he could not bear it. He sank back against the hedge. 'It is over!' he said. 'He ruins us all!'

The millwright moved on, waving his stick triumphantly, and the two brothers stood still. They could see his drab figure stalking along the path, and over his head the lights from the conservatory of Narrobourne House, inside which Albert Fellmer might possibly be sitting with Rosa at that moment, holding her hand, and asking her to share his home with him.

The staggering whity-brown form, advancing to put a blot on all this, had been diminishing in the shade; and now suddenly disappeared beside a weir. There was the noise of a flounce in the water.

'He has fallen in!' said Cornelius, starting forward to run for the place at which his father had vanished.

Joshua, awaking from the stupefied reverie into which he had sunk, rushed to the other's side before he had taken ten steps. 'Stop, stop, what are you thinking of?' he whispered hoarsely, grasping Cornelius's arm.

'Pulling him out!'

'Yes, yes – so am I. But – wait a moment—'

'But, Joshua!'

'Her life and happiness, you know – Cornelius – and your reputation and mine – and our chance of rising together, all three—'

He clutched his brother's arm to the bone; and as they stood breathless the splashing and floundering in the weir continued; over it they saw the hopeful lights from the manor-house conservatory winking through the trees as their bare branches waved to and fro. In their pause there had been time to save him twice over.

The floundering and splashing grew weaker, and they could hear gurgling words: 'Help – I'm drownded! Rosie – Rosie!'

'We'll go – we *must* save him. O Joshua!'

'Yes, yes! we must!'

Still they did not move, but waited, holding each other, each thinking the same thought. Weights of lead seemed to be affixed to their feet, which would no longer obey their wills. The mead became silent.

Over it they fancied they could see figures moving in the conservatory. The air up there seemed to emit gentle kisses.

Cornelius started forward at last, and Joshua almost simultaneously. Two or three minutes brought them to the brink of the stream. At first they could see nothing in the water, though it was not so deep nor the night so dark but that their father's light kerseymere coat would have been visible if he had lain at the bottom. Joshua looked this way and that.

'He has drifted into the culvert,' he said.

Below the foot-bridge of the weir the stream suddenly narrowed to half its width, to pass under a barrel arch or culvert constructed for waggons to cross into the middle of the mead in haymaking time. It being at present the season of high water the arch was full to the crown, against which the ripples clucked every now and then. At this point he had just caught sight of a pale object slipping under. In a moment it was gone.

They went to the lower end, but nothing emerged. For a long time they tried at both ends to effect some communication with the interior, but to no purpose.

'We ought to have come sooner!' said the conscience-stricken Cornelius, when they were quite exhausted, and dripping wet.

'I suppose we ought,' replied Joshua heavily. He perceived his father's walking-stick on the bank; hastily picking it up he stuck it into the mud among the sedge. Then they went on.

'Shall we – say anything about this accident?' whispered Cornelius as they approached the door of Joshua's house.

'What's the use? It can do no good. We must wait until he is found.'

They went indoors and changed their clothes; after which they started for the manor-house, reaching it about ten o'clock. Besides their sister there were only three guests; an adjoining landowner and his wife, and the infirm old rector.

Rosa, although she had parted from them so recently, grasped their hands in an ecstatic, brimming, joyful manner, as if she had not seen them for years. 'You look pale,' she said.

The brothers answered that they had had a long walk, and were somewhat tired. Everybody in the room seemed charged full with some sort of interesting knowledge: the squire's neighbour and neighbour's wife looked wisely around; and Fellmer himself played the part of host with a preoccupied bearing which approached fervour. They left at eleven, not accepting the carriage offered, the distance being so short and the roads dry. The squire came rather further into the dark with them than he need have done, and wished Rosa good-night in a mysterious manner, slightly apart from the rest.

When they were walking along Joshua said, with a desperate attempt at joviality, 'Rosa, what's going on?'

'O, I—' she began between a gasp and a bound. 'He—'

'Never mind – if it disturbs you.'

She was so excited that she could not speak connectedly at first, the practised air which she had brought home with her having disappeared. Calming herself she added, 'I am not disturbed, and nothing has happened. Only he said he wanted to ask me *something*, some day; and I said never mind that now. He hasn't asked yet, and is coming to speak to you about it. He would have done so to-night, only I asked him not to be in a hurry. But he will come to-morrow, I am sure!'

V

It was summer-time, six months later, and mowers and haymakers were at work in the meads. The manor-house, being opposite them, frequently formed a peg for conversation during these operations; and the doings of the squire, and the squire's young wife, the curate's sister – who was at present the admired of most of them, and the interest of all – met with their due amount of criticism.

Rosa was happy, if ever woman could be said to be so. She had not learnt the fate of her father, and sometimes wondered – perhaps with a sense of relief – why he did not write to her from his supposed home in Canada. Her brother Joshua had been presented to a living in a small town, shortly after her marriage, and Cornelius had thereupon succeeded to the vacant curacy of Narrobourne.

These two had awaited in deep suspense the discovery of their father's body; and yet the discovery had not been made. Every day they expected a man or a boy to run up from the meads with the intelligence; but he had never come. Days had accumulated to weeks and months; the wedding had come and gone: Joshua had tolled and read himself in at his new parish; and never a shout of amazement over the millwright's remains.

But now, in June, when they were mowing the meads, the hatches had to be drawn and the water let out of its channels for the convenience of the mowers. It was thus that the discovery was made. A man, stooping low with his scythe, caught a view of the culvert lengthwise, and saw something entangled in the recently bared weeds of its bed. A day or two after there was an inquest; but the body was unrecognizable. Fish and flood had been busy with the millwright; he had no watch or marked article which could be identified; and a verdict of the accidental drowning of a person unknown settled the matter.

As the body was found in Narrobourne parish, there it had to be buried. Cornelius wrote to Joshua, begging him to come and read the service, or to send some one; he himself could not do it. Rather than let in a stranger Joshua came, and silently scanned the coroner's order handed him by the undertaker: –

'I, Henry Giles, Coroner for the Mid-Division of Outer Wessex, do hereby order the Burial of the Body now shown to the Inquest Jury as the Body of an Adult Male Person Unknown . . .,' etc.

Joshua Halborough got through the service in some way, and rejoined his brother Cornelius at his house. Neither accepted an invitation to lunch at their sister's; they wished to discuss parish matters together. In the afternoon she came down, though they had already called on her, and had not expected to see her again. Her bright eyes, brown hair, flowery bonnet, lemon-coloured gloves, and flush beauty, were like an irradiation into the apartment, which they in their gloom could hardly bear.

'I forgot to tell you,' she said, 'of a curious thing which happened to me a month or two before my marriage – something which I have thought may have had a connection with the accident to the poor man you have buried to-day. It was on that evening I was at the manor-house waiting for you to fetch me; I was in the winter-garden with Albert, and we were silent together, when we fancied we heard a cry in the distant meadow. We opened the door, and while Albert ran to fetch his hat, leaving me standing there, the cry was repeated, and my excited senses made me think I heard my own name. When Albert came back all was silent, and we decided that it was only a drunken shout, and not a cry for help. We both forgot the incident, and it never has occurred to me till since the funeral to-day that it might have been this stranger's cry. The name of course was only fancy, or he might have had a wife or child with a name something like mine, poor man!'

When she was gone the brothers were silent till Cornelius said, 'Now mark this, Joshua. Sooner or later she'll know.'

'How?'

'From one of us. Do you think human hearts are iron-cased safes, that you suppose we can keep this secret for ever?'

'Yes, I think they are, sometimes,' said Joshua.

'No. It will out. We shall tell.'

'What, and ruin her – kill her? Disgrace her children, and pull down the whole auspicious house of Fellmer about our ears? No! May I – drown where he was drowned before I do it! Never, never. Surely you can say the same, Cornelius!'

Cornelius seemed fortified, and no more was said. For a long time after that day he did not see Joshua, and before the next year was out a son and heir was born to the Fellmers. The villagers rang the three bells every evening for a week and more, and were made merry by Mr Fellmer's ale; and when the christening came on Joshua paid Narrobourne another visit.

Among all the people who assembled on that day the brother clergymen were the least interested. Their minds were haunted by a spirit in kerseymere. In the evening they walked together in the fields.

'She's all right,' said Joshua. 'But here are you doing journey-work, Cornelius, and likely to continue at it till the end of the day, as far as I can see. I, too, with my petty living – what am I after all? . . . To tell the truth, the Church is a poor forlorn hope for people without influence, particularly when their enthusiasm begins to flag. A social regenerator has a better chance outside, where he is unhampered by dogma and tradition. As for me, I would rather have gone on mending mills, with my crust of bread and liberty.'

Almost automatically they had bent their steps along the margin of the river; they now paused. They were standing on the brink of the well-known weir. There were the hatches, there was the culvert; they could see the pebbly bed of the stream through the pellucid water. The notes of the church-bells were audible, still jangled by the enthusiastic villagers.

'Why, see – it was there I hid his walking-stick!' said Joshua, looking towards the sedge. The next moment, during a passing breeze, something flashed white on the spot to which the attention of Cornelius was drawn.

From the sedge rose a straight little silver-poplar, and it was the leaves of this sapling which caused the flicker of whiteness.

'His walking-stick has grown!' Joshua added. 'It was a rough one – cut from the hedge, I remember.'

At every puff of wind the tree turned white, till they could not bear to look at it; and they walked away.

'I see him every night,' Cornelius murmured. . . . 'Ah, we read our *Hebrews* to little account, Jos! Ὑπέμεινε σταυρὸν, αἰσχύνης καταφρονήσας. To have *endured* the cross, *despising* the shame – there lay greatness! But now I often feel that I should like to put an end to trouble here in this selfsame spot.'

'I have thought of it myself,' said Joshua.

'Perhaps we shall, some day,' murmured his brother.

'Perhaps,' said Joshua moodily.

With that contingency to consider in the silence of their nights and days they bent their steps homewards.

December 1888

On the Western Circuit

I

THE man who played the disturbing part in the two quiet feminine lives hereunder depicted – no great man, in any sense, by the way – first had knowledge of them on an October evening, in the city of Melchester. He had been standing in the Close, vainly endeavouring to gain amid the darkness a glimpse of the most homogeneous pile of mediæval architecture in England, which towered and tapered from the damp and level sward in front of him. While he stood the presence of the Cathedral walls was revealed rather by the ear than by the eyes; he could not see them, but they reflected sharply a roar of sound which entered the Close by a street leading from the city square, and, falling upon the building, was flung back upon him.

He postponed till the morrow his attempt to examine the deserted edifice, and turned his attention to the noise. It was compounded of steam barrel-organs, the clanging of gongs, the ringing of hand-bells, the clack of rattles, and the undistinguishable shouts of men. A lurid light hung in the air in the direction of the tumult. Thitherward he went, passing under the arched gateway, along a straight street, and into the square.

He might have searched Europe over for a greater contrast between juxtaposed scenes. The spectacle was that of the eighth chasm of the Inferno as to colour and flame, and, as to mirth, a development of the Homeric heaven. A smoky glare, of the complexion of brass-filings, ascended from the fiery tongues of innumerable naphtha lamps affixed to booths, stalls, and other temporary erections which crowded the spacious market-square. In front of this irradiation scores of human figures, more or less in profile, were darting athwart and across, up, down, and around, like gnats against a sunset.

Their motions were so rhythmical that they seemed to be moved by machinery. And it presently appeared that they were moved by machinery indeed; the figures being those of the patrons of swings, see-saws, flying-leaps, above all of the three steam roundabouts which occupied the centre of the position. It was from the latter that the din of steam-organs came.

Throbbing humanity in full light was, on second thoughts, better than architecture in the dark. The young man, lighting a short pipe, and putting his hat on one side and one hand in his pocket, to throw himself into harmony with his new environment, drew near to the largest and most patronized of the steam circuses, as the roundabouts were called by their owners. This was one of brilliant finish, and it was now in full revolution. The musical instrument around which and to whose tones the riders revolved, directed its trumpet-mouths of brass upon the young man, and the long plate-glass mirrors set at angles, which revolved with the machine, flashed the gyrating personages and hobby-horses kaleidoscopically into his eyes.

It could now be seen that he was unlike the majority of the crowd. A gentlemanly young fellow, one of the species found in large towns only, and London particularly, built on delicate lines, well, though not fashionably dressed, he appeared to belong to the professional class; he had nothing square or practical about his look, much that was curvilinear and sensuous. Indeed, some would have called him a man not altogether typical of the middle-class male of a century wherein sordid ambition is the master-passion that seems to be taking the time-honoured place of love.

The revolving figures passed before his eyes with an unexpected and quiet grace in a throng whose natural movements did not suggest gracefulness or quietude as a rule. By some contrivance there was imparted to each of the hobby-horses a motion which was really the triumph and perfection of roundabout inventiveness – a galloping rise and fall, so timed that, of each pair of steeds, one was on the spring while the other was on the pitch. The riders were quite fascinated by these equine undulations in this most delightful holiday-game of our times. There were riders as young as six, and as old as sixty years, with every age between. At first it was difficult to catch a personality, but by and by the observer's eyes centred on the prettiest girl out of the several pretty ones revolving.

It was not that one with the light frock and light hat whom he had been at first attracted by; no, it was the one with the black cape, gray skirt, light gloves and – no, not even she, but the one behind her; she with the crimson skirt, dark jacket, brown hat and brown gloves. Unmistakably that was the prettiest girl.

Having finally selected her, this idle spectator studied her as well as he was able during each of her brief transits across his visual field. She was absolutely unconscious of everything save the act of riding: her features were rapt in an ecstatic dreaminess; for the moment she did not know her age or her history or her lineaments, much less her troubles. He himself was full of vague latter-day glooms and popular melancholies, and it was a refreshing sensation to behold this young thing then and there, absolutely as happy as if she were in a Paradise.

Dreading the moment when the inexorable stoker, grimily lurking behind the glittering rococo-work, should decide that this set of riders had had their pennyworth, and bring the whole concern of steam-engine, horses, mirrors, trumpets, drums, cymbals, and such-like to pause and silence, he waited for her every reappearance, glancing indifferently over the intervening forms, including the two plainer girls, the old woman and child, the two youngsters, the newly-married couple, the old man with a clay pipe, the sparkish youth with a ring, the young ladies in the chariot, the pair of journeyman-carpenters, and others, till his select country beauty followed on again in her place. He had never seen a fairer product of nature, and at each round she made a deeper mark in his sentiments. The stoppage then came, and the sighs of the riders were audible.

He moved round to the place at which he reckoned she would alight; but she retained her seat. The empty saddles began to refill, and she plainly was deciding to have another turn. The young man drew up to the side of her steed, and pleasantly asked her if she had enjoyed her ride.

'O yes!' she said, with dancing eyes. 'It has been quite unlike anything I have ever felt in my life before!'

It was not difficult to fall into conversation with her. Unreserved – too unreserved – by nature, she was not experienced enough to be reserved by art, and after a little coaxing she answered his remarks readily. She had come to live in Melchester from a village on the Great Plain, and this was the first time that she had ever seen a steam-circus; she could not understand how such wonderful machines were made. She had come to the city on the invitation of Mrs Harnham, who had taken her into her household to train her as a servant, if she showed any aptitude.

Mrs Harnham was a young lady who before she married had been Miss
Edith White, living in the country near the speaker's cottage; she was
now very kind to her through knowing her in childhood so well. She
was even taking the trouble to educate her. Mrs Harnham was the only
friend she had in the world, and being without children had wished to
have her near her in preference to anybody else, though she had only
lately come; allowed her to do almost as she liked, and to have a holiday
whenever she asked for it. The husband of this kind young lady was a
rich wine-merchant of the town, but Mrs Harnham did not care much
about him. In the daytime you could see the house from where they
were talking. She, the speaker, liked Melchester better than the lonely
country, and she was going to have a new hat for next Sunday that was
to cost fifteen and ninepence.

Then she inquired of her acquaintance where he lived, and he told
her in London, that ancient and smoky city, where everybody lived who
lived at all, and died because they could not live there. He came into
Wessex two or three times a year for professional reasons; he had arrived
from Wintoncester yesterday, and was going on into the next county in
a day or two. For one thing he did like the country better than the town,
and it was because it contained such girls as herself.

Then the pleasure-machine started again, and, to the light-hearted
girl, the figure of the handsome young man, the market-square with its
lights and crowd, the houses beyond, and the world at large, began
moving round as before, countermoving in the revolving mirrors on her
right hand, she being as it were the fixed point in an undulating,
dazzling, lurid universe, in which loomed forward most prominently of
all the form of her late interlocutor. Each time that she approached the
half of her orbit that lay nearest him they gazed at each other with smiles,
and with that unmistakable expression which means so little at the
moment, yet so often leads up to passion, heartache, union, disunion,
devotion, overpopulation, drudgery, content, resignation, despair.

When the horses slowed anew he stepped to her side and proposed
another heat. 'Hang the expense for once,' he said. 'I'll pay!'

She laughed till the tears came.

'Why do you laugh, dear?' said he.

'Because – you are so genteel that you must have plenty of money,
and only say that for fun!' she returned.

'Ha-ha!' laughed the young man in unison, and gallantly producing
his money she was enabled to whirl on again.

As he stood smiling there in the motley crowd, with his pipe in his hand, and clad in the rough pea-jacket and wideawake that he had put on for his stroll, who would have supposed him to be Charles Bradford Raye, Esquire, stuff-gownsman, educated at Wintoncester, called to the Bar at Lincoln's Inn, now going the Western Circuit, merely detained in Melchester by a small arbitration after his brethren had moved on to the next county-town?

II

The square was overlooked from its remoter corner by the house of which the young girl had spoken, a dignified residence of considerable size, having several windows on each floor. Inside one of these, on the first floor, the apartment being a large drawing-room, sat a lady, in appearance from twenty-eight to thirty years of age. The blinds were still undrawn, and the lady was absently surveying the weird scene without, her cheek resting on her hand. The room was unlit from within, but enough of the glare from the market-place entered it to reveal the lady's face. She was what is called an interesting creature rather than a handsome woman; dark-eyed, thoughtful, and with sensitive lips.

A man sauntered into the room from behind and came forward.

'O, Edith, I didn't see you,' he said. 'Why are you sitting here in the dark?'

'I am looking at the fair,' replied the lady in a languid voice.

'Oh? Horrid nuisance every year! I wish it could be put a stop to.'

'I like it.'

'H'm. There's no accounting for taste.'

For a moment he gazed from the window with her, for politeness' sake, and then went out again.

In a few minutes she rang.

'Hasn't Anna come in?' asked Mrs Harnham.

'No, m'm.'

'She ought to be in by this time. I meant her to go for ten minutes only.'

'Shall I go and look for her, m'm?' said the housemaid alertly.

'No. It is not necessary: she is a good girl and will come soon.'

However, when the servant had gone Mrs Harnham arose, went up to her room, cloaked and bonneted herself, and proceeded downstairs, where she found her husband.

'I want to see the fair,' she said; 'and I am going to look for Anna. I have made myself responsible for her, and must see she comes to no harm. She ought to be indoors. Will you come with me?'

'Oh, she's all right. I saw her on one of those whirligig things, talking to her young man as I came in. But I'll go if you wish, though I'd rather go a hundred miles the other way.'

'Then please do so. I shall come to no harm alone.'

She left the house and entered the crowd which thronged the market-place, where she soon discovered Anna, seated on the revolving horse. As soon as it stopped Mrs Harnham advanced and said severely, 'Anna, how can you be such a wild girl? You were only to be out for ten minutes.'

Anna looked blank, and the young man, who had dropped into the background, came to help her alight.

'Please don't blame her,' he said politely. 'It is my fault that she has stayed. She looked so graceful on the horse that I induced her to go round again. I assure you that she has been quite safe.'

'In that case I'll leave her in your hands,' said Mrs Harnham, turning to retrace her steps.

But this for the moment it was not so easy to do. Something had attracted the crowd to a spot in their rear, and the wine-merchant's wife, caught by its sway, found herself pressed against Anna's acquaintance without power to move away. Their faces were within a few inches of each other, his breath fanned her cheek as well as Anna's. They could do no other than smile at the accident; but neither spoke, and each waited passively. Mrs Harnham then felt a man's hand clasping her fingers, and from the look of consciousness on the young fellow's face she knew the hand to be his: she also knew that from the position of the girl he had no other thought than that the imprisoned hand was Anna's. What prompted her to refrain from undeceiving him she could hardly tell. Not content with holding the hand, he playfully slipped two of his fingers inside her glove, against her palm. Thus matters continued till the pressure lessened; but several minutes passed before the crowd thinned sufficiently to allow Mrs Harnham to withdraw.

'How did they get to know each other, I wonder?' she mused as she retreated. 'Anna is really very forward – and he very wicked and nice.'

She was so gently stirred with the stranger's manner and voice, with the tenderness of his idle touch, that instead of re-entering the house she turned back again and observed the pair from a screened nook.

Really she argued (being little less impulsive than Anna herself) it was very excusable in Anna to encourage him, however she might have contrived to make his acquaintance; he was so gentlemanly, so fascinating, had such beautiful eyes. The thought that he was several years her junior produced a reasonless sigh.

At length the couple turned from the roundabout towards the door of Mrs Harnham's house, and the young man could be heard saying that he would accompany her home. Anna, then, had found a lover, apparently a very devoted one. Mrs Harnham was quite interested in him. When they drew near the door of the wine-merchant's house, a comparatively deserted spot by this time, they stood invisible for a little while in the shadow of a wall, where they separated, Anna going on to the entrance, and her acquaintance returning across the square.

'Anna,' said Mrs Harnham, coming up. 'I've been looking at you! That young man kissed you at parting, I am almost sure.'

'Well,' stammered Anna; 'he said, if I didn't mind – it would do me no harm, and – and – him a great deal of good!'

'Ah, I thought so! And he was a stranger till tonight?'

'Yes, ma'am.'

'Yet I warrant you told him your name and everything about yourself?'

'He asked me.'

'But he didn't tell you his?'

'Yes, ma'am, he did!' cried Anna victoriously. 'It is Charles Bradford, of London.'

'Well, if he's respectable, of course I've nothing to say against your knowing him,' remarked her mistress, prepossessed, in spite of general principles, in the young man's favour. 'But I must reconsider all that, if he attempts to renew your acquaintance. A country-bred girl like you, who has never lived in Melchester till this month, who had hardly ever seen a black-coated man till you came here, to be so sharp as to capture a young Londoner like him!'

'I didn't capture him. I didn't do anything,' said Anna, in confusion.

When she was indoors and alone Mrs Harnham thought what a well-bred and chivalrous young man Anna's companion had seemed. There had been a magic in his wooing touch of her hand; and she wondered how he had come to be attracted by the girl.

The next morning the emotional Edith Harnham went to the usual week-day service in Melchester cathedral. In crossing the Close through the fog she again perceived him who had interested her the previous evening, gazing up thoughtfully at the high-piled architecture of the nave: and as soon as she had taken her seat he entered and sat down in a stall opposite hers.

He did not particularly heed her; but Mrs Harnham was continually occupying her eyes with him, and wondered more than ever what had attracted him in her unfledged maid-servant. The mistress was almost as unaccustomed as the maiden herself to the end-of-the-age young man, or she might have wondered less. Raye, having looked about him a while, left abruptly, without regard to the service that was proceeding; and Mrs Harnham – lonely, impressionable creature that she was – took no further interest in praising the Lord. She wished she had married a London man who knew the subtleties of love-making as they were evidently known to him who had mistakenly caressed her hand.

III

The calendar at Melchester had been light, occupying the court only a few hours; and the assizes at Casterbridge, the next county-town on the Western Circuit, having no business for Raye, he had not gone thither. At the next town after that they did not open till the following Monday, trials to begin on Tuesday morning. In the natural order of things Raye would have arrived at the latter place on Monday afternoon; but it was not till the middle of Wednesday that his gown and gray wig, curled in tiers, in the best fashion of Assyrian bas-reliefs, were seen blowing and bobbing behind him as he hastily walked up the High Street from his lodgings. But though he entered the assize building there was nothing for him to do, and sitting at the blue baize table in the well of the court, he mended pens with a mind far away from the case in progress. Thoughts of unpremeditated conduct, of which a week earlier he would not have believed himself capable, threw him into a mood of dissatisfied depression.

He had contrived to see again the pretty rural maiden Anna, the day after the fair, had walked out of the city with her to the earthworks of Old Melchester, and feeling a violent fancy for her, had remained in Melchester all Sunday, Monday, and Tuesday; by persuasion obtaining walks and meetings with the girl six or seven times during the interval; had in brief won her, body and soul.

He supposed it must have been owing to the seclusion in which he had lived of late in town that he had given way so unrestrainedly to a passion for an artless creature whose inexperience had, from the first, led her to place herself unreservedly in his hands. Much he deplored trifling with her feelings for the sake of a passing desire; and he could only hope that she might not live to suffer on his account.

She had begged him to come to her again; entreated him; wept. He had promised that he would do so, and he meant to carry out that promise. He could not desert her now. Awkward as such unintentional connections were, the interspace of a hundred miles – which to a girl of her limited capabilities was like a thousand – would effectually hinder this summer fancy from greatly encumbering his life; while thought of her simple love might do him the negative good of keeping him from idle pleasures in town when he wished to work hard. His circuit journeys would take him to Melchester three or four times a year; and then he could always see her.

The pseudonym, or rather partial name, that he had given her as his before knowing how far the acquaintance was going to carry him, had been spoken on the spur of the moment, without any ulterior intention whatever. He had not afterwards disturbed Anna's error, but on leaving her he had felt bound to give her an address at a stationer's not far from his chambers, at which she might write to him under the initials 'C.B.'

In due time Raye returned to his London abode, having called at Melchester on his way and spent a few additional hours with his fascinating child of nature. In town he lived monotonously every day. Often he and his rooms were enclosed by a tawny fog from all the world besides, and when he lighted the gas to read or write by, his situation seemed so unnatural that he would look into the fire and think of that trusting girl at Melchester again and again. Often, oppressed by absurd fondness for her, he would enter the dim religious nave of the Law Courts by the north door, elbow other juniors habited like himself, and like him unretained; edge himself into this or that crowded court where a sensational case was going on, just as if he were in it, though the police officers at the door knew as well as he knew himself that he had no more concern with the business in hand than the patient idlers at the gallery-door outside, who had waited to enter since eight in the morning because, like him, they belonged to the classes that live on expectation. But he would do these things to no purpose, and think how greatly the characters in such scenes contrasted with the pink and breezy Anna.

An unexpected feature in that peasant maiden's conduct was that she had not as yet written to him, though he had told her she might do so if she wished. Surely a young creature had never before been so reticent in such circumstances. At length he sent her a brief line, positively requesting her to write. There was no answer by the return post, but the day after a letter in a neat feminine hand, and bearing the Melchester post-mark, was handed to him by the stationer.

The fact alone of its arrival was sufficient to satisfy his imaginative sentiment. He was not anxious to open the epistle, and in truth did not begin to read it for nearly half-an-hour, anticipating readily its terms of passionate retrospect and tender adjuration. When at last he turned his feet to the fireplace and unfolded the sheet, he was surprised and pleased to find that neither extravagance nor vulgarity was there. It was the most charming little missive he had ever received from woman. To be sure the language was simple and the ideas were slight; but it was so self-possessed; so purely that of a young girl who felt her womanhood to be enough for her dignity that he read it through twice. Four sides were filled, and a few lines written across, after the fashion of former days; the paper, too, was common, and not of the latest shade and surface. But what of those things ? He had received letters from women who were fairly called ladies, but never so sensible, so human a letter as this. He could not single out any one sentence and say it was at all remarkable or clever; the *ensemble* of the letter it was which won him; and beyond the one request that he would write or come to her again soon there was nothing to show her sense of a claim upon him.

To write again and develop a correspondence was the last thing Raye would have preconceived as his conduct in such a situation; yet he did send a short, encouraging line or two, signed with his pseudonym, in which he asked for another letter, and cheeringly promised that he would try to see her again on some near day, and would never forget how much they had been to each other during their short acquaintance.

IV

To return now to the moment at which Anna, at Melchester, had received Raye's letter.

It had been put into her own hand by the postman on his morning rounds. She flushed down to her neck on receipt of it, and turned it over and over. 'It is mine?' she said.

'Why, yes, can't you see it is?' said the postman, smiling as he guessed the nature of the document and the cause of the confusion.

'O yes, of course!' replied Anna, looking at the letter, forcedly tittering, and blushing still more.

Her look of embarrassment did not leave her with the postman's departure. She opened the envelope, kissed its contents, put away the letter in her pocket, and remained musing till her eyes filled with tears.

A few minutes later she carried up a cup of tea to Mrs Harnham in her bed-chamber. Anna's mistress looked at her, and said: 'How dismal you seem this morning, Anna. What's the matter?'

'I'm not dismal. I'm glad; only I—' She stopped to stifle a sob.

'Well?'

'I've got a letter – and what good is it to me, if I can't read a word in it!'

'Why, I'll read it, child, if necessary.'

'But this is from somebody – I don't want anybody to read it but myself!' Anna murmured.

'I shall not tell anybody. Is it from that young man?'

'I think so.' Anna slowly produced the letter, saying: 'Then will you read it to me, ma'am?'

This was the secret of Anna's embarrassment and flutterings. She could neither read nor write. She had grown up under the care of an aunt by marriage, at one of the lonely hamlets on the Great Mid-Wessex Plain where, even in days of national education, there had been no school within a distance of two miles. Her aunt was an ignorant woman; there had been nobody to investigate Anna's circumstances, nobody to care about her learning the rudiments; though, as often in such cases, she had been well fed and clothed and not unkindly treated. Since she had come to live at Melchester with Mrs Harnham, the latter, who took a kindly interest in the girl, had taught her to speak correctly, in which accomplishment Anna showed considerable readiness, as is not unusual with the illiterate; and soon became quite fluent in the use of her mistress's phraseology. Mrs Harnham also insisted upon her getting a spelling and copy book, and beginning to practise in these. Anna was slower in this branch of her education, and meanwhile here was the letter.

Edith Harnham's large dark eyes expressed some interest in the contents, though, in her character of mere interpreter, she threw into her tone as much as she could of mechanical passiveness. She read the short epistle on to its concluding sentence, which idly requested Anna to send him a tender answer.

'Now – you'll do it for me, won't you, dear mistress?' said Anna eagerly. 'And you'll do it as well as ever you can, please? Because I couldn't bear him to think I am not able to do it myself. I should sink into the earth with shame if he knew that!'

From some words in the letter Mrs Harnham was led to ask questions, and the answers she received confirmed her suspicions. Deep concern filled Edith's heart at perceiving how the girl had committed her happiness to the issue of this new-sprung attachment. She blamed herself for not interfering in a flirtation which had resulted so seriously for the poor little creature in her charge; though at the time of seeing the pair together she had a feeling that it was hardly within her province to nip young affection in the bud. However, what was done could not be undone, and it behoved her now, as Anna's only protector, to help her as much as she could. To Anna's eager request that she, Mrs Harnham, should compose and write the answer to this young London man's letter, she felt bound to accede, to keep alive his attachment to the girl if possible; though in other circumstances she might have suggested the cook as an amanuensis.

A tender reply was thereupon concocted, and set down in Edith Harnham's hand. This letter it had been which Raye had received and delighted in. Written in the presence of Anna it certainly was, and on Anna's humble note-paper, and in a measure indited by the young girl; but the life, the spirit, the individuality, were Edith Harnham's.

'Won't you at least put your name yourself?' she said. 'You can manage to write that by this time?'

'No, no,' said Anna, shrinking back. 'I should do it so bad. He'd be ashamed of me, and never see me again!'

The note, so prettily requesting another from him, had, as we have seen, power enough in its pages to bring one. He declared it to be such a pleasure to hear from her that she must write every week. The same process of manufacture was accordingly repeated by Anna and her mistress, and continued for several weeks in succession; each letter being penned and suggested by Edith, the girl standing by; the answer read and commented on by Edith, Anna standing by and listening again.

Late on a winter evening, after the dispatch of the sixth letter, Mrs

Harnham was sitting alone by the remains of her fire. Her husband had retired to bed, and she had fallen into that fixity of musing which takes no count of hour or temperature. The state of mind had been brought about in Edith by a strange thing which she had done that day. For the first time since Raye's visit Anna had gone to stay over a night or two with her cottage friends on the Plain, and in her absence had arrived, out of its time, a letter from Raye. To this Edith had replied on her own responsibility, from the depths of her own heart, without waiting for her maid's collaboration. The luxury of writing to him what would be known to no consciousness but his was great, and she had indulged herself therein.

Why was it a luxury?

Edith Harnham led a lonely life. Influenced by the belief of the British parent that a bad marriage with its aversions is better than free woman-hood with its interests, dignity, and leisure, she had consented to marry the elderly wine-merchant as a *pis aller*, at the age of seven-and-twenty – some three years before this date – to find afterwards that she had made a mistake. That contract had left her still a woman whose deeper nature had never been stirred.

She was now clearly realizing that she had become possessed to the bottom of her soul with the image of a man to whom she was hardly so much as a name. From the first he had attracted her by his looks and voice; by his tender touch; and, with these as generators, the writing of letter after letter and the reading of their soft answers had insensibly developed on her side an emotion which fanned his; till there had resulted a magnetic reciprocity between the correspondents, notwith-standing that one of them wrote in a character not her own. That he had been able to seduce another woman in two days was his crowning though unrecognized fascination for her as the she-animal.

They were her own impassioned and pent-up ideas – lowered to monosyllabic phraseology in order to keep up the disguise – that Edith put into letters signed with another name, much to the shallow Anna's delight, who, unassisted, could not for the world have conceived such pretty fancies for winning him, even had she been able to write them. Edith found that it was these, her own foisted-in sentiments, to which the young barrister mainly responded. The few sentences occasionally added from Anna's own lips made apparently no impression upon him.

The letter-writing in her absence Anna never discovered; but on her return the next morning she declared she wished to see her lover about something at once, and begged Mrs Harnham to ask him to come.

There was a strange anxiety in her manner which did not escape Mrs Harnham, and ultimately resolved itself into a flood of tears. Sinking down at Edith's knees, she made confession that the result of her relations with her lover it would soon become necessary to disclose.

Edith Harnham was generous enough to be very far from inclined to cast Anna adrift at this conjuncture. No true woman ever is so inclined from her own personal point of view, however prompt she may be in taking such steps to safeguard those dear to her. Although she had written to Raye so short a time previously, she instantly penned another Anna-note hinting clearly though delicately the state of affairs.

Raye replied by a hasty line to say how much he was concerned at her news: he felt that he must run down to see her almost immediately.

But a week later the girl came to her mistress's room with another note, which on being read informed her that after all he could not find time for the journey. Anna was broken with grief; but by Mrs Harnham's counsel strictly refrained from hurling at him the reproaches and bitterness customary from young women so situated. One thing was imperative: to keep the young man's romantic interest in her alive. Rather therefore did Edith, in the name of her *protégée*, request him on no account to be distressed about the looming event, and not to inconvenience himself to hasten down. She desired above everything to be no weight upon him in his career, no clog upon his high activities. She had wished him to know what had befallen: he was to dismiss it again from his mind. Only he must write tenderly as ever, and when he should come again on the spring circuit it would be soon enough to discuss what had better be done.

It may well be supposed that Anna's own feelings had not been quite in accord with these generous expressions; but the mistress's judgment had ruled, and Anna had acquiesced. 'All I want is that *niceness* you can so well put into your letters, my dear, dear mistress, and that I can't for the life o' me make up out of my own head; though I mean the same thing and feel it exactly when you've written it down!'

When the letter had been sent off, and Edith Harnham was left alone, she bowed herself on the back of her chair and wept.

'I wish his child was mine – I wish it was!' she murmured. 'Yet how can I say such a wicked thing!'

V

The letter moved Raye considerably when it reached him. The intelligence itself had affected him less than her unexpected manner of treating him in relation to it. The absence of any word of reproach, the devotion to his interests, the self-sacrifice apparent in every line, all made up a nobility of character that he had never dreamt of finding in womankind.

'God forgive me!' he said tremulously. 'I have been a wicked wretch. I did not know she was such a treasure as this!'

He reassured her instantly – declaring that he would not of course desert her, that he would provide a home for her somewhere. Meanwhile she was to stay where she was as long as her mistress would allow her.

But a misfortune supervened in this direction. Whether an inkling of Anna's circumstances reached the knowledge of Mrs Harnham's husband or not cannot be said, but the girl was compelled, in spite of Edith's entreaties, to leave the house. By her own choice she decided to go back for a while to the cottage on the Plain. This arrangement led to a consultation as to how the correspondence should be carried on; and in the girl's inability to continue personally what had been begun in her name, and in the difficulty of their acting in concert as heretofore, she requested Mrs Harnham – the only well-to-do friend she had in the world – to receive the letters and reply to them off-hand, sending them on afterwards to herself on the Plain, where she might at least get some neighbour to read them to her, if a trustworthy one could be met with. Anna and her box then departed for the Plain.

Thus it befell that Edith Harnham found herself in the strange position of having to correspond, under no supervision by the real woman, with a man not her husband, in terms which were virtually those of a wife, concerning a corporeal condition that was not Edith's at all; the man being one for whom, mainly through the sympathies involved in playing this part, she secretly cherished a predilection, subtle and imaginative truly, but strong and absorbing. She opened each letter, read it as if intended for herself, and replied from the promptings of her own heart and no other.

Throughout this correspondence, carried on in the girl's absence, the high-strung Edith Harnham lived in the ecstasy of fancy; the vicarious intimacy engendered such a flow of passionateness as was never exceeded.

For conscience' sake Edith at first sent on each of his letters to Anna, and even rough copies of her replies; but later on these so-called copies were much abridged, and many letters on both sides were not sent on at all.

Though sensuous, and, superficially at least, infested with the self-indulgent vices of artificial society, there was a substratum of honesty and fairness in Raye's character. He had really a tender regard for the country girl, and it grew more tender than ever when he found her apparently capable of expressing the deepest sensibilities in the simplest words. He meditated, he wavered, and finally resolved to consult his sister, a maiden lady much older than himself, of lively sympathies and good intent. In making this confidence he showed her some of the letters.

'She seems fairly educated,' Miss Raye observed. 'And bright in ideas. She expresses herself with a taste that must be innate.'

'Yes. She writes very prettily, doesn't she, thanks to these elementary schools?'

'One is drawn out towards her, in spite of one's self, poor thing.'

The upshot of the discussion was that though he had not been directly advised to do it, Raye wrote, in his real name, what he would never have decided to write on his own responsibility; namely, that he could not live without her, and would come down in the spring and shelve her looming difficulty by marrying her.

This bold acceptance of the situation was made known to Anna by Mrs Harnham driving out immediately to the cottage on the Plain. Anna jumped for joy like a little child. And poor, crude directions for answering appropriately were given to Edith Harnham, who on her return to the city carried them out with warm intensifications.

'O!' she groaned, as she threw down the pen. 'Anna – poor good little fool – hasn't intelligence enough to appreciate him! How should she? While I – don't bear his child!'

It was now February. The correspondence had continued altogether for four months, and the next letter from Raye contained incidentally a statement of his position and prospects. He said that in offering to wed her he had, at first, contemplated the step of retiring from a profession which hitherto had brought him very slight emolument, and which, to speak plainly, he had thought might be difficult of practice after his union with her. But the unexpected mines of brightness and warmth that her letters had disclosed to be lurking in her sweet nature had led him to abandon that somewhat sad prospect. He felt sure that, with her powers of development, after a little private training in the social forms of London under his supervision, and a little help from a governess if necessary, she would make as good a professional man's wife as could be desired, even if he should rise to the woolsack. Many a Lord Chancellor's wife had been less intuitively a lady than she had shown herself to be in her lines to him.

'O – poor fellow, poor fellow!' mourned Edith Harnham.

Her distress now raged as high as her infatuation. It was she who had wrought him to this pitch – to a marriage which meant his ruin; yet she could not, in mercy to her maid, do anything to hinder his plan. Anna was coming to Melchester that week, but she could hardly show the girl this last reply from the young man; it told too much of the second individuality that had usurped the place of the first.

Anna came, and her mistress took her into her own room for privacy. Anna began by saying with some anxiety that she was glad the wedding was so near.

'O, Anna!' replied Mrs Harnham. 'I think we must tell him all – that I have been doing your writing for you? – lest he should not know it till after you become his wife, and it might lead to dissension and recriminations—'

'O, mis'ess, dear mis'ess – please don't tell him now!' cried Anna in distress. 'If you were to do it, perhaps he would not marry me; and what should I do then? It would be terrible what would come to me! And I am getting on with my writing, too. I have brought with me the copybook you were so good as to give me, and I practise every day, and though it is so, so hard, I shall do it well at last, I believe, if I keep on trying.'

Edith looked at the copybook. The copies had been set by herself, and such progress as the girl had made was in the way of grotesque facsimile of her mistress's hand. But even if Edith's flowing caligraphy were reproduced the inspiration would be another thing.

'You do it so beautifully,' continued Anna, 'and say all that I want to say so much better than I could say it, that I do hope you won't leave me in the lurch just now!'

'Very well,' replied the other. 'But I – but I thought I ought not to go on!'

'Why?'

Her strong desire to confide her sentiments led Edith to answer truly:

'Because of its effect upon me.'

'But it *can't* have any!'

'Why, child?'

'Because you are married already!' said Anna with lucid simplicity.

'Of course it can't,' said her mistress hastily; yet glad, despite her conscience, that two or three outpourings still remained to her. 'But you must concentrate your attention on writing your name as I write it here.'

VI

Soon Raye wrote about the wedding. Having decided to make the best of what he feared was a piece of romantic folly, he had acquired more zest for the grand experiment. He wished the ceremony to be in London, for greater privacy. Edith Harnham would have preferred it at Melchester; Anna was passive. His reasoning prevailed, and Mrs Harnham threw herself with mournful zeal into the preparations for Anna's departure. In a last desperate feeling that she must at every hazard be in at the death of her dream, and see once again the man who by a species of telepathy had exercised such an influence on her, she offered to go up with Anna and be with her through the ceremony – 'to see the end of her', as her mistress put it with forced gaiety; an offer which the girl gratefully accepted; for she had no other friend capable of playing the part of companion and witness, in the presence of a gentlemanly bridegroom, in such a way as not to hasten an opinion that he had made an irremediable social blunder.

It was a muddy morning in March when Raye alighted from a four-wheel cab at the door of a registry-office in the S.W. district of London, and carefully handed down Anna and her companion Mrs Harnham. Anna looked attractive in the somewhat fashionable clothes which Mrs Harnham had helped her to buy, though not quite so attractive as, an innocent child, she had appeared in her country gown on the back of the wooden horse at Melchester Fair.

Mrs Harnham had come up this morning by an early train, and a young man – a friend of Raye's – having met them at the door, all four entered the registry-office together. Till an hour before this time Raye had never known the wine-merchant's wife, except at that first casual encounter, and in the flutter of the performance before them he had little opportunity for more than a brief acquaintance. The contract of marriage at a registry is soon got through; but somehow, during its progress, Raye discovered a strange and secret gravitation between himself and Anna's friend.

The formalities of the wedding – or rather ratification of a previous union – being concluded, the four went in one cab to Raye's lodgings, newly taken in a new suburb in preference to a house, the rent of which he could ill afford just then. Here Anna cut the little cake which Raye had bought at a pastrycook's on his way home from Lincoln's Inn the night before. But she did not do much besides. Raye's friend was obliged to depart almost immediately, and when he had left the only ones virtually present were Edith and Raye, who exchanged ideas with much animation. The conversation was indeed theirs only, Anna being as a domestic animal who humbly heard but understood not. Raye seemed startled in awakening to this fact, and began to feel dissatisfied with her inadequacy.

At last, more disappointed than he cared to own, he said, 'Mrs Harnham, my darling is so flurried that she doesn't know what she is doing or saying. I see that after this event a little quietude will be necessary before she gives tongue to that tender philosophy which she used to treat me to in her letters.'

They had planned to start early that afternoon for Knollsea, to spend the few opening days of their married life there, and as the hour for departure was drawing near Raye asked his wife if she would go to the writing-desk in the next room and scribble a little note to his sister, who had been unable to attend through indisposition, informing her that the ceremony was over, thanking her for her little present, and hoping to know her well now that she was the writer's sister as well as Charles's.

'Say it in the pretty poetical way you know so well how to adopt,' he added, 'for I want you particularly to win her, and both of you to be dear friends.'

Anna looked uneasy, but departed to her task, Raye remaining to talk to their guest. Anna was a long while absent, and her husband suddenly rose and went to her.

He found her still bending over the writing-table, with tears brimming up in her eyes; and he looked down upon the sheet of note-paper with some interest, to discover with what tact she had expressed her good-will in the delicate circumstances. To his surprise she had progressed but a few lines, in the characters and spelling of a child of eight, and with the ideas of a goose.

'Anna,' he said, staring; 'what's this?'

'It only means – that I can't do it any better!' she answered, through her tears.

'Eh? Nonsense!'

'I can't!' she insisted, with miserable, sobbing hardihood. 'I – I – didn't write those letters, Charles! I only told *her* what to write! And not always that! But I am learning, O so fast, my dear, dear husband! And you'll forgive me, won't you, for not telling you before?' She slid to her knees, abjectly clasped his waist and laid her face against him.

He stood a few moments, raised her, abruptly turned, and shut the door upon her, rejoining Edith in the drawing-room. She saw that something untoward had been discovered, and their eyes remained fixed on each other.

'Do I guess rightly?' he asked, with wan quietude. '*You* were her scribe through all this?'

'It was necessary,' said Edith.

'Did she dictate every word you ever wrote to me?'

'Not every word.'

'In fact, very little?'

'Very little.'

'You wrote a great part of those pages every week from your own conceptions, though in her name!'

'Yes.'

'Perhaps you wrote many of the letters when you were alone, without communication with her?'

'I did.'

He turned to the bookcase, and leant with his hand over his face; and Edith, seeing his distress, became white as a sheet.

'You have deceived me – ruined me!' he murmured.

'O, don't say it!' she cried in her anguish, jumping up and putting her hand on his shoulder. 'I can't bear that!'

'Delighting me deceptively! Why did you do it – *why* did you!'

'I began doing it in kindness to her! How could I do otherwise than try to save such a simple girl from misery? But I admit that I continued it for pleasure to myself.'

Raye looked up. 'Why did it give you pleasure?' he asked.

'I must not tell,' she said.

He continued to regard her, and saw that her lips suddenly began to quiver under his scrutiny, and her eyes to fill and droop. She started aside, and said that she must go to the station to catch the return train: could a cab be called immediately?

But Raye went up to her, and took her unresisting hand. 'Well, to think of such a thing as this!' he said. 'Why, you and I are friends – lovers – devoted lovers – by correspondence!'

'Yes; I suppose.'

'More.'

'More?'

'Plainly more. It is no use blinking that. Legally I have married her – God help us both! – in soul and spirit I have married you, and no other woman in the world!'

'Hush!'

'But I will not hush! Why should you try to disguise the full truth, when you have already owned half of it? Yes, it is between you and me that the bond is – not between me and her! Now I'll say no more. But, O my cruel one, I think I have one claim upon you!'

She did not say what, and he drew her towards him, and bent over her. 'If it was all pure invention in those letters,' he said emphatically, 'give me your cheek only. If you meant what you said, let it be lips. It is for the first and last time, remember!'

She put up her mouth, and he kissed her long. 'You forgive me?' she said, crying.

'Yes.'

'But you are ruined!'

'What matter!' he said, shrugging his shoulders. 'It serves me right!'

She withdrew, wiped her eyes, entered and bade good-bye to Anna, who had not expected her to go so soon, and was still wrestling with the letter. Raye followed Edith downstairs, and in three minutes she was in a hansom driving to the Waterloo station.

He went back to his wife. 'Never mind the letter, Anna, to-day,' he said gently. 'Put on your things. We, too, must be off shortly.'

The simple girl, upheld by the sense that she was indeed married, showed her delight at finding that he was as kind as ever after the disclosure. She did not know that before his eyes he beheld as it were a galley, in which he, the fastidious urban, was chained to work for the remainder of his life, with her, the unlettered peasant, chained to his side.

Edith travelled back to Melchester that day with a face that showed the very stupor of grief, her lips still tingling from the desperate pressure of his kiss. The end of her impassioned dream had come. When at dusk she reached the Melchester station her husband was there to meet her, but in his perfunctoriness and her preoccupation they did not see each other, and she went out of the station alone.

She walked mechanically homewards without calling a fly. Entering, she could not bear the silence of the house, and went up in the dark to where Anna had slept, where she remained thinking awhile. She then returned to the drawing-room, and not knowing what she did, crouched down upon the floor.

'I have ruined him!' she kept repeating. 'I have ruined him; because I would not deal treacherously towards her!'

In the course of half an hour a figure opened the door of the apartment.

'Ah – who's that?' she said, starting up, for it was dark.

'Your husband – who should it be?' said the worthy merchant.

'Ah – my husband! – I forgot I had a husband!' she whispered to herself.

'I missed you at the station,' he continued. 'Did you see Anna safely tied up? I hope so, for 'twas time.'

'Yes – Anna is married.'

Simultaneously with Edith's journey home Anna and her husband were sitting at the opposite windows of a second-class carriage which sped along to Knollsea. In his hand was a pocket-book full of creased sheets closely written over. Unfolding them one after another he read them in silence, and sighed.

'What are you doing, dear Charles?' she said timidly from the other window, and drew nearer to him as if he were a god.

'Reading over all those sweet letters to me signed "Anna",' he replied with dreary resignation.

Autumn 1891

To Please His Wife

THE interior of St James's Church, in Havenpool Town, was slowly darkening under the close clouds of a winter afternoon. It was Sunday: service had just ended, the face of the parson in the pulpit was buried in his hands, and the congregation, with a cheerful sigh of release, were rising from their knees to depart.

For the moment the stillness was so complete that the surging of the sea could be heard outside the harbour-bar. Then it was broken by the footsteps of the clerk going towards the west door to open it in the usual manner for the exit of the assembly. Before, however, he had reached the doorway, the latch was lifted from without, and the dark figure of a man in a sailor's garb appeared against the light.

The clerk stepped aside, the sailor closed the door gently behind him, and advanced up the nave till he stood at the chancel-step. The parson looked up from the private little prayer which, after so many for the parish, he quite fairly took for himself, rose to his feet, and stared at the intruder.

'I beg your pardon, sir,' said the sailor, addressing the minister in a voice distinctly audible to all the congregation. 'I have come here to offer thanks for my narrow escape from shipwreck. I am given to understand that it is a proper thing to do, if you have no objection?'

The parson, after a moment's pause, said hesitatingly, 'I have no objection; certainly. It is usual to mention any such wish before service, so that the proper words may be used in the General Thanksgiving. But, if you wish, we can read from the form for use after a storm at sea.'

'Ay, sure; I ain't particular,' said the sailor.

The clerk thereupon directed the sailor to the page in the prayer-book where the collect of thanksgiving would be found, and the rector began reading it, the sailor kneeling where he stood, and repeating it after him word by word in a distinct voice. The people, who had remained agape and motionless at the proceeding, mechanically knelt down likewise; but they continued to regard the isolated form of the sailor who, in the precise middle of the chancel-step, remained fixed on his knees, facing the east, his hat beside him, his hands joined, and he quite unconscious of his appearance in their regard.

When his thanksgiving had come to an end he rose; the people rose also; and all went out of church together. As soon as the sailor emerged, so that the remaining daylight fell upon his face, old inhabitants began to recognize him as no other than Shadrach Jolliffe, a young man who had not been seen at Havenpool for several years. A son of the town, his parents had died when he was quite young, on which account he had early gone to sea, in the Newfoundland trade.

He talked with this and that townsman as he walked, informing them that, since leaving his native place years before, he had become captain and owner of a small coasting-ketch, which had providentially been saved from the gale as well as himself. Presently he drew near to two girls who were going out of the churchyard in front of him; they had been sitting in the nave at his entry, and had watched his doings with deep interest, afterwards discussing him as they moved out of church together. One was a slight and gentle creature; the other a tall, large-framed, deliberative girl. Captain Jolliffe regarded the loose curls of their hair, their backs and shoulders, down to their heels, for some time.

'Who may them two maids be?' he whispered to his neighbour.

'The little one is Emily Hanning; the tall one Joanna Phippard.'

'Ah! I recollect 'em now, to be sure.'

He advanced to their elbow, and genially stole a gaze at them.

'Emily, you don't know me?' said the sailor, turning his beaming brown eyes on her.

'I think I do, Mr Jolliffe,' said Emily shyly.

The other girl looked straight at him with her dark eyes.

'The face of Miss Joanna I don't call to mind so well,' he continued. 'But I know her beginnings and kindred.'

They walked and talked together, Jolliffe narrating particulars of his late narrow escape, till they reached the corner of Sloop Lane, in which Emily Hanning dwelt, when, with a nod and smile, she left them. Soon the sailor parted also from Joanna, and, having no especial errand or appointment, turned back towards Emily's house. She lived with her father, who called himself an accountant, the daughter, however, keeping a little stationery-shop as a supplemental provision for the gaps of his somewhat uncertain business. On entering Jolliffe found father and daughter about to begin tea.

'O, I didn't know it was tea-time,' he said. 'Ay, I'll have a cup with much pleasure.'

He remained to tea and long afterwards, telling more tales of his seafaring life. Several neighbours called to listen, and were asked to come in. Somehow Emily Hanning lost her heart to the sailor that Sunday night, and in the course of a week or two there was a tender understanding between them.

One moonlight evening in the next month Shadrach was ascending out of the town by the long straight road eastward, to an elevated suburb where the more fashionable houses stood – if anything near this ancient port could be called fashionable – when he saw a figure before him whom, from her manner of glancing back, he took to be Emily. But, on coming up, he found she was Joanna Phippard. He gave a gallant greeting, and walked beside her.

'Go along,' she said, 'or Emily will be jealous!'

He seemed not to like the suggestion, and remained.

What was said and what was done on that walk never could be clearly recollected by Shadrach; but in some way or other Joanna contrived to wean him away from her gentler and younger rival. From that week onwards, Jolliffe was seen more and more in the wake of Joanna Phippard and less in the company of Emily, and it was soon rumoured about the quay that old Jolliffe's son, who had come home from sea, was going to be married to the former young woman, to the great disappointment of the latter.

Just after this report had gone about, Joanna dressed herself for a walk one morning, and started for Emily's house in the little cross-street. Intelligence of the deep sorrow of her friend on account of the loss of Shadrach had reached her ears also, and her conscience reproached her for winning him away.

Joanna was not altogether satisfied with the sailor. She liked his attentions, and she coveted the dignity of matrimony; but she had never been deeply in love with Jolliffe. For one thing, she was ambitious, and socially his position was hardly so good as her own, and there was always the chance of an attractive woman mating considerably above her. It had long been in her mind that she would not strongly object to give him back again to Emily if her friend felt so very badly about him. To this end she had written a letter of renunciation to Shadrach, which letter she carried in her hand, intending to send it if personal observation of Emily convinced her that her friend was suffering.

Joanna entered Sloop Lane and stepped down into the stationery-shop, which was below the pavement level. Emily's father was never at home at this hour of the day, and it seemed as though Emily were not at home either, for the visitor could make nobody hear. Customers came so seldom hither that a five minutes' absence of the proprietor counted for little. Joanna waited in the little shop, where Emily had tastefully set out – as women can – articles in themselves of slight value, so as to obscure the meagreness of the stock-in-trade; till she saw a figure pausing without the window apparently absorbed in the contemplation of the sixpenny books, packets of paper, and prints hung on a string. It was Captain Shadrach Jolliffe, peering in to ascertain if Emily were there alone. Moved by an impulse of reluctance to meet him in a spot which breathed of Emily, Joanna slipped through the door that communicated with the parlour at the back. She had frequently done so before, for in her friendship with Emily she had the freedom of the house without ceremony.

Jolliffe entered the shop. Through the thin blind which screened the glass partition she could see that he was disappointed at not finding Emily there. He was about to go out again, when Emily's form darkened the doorway, hastening home from some errand. At sight of Jolliffe she started back as if she would have gone out again.

'Don't run away, Emily; don't!' said he. 'What can make 'ee afraid?'

'I'm not afraid, Captain Jolliffe. Only – only I saw you all of a sudden, and – it made me jump!' Her voice showed that her heart had jumped even more than the rest of her.

'I just called as I was passing,' he said.

'For some paper?' She hastened behind the counter.

'No, no, Emily; why do you get behind there? Why not stay by me? You seem to hate me.'

'I don't hate you. How can I?'

'Then come out, so that we can talk like Christians.'

Emily obeyed with a fitful laugh, till she stood again beside him in the open part of the shop.

'There's a dear,' he said.

'You mustn't say that, Captain Jolliffe; because the words belong to somebody else.'

'Ah! I know what you mean. But, Emily, upon my life I didn't know till this morning that you cared one bit about me, or I should not have done as I have done. I have the best of feelings for Joanna, but I know that from the beginning she hasn't cared for me more than in a friendly way; and I see now the one I ought to have asked to be my wife. You know, Emily, when a man comes home from sea after a long voyage he's as blind as a bat – he can't see who's who in women. They are all alike to him, beautiful creatures, and he takes the first that comes easy, without thinking if she loves him, or if he might not soon love another better than her. From the first I inclined to you most, but you were so backward and shy that I thought you didn't want me to bother 'ee, and so I went to Joanna.'

'Don't say any more, Mr Jolliffe, don't!' said she, choking. 'You are going to marry Joanna next month, and it is wrong to – to—'

'O, Emily, my darling!' he cried, and clasped her little figure in his arms before she was aware.

Joanna, behind the curtain, turned pale, tried to withdraw her eyes, but could not.

'It is only you I love as a man ought to love the woman he is going to marry; and I know this from what Joanna has said, that she will willingly let me off! She wants to marry higher, I know, and only said "Yes" to me out of kindness. A fine, tall girl like her isn't the sort for a plain sailor's wife; you be the best suited for that.'

He kissed her and kissed her again, her flexible form quivering in the agitation of his embrace.

'I wonder – are you sure – Joanna is going to break off with you? O, are you sure? Because—'

'I know she would not wish to make us miserable. She will release me.'

'O, I hope – I hope she will! Don't stay any longer, Captain Jolliffe!'

He lingered, however, till a customer came for a penny stick of sealing-wax, and then he withdrew.

Green envy had overspread Joanna at the scene. She looked about for a way of escape. To get out without Emily's knowledge of her visit was indispensable. She crept from the parlour into the passage, and thence to the back door of the house, where she let herself noiselessly into the street.

The sight of that caress had reversed all her resolutions. She could not let Shadrach go. Reaching home she burnt the letter, and told her mother that if Captain Jolliffe called she was too unwell to see him.

Shadrach, however, did not call. He sent her a note expressing in simple language the state of his feelings; and asked to be allowed to take advantage of the hints she had given him that her affection, too, was little more than friendly, by cancelling the engagement.

Looking out upon the harbour and the island beyond he waited and waited in his lodgings for an answer that did not come. The suspense grew to be so intolerable that after dark he went up the High Street. He could not resist calling at Joanna's to learn his fate.

Her mother said her daughter was too unwell to see him, and to his questioning admitted that it was in consequence of a letter received from himself, which had distressed her deeply.

'You know what it was about, perhaps, Mrs Phippard?' he said.

Mrs Phippard owned that she did, adding that it put them in a very painful position. Thereupon Shadrach, fearing that he had been guilty of an enormity, explained that if his letter had pained Joanna it must be owing to a misunderstanding, since he had thought it would be a relief to her. If otherwise, he would hold himself bound by his word, and she was to think of the letter as never having been written.

Next morning he received an oral message from the young woman, asking him to fetch her home from a meeting that evening. This he did, and while walking from the Town Hall to her door, with her hand in his arm, she said:

'It is all the same as before between us, isn't it, Shadrach? Your letter was sent in mistake?'

'It is all the same as before,' he answered, 'if you say it must be.'

'I wish it to be,' she murmured, with hard lineaments, as she thought of Emily.

Shadrach was a religious and scrupulous man, who respected his word as his life. Shortly afterwards the wedding took place, Jolliffe having conveyed to Emily as gently as possible the error he had fallen into when estimating Joanna's mood as one of indifference.

II

A month after the marriage Joanna's mother died, and the couple were obliged to turn their attention to very practical matters. Now that she was left without a parent, Joanna could not bear the notion of her husband going to sea again, but the question was, What could he do at home? They finally decided to take on a small grocer's shop in High Street, the goodwill and stock of which were waiting to be disposed of at that time. Shadrach knew nothing of shopkeeping, and Joanna very little, but they hoped to learn.

To the management of this grocery business they now devoted all their energies, and continued to conduct it for many succeeding years, without great success. Two sons were born to them, whom their mother loved to idolatry, although she had never passionately loved her husband; and she lavished upon them all her forethought and care. But the shop did not thrive, and the large dreams she had entertained of her sons' education and career became attenuated in the face of realities. Their schooling was of the plainest, but, being by the sea, they grew alert in all such nautical arts and enterprises as were attractive to their age.

The great interest of the Jolliffes' married life, outside their own immediate household, had lain in the marriage of Emily. By one of those odd chances which lead those that lurk in unexpected corners to be discovered, while the obvious are passed by, the gentle girl had been seen and loved by a thriving merchant of the town, a widower, some years older than herself, though still in the prime of life. At first Emily had declared that she never, never could marry anyone; but Mr Lester had quietly persevered, and had at last won her reluctant assent. Two children also were the fruits of this union, and, as they grew and prospered, Emily declared that she had never supposed that she could live to be so happy.

The worthy merchant's home, one of those large, substantial brick mansions frequently jammed up in old-fashioned towns, faced directly on the High Street, nearly opposite to the grocery shop of the Jolliffes, and it now became the pain of Joanna to behold the woman whose place she had usurped out of pure covetousness, looking down from her position of comparative wealth upon the humble shop-window with its dusty sugar-loaves, heaps of raisins, and canisters of tea, over which it was her own lot to preside. The business having so dwindled, Joanna was obliged to serve in the shop herself, and it galled and mortified her that Emily Lester, sitting in her large drawing-room over the way, could witness her own dancings up and down behind the counter at the beck and call of wretched twopenny customers, whose patronage she was driven to welcome gladly; persons to whom she was compelled to be civil in the street, while Emily was bounding along with her children and her governess, and conversing with the genteelest people of the town and neighbourhood. This was what she had gained by not letting Shadrach Jolliffe, whom she had so faintly loved, carry his affection elsewhere.

Shadrach was a good and honest man, and he had been faithful to her in heart and in deed. Time had clipped the wings of his love for Emily in his devotion to the mother of his boys; he had quite lived down that impulsive earlier fancy, and Emily had become in his regard nothing more than a friend. It was the same with Emily's feelings for him. Possibly, had she found the least cause for jealousy, Joanna would almost have been better satisfied. It was in the absolute acquiescence of Emily and Shadrach in the results she herself had contrived that her discontent found nourishment.

Shadrach was not endowed with the narrow shrewdness necessary for developing a retail business in the face of many competitors. Did a customer inquire if the grocer could really recommend the wondrous substitute for eggs which a persevering bagman had forced into his stock, he would answer that 'when you did not put eggs into a pudding it was difficult to taste them there'; and when he was asked if his 'real Mocha coffee' was real Mocha, he would say grimly, 'as understood in small shops'. The way to wealth was not by this route.

One summer day, when the big brick house opposite was reflecting the oppressive sun's heat into the shop, and nobody was present but husband and wife, Joanna looked across at Emily's door, where a wealthy visitor's carriage had drawn up. Traces of patronage had been visible in Emily's manner of late.

'Shadrach, the truth is, you are not a business-man,' his wife sadly murmured. 'You were not brought up to shopkeeping, and it is impossible for a man to make a fortune at an occupation he has jumped into, as you did into this.'

Jolliffe agreed with her, in this as in everything else. 'Not that I care a rope's end about making a fortune,' he said cheerfully. 'I am happy enough, and we can rub on somehow.'

She looked again at the great house through the screen of bottled pickles.

'Rub on – yes,' she said bitterly. 'But see how well off Emmy Lester is, who used to be so poor! Her boys will go to College, no doubt; and think of yours – obliged to go to the Parish School!'

Shadrach's thoughts had flown to Emily.

'Nobody,' he said good-humouredly, 'ever did Emily a better turn than you did, Joanna, when you warned her off me and put an end to that little simpering nonsense between us, so as to leave it in her power to say "Aye" to Lester when he came along.'

This almost maddened her.

'Don't speak of bygones!' she implored, in stern sadness. 'But think, for the boys' and my sake, if not for your own, what are we to do to get richer?'

'Well,' he said, becoming serious, 'to tell the truth, I have always felt myself unfit for this business, though I've never liked to say so. I seem to want more room for sprawling; a more open space to strike out in than here among friends and neighbours. I could get rich as well as any man, if I tried my own way.'

'I wish you would! What is your way?'

'To go to sea again.'

She had been the very one to keep him at home, hating the semi-widowed existence of sailors' wives. But her ambition checked her instincts now, and she said:

'Do you think success really lies that way?'

'I am sure it lies in no other.'

'Do you want to go, Shadrach?'

'Not for the pleasure of it, I can tell 'ee. There's no such pleasure at sea, Joanna, as I can find in my back parlour here. To speak honest, I have no love for the brine. I never had much. But if it comes to a question of a fortune for you and the lads, it is another thing. That's the only way to it for one born and bred a seafarer as I.'

'Would it take long to earn?'

'Well, that depends; perhaps not.'

The next morning Shadrach pulled from a chest of drawers the nautical jacket he had worn during the first months of his return, brushed out the moths, donned it, and walked down to the quay. The port still did a fair business in the Newfoundland trade, though not so much as formerly.

It was not long after this that he invested all he possessed in purchasing a part-ownership in a brig, of which he was appointed captain. A few months were passed in coast-trading, during which interval Shadrach wore off the land-rust that had accumulated upon him in his grocery phase; and in the spring the brig sailed for Newfoundland.

Joanna lived on at home with her sons, who were now growing up into strong lads, and occupying themselves in various ways about the harbour and quay.

'Never mind, let them work a little,' their fond mother said to herself. 'Our necessities compel it now, but when Shadrach comes home they will be only seventeen and eighteen, and they shall be removed from the port, and their education thoroughly taken in hand by a tutor; and with the money they'll have they will perhaps be as near to gentlemen as Emmy Lester's precious two, with their algebra and their Latin!'

The date for Shadrach's return drew near and arrived, and he did not appear. Joanna was assured that there was no cause for anxiety, sailing-ships being so uncertain in their coming; which assurance proved to be well grounded, for late one wet evening, about a month after the calculated time, the ship was announced as at hand, and presently the slip-slop step of Shadrach as the sailor sounded in the passage, and he entered. The boys had gone out and had missed him, and Joanna was sitting alone.

As soon as the first emotion of reunion between the couple had passed, Jolliffe explained the delay as owing to a small speculative contract, which had produced good results.

'I was determined not to disappoint 'ee,' he said; 'and I think you'll own that I haven't!'

With this he pulled out an enormous canvas bag, full and rotund as the money-bag of the giant whom Jack slew, untied it, and shook the contents out into her lap as she sat in her low chair by the fire. A mass of sovereigns and guineas (there were guineas on the earth in those days) fell into her lap with a sudden thud, weighing down her gown to the floor.

'There!' said Shadrach complacently. 'I told 'ee, dear, I'd do it; and have I done it or no?'

Somehow her face, after the first excitement of possession, did not retain its glory.

'It is a lot of gold, indeed,' she said. 'And – is this *all*?'

'All? Why, dear Joanna, do you know you can count to three hundred in that heap? It is a fortune!'

'Yes – yes. A fortune – judged by sea; but judged by land—'

However, she banished considerations of the money for the nonce. Soon the boys came in, and next Sunday Shadrach returned thanks to God – this time by the more ordinary channel of the italics in the General Thanksgiving. But a few days after, when the question of investing the money arose, he remarked that she did not seem so satisfied as he had hoped.

'Well, you see, Shadrach,' she answered, '*we* count by hundreds; *they* count by thousands' (nodding towards the other side of the street). 'They have set up a carriage and pair since you left.'

'O, have they?'

'My dear Shadrach, you don't know how the world moves. However, we'll do the best we can with it. But they are rich, and we are poor still!'

The greater part of a year was desultorily spent. She moved sadly about the house and shop, and the boys were still occupying themselves in and around the harbour.

'Joanna,' he said, one day, 'I see by your movements that it is not enough.'

'It is not enough,' said she. 'My boys will have to live by steering the ships that the Lesters own; and I was once above her!'

Jolliffe was not an argumentative man, and he only murmured that he thought he would make another voyage. He meditated for several days, and coming home from the quay one afternoon said suddenly:

'I could do it for 'ee, dear, in one more trip, for certain, if – if—'

'Do what, Shadrach?'

'Enable 'ee to count by thousands instead of hundreds.'

'If what?'

'If I might take the boys.'

She turned pale.

'Don't say that, Shadrach,' she answered hastily.

'Why?'

'I don't like to hear it! There's danger at sea. I want them to be something genteel, and no danger to them. I couldn't let them risk their lives at sea. O, I couldn't ever, ever!'

'Very well, dear, it shan't be done.'

Next day, after a silence, she asked a question:

'If they were to go with you it would make a great deal of difference, I suppose, to the profit?'

' 'Twould treble what I should get from the venture single-handed. Under my eye they would be as good as two more of myself.'

Later on she said: 'Tell me more about this.'

'Well, the boys are almost as clever as master-mariners in handling a craft, upon my life! There isn't a more cranky place in the Northern Seas than about the sandbanks of this harbour, and they've practised

here from their infancy. And they are so steady. I couldn't get their
steadiness and their trustworthiness in half a dozen men twice their age.'

'And is it *very* dangerous at sea; now, too, there are rumours of war?'
she asked uneasily.

'O, well, there be risks. Still. . . .'

The idea grew and magnified, and the mother's heart was crushed and
stifled by it. Emmy was growing *too* patronizing; it could not be borne.
Shadrach's wife could not help nagging him about their comparative
poverty. The young men, amiable as their father, when spoken to on
the subject of a voyage of enterprise, were quite willing to embark; and
though they, like their father, had no great love for the sea, they became
quite enthusiastic when the proposal was detailed.

Everything now hung upon their mother's assent. She withheld it
long, but at last gave the word: the young men might accompany their
father. Shadrach was unusually cheerful about it: Heaven had preserved
him hitherto, and he had uttered his thanks. God would not forsake
those who were faithful to him.

All that the Jolliffes possessed in the world was put into the enterprise.
The grocery stock was pared down to the least that possibly could afford
a bare sustenance to Joanna during the absence, which was to last
through the usual 'New-f'nland spell'. How she would endure the
weary time she hardly knew, for the boys had been with her formerly;
but she nerved herself for the trial.

The ship was laden with boots and shoes, ready-made clothing,
fishing-tackle, butter, cheese, cordage, sailcloth, and many other
commodities; and was to bring back oil, furs, skins, fish, cranberries,
and what else came to hand. But much speculative trading to other ports
was to be undertaken between the voyages out and homeward, and
thereby much money made.

III

The brig sailed on a Monday morning in spring; but Joanna did not
witness its departure. She could not bear the sight that she had been the
means of bringing about. Knowing this, her husband told her overnight
that they were to sail some time before noon next day; hence when,
awakening at five the next morning, she heard them bustling about
downstairs, she did not hasten to descend, but lay trying to nerve herself

for the parting, imagining they would leave about nine, as her husband had done on his previous voyage. When she did descend she beheld words chalked upon the sloping face of the bureau; but no husband or sons. In the hastily-scrawled lines Shadrach said they had gone off thus not to pain her by a leave-taking; and the sons had chalked under his words: 'Good-bye, mother!'

She rushed to the quay, and looked down the harbour towards the blue rim of the sea, but she could only see the masts and bulging sails of the *Joanna;* no human figures. ' 'Tis I have sent them!' she said wildly, and burst into tears. In the house the chalked 'Good-bye' nearly broke her heart. But when she had re-entered the front room, and looked across at Emily's, a gleam of triumph lit her thin face at her anticipated release from the thraldom of subservience.

To do Emily Lester justice, her assumption of superiority was mainly a figment of Joanna's brain. That the circumstances of the merchant's wife were more luxurious than Joanna's, the former could not conceal; though whenever the two met, which was not very often now, Emily endeavoured to subdue the difference by every means in her power.

The first summer lapsed away; and Joanna meagrely maintained herself by the shop, which now consisted of little more than a window and a counter. Emily was, in truth, her only large customer; and Mrs Lester's kindly readiness to buy anything and everything without questioning the quality had a sting of bitterness in it, for it was the uncritical attitude of a patron, and almost of a donor. The long dreary winter moved on; the face of the bureau had been turned to the wall to protect the chalked words of farewell, for Joanna could never bring herself to rub them out; and she often glanced at them with wet eyes. Emily's handsome boys came home for the Christmas holidays; the University was talked of for them; and still Joanna subsisted as it were with held breath, like a person submerged. Only one summer more, and the 'spell' would end. Towards the close of the time Emily called on her quondam friend. She had heard that Joanna began to feel anxious; she had received no letter from husband or sons for some months. Emily's silks rustled arrogantly when, in response to Joanna's almost dumb invitation, she squeezed through the opening of the counter and into the parlour behind the shop.

'*You* are all success, and *I* am all the other way!' said Joanna.

'But why do you think so?' said Emily. 'They are to bring back a fortune, I hear.'

'Ah! will they come? The doubt is more than a woman can bear. All three in one ship – think of that! And I have not heard of them for months!'

'But the time is not up. You should not meet misfortune half-way.'

'Nothing will repay me for the grief of their absence!'

'Then why did you let them go? You were doing fairly well.'

'I *made* them go!' she said, turning vehemently upon Emily. 'And I'll tell you why! I could not bear that we should be only muddling on, and you so rich and thriving! Now I have told you, and you may hate me if you will!'

'I shall never hate you, Joanna.'

And she proved the truth of her words afterwards. The end of autumn came, and the brig should have been in port; but nothing like the *Joanna* appeared in the channel between the sands, It was now really time to be uneasy. Joanna Jolliffe sat by the fire, and every gust of wind caused her a cold thrill. She had always feared and detested the sea; to her it was a treacherous, restless, slimy creature, glorying in the griefs of women. 'Still,' she said, 'they *must* come!'

She recalled to her mind that Shadrach had said before starting that if they returned safe and sound, with success crowning their enterprise, he would go as he had gone after his shipwreck, and kneel with his sons in the church, and offer sincere thanks for their deliverance. She went to church regularly morning and afternoon, and sat in the most forward pew, nearest the chancel-step. Her eyes were mostly fixed on that step, where Shadrach had knelt in the bloom of his young manhood: she knew to an inch the spot which his knees had pressed twenty winters before; his outline as he had knelt, his hat on the step beside him. God was good. Surely her husband must kneel there again: a son on each side as he had said; George just here, Jim just there. By long watching the spot as she worshipped became as if she saw the three returned ones there kneeling; the two slim outlines of her boys, the more bulky form between them; their hands clasped, their heads shaped against the eastern wall. The fancy grew almost to an hallucination; she could never turn her worn eyes to the step without seeing them there.

Nevertheless they did not come. Heaven was merciful, but it was not yet pleased to relieve her soul. This was her purgation for the sin of making them the slaves of her ambition. But it became more than purgation soon, and her mood approached despair. Months had passed since the brig had been due, but it had not returned.

Joanna was always hearing or seeing evidences of their arrival. When on the hill behind the port, whence a view of the open Channel could be obtained, she felt sure that a little speck on the horizon, breaking the eternally level waste of waters southward, was the truck of the *Joanna*'s mainmast. Or when indoors, a shout or excitement of any kind at the corner of the Town Cellar, where the High Street joined the Quay, caused her to spring to her feet and cry: ' 'Tis they!'

But it was not. The visionary forms knelt every Sunday afternoon on the chancel-step, but not the real. Her shop had, as it were, eaten itself hollow. In the apathy which had resulted from her loneliness and grief she had ceased to take in the smallest supplies, and thus had sent away her last customer.

In this strait Emily Lester tried by every means in her power to aid the afflicted woman; but she met with constant repulses.

'I don't like you! I can't bear to see you!' Joanna would whisper hoarsely when Emily came to her and made advances.

'But I want to help and soothe you, Joanna,' Emily would say.

'You are a lady, with a rich husband and fine sons! What can you want with a bereaved crone like me!'

'Joanna, I want this: I want you to come and live in my house, and not stay alone in this dismal place any longer.'

'And suppose they come and don't find me at home? You wish to separate me and mine! No, I'll stay here. I don't like you, and I can't thank you, whatever kindness you do me!'

However, as time went on Joanna could not afford to pay the rent of the shop and house without an income. She was assured that all hope of the return of Shadrach and his sons was vain, and she reluctantly consented to accept the asylum of the Lesters' house. Here she was allotted a room of her own on the second floor, and went and came as she chose, without contact with the family. Her hair greyed and whitened, deep lines channelled her forehead, and her form grew gaunt and stooping. But she still expected the lost ones, and when she met Emily on the staircase she would say morosely: 'I know why you've got me here! They'll come, and be disappointed at not finding me at home, and perhaps go away again; and then you'll be revenged for my taking Shadrach away from 'ee!'

Emily Lester bore these reproaches from the grief-stricken soul. She was sure – all the people of Havenpool were sure – that Shadrach and his sons had gone to the bottom. For years the vessel had been given up as lost. Nevertheless, when awakened at night by any noise, Joanna would rise from bed and glance at the shop opposite by the light from the flickering lamp, to make sure it was not they.

It was a damp and dark December night, six years after the departure of the brig *Joanna*. The wind was from the sea, and brought up a fishy mist which mopped the face like moist flannel. Joanna had prayed her usual prayer for the absent ones with more fervour and confidence than she had felt for months, and had fallen asleep about eleven. It must have been between one and two when she suddenly started up. She had certainly heard steps in the street, and the voices of Shadrach and her sons calling at the door of the grocery shop. She sprang out of bed, and, hardly knowing what clothing she dragged on herself, hastened down Emily's large and carpeted staircase, put the candle on the hall-table, unfastened the bolts and chain, and stepped into the street. The mist, blowing up the street from the Quay, hindered her seeing the shop, although it was so near; but she had crossed to it in a moment. How was it? Nobody stood there. The wretched woman walked wildly up and down with her bare feet – there was not a soul. She returned and knocked with all her might at the door which had once been her own – they might have been admitted for the night, unwilling to disturb her till the morning. It was not till several minutes had elapsed that the young man who now kept the shop looked out of an upper window, and saw the skeleton of something human standing below half-dressed.

'Has anybody come?' asked the form.

'O, Mrs Jolliffe, I didn't know it was you,' said the young man kindly, for he was aware how her baseless expectations moved her. 'No; nobody has come.'

June 1891

The Fiddler of the Reels

'TALKING of Exhibitions, World's Fairs, and what not,' said the old gentleman, 'I would not go round the corner to see a dozen of them nowadays. The only exhibition that ever made, or ever will make, any impression upon my imagination was the first of the series, the parent of them all, and now a thing of old times – the Great Exhibition of 1851, in Hyde Park, London. None of the younger generation can realize the sense of novelty it produced in us who were then in our prime. A noun substantive went so far as to become an adjective in honour of the occasion. It was "exhibition" hat, "exhibition" razor-strop, "exhibition" watch; nay, even "exhibition" weather, "exhibition" spirits, sweethearts, babies, wives – for the time.

'For South Wessex, the year formed in many ways an extraordinary chronological frontier or transit-line, at which there occurred what one might call a precipice in Time. As in a geological "fault", we had presented to us a sudden bringing of ancient and modern into absolute contact, such as probably in no other single year since the Conquest was ever witnessed in this part of the country.'

These observations led us onward to talk of the different personages, gentle and simple, who lived and moved within our narrow and peaceful horizon at that time; and of three people in particular, whose queer little history was oddly touched at points by the Exhibition, more concerned with it than that of anybody else who dwelt in those outlying shades of the world, Stickleford, Mellstock, and Egdon. First in prominence among these three came Wat Ollamoor – if that were his real name – whom the seniors in our party had known well.

He was a woman's man, they said, – supremely so – externally little else. To men he was not attractive; perhaps a little repulsive at times. Musician, dandy, and company-man in practice; veterinary surgeon in theory, he lodged awhile in Mellstock village, coming from nobody knew where; though some said his first appearance in this neighbour-hood had been as fiddle-player in a show at Greenhill Fair.

Many a worthy villager envied him his power over unsophisticated maidenhood – a power which seemed sometimes to have a touch of the weird and wizardly in it. Personally he was not ill-favoured, though rather un-English, his complexion being a rich olive, his rank hair dark and rather clammy – made still clammier by secret ointments, which, when he came fresh to a party, caused him to smell like 'boys'-love' (southernwood) steeped in lamp-oil. On occasion he wore curls – a double row – running almost horizontally around his head. But as these were sometimes noticeably absent, it was concluded that they were not altogether of Nature's making. By girls whose love for him had turned to hatred he had been nicknamed 'Mop', from this abundance of hair, which was long enough to rest upon his shoulders; as time passed the name more and more prevailed.

His fiddling possibly had the most to do with the fascination he exercised, for, to speak fairly, it could claim for itself a most peculiar and personal quality, like that in a moving preacher. There were tones in it which bred the immediate conviction that indolence and averseness to systematic application were all that lay between 'Mop' and the career of a second Paganini.

While playing he invariably closed his eyes; using no notes, and, as it were, allowing the violin to wander on at will into the most plaintive passages ever heard by rustic man. There was a certain lingual character in the supplicatory expressions he produced, which would wellnigh have drawn an ache from the heart of a gate-post. He could make any child in the parish, who was at all sensitive to music, burst into tears in a few minutes by simply fiddling one of the old dance-tunes he almost entirely affected – country jigs, reels, and 'Favourite Quick Steps' of the last century – some mutilated remains of which even now reappear as nameless phantoms in new quadrilles and gallops, where they are recognized only by the curious, or by such old-fashioned and far-between people as have been thrown with men like Wat Ollamoor in their early life.

His date was a little later than that of the old Mellstock quire-band which comprised the Dewys, Mail, and the rest – in fact, he did not rise above the horizon thereabout till those well-known musicians were dis-banded as ecclesiastical functionaries. In their honest love of thorough-ness they despised the new man's style. Theophilus Dewy (Reuben the tranter's younger brother) used to say there was no 'plumness' in it – no bowing, no solidity – it was all fantastical. And probably this was true. Anyhow, Mop had, very obviously, never bowed a note of church-music from his birth; he never once sat in the gallery of Mellstock Church where the others had tuned their venerable psalmody so many hundreds of times; had never, in all likelihood, entered a church at all. All were devil's tunes in his repertory. 'He could no more play the Wold Hundredth to his true time than he could play the brazen serpent,' the tranter would say. (The brazen serpent was supposed in Mellstock to be a musical instrument particularly hard to blow.)

Occasionally Mop could produce the aforesaid moving effect upon the souls of grown-up persons, especially young women of fragile and responsive organization. Such an one was Car'line Aspent. Though she was already engaged to be married before she met him, Car'line, of them all, was the most influenced by Mop Ollamoor's heart-stealing melodies, to her discomfort, nay, positive pain and ultimate injury. She was a pretty, invocating, weak-mouthed girl, whose chief defect as a companion with her sex was a tendency to peevishness now and then. At this time she was not a resident in Mellstock parish where Mop lodged, but lived some miles off at Stickleford, further down the river.

How and where she first made acquaintance with him and his fiddling is not truly known, but the story was that it either began or was developed on one spring evening, when, in passing through Lower Mellstock, she chanced to pause on the bridge near his house to rest herself, and languidly leaned over the parapet. Mop was standing on his door-step, as was his custom, spinning the insidious thread of semi- and demi-semiquavers from the E string of his fiddle for the benefit of passers-by, and laughing as the tears rolled down the cheeks of the little children hanging around him. Car'line pretended to be engrossed with the rippling of the stream under the arches, but in reality she was listening, as he knew. Presently the aching of the heart seized her simultaneously with a wild desire to glide airily in the mazes of an infinite dance. To shake off the fascination she resolved to go on, although it would be necessary to pass him as he played. On stealthily glancing ahead at the performer, she found to her relief that his eyes were closed in abandonment to instrumentation, and she strode on boldly. But when closer her step grew timid, her tread convulsed itself more and more accordantly with the time of the melody, till she very nearly danced along. Gaining another glance at him when immediately opposite, she saw that *one* of his eyes was open, quizzing her as he smiled at her emotional state. Her gait could not divest itself of its compelled capers till she had gone a long way past the house; and Car'line was unable to shake off the strange infatuation for hours.

After that day, whenever there was to be in the neighbourhood a dance to which she could get an invitation, and where Mop Ollamoor was to be the musician, Car'line contrived to be present, though it sometimes involved a walk of several miles; for he did not play so often in Stickleford as elsewhere.

The next evidences of his influence over her were singular enough, and it would require a neurologist to fully explain them. She would be sitting quietly, any evening after dark, in the house of her father, the parish clerk, which stood in the middle of Stickleford village street, this being the highroad between Lower Mellstock and Moreford, five miles eastward. Here, without a moment's warning, and in the midst of a general conversation between her father, sister, and the young man before alluded to, who devotedly wooed her in ignorance of her infatuation, she would start from her seat in the chimney-corner as if she had received a galvanic shock, and spring convulsively towards the ceiling; then she would burst into tears, and it was not till some half-hour had passed that she grew calm as usual. Her father, knowing her hysterical tendencies, was always excessively anxious about this trait in his youngest girl, and feared the attack to be a species of epileptic fit. Not so her sister Julia. Julia had found out what was the cause. At the moment before the jumping, only an exceptionally sensitive ear situated in the chimney-nook could have caught from down the flue the beat of a man's footstep along the highway without. But it was in that footfall, for which she had been waiting, that the origin of Car'line's involuntary springing lay. The pedestrian was Mop Ollamoor, as the girl well knew; but his business that way was not to visit her; he sought another woman whom he spoke of as his Intended, and who lived at Moreford, two miles further on. On one, and only one, occasion did it happen that Car'line could not control her utterance; it was when her sister alone chanced to be present. 'O – O – O –!' she cried. 'He's going to *her*, and not coming to *me*!'

To do the fiddler justice, he had not at first thought greatly of, or spoken much to, this girl of impressionable mould. But he had soon found out her secret, and could not resist a little by-play with her too easily hurt heart, as an interlude between his more serious lovemakings at Moreford. The two became well acquainted, though only by stealth, hardly a soul in Stickleford except her sister, and her lover Ned Hipcroft, being aware of the attachment. Her father disapproved of her coldness to Ned; her sister, too, hoped she might get over this nervous passion for a man of whom so little was known. The ultimate result was that Car'line's manly and simple wooer Edward found his suit becoming practically hopeless. He was a respectable mechanic, in a far sounder position than Mop the nominal horse-doctor; but when, before leaving her, Ned put his flat and final question, would she marry him, then and there, now or never, it was with little expectation of obtaining more than the negative she gave him. Though her father supported him and her sister supported him, he could not play the fiddle so as to draw your soul out of your body like a spider's thread, as Mop did, till you felt as limp as withywind and yearned for something to cling to. Indeed, Hipcroft had not the slightest ear for music; could not sing two notes in tune, much less play them.

The No he had expected and got from her, in spite of a preliminary encouragement, gave Ned a new start in life. It had been uttered in such a tone of sad entreaty that he resolved to persecute her no more; she should not even be distressed by a sight of his form in the distant perspective of the street and lane. He left the place, and his natural course was to London.

The railway to South Wessex was in process of construction, but it was not as yet opened for traffic; and Hipcroft reached the capital by a six days' trudge on foot, as many a better man had done before him. He was one of the last of the artisan class who used that now extinct method of travel to the great centres of labour, so customary then from time immemorial.

In London he lived and worked regularly at his trade. More fortunate than many, his disinterested willingness recommended him from the first. During the ensuing four years he was never out of employment. He neither advanced nor receded in the modern sense; he improved as a workman, but he did not shift one jot in social position. About his love for Car'line he maintained a rigid silence. No doubt he often thought of her; but being always occupied, and having no relations at Stickleford, he held no communication with that part of the country, and showed no desire to return. In his quiet lodging in Lambeth he moved about after working-hours with the facility of a woman, doing his own cooking, attending to his stocking-heels, and shaping himself by degrees to a lifelong bachelorhood. For this conduct one is bound to advance the canonical reason that time could not efface from his heart the image of little Car'line Aspent – and it may be in part true; but there was also the inference that his was a nature not greatly dependent upon the ministrations of the other sex for its comforts.

The fourth year of his residence as a mechanic in London was the year of the Hyde-Park Exhibition already mentioned, and at the construction of this huge glass-house, then unexampled in the world's history, he worked daily. It was an era of great hope and activity among the nations and industries. Though Hipcroft was, in his small way, a central man in the movement, he plodded on with his usual outward placidity. Yet for him, too, the year was destined to have its surprises, for when the bustle of getting the building ready for the opening day was past, the ceremonies had been witnessed, and people were flocking thither from all parts of the globe, he received a letter from Car'line. Till that day the silence of four years between himself and Stickleford had never been broken.

She informed her old lover, in an uncertain penmanship which suggested a trembling hand, of the trouble she had been put to in ascertaining his address, and then broached the subject which had prompted her to write. Four years ago, she said with the greatest delicacy of which she was capable, she had been so foolish as to refuse him. Her wilful wrong-headedness had since been a grief to her many times, and of late particularly. As for Mr Ollamoor, he had been absent almost as long as Ned – she did not know where. She would gladly marry Ned now if he were to ask her again, and be a tender little wife to him till her life's end.

A tide of warm feeling must have surged through Ned Hipcroft's frame on receipt of this news, if we may judge by the issue. Unquestionably he loved her still, even if not to the exclusion of every other happiness. This from his Car'line, she who had been dead to him these many years, alive to him again as of old, was in itself a pleasant, gratifying thing. Ned had grown so resigned to, or satisfied with, his lonely lot, that he probably would not have shown much jubilation at anything. Still, a certain ardour of preoccupation, after his first surprise, revealed how deeply her confession of faith in him had stirred him. Measured and methodical in his ways, he did not answer the letter that day, nor the next, nor the next. He was having 'a good think'. When he did answer it, there was a great deal of sound reasoning mixed in with the unmistakable tenderness of his reply; but the tenderness itself was sufficient to reveal that he was pleased with her straightforward frankness; that the anchorage she had once obtained in his heart was renewable, if it had not been continuously firm.

He told her – and as he wrote his lips twitched humorously over the few gentle words of raillery he indited among the rest of his sentences – that it was all very well for her to come round at this time of day. Why wouldn't she have him when he wanted her? She had no doubt learned that he was not married, but suppose his affections had since been fixed on another? She ought to beg his pardon. Still, he was not the man to forget her. But considering how he had been used, and what he had suffered, she could not quite expect him to go down to Stickleford and fetch her. But if she would come to him, and say she was sorry, as was only fair; why, yes, he would marry her, knowing what a good little woman she was at the core. He added that the request for her to come to him was a less one to make than it would have been when he first left Stickleford, or even a few months ago; for the new railway into South Wessex was now open, and there had just begun to be run wonderfully contrived special trains, called excursion-trains, on account of the Great Exhibition; so that she could come up easily alone.

She said in her reply how good it was of him to treat her so generously, after her hot-and-cold treatment of him; that though she felt frightened at the magnitude of the journey, and was never as yet in a railway-train, having only seen one pass at a distance, she embraced his offer with all her heart; and would, indeed, own to him how sorry she was, and beg his pardon, and try to be a good wife always, and make up for lost time.

The remaining details of when and where were soon settled, Car'line informing him, for her ready identification in the crowd, that she would be wearing 'my new sprigged-laylock cotton gown', and Ned gaily responding that, having married her the morning after her arrival, he would make a day of it by taking her to the Exhibition. One early summer afternoon, accordingly, he came from his place of work, and hastened towards Waterloo Station to meet her. It was as wet and chilly as an English June day can occasionally be, but as he waited on the platform in the drizzle he glowed inwardly, and seemed to have something to live for again.

The 'excursion-train' – an absolutely new departure in the history of travel – was still a novelty on the Wessex line, and probably everywhere. Crowds of people had flocked to all the stations on the way up to witness the unwonted sight of so long a train's passage, even where they did not take advantage of the opportunity it offered. The seats for the humbler class of travellers in these early experiments in steam-locomotion, were open trucks, without any protection whatever from the wind and rain; and damp weather having set in with the afternoon, the unfortunate occupants of these vehicles were, on the train drawing up at the London terminus, found to be in a pitiable condition from their long journey; blue-faced, stiff-necked, sneezing, rain-beaten, chilled to the marrow, many of the men being hatless; in fact, they resembled people who had been out all night in an open boat on a rough sea, rather than inland excursionists for pleasure. The women had in some degree protected themselves by turning up the skirts of their gowns over their heads, but as by this arrangement they were additionally exposed about the hips, they were all more or less in a sorry plight.

In the bustle and crush of alighting forms of both sexes which followed the entry of the huge concatenation into the station, Ned Hipcroft soon discerned the slim little figure his eye was in search of, in the sprigged lilac, as described. She came up to him with a frightened smile – still pretty, though so damp, weather-beaten, and shivering from long exposure to the wind.

'O Ned!' she sputtered, 'I – I—' He clasped her in his arms and kissed her, whereupon she burst into a flood of tears.

'You are wet, my poor dear! I hope you'll not get cold,' he said. And surveying her and her multifarious surrounding packages, he noticed that by the hand she led a toddling child – a little girl of three or so – whose hood was as clammy and tender face as blue as those of the other travellers.

'Who is this – somebody you know?' asked Ned curiously.

'Yes, Ned. She's mine.'

'Yours?'

'Yes – my own.'

'Your own child?'

'Yes!'

'But who's the father?'

'The young man I had after you courted me.'

'Well – as God's in—'

'Ned, I didn't name it in my letter, because, you see, it would have been so hard to explain! I thought that when we met I could tell you how she happened to be born, so much better than in writing! I hope you'll excuse it this once, dear Ned, and not scold me, now I've come so many, many miles!'

'This means Mr Mop Ollamoor, I reckon!' said Hipcroft, gazing palely at them from the distance of the yard or two to which he had withdrawn with a start.

Car'line gasped. 'But he's been gone away for years!' she supplicated. 'And I never had a young man before! And I was so onlucky to be catched the first time he took advantage o' me, though some of the girls down there go on like anything!'

Ned remained in silence, pondering.

'You'll forgive me, dear Ned?' she added, beginning to sob outright. 'I haven't taken 'ee in after all, because – because you can pack us back again, if you want to; though 'tis hundreds o' miles, and so wet, and night a-coming on, and I with no money!'

'What the devil can I do!' Hipcroft groaned.

A more pitiable picture than the pair of helpless creatures presented was never seen on a rainy day, as they stood on the great, gaunt, puddled platform, a whiff of drizzle blowing under the roof upon them now and then; the pretty attire in which they had started from Stickleford in the early morning bemuddled and sodden, weariness on their faces, and fear of him in their eyes; for the child began to look as if she thought she too had done some wrong, remaining in an appalled silence till the tears rolled down her chubby cheeks.

'What's the matter, my little maid?' said Ned mechanically.

'I do want to go home!' she let out, in tones that told of a bursting heart. 'And my totties be cold, an' I shan't have no bread an' butter no more!'

'I don't know what to say to it all!' declared Ned, his own eye moist as he turned and walked a few steps with his head down; then regarded them again point-blank. From the child escaped troubled breaths and silently welling tears.

'Want some bread and butter, do 'ee?' he said, with factitious hardness.

'Ye-e-s!'

'Well, I dare say I can get 'ee a bit! Naturally, you must want some. And you, too, for that matter, Car'line.'

'I do feel a little hungered. But I can keep it off,' she murmured.

'Folk shouldn't do that,' he said gruffly. . . . 'There, come along!' He caught up the child, as he added, 'You must bide here to-night, anyhow, I s'pose! What can you do otherwise? I'll get 'ee some tea and victuals; and as for this job, I'm sure I don't know what to say! This is the way out.'

They pursued their way, without speaking, to Ned's lodgings, which were not far off. There he dried them and made them comfortable, and prepared tea; they thankfully sat down. The ready-made household of which he suddenly found himself the head imparted a cosy aspect to his room, and a paternal one to himself. Presently he turned to the child and kissed her now blooming cheeks; and, looking wistfully at Car'line, kissed her also.

'I don't see how I can send you back all them miles,' he growled, 'now you've come all the way o' purpose to join me. But you must trust me, Car'line, and show you've real faith in me. Well, do you feel better now, my little woman?'

The child nodded beamingly, her mouth being otherwise occupied.

'I did trust you, Ned, in coming; and I shall always!'

Thus, without any definite agreement to forgive her, he tacitly acquiesced in the fate that Heaven had sent him; and on the day of their marriage (which was not quite so soon as he had expected it could be, on account of the time necessary for banns) he took her to the Exhibition when they came back from church, as he had promised. While standing near a large mirror in one of the courts devoted to furniture, Car'line started, for in the glass appeared the reflection of a form exactly resembling Mop Ollamoor's – so exactly, that it seemed impossible to believe anybody but that artist in person to be the original. On passing round the objects which hemmed in Ned, her, and the child from a direct view, no Mop was to be seen. Whether he were really in London or not at that time was never known; and Car'line always stoutly denied that her readiness to go and meet Ned in town arose from any rumour that Mop had also gone thither; which denial there was no reasonable ground for doubting.

And then the year glided away, and the Exhibition folded itself up and became a thing of the past. The park trees that had been enclosed for six months were again exposed to the winds and storms, and the sod grew green anew. Ned found that Car'line resolved herself into a very good wife and companion, though she had made herself what is called cheap to him; but in that she was like another domestic article, a cheap tea-pot, which often brews better tea than a dear one. One autumn Hipcroft found himself with but little work to do, and a prospect of less for the winter. Both being country born and bred, they fancied they would like to live again in their natural atmosphere. It was accordingly decided between them that they should leave the pent-up London lodging, and that Ned should seek out employment near his native place, his wife and her daughter staying with Car'line's father during the search for occupation and an abode of their own.

Tinglings of pride pervaded Car'line's spasmodic little frame as she journeyed down with Ned to the place she had left two or three years before, in silence and under a cloud. To return to where she had once been despised, a smiling London wife with a distinct London accent, was a triumph which the world did not witness every day.

The train did not stop at the petty roadside station that lay nearest to Stickleford, and the trio went on to Casterbridge. Ned thought it a good opportunity to make a few preliminary inquiries for employment at workshops in the borough where he had been known; and feeling cold from her journey, and it being dry underfoot and only dusk as yet, with a moon on the point of rising, Car'line and her little girl walked on towards Stickleford, leaving Ned to follow at a quicker pace, and pick her up at a certain half-way house, widely known as an inn.

The woman and child pursued the well-remembered way comfortably enough, though they were both becoming wearied. In the course of three miles they had passed Heedless-William's Pond, the familiar landmark by Bloom's End, and were drawing near the Quiet Woman, a lone roadside hostel on the lower verge of the Egdon Heath, since and for many years abolished. In stepping up towards it Car'line heard more voices within than had formerly been customary at such an hour, and she learned that an auction of fat stock had been held near the spot that afternoon. The child would be the better for a rest as well as herself, she thought, and she entered.

The guests and customers overflowed into the passage, and Car'line had no sooner crossed the threshold than a man whom she remembered by sight came forward with a glass and mug in his hands towards a friend leaning against the wall; but, seeing her, very gallantly offered her a drink of the liquor, which was gin-and-beer hot, pouring her out a tumblerful and saying, in a moment or two: 'Surely, 'tis little Car'line Aspent that was – down at Stickleford?'

She assented, and, though she did not exactly want this beverage, she drank it since it was offered, and her entertainer begged her to come in further and sit down. Once within the room she found that all the persons present were seated close against the walls, and there being a chair vacant she did the same. An explanation of their position occurred the next moment. In the opposite corner stood Mop, rosining his bow and looking just the same as ever. The company had cleared the middle of the room for dancing, and they were about to dance again. As she wore a veil to keep off the wind she did not think he had recognized her, or could possibly guess the identity of the child; and to her satisfied surprise she found that she could confront him quite calmly – mistress of herself in the dignity her London life had given her. Before she had quite emptied her glass the dance was called, the dancers formed in two lines, the music sounded, and the figure began.

Then matters changed for Car'line. A tremor quickened itself to life in her, and her hand so shook that she could hardly set down her glass. It was not the dance nor the dancers, but the notes of that old violin which thrilled the London wife, these having still all the witchery that she had so well known of yore, and under which she had used to lose her power of independent will. How it all came back! There was the fiddling figure against the wall; the large, oily, mop-like head of him, and beneath the mop the face with closed eyes.

After the first moments of paralyzed reverie the familiar tune in the familiar rendering made her laugh and shed tears simultaneously. Then a man at the bottom of the dance, whose partner had dropped away, stretched out his hand and beckoned to her to take the place. She did not want to dance; she entreated by signs to be left where she was, but she was entreating of the tune and its player rather than of the dancing man. The saltatory tendency which the fiddler and his cunning instrument had ever been able to start in her was seizing Car'line just as it had done in earlier years, possibly assisted by the gin-and-beer hot. Tired as she was she grasped her little girl by the hand, and plunging in at the bottom of the figure, whirled about with the rest. She found that her companions were mostly people of the neighbouring hamlets and farms – Bloom's End, Mellstock, Lewgate, and elsewhere; and by degrees she was recognized as she convulsively danced on, wishing that Mop would cease and let her heart rest from the aching he caused, and her feet also.

After long and many minutes the dance ended, when she was urged to fortify herself with more gin-and-beer; which she did, feeling very weak and overpowered with hysteric emotion. She refrained from unveiling, to keep Mop in ignorance of her presence, if possible. Several of the guests having left, Car'line hastily wiped her lips and also turned to go; but, according to the account of some who remained, at that very moment a five-handed reel was proposed, in which two or three begged her to join.

She declined on the plea of being tired and having to walk to Stickleford, when Mop began aggressively tweedling 'My Fancy-Lad', in D major, as the air to which the reel was to be footed. He must have recognized her, though she did not know it, for it was the strain of all seductive strains which she was least able to resist – the one he had played when she was leaning over the bridge at the date of their first acquaintance. Car'line stepped despairingly into the middle of the room with the other four.

Reels were resorted to hereabouts at this time by the more robust spirits, for the reduction of superfluous energy which the ordinary figure-dances were not powerful enough to exhaust. As everybody knows, or does not know, the five reelers stood in the form of a cross, the reel being performed by each line of three alternately, the persons who successively came to the middle place dancing in both directions. Car'line soon found herself in this place, the axis of the whole performance, and could not get out of it, the tune turning into the first part without giving her opportunity. And now she began to suspect that Mop did know her, and was doing this on purpose, though whenever she stole a glance at him his closed eyes betokened obliviousness to everything outside his own brain. She continued to wend her way through the figure of 8 that was formed by her course, the fiddler introducing into his notes the wild and agonizing sweetness of a living voice in one too highly wrought; its pathos running high and running low in endless variation, projecting through her nerves excruciating spasms, a sort of blissful torture. The room swam; the tune was endless; and in about a quarter of an hour the only other woman in the figure dropped out exhausted, and sank panting on a bench.

The reel instantly resolved itself into a four-handed one. Car'line would have given anything to leave off; but she had, or fancied she had, no power, while Mop played such tunes; and thus another ten minutes slipped by, a haze of dust now clouding the candles, the floor being of stone, sanded. Then another dancer fell out – one of the men – and went into the passage in a frantic search for liquor. To turn the figure into a three-handed reel was the work of a second, Mop modulating at the same time into 'The Fairy Dance', as better suited to the contracted movement, and no less one of those foods of love which, as manufactured by his bow, had always intoxicated her.

In a reel for three there was no rest whatever, and four or five minutes were enough to make her remaining two partners, now thoroughly blown, stamp their last bar, and, like their predecessors, limp off into the next room to get something to drink. Car'line, half-stifled inside her veil, was left dancing alone, the apartment now being empty of everybody save herself, Mop, and their little girl.

She flung up the veil, and cast her eyes upon him, as if imploring him to withdraw himself and his acoustic magnetism from the atmosphere. Mop opened one of his own orbs, as though for the first time, fixed it peeringly upon her, and smiling dreamily, threw into his strains the reserve of expression which he could not afford to waste on a big and noisy dance. Crowds of little chromatic subtleties, capable of drawing tears from a statue, proceeded straightway from the ancient fiddle, as if it were dying of the emotion which had been pent up within it ever since its banishment from some Italian or German city where it first took shape and sound. There was that in the look of Mop's one dark eye which said: 'You cannot leave off, dear, whether you would or no!' and it bred in her a paroxysm of desperation that defied him to tire her down.

She thus continued to dance alone, defiantly as she thought, but in truth slavishly and abjectly, subject to every wave of the melody, and probed by the gimlet-like gaze of her fascinator's open eye; keeping up at the same time a feeble smile in his face, as a feint to signify it was still her own pleasure which led her on. A terrified embarrassment as to what she could say to him if she were to leave off, had its unrecognized share in keeping her going. The child, who was beginning to be distressed by the strange situation, came up and whimpered: 'Stop, mother, stop, and let's go home!' as she seized Car'line's hand.

Suddenly Car'line sank staggering to the floor, and rolling over on her face, prone she remained. Mop's fiddle thereupon emitted an elfin shriek of finality; stepping quickly down from the nine-gallon beer-cask which had formed his rostrum, he went to the little girl, who disconsolately bent over her mother.

The guests who had gone into the back room for liquor and change of air, hearing something unusual, trooped back hitherward, where they endeavoured to revive poor, weak Car'line by blowing her with the bellows and opening the window. Ned, her husband, who had been

detained in Casterbridge, as aforesaid, came along the road at this
juncture, and hearing excited voices through the open casement, and,
to his great surprise, the mention of his wife's name, he entered amid the
rest upon the scene. Car'line was now in convulsions, weeping violently,
and for a long time nothing could be done with her. While he was
sending for a cart to take her onward to Stickleford Hipcroft anxiously
inquired how it had all happened; and then the assembly explained that
a fiddler formerly known in the locality had lately visited his old haunts,
and had taken upon himself without invitation to play that evening at
the inn and raise a dance.

Ned demanded the fiddler's name, and they said Ollamoor.

'Ah!' exclaimed Ned, looking round him. 'Where is he, and where –
where's my little girl?'

Ollamoor had disappeared, and so had the child. Hipcroft was in
ordinary a quiet and tractable fellow, but a determination which was to
be feared settled in his face now. 'Blast him!' he cried. 'I'll beat his
skull in for'n, if I swing for it to-morrow!'

He had rushed to the poker which lay on the hearth, and hastened
down the passage, the people following. Outside the house, on the
other side of the highway, a mass of dark heath-land rose sullenly upward to its not easily accessible interior, a ravined plateau, whereon
jutted into the sky, at the distance of a couple of miles, the fir-woods of
Mistover backed by the Yalbury coppices – a place of Dantesque gloom
at this hour, which would have afforded secure hiding for a battery of
artillery, much less a man and a child.

Some other men plunged thitherward with him, and more went along
the road. They were gone about twenty minutes altogether, returning
without result to the inn. Ned sat down in the settle, and clasped his
forehead with his hands.

'Well – what a fool the man is, and hev been all these years, if he
thinks the child his, as a' do seem to!' they whispered. 'And everybody
else knowing otherwise!'

'No, I don't think 'tis mine!' cried Ned hoarsely, as he looked up
from his hands. 'But she *is* mine, all the same! Ha'n't I nussed her?
Ha'n't I fed her and teached her? Ha'n't I played wi' her? O, little
Carry – gone with that rogue – gone!'

'You ha'n't lost your mis'ess, anyhow,' they said to console him.
'She's throwed up the sperrits, and she is feeling better, and she's more
to 'ee than a child that isn't yours.'

'She isn't! She's not so particular much to me, especially now she's lost the little maid! But Carry's the whole world to me!'

'Well, ver' like you'll find her to-morrow.'

'Ah – but shall I? Yet he *can't* hurt her – surely he can't! Well – how's Car'line now? I am ready. Is the cart here?'

She was lifted into the vehicle, and they sadly lumbered on toward Stickleford. Next day she was calmer; but the fits were still upon her; and her will seemed shattered. For the child she appeared to show singularly little anxiety, though Ned was nearly distracted by his passionate paternal love for a child not his own. It was nevertheless quite expected that the impish Mop would restore the lost one after a freak of a day or two; but time went on, and neither he nor she could be heard of, and Hipcroft murmured that perhaps he was exercising upon her some unholy musical charm, as he had done upon Car'line herself. Weeks passed, and still they could obtain no clue either to the fiddler's whereabouts or to the girl's; and how he could have induced her to go with him remained a mystery.

Then Ned, who had obtained only temporary employment in the neighbourhood, took a sudden hatred towards his native district, and a rumour reaching his ears through the police that a somewhat similar man and child had been seen at a fair near London, he playing a violin, she dancing on stilts, a new interest in the capital took possession of Hipcroft with an intensity which would scarcely allow him time to pack before returning thither. He did not, however, find the lost one, though he made it the entire business of his over-hours to stand about in by-streets in the hope of discovering her, and would start up in the night, saying, 'That rascal's torturing her to maintain him!' To which his wife would answer peevishly, 'Don't 'ee raft yourself so, Ned! You prevent my getting a bit o' rest! He won't hurt her!' and fall asleep again.

That Carry and her father had emigrated to America was the general opinion; Mop, no doubt, finding the girl a highly desirable companion when he had trained her to keep him by her earnings as a dancer. There, for that matter, they may be performing in some capacity now, though he must be an old scamp verging on three-score-and-ten, and she a woman of four-and-forty.

May 1893

A Few Crusted Characters

INTRODUCTION

IT is a Saturday afternoon of blue and yellow autumn-time, and the scene is the High Street of a well-known market-town. A large carrier's van stands in the quadrangular fore-court of the White Hart Inn, upon the sides of its spacious tilt being painted, in weather-beaten letters: 'Burthen, Carrier to Longpuddle'. These vans, so numerous hereabout, are a respectable, if somewhat lumbering, class of conveyance, much resorted to by decent travellers not overstocked with money, the better among them roughly corresponding to the old French *diligences*.

The present one is timed to leave the town at four in the afternoon precisely, and it is now half-past three by the clock in the turret at the top of the street. In a few seconds errand-boys from the shops begin to arrive with packages, which they fling into the vehicle, and turn away whistling, and care for the packages no more. At twenty minutes to four an elderly woman places her basket upon the shafts, slowly mounts, takes up a seat inside, and folds her hands and her lips. She has secured her corner for the journey, though there is as yet no sign of a horse being put in, nor of a carrier. At the three-quarters, two other women arrive, in whom the first recognizes the postmistress of Upper Longpuddle and the registrar's wife, they recognizing her as the aged groceress of the same village. At five minutes to the hour there approach Mr Profitt, the schoolmaster, in a soft felt hat, and Christopher Twink, the master-thatcher; and as the hour strikes there rapidly drop in the parish clerk and his wife, the seedsman and his aged father, the registrar; also Mr

Day, the world-ignored local landscape-painter, an elderly man who resides in his native place, and has never sold a picture outside it, though his pretensions to art have been nobly supported by his fellow-villagers, whose confidence in his genius has been as remarkable as the outer neglect of it, leading them to buy his paintings so extensively (at the price of a few shillings each, it is true) that every dwelling in the parish exhibits three or four of those admired productions on its walls.

Burthen, the carrier, is by this time seen bustling round the vehicle; the horses are put in, the proprietor arranges the reins and springs up into his seat as if he were used to it – which he is.

'Is everybody here?' he asks preparatorily over his shoulder to the passengers within.

As those who were not there did not reply in the negative the muster was assumed to be complete, and after a few hitches and hindrances the van with its human freight was got under way. It jogged on at an easy pace till it reached the bridge which formed the last outpost of the town. The carrier pulled up suddenly.

'Bless my soul!' he said, 'I've forgot the curate!'

All who could do so gazed from the little back-window of the van, but the curate was not in sight.

'Now I wonder where that there man is?' continued the carrier.

'Poor man, he ought to have a living at his time of life.'

'And he ought to be punctual,' said the carrier. ' "Four o'clock sharp is my time for starting," I said to 'en. And he said, "I'll be there." Now he's not here; and as a serious old church-minister he ought to be as good as his word. Perhaps Mr Flaxton knows, being in the same line of life?' He turned to the parish clerk.

'I was talking an immense deal with him, that's true, half an hour ago,' replied that ecclesiastic, as one of whom it was no erroneous supposition that he should be on intimate terms with another of the cloth. 'But he didn't say he would be late.'

The discussion was cut off by the appearance round the corner of the van of rays from the curate's spectacles, followed hastily by his face and a few white whiskers, and the swinging tails of his long gaunt coat. Nobody reproached him, seeing how he was reproaching himself; and he entered breathlessly and took his seat.

'Now be we all here?' said the carrier again. They started a second time, and moved on till they were about three hundred yards out of the town, and had nearly reached the second bridge, behind which, as every native remembers, the road takes a turn, and travellers by this highway disappear finally from the view of gazing burghers.

'Well, as I'm alive!' cried the postmistress from the interior of the conveyance, peering through the little square back-window along the road townward.

'What ?' said the carrier.

'A man hailing us!'

Another sudden stoppage. 'Somebody else?' the carrier asked.

'Ay, sure!' All waited silently, while those who could gaze out did so.

'Now, who can that be?' Burthen continued. 'I just put it to ye, neighbours, can any man keep time with such hindrances? Bain't we full a'ready? Who in the world can the man be?'

'He's a sort of gentleman,' said the schoolmaster, his position commanding the road more comfortably than that of his comrades.

The stranger, who had been holding up his umbrella to attract their notice, was walking forward leisurely enough, now that he found, by their stopping, that it had been secured. His clothes were decidedly not of a local cut, though it was difficult to point out any particular mark of difference. In his left hand he carried a small leather travelling-bag. As soon as he had overtaken the van he glanced at the inscription on its side, as if to assure himself that he had hailed the right conveyance, and asked if they had room.

The carrier replied that though they were pretty well laden he supposed they could carry one more, whereupon the stranger mounted, and took the seat cleared for him within. And then the horses made another move, this time for good, and swung along with their burden of fourteen souls all told.

'You bain't one of these parts, sir?' said the carrier. 'I could tell that as far as I could see 'ee.'

'Yes, I am one of these parts,' said the stranger.

'Oh? H'm.'

The silence which followed seemed to imply a doubt of the truth of the new-comer's assertion. 'I was speaking of Upper Longpuddle, more particular,' continued the carrier hardily, 'and I think I know most faces of that valley.'

'I was born at Longpuddle, and nursed at Longpuddle, and my father and grandfather before me,' said the passenger quietly.

'Why, to be sure,' said the aged groceress in the background, 'it isn't John Lackland's son – never – it can't be – he who went to foreign parts five-and-thirty years ago with his wife and family? Yet – what do I hear? – that's his father's voice!'

'That's the man,' replied the stranger. 'John Lackland was my father, and I am John Lackland's son. Five-and-thirty years ago, when I was a boy of eleven, my parents emigrated across the seas, taking me and my sister with them. Kytes's boy Tony was the one who drove us and our belongings to Casterbridge on the morning we left; and his was the last Longpuddle face I saw. We sailed the same week across the ocean, and there we've been ever since, and there I've left those I went with – all three.'

'Alive or dead?'

'Dead,' he replied in a low voice. 'And I have come back to the old place, having nourished a thought – not a definite intention, but just a thought – that I should like to return here in a year or two, to spend the remainder of my days.'

'Married man, Mr Lackland?'

'No.'

'And have the world used 'ee well, sir – or rather John, knowing 'ee as a child? In these rich new countries that we hear of so much, you've got rich with the rest?'

'I am not very rich,' Mr Lackland said. 'Even in new countries, you know, there are failures. The race is not always to the swift, nor the battle to the strong; and even if it sometimes is, you may be neither swift nor strong. However, that's enough about me. Now, having answered your inquiries, you must answer mine; for being in London, I have come down here entirely to discover what Longpuddle is looking like, and who are living there. That was why I preferred a seat in your van to hiring a carriage for driving across.'

'Well, as for Longpuddle, we rub on there much as usual. Old figures have dropped out o' their frames, so to speak it, and new ones have been put in their places. You mentioned Tony Kytes as having been the one to drive your family and your goods to Casterbridge in his father's waggon when you left. Tony is, I believe, living still, but not at Longpuddle. He went away and settled at Lewgate, near Mellstock, after his marriage. Ah, Tony was a sort o' man!'

'His character had hardly come out when I knew him.'

'No. But 'twas well enough, as far as that goes – except as to women. I shall never forget his courting – never!'

The returned villager waited silently, and the carrier went on: –

TONY KYTES, THE ARCH-DECEIVER

'I shall never forget Tony's face. 'Twas a little, round, firm, tight face, with a seam here and there left by the smallpox, but not enough to hurt his looks in a woman's eye, though he'd had it badish when he was a boy. So very serious looking and unsmiling 'a was, that young man, that it really seemed as if he couldn't laugh at all without great pain to his conscience. He looked very hard at a small speck in your eye when talking to 'ee. And there was no more sign of a whisker or beard on Tony Kytes's face than on the palm of my hand. He used to sing "The Tailor's Breeches" with a religious manner, as if it were a hymn: –

' "O the petticoats went off, and the breeches they went on!"

and all the rest of the scandalous stuff. He was quite the women's favourite, and in return for their likings he loved 'em in shoals.

'But in course of time Tony got fixed down to one in particular, Milly Richards, a nice, light, small, tender little thing; and it was soon said that they were engaged to be married. One Saturday he had been to market to do business for his father, and was driving home the waggon in the afternoon. When he reached the foot of the very hill we shall be going over in ten minutes who should he see waiting for him at the top but Unity Sallet, a handsome girl, one of the young women he'd been very tender towards before he'd got engaged to Milly.

'As soon as Tony came up to her she said, "My dear Tony, will you give me a lift home?"

' "That I will, darling," said Tony. "You don't suppose I could refuse 'ee?"

'She smiled a smile, and up she hopped, and on drove Tony.

' "Tony," she says, in a sort of tender chide, "why did ye desert me for that other one? In what is she better than I? I should have made 'ee a finer wife, and a more loving one, too. 'Tisn't girls that are so easily won at first that are the best. Think how long we've known each other – ever since we were children almost – now haven't we, Tony?"

' "Yes, that we have," says Tony, a-struck with the truth o't.

' "And you've never seen anything in me to complain of, have ye, Tony? Now tell the truth to me!"

' "I never have, upon my life," says Tony.

' "And – can you say I'm not pretty, Tony? Now look at me!"

'He let his eyes light upon her for a long while. "I really can't," says he. "In fact, I never knowed you was so pretty before!"

' "Prettier than she?"

'What Tony would have said to that nobody knows, for before he could speak, what should he see ahead, over the hedge past the turning, but a feather he knew well – the feather in Milly's hat – she to whom he had been thinking of putting the question as to giving out the banns that very week.

' "Unity," says he, as mild as he could, "here's Milly coming. Now I shall catch it mightily if she sees 'ee riding here with me; and if you get down she'll be turning the corner in a moment, and, seeing 'ee in the road, she'll know we've been coming on together. Now, dearest Unity, will ye, to avoid all unpleasantness, which I know ye can't bear any more than I, will ye lie down in the back part of the waggon, and let me cover you over with the tarpaulin till Milly has passed? It will all be done in a minute. Do! – and I'll think over what we've said, and per- haps I shall put a loving question to you after all, instead of to Milly. 'Tisn't true that it is all settled between her and me."

'Well, Unity Sallet agreed, and lay down at the back end of the waggon, and Tony covered her over, so that the waggon seemed to be empty but for the loose tarpaulin; and then he drove on to meet Milly.

' "My dear Tony!" cries Milly, looking up with a little pout at him as he came near. "How long you've been coming home! Just as if I didn't live at Upper Longpuddle at all! And I've come to meet you as you asked me to do, and to ride back with you, and talk over our future home – since you asked me, and I promised. But I shouldn't have come else, Mr Tony!"

' "Ay, my dear, I did ask 'ee – to be sure I did, now I think of it – but I had quite forgot it. To ride back with me, did you say, dear Milly?"

' "Well, of course! What can I do else? Surely you don't want me to walk, now I've come all this way?"

' "O no, no! I was thinking you might be going on to town to meet your mother. I saw her there – and she looked as if she might be expecting 'ee."

' "O no; she's just home. She came across the fields, and so got back before you."

' "Ah! I didn't know that," says Tony. And there was no help for it but to take her up beside him.

'They talked on very pleasantly, and looked at the trees, and beasts, and birds, and insects, and at the ploughmen at work in the fields, till presently who should they see looking out of the upper window of a house that stood beside the road they were following, but Hannah Jolliver, another young beauty of the place at that time, and the very first woman that Tony had fallen in love with – before Milly and before Unity, in fact – the one that he had almost arranged to marry instead of Milly. She was a much more dashing girl than Milly Richards, though he'd not thought much of her of late. The house Hannah was looking from was her aunt's.

' "My dear Milly – my coming wife, as I may call 'ee," says Tony in his modest way, and not so loud that Unity could overhear, "I see a young woman a-looking out of window, who I think may accost me. The fact is, Milly, she had a notion that I was wishing to marry her, and since she's discovered I've promised another, and a prettier than she, I'm rather afeared of her temper if she sees us together. Now, Milly, would you do me a favour – my coming wife, as I may say ?"

' "Certainly, dearest Tony," says she.

' "Then would ye creep under the empty sacks just here in the front of the waggon, and hide there out of sight till we've passed the house ? She hasn't seen us yet. You see, we ought to live in peace and goodwill since 'tis almost Christmas, and 'twill prevent angry passions rising, which we always should do."

' "I don't mind, to oblige you, Tony," Milly said; and though she didn't care much about doing it, she crept under, and crouched down just behind the seat, Unity being snug at the other end. So they drove on till they got near the road-side cottage. Hannah had soon seen him coming, and waited at the window, looking down upon him. She tossed her head a little disdainful and smiled off-hand.

' "Well, aren't you going to be civil enough to ask me to ride home with you!" she says, seeing that he was for driving past with a nod and a smile.

' "Ah, to be sure! What was I thinking of ?" said Tony, in a flutter. "But you seem as if you was staying at your aunt's ?"

' "No, I am not," she said. "Don't you see I have my bonnet and jacket on ? I have only called to see her on my way home. How can you be so stupid, Tony ?"

' "In that case – ah – of course you must come along wi' me," says Tony, feeling a dim sort of sweat rising up inside his clothes. And he reined in the horse, and waited till she'd come downstairs, and then helped her up beside him, her feet outside. He drove on again, his face as long as a face that was a round one by nature well could be.

'Hannah looked round sideways into his eyes. "This is nice, isn't it, Tony?" she says. "I like riding with you."

'Tony looked back into her eyes. "And I with you," he said after a while. In short, having considered her, he warmed up, and the more he looked at her the more he liked her, till he couldn't for the life of him think why he had ever said a word about marriage to Milly or Unity while Hannah Jolliver was in question. So they sat a little closer and closer, their feet upon the foot-board and their shoulders touching, and Tony thought over and over again how handsome Hannah was. He spoke tenderer and tenderer, and called her "dear Hannah" in a whisper at last.

' "You've settled it with Milly by this time, I suppose?" said she.

' "N-no, not exactly."

' "What? How low you talk, Tony."

' "Yes – I've a kind of hoarseness. I said, not exactly."

' "I suppose you mean to?"

' "Well, as to that—" His eyes rested on her face, and hers on his. He wondered how he could have been such a fool as not to follow up Hannah. "My sweet Hannah!" he bursts out, taking her hand, not being really able to help it, and forgetting Milly and Unity, and all the world besides. "Settled it? I don't think I have!"

' "Hark!" says Hannah.

' "What?" says Tony, letting go her hand.

' "Surely I heard a sort of little screaming squeak under those sacks? Why, you've been carrying corn, and there's mice in this waggon, I declare!" She began to haul up the tails of her gown.

' "O no, 'tis the axle," said Tony in an assuring way. "It do go like that sometimes in dry weather."

' "Perhaps it was. . . . Well, now, to be quite honest, dear Tony, do you like her better than me? Because – because, although I've held off so independent, I'll own at last that I do like 'ee, Tony, to tell the truth; and I wouldn't say no if you asked me – you know what."

'Tony was so won over by this pretty offering mood of a girl who had been quite the reverse (Hannah had a backward way with her at times, if you can mind) that he just glanced behind, and then whispered very

soft, "I haven't quite promised her, and I think I can get out of it, and
ask you that question you speak of."

' "Throw over Milly? – all to marry me! How delightful!" broke out
Hannah, quite loud, clapping her hands.

'At this there was a real squeak – an angry, spiteful squeak, and
afterward a long moan, as if something had broke its heart, and a movement of the empty sacks.

' "Something's there!" said Hannah, starting up.

' "It's nothing really," says Tony in a soothing voice, and praying
inwardly for a way out of this. "I wouldn't tell 'ee at first, because I
wouldn't frighten 'ee. But, Hannah, I've really a couple of ferrets in a
bag under there, for rabbiting, and they quarrel sometimes. I don't
wish it knowed, as 'twould be called poaching. Oh, they can't get out,
bless 'ee – you are quite safe! And – and – what a fine day it is, isn't it,
Hannah, for this time of year? Be you going to market next Saturday?
How is your aunt now?" And so on, says Tony, to keep her from talking
any more about love in Milly's hearing.

'But he found his work cut out for him, and wondering again how he
should get out of this ticklish business, he looked about for a chance.
Nearing home he saw his father in a field not far off, holding up his
hand as if he wished to speak to Tony.

' "Would you mind taking the reins a moment, Hannah," he said,
much relieved, "while I go and find out what father wants?"

'She consented, and away he hastened into the field, only too glad to
get breathing time. He found that his father was looking at him with
rather a stern eye.

' "Come, come, Tony," says old Mr Kytes, as soon as his son was
alongside him, "this won't do, you know."

' "What?" says Tony.

' "Why, if you mean to marry Milly Richards, do it, and there's an
end o't. But don't go driving about the country with Jolliver's daughter
and making a scandal. I won't have such things done."

' "I only asked her – that is, she asked me, to ride home."

' "She? Why, now, if it had been Milly, 'twould have been quite
proper; but you and Hannah Jolliver going about by yourselves—"

' "Milly's there, too, father."

' "Milly? Where?"

' "Under the corn-sacks! Yes, the truth is, father, I've got rather into
a nunnywatch, I'm afeared! Unity Sallet is there, too – yes, at the other

end, under the tarpaulin. All three are in that waggon, and what to do with 'em I know no more than the dead! The best plan is, as I'm thinking, to speak out loud and plain to one of 'em before the rest, and that will settle it; not but what 'twill cause 'em to kick up a bit of a miff, for certain. Now which would you marry, father, if you was in my place?"

' "Whichever of 'em did *not* ask to ride with thee."

' "That was Milly, I'm bound to say, as she only mounted by my invitation. But Milly—"

' "Then stick to Milly, she's the best. . . . But look at that!"

'His father pointed toward the waggon. "She can't hold that horse in. You shouldn't have left the reins in her hands. Run on and take the horse's head, or there'll be some accident to them maids!"

'Tony's horse, in fact, in spite of Hannah's tugging at the reins, had started on his way at a brisk walking pace, being very anxious to get back to the stable, for he had had a long day out. Without another word Tony rushed away from his father to overtake the horse.

'Now of all things that could have happened to wean him from Milly there was nothing so powerful as his father's recommending her. No; it could not be Milly, after all. Hannah must be the one, since he could not marry all three as he longed to do. This he thought while running after the waggon. But queer things were happening inside it.

'It was, of course, Milly who had screamed under the sack-bags, being obliged to let off her bitter rage and shame in that way at what Tony was saying, and never daring to show, for very pride and dread o' being laughed at, that she was in hiding. She became more and more restless, and in twisting herself about, what did she see but another woman's foot and white stocking close to her head. It quite frightened her, not knowing that Unity Sallet was in the waggon likewise. But after the fright was over she determined to get to the bottom of all this, and she crept and crept along the bed of the waggon, under the tarpaulin, like a snake, when lo and behold she came face to face with Unity.

' "Well, if this isn't disgraceful!" says Milly in a raging whisper to Unity.

' "'Tis," says Unity, "to see you hiding in a young man's waggon like this, and no great character belonging to either of ye!"

' "Mind what you are saying!" replied Milly, getting louder. "I am engaged to be married to him, and haven't I a right to be here? What right have you, I should like to know? What has he been promising you? A pretty lot of nonsense, I expect! But what Tony says to other women is all mere wind, and no concern to me!"

' "Don't you be too sure!" says Unity. "He's going to have Hannah, and not you, nor me either; I could hear that."

'Now at these strange voices sounding from under the cloth Hannah was thunderstruck a'most into a swound; and it was just at this time that the horse moved on. Hannah tugged away wildly, not knowing what she was doing; and as the quarrel rose louder and louder Hannah got so horrified that she let go the reins altogether. The horse went on at his own pace, and coming to the corner where we turn round to drop down the hill to Lower Longpuddle he turned too quick, the off wheels went up the bank, the waggon rose sideways till it was quite on edge upon the near axles, and out rolled the three maidens into the road in a heap. The horse looked round and stood still.

'When Tony came up, frightened and breathless, he was relieved enough to see that neither of his darlings was hurt, beyond a few scratches from the brambles of the hedge. But he was rather alarmed when he heard how they were going on at one another.

' "Don't ye quarrel, my dears – don't ye!" says he, taking off his hat out of respect to 'em. And then he would have kissed them all round, as fair and square as a man could, but they were in too much of a taking to let him, and screeched and sobbed till they was quite spent.

' "Now I'll speak out honest, because I ought to," says Tony, as soon as he could get heard. "And this is the truth," says he. "I've asked Hannah to be mine, and she is willing, and we are going to put up the banns next—"

'Tony had not noticed that Hannah's father was coming up behind, nor had he noticed that Hannah's face was beginning to bleed from the scratch of a bramble. Hannah had seen her father, and had run to him, crying worse than ever.

' "My daughter is *not* willing, sir!" says Mr Jolliver hot and strong. "Be you willing, Hannah? I ask ye to have spirit enough to refuse him, if yer virtue is left to 'ee and you run no risk?"

' "She's as sound as a bell for me, that I'll swear!" says Tony, flaring up. "And so's the others, come to that, though you may think it an onusual thing in me!"

' "I have spirit, and I do refuse him!" says Hannah, partly because her father was there, and partly, too, in a tantrum because of the discovery, and the scar that might be left on her face. "Little did I think when I was so soft with him just now that I was talking to such a false deceiver!"

' "What, you won't have me, Hannah?" says Tony, his jaw hanging down like a dead man's.

' "Never – I would sooner marry no – nobody at all!" she gasped out, though with her heart in her throat, for she would not have refused Tony if he had asked her quietly, and her father had not been there, and her face had not been scratched by the bramble. And having said that, away she walked upon her father's arm, thinking and hoping he would ask her again.

'Tony didn't know what to say next. Milly was sobbing her heart out; but as his father had strongly recommended her he couldn't feel inclined that way. So he turned to Unity.

' "Well, will you, Unity dear, be mine?" he says.

' "Take her leavings? Not I!" says Unity. "I'd scorn it!" And away walks Unity Sallet likewise, though she looked back when she'd gone some way, to see if he was following her.

'So there at last were left Milly and Tony by themselves, she crying in watery streams, and Tony looking like a tree struck by lightning.

' "Well, Milly," he says at last, going up to her, "it do seem as if fate had ordained that it should be you and I, or nobody. And what must be must be, I suppose. Hey, Milly?"

' "If you like, Tony. You didn't really mean what you said to them?"

' "Not a word of it!" declares Tony, bringing down his fist upon his palm.

'And then he kissed her, and put the waggon to rights, and they mounted together; and their banns were put up the very next Sunday. I was not able to go to their wedding, but it was a rare party they had, by all account. Everybody in Longpuddle was there almost; you among the rest, I think, Mr Flaxton?' The speaker turned to the parish clerk.

'I was,' said Mr Flaxton. 'And that party was the cause of a very curious change in some other people's affairs; I mean in Steve Hardcome's and his cousin James's.'

'Ah! the Hardcomes,' said the stranger. 'How familiar that name is to me! What of them?'

The clerk cleared his throat and began: –

THE HISTORY OF THE HARDCOMES

'Yes, Tony's was the very best wedding-randy that ever I was at; and
I've been at a good many, as you may suppose' – turning to the newly-
arrived one – 'having, as a church-officer, the privilege to attend all
christening, wedding, and funeral parties – such being our Wessex
custom.

' 'Twas on a frosty night in Christmas week, and among the folk
invited were the said Hardcomes o' Climmerston – Steve and James –
first cousins, both of them small farmers, just entering into business on
their own account. With them came, as a matter of course, their intended
wives, two young women of the neighbourhood, both very pretty and
sprightly maidens, and numbers of friends from Abbot's-Cernel, and
Weatherbury, and Mellstock, and I don't know where – a regular house-
ful.

'The kitchen was cleared of furniture for dancing, and the old folk
played at "Put" and "All-fours" in the parlour, though at last they gave
that up to join in the dance. The top of the figure was by the large front
window of the room, and there were so many couples that the lower
part of the figure reached through the door at the back, and into the
darkness of the out-house; in fact, you couldn't see the end of the row
at all, and 'twas never known exactly how long that dance was, the
lowest couples being lost among the faggots and brushwood in the out-
house.

'When we had danced a few hours, and the crowns of we taller men
were swelling into lumps with bumping the beams of the ceiling, the
first fiddler laid down his fiddle-bow, and said he should play no more,
for he wished to dance. And in another hour the second fiddler laid
down his, and said he wanted to dance, too; so there was only the third
fiddler left, and he was a' old, veteran man, very weak in the wrist.
However, he managed to keep up a faltering tweedle-dee; but there
being no chair in the room, and his knees being as weak as his wrists, he
was obliged to sit upon as much of the little corner-table as projected
beyond the corner-cupboard fixed over it, which was not a very wide
seat for a man advanced in years.

'Among those who danced most continually were the two engaged
couples, as was natural to their situation. Each pair was very well
matched, and very unlike the other. James Hardcome's intended was

called Emily Darth, and both she and James were gentle, nice-minded, in-door people, fond of a quiet life. Steve and his chosen, named Olive Pawle, were different; they were of a more bustling nature, fond of racketing about and seeing what was going on in the world. The two couples had arranged to get married on the same day, and that not long thence; Tony's wedding being a sort of stimulant, as is often the case; I've noticed it professionally many times.

'They danced with such a will as only young people in that stage of courtship can dance; and it happened that as the evening wore on James had for his partner Stephen's plighted one, Olive, at the same time that Stephen was dancing with James's Emily. It was noticed that in spite o' the exchange the young men seemed to enjoy the dance no less than before. By and by they were treading another tune in the same changed order as we had noticed earlier, and though at first each one had held the other's mistress strictly at half-arm's length, lest there should be shown any objection to too close quarters by the lady's proper man, as time passed there was a little more closeness between 'em; and presently a little more closeness still.

'The later it got the more did each of the two cousins dance with the wrong young girl, and the tighter did he hold her to his side as he whirled her round; and, what was very remarkable, neither seemed to mind what the other was doing. The party began to draw towards its end, and I saw no more that night, being one of the first to leave, on account of my morning's business. But I learnt the rest of it from those that knew.

'After finishing a particularly warming dance with the changed partners, as I've mentioned, the two young men looked at one another, and in a moment or two went out into the porch together.

' "James," says Steve, "what were you thinking of when you were dancing with my Olive?"

' "Well," said James, "perhaps what you were thinking of when you were dancing with my Emily."

' "I was thinking," said Steve, with some hesitation, "that I wouldn't mind changing for good and all!"

' "It was what I was feeling likewise," said James.

' "I willingly agree to it, if you think we could manage it."

' "So do I. But what would the girls say?"

' " 'Tis my belief," said Steve, "that they wouldn't particularly object. Your Emily clung as close to me as if she already belonged to me, dear girl."

' "And your Olive to me," says James. "I could feel her heart beating like a clock."

'Well, they agreed to put it to the girls when they were all four walking home together. And they did so. When they parted that night the exchange was decided on – all having been done under the hot excitement of that evening's dancing. Thus it happened that on the following Sunday morning, when the people were sitting in church with mouths wide open to hear the names published as they had expected, there was no small amazement to hear them coupled the wrong way, as it seemed. The congregation whispered, and thought the parson had made a mistake; till they discovered that his reading of the names was verily the true way. As they had decided, so they were married, each one to the other's original property.

'Well, the two couples lived on for a year or two ordinarily enough, till the time came when these young people began to grow a little less warm to their respective spouses, as is the rule of married life; and the two cousins wondered more and more in their hearts what had made 'em so mad at the last moment to marry crosswise as they did, when they might have married straight, as was planned by Nature, and as they had fallen in love. 'Twas Tony's party that had done it, plain enough, and they half wished they had never gone there. James, being a quiet, fireside, perusing man, felt at times a wide gap between himself and Olive, his wife, who loved riding and driving and outdoor jaunts to a degree; while Steve, who was always knocking about hither and thither, had a very domestic wife, who worked samplers, and made hearthrugs, scarcely ever wished to cross the threshold, and only drove out with him to please him.

'However, they said very little about this mismating to any of their acquaintances, though sometimes Steve would look at James's wife, and sigh, and James would look at Steve's wife and do the same. Indeed, at last the two men were frank enough towards each other not to mind mentioning it quietly to themselves, in a long-faced, sorry-smiling, whimsical sort of way, and would shake their heads together over their foolishness in upsetting a well-considered choice on the strength of an hour's fancy in the whirl and wildness of a dance. Still, they were sensible and honest young fellows enough, and did their best to make shift with their lot as they had arranged it, and not to repine at what could not now be altered or mended.

'So things remained till one fine summer day they went for their yearly little outing together, as they had made it their custom to do for a long while past. This year they chose Budmouth-Regis as the place to spend their holiday in; and off they went in their best clothes at nine o'clock in the morning.

'When they had reached Budmouth-Regis they walked two and two along the shore – their new boots going squeakity-squash upon the clammy velvet sands. I can seem to see 'em now! Then they looked at the ships in the harbour; and then went up to the Look-out; and then had dinner at an inn, and then again walked two and two, squeakity-squash, upon the velvet sands. As evening drew on they sat on one of the public seats upon the Esplanade, and listened to the band; and then they said, "What shall we do next?"

' "Of all things," said Olive (Mrs James Hardcome, that is), "I should like to row in the bay! We could listen to the music from the water as well as from here, and have the fun of rowing besides."

' "The very thing; so should I," says Stephen, his tastes being always like hers.'

Here the clerk turned to the curate.

'But you, sir, know the rest of the strange particulars of that strange evening of their lives better than anybody else, having had much of it from their own lips, which I had not; and perhaps you'll oblige the gentleman?'

'Certainly, if it is wished,' said the curate. And he took up the clerk's tale: –

'Stephen's wife hated the sea, except from land, and couldn't bear the thought of going into a boat. James, too, disliked the water, and said that for his part he would much sooner stay on and listen to the band in the seat they occupied, though he did not wish to stand in his wife's way if she desired a row. The end of the discussion was that James and his cousin's wife Emily agreed to remain where they were sitting and enjoy the music, while they watched the other two hire a boat just beneath, and take their water-excursion of half an hour or so, till they should choose to come back and join the sitters on the Esplanade; when they would all start homeward together.

'Nothing could have pleased the other two restless ones better than this arrangement; and Emily and James watched them go down to the boatman below and choose one of the little yellow skiffs, and walk carefully out upon the little plank that was laid on trestles to enable them to

get alongside the craft. They saw Stephen hand Olive in, and take his
seat facing her; when they were settled they waved their hands to the
couple watching them, and then Stephen took the pair of sculls and
pulled off to the tune beat by the band, she steering through the other
boats skimming about, for the sea was as smooth as glass that evening,
and pleasure-seekers were rowing everywhere.

' "How pretty they look moving on, don't they?" said Emily to
James (as I've been assured). "They both enjoy it equally. In everything
their likings are the same."

' "That's true," said James.

' "They would have made a handsome pair if they had married," said
she.

' "Yes," said he. " 'Tis a pity we should have parted 'em."

' "Don't talk of that, James," said she. "For better or for worse we
decided to do as we did, and there's an end of it."

'They sat on after that without speaking, side by side, and the band
played as before; the people strolled up and down; and Stephen and
Olive shrank smaller and smaller as they shot straight out to sea. The
two on shore used to relate how they saw Stephen stop rowing a moment,
and take off his coat to get at his work better; but James's wife sat quite
still in the stern, holding the tiller-ropes by which she steered the boat.
When they had got very small indeed she turned her head to shore.

' "She is waving her handkerchief to us," said Stephen's wife, who
thereupon pulled out her own, and waved it as a return signal.

'The boat's course had been a little awry while Mrs James neglected
her steering to wave her handkerchief to her husband and Mrs Stephen;
but now the light skiff went straight onward again, and they could
soon see nothing more of the two figures it contained than Olive's light
mantle and Stephen's white shirt-sleeves behind.

'The two on the shore talked on. " 'Twas very curious – our changing
partners at Tony Kytes's wedding," Emily declared. "Tony was of a
fickle nature by all account, and it really seemed as if his character had
infected us that night. Which of you two was it that first proposed not to
marry as we were engaged?"

' "H'm – I can't remember at this moment," says James. "We talked
it over, you know; and no sooner said than done."

' " " 'Twas the dancing," said she. "People get quite crazy sometimes
in a dance."

' "They do," he owned.

' "James – do you think they care for one another still?" asks Mrs Stephen.

'James Hardcome mused and admitted that perhaps a little tender feeling might flicker up in their hearts for a moment now and then. "Still, nothing of any account," he said.

' "I sometimes think that Olive is in Steve's mind a good deal," murmurs Mrs Stephen; "particularly when she pleases his fancy by riding past our window at a gallop on one of the draught-horses. . . . I never could do anything of that sort; I could never get over my fear of a horse."

' "And I am no horseman, though I pretend to be on her account," murmured James Hardcome. "But isn't it almost time for them to turn and sweep round to the shore, as the other boating folk have done? I wonder what Olive means by steering away straight to the horizon like that? She has hardly swerved from a direct line seaward since they started."

' "No doubt they are talking, and don't think of where they are going," suggests Stephen's wife.

' "Perhaps so," said James. "I didn't know Steve could row like that."

' "O yes," says she. "He often comes here on business, and generally has a pull round the bay."

' "I can hardly see the boat or them," says James again; "and it is getting dark."

'The heedless pair afloat now formed a mere speck in the films of the coming night, which thickened apace, till it completely swallowed up their distant shapes. They had disappeared while still following the same straight course away from the world of land-livers, as if they were intending to drop over the sea-edge into space, and never return to earth again.

'The two on the shore continued to sit on, punctually abiding by their agreement to remain on the same spot till the others returned. The Esplanade lamps were lit one by one, the bandsmen folded up their stands and departed, the yachts in the bay hung out their riding lights, and the little boats came back to shore one after another, their hirers walking on to the sands by the plank they had climbed to go afloat; but among these Stephen and Olive did not appear.

' "What a time they are!" said Emily. "I am getting quite chilly. I did not expect to have to sit so long in the evening air."

'Thereupon James Hardcome said that he did not require his overcoat, and insisted on lending it to her.

'He wrapped it round Emily's shoulders.

' "Thank you, James," she said. "How cold Olive must be in that thin jacket!"

'He said he was thinking so, too. "Well, they are sure to be quite close at hand by this time, though we can't see 'em. The boats are not all in yet. Some of the rowers are fond of paddling along the shore to finish out their hour of hiring."

' "Shall we walk by the edge of the water," said she, "to see if we can discover them?"

'He assented, reminding her that they must not lose sight of the seat, lest the belated pair should return and miss them, and be vexed that they had not kept the appointment.

'They walked a sentry-beat up and down the sands immediately opposite the seat; and still the others did not come. James Hardcome at last went to the boatman, thinking that after all his wife and cousin might have come in under shadow of the dusk without being perceived, and might have forgotten the appointment at the bench.

' "All in?" asked James.

' "All but one boat," said the lessor. "I can't think where that couple is keeping to. They might run foul of something or other in the dark."

'Again Stephen's wife and Olive's husband waited, with more and more anxiety. But no little yellow boat returned. Was it possible they could have landed further down the Esplanade?

' "It may have been done to escape paying," said the boat-owner. "But they didn't look like people who would do that."

'James Hardcome knew that he could found no hope on such a reason as that. But now, remembering what had been casually discussed between Steve and himself about their wives from time to time, he admitted for the first time the possibility that their old tenderness had been revived by their face-to-face position more strongly than either had anticipated at starting – the excursion having been so obviously undertaken for the pleasure of the performance only – and that they had landed at some steps he knew of further down towards the pier, to be longer alone together.

'Still he disliked to harbour the thought, and would not mention its existence to his companion. He merely said to her, "Let us walk further on."

'They did so, and lingered between the boat-stage and the pier till Stephen Hardcome's wife was uneasy, and was obliged to accept James's offered arm. Thus the night advanced. Emily was presently so worn out by fatigue that James felt it necessary to conduct her home; there was, too, a remote chance that the truants had landed in the harbour on the other side of the town, or elsewhere, and hastened home in some unexpected way, in the belief that their consorts would not have waited so long.

'However, he left a direction in the town that a look-out should be kept, though this was arranged privately, the bare possibility of an elopement being enough to make him reticent; and, full of misgivings, the two remaining ones hastened to catch the last train out of Budmouth-Regis; and when they got to Casterbridge drove back to Upper Longpuddle.'

'Along this very road as we do now,' remarked the parish clerk.

'To be sure – along this very road,' said the curate. 'However, Stephen and Olive were not at their homes; neither had entered the village since leaving it in the morning. Emily and James Hardcome went to their respective dwellings to snatch a hasty night's rest, and at daylight the next morning they drove again to Casterbridge and entered the Budmouth train, the line being just opened.

'Nothing had been heard of the couple there during this brief absence. In the course of a few hours some young men testified to having seen such a man and woman rowing in a frail hired craft, the head of the boat kept straight to sea; they had sat looking in each other's faces as if they were in a dream, with no consciousness of what they were doing, or whither they were steering. It was not till late that day that more tidings reached James's ears. The boat had been found drifting bottom upward a long way from land. In the evening the sea rose somewhat, and a cry spread through the town that two bodies were cast ashore in Lulwind Bay, several miles to the eastward. They were brought to Budmouth, and inspection revealed them to be the missing pair. It was said that they had been found tightly locked in each other's arms, his lips upon hers, their features still wrapt in the same calm and dream-like repose which had been observed in their demeanour as they had glided along.

'Neither James nor Emily questioned the original motives of the unfortunate man and woman in putting to sea. They were both above suspicion as to intention. Whatever their mutual feelings might have led them on to, underhand behaviour at starting was foreign to the nature of either. Conjecture pictured that they might have fallen into tender reverie while gazing each into a pair of eyes that had formerly flashed for him and her alone, and, unwilling to avow what their mutual sentiments were, they had done no more than continue thus, oblivious of time and space, till darkness suddenly overtook them far from land. But nothing was truly known. It had been their destiny to die thus. The two halves, intended by Nature to make the perfect whole, had failed in that result during their lives, though "in their death they were not divided". Their bodies were brought home, and buried on one day. I remember that, on looking round the churchyard while reading the service, I observed nearly all the parish at their funeral.'

'It was so, sir,' said the clerk.

'The remaining two,' continued the curate (whose voice had grown husky while relating the lovers' sad fate), 'were a more thoughtful and far-seeing, though less romantic, couple than the first. They were now mutually bereft of a companion, and found themselves by this accident in a position to fulfil their destiny according to Nature's plan and their own original and calmly-formed intention. James Hardcome took Emily to wife in the course of a year and a half; and the marriage proved in every respect a happy one. I solemnized the service, Hardcome having told me, when he came to give notice of the proposed wedding, the story of his first wife's loss almost word for word as I have told it to you.'

'And are they living in Longpuddle still?' asked the new-comer.

'O no, sir,' interposed the clerk. 'James has been dead these dozen years, and his mis'ess about six or seven. They had no children. William Privett used to be their odd man till he died.'

'Ah – William Privett! He dead, too? – dear me!' said the other. 'All passed away!'

'Yes, sir. William was much older than I. He'd ha' been over eighty if he had lived till now.'

'There was something very strange about William's death – very strange indeed!' sighed a melancholy man in the back of the van. It was the seedsman's father, who had hitherto kept silence.

'And what might that have been?' asked Mr Lackland.

THE SUPERSTITIOUS MAN'S STORY

'William, as you may know, was a curious, silent man; you could feel
when he came near 'ee; and if he was in the house or anywhere behind
your back without your seeing him, there seemed to be something
clammy in the air, as if a cellar door was opened close by your elbow.
Well, one Sunday, at a time that William was in very good health to all
appearance, the bell that was ringing for church went very heavy all of
a sudden; the sexton, who told me o't, said he'd not known the bell go
so heavy in his hand for years – and he feared it meant a death in the
parish. That was on the Sunday, as I say. During the week after, it
chanced that William's wife was staying up late one night to finish her
ironing, she doing the washing for Mr and Mrs Hardcome. Her husband
had finished his supper and gone to bed as usual some hour or two
before. While she ironed she heard him coming downstairs; he stopped
to put on his boots at the stair-foot, where he always left them, and then
came on into the living-room where she was ironing, passing through it
towards the door, this being the only way from the staircase to the outside of the house. No word was said on either side, William not being a
man given to much speaking, and his wife being occupied with her work.
He went out and closed the door behind him. As her husband had now
and then gone out in this way at night before when unwell, or unable to
sleep for want of a pipe, she took no particular notice, and continued at
her ironing. This she finished shortly after, and as he had not come in
she waited a while for him, putting away the irons and things, and
preparing the table for his breakfast in the morning. Still he did not
return, and supposing him not far off, and wanting to get to bed herself,
tired as she was, she left the door unbarred and went to the stairs, after
writing on the back of the door with chalk: *Mind and do the door*
(because he was a forgetful man).

'To her great surprise, and I might say alarm, on reaching the foot
of the stairs his boots were standing there as they always stood when he
had gone to rest; going up to their chamber she found him in bed sleeping as sound as a rock. How he could have got back again without her
seeing or hearing him was beyond her comprehension. It could only
have been by passing behind her very quietly while she was bumping
with the iron. But this notion did not satisfy her: it was surely impossible

that she should not have seen him come in through a room so small. She could not unravel the mystery, and felt very queer and uncomfortable about it. However, she would not disturb him to question him then, and went to bed herself.

'He rose and left for his work very early the next morning, before she was awake, and she waited his return to breakfast with much anxiety for an explanation, for thinking over the matter by daylight made it seem only the more startling. When he came in to the meal he said, before she could put her question, "What's the meaning of them words chalked on the door?"

'She told him, and asked him about his going out the night before. William declared that he had never left the bedroom after entering it, having in fact undressed, lain down, and fallen asleep directly, never once waking till the clock struck five, and he rose up to go to his labour.

'Betty Privett was as certain in her own mind that he did go out as she was of her own existence, and was little less certain that he did not return. She felt too disturbed to argue with him, and let the subject drop as though she must have been mistaken. When she was walking down Longpuddle street later in the day she met Jim Weedle's daughter Nancy, and said, "Well, Nancy, you do look sleepy to-day!"

' "Yes, Mrs Privett," says Nancy. "Now don't tell anybody, but I don't mind letting you know what the reason o't is. Last night, being Old Midsummer Eve, some of us went to church porch, and didn't get home till near one."

' "Did ye?" says Mrs Privett. "Old Midsummer yesterday, was it? Faith I didn't think whe'r 'twas Midsummer or Michaelmas; I'd too much work to do."

' "Yes. And we were frightened enough, I can tell 'ee, by what we saw."

' "What did ye see?"

'(You may not remember, sir, having gone off to foreign parts so young, that on Midsummer Night it is believed hereabout that the faint shapes of all the folk in the parish who are going to be at death's door within the year can be seen entering the church. Those who get over their illness come out again after a while; those that are doomed to die do not return.)

' "What did you see?" asked William's wife.

' "Well," says Nancy, backwardly – "we needn't tell what we saw, or who we saw."

' "You saw my husband," says Betty Privett, in a quiet way.

' "Well, since you put it so," says Nancy, hanging fire, "we – thought we did see him; but it was darkish, and we was frightened, and of course it might not have been he."

' "Nancy, you needn't mind letting it out, though 'tis kept back in kindness. And he didn't come out of church again: I know it as well as you."

'Nancy did not answer yes or no to that, and no more was said. But three days after, William Privett was mowing with John Chiles in Mr Hardcome's meadow, and in the heat of the day they sat down to eat their bit o' nunch under a tree, and empty their flagon. Afterwards both of 'em fell asleep as they sat. John Chiles was the first to wake, and as he looked towards his fellow-mower he saw one of those great white miller's-souls as we call 'em – that is to say, a miller-moth – come from William's open mouth while he slept, and fly straight away. John thought it odd enough, as William had worked in a mill for several years when he was a boy. He then looked at the sun, and found by the place o't that they had slept a long while, and as William did not wake, John called to him and said it was high time to begin work again. He took no notice, and then John went up and shook him, and found he was dead.

'Now on that very day old Philip Hookhorn was down at Longpuddle Spring dipping up a pitcher of water; and as he turned away, who should he see coming down to the spring on the other side but William, looking very pale and odd. This surprised Philip Hookhorn very much, for years before that time William's little son – his only child – had been drowned in that spring while at play there, and this had so preyed upon William's mind that he'd never been seen near the spring afterwards, and had been known to go half a mile out of his way to avoid the place. On inquiry, it was found that William in body could not have stood by the spring, being in the mead two miles off; and it also came out that the time at which he was seen at the spring was the very time when he died.'

'A rather melancholy story,' observed the emigrant, after a minute's silence.

'Yes, yes. Well, we must take ups and downs together,' said the seeds-man's father.

'You don't know, Mr Lackland, I suppose, what a rum start that was between Andrey Satchel and Jane Vallens and the pa'son and clerk o'

Scrimpton?' said the master-thatcher, a man with a spark of subdued liveliness in his eye, who had hitherto kept his attention mainly upon small objects a long way ahead, as he sat in front of the van with his feet outside. 'Theirs was a queerer experience of a pa'son and clerk than some folks get, and may cheer 'ee up a little after this dampness that's been flung over yer soul.'

The returned one replied that he knew nothing of the history, and should be happy to hear it, quite recollecting the personality of the man Satchel.

'Ah, no; this Andrey Satchel is the son of the Satchel that you knew; this one has not been married more than two or three years, and 'twas at the time o' the wedding that the accident happened that I could tell 'ee of, or anybody else here, for that matter.'

'No, no; you must tell it, neighbour, if anybody,' said several; a request in which Mr Lackland joined, adding that the Satchel family was one he had known well before leaving home.

'I'll just mention, as you be a stranger,' whispered the carrier to Lackland, 'that Christopher's stories will bear pruning.'

The emigrant nodded.

'Well, I can soon tell it,' said the master-thatcher, schooling himself to a tone of actuality. 'Though as it has more to do with the pa'son and clerk than with Andrey himself, it ought to be told by a better church-man than I.'

ANDREY SATCHEL AND THE PARSON AND CLERK

'It all arose, you must know, from Andrey being fond of a drop of drink at that time – though he's a sober enough man now by all account, so much the better for him. Jane, his bride, you see, was somewhat older than Andrey; how much older I don't pretend to say; she was not one of our parish, and the register alone may be able to tell that. But, at any rate, her being a little ahead of her young man in mortal years, coupled with other bodily circumstances owing to that young man – '

('Ah, poor thing!' sighed the women.)

' – made her very anxious to get the thing done before he changed his mind; and 'twas with a joyful countenance (they say) that she, with Andrey and his brother and sister-in-law, marched off to church one

November morning as soon as 'twas day a'most to be made one with Andrey for the rest of her life. He had left our place long before it was light, and the folks that were up all waved their lanterns at him, and flung up their hats as he went.

'The church of her parish was a mile and more from where she lived, and, as it was a wonderful fine day for the time of year, the plan was that as soon as they were married they would make out a holiday by driving straight off to Port Bredy, to see the ships and the sea and the sojers, instead of coming back to a meal at the house of the distant relation she lived wi', and moping about there all the afternoon.

'Well, some folks noticed that Andrey walked with rather wambling steps to church that morning; the truth o't was that his nearest neighbour's child had been christened the day before, and Andrey, having stood godfather, had stayed all night keeping up the christening, for he had said to himself, "Not if I live to be a thousand shall I again be made a godfather one day, and a husband the next, and perhaps a father the next, and therefore I'll make the most of the blessing." So that when he started from home in the morning he had not been in bed at all. The result was, as I say, that when he and his bride-to-be walked up the church to get married, the pa'son (who was a very strict man inside the church, whatever he was outside) looked hard at Andrey, and said, very sharp:

' "How's this, my man? You are in liquor. And so early, too. I'm ashamed of you!"

' "Well, that's true, sir," says Andrey. "But I can walk straight enough for practical purposes. I can walk a chalk line," he says (meaning no offence), "as well as some other folk: and " – (getting hotter) – "I reckon that if you, Pa'son Billy Toogood, had kept up a christening all night so thoroughly as I have done, you wouldn't be able to stand at all; d— me if you would!"

'This answer made Pa'son Billy – as they used to call him – rather spitish, not to say hot, for he was a warm-tempered man if provoked, and he said, very decidedly: "Well, I cannot marry you in this state; and I will not! Go home and get sober!" And he slapped the book together like a rat-trap.

'Then the bride burst out crying as if her heart would break, for very fear that she would lose Andrey after all her hard work to get him, and begged and implored the pa'son to go on with the ceremony. But no.

' "I won't be a party to your solemnizing matrimony with a tipsy man," says Mr Toogood. "It is not right and decent. I am sorry for you, my young woman, seeing the condition you are in, but you'd better go home again. I wonder how you could think of bringing him here drunk like this!"

' "But if – if he don't come drunk he won't come at all, sir!" she says, through her sobs.

' "I can't help that," says the pa'son; and plead as she might, it did not move him. Then she tried him another way.

' "Well, then, if you'll go home, sir, and leave us here, and come back to the church in an hour or two, I'll undertake to say that he shall be as sober as a judge," she cries. "We'll bide here, with your permission; for if he once goes out of this here church unmarried, all Van Amburgh's horses won't drag him back again!"

' "Very well," says the parson. "I'll give you two hours, and then I'll return."

' "And please, sir, lock the door, so that we can't escape!" says she.

' "Yes," says the parson.

' "And let nobody know that we are here."

'The pa'son then took off his clane white surplice, and went away; and the others consulted upon the best means for keeping the matter a secret, which it was not a very hard thing to do, the place being so lonely, and the hour so early. The witnesses, Andrey's brother and brother's wife, neither one o' which cared about Andrey's marrying Jane, and had come rather against their will, said they couldn't wait two hours in that hole of a place, wishing to get home to Longpuddle before dinner-time. They were altogether so crusty that the clerk said there was no difficulty in their doing as they wished. They could go home as if their brother's wedding had actually taken place and the married couple had gone onward for their day's pleasure jaunt to Port Bredy as intended. He, the clerk, and any casual passer-by would act as witnesses when the pa'son came back.

'This was agreed to, and away Andrey's relations went, nothing loath, and the clerk shut the church door and prepared to lock in the couple. The bride went up and whispered to him, with her eyes a-streaming still.

' "My dear good clerk," she says, "if we bide here in the church, folk may see us through the windows, and find out what has happened; and 'twould cause such a talk and scandal that I never should get over it:

and perhaps, too, dear Andrey might try to get out and leave me! Will ye lock us up in the tower, my dear good clerk?" she says. "I'll tole him in there if you will."

'The clerk had no objection to do this to oblige the poor young woman, and they toled Andrey into the tower, and the clerk locked 'em both up straightway, and then went home, to return at the end of the two hours.

'Pa'son Toogood had not been long in his house after leaving the church when he saw a gentleman in pink and top-boots ride past his windows, and with a sudden flash of heat he called to mind that the hounds met that day just on the edge of his parish. The pa'son was one who dearly loved sport, and much he longed to be there.

'In short, except o' Sundays and at tide-times in the week, Pa'son Billy was the life o' the hunt. 'Tis true that he was poor, and that he rode all of a heap, and that his black mare was rat-tailed and old, and his tops older, and all over of one colour, whitey-brown, and full o' cracks. But he'd been in at the death of three thousand foxes. And – being a bachelor man – every time he went to bed in summer he used to open the bed at bottom and crawl up head foremost, to mind en of the coming winter and the good sport he'd have, and the foxes going to earth. And whenever there was a christening at the Squire's, and he had dinner there afterwards, as he always did, he never failed to christen the chiel over again in a bottle of port wine.

'Now the clerk was the pa'son's groom and gardener and general manager, and had just got back to his work in the garden when he, too, saw the hunting man pass, and presently saw lots more of 'em, noblemen and gentry, and then he saw the hounds, the huntsman, Jim Treadhedge, the whipper-in, and I don't know who besides. The clerk loved going to cover as frantical as the pa'son, so much so that whenever he saw or heard the pack he could no more rule his feelings than if they were the winds of heaven. He might be bedding, or he might be sowing – all was forgot. So he throws down his spade and rushes in to the pa'son, who was by this time as frantical to go as he.

' "That there mare of yours, sir, do want exercise bad, very bad, this morning!" the clerk says, all of a tremble. "Don't ye think I'd better trot her round the downs for an hour, sir?"

' "To be sure, she does want exercise badly. I'll trot her round myself," says the pa'son.

' "Oh – you'll trot her yerself? Well, there's the cob, sir. Really that cob is getting oncontrollable through biding in a stable so long! If you wouldn't mind my putting on the saddle—"

' "Very well. Take him out, certainly," says the pa'son, never caring what the clerk did so long as he himself could get off immediately. So, scrambling into his riding-boots and breeches as quick as he could, he rode off towards the meet, intending to be back in an hour. No sooner was he gone than the clerk mounted the cob, and was off after him. When the pa'son got to the meet he found a lot of friends, and was as jolly as he could be: the hounds found a'most as soon as they threw off, and there was great excitement. So, forgetting that he had meant to go back at once, away rides the pa'son with the rest o' the hunt, all across the fallow ground that lies between Lippet Wood and Green's Copse; and as he galloped he looked behind for a moment, and there was the clerk close to his heels.

' "Ha, ha, clerk – you here?" he says.

' "Yes, sir, here be I," says t'other.

' "Fine exercise for the horses!"

' "Ay, sir – hee, hee!" says the clerk.

'So they went on and on, into Green's Copse, then across to Higher Jirton; then on across this very turnpike-road to Waterston Ridge, then away towards Yalbury Wood: up hill and down dale, like the very wind, the clerk close to the pa'son, and the pa'son not far from the hounds. Never was there a finer run knowed with that pack than they had that day; and neither pa'son nor clerk thought one word about the unmarried couple locked up in the church tower waiting to get j'ined.

' "These hosses of yours, sir, will be much improved by this!" says the clerk as he rode along, just a neck behind the pa'son. " 'Twas a happy thought of your reverent mind to bring 'em out to-day. Why, it may be frosty and slippery in a day or two, and then the poor things mid not be able to leave the stable for weeks."

' "They may not, they may not, it is true. A merciful man is merciful to his beast," says the pa'son.

' "Hee, hee!" says the clerk, glancing sly into the pa'son's eye.

' "Ha, ha!" says the pa'son, a-glancing back into the clerk's. "Halloo!" he shouts, as he sees the fox break cover at that moment.

' "Halloo!" cries the clerk. "There he goes! Why, dammy, there's two foxes—"

' "Hush, clerk, hush! Don't let me hear that word again! Remember our calling."

' "True, sir, true. But really, good sport do carry away a man so, that he's apt to forget his high persuasion!" And the next minute the corner of the clerk's eye shot again into the corner of the pa'son's, and the pa'son's back again to the clerk's. "Hee, hee!" said the clerk.

' "Ha, ha!" said Pa'son Toogood.

' "Ah, sir," says the clerk again, "this is better than crying Amen to your Ever-and-ever on a winter's morning!"

' "Yes, indeed, clerk! To everything there's a season," says Pa'son Toogood, quite pat, for he was a learned Christian man when he liked, and had chapter and ve'se at his tongue's end, as a pa'son should.

'At last, late in the day, the hunting came to an end by the fox running into a' old woman's cottage, under her table, and up the clock-case. The pa'son and clerk were among the first in at the death, their faces a-staring in at the old woman's winder, and the clock striking as he'd never been heard to strik' before. Then came the question of finding their way home.

'Neither the pa'son nor the clerk knowed how they were going to do this, for their beasts were wellnigh tired down to the ground. But they started back-along as well as they could, though they were so done up that they could only drag along at a' amble, and not much of that at a time.

' "We shall never, never get there!" groaned Mr Toogood, quite bowed down.

' "Never!" groans the clerk. " 'Tis a judgment upon us for our iniquities!"

' "I fear it is," murmurs the pa'son.

'Well, 'twas quite dark afore they entered the pa'sonage gate, having crept into the parish as quiet as if they'd stole a hammer, little wishing their congregation to know what they'd been up to all day long. And as they were so dog-tired, and so anxious about the horses, never once did they think of the unmarried couple. As soon as ever the horses had been stabled and fed, and the pa'son and clerk had had a bit and a sup theirselves, they went to bed.

'Next morning when Pa'son Toogood was at breakfast, thinking of the glorious sport he'd had the day before, the clerk came in a hurry to the door and asked to see him.

' "It has just come into my mind, sir, that we've forgot all about the couple that we was to have married yesterday!"

'The half-chawed victuals dropped from the pa'son's mouth as if he'd been shot. "Bless my soul," says he, "so we have! How very awkward"!

' "It is, sir; very. Perhaps we've ruined the 'ooman!"

' "Ah – to be sure – I remember! She ought to have been married before."

' "If anything has happened to her up in that there tower, and no doctor or nuss – " '

('Ah – poor thing!' sighed the women.)

' " – 'twill be a quarter-sessions matter for us, not to speak of the disgrace to the Church!"

' "Good God, clerk, don't drive me wild!" says the pa'son. "Why the hell didn't I marry 'em, drunk or sober!" (Pa'sons used to cuss in them days like plain honest men.) "Have you been to the church to see what happened to them, or inquired in the village?"

' "Not I, sir! It only came into my head a moment ago, and I always like to be second to you in church matters. You could have knocked me down with a sparrow's feather when I thought o't, sir; I assure 'ee you could!"

'Well, the pa'son jumped up from his breakfast, and together they went off to the church.

' "It is not at all likely that they are there now," says Mr Toogood, as they went; "and indeed I hope they are not. They be pretty sure to have escaped and gone home."

'However, they opened the church-hatch, entered the churchyard, and looking up at the tower there they seed a little small white face at the belfry-winder, and a little small hand waving. 'Twas the bride

' "God my life, clerk," says Mr Toogood. "I don't know how to face 'em!" And he sank down upon a tombstone. "How I wish I hadn't been so cussed particular!"

' "Yes – 'twas a pity we didn't finish it when we'd begun," the clerk said. "Still, since the feelings of your holy priestcraft wouldn't let ye, the couple must put up with it."

' "True, clerk, true! Does she look as if anything premature had took place?"

' "I can't see her no lower down than her arm-pits, sir."

' "Well – how do her face look?"

' "It do look mighty white!"

' "Well, we must know the worst! Dear me, how the small of my back do ache from that ride yesterday! . . . But to more godly business!"

'They went on into the church, and unlocked the tower stairs, and immediately poor Jane and Andrey busted out like starved mice from a cupboard, Andrey limp and sober enough now, and his bride pale and cold, but otherwise as usual.

' "What," says the pa'son with a great breath of relief, "you haven't been here ever since?"

' "Yes, we have, sir!" says the bride, sinking down upon a seat in her weakness. "Not a morsel, wet or dry, have we had since! It was impossible to get out without help, and here we've stayed!"

' "But why didn't you shout, good souls?" said the pa'son.

' "She wouldn't let me," says Andrey.

' "Because we were so ashamed at what had led to it," sobs Jane. "We felt that if it were noised abroad it would cling to us all our lives! Once or twice Andrey had a good mind to toll the bell, but then he said: 'No; I'll starve first. I won't bring disgrace on my name and yours, my dear.' And so we waited and waited, and walked round and round; but never did you come till now!"

' "To my regret!" says the pa'son. "Now, then, we will soon get it over."

' "I – I should like some victuals," said Andrey; " 'twould gie me courage to do it, if it is only a crust o' bread and a' onion; for I am that leery that I can feel my stomach rubbing against my backbone."

' "I think we had better get it done," said the bride, a bit anxious in manner; "since we are all here convenient, too!"

'Andrey gave way about the victuals, and the clerk called in a second witness who wouldn't be likely to gossip about it, and soon the knot was tied, and the bride looked smiling and calm forthwith, and Andrey limper than ever.

' "Now," said Pa'son Toogood, "you two must come to my house, and have a good lining put to your insides before you go a step further."

'They were very glad of the offer, and went out of the churchyard by one path while the pa'son and clerk went out by the other, and so did not attract notice, it being still early. They entered the rectory as if they'd just come back from their trip to Port Bredy; and then they knocked in the victuals and drink till they could hold no more.

'It was a long while before the story of what they had gone through was known, but it was talked of in time, and they themselves laugh over it now; though what Jane got for her pains was no great bargain after all. 'Tis true she saved her name.'

*

'Was that the same Andrey who went to the squire's house as one of the Christmas fiddlers ?' asked the seedsman.

'No, no,' replied Mr Profitt, the schoolmaster. 'It was his father did that. Ay, it was all owing to his being such a man for eating and drinking.' Finding that he had the ear of the audience, the schoolmaster continued without delay: –

OLD ANDREY'S EXPERIENCE AS A MUSICIAN

'I was one of the quire-boys at that time, and we and the players were to appear at the manor-house as usual that Christmas week, to play and sing in the hall to the Squire's people and visitors (among 'em being the archdeacon, Lord and Lady Baxby, and I don't know who); afterwards going, as we always did, to have a good supper in the servants' hall. Andrew knew this was the custom, and meeting us when we were starting to go, he said to us: "Lord, how I should like to join in that meal of beef, and turkey, and plum-pudding, and ale, that you happy ones be going to just now! One more or less will make no difference to the Squire. I am too old to pass as a singing boy, and too bearded to pass as a singing girl; can ye lend me a fiddle, neighbours, that I may come with ye as a bandsman ?"

'Well, we didn't like to be hard upon him, and lent him an old one, though Andrew knew no more of music than the Giant o' Cernel; and armed with the instrument he walked up to the Squire's house with the others of us at the time appointed, and went in boldly, his fiddle under his arm. He made himself as natural as he could in opening the music-books and moving the candles to the best points for throwing light upon the notes; and all went well till we had played and sung "While shepherds watch", and "Star, arise", and "Hark the glad sound". Then the Squire's mother, a tall gruff old lady, who was much interested in church-music, said quite unexpectedly to Andrew: "My man, I see you don't play your instrument with the rest. How is that ?"

'Every one of the quire was ready to sink into the earth with concern at the fix Andrew was in. We could see that he had fallen into a cold sweat, and how he would get out of it we did not know.

' "I've had a misfortune, mem," he says, bowing as meek as a child. "Coming along the road I fell down and broke my bow."

' "O, I am sorry to hear that," says she. "Can't it be mended ?"

' "O no, mem," says Andrew. " 'Twas broke all to splinters."

' "I'll see what I can do for you," says she.

'And then it seemed all over, and we played "Rejoice, ye drowsy mortals all", in D and two sharps. But no sooner had we got through it than she says to Andrew:

' "I've sent up into the attic, where we have some old musical instruments, and found a bow for you." And she hands the bow to poor wretched Andrew, who didn't even know which end to take hold of. "Now we shall have the full accompaniment," says she.

'Andrew's face looked as if it were made of rotten apple as he stood in the circle of players in front of his book; for if there was one person in the parish that everybody was afraid of, 'twas this hook-nosed old lady. However, by keeping a little behind the next man he managed to make pretence of beginning, sawing away with his bow without letting it touch the strings, so that it looked as if he were driving into the tune with heart and soul. 'Tis a question if he wouldn't have got through all right if one of the Squire's visitors (no other than the archdeacon) hadn't noticed that he held the fiddle upside down, the nut under his chin, and the tail-piece in his hand; and they began to crowd round him, thinking 'twas some new way of performing.

'This revealed everything; the Squire's mother had Andrew turned out of the house as a vile impostor, and there was great interruption to the harmony of the proceedings, the Squire declaring he should have notice to leave his cottage that day fortnight. However, when we got to the servants' hall there sat Andrew, who had been let in at the back door by the orders of the Squire's wife, after being turned out at the front by the orders of the Squire, and nothing more was heard about his leaving his cottage. But Andrew never performed in public as a musician after that night; and now he's dead and gone, poor man, as we all shall be!'

'I had quite forgotten the old choir, with their fiddles and bass-viols,' said the home-comer, musingly. 'Are they still going on the same as of old?'

'Bless the man!' said Christopher Twink, the master-thatcher; 'why, they've been done away with these twenty year. A young teetotaller plays the organ in church now, and plays it very well; though 'tis not quite such good music as in old times, because the organ is one of them that go with a winch, and the young teetotaller says he can't always throw the proper feeling into the tune without wellnigh working his arms off.'

'Why did they make the change, then?'

'Well, partly because of fashion, partly because the old musicians got into a sort of scrape. A terrible scrape 'twas, too – wasn't it, John? I shall never forget it – never! They lost their character as officers of the church as complete as if they'd never had any character at all.'

'That was very bad for them.'

'Yes.' The master-thatcher attentively regarded past times as if they lay about a mile off, and went on: –

ABSENT-MINDEDNESS IN A PARISH CHOIR

'It happened on Sunday after Christmas – the last Sunday ever they played in Longpuddle church gallery, as it turned out, though they didn't know it then. As you may know, sir, the players formed a very good band – almost as good as the Mellstock parish players that were led by the Dewys; and that's saying a great deal. There was Nicholas Puddingcome, the leader, with the first fiddle; there was Timothy Thomas, the bass-viol man; John Biles, the tenor fiddler, Dan'l Horn-head, with the serpent; Robert Dowdle, with the clarionet; and Mr Nicks, with the oboe – all sound and powerful musicians, and strong-winded men – they that blowed. For that reason they were very much in demand Christmas week for little reels and dancing parties: for they could turn a jig or a hornpipe out of hand as well as ever they could turn out a psalm, and perhaps better, not to speak irreverent. In short, one half-hour they could be playing a Christmas carol in the Squire's hall to the ladies and gentlemen, and drinking tay and coffee with 'em as modest as saints; and the next, at The Tinker's Arms, blazing away like wild horses with the "Dashing White Sergeant" to nine couple of dancers and more, and swallowing rum-and-cider hot as flame.

'Well, this Christmas they'd been out to one rattling randy after another every night, and had got next to no sleep at all. Then came the Sunday after Christmas, their fatal day. 'Twas so mortal cold that year that they could hardly sit in the gallery; for though the congregation down in the body of the church had a stove to keep off the frost, the players in the gallery had nothing at all. So Nicholas said at morning service, when 'twas freezing an inch an hour, "Please the Lord I won't stand this numbing weather no longer: this afternoon we'll have some-thing in our insides to make us warm, if it cost a king's ransom."

'So he brought a gallon of hot brandy and beer, ready mixed, to church with him in the afternoon, and by keeping the jar well wrapped up in Timothy Thomas's bass-viol bag it kept drinkably warm till they wanted it, which was just a thimbleful in the Absolution, and another after the Creed, and the remainder at the beginning o' the sermon. When they'd had the last pull they felt quite comfortable and warm, and as the sermon went on – most unfortunately for 'em it was a long one that afternoon – they fell asleep, every man jack of 'em; and there they slept on as sound as rocks.

' 'Twas a very dark afternoon, and by the end of the sermon all you could see of the inside of the church were the pa'son's two candles alongside of him in the pulpit, and his spaking face behind 'em. The sermon being ended at last, the pa'son gie'd out the Evening Hymn. But no quire set about sounding up the tune, and the people began to turn their heads to learn the reason why, and then Levi Limpet, a boy who sat in the gallery, nudged Timothy and Nicholas, and said, "Begin! begin!"

' "Hey? what?" says Nicholas, starting up; and the church being so dark and his head so muddled he thought he was at the party they had played at all the night before, and away he went, bow and fiddle, at "The Devil among the Tailors", the favourite jig of our neighbourhood at that time. The rest of the band, being in the same state of mind and nothing doubting, followed their leader with all their strength, according to custom. They poured out that there tune till the lower bass notes of "The Devil among the Tailors" made the cobwebs in the roof shiver like ghosts; then Nicholas, seeing nobody moved, shouted out as he scraped (in his usual commanding way at dances when the folk didn't know the figures), "Top couples cross hands! And when I make the fiddle squeak at the end, every man kiss his pardner under the mistletoe!"

'The boy Levi was so frightened that he bolted down the gallery stairs and out homeward like lightning. The pa'son's hair fairly stood on end when he heard the evil tune raging through the church, and thinking the quire had gone crazy he held up his hand and said: "Stop, stop, stop! Stop, stop! What's this?" But they didn't hear'n for the noise of their own playing, and the more he called the louder they played.

'Then the folks came out of their pews, wondering down to the ground, and saying: "What do they mean by such wickedness! We shall be consumed like Sodom and Gomorrah!"

'And the Squire, too, came out of his pew lined wi' green baize, where lots of lords and ladies visiting at the house were worshipping along with him, and went and stood in front of the gallery, and shook his fist in the musicians' faces, saying, "What! In this reverent edifice! What!"

'And at last they heard'n through their playing, and stopped.

' "Never such an insulting, disgraceful thing – never!" says the Squire, who couldn't rule his passion.

' "Never!" says the pa'son, who had come down and stood beside him.

' "Not if the Angels of Heaven," says the Squire (he was a wickedish man, the Squire was, though now for once he happened to be on the Lord's side) – "not if the Angels of Heaven come down," he says, "shall one of you villainous players ever sound a note in this church again; for the insult to me, and my family, and my visitors, and the pa'son, and God Almighty, that you've a-perpetrated this afternoon!"

'Then the unfortunate church band came to their senses, and remembered where they were; and 'twas a sight to see Nicholas Pudding-come and Timothy Thomas and John Biles creep down the gallery stairs with their fiddles under their arms, and poor Dan'l Hornhead with his serpent, and Robert Dowdle with his clarionet, all looking as little as ninepins; and out they went. The pa'son might have forgi'ed 'em when he learned the truth o't, but the Squire would not. That very week he sent for a barrel-organ that would play two-and-twenty new psalm-tunes, so exact and particular that, however sinful inclined you was, you could play nothing but psalm-tunes whatsomever. He had a really respectable man to turn the winch, as I said, and the old players played no more.'

'And, of course, my old acquaintance, the annuitant, Mrs Winter, who always seemed to have something on her mind, is dead and gone?' said the home-comer, after a long silence.

Nobody in the van seemed to recollect the name.

'O yes, she must be dead long since: she was seventy when I as a child knew her,' he added.

'I can recollect Mrs Winter very well, if nobody else can,' said the aged groceress. 'Yes, she's been dead these five-and-twenty year at least. You knew what it was upon her mind, sir, that gave her that hollow-eyed look, I suppose?'

'It had something to do with a son of hers, I think I once was told. But I was too young to know particulars.'

The groceress sighed as she conjured up a vision of days long past. 'Yes,' she murmured, 'it had all to do with a son.' Finding that the van was still in a listening mood, she spoke on: –

THE WINTERS AND THE PALMLEYS

'To go back to the beginning – if one must – there were two women in the parish when I was a child, who were to a certain extent rivals in good looks. Never mind particulars, but in consequence of this they were at daggers-drawn, and they did not love each other any better when one of them tempted the other's lover away from her and married him. He was a young man of the name of Winter, and in due time they had a son.

'The other woman did not marry for many years: but when she was about thirty a quiet man named Palmley asked her to be his wife, and she accepted him. You don't mind when the Palmleys were Longpuddle folk, but I do well. She had a son also, who was, of course, nine or ten years younger than the son of the first. The child proved to be of rather weak intellect, though his mother loved him as the apple of her eye.

'This woman's husband died when the child was eight years old, and left his widow and boy in poverty. Her former rival, also a widow now, but fairly well provided for, offered for pity's sake to take the child as errand-boy, small as he was, her own son, Jack, being hard upon seventeen. Her poor neighbour could do no better than let the child go there. And to the richer woman's house little Palmley straightway went.

'Well, in some way or other – how, it was never exactly known – the thriving woman, Mrs Winter, sent the little boy with a message to the next village one December day, much against his will. It was getting dark, and the child prayed to be allowed not to go, because he would be afraid coming home. But the mistress insisted, more out of thoughtlessness than cruelty, and the child went. On his way back he had to pass through Yalbury Wood, and something came out from behind a tree and frightened him into fits. The child was quite ruined by it; he became quite a drivelling idiot, and soon afterward died.

'Then the other woman had nothing left to live for, and vowed vengeance against that rival who had first won away her lover, and now had been the cause of her bereavement. This last affliction was certainly not intended by her thriving acquaintance, though it must be owned that when it was done she seemed but little concerned. Whatever vengeance poor Mrs Palmley felt, she had no opportunity of carrying it out, and time might have softened her feelings into forgetfulness of her supposed wrongs as she dragged on her lonely life. So matters stood when, a year after the death of the child, Mrs Palmley's niece, who had been born and bred in the city of Exonbury, came to live with her.

'This young woman – Miss Harriet Palmley – was a proud and handsome girl, very well brought up, and more stylish and genteel than the people of our village, as was natural, considering where she came from. She regarded herself as much above Mrs Winter and her son in position as Mrs Winter and her son considered themselves above poor Mrs Palmley. But love is an unceremonious thing, and what in the world should happen but that young Jack Winter must fall woefully and wildly in love with Harriet Palmley almost as soon as he saw her.

'She, being better educated than he, and caring nothing for the village notion of his mother's superiority to her aunt, did not give him much encouragement. But Longpuddle being no very large world, the two could not help seeing a good deal of each other while she was staying there, and, disdainful young woman as she was, she did seem to take a little pleasure in his attentions and advances.

'One day when they were picking apples together, he asked her to marry him. She had not expected anything so practical as that at so early a time, and was led by her surprise into a half-promise; at any rate, she did not absolutely refuse him, and accepted some little presents that he made her.

'But he saw that her view of him was rather as a simple village lad than as a young man to look up to, and he felt that he must do something bold to secure her. So he said one day, "I am going away, to try to get into a better position than I can get here." In two or three weeks he wished her good-bye, and went away to Monksbury, to superintend a farm, with a view to start as a farmer himself; and from there he wrote regularly to her, as if their marriage were an understood thing.

'Now Harriet liked the young man's presents and the admiration of his eyes; but on paper he was less attractive to her. Her mother had been a schoolmistress, and Harriet had besides a natural aptitude for pen-and-ink work, in days when to be a ready writer was not such a common thing as it is now, and when actual handwriting was valued as an accomplishment in itself. Jack Winter's performances in the shape of love-letters quite jarred her city nerves and her finer taste, and when she answered one of them, in the lovely running hand that she took such pride in, she very strictly and loftily bade him to practise with a pen and spelling-book if he wished to please her. Whether he listened to her request or not nobody knows, but his letters did not improve. He ventured to tell her in his clumsy way that if her heart were more warm towards him she would not be so nice about his handwriting and spelling; which indeed was true enough.

'Well, in Jack's absence the weak flame that had been set alight in Harriet's heart soon sank low, and at last went out altogether. He wrote and wrote, and begged and prayed her to give a reason for her coldness; and then she told him plainly that she was town born, and he was not sufficiently well educated to please her.

'Jack Winter's want of pen-and-ink training did not make him less thin-skinned than others; in fact, he was terribly tender and touchy about anything. This reason that she gave for finally throwing him over grieved him, shamed him, and mortified him more than can be told in these times, the pride of that day in being able to write with beautiful flourishes, and the sorrow at not being able to do so, raging so high. Jack replied to her with an angry note, and then she hit back with smart little stings, telling him how many words he had misspelt in his last letter, and declaring again that this alone was sufficient justification for any woman to put an end to an understanding with him. Her husband must be a better scholar.

'He bore her rejection of him in silence, but his suffering was sharp – all the sharper in being untold. She communicated with Jack no more; and as his reason for going out into the world had been only to provide a home worthy of her, he had no further object in planning such a home now that she was lost to him. He therefore gave up the farming occupation by which he had hoped to make himself a master-farmer, and left the spot to return to his mother.

'As soon as he got back to Longpuddle he found that Harriet had already looked wi' favour upon another lover. He was a young road-contractor, and Jack could not but admit that his rival was both in manners and scholarship much ahead of him. Indeed, a more sensible match for the beauty who had been dropped into the village by fate could hardly have been found than this man, who could offer her so much better a chance than Jack could have done, with his uncertain future and narrow abilities for grappling with the world. The fact was so clear to him that he could hardly blame her.

'One day by accident Jack saw on a scrap of paper the handwriting of Harriet's new beloved. It was flowing like a stream, well spelt, the work of a man accustomed to the ink-bottle and the dictionary, of a man already called in the parish a good scholar. And then it struck all of a sudden into Jack's mind what a contrast the letters of this young man must make to his own miserable old letters, and how ridiculous they must make his lines appear. He groaned and wished he had never written to her, and wondered if she had ever kept his poor performances. Possibly she had kept them, for women are in the habit of doing that, he thought, and whilst they were in her hands there was always a chance of his honest, stupid love-assurances to her being joked over by Harriet with her present lover, or by anybody who should accidentally uncover them.

'The nervous, moody young man could not bear the thought of it, and at length decided to ask her to return them, as was proper when engagements were broken off. He was some hours in framing, copying, and recopying the short note in which he made his request, and having finished it he sent it to her house. His messenger came back with the answer, by word of mouth, that Miss Palmley bade him say she should not part with what was hers, and wondered at his boldness in troubling her.

'Jack was much affronted at this, and determined to go for his letters himself. He chose a time when he knew she was at home, and knocked and went in without much ceremony; for though Harriet was so high and mighty, Jack had small respect for her aunt, Mrs Palmley, whose little child had been his boot-cleaner in earlier days. Harriet was in the room, this being the first time they had met since she had jilted him. He asked for his letters with a stern and bitter look at her.

'At first she said he might have them for all that she cared, and took them out of the bureau where she kept them. Then she glanced over the outside one of the packet, and suddenly altering her mind, she told him shortly that his request was a silly one, and slipped the letters into her aunt's work-box, which stood open on the table, locking it and saying with a bantering laugh that of course she thought it best to keep 'em, since they might be useful to produce as evidence that she had good cause for declining to marry him.

'He blazed up hot. "Give me those letters!" he said. "They are mine!"

' "No, they are not," she replied; "they are mine."

' "Whos'ever they are I want them back," says he. "I don't want to be made sport of for my penmanship: you've another young man now! He has your confidence, and you pour all your tales into his ear. You'll be showing them to him!"

' "Perhaps," said my lady Harriet, with calm coolness, like the heartless woman that she was.

'Her manner so maddened him that he made a step towards the workbox, but she snatched it up, locked it in the bureau, and turned upon him triumphant. For a moment he seemed to be going to wrench the key of the bureau out of her hand; but he stopped himself, and swung round upon his heel and went away.

'When he was out-of-doors alone, and it got night, he walked about restless, and stinging with the sense of being beaten at all points by her. He could not help fancying her telling her new lover or her acquaintances of this scene with himself, and laughing with them over those poor blotted, crooked lines of his that he had been so anxious to obtain. As the evening passed on he worked himself into a dogged resolution to have them back at any price, come what might.

'At the dead of night he came out of his mother's house by the back door, and creeping through the garden hedge went along the field adjoining till he reached the back of her aunt's dwelling. The moon struck bright and flat upon the walls, 'twas said, and every shiny leaf of the creepers was like a little looking-glass in the rays. From long acquaintance Jack knew the arrangement and position of everything in Mrs Palmley's house as well as in his own mother's. The back window close to him was a casement with little leaded squares, as it is to this day, and was, as now, one of two lighting the sitting-room. The other, being in front, was closed up with shutters, but this back one had not even a blind, and the moonlight as it streamed in showed every article of the furniture to him outside. To the right of the room is the fireplace, as you may remember; to the left was the bureau at that time; inside the bureau was Harriet's work-box, as he supposed (though it was really her aunt's), and inside the work-box were his letters. Well, he took out his pocket-knife, and without noise lifted the leading of one of the panes, so that he could take out the glass, and putting his hand through the hole he unfastened the casement, and climbed in through the opening. All the household – that is to say, Mrs Palmley, Harriet, and the little maidservant – were asleep. Jack went straight to the bureau, so he said, hoping it might have been unfastened again – it not being kept locked in ordinary – but Harriet had never unfastened it since she secured her letters there the day before. Jack told afterward how he thought of her asleep upstairs, caring nothing for him, and of the way she had made sport of him and of his letters; and having advanced so far, he was not to be hindered now. By forcing the large blade of his knife under the flap of the bureau, he burst the weak lock; within was the rosewood work-box just as she had placed it in her hurry to keep it from him. There being no time to spare for getting the letters out of it then, he took it under his arm, shut the bureau, and made the best of his way out of the house, latching the casement behind him, and refixing the pane of glass in its place.

'Winter found his way back to his mother's as he had come, and being dog-tired, crept upstairs to bed, hiding the box till he could destroy its contents. The next morning early he set about doing this, and carried it to the linhay at the back of his mother's dwelling. Here by the hearth he opened the box, and began burning one by one the letters that had cost him so much labour to write and shame to think of, meaning to return the box to Harriet, after repairing the slight damage he had caused it by opening it without a key, with a note – the last she would ever receive from him – telling her triumphantly that in refusing to return what he had asked for she had calculated too surely upon his submission to her whims.

'But on removing the last letter from the box he received a shock; for underneath it, at the very bottom, lay money – several golden guineas – "Doubtless Harriet's pocket-money," he said to himself; though it was not, but Mrs Palmley's. Before he had got over his qualms at this discovery he heard footsteps coming through the house-passage to where he was. In haste he pushed the box and what was in it under some brushwood which lay in the linhay; but Jack had been already seen. Two constables entered the out-house, and seized him as he knelt before the fireplace, securing the work-box and all it contained at the same moment. They had come to apprehend him on a charge of breaking into the dwelling-house of Mrs Palmley on the night preceding; and almost before the lad knew what had happened to him they were leading him along the lane that connects that end of the village with this turnpike-road, and along they marched him between 'em all the way to Casterbridge jail.

'Jack's act amounted to night burglary – though he had never thought of it – and burglary was felony, and a capital offence in those days. His figure had been seen by some one against the bright wall as he came away from Mrs Palmley's back window, and the box and money were found in his possession, while the evidence of the broken bureau-lock and tinkered window-pane was more than enough for circumstantial detail. Whether his protestation that he went only for his letters, which he believed to be wrongfully kept from him, would have availed him anything if supported by other evidence I do not know; but the one person who could have borne it out was Harriet, and she acted entirely under the sway of her aunt. That aunt was deadly towards Jack Winter. Mrs Palmley's time had come. Here was her revenge upon the woman who had first won away her lover, and next ruined and deprived her of her heart's treasure – her little son. When the assize week drew on, and Jack had to stand his trial, Harriet did not appear in the case at all, which was allowed to take its course, Mrs Palmley testifying to the general facts of the burglary. Whether Harriet would have come forward if Jack had appealed to her is not known; possibly she would have done it for pity's sake; but Jack was too proud to ask a single favour of a girl who had jilted him; and he let her alone. The trial was a short one, and the death sentence was passed.

'The day o' young Jack's execution was a cold dusty Saturday in March. He was so boyish and slim that they were obliged in mercy to hang him in the heaviest fetters kept in the jail, lest his heft should not break his neck, and they weighed so upon him that he could hardly drag himself up to the drop. At that time the gover'ment was not strict about burying the body of an executed person within the precincts of the prison, and at the earnest prayer of his poor mother his body was allowed to be brought home. All the parish waited at their cottage doors in the evening for its arrival: I remember how, as a very little girl, I stood by my mother's side. About eight o'clock, as we hearkened on our door-stones in the cold bright starlight, we could hear the faint crackle of a waggon from the direction of the turnpike-road. The noise was lost as the waggon dropped into a hollow, then it was plain again as it lumbered down the next long incline, and presently it entered Longpuddle. The coffin was laid in the belfry for the night, and the next day, Sunday, between the services, we buried him. A funeral sermon was preached the same afternoon, the text chosen being, "He was the only son of his mother, and she was a widow." . . . Yes, they were cruel times!

'As for Harriet, she and her lover were married in due time; but by all account her life was no jocund one. She and her good-man found that

they could not live comfortably at Longpuddle, by reason of her connection with Jack's misfortunes, and they settled in a distant town, and
were no more heard of by us; Mrs Palmley, too, found it advisable to
join 'em shortly after. The dark-eyed, gaunt old Mrs Winter, remembered
by the emigrant gentleman here, was, as you will have foreseen, the Mrs
Winter of this story; and I can well call to mind how lonely she was,
how afraid the children were of her, and how she kept herself as a
stranger among us, though she lived so long.'

'Longpuddle has had her sad experiences as well as her sunny ones,'
said Mr Lackland.
    'Yes, yes. But I am thankful to say not many like that, though good
and bad have lived among us.'
    'There was Georgy Crookhill – he was one of the shady sort, as I have
reason to know,' observed the registrar, with the manner of a man who
would like to have his say also.
    'I used to hear what he was as a boy at school.'
    'Well, as he began so he went on. It never got so far as a hanging
matter with him, to be sure; but he had some narrow escapes of penal
servitude; and once it was a case of the biter bit.'

INCIDENT IN THE LIFE OF MR GEORGE
CROOKHILL

'One day,' the registrar continued, 'Georgy was ambling out of Melchester on a miserable screw, the fair being just over, when he saw in
front of him a fine-looking young farmer riding out of the town in the
same direction. He was mounted on a good strong handsome animal,
worth fifty guineas if worth a crown. When they were going up Bissett
Hill, Georgy made it his business to overtake the young farmer. They
passed the time o' day to one another; Georgy spoke of the state of the
roads, and jogged alongside the well-mounted stranger in very friendly
conversation. The farmer had not been inclined to say much to Georgy
at first, but by degrees he grew quite affable, too – as friendly as Georgy
was towards him. He told Crookhill that he had been doing business at
Melchester fair, and was going on as far as Shottsford-Forum that night,
so as to reach Casterbridge market the next day. When they came to
Woodyates Inn they stopped to bait their horses, and agreed to drink

together; with this they got more friendly than ever, and on they went again. Before they had nearly reached Shottsford it came on to rain, and as they were now passing through the village of Trantridge, and it was quite dark, Georgy persuaded the young farmer to go no further that night; the rain would most likely give them a chill. For his part he had heard that the little inn here was comfortable, and he meant to stay. At last the young farmer agreed to put up there also; and they dismounted, and entered, and had a good supper together, and talked over their affairs like men who had known and proved each other a long time. When it was the hour for retiring they went upstairs to a double-bedded room which Georgy Crookhill had asked the landlord to let them share, so sociable were they.

'Before they fell asleep they talked across the room about one thing and another, running from this to that till the conversation turned upon disguises, and changing clothes for particular ends. The farmer told Georgy that he had often heard tales of people doing it; but Crookhill professed to be very ignorant of all such tricks; and soon the young farmer sank into slumber.

'Early in the morning, while the tall young farmer was still asleep (I tell the story as 'twas told me), honest Georgy crept out of his bed by stealth, and dressed himself in the farmer's clothes, in the pockets of the said clothes being the farmer's money. Now though Georgy particularly wanted the farmer's nice clothes and nice horse, owing to a little transaction at the fair which made it desirable that he should not be too easily recognized, his desires had their bounds: he did not wish to take his young friend's money, at any rate more of it than was necessary for paying his bill. This he abstracted, and leaving the farmer's purse containing the rest on the bedroom table, went downstairs. The inn folks had not particularly noticed the faces of their customers, and the one or two who were up at this hour had no thought but that Georgy was the farmer; so when he had paid the bill very liberally, and said he must be off, no objection was made to his getting the farmer's horse saddled for himself; and he rode away upon it as if it were his own.

'About half an hour after, the young farmer awoke, and looking across the room saw that his friend Georgy had gone away in clothes which didn't belong to him, and had kindly left for himself the seedy ones worn by Georgy. At this he sat up in a deep thought for some time, instead of hastening to give an alarm. "The money, the money is gone," he said to himself, "and that's bad. But so are the clothes."

'He then looked upon the table and saw that the money, or most of it, had been left behind.

' "Ha, ha, ha!" he cried, and began to dance about the room. "Ha, ha, ha!" he said again, and made beautiful smiles to himself in the shaving-glass and in the brass candlestick; and then swung about his arms for all the world as if he were going through the sword exercise.

'When he had dressed himself in Georgy's clothes and gone downstairs, he did not seem to mind at all that they took him for the other; and even when he saw that he had been left a bad horse for a good one, he was not inclined to cry out. They told him his friend had paid the bill, at which he seemed much pleased, and without waiting for breakfast he mounted Georgy's horse and rode away likewise, choosing the nearest by-lane in preference to the highroad, without knowing that Georgy had chosen that by-lane also.

'He had not trotted more than two miles in the personal character of Georgy Crookhill when, suddenly rounding a bend that the lane made thereabout, he came upon a man struggling in the hands of two village constables. It was his friend Georgy, the borrower of his clothes and horse. But so far was the young farmer from showing any alacrity in rushing forward to claim his property that he would have turned the poor beast he rode into the wood adjoining, if he had not been already perceived. ' "Help, help, help!" cried the constables. "Assistance in the name of the Crown!"

'The young farmer could do nothing but ride forward. "What's the matter?" he inquired, as coolly as he could.

' "A deserter – a deserter!" said they. "One who's to be tried by court-martial and shot without parley. He deserted from the Dragoons at Cheltenham some days ago, and was tracked; but the search-party can't find him anywhere, and we told 'em if we met him we'd hand him on to 'em forthwith. The day after he left the barracks the rascal met a respectable farmer and made him drunk at an inn, and told him what a fine soldier he would make, and coaxed him to change clothes, to see how well a military uniform would become him. This the simple farmer did; when our deserter said that for a joke he would leave the room and go to the landlady, to see if she would know him in that dress. He never came back, and Farmer Jollice found himself in soldier's clothes, the money in his pockets gone, and, when he got to the stable, his horse gone, too."

' "A scoundrel!" says the young man in Georgy's clothes. "And is this the wretched caitiff?" (pointing to Georgy).

' "No, no!" cries Georgy, as innocent as a babe of this matter of the soldier's desertion. "He's the man! He was wearing Farmer Jollice's suit o' clothes, and he slept in the same room wi' me, and brought up the subject of changing clothes, which put it into my head to dress myself in his suit before he was awake. He's got on mine!"

' "D'ye hear the villain?" groans the tall young man to the constables. "Trying to get out of his crime by charging the first innocent man with it that he sees! No, master soldier – that won't do!"

' "No, no! That won't do!" the constables chimed in. "To have the impudence to say such as that, when we caught him in the act almost! But, thank God, we've got the handcuffs on him at last."

' "We have, thank God," said the tall young man. "Well, I must move on. Good luck to ye with your prisoner!" And off he went, as fast as his poor jade would carry him.

'The constables then, with Georgy handcuffed between 'em, and leading the horse, marched off in the other direction, towards the village where they had been accosted by the escort of soldiers sent to bring the deserter back, Georgy groaning: "I shall be shot, I shall be shot!" They had not gone more than a mile before they met them.

' "Hoi, there!" says the head constable.

' "Hoi, yerself!" says the corporal in charge.

' "We've got your man," says the constable.

' "Where?" says the corporal.

' "Here, between us," said the constable. "Only you don't recognize him out o' uniform."

'The corporal looked at Georgy hard enough; then shook his head and said he was not the absconder.

' "But the absconder changed clothes with Farmer Jollice, and took his horse; and this man has 'em, d'ye see!"

' " 'Tis not our man," said the soldiers. "He's a tall young fellow with a mole on his right cheek, and a military bearing, which this man decidedly has not."

' "I told the two officers of justice that 'twas the other!" pleaded Georgy. "But they wouldn't believe me."

'And so it became clear that the missing dragoon was the tall young farmer, and not Georgy Crookhill – a fact which Farmer Jollice himself corroborated when he arrived on the scene. As Georgy had only robbed the robber, his sentence was comparatively light. The deserter from the Dragoons was never traced: his double shift of clothing having been of the greatest advantage to him in getting off; though he left Georgy's horse behind him a few miles ahead, having found the poor creature more hindrance than aid.'

The man from abroad seemed to be less interested in the questionable characters of Longpuddle and their strange adventures than in the ordinary inhabitants and the ordinary events, though his local fellow-travellers preferred the former as subjects of discussion. He now for the first time asked concerning young persons of the opposite sex – or rather those who had been young when he left his native land. His informants, adhering to their own opinion that the remarkable was better worth telling than the ordinary, would not allow him to dwell upon the simple chronicles of those who had merely come and gone. They asked him if he remembered Netty Sargent.

'Netty Sargent – I do, just remember her. She was a young woman living with her uncle when I left, if my childish recollection may be trusted.'

'That was the maid. She was a oneyer, if you like, sir. Not any harm in her, you know, but up to everything. You ought to hear how she got the copyhold of her house extended. Oughtn't he, Mr Day?'

'He ought,' replied the world-ignored old painter.

'Tell him, Mr Day. Nobody can do it better than you, and you know the legal part better than some of us.'

Day apologized, and began: –

NETTY SARGENT'S COPYHOLD

'She continued to live with her uncle, in the lonely house by the copse, just as at the time you knew her; a tall spry young woman. Ah, how well one can remember her black hair and dancing eyes at that time, and her sly way of screwing up her mouth when she meant to tease ye! Well, she was hardly out of short frocks before the chaps were after her, and by long and by late she was courted by a young man whom perhaps you did not know – Jasper Cliff was his name – and, though she might have had many a better fellow, he so greatly took her fancy that 'twas Jasper or nobody for her. He was a selfish customer, always thinking less of what he was going to do than of what he was going to gain by his doings. Jasper's eyes might have been fixed upon Netty, but his mind was upon her uncle's house; though he was fond of her in his way – I admit that.

'This house, built by her great-great-grandfather, with its garden and little field, was copyhold – granted upon lives in the old way, and had been so granted for generations. Her uncle's was the last life upon the property; so that at his death, if there was no admittance of new lives, it would all fall into the hands of the lord of the manor. But 'twas easy to admit – a slight "fine", as 'twas called, of a few pounds, was enough to entitle him to a new deed o' grant by the custom of the manor; and the lord could not hinder it.

'Now there could be no better provision for his niece and only relative than a sure house over her head, and Netty's uncle should have seen to the renewal in time, owing to the peculiar custom of forfeiture by the dropping of the last life before the new fine was paid; for the Squire was very anxious to get hold of the house and land; and every Sunday when the old man came into the church and passed the Squire's pew, the Squire would say, "A little weaker in his knees, a little crookeder in his back – and the re-admittance not applied for: ha! ha! I shall be able to make a complete clearing of that corner of the manor some day!"

' 'Twas extraordinary, now we look back upon it, that old Sargent should have been so dilatory; yet some people are like it; and he put off calling at the Squire's agent's office with the fine week after week, saying to himself, "I shall have more time next market-day than I have now." One unfortunate hindrance was that he didn't very well like Jasper Cliff, and as Jasper kept urging Netty, and Netty on that account kept urging her uncle, the old man was inclined to postpone the relieving as long as he could, to spite the selfish young lover. At last old Mr Sargent fell ill, and then Jasper could bear it no longer: he produced the fine-money himself, and handed it to Netty, and spoke to her plainly.

' "You and your uncle ought to know better. You should press him more. There's the money. If you let the house and ground slip between ye, I won't marry; hang me if I will! For folks won't deserve a husband that can do such things."

'The worried girl took the money and went home, and told her uncle that it was no house no husband for her. Old Mr Sargent pooh-poohed the money, for the amount was not worth consideration, but he did now bestir himself, for he saw she was bent upon marrying Jasper, and he did not wish to make her unhappy, since she was so determined. It was much to the Squire's annoyance that he found Sargent had moved in the matter at last; but he could not gainsay it, and the documents were prepared (for on this manor the copyholders had writings with their holdings, though on some manors they had none). Old Sargent being now too feeble to go to the agent's house, the deed was to be brought to his house signed, and handed over as a receipt for the money; the counterpart to be signed by Sargent, and sent back to the Squire.

'The agent had promised to call on old Sargent for this purpose at five o'clock, and Netty put the money into her desk to have it close at hand. While doing this she heard a slight cry from her uncle, and turning round, saw that he had fallen forward in his chair. She went and lifted him, but he was unconscious; and unconscious he remained. Neither medicine nor stimulants would bring him to himself. She had been told that he might possibly go off in that way, and it seemed as if the end had come. Before she had started for the doctor his face and extremities grew quite cold and white, and she saw that help would be useless. He was stone-dead.

'Netty's situation rose upon her distracted mind in all its seriousness. The house, garden, and field were lost – by a few hours – and with them a home for herself and her lover. She would not think so meanly of Jasper as to suppose that he would adhere to the resolution declared in a moment of impatience; but she trembled, nevertheless. Why could not her uncle have lived a couple of hours longer, since he had lived so long? It was now past three o'clock; at five the agent was to call, and, if all had gone well, by ten minutes past five the house and holding would have been securely hers for her own and Jasper's lives, these being two of the three proposed to be added by paying the fine. How that wretched old Squire would rejoice at getting the little tenancy into his hands! He did not really require it, but constitutionally hated these tiny copyholds and leaseholds and freeholds, which made islands of independence in the fair, smooth ocean of his estates.

'Then an idea struck into the head of Netty how to accomplish her object in spite of her uncle's negligence. It was a dull December afternoon: and the first step in her scheme – so the story goes, and I see no reason to doubt it—'

' 'Tis true as the light,' affirmed Christopher Twink. 'I was just passing by.'

'The first step in her scheme was to fasten the outer door, to make sure of not being interrupted. Then she set to work by placing her uncle's small, heavy oak table before the fire; then she went to her uncle's corpse, sitting in the chair as he had died – a stuffed arm-chair, on casters, and rather high in the seat, so it was told me – and wheeled the chair, uncle and all, to the table, placing him with his back towards the window, in the attitude of bending over the said oak table, which I knew as a boy as well as I know any piece of furniture in my own house. On the table she laid the large family Bible open before him, and placed his forefinger on the page; and then she opened his eyelids a bit, and put on him his spectacles, so that from behind he appeared for all the world as if he were reading the Scriptures. Then she unfastened the door and sat down, and when it grew dark she lit a candle, and put it on the table beside her uncle's book.

'Folk may well guess how the time passed with her till the agent came, and how, when his knock sounded upon the door, she nearly started out of her skin – at least that's as it was told me. Netty promptly went to the door.

' "I am sorry, sir," she says, under her breath; "my uncle is not so well to-night, and I'm afraid he can't see you."

' "H'm! – that's a pretty tale," says the steward. "So I've come all this way about this trumpery little job for nothing!"

' "O no, sir – I hope not," says Netty. "I suppose the business of granting the new deed can be done just the same?"

' "Done? Certainly not. He must pay the renewal money, and sign the parchment in my presence."

'She looked dubious. "Uncle is so dreadful nervous about law business," says she, "that, as you know, he's put it off and put it off for years; and now to-day really I've feared it would verily drive him out of his mind. His poor three teeth quite chattered when I said to him that you would be here soon with the parchment writing. He always was afraid of agents, and folks that come for rent, and such-like."

' "Poor old fellow – I'm sorry for him. Well, the thing can't be done unless I see him and witness his signature."

' "Suppose, sir, that you see him sign, and he don't see you looking at him? I'd soothe his nerves by saying you weren't strict about the form of witnessing, and didn't wish to come in. So that it was done in your bare presence it would be sufficient, would it not? As he's such an old, shrinking, shivering man, it would be a great considerateness on your part if that would do."

' "In my bare presence would do, of course – that's all I come for. But how can I be a witness without his seeing me?"

' "Why, in this way, sir; if you'll oblige me by just stepping here." She conducted him a few yards to the left, till they were opposite the parlour window. The blind had been left up purposely, and the candle-light shone out upon the garden bushes. Within the agent could see, at the other end of the room, the back and side of the old man's head, and his shoulders and arm, sitting with the book and candle before him, and his spectacles on his nose, as she had placed him.

' "He's reading his Bible, as you see, sir," she says, quite in her meekest way.

' "Yes. I thought he was a careless sort of man in matters of religion?"

' "He always was fond of his Bible," Netty assured him. "Though I think he's nodding over it just at this moment. However, that's natural in an old man, and unwell. Now you could stand here and see him sign, couldn't you, sir, as he's such an invalid?"

' "Very well," said the agent, lighting a cigar. "You have ready by you the merely nominal sum you'll have to pay for the admittance, of course?"

' "Yes," said Netty. "I'll bring it out." She fetched the cash, wrapped in paper, and handed it to him, and when he had counted it the steward took from his breast pocket the precious parchments and gave one to her to be signed.

' "Uncle's hand is a little paralyzed," she said. "And what with his being half asleep, too, really I don't know what sort of a signature he'll be able to make."

' "Doesn't matter, so that he signs."

' "Might I hold his hand?"

' "Ay, hold his hand, my young woman – that will be near enough."

'Netty re-entered the house, and the agent continued smoking outside the window. Now came the ticklish part of Netty's performance. The steward saw her put the inkhorn – "horn", says I in my old-fashioned way – the inkstand, before her uncle, and touch his elbow as if to arouse him, and speak to him, and spread out the deed; when she had pointed to show him where to sign she dipped the pen and put it into his hand. To hold his hand she artfully stepped behind him, so that the agent could only see a little bit of his head, and the hand she held; but he saw the old man's hand trace his name on the document. As soon as 'twas done she came out to the steward with the parchment in her hand, and the steward signed as witness by the light from the parlour window. Then he gave her the deed signed by the Squire, and left; and next morning Netty told the neighbours that her uncle was dead in his bed.'

'She must have undressed him and put him there.'

'She must. O, that girl had a nerve, I can tell ye! Well, to cut a long story short, that's how she got back the house and field that were, strictly speaking, gone from her; and by getting them, got her a husband.

'Every virtue has its reward, they say. Netty had hers for her ingenious contrivance to gain Jasper. Two years after they were married he took to beating her – not hard, you know; just a smack or two, enough to set her in a temper, and let out to the neighbours what she had done to win him, and how she repented of her pains. When the old Squire was dead, and his son came into the property, this confession of hers began to be whispered about. But Netty was a pretty young woman, and the Squire's son was a pretty young man at that time, and wider-minded than his father, having no objection to little holdings; and he never took any proceedings against her.'

There was now a lull in the discourse, and soon the van descended the hill leading into the long straggling village. When the houses were reached the passengers dropped off one by one, each at his or her own door. Arrived at the inn, the returned emigrant secured a bed, and having eaten a light meal, sallied forth upon the scene he had known so well in his early days. Though flooded with the light of the rising moon, none of the objects wore the attractiveness in this their real presentation that had ever accompanied their images in the field of his imagination when he was more than two thousand miles removed from them. The peculiar charm attaching to an old village in an old country, as seen by the eyes of an absolute foreigner, was lowered in his case by magnified expectations from infantine memories. He walked on, looking at this chimney and that old wall, till he came to the churchyard, which he entered.

The head-stones, whitened by the moon, were easily decipherable; and now for the first time Lackland began to feel himself amid the village community that he had left behind him five-and-thirty years before. Here, beside the Sallets, the Darths, the Pawles, the Privetts, the Sargents, and others of whom he had just heard, were names he remembered even better than those: the Jickses, and the Crosses, and the Knights, and the Olds. Doubtless representatives of these families, or some of them, were yet among the living; but to him they would all be as strangers. Far from finding his heart ready-supplied with roots and tendrils here, he perceived that in returning to this spot it would be incumbent upon him to re-establish himself from the beginning, precisely as though he had never known the place, nor it him. Time had not condescended to wait his pleasure, nor local life his greeting.

The figure of Mr Lackland was seen at the inn, and in the village street, and in the fields and lanes about Upper Longpuddle, for a few days after his arrival, and then, ghost-like, it silently disappeared. He had told some of the villagers that his immediate purpose in coming had been fulfilled by a sight of the place, and by conversation with its inhabitants; but that his ulterior purpose – of coming to spend his latter days among them – would probably never be carried out. It is now a dozen or fifteen years since his visit was paid, and his face has not again been seen.

March 1891

A CHANGED MAN AND OTHER TALES

Prefatory Note to 'A Changed Man' and Other Tales

I REPRINT in this volume, for what they may be worth, a dozen minor novels that have been published in the periodical press at various dates in the past, in order to render them accessible to readers who desire to have them in the complete series issued by my publishers. For aid in reclaiming some of the narratives I express my thanks to the proprietors and editors of the newspapers and magazines in whose pages they first appeared.

August 1913   T.H.

A Changed Man

I

THE person who, next to the actors themselves, chanced to know most of their story, lived just below 'Top o' Town' (as the spot was called) in an old substantially-built house, distinguished among its neighbours by having an oriel window on the first floor, whence could be obtained a raking view of the High Street, west and east, the former including Laura's dwelling, the end of the Town Avenue hard by (in which were played the odd pranks hereafter to be mentioned), the Port-Bredy road rising westwards, and the turning that led to the cavalry barracks where the Captain was quartered. Looking eastward down the town from the same favoured gazebo, the long perspective of houses declined and dwindled till they merged in the highway across the moor. The white riband of road disappeared over Grey's Bridge a quarter of a mile off, to plunge into innumerable rustic windings, shy shades, and solitary undulations up hill and down dale for one hundred and twenty miles till it exhibited itself at Hyde Park Corner as a smooth bland surface in touch with a busy and fashionable world.

To the barracks aforesaid had recently arrived the —th Hussars, a regiment new to the locality. Almost before any acquaintance with its members had been made by the townspeople, a report spread that they were a 'crack' body of men, and had brought a splendid band. For some reason or other the town had not been used as the headquarters of cavalry for many years, the various troops stationed there having consisted of casual detachments only; so that it was with a sense of honour that everybody – even the small furniture-broker from whom the married troopers hired tables and chairs – received the news of their crack quality.

In those days the Hussar regiments still wore over the left shoulder that attractive attachment, or frilled half-coat, hanging loosely behind like the wounded wing of a bird, which was called the pelisse, though it was known among the troopers themselves as a 'sling-jacket'. It added amazingly to their picturesqueness in women's eyes, and, indeed, in the eyes of men also.

The burgher who lived in the house with the oriel window sat during a great many hours of the day in that projection, for he was an invalid, and time hung heavily on his hands unless he maintained a constant interest in proceedings without. Not more than a week after the arrival of the Hussars his ears were assailed by the shout of one schoolboy to another in the street below.

'Have 'ee heard this about the Hussars? They are haunted! Yes – a ghost troubles 'em; he has followed 'em about the world for years.'

A haunted regiment: that was a new idea for either invalid or stalwart. The listener in the oriel came to the conclusion that there were some lively characters among the —th Hussars.

He made Captain Maumbry's acquaintance in an informal manner at an afternoon tea to which he went in a wheeled chair – one of the very rare outings that the state of his health permitted. Maumbry showed himself to be a handsome man of twenty-eight or thirty, with an attractive hint of wickedness in his manner that was sure to make him adorable with good young women. The large dark eyes that lit his pale face expressed this wickedness strongly, though such was the adaptability of their rays that one could think they might have expressed sadness or seriousness just as readily, if he had had a mind for such.

An old and deaf lady who was present asked Captain Maumbry bluntly: 'What's this we hear about you? They say your regiment is haunted.'

The Captain's face assumed an aspect of grave, even sad, concern. 'Yes,' he replied, 'it is too true.'

Some younger ladies smiled till they saw how serious he looked, when they looked serious likewise.

'Really?' said the old lady.

'Yes. We naturally don't wish to say much about it.'

'No, no; of course not. But – how haunted?'

'Well; the – *thing*, as I'll call it, follows us. In country quarters or town, abroad or at home, it's just the same.'

'How do you account for it?'

'H'm.' Maumbry lowered his voice. 'Some crime committed by certain of our regiment in past years, we suppose.'

'Dear me. . . . How very horrid, and singular!'

'But, as I said, we don't speak of it much.'

'No . . . no.'

When the Hussar was gone, a young lady, disclosing a long-suppressed interest, asked if the ghost had been seen by any of the town.

The lawyer's son, who always had the latest borough news, said that, though it was seldom seen by anyone but the Hussars themselves, more than one townsman and woman had already set eyes on it, to his or her terror. The phantom mostly appeared very late at night, under the dense trees of the town-avenue nearest the barracks. It was about ten feet high; its teeth chattered with a dry naked sound, as if they were those of a skeleton; and its hip-bones could be heard grating in their sockets.

During the darkest weeks of winter several timid persons were seriously frightened by the object answering to this cheerful description, and the police began to look into the matter. Whereupon the appearances grew less frequent, and some of the Boys of the regiment thankfully stated that they had not been so free from ghostly visitation for years as they had become since their arrival in Casterbridge.

This playing at ghosts was the most innocent of the amusements indulged in by the choice young spirits who inhabited the lichened, red-brick building at the top of the town bearing 'W.D.' and a broad arrow on its quoins. Far more serious escapades – levities relating to love, wine, cards, betting – were talked of, with no doubt more or less of exaggeration. That the Hussars, Captain Maumbry included, were the cause of bitter tears to several young women of the town and country is unquestionably true, despite the fact that the gaieties of the young men wore a more staring colour in this old-fashioned place than they would have done in a large and modern city.

II

Regularly once a week they rode out in marching order.

Returning up the town on one of these occasions, the romantic pelisse flapping behind each horseman's shoulder in the soft south-west wind, Captain Maumbry glanced up at the oriel. A mutual nod was exchanged between him and the person who sat there reading. The reader and a friend in the room with him followed the troop with their eyes all the way up the street, till, when the soldiers were opposite the house in which Laura lived, that young lady became discernible in the balcony.

'They are engaged to be married, I hear,' said the friend.

'Who – Maumbry and Laura? Never – so soon?'

'Yes.'

'He'll never marry. Several girls have been mentioned in connection with his name. I am sorry for Laura.'

'Oh, but you needn't be. They are excellently matched.'

'She's only one more.'

'She's one more, and more still. She has regularly caught him. She is a born player of the game of hearts, and she knew how to beat him in his own practices. If there is one woman in the town who has any chance of holding her own and marrying him, she is that woman.'

This was true, as it turned out. By natural proclivity Laura had from the first entered heart and soul into military romance as exhibited in the plots and characters of those living exponents of it who came under her notice. From her earliest young womanhood civilians, however promising, had no chance of winning her interest if the meanest warrior were within the horizon. It may be that the position of her uncle's house (which was her home) at the corner of West Street nearest the barracks, the daily passing of the troops, the constant blowing of trumpet-calls a furlong from her windows, coupled with the fact that she knew nothing of the inner realities of military life, and hence idealized it, had also helped her mind's original bias for thinking men-at-arms the only ones worthy of a woman's heart.

Captain Maumbry was a typical prize; one whom all surrounding maidens had coveted, ached for, angled for, wept for, had by her judicious management become subdued to her purpose; and in addition to the pleasure of marrying the man she loved, Laura had the joy of feeling herself hated by the mothers of all the marriageable girls of the neighbourhood.

The man in the oriel went to the wedding; not as a guest, for at this time he was but slightly acquainted with the parties; but mainly because the church was close to his house; partly, too, for a reason which moved many others to be spectators of the ceremony; a subconsciousness that, though the couple might be happy in their experiences, there was sufficient possibility of their being otherwise to colour the musings of an onlooker with a pleasing pathos of conjecture. He could on occasion do a pretty stroke of rhyming in those days, and he beguiled the time of

waiting by pencilling on a blank page of his prayer-book a few lines
which, though kept private then, may be given here: –

AT A HASTY WEDDING
(*Triolet*)

If hours be years the twain are blest,
    For now they solace swift desire
By lifelong ties that tether zest
    If hours be years. The twain are blest
Do eastern suns slope never west,
    Nor pallid ashes follow fire.
If hours be years the twain are blest,
    For now they solace swift desire.

As if, however, to falsify all prophecies, the couple seemed to find in
marriage the secret of perpetuating the intoxication of a courtship which,
on Maumbry's side at least, had opened without serious intent. During
the winter following they were the most popular pair in and about
Casterbridge – nay, in South Wessex itself. No smart dinner in the
country houses of the younger and gayer families within driving distance
of the borough was complete without their lively presence; Mrs
Maumbry was the blithest of the whirling figures at the county ball;
and when followed that inevitable incident of garrison-town life, an
amateur dramatic entertainment, it was just the same. The acting was
for the benefit of such and such an excellent charity – nobody cared
what, provided the play were played – and both Captain Maumbry and
his wife were in the piece, having been in fact, by mutual consent, the
originators of the performance. And so with laughter, and thoughtlessness, and movement, all went merrily. There was a little backwardness
in the bill-paying of the couple; but in justice to them it must be added
that sooner or later all owings were paid.

III

At the chapel-of-ease attended by the troops there arose above the edge
of the pulpit one Sunday an unknown face. This was the face of a new
curate. He placed upon the desk, not the familiar sermon book, but
merely a Bible. The person who tells these things was not present at that
service, but he soon learnt that the young curate was nothing less than
a great surprise to his congregation; a mixed one always, for though the

Hussars occupied the body of the building, its nooks and corners were crammed with civilians, whom, up to the present, even the least uncharitable would have described as being attracted thither less by the services than by the soldiery.

Now there arose a second reason for squeezing into an already overcrowded church. The persuasive and gentle eloquence of Mr Sainway operated like a charm upon those accustomed only to the higher and drier styles of preaching, and for a time the other churches of the town were thinned of their sitters.

At this point in the nineteenth century the sermon was the sole reason for churchgoing amongst a vast body of religious people. The liturgy was a formal preliminary, which, like the Royal proclamation in a court of assize, had to be got through before the real interest began; and on reaching home the question was simply: Who preached, and how did he handle his subject? Even had an archbishop officiated in the service proper nobody would have cared much about what was said or sung. People who had formerly attended in the morning only began to go in the evening, and even to the special addresses in the afternoon.

One day when Captain Maumbry entered his wife's drawing-room, filled with hired furniture, she thought he was somebody else, for he had not come upstairs humming the most catching air afloat in musical circles or in his usual careless way.

'What's the matter, Jack?' she said without looking up from a note she was writing.

'Well – not much, that I know.'

'O, but there is,' she murmured as she wrote.

'Why – this cursed new lath in a sheet – I mean the new parson! He wants us to stop the band-playing on Sunday afternoons.'

Laura looked up aghast.

'Why, it is the one thing that enables the few rational beings hereabouts to keep alive from Saturday to Monday!'

'He says all the town flock to the music and don't come to the service, and that the pieces played are profane, or mundane, or inane, or something – not what ought to be played on Sunday. Of course 'tis Lautmann who settles those things.'

Lautmann was the bandmaster.

The barrack-green on Sunday afternoons had, indeed, become the promenade of a great many townspeople cheerfully inclined, many even of those who attended in the morning at Mr Sainway's service; and little boys who ought to have been listening to the curate's afternoon lecture were too often seen rolling upon the grass and making faces behind the more dignified listeners.

Laura heard no more about the matter, however, for two or three weeks, when suddenly remembering it she asked her husband if any further objections had been raised.

'O – Mr Sainway. I forgot to tell you. I've made his acquaintance. He is not a bad sort of man.'

Laura asked if either Maumbry or some others of the officers did not give the presumptuous curate a good setting down for his interference.

'O well – we've forgotten that. He's a stunning preacher, they tell me.'

The acquaintance developed apparently, for the Captain said to her a little later on, 'There's a good deal in Sainway's argument about having no band on Sunday afternoons. After all, it is close to his church. But he doesn't press his objections unduly.'

'I am surprised to hear you defend him!'

'It was only a passing thought of mine. We naturally don't wish to offend the inhabitants of the town if they don't like it.'

'But they do.'

The invalid in the oriel never clearly gathered the details of progress in this conflict of lay and clerical opinion; but so it was that, to the disappointment of musicians, the grief of out-walking lovers, and the regret of the junior population of the town and country round, the band-playing on Sunday afternoons ceased in Casterbridge barrack-square.

By this time the Maumbrys had frequently listened to the preaching of the gentle if narrow-minded curate; for these light-natured, hit-or-miss, rackety people went to church like others for respectability's sake. None so orthodox as your unmitigated worldling. A more remarkable event was the sight to the man in the window of Captain Maumbry and Mr Sainway walking down the High Street in earnest conversation. On his mentioning this fact to a caller he was assured that it was a matter of common talk that they were always together.

The observer would soon have learnt this with his own eyes if he had not been told. They began to pass together nearly every day. Hitherto Mrs Maumbry, in fashionable walking clothes, had usually been her husband's companion; but this was less frequent now. The close and singular friendship between the two men went on for nearly a year, when

Mr Sainway was presented to a living in a densely-populated town in the midland counties. He bade the parishioners of his old place a reluctant farewell and departed, the touching sermon he preached on the occasion being published by the local printer. Everybody was sorry to lose him; and it was with genuine grief that his Casterbridge congregation learnt later on that soon after his induction to his benefice, during some bitter weather, he had fallen seriously ill of inflammation of the lungs, of which he eventually died.

We now get below the surface of things. Of all who had known the dead curate, none grieved for him like the man who on his first arrival had called him a 'lath in a sheet'. Mrs Maumbry had never greatly sympathized with the impressive parson; indeed, she had been secretly glad that he had gone away to better himself. He had considerably diminished the pleasures of a woman by whom the joys of earth and good company had been appreciated to the full. Sorry for her husband in his loss of a friend who had been none of hers, she was yet quite unprepared for the sequel.

'There is something that I have wanted to tell you lately, dear,' he said one morning at breakfast with hesitation. 'Have you guessed what it is?'

She had guessed nothing.

'That I think of retiring from the army.'

'What!'

'I have thought more and more of Sainway since his death, and of what he used to say to me so earnestly. And I feel certain I shall be right in obeying a call within me to give up this fighting trade and enter the Church.'

'What – be a parson?'

'Yes.'

'But what should I do?'

'Be a parson's wife.'

'Never!' she affirmed.

'But how can you help it?'

'I'll run away rather!' she said vehemently.

'No, you mustn't,' Maumbry replied, in the tone he used when his mind was made up. 'You'll get accustomed to the idea, for I am constrained to carry it out, though it is against my worldly interests. I am forced on by a Hand outside me to tread in the steps of Sainway.'

'Jack,' she asked, with calm pallor and round eyes; 'do you mean to say seriously that you are arranging to be a curate instead of a soldier?'

'I might say a curate *is* a soldier – of the church militant; but I don't want to offend you with doctrine. I distinctly say, yes.'

Late one evening, a little time onward, he caught her sitting by the dim firelight in her room. She did not know he had entered; and he found her weeping. 'What are you crying about, poor dearest?' he said.

She started. 'Because of what you have told me!'

The Captain grew very unhappy; but he was undeterred.

In due time the town learnt, to its intense surprise, that Captain Maumbry had retired from the —th Hussars and gone to Fountall Theological College to prepare for the ministry.

IV

'O, the pity of it! Such a dashing soldier – so popular – such an acquisition to the town – the soul of social life here! And now!... One should not speak ill of the dead, but that dreadful Mr Sainway – it was too cruel of him!'

This is a summary of what was said when Captain, now the Reverend, John Maumbry was enabled by circumstances to indulge his heart's desire of returning to the scene of his former exploits in the capacity of a minister of the Gospel. A low-lying district of the town, which at that date was crowded with impoverished cottagers, was crying for a curate, and Mr Maumbry generously offered himself as one willing to undertake labours that were certain to produce little result, and no thanks, credit, or emolument.

Let the truth be told about him as a clergyman; he proved to be anything but a brilliant success. Painstaking, single-minded, deeply in earnest as all could see, his delivery was laboured, his sermons were dull to listen to, and alas, too, too long. Even the dispassionate judges who sat by the hour in the bar-parlour of the White Hart – an inn standing at the dividing line between the poor quarter aforesaid and the fashionable quarter of Maumbry's former triumphs, and hence affording a position of strict impartiality – agreed in substance with the young ladies to the westward, though their views were somewhat more tersely expressed: 'Surely, God A'mighty spwiled a good sojer to make a bad pa'son when He shifted Cap'n Ma'mbry into a sarpless!'

The latter knew that such things were said, but he pursued his daily labours in and out of the hovels with serene unconcern.

It was about this time that the invalid in the oriel became more than a mere bowing acquaintance of Mrs Maumbry's. She had returned to the town with her husband, and was living with him in a little house in the centre of his circle of ministration, when by some means she became one of the invalid's visitors. After a general conversation while sitting in his room with a friend of both, an incident led up to the matter that still rankled deeply in her soul. Her face was now paler and thinner than it had been; even more attractive, her disappointments having inscribed themselves as meek thoughtfulness on a look that was once a little frivolous. The two ladies had called to be allowed to use the window for observing the departure of the Hussars, who were leaving for barracks much nearer to London.

The troopers turned the corner of Barrack Road into the top of High Street, headed by their band playing 'The girl I left behind me' (which was formerly always the tune for such times, though it is now nearly disused). They came and passed the oriel, where an officer or two, looking up and discovering Mrs Maumbry, saluted her, whose eyes filled with tears as the notes of the band waned away. Before the little group had recovered from that sense of the romantic which such spectacles impart, Mr Maumbry came along the pavement. He probably had bidden his former brethren-in-arms a farewell at the top of the street, for he walked from that direction in his rather shabby clerical clothes, and with a basket on his arm which seemed to hold some purchases he had been making for his poorer parishioners. Unlike the soldiers he went along quite unconscious of his appearance or of the scene around.

The contrast was too much for Laura. With lips that now quivered, she asked the invalid what he thought of the change that had come to her.

It was difficult to answer, and with a wilfulness that was too strong in her she repeated the question.

'Do you think,' she added, 'that a woman's husband has a right to do such a thing, even if he does feel a certain call to it?'

Her listener sympathized too largely with both of them to be anything but unsatisfactory in his reply. Laura gazed longingly out of the window towards the thin dusty line of Hussars, now smalling towards the Mellstock Ridge. 'I,' she said, 'who should have been in their van on the way to London, am doomed to fester in a hole in Durnover Lane!'

Many events had passed and many rumours had been current concerning her before the invalid saw her again after her leave-taking that day.

V

Casterbridge had known many military and civil episodes; many happy times, and times less happy; and now came the time of her visitation. The scourge of cholera had been laid on the suffering country, and the low-lying purlieus of this ancient borough had more than their share of the infliction. Mixen Lane, in the Durnover quarter, and in Maumbry's parish, was where the blow fell most heavily. Yet there was a certain mercy in its choice of a date, for Maumbry was the man for such an hour.

The spread of the epidemic was so rapid that many left the town and took lodgings in the villages and farms. Mr Maumbry's house was close to the most infected street, and he himself was occupied morn, noon, and night in endeavours to stamp out the plague and in alleviating the sufferings of the victims. So, as a matter of ordinary precaution, he decided to isolate his wife somewhere away from him for a while.

She suggested a village by the sea, near Budmouth Regis, and lodgings were obtained for her at Creston, a spot divided from the Casterbridge valley by a high ridge that gave it quite another atmosphere, though it lay no more than six miles off.

Thither she went. While she was rusticating in this place of safety, and her husband was slaving in the slums, she struck up an acquaintance with a lieutenant in the —st Foot, a Mr Vannicock, who was stationed with his regiment at the Budmouth infantry barracks. As Laura frequently sat on the shelving beach, watching each thin wave slide up to her, and hearing, without heeding, its gnaw at the pebbles in its retreat, he often took a walk that way.

The acquaintance grew and ripened. Her situation, her history, her beauty, her age - a year or two above his own - all tended to make an impression on the young man's heart, and a reckless flirtation was soon in blithe progress upon that lonely shore.

It was said by her detractors afterwards that she had chosen her lodging to be near this gentleman, but there is reason to believe that she had never seen him till her arrival there. Just now Casterbridge was so deeply occupied with its own sad affairs - a daily burying of the dead

and destruction of contaminated clothes and bedding – that it had little
inclination to promulgate such gossip as may have reached its ears on
the pair. Nobody long considered Laura in the tragic cloud which over-
hung all.

Meanwhile, on the Budmouth side of the hill the very mood of men
was in contrast. The visitation there had been slight and much earlier,
and normal occupations and pastimes had been resumed. Mr Maumbry
had arranged to see Laura twice a week in the open air, that she might
run no risk from him; and, having heard nothing of the faint rumour,
he met her as usual one dry and windy afternoon on the summit of the
dividing hill, near where the high road from town to town crosses the
old Ridgeway at right angles.

He waved his hand, and smiled as she approached, shouting to her:
'We will keep this wall between us, dear.' (Walls formed the field-fences
here.) 'You mustn't be endangered. It won't be for long, with God's
help!'

'I will do as you tell me, Jack. But you are running too much
risk yourself, aren't you? I get little news of you; but I fancy you
are.'

'Not more than others.'

Thus somewhat formally they talked, an insulating wind beating the
wall between them like a mill-weir.

'But you wanted to ask me something?' he added.

'Yes. You know we are trying in Budmouth to raise some money for
your sufferers; and the way we have thought of is by a dramatic performance. They want me to take a part.'

His face saddened. 'I have known so much of that sort of thing, and all
that accompanies it! I wish you had thought of some other way.'

She said lightly that she was afraid it was all settled. 'You object to
my taking a part, then? Of course—'

He told her that he did not like to say he positively objected. He
wished they had chosen an oratorio, or lecture, or anything more in
keeping with the necessity it was to relieve.

'But,' said she impatiently, 'people won't come to oratorios or
lectures! They will crowd to comedies and farces.'

'Well, I cannot dictate to Budmouth how it shall earn the money it is
going to give us. Who is getting up this performance?'

'The boys of the —st.'

'Ah, yes; our old game!' replied Mr Maumbry. 'The grief of Casterbridge is the excuse for their frivolity. Candidly, dear Laura, I wish you wouldn't play in it. But I don't forbid you to. I leave the whole to your judgment.'

The interview ended, and they went their ways northward and southward. Time disclosed to all concerned that Mrs Maumbry played in the comedy as the heroine, the lover's part being taken by Mr Vannicock.

VI

Thus was helped on an event which the conduct of the mutually-attracted ones had been generating for some time.

It is unnecessary to give details. The —st Foot left for Bristol, and this precipitated their action. After a week of hesitation she agreed to leave her home at Creston and meet Vannicock on the ridge hard by, and to accompany him to Bath, where he had secured lodgings for her, so that she would be only about a dozen miles from his quarters.

Accordingly, on the evening chosen, she laid on her dressing-table a note for her husband, running thus: –

DEAR JACK, – I am unable to endure this life any longer, and I have resolved to put an end to it. I told you I should run away if you persisted in being a clergyman, and now I am doing it. One cannot help one's nature. I have resolved to throw in my lot with Mr Vannicock, and I hope rather than expect you will forgive me. – L.

Then, with hardly a scrap of luggage, she went, ascending to the ridge in the dusk of early evening. Almost on the very spot where her husband had stood at their last tryst she beheld the outline of Vannicock, who had come all the way from Bristol to fetch her.

'I don't like meeting here – it is so unlucky!' she cried to him. 'For God's sake let us have a place of our own. Go back to the milestone, and I'll come on.'

He went back to the milestone that stands on the north slope of the ridge, where the old and new roads diverge, and she joined him there.

She was taciturn and sorrowful when he asked her why she would not meet him on the top. At last she inquired how they were going to travel.

He explained that he proposed to walk to Mellstock Hill, on the other side of Casterbridge, where a fly was waiting to take them by a cross-cut into the Ivell Road, and onward to that town. The Bristol railway was open to Ivell.

This plan they followed, and walked briskly through the dull gloom till they neared Casterbridge, which place they avoided by turning to the right at the Roman Amphitheatre and bearing round to Durnover Cross. Thence the way was solitary and open across the moor to the hill whereon the Ivell fly awaited them.

'I have noticed for some time,' she said, 'a lurid glare over the Durnover end of the town. It seems to come from somewhere about Mixen Lane.'

'The lamps,' he suggested.

'There's not a lamp as big as a rushlight in the whole lane. It is where the cholera is worst.'

By Standfast Corner, a little beyond the Cross, they suddenly obtained an end view of the lane. Large bonfires were burning in the middle of the way, with a view to purifying the air; and from the wretched tenements with which the lane was lined in those days persons were bringing out bedding and clothing. Some was thrown into the fires, the rest placed in wheel-barrows and wheeled into the moor directly in the track of the fugitives.

They followed on, and came up to where a vast copper was set in the open air. Here the linen was boiled and disinfected. By the light of the lanterns Laura discovered that her husband was standing by the copper, and that it was he who unloaded the barrow and immersed its contents. The night was so calm and muggy that the conversation by the copper reached her ears.

'Are there many more loads to-night?'

'There's the clothes o' they that died this afternoon, sir. But that might bide till to-morrow, for you must be tired out.'

'We'll do it at once, for I can't ask anybody else to undertake it. Overturn that load on the grass and fetch the rest.'

The man did so and went off with the barrow. Maumbry paused for a moment to wipe his face, and resumed his homely drudgery amid this squalid and reeking scene, pressing down and stirring the contents of the copper, with what looked like an old rolling-pin. The steam therefrom, laden with death, travelled in a low trail across the meadow.

Laura spoke suddenly: 'I won't go to-night after all. He is so tired, and I must help him. I didn't know things were so bad as this!'

Vannicock's arm dropped from her waist, where it had been resting as they walked. 'Will you leave?' she asked.

'I will if you say I must. But I'd rather help too.' There was no expostulation in his tone.

Laura had gone forward. 'Jack,' she said, 'I am come to help!'

The weary curate turned and held up the lantern. 'O – what, is it you, Laura?' he asked in surprise. 'Why did you come into this? You had better go back – the risk is great.'

'But I want to help you, Jack. Please let me help! I didn't come by myself – Mr Vannicock kept me company. He will make himself useful too, if he's not gone on. Mr Vannicock!'

The young lieutenant came forward reluctantly. Mr Maumbry spoke formally to him, adding as he resumed his labour, 'I thought the —st Foot had gone to Bristol.'

'We have. But I have run down again for a few things.'

The two newcomers began to assist, Vannicock placing on the ground the small bag containing Laura's toilet articles that he had been carrying. The barrow-man soon returned with another load, and all continued work for nearly a half-hour, when a coachman came out from the shadows to the north.

'Beg pardon, sir,' he whispered to Vannicock, 'but I've waited so long on Mellstock hill that at last I drove down to the turnpike; and seeing the light here, I ran on to find out what had happened.'

Lieutenant Vannicock told him to wait a few minutes, and the last barrow-load was got through. Mr Maumbry stretched himself and breathed heavily, saying, 'There; we can do no more.'

As if from the relaxation of effort he seemed to be seized with violent pain. He pressed his hands to his sides and bent forward.

'Ah! I think it has got hold of me at last,' he said with difficulty. 'I must try to get home. Let Mr Vannicock take you back, Laura.'

He walked a few steps, they helping him, but was obliged to sink down on the grass.

'I am – afraid – you'll have to send for a hurdle, or shutter, or something,' he went on feebly, 'or try to get me into the barrow.'

But Vannicock had called to the driver of the fly, and they waited until it was brought on from the turnpike hard by. Mr Maumbry was placed therein. Laura entered with him, and they drove to his humble residence near the Cross, where he was got upstairs.

Vannicock stood outside by the empty fly a while, but Laura did not reappear. He thereupon entered the fly and told the driver to take him back to Ivell.

VII

Mr Maumbry had over-exerted himself in the relief of the suffering poor, and fell a victim – one of the last – to the pestilence which had carried off so many. Two days later he lay in his coffin.

Laura was in the room below. A servant brought in some letters, and she glanced them over. One was the note from herself to Maumbry, informing him that she was unable to endure life with him any longer and was about to elope with Vannicock. Having read the letter she took it upstairs to where the dead man was, and slipped it into his coffin. The next day she buried him.

She was now free.

She shut up his house at Durnover Cross and returned to her lodgings at Creston. Soon she had a letter from Vannicock, and six weeks after her husband's death her lover came to see her.

'I forgot to give you back this – that night,' he said presently, handing her the little bag she had taken as her whole luggage when leaving.

Laura received it and absently shook it out. There fell upon the carpet her brush, comb, slippers, nightdress, and other simple necessaries for a journey. They had an intolerably ghastly look now, and she tried to cover them.

'I can now,' he said, 'ask you to belong to me legally – when a proper interval has gone – instead of as we meant.'

There was languor in his utterance, hinting at a possibility that it was perfunctorily made. Laura picked up her articles, answering that he certainly could so ask her – she was free. Yet not her expression either could be called an ardent response. Then she blinked more and more quickly and put her handkerchief to her face. She was weeping violently.

He did not move or try to comfort her in any way. What had come between them? No living person. They had been lovers. There was now no material obstacle whatever to their union. But there was the insistent shadow of that unconscious one; the thin figure of him, moving to and fro in front of the ghastly furnace in the gloom of Durnover Moor.

Yet Vannicock called upon Laura when he was in the neighbourhood, which was not often; but in two years, as if on purpose to further the marriage which everybody was expecting, the —st Foot returned to Budmouth Regis.

Thereupon the two could not help encountering each other at times. But whether because the obstacle had been the source of the love, or from a sense of error, and because Mrs Maumbry bore a less attractive look as a widow than before, their feelings seemed to decline from their former incandescence to a mere tepid civility. What domestic issues supervened in Vannicock's further story the man in the oriel never knew; but Mrs Maumbry lived and died a widow.

1900

The Waiting Supper

I

WHOEVER had perceived the yeoman standing on Squire Everard's lawn in the dusk of that October evening fifty years ago, might have said at first sight that he was loitering there from idle curiosity. For a large five-light window of the manor-house in front of him was unshuttered and uncurtained, so that the illuminated room within could be scanned almost to its four corners. Obviously nobody was ever expected to be in this part of the grounds after nightfall.

The apartment thus swept by an eye from without was occupied by two persons; they were sitting over dessert, the tablecloth having been removed in the old-fashioned way. The fruits were local, consisting of apples, pears, nuts, and such other products of the summer as might be presumed to grow on the estate. There was strong ale and rum on the table, and but little wine. Moreover, the appointments of the dining-room were simple and homely even for the date, betokening a countrified household of the smaller gentry, without much wealth or ambition – formerly a numerous class, but now in great part ousted by the territorial landlords.

One of the two sitters was a young lady in white muslin, who listened somewhat impatiently to the remarks of her companion, an elderly, rubicund personage, whom the merest stranger could have pronounced to be her father. The watcher envinced no signs of moving, and it became evident that affairs were not so simple as they first had seemed. The tall farmer was in fact no accidental spectator, and he stood by premeditation close to the trunk of a tree, so that had any traveller passed along the road without the park gate, or even round the lawn to the door, that person would scarce have noticed the other, notwithstanding that the gate was quite near at hand, and the park little larger than a paddock. There was still light enough in the western heaven to brighten faintly one side of the man's face, and to show against the trunk of the tree behind the admirable cut of his profile; also to reveal that the front of the manor-house, small though it seemed, was solidly built of stone in that never-to-be-surpassed style for the English country residence – the mullioned and transomed Elizabethan.

The lawn, although neglected, was still as level as a bowling-green – which indeed it might once have served for; and the blades of grass before the window were raked by the candle-shine, which stretched over them so far as to touch the yeoman's face in front.

Within the dining-room there were also, with one of the twain, the same signs of a hidden purpose that marked the farmer. The young lady's mind was straying as clearly into the shadows as that of the loiterer was fixed upon the room – nay, it could be said that she was quite conscious of his presence outside. Impatience caused her foot to beat silently on the carpet, and she more than once rose to leave the table. This proceeding was checked by her father, who would put his hand upon her shoulder and unceremoniously press her down into her chair, till he should have concluded his observations. Her replies were brief enough, and there was factitiousness in her smiles of assent to his views. A small iron casement between two of the mullions was open, and some occasional words of the dialogue were audible without.

'As for drains – how can I put in drains? The pipes don't cost much, that's true; but the labour in sinking the trenches is ruination. And then the gates – they should be hung to stone posts, otherwise there's no keeping them up through harvest.' The Squire's voice was strongly toned with the local accent, so that he said 'draïns' and 'geäts' like the rustics on his estate.

The landscape without grew darker, and the young man's figure seemed to be absorbed into the trunk of the tree. The small stars filled in between the larger, the nebulæ between the small stars, the trees quite lost their voice; and if there was still a sound, it was from the cascade of a stream which stretched along under the trees that bounded the lawn on its northern side.

At last the young girl did get to her feet and secure her retreat. 'I have something to do, papa,' she said. 'I shall not be in the drawing-room just yet.'

'Very well,' replied he. 'Then I won't hurry.' And closing the door behind her, he drew his decanters together and settled down in his chair.

Three minutes after that a woman's shape emerged from the drawing-room window, and passing through a wall-door to the entrance front, came across the grass. She kept well clear of the dining-room window, but enough of its light fell on her to show, escaping from the dark-hooded cloak that she wore, stray verges of the same light dress which had figured but recently at the dinner-table. The hood was contracted tight about her face with a drawing-string, making her countenance small and baby-like, and lovelier even than before.

Without hesitation she brushed across the grass to the tree under which the young man stood concealed. The moment she had reached him he enclosed her form with his arm. The meeting and embrace, though by no means formal, were yet not passionate; the whole proceeding was that of persons who had repeated the act so often as to be unconscious of its performance. She turned within his arm, and faced in the same direction with himself, which was towards the window; and thus they stood without speaking, the back of her head leaning against his shoulder. For a while each seemed to be thinking his and her diverse thoughts.

'You have kept me waiting a long time, dear Christine,' he said at last. 'I wanted to speak to you particularly, or I should not have stayed. How came you to be dining at this time o' night?'

'Father has been out all day, and dinner was put back till six. I know I have kept you; but, Nicholas, how can I help it sometimes, if I am not to run any risk? My poor father insists upon my listening to all he has to say; since my brother left he has had nobody else to listen to him; and to-night he was particularly tedious on his usual topics – draining, and tenant-farmers, and the village people. I must take daddy to London; he gets so narrow always staying here.'

'And what did you say to it all?'

'Well, I took the part of the tenant-farmers, of course, as the beloved of one should in duty do.' There followed a little break or gasp, implying a strangled sigh.

'You are sorry you have encouraged that beloving one?'

'O no, Nicholas. . . . What is it you want to see me for particularly?'

'I know you *are* sorry, as time goes on, and everything is at a deadlock, with no prospect of change, and your rural swain loses his freshness! Only think, this secret understanding between us has lasted near three year, ever since you was a little over sixteen.'

'Yes; it has been a long time.'

'And I an untamed, uncultivated man, who has never seen London, and knows nothing about society at all.'

'Not uncultivated, dear Nicholas. Untravelled, socially unpractised, if you will,' she said, smiling. 'Well, I did sigh; but not because I regret being your promised one. What I do sometimes regret is that the scheme, which my meetings with you are but a part of, has not been carried out completely. You said, Nicholas, that if I consented to swear to keep faith with you, you would go away and travel, and see nations, and peoples, and cities, and take a professor with you, and study books and art, simultaneously with your study of men and manners; and then come back at the end of two years, when I should find that my father would by no means be indisposed to accept you as a son-in-law. You said your reason for wishing to get my promise before starting was that your mind would then be more at rest when you were far away, and so could give itself more completely to knowledge than if you went as my unaccepted lover only, fuming with anxiety as to how I should be when you came back. I saw how reasonable that was; and solemnly swore myself to you in consequence. But instead of going to see the world you stay on and on here to see me.'

'And you don't want me to see you?'

'Yes – no – it is not that. It is that I have latterly felt frightened at what I am doing when not in your actual presence. It seems so wicked not to tell my father that I have a lover close at hand, within touch and view of both of us; whereas if you were absent my conduct would not seem quite so treacherous. The realities would not stare at one so. You would be a pleasant dream to me, which I should be free to indulge in without reproach of my conscience; I should live in hopeful expectation of your returning fully qualified to boldly claim me of my father. There, I have been terribly frank, I know.'

He in his turn had lapsed into gloomy breathings now. 'I did plan it as you state,' he answered. 'I did mean to go away the moment I had your promise. But, dear Christine, I did not foresee two or three things. I did not know what a lot of pain it would cost to tear myself from you. And I did not know that my stingy uncle – heaven forgive me calling him so! – would so flatly refuse to advance me money for my purpose – the scheme of travelling with a first-rate tutor costing a formidable sum o' money. You have no idea what it would cost!'

'But I have said that I'll find the money.'

'Ah, there,' he returned, 'you have hit a sore place. To speak truly, dear, I would rather stay unpolished a hundred years than take your money.'

'But why? Men continually use the money of the women they marry.'

'Yes; but not till afterwards. No man would like to touch your money at present, and I should feel very mean if I were to do so in present circumstances. That brings me to what I was going to propose. But no – upon the whole I will not propose it now.'

'Ah! I would guarantee expenses, and you won't let me! The money is my personal possession: it comes to me from my late grandfather, and not from my father at all.'

He laughed forcedly and pressed her hand. 'There are more reasons why I cannot tear myself away,' he added. 'What would become of my uncle's farming? Six hundred acres in this parish, and five hundred in the next – a constant traipsing from one farm to the other; he can't be in two places at once. Still, that might be got over if it were not for the other matters. Besides, dear, I still should be a little uneasy, even though I have your promise, lest somebody should snap you up away from me.'

'Ah, you should have thought of that before. Otherwise I have committed myself for nothing.'

'I should have thought of it,' he answered gravely. 'But I did not. There lies my fault, I admit it freely. Ah, if you would only commit yourself a little more, I might at least get over that difficulty! But I won't ask you. You have no idea how much you are to me still; you could not argue so coolly if you had. What property belongs to you I hate the very sound of; it is you I care for. I wish you hadn't a farthing in the world but what I could earn for you!'

'I don't altogether wish that,' she murmured.

'I wish it, because it would have made what I was going to propose much easier to do than it is now. Indeed I will not propose it, although I came on purpose, after what you have said in your frankness.'

'Nonsense, Nic. Come, tell me. How can you be so touchy?'

'Look at this then, Christine dear.' He drew from his breast-pocket a sheet of paper and unfolded it, when it was observable that a seal dangled from the bottom.

'What is it?' She held the paper sideways, so that what there was of window-light fell on its surface. 'I can only read the Old English letters – why – our names! Surely it is not a marriage-licence?'

'It is.'

She trembled. 'O Nic! how could you do this – and without telling me!'

'Why should I have thought I must tell you? You had not spoken "frankly" then as you have now. We have been all to each other more than these two years, and I thought I would propose that we marry privately, and that I then leave you on the instant. I would have taken my travelling-bag to church, and you would have gone home alone. I should not have started on my adventures in the brilliant manner of our original plan, but should have roughed it a little at first; my great gain would have been that the absolute possession of you would have enabled me to work with spirit and purpose, such as nothing else could do. But I dare not ask you now – so frank as you have been.'

She did not answer. The document he had produced gave such unexpected substantiality to the venture with which she had so long toyed as a vague dream merely, that she was, in truth, frightened a little. 'I – don't know about it!' she said.

'Perhaps not. Ah, my little lady, you are wearying of me!'

'No, Nic,' responded she, creeping closer. 'I am not. Upon my word, and truth, and honour, I am not, Nic.'

'A mere tiller of the soil, as I should be called,' he continued, without heeding her. 'And you – well, a daughter of one of the – I won't say oldest families, because that's absurd, all families are the same age – one of the longest chronicled families about here, whose name is actually the name of the place.'

'That's not much, I am sorry to say! My poor brother – but I won't speak of that. . . . Well,' she murmured mischievously, after a pause, 'you certainly would not need to be uneasy if I were to do this that you want me to do. You would have me safe enough in your trap then; I couldn't get away!'

'That's just it!' he said vehemently. 'It *is* a trap – you feel it so, and that though you wouldn't be able to get away from me you might particularly wish to! Ah, if I had asked you two years ago you would have agreed instantly. But I thought I was bound to wait for the proposal to come from you as the superior!'

'Now you are angry, and take seriously what I meant purely in fun. You don't know me even yet! To show you that you have not been mistaken in me, I *do* propose to carry out this licence. I'll marry you, dear Nicholas, to-morrow morning.'

'Ah, Christine! I am afraid I have stung you on to this, so that I cannot—'

'No, no, no!' she hastily rejoined, and there was something in her tone which suggested that she had been put upon her mettle and would not flinch. 'Take me whilst I am in the humour. What church is the licence for?'

'That I've not looked to see – why, our parish church here, of course. Ah, then we cannot use it! We dare not be married here.'

'We do dare,' said she. 'And we will too, if you'll be there.'

'*If* I'll be there!'

They speedily came to an agreement that he should be in the church-porch at ten minutes to eight on the following morning, awaiting her; and that, immediately after the conclusion of the service which would make them one, Nicholas should set out on his long-deferred educational tour, towards the cost of which she was resolving to bring a substantial subscription with her to church. Then, slipping from him, she went indoors by the way she had come, and Nicholas bent his steps home-wards.

II

Instead of leaving the spot by the gate, he flung himself over the fence, and pursued a direction towards the river under the trees. And it was now, in his lonely progress, that he showed for the first time outwardly that he was not altogether unworthy of her. He wore long water-boots reaching above his knees, and, instead of making a circuit to find a bridge by which he might cross the Froom – the river aforesaid – he made straight for the point whence proceeded the low roar that was at this hour the only evidence of the stream's existence. He speedily stood on the verge of the waterfall which caused the noise, and stepping into the water at the top of the fall, waded through with the sure tread of one who knew every inch of his footing, even though the canopy of trees rendered the darkness almost absolute, and a false step would have precipitated him into the pool beneath. Soon reaching the boundary of the grounds, he continued in the same direct line to traverse the alluvial valley, full of brooks and tributaries to the main stream – in former times quite impassable, and impassable in winter, now. Sometimes he would cross a deep gully on a plank not wider than the hand; at another

time he ploughed his way through beds of spear-grass, where at a few
feet to the right or left he might have been sucked down into a morass.
At last he reached firm land on the other side of this watery tract, and
came to his house on the rise behind – Elsenford – an ordinary farm-
stead, from the back of which rose indistinct breathings, belchings, and
snortings, the rattle of halters, and other familiar features of an agri-
culturist's home.

While Nicholas Long was packing his bag in an upper room of this
dwelling, Miss Christine Everard sat at a desk in her own chamber at
Froom-Everard manor-house, looking with pale fixed countenance at
the candles.

'I ought – I must now!' she whispered to herself. 'I should not have
begun it if I had not meant to carry it through! It runs in the blood of
us, I suppose.' She alluded to a fact unknown to her lover, the clandestine
marriage of an aunt under circumstances somewhat similar to the
present. In a few minutes she had penned the following note: –

October 13, 183–

DEAR MR BEALAND, – Can you make it convenient to yourself to meet
me at the Church to-morrow morning at eight? I name the early
hour because it would suit me better than later on in the day. You
will find me in the chancel, if you can come. An answer yes or no by
the bearer of this will be sufficient.

CHRISTINE EVERARD

She sent the note to the rector immediately, waiting at a small side-
door of the house till she heard the servant's footsteps returning along
the lane, when she went round and met him in the passage. The rector
had taken the trouble to write a line, and answered that he would meet
her with pleasure.

A dripping fog which ushered in the next morning was highly favourable
to the scheme of the pair. At that time of the century Froom-Everard
House had not been altered and enlarged; the public lane passed close
under its walls; and there was a door opening directly from one of
the old parlours – the south parlour, as it was called – into the lane which
led to the village. Christine came out this way, and after following the
lane for a short distance entered upon a path within a belt of plantation,
by which the church could be reached privately. She even avoided the
churchyard gate, walking along to a place where the turf without the
low wall rose into a mound, enabling her to mount upon the coping and

spring down inside. She crossed the wet graves, and so glided round to
the door. He was there, with his bag in his hand. He kissed her with a
sort of surprise, as if he had expected that at the last moment her heart
would fail her.

Though it had not failed her, there was, nevertheless, no great ardour
in Christine's bearing – merely the momentum of an antecedent impulse. They went up the aisle together, the bottle-green glass of the old
lead quarries admitting but little light at that hour, and under such an
atmosphere. They stood by the altar-rail in silence, Christine's skirt
visibly quivering at each beat of her heart.

Presently a quick step ground upon the gravel, and Mr Bealand came
round by the front. He was a quiet bachelor, courteous towards
Christine, and not at first recognizing in Nicholas a neighbouring yeoman (for he lived aloofly in the next parish), advanced to her without
revealing any surprise at her unusual request. But in truth he was
surprised, the keen interest taken by many country young women at the
present day in church decoration and festivals being then unknown.

'Good morning,' he said; and repeated the same words to Nicholas
more mechanically.

'Good morning,' she replied gravely. 'Mr Bealand, I have a serious
reason for asking you to meet me – us, I may say. We wish you to marry
us.'

The rector's gaze hardened to fixity, rather between than upon either
of them, and he neither moved nor replied for some time.

'Ah!' he said at last.

'And we are quite ready.'

'I had no idea—'

'It has been kept rather private,' she said calmly.

'Where are your witnesses ?'

'They are outside in the meadow, sir. I can call them in a moment,'
said Nicholas.

'Oh – I see it is – Mr Nicholas Long,' said Mr Bealand, and turning
again to Christine, 'Does your father know of this ?'

'Is it necessary that I should answer that question, Mr Bealand ?'

'I am afraid it is – highly necessary.'

Christine began to look concerned.

'Where is the licence ?' the rector asked; 'since there have been no
banns.'

Nicholas produced it, Mr Bealand read it, an operation which occupied him several minutes – or at least he made it appear so; till Christine said impatiently, 'We are quite ready, Mr Bealand. Will you proceed? Mr Long has to take a journey of a great many miles to-day.'

'And you?'

'No. I remain.'

Mr Bealand assumed firmness. 'There is something wrong in this,' he said. 'I cannot marry you without your father's presence.'

'But have you a right to refuse us?' interposed Nicholas. 'I believe we are in a position to demand your fulfilment of our request.'

'No, you are not! Is Miss Everard of age? I think not. I think she is months from being so. Eh, Miss Everard?'

'Am I bound to tell that?'

'Certainly. At any rate you are bound to write it. Meanwhile I refuse to solemnize the service. And let me entreat you two young people to do nothing so rash as this, even if by going to some strange church, you may do so without discovery. The tragedy of marriage—'

'Tragedy?'

'Certainly. It is full of crises and catastrophes, and ends with the death of one of the actors. The tragedy of marriage, as I was saying, is one I shall not be a party to your beginning with such light hearts, and I shall feel bound to put your father on his guard, Miss Everard. Think better of it, I entreat you! Remember the proverb "Marry in haste and repent at leisure." '

Christine, spurred by opposition, almost stormed at him. Nicholas implored; but nothing would turn that obstinate rector. She sat down and reflected. By-and-by she confronted Mr Bealand.

'Our marriage is not to be this morning, I see,' she said. 'Now grant me one favour, and in return I'll promise you to do nothing rashly. Do not tell my father a word of what has happened here.'

'I agree – if you undertake not to elope.'

She looked at Nicholas, and he looked at her. 'Do you wish me to elope, Nic?' she asked.

'No,' he said.

So the compact was made, and they left the church singly, Nicholas remaining till the last, and closing the door. On his way home, carrying the well-packed bag which was just now to go no further, the two men who were mending water-carriers in the meadows approached the hedge, as if they had been on the alert all the time.

'You said you mid want us for zummat, sir?'

'All right – never mind,' he answered, through the hedge. 'I did not require you after all.'

III

At a manor not far away there lived a queer and primitive couple who had lately been blessed with a son and heir. The christening took place during the week under notice, and this had been followed by a feast to the parishioners. Christine's father, one of the same generation and kind, had been asked to drive over and assist in the entertainment, and Christine, as a matter of course, accompanied him.

When they reached Athelhall, as the house was called, they found the usually quiet nook a lively spectacle. Tables had been spread in the apartment which lent its name to the whole building – the hall proper – covered with a fine open-timbered roof, whose braces, purlins, and rafters made a brown thicket of oak overhead. Here tenantry of all ages sat with their wives and families, and the servants were assisted in their ministrations by the sons and daughters of the owner's friends and neighbours. Christine lent a hand among the rest.

She was holding a plate in each hand towards a huge brown platter of baked rice-pudding, from which a footman was scooping a large spoonful, when a voice reached her ear over her shoulder: 'Allow me to hold them for you.'

Christine turned, and recognized in the speaker the nephew of the entertainer, a young man from London, whom she had already met on two or three occasions. She accepted the proffered help, and from that moment, whenever he passed her in their marchings to and fro during the remainder of the serving, he smiled acquaintance. When their work was done, he improved the few words into a conversation. He plainly had been attracted by her fairness.

Bellston was a self-assured young man, not particularly good-looking, with more colour in his skin than even Nicholas had. He had flushed a little in attracting her notice, though the flush had nothing of nervousness in it – the air with which it was accompanied making it curiously suggestive of a flush of anger; and even when he laughed it was difficult to banish that fancy.

The late autumn sunlight streamed in through the window panes upon the heads and shoulders of the venerable patriarchs of the hamlet, and upon the middle-aged, and upon the young; upon men and women who had played out, or were to play, tragedies or tragi-comedies in that nook of civilization not less great, essentially, than those which, enacted on more central arenas, fix the attention of the world. One of the party was a cousin of Nicholas Long's, who sat with her husband and children.

To make himself as locally harmonious as possible, Mr Bellston remarked to his companion on the scene –

'It does one's heart good,' he said, 'to see these simple peasants enjoying themselves.'

'O Mr Bellston!' exclaimed Christine; 'don't be too sure about that word "simple"! You little think what they see and meditate! Their reasonings and emotions are as complicated as ours.'

She spoke with a vehemence which would have been hardly present in her words but for her own relation to Nicholas. The sense of that produced in her a nameless depression thenceforward. The young man, however, still followed her up.

'I am glad to hear you say it,' he returned warmly. 'I was merely attuning myself to your mood, as I thought. The real truth is that I know more of the Parthians, and Medes, and dwellers in Mesopotamia – almost of any people, indeed – than of the English rustics. Travel and exploration are my profession, not the study of the British peasantry.'

Travel. There was sufficient coincidence between his declaration and the course she had urged upon her lover, to lend Bellston's account of himself a certain interest in Christine's ears. He might perhaps be able to tell her something that would be useful to Nicholas, if their dream were carried out. A door opened from the hall into the garden, and she somehow found herself outside, chatting with Mr Bellston on this topic, till she thought that upon the whole she liked the young man. The garden being his uncle's, he took her round it with an air of proprietorship; and they went on amongst the Michaelmas daisies and chrysanthemums, and through a door to the fruit-garden. A green-house was open, and he went in and cut her a bunch of grapes.

'How daring of you! They are your uncle's.'

'O, he don't mind – I do anything here. A rough old buffer, isn't he?'

She was thinking of her Nic, and felt that, by comparison with her present acquaintance, the farmer more than held his own as a fine and intelligent fellow; but the harmony with her own existence in little things, which she found here, imparted an alien tinge to Nicholas just now. The latter, idealized by moonlight, or a thousand miles of distance, was altogether a more romantic object for a woman's dream than this smart new-lacquered man; but in the sun of afternoon, and amid a surrounding company, Mr Bellston was a very tolerable companion.

When they re-entered the hall, Bellston entreated her to come with him up a spiral stair in the thickness of the wall, leading to a passage and gallery whence they could look down upon the scene below. The people had finished their feast, the newly-christened baby had been exhibited, and a few words having been spoken to them they began, amid a racketing of forms, to make for the greensward without, Nicholas's cousin and cousin's wife and cousin's children among the rest. While they were filing out, a voice was heard calling –

'Hullo! – here, Jim; where are you?' said Bellston's uncle. The young man descended, Christine following at leisure.

'Now will ye be a good fellow,' the Squire continued, 'and set them going outside in some dance or other that they know? I'm dog-tired, and I want to have a vew words with Mr Everard before we join 'em – hey, Everard? They are shy till somebody starts 'em; afterwards they'll keep gwine brisk enough.'

'Ay, that they wool,' said Squire Everard.

They followed to the lawn; and here it proved that James Bellston was as shy, or rather as averse, as any of the tenantry themselves, to acting the part of fugleman. Only the parish people had been at the feast, but outlying neighbours had now strolled in for a dance.

'They want "Speed the Plough",' said Bellston, coming up breathless. 'It must be a country dance, I suppose? Now, Miss Everard, do have pity upon me. I am supposed to lead off; but really I know no more about speeding the plough than a child just born! Would you take one of the villagers? – just to start them, my uncle says. Suppose you take that handsome young farmer over there – I don't know his name, but I dare say you do – and I'll come on with one of the dairyman's daughters as a second couple.'

Christine turned in the direction signified, and changed colour – though in the shade nobody noticed it. 'Oh, yes – I know him,' she said coolly. 'He is from near our own place – Mr Nicholas Long.'

'That's capital – then you can easily make him stand as first couple with you. Now I must pick up mine.'

'I – I think I'll dance with you, Mr Bellston,' she said with some trepidation. 'Because, you see,' she explained eagerly, 'I know the figure and you don't – so that I can help you; while Nicholas Long, I know, is familiar with the figure, and that will make two couples who know it – which is necessary, at least.'

Bellston showed his gratification by one of his angry-pleasant flushes – he had hardly dared to ask for what she proffered freely; and having requested Nicholas to take the dairyman's daughter, led Christine to her place, Long promptly stepping up second with his charge. There were grim silent depths in Nic's character; a small deedy spark in his eye, as it caught Christine's, was all that showed his consciousness of her. Then the fiddlers began – the celebrated Mellstock fiddlers who, given free stripping, could play from sunset to dawn without turning a hair. The couples wheeled and swung, Nicholas taking Christine's hand in the course of business with the figure, when she waited for him to give it a little squeeze; but he did not.

Christine had the greatest difficulty in steering her partner through the maze, on account of his self-will, and when at last they reached the bottom of the long line, she was breathless with her hard labour. Resting here, she watched Nic and his lady; and, though she had decidedly cooled off in these later months, began to admire him anew. Nobody knew these dances like him, after all, or could do anything of this sort so well. His performance with the dairyman's daughter so won upon her, that when 'Speed the Plough' was over she contrived to speak to him.

'Nic, you are to dance with me next time.'

He said he would, and presently asked her in a formal public manner, lifting his hat gallantly. She showed a little backwardness, which he quite understood, and allowed him to lead her to the top, a row of enormous length appearing below them as if by magic as soon as they had taken their places. Truly the Squire was right when he said that they only wanted starting.

'What is it to be?' whispered Nicholas.

She turned to the band. ' "The Honeymoon",' she said.

And then they trod the delightful last-century measure of that name, which if it had ever been danced better, was never danced with more zest. The perfect responsiveness which their tender acquaintance threw into the motions of Nicholas and his partner lent to their gyrations the fine adjustment of two interacting parts of a single machine. The excitement of the movement carried Christine back to the time – the unreflecting passionate time, about two years before – when she and

Nic had been incipient lovers only; and it made her forget the carking anxieties, the vision of social breakers ahead, that had begun to take the gilding off her position now. Nicholas, on his part, had never ceased to be a lover; no personal worries had as yet made him conscious of any staleness, flatness, or unprofitableness in his admiration of Christine.

'Not quite so wildly, Nic,' she whispered. 'I don't object personally; but they'll notice us. How came you here?'

'I heard that you had driven over; and I set out – on purpose for this.'

'What – you have walked?'

'Yes. If I had waited for one of uncle's horses I should have been too late.'

'Five miles here and five back – ten miles on foot – merely to dance!'

'With you. What made you think of this old "Honeymoon" thing?'

'O! it came into my head when I saw you, as what would have been a reality with us if you had not been stupid about that licence, and had got it for a distant church.'

'Shall we try again?'

'No – I don't know. I'll think it over.'

The villagers admired their grace and skill, as the dancers themselves perceived; but they did not know what accompanied that admiration in one spot, at least.

'People who wonder they can foot it so featly together should know what some others think,' a waterman was saying to his neighbour. 'Then their wonder would be less.'

His comrade asked for information.

'Well – really I hardly believe it – but 'tis said they be man and wife. Yes, sure – went to church and did the job a'most afore 'twas light one morning. But mind, not a word of this; for 'twould be the loss of a winter's work to me if I had spread such a report and it were not true.'

When the dance had ended she rejoined her own section of the company. Her father and Mr Bellston the elder had now come out from the house, and were smoking in the background. Presently she found that her father was at her elbow.

'Christine, don't dance too often with young Long – as a mere matter of prudence, I mean, as volk might think it odd, he being one of our own neighbouring farmers. I should not mention this to 'ee if he were an ordinary young fellow; but being superior to the rest it behoves you to be careful.'

'Exactly, papa,' said Christine.

But the revived sense that she was deceiving him threw a damp over her spirits. 'But, after all,' she said to herself, 'he is a young man of Elsenford, handsome, able, and the soul of honour; and I am a young woman of the adjoining parish, who have been constantly thrown into communication with him. Is it not, by Nature's rule, the most proper thing in the world that I should marry him, and is it not an absurd conventional regulation which says that such a union would be wrong?'

It may be concluded that the strength of Christine's large-minded argument was rather an evidence of weakness than of strength in the passion it concerned, which had required neither argument nor reasoning of any kind for its maintenance when full and flush in its early days.

When driving home in the dark with her father she sank into pensive silence. She was thinking of Nicholas having to trudge on foot all those miles back after his exertions on the sward. Mr Everard, arousing himself from a nap, said suddenly, 'I have something to mention to 'ee, by George – so I have, Chris! You probably know what it is?'

She expressed ignorance, wondering if her father had discovered anything of her secret.

'Well, according to *him* you know it. But I will tell 'ee. Perhaps you noticed young Jim Bellston walking me off down the lawn with him? – whether or no, we walked together a good while; and he informed me that he wanted to pay his addresses to 'ee. I naturally said that it depended upon yourself; and he replied that you were willing enough; you had given him particular encouragement – showing your preference for him by specially choosing him for your partner – hey? "In that case," says I, "go on and conquer – settle it with her – I have no objection." The poor fellow was very grateful, and in short, there we left the matter. He'll propose to-morrow.'

She saw now to her dismay what James Bellston had read as encouragement. 'He has mistaken me altogether,' she said. 'I had no idea of such a thing.'

'What, you won't have him?'

'Indeed, I cannot!'

'Chrissy,' said Mr Everard with emphasis, 'there's *noo*body whom I should so like you to marry as that young man. He's a thoroughly clever fellow, and fairly well provided for. He's travelled all over the temperate zone; but he says that directly he marries he's going to give up all that, and be a regular stay-at-home. You would be nowhere safer than in his hands.'

'It is true,' she answered. 'He *is* a highly desirable match, and I *should* be well provided for, and probably very safe in his hands.'

'Then don't be skittish, and stand-to.'

She had spoken from her conscience and understanding, and not to please her father. As a reflecting woman she believed that such a marriage would be a wise one. In great things Nicholas was closest to her nature in little things Bellston seemed immeasurably nearer than Nic; and life was made up of little things.

Altogether the firmament looked black for Nicholas Long, notwithstanding her half-hour's ardour for him when she saw him dancing with the dairyman's daughter. Most great passions, movements, and beliefs - individual and national - burst during their decline into a temporary irradiation, which rivals their original splendour; and then they speedily become extinct. Perhaps the dance had given the last flare-up to Christine's love. It seemed to have improvidently consumed for it immediate purpose all her ardour forwards, so that for the future there was nothing left but frigidity.

Nicholas had certainly been very foolish about that licence!

IV

This laxity of emotional tone was further increased by an incident when, two days later, she kept an appointment with Nicholas in the Sallows. The Sallows was an extension of shrubberies and plantation along the banks of the Froom, accessible from the lawn of Froom Everard House only, except by wading through the river at the waterfall or elsewhere. Near the brink was a thicket of box in which a trunk lay prostrate; this had been once or twice their trysting-place, though it was by no means a safe one; and it was here she sat awaiting him now.

The noise of the stream muffled any sound of footsteps, and it was before she was aware of his approach that she looked up and saw him wading across at the top of the waterfall.

Noontide lights and dwarfed shadows always banished the romantic aspect of her love for Nicholas. Moreover, something new had occurred to disturb her; and if ever she had regretted giving way to a tenderness for him - which perhaps she had not done with any distinctness - she regretted it now. Yet in the bottom of their hearts those two were excellently paired, the very twin halves of a perfect whole; and their love was pure. But at this hour surfaces showed garishly, and obscured the depths. Probably her regret appeared in her face.

He walked up to her without speaking, the water running from his boots; and, taking one of her hands in each of his own, looked narrowly into her eyes.

'Have you thought it over?'

'What?'

'Whether we shall try again; you remember saying you would at the dance?'

'Oh, I had forgotten that!'

'You are sorry we tried at all!' he said accusingly.

'I am not so sorry for the fact as for the rumours,' she said.

'Ah! rumours?'

'They say we are already married.'

'Who?'

'I cannot tell exactly. I heard some whispering to that effect. Somebody in the village told one of the servants, I believe. This man said that he was crossing the churchyard early on that unfortunate foggy morning, and heard voices in the chancel, and peeped through the window as well as the dim panes would let him; and there he saw you and me and Mr Bealand, and so on; but thinking his surmises would be dangerous knowledge, he hastened on. And so the story got afloat. Then your aunt, too—'

'Good Lord! – what has she done?'

'The story was told her, and she said proudly, "O yes, it is true enough. I have seen the licence. But it is not to be known yet." '

'Seen the licence? How the—'

'Accidentally, I believe, when your coat was hanging somewhere.'

The information, coupled with the infelicitous word 'proudly', caused Nicholas to flush with mortification. He knew that it was in his aunt's nature to make a brag of that sort; but worse than the brag was the fact that this was the first occasion on which Christine had deigned to show her consciousness that such a marriage would be a source of pride to his relatives – the only two he had in the world.

'You are sorry, then, even to be thought my wife, much less to be it.' He dropped her hand, which fell lifelessly.

'It is not sorry exactly, dear Nic. But I feel uncomfortable and vexed, that after screwing up my courage, my fidelity, to the point of going to church, you should have so muddled – managed the matter that it has ended in neither one thing nor the other. How can I meet acquaintances, when I don't know what they are thinking of me?'

'Then, dear Christine, let us mend the muddle. I'll go away for a few days and get another licence, and you can come to me.'

She shrank from this perceptibly. 'I cannot screw myself up to it a second time,' she said. 'I am sure I cannot! Besides, I promised Mr Bealand. And yet how can I continue to see you after such a rumour? We shall be watched now, for certain.'

'Then don't see me.'

'I fear I must not for the present. Altogether—'

'What?'

'I am very depressed.'

These views were not very inspiriting to Nicholas, as he construed them. It may indeed have been possible that he construed them wrongly, and should have insisted upon her making the rumour true. Unfortunately, too, he had come to her in a hurry through brambles and briars, water and weed, and the shaggy wildness which hung about his appearance at this fine and correct time of day lent an impracticability to the look of him.

'You blame me – you repent your courses – you repent that you ever, ever owned anything to me!'

'No, Nicholas, I do not repent that,' she returned gently, though with firmness. 'But I think that you ought not to have got that licence without asking me first; and I also think that you ought to have known how it would be if you lived on here in your present position, and made no effort to better it. I can bear whatever comes, for social ruin is not personal ruin or even personal disgrace. But as a sensible, new-risen poet says, whom I have been reading this morning: –

> The world and its ways have a certain worth:
> And to press a point while these oppose
> Were simple policy. Better wait.

As soon as you had got my promise, Nic, you should have gone away – yes – and made a name, and come back to claim me. That was my silly girlish dream about my hero.'

'Perhaps I can do as much yet! And would you have indeed liked better to live away from me for family reasons, than to run a risk in seeing me for affection's sake? O what a cold heart it has grown! If I had been a prince, and you a dairymaid, I'd have stood by you in the face of the world!'

She shook her head. 'Ah – you don't know what society is – you don't know.'

'Perhaps not. Who was that strange gentleman of about seven-and-twenty I saw at Mr Bellston's christening feast?'

'Oh – that was his nephew James. Now he is a man who has seen an unusual extent of the world for his age. He is a great traveller, you know.'

'Indeed.'

'In fact an explorer. He is very entertaining.'

'No doubt.'

Nicholas received no shock of jealousy from her announcement. He knew her so well that he could see she was not in the least in love with Bellston. But he asked if Bellston were going to continue his explorations.

'Not if he settles in life. Otherwise he will, I suppose.'

'Perhaps I could be a great explorer, too, if I tried.'

'You could, I am sure.'

They sat apart, and not together; each looking afar off at vague objects, and not in each other's eyes. Thus the sad autumn afternoon waned, while the waterfall hissed sarcastically of the inevitableness of the unpleasant. Very different this from the time when they had first met there.

The nook was most picturesque; but it looked horridly common and stupid now. Their sentiment had set a colour hardly less visible than a material one on surrounding objects, as sentiment must where life is but thought. Nicholas was as devoted as ever to the fair Christine; but unhappily he too had moods and humours, and the division between them was not closed.

She had no sooner got indoors and sat down to her work-table than her father entered the drawing-room. She handed him his newspaper; he took it without a word, went and stood on the hearthrug, and flung the paper on the floor.

'Christine, what's the meaning of this terrible story? I was just on my way to look at the register.'

She looked at him without speech.

'You have married – Nicholas Long?'

'No, father.'

'No? Can you say no in the face of such facts as I have been put in possession of?'

'Yes.'

'But – the note you wrote to the rector – and the going to church?'

She briefly explained that their attempt had failed.

'Ah! Then this is what that dancing meant, was it? By —, it makes me —. How long has this been going on, may I ask?'

'This what?'

'What, indeed! Why, making him your beau. Now listen to me. All's well that ends well; from this day, madam, this moment, he is to be nothing more to you. You are not to see him. Cut him adrift instantly! I only wish his volk were on my farm – out they should go, or I would know the reason why. However, you are to write him a letter to this effect at once.'

'How can I cut him adrift?'

'Why not? You must, my good maid!'

'Well, though I have not actually married him, I have solemnly sworn to be his wife when he comes home from abroad to claim me. It would be gross perjury not to fulfil my promise. Besides, no woman can go to church with a man to deliberately solemnize matrimony, and refuse him afterwards, if he does nothing wrong meanwhile.'

The uttered sound of her strong conviction seemed to kindle in Christine a livelier perception of all its bearings than she had known while it had lain unformulated in her mind. For when she had done speaking she fell down on her knees before her father, covered her face, and said, 'Please, please forgive me, papa! How *could* I do it without letting you know! I don't know, I don't know!'

When she looked up she found that, in the turmoil of his mind, her father was moving about the room. 'You are within an ace of ruining yourself, ruining me, ruining us all!' he said. 'You are nearly as bad as your brother, begad!'

'Perhaps I am – yes – perhaps I am!'

'That I should father such a harum-scarum brood!'

'It is very bad; but Nicholas—'

'He's a scoundrel!'

'He is *not* a scoundrel!' cried she, turning quickly. 'He's as good and worthy as you or I, or anybody bearing our name, or any nobleman in the kingdom, if you come to that! Only – only' – she could not continue the argument on those lines. 'Now, father, listen!' she sobbed: 'if you taunt me I'll go off and join him at his farm this very day, and marry him to-morrow, that's what I'll do!'

'I don't taant ye!'

'I wish to avoid unseemliness as much as you.'

She went away. When she came back a quarter of an hour later, thinking to find the room empty, he was standing there as before, never having apparently moved. His manner had quite changed. He seemed to take a resigned and entirely different view of circumstances.

'Christine, here's a paragraph in the paper hinting at a secret wedding, and I'm blazed if it don't point to you. Well, since this was to happen, I'll bear it, and not complain. All volk have crosses, and this is one of mine. Well, this is what I've got to say – I feel that you must carry out this attempt at marrying Nicholas Long. Faith, you must! The rumour will become a scandal if you don't – that's my view. I have tried to look at the brightest side of the case. Nicholas Long is a young man superior to most of his class, and fairly presentable. And he's not poor – at least his uncle is not. I believe the old muddler could buy me up any day. However, a farmer's wife you must be, as far as I can see. As you've made your bed, so ye must lie. Parents propose, and ungrateful children dispose. You shall marry him, and immediately.'

Christine hardly knew what to make of this. 'He is quite willing to wait, and so am I. We can wait for two or three years, and then he will be as worthy as—'

'You must marry him. And the sooner the better, if 'tis to be done at all. . . . And yet I did wish you could have been Jim Bellston's wife. I did wish it! But no.'

'I, too, wished it and do still, in one sense,' she returned gently. His moderation had won her out of her defiant mood, and she was willing to reason with him.

'You do?' he said, surprised.

'I see that in a worldly sense my conduct with Mr Long may be considered a mistake.'

'H'm – I am glad to hear that – after my death you may see it more clearly still; and you won't have long to wait, to my reckoning.'

She fell into bitter repentance, and kissed him in her anguish. 'Don't say that!' she cried. 'Tell me what to do?'

'If you'll leave me for an hour or two I'll think. Drive to the market and back – the carriage is at the door – and I'll try to collect my senses. Dinner can be put back till you return.'

In a few minutes she was dressed, and the carriage bore her up the hill which divided the village and manor from the market-town.

V

A quarter of an hour brought her into the High Street, and for want of a more important errand she called at the harness-maker's for a dog-collar that she required.

It happened to be market-day, and Nicholas, having postponed the engagements which called him thither to keep the appointment with her in the Sallows, rushed off at the end of the afternoon to attend to them as well as he could. Arriving thus in a great hurry on account of the lateness of the hour, he still retained the wild, amphibious appearance which had marked him when he came up from the meadows to her side – an exceptional condition of things which had scarcely ever before occurred. When she crossed the pavement from the shop door, the shopman bowing and escorting her to the carriage, Nicholas chanced to be standing at the road-waggon office, talking to the master of the waggons. There were a good many people about, and those near paused and looked at her transit, in the full stroke of the level October sun, which went under the brims of their hats, and pierced through their button-holes. From the group she heard murmured the words: 'Mrs Nicholas Long'.

The unexpected remark, not without distinct satire in its tone, took her so greatly by surprise that she was confounded. Nicholas was by this time nearer, though coming against the sun he had not yet perceived her. Influenced by her father's lecture, she felt angry with him for being there and causing this awkwardness. Her notice of him was therefore slight, supercilious perhaps, slurred over; and her vexation at his presence showed distinctly in her face as she sat down in her seat. Instead of catching his waiting eye, she positively turned her head away.

A moment after she was sorry she had treated him so; but he was gone.

Reaching home she found on her dressing-table a note from her father. The statement was brief:

I have considered and am of the same opinion. You must marry him. He can leave home at once and travel as proposed. I have

written to him to this effect. I don't want any victuals, so don't
wait dinner for me.

Nicholas was the wrong kind of man to be blind to his Christine's
mortification, though he did not know its entire cause. He had lately
foreseen something of this sort as possible.

'It serves me right,' he thought, as he trotted homeward. 'It was
absurd – wicked of me to lead her on so. The sacrifice would have been
too great – too cruel!' And yet, though he thus took her part, he flushed
with indignation every time he said to himself, 'She is ashamed of
me!'

On the ridge which overlooked Froom-Everard he met a neighbour of
his – a stock-dealer – in his gig, and they drew rein and exchanged a
few words. A part of the dealer's conversation had much meaning for
Nicholas.

'I've had occasion to call on Squire Everard,' the former said; 'but
he couldn't see me on account of being quite knocked up at some bad
news he has heard.'

Nicholas rode on past Froom-Everard to Elsenford Farm, pondering.
He had new and startling matter for thought as soon as he got there.
The Squire's note had arrived. At first he could not credit its import;
then he saw further, took in the tone of the letter, saw the writer's
contempt behind the words, and understood that the letter was written
as by a man hemmed into a corner. Christine was defiantly – insultingly –
hurled at his head. He was accepted because he was so despised.

And yet with what respect he had treated her and hers! Now he was
reminded of what an agricultural friend had said years ago, seeing the
eyes of Nicholas fixed on Christine as on an angel when she passed:
'Better a little fire to warm 'ee than a great one to burn 'ee. No good can
come of throwing your heart there.' He went into the mead, sat down,
and asked himself four questions:

1. How could she live near her acquaintance as his wife, even in his
absence, without suffering martyrdom from the stings of their contempt?

2. Would not this entail total estrangement between Christine and her
family also, and her own consequent misery?

3. Must not such isolation extinguish her affection for him?

4. Supposing that her father rigged them out as colonists and sent
them off to America, was not the effect of such exile upon one of her
gentle nurture likely to be as the last?

In short, whatever they should embark in together would be cruelty to her, and his death would be a relief. It would, indeed, in one aspect be a relief to her now, if she were so ashamed of him as she had appeared to be that day. Were he dead, this little episode with him would fade away like a dream.

Mr Everard was a good-hearted man at bottom, but to take his enraged offer seriously was impossible. Obviously it was hotly made in his first bitterness at what he had heard. The least thing that he could do would be to go away and never trouble her more. To travel and learn and come back in two years, as mapped out in their first sanguine scheme, required a staunch heart on her side, if the necessary expenditure of time and money were to be afterwards justified; and it were folly to calculate on that when he had seen to-day that her heart was failing her already. To travel and disappear and not be heard of for many years would be a far more independent stroke, and it would leave her entirely unfettered. Perhaps he might rival in this kind the accomplished Mr Bellston, of whose journeyings he had heard so much.

He sat and sat, and the fog rose out of the river, enveloping him like a fleece; first his feet and knees, then his arms and body, and finally submerging his head. When he had come to a decision he went up again into the homestead. He would be independent, if he died for it, and he would free Christine. Exile was the only course. The first step was to inform his uncle of his determination.

Two days later Nicholas was on the same spot in the mead, at almost the same hour of eve. But there was no fog now; a blusterous autumn wind had ousted the still, golden days and misty nights; and he was going, full of purpose, in the opposite direction. When he had last entered the mead he was an inhabitant of the Froom valley; in forty-eight hours he had severed himself from that spot as completely as if he had never belonged to it. All that appertained to him in the Froom valley now was circumscribed by the portmanteau in his hand.

In making his preparations for departure he had unconsciously held a faint, foolish hope that she would communicate with him and make up their estrangement in some soft womanly way. But she had given no signal, and it was too evident to him that her latest mood had grown to be her fixed one, proving how well-founded had been his impulse to set her free.

He entered the Sallows, found his way in the dark to the garden-door of the house, slipped under it a note to tell her of his departure, and explaining its true reason to be a consciousness of her growing feeling

that he was an encumbrance and a humiliation. Of the direction of his
journey and of the date of his return he said nothing.

His course now took him into the high road, which he pursued for
some miles in a north-easterly direction, still spinning the thread of sad
inferences, and asking himself why he should ever return. At daybreak
he stood on the hill above Shottsford-Forum, and awaited a coach which
passed about this time along that highway towards Melchester and
London.

VI

Some fifteen years after the date of the foregoing incidents, a man who
had dwelt in far countries, and viewed many cities, arrived at Roy-
Town, a roadside hamlet on the old western turnpike road, not five
miles from Froom-Everard, and put up at the Buck's Head, an isolated
inn at that spot. He was still barely of middle age, but it could be seen
that a haze of gray was settling upon the locks of his hair, and that his
face had lost colour and curve, as if by exposure to bleaching climates
and strange atmospheres, or from ailments incidental thereto. He seemed
to observe little around him, by reason of the intrusion of his musings
upon the scene. In truth Nicholas Long was just now the creature of old
hopes and fears consequent upon his arrival – this man who once had not
cared if his name were blotted out from that district. The evening light
showed wistful lines which he could not smooth away by the worldling's
gloss of nonchalance that he had learnt to fling over his face.

The Buck's Head was a somewhat unusual place for a man of this
sort to choose as a house of sojourn in preference to some Casterbridge
inn four miles further on. Before he left home it had been a lively old
tavern at which High-flyers, and Heralds, and Tally-hoes had changed
horses on their stages up and down the country; but now the house was
rather cavernous and chilly, the stable-roofs were hollow-backed, the
landlord was asthmatic, and the traffic gone.

He arrived in the afternoon, and when he had sent back the fly and
was having a nondescript meal, he put a question to the waiting-maid
with a mien of indifference.

'Squire Everard, of Froom-Everard Manor, has been dead some years,
I believe?'

She replied in the affirmative.

'And are any of the family left there still?'

'O no, bless you, sir! They sold the place years ago – Squire Everard's son did – and went away. I've never heard where they went to. They came quite to nothing.'

'Never heard anything of the young lady – the Squire's daughter?'

'No. You see 'twas before I came to these parts.'

When the waitress left the room, Nicholas pushed aside his plate and gazed out of the window. He was not going over into the Froom valley altogether on Christine's account, but she had greatly animated his motive in coming that way. Anyhow he would push on there now that he was so near, and not ask questions here where he was liable to be wrongly informed. The fundamental inquiry he had not ventured to make – whether Christine had married before the family went away. He had abstained because of an absurd dread of extinguishing hopeful surmise. That the Everards had left their old home was bad enough intelligence for one day.

Rising from the table he put on his hat and went out, ascending towards the upland which divided this district from his native vale. The first familiar feature that met his eye was a little spot on the distant sky – a clump of trees standing on a barrow which surmounted a yet more remote upland – a point where, in his childhood, he had believed people could stand and see America. He reached the further verge of the plateau on which he had entered. Ah, there was the valley – a greenish-gray stretch of colour – still looking placid and serene, as though it had not much missed him. If Christine was no longer there, why should he pause over it this evening? His uncle and aunt were dead, and to-morrow would be soon enough to inquire for remoter relatives. Thus, disinclined to go further, he turned to retrace his way to the inn.

In the backward path he now perceived the figure of a woman, who had been walking at a distance behind him; and as she drew nearer he began to be startled. Surely, despite the variations introduced into that figure by changing years, its ground-lines were those of Christine?

Nicholas had been sentimental enough to write to Christine immediately on landing at Southampton a day or two before this, addressing his letter at a venture to the old house, and merely telling her that he planned to reach the Roy-Town inn on the present afternoon. The news of the scattering of the Everards had dissipated his hope of hearing of her; but here she was.

So they met – there, alone, on the open down by a pond, just as if the meeting had been carefully arranged.

She threw up her veil. She was still beautiful, though the years had touched her; a little more matronly – much more homely. Or was it only that he was much less homely now – a man of the world – the sense of homeliness being relative? Her face had grown to be pre-eminently of the sort that would be called interesting. Her habiliments were of a demure and sober cast, though she was one who had used to dress so airily and so gaily. Years had laid on a few shadows too in this.

'I received your letter,' she said, when the momentary embarrassment of their first approach had passed. 'And I thought I would walk across the hills to-day, as it was fine. I have just called at the inn, and they told me you were out. I was now on my way homeward.'

He hardly listened to this, though he intently gazed at her. 'Christine,' he said, 'one word. Are you free?'

'I – I am in a certain sense,' she replied, colouring.

The announcement had a magical effect. The intervening time between past and present closed up for him, and moved by an impulse which he had combated for fifteen years, he seized her two hands and drew her towards him.

She started back, and became almost a mere acquaintance. 'I have to tell you,' she gasped, 'that I have – been married.'

Nicholas's rose-coloured dream was immediately toned down to a grayish tinge.

'I did not marry till many years after you had left,' she continued in the humble tones of one confessing to a crime. 'Oh Nic,' she cried reproachfully, 'how could you stay away so long?'

'Whom did you marry?'

'Mr Bellston.'

'I – ought to have expected it.' He was going to add, 'And is he dead?' but he checked himself. Her dress unmistakably suggested widowhood; and she had said she was free.

'I must now hasten home,' said she. 'I felt that, considering my shortcomings at our parting so many years ago, I owed you the initiative now.'

'There is some of your old generosity in that. I'll walk with you, if I may. Where are you living, Christine?'

'In the same house, but not on the old conditions. I have part of it on lease; the farmer now tenanting the premises found the whole more than he wanted, and the owner allowed me to keep what rooms I chose. I am poor now, you know, Nicholas, and almost friendless. My brother sold the Froom-Everard estate when it came to him, and the person who bought it turned our home into a farmhouse. Till my father's death my husband and I lived in the manor-house with him, so that I have never lived away from the spot.'

She was poor. That, and the change of name, sufficiently accounted for the inn-servant's ignorance of her continued existence within the walls of her old home.

It was growing dusk, and he still walked with her. A woman's head arose from the declivity before them, and as she drew nearer, Christine asked him to go back. 'This is the wife of the farmer who shares the house,' she said. 'She is accustomed to come out and meet me whenever I walk far and am benighted. I am obliged to walk everywhere now.'

The farmer's wife, seeing that Christine was not alone, paused in her advance, and Nicholas said, 'Dear Christine, if you are obliged to do these things, I am not, and what wealth I can command you may command likewise. They say rolling stones gather no moss; but they gather dross sometimes. I was one of the pioneers to the gold-fields, you know, and made a sufficient fortune there for my wants. What is more, I kept it. When I had done this I was coming home, but hearing of my uncle's death I changed my plan, travelled, speculated, and increased my fortune. Now, before we part: you remember you stood with me at the altar once, and therefore I speak with less preparation than I should otherwise use. Before we part then I ask, shall another again intrude between us? Or shall we complete the union we began?'

She trembled – just as she had done at that very minute of standing with him in the church, to which he had recalled her mind. 'I will not enter into that now, dear Nicholas,' she replied. 'There will be more to talk of and consider first – more to explain, which it would have spoiled this meeting to have entered into now.'

'Yes, yes; but—'

'Further than the brief answer I first gave, Nic, don't press me to-night. I still have the old affection for you, or I should not have sought you. Let that suffice for the moment.'

'Very well, dear one. And when shall I call to see you?'

'I will write and fix an hour. I will tell you everything of my history then.'

And thus they parted, Nicholas feeling that he had not come here fruitlessly. When she and her companion were out of sight he retraced his steps to Roy-Town, where he made himself as comfortable as he could in the deserted old inn of his boyhood's days. He missed her companionship this evening more than he had done at any time during the whole fifteen years; and it was as though instead of separation there had been constant communion with her throughout that period. The tones of her voice had stirred his heart in a nook which had lain stagnant ever since he last heard them. They recalled the woman to whom he had once lifted his eyes as to a goddess. Her announcement that she had been another's came as a little shock to him, and he did not now lift his eyes to her in precisely the same way as he had lifted them at first. But he forgave her for marrying Bellston; what could he expect after fifteen years?

He slept at Roy-Town that night, and in the morning there was a short note from her, repeating more emphatically her statement of the previous evening – that she wished to inform him clearly of her circumstances, and to calmly consider with him the position in which she was placed. Would he call upon her on Sunday afternoon, when she was sure to be alone?

'Nic,' she wrote on, 'what a cosmopolite, you are! I expected to find my old yeoman still; but I was quite awed in the presence of such a citizen of the world. Did I seem rusty and unpractised? Ah – you seemed so once to me!'

Tender playful words; the old Christine was in them. She said Sunday afternoon, and it was now only Saturday morning. He wished she had said to-day; that short revival of her image had vitalized to sudden heat feelings that had almost been stilled. Whatever she might have to explain as to her position – and it was awkwardly narrowed, no doubt – he could not give her up. Miss Everard or Mrs Bellston, what mattered it? – she was the same Christine.

He did not go outside the inn all Saturday. He had no wish to see or do anything but to await the coming interview. So he smoked, and read the local newspaper of the previous week, and stowed himself in the chimney-corner. In the evening he felt that he could remain indoors no longer, and the moon being near the full, he started from the inn on foot in the same direction as that of yesterday, with the view of contemplating the old village and its precincts, and hovering round her house under the cloak of night.

With a stout stick in his hand he climbed over the five miles of upland in a comparatively short space of time. Nicholas had seen many strange lands and trodden many strange ways since he last walked that path, but as he trudged he seemed wonderfully like his old self, and had not the slightest difficulty in finding the way. In descending to the meads the streams perplexed him a little, some of the old foot-bridges having been removed; but he ultimately got across the larger water-courses, and pushed on to the village, avoiding her residence for the moment, lest she should encounter him, and think he had not respected the time of her appointment.

He found his way to the churchyard, and first ascertained where lay the two relations he had left alive at his departure; then he observed the gravestones of other inhabitants with whom he had been well acquainted, till by degrees he seemed to be in the society of all the elder Froom-Everard population, as he had known the place. Side by side as they had lived in his day here were they now. They had moved house in mass.

But no tomb of Mr Bellston was visible, though, as he had lived at the manor-house, it would have been natural to find it here. In truth Nicholas was more anxious to discover that than anything, being curious to know how long he had been dead. Seeing from the glimmer of a light in the church that somebody was there cleaning for Sunday he entered, and looked round upon the walls as well as he could. But there was no monument to her husband, though one had been erected to the Squire.

Nicholas addressed the young man who was sweeping. 'I don't see any monument or tomb to the late Mr Bellston?'

'O no, sir; you won't see that,' said the young man drily.

'Why, pray?'

'Because he's not buried here. He's not Christian-buried anywhere, as far as we know. In short, perhaps he's not buried at all; and between ourselves, perhaps he's alive.'

Nicholas sank an inch shorter. 'Ah,' he answered.

'Then you don't know the peculiar circumstances, sir?'

'I am a stranger here – as to late years.'

'Mr Bellston was a traveller – an explorer – it was his calling; you may have heard his name as such?'

'I remember.' Nicholas recalled the fact that this very bent of Mr Bellston's was the incentive to his own roaming.

'Well, when he married he came and lived here with his wife and his wife's father, and said he would travel no more. But after a time he got weary of biding quiet here, and weary of her – he was not a good husband to the young lady by any means – and he betook himself again to his old trick of roving – with her money. Away he went, quite out of the realm of human foot, into the bowels of Asia, and never was heard of more. He was murdered, it is said, but nobody knows; though as that was nine years ago he's dead enough in principle, if not in corporation. His widow lives quite humble, for between her husband and her brother she's left in very lean pasturage.'

Nicholas went back to the Buck's Head without hovering round her dwelling. This then was the explanation which she had wanted to make. Not dead, but missing. How could he have expected that the first fair promise of happiness held out to him would remain untarnished? She had said that she was free; and legally she was free, no doubt. Moreover, from her tone and manner he felt himself justified in concluding that she would be willing to run the risk of a union with him, in the improbability of her husband's existence. Even if that husband lived, his return was not a likely event, to judge from his character. A man who could spend her money on his own personal adventures would not be anxious to disturb her poverty after such a lapse of time.

Well, the prospect was not so unclouded as it had seemed. But could he, even now, give up Christine?

VII

Two months more brought the year nearly to a close, and found Nicholas Long tenant of a spacious house in the market-town nearest to Froom-Everard. A man of means, genial character, and a bachelor, he was an object of great interest to his neighbours, and to his neighbours' wives and daughters. But he took little note of this, and had made it his business to go twice a week, no matter what the weather, to the now farmhouse at Froom-Everard, a wing of which had been retained as the refuge of Christine. He always walked, to give no trouble in putting up a horse to a housekeeper whose staff was limited.

The two had put their heads together on the situation, had gone to a solicitor, had balanced possibilities, and had resolved to make the plunge of matrimony. 'Nothing venture, nothing have,' Christine had said, with some of her old audacity.

With almost gratuitous honesty they had let their intentions be widely known. Christine, it is true, had rather shrunk from publicity at first; but Nicholas argued that their boldness in this respect would have good results. With his friends he held that there was not the slightest probability of her being other than a widow, and a challenge to the missing man now, followed by no response, would stultify any unpleasant remarks which might be thrown at her after their union. To this end a paragraph was inserted in the Wessex papers, announcing that their marriage was proposed to be celebrated on such and such a day in December.

His periodic walks along the south side of the valley to visit her were among the happiest experiences of his life. The yellow leaves falling around him in the foreground, the well-watered meads on the left hand, and the woman he loved awaiting him at the back of the scene, promised a future of much serenity, as far as human judgment could foresee. On arriving, he would sit with her in the 'parlour' of the wing she retained, her general sitting-room, where the only relics of her early surroundings were an old clock from the other end of the house, and her own piano. Before it was quite dark they would stand, hand in hand, looking out of the window across the flat turf to the dark clump of trees which hid further view from their eyes.

'Do you wish you were still mistress here, dear?' he once said.

'Not at all,' said she cheerfully. 'I have a good enough room, and a good enough fire, and a good enough friend. Besides, my latter days as mistress of the house were not happy ones, and they spoilt the place for me. It was a punishment for my faithlessness. Nic, you do forgive me? Really you do?'

The twenty-third of December, the eve of the wedding-day, had arrived at last in the train of such uneventful ones as these. Nicholas had arranged to visit her that day a little later than usual, and see that everything was ready with her for the morrow's event and her removal to his house; for he had begun to look after her domestic affairs, and to lighten as much as possible the duties of her house-keeping.

He was to come to an early supper, which she had arranged to take the place of a wedding-breakfast next day – the latter not being feasible in her present situation. An hour or so after dark the wife of the farmer who lived in the other part of the house entered Christine's parlour to lay the cloth.

'What with getting the ham skinned, and the black-puddings hotted up,' she said, 'it will take me all my time before he's here, if I begin this minute.'

'I'll lay the table myself,' said Christine, jumping up. 'Do you attend to the cooking.'

'Thank you, ma'am. And perhaps 'tis no matter, seeing that it is the last night you'll have to do such work. I knew this sort of life wouldn't last long for 'ee, being born to better things.'

'It has lasted rather long, Mrs Wake. And if he had not found me out it would have lasted all my days.'

'But he did find you out.'

'He did. And I'll lay the cloth immediately.'

Mrs Wake went back to the kitchen, and Christine began to bustle about. She greatly enjoyed preparing this table for Nicholas and herself with her own hands. She took artistic pleasure in adjusting each article to its position, as if half-an-inch error were a point of high importance. Finally she placed the two candles where they were to stand, and sat down by the fire.

Mrs Wake re-entered and regarded the effect. 'Why not have another candle or two, ma'am?' she said. ' 'Twould make it livelier. Say four.'

'Very well,' said Christine, and four candles were lighted. 'Really,' she added, surveying them, 'I have been now so long accustomed to little economies that they look quite extravagant.'

'Ah, you'll soon think nothing of forty in his grand new house! Shall I bring in supper directly he comes, ma'am?'

'No, not for half-an-hour; and, Mrs Wake, you and Betsy are busy in the kitchen, I know; so when he knocks don't disturb yourselves; I can let him in.'

She was again left alone, and, as it still wanted some time to Nicholas's appointment, she stood by the fire, looking at herself in the glass over the mantel. Reflectively raising a lock of her hair just above her temple she uncovered a small scar. That scar had a history. The terrible temper of her late husband – those sudden moods of irascibility which had made even his friendly excitements look like anger – had once caused him to set that mark upon her with the bezel of a ring he wore. He declared that the whole thing was an accident. She was a woman and kept her own opinion.

Christine then turned her back to the glass and scanned the table and the candles, shining one at each corner like types of the four Evangelists, and thought they looked too assuming – too confident. She glanced up at the clock, which stood also in this room, there not being space enough for it in the passage. It was nearly seven, and she expected Nicholas at half-past. She liked the company of this venerable article in her lonely life: its tickings and whizzings were a sort of conversation. It now began to strike the hour. At the end something grated slightly. Then, without any warning, the clock slowly inclined forward and fell at full length upon the floor.

The crash brought the farmer's wife rushing into the room. Christine had wellnigh sprung out of her shoes. Mrs Wake's enquiry what had happened was answered by the evidence of her own eyes.

'How did it occur?' she said.

'I cannot say; it was not firmly fixed, I suppose. Dear me, how sorry I am! My dear father's hall-clock! And now I suppose it is ruined.'

Assisted by Mrs Wake, she lifted the clock. Every inch of glass was, of course, shattered, but very little harm besides appeared to be done. They propped it up temporarily, though it would not go again.

Christine had soon recovered her composure, but she saw that Mrs Wake was gloomy. 'What does it mean, Mrs Wake?' she said. 'Is it ominous?'

'It is a sign of a violent death in the family.'

'Don't talk of it. I don't believe such things; and don't mention it to Mr Long when he comes. *He*'s not in the family yet, you know.'

'O no, it cannot refer to him,' said Mrs Wake musingly.

'Some remote cousin, perhaps,' observed Christine, no less willing to humour her than to get rid of a shapeless dread which the incident had caused in her own mind. 'And – supper is almost ready, Mrs Wake?'

'In three-quarters of an hour.'

Mrs Wake left the room, and Christine sat on. Though it still wanted fifteen minutes to the hour at which Nicholas had promised to be there, she began to grow impatient. After the accustomed ticking the dead silence was oppressive. But she had not to wait so long as she had expected; steps were heard approaching the door, and there was a knock.

Christine was already there to open it. The entrance had no lamp, but it was not particularly dark out of doors. She could see the outline of a man, and cried cheerfully, 'You are early; it is very good of you.'

'I beg pardon. It is not Mr Bellston himself – only a messenger with his bag and greatcoat. But he will be here soon.'

The voice was not the voice of Nicholas, and the intelligence was strange. 'I – I don't understand. Mr Bellston?' she faintly replied.

'Yes, ma'am. A gentleman – a stranger to me – gave me these things at Casterbridge station to bring on here, and told me to say that Mr Bellston had arrived there, and is detained for half-an-hour, but will be here in the course of the evening.'

She sank into a chair. The porter put a small battered portmanteau on the floor, the coat on a chair, and looking into the room at the spread table said, 'If you are disappointed, ma'am, that your husband (as I s'pose he is) is not come, I can assure you he'll soon be here. He's stopped to get a shave, to my thinking, seeing he wanted it. What he said was that I could tell you he had heard the news in Ireland, and would have come sooner, his hand being forced; but was hindered crossing by the weather, having took passage in a sailing vessel. What news he meant he didn't say.'

'Ah, yes,' she faltered. It was plain that the man knew nothing of her intended re-marriage.

Mechanically rising and giving him a shilling, she answered to his 'good-night', and he withdrew, the beat of his footsteps lessening in the distance. She was alone; but in what a solitude.

Christine stood in the middle of the hall, just as the man had left her, in the gloomy silence of the stopped clock within the adjoining room, till she aroused herself, and turning to the portmanteau and greatcoat brought them to the light of the candles, and examined them. The portmanteau bore painted upon it the initials 'J.B.' in white letters – the well-known initials of her husband.

She examined the greatcoat. In the breast-pocket was an empty spirit flask, which she firmly fancied she recognized as the one she had filled many times for him when he was living at home with her.

She turned desultorily hither and thither, until she heard another tread without, and there came a second knocking at the door. She did not respond to it; and Nicholas – for it was he – thinking that he was not heard by reason of a concentration on to-morrow's proceedings, opened the door softly, and came on to the door of her room, which stood un-closed, just as it had been left by the Casterbridge porter.

Nicholas uttered a blithe greeting, cast his eye round the parlour, which with its tall candles, blazing fire, snow-white cloth, and prettily-spread table, formed a cheerful spectacle enough for a man who had been walking in the dark for an hour.

'My bride – almost, at last!' he cried, encircling her with his arms.

Instead of responding, her figure became limp, frigid, heavy; her head fell back, and he found that she had fainted.

It was natural, he thought. She had had many little worrying matters to attend to, and but slight assistance. He ought to have seen more effectually to her affairs; the closeness of the event had over-excited her.

Nicholas kissed her unconscious face – more than once, little thinking what news it was that had changed its aspect. Loth to call Mrs Wake, he carried Christine to a couch and laid her down. This had the effect of reviving her. Nicholas bent and whispered in her ear, 'Lie quiet, dearest, no hurry; and dream, dream, dream of happy days. It is only I. You will soon be better.' He held her by the hand.

'No, no, no!' she said, with a stare. 'O, how can this be?'

Nicholas was alarmed and perplexed, but the disclosure was not long delayed. When she had sat up, and by degrees made the stunning event known to him, he stood as if transfixed.

'Ah – is it so?' said he. Then, becoming quite meek, 'And why was he so cruel as to – delay his return till now?'

She dutifully recited the explanation her husband had given her through the messenger; but her mechanical manner of telling it showed how much she doubted its truth. It was too unlikely that his arrival at such a dramatic moment should not be a contrived surprise, quite of a piece with his previous dealings towards her.

'But perhaps it may be true – and he may have become kind now – not as he used to be,' she faltered. 'Yes, perhaps, Nicholas, he is an altered man – we'll hope he is. I suppose I ought not to have listened to my legal advisers, and assumed his death so surely! Anyhow, I am roughly received back into – the right way!'

Nicholas burst out bitterly: 'O what too, too honest fools we were! – to so court daylight upon our intention by putting that announcement in the papers! Why could we not have married privately, and gone away, so that he would never have known what had become of you, even if he had returned? Christine, he has done it to. . . . But I'll say no more. Of course we – might fly now.'

'No, no; we might not,' said she hastily.

'Very well. But this is hard to bear! "When I looked for good then evil came unto me, and when I waited for light there came darkness." So once said a sorely tried man in the land of Uz, and so say I now! . . . I wonder if he is almost here at this moment?'

She told him she supposed Bellston was approaching by the path across the fields, having sent on his greatcoat, which he would not want walking.

'And is this meal laid for him, or for me?'

'It was laid for you.'

'And it will be eaten by him?'

'Yes.'

'Christine, are you *sure* that he is come, or have you been sleeping over the fire and dreaming it?'

She pointed anew to the portmanteau with the initials 'J.B.', and to the coat beside it.

'Well, good-bye – good-bye! Curse that parson for not marrying us fifteen years ago!'

It is unnecessary to dwell further upon that parting. There are scenes wherein the words spoken do not even approximate to the level of the mental communion between the actors. Suffice it to say that part they did, and quickly; and Nicholas, more dead than alive, went out of the house homewards.

Why had he ever come back? During his absence he had not cared for Christine as he cared now. If he had been younger he might have felt tempted to descend into the meads instead of keeping along their edge. The Froom was down there, and he knew of quiet pools in that stream to which death would come easily. But he was too old to put an end to himself for such a reason as love; and another thought, too, kept him from seriously contemplating any desperate act. His affection for her was strongly protective, and in the event of her requiring a friend's support in future troubles there was none but himself left in the world to afford it. So he walked on.

Meanwhile Christine had resigned herself to circumstances. A resolve to continue worthy of her history and of her family lent her heroism and dignity. She called Mrs Wake, and explained to that worthy woman as much of what had occurred as she deemed necessary. Mrs Wake was too amazed to reply; she retreated slowly, her lips parted; till at the door she said with a dry mouth, 'And the beautiful supper, ma'am?'

'Serve it when he comes.'

'When Mr Bellston – yes, ma'am, I will.' She still stood gazing, as if she could hardly take in the order.

'That will do, Mrs Wake. I am much obliged to you for all your kindness.' And Christine was left alone again, and then she wept.

She sat down and waited. That awful silence of the stopped clock began anew, but she did not mind it now. She was listening for a footfall in a state of mental tensity which almost took away from her the power of motion. It seemed to her that the natural interval for her husband's journey thither must have expired; but she was not sure, and waited on.

Mrs Wake again came in. 'You have not rung for supper—'

'He is not yet come, Mrs Wake. If you want to go to bed, bring in the supper and set it on the table. It will be nearly as good cold. Leave the door unbarred.'

Mrs Wake did as was suggested, made up the fire, and went away. Shortly afterwards Christine heard her retire to her chamber. But Christine still sat on, and still her husband postponed his entry.

She aroused herself once or twice to freshen the fire, but was ignorant how the night was going. Her watch was upstairs, and she did not make the effort to go up to consult it. In her seat she continued; and still the supper waited, and still he did not come.

At length she was so nearly persuaded that the arrival of his things must have been a dream after all, that she again went over to them, felt them, and examined them. His they unquestionably were; and their forwarding by the porter had been quite natural. She sighed and sat down again.

Presently she fell into a doze, and when she again became conscious she found that the four candles had burned into their sockets and gone out. The fire still emitted a feeble shine. Christine did not take the trouble to get more candles, but stirred the fire and sat on.

After a long period she heard a creaking of the chamber floor and stairs at the other end of the house, and knew that the farmer's family were getting up. By-and-by Mrs Wake entered the room, candle in hand, bouncing open the door in her morning manner, obviously without any expectation of finding a person there.

'Lord-a-mercy! What, sitting here again, ma'am?'

'Yes, I am sitting here still.'

'You've been there ever since last night?'

'Yes.'

'Then—'

'He's not come.'

'Well, he won't come at this time o' morning,' said the farmer's wife. 'Do 'ee get on to bed, ma'am. You must be shrammed to death!'

It occurred to Christine now that possibly her husband had thought better of obtruding himself upon her company within an hour of revealing his existence to her, and had decided to pay a more formal visit next day. She therefore adopted Mrs Wake's suggestion and retired.

VIII

Nicholas had gone straight home, neither speaking to nor seeing a soul. From that hour a change seemed to come over him. He had ever possessed a full share of self-consciousness; he had been readily piqued, had shown an unusual dread of being personally obtrusive. But now his sense of self, as an individual provoking opinion, appeared to leave him. When, therefore, after a day or two of seclusion, he came forth again, and the few acquaintances he had formed in the town condoled with him on what had happened, and pitied his haggard looks, he did not shrink from their regard as he would have done formerly, but took their sympathy as it would have been accepted by a child.

It reached his ears that Bellston had not appeared on the evening of his arrival at any hotel in the town or neighbourhood, or entered his wife's house at all. 'That's a part of his cruelty,' thought Nicholas. And when two or three days had passed, and still no account came to him of Bellston having joined her, he ventured to set out for Froom-Everard.

Christine was so shaken that she was obliged to receive him as she lay on a sofa, beside the square table which was to have borne their evening feast. She fixed her eyes wistfully upon him, and smiled a sad smile.

'He has not come?' said Nicholas under his breath.

'He has not.'

Then Nicholas sat beside her, and they talked on general topics merely like saddened old friends. But they could not keep away the subject of Bellston, their voices dropping as it forced its way in. Christine, no less than Nicholas, knowing her husband's character, inferred that, having stopped her game, as he would have phrased it, he was taking things leisurely, and, finding nothing very attractive in her limited mode of living, was meaning to return to her only when he had nothing better to do.

The bolt which laid low their hopes had struck so recently that they could hardly look each other in the face when speaking that day. But when a week or two had passed, and all the horizon still remained as vacant of Bellston as before, Nicholas and she could talk of the event with calm wonderment. Why had he come, to go again like this?

And then there set in a period of resigned surmise, during which

So like, so very like, was day to day,

that to tell of one of them is to tell of all. Nicholas would arrive between three and four in the afternoon, a faint trepidation influencing his walk as he neared her door. He would knock; she would always reply in person, having watched for him from the window. Then he would whisper –

'He has not come?'

'He has not,' she would say.

Nicholas would enter then, and she being ready bonneted, they would walk into the Sallows together as far as to the spot which they had frequently made their place of appointment in their youthful days. A plank bridge, which Bellston had caused to be thrown over the stream during his residence with her in the manor-house, was now again removed, and all was just the same as in Nicholas's time, when he had been accustomed to wade across on the edge of the cascade and come up to her like a merman from the deep. Here on the felled trunk, which still lay rotting in its old place, they would now sit, gazing at the descending sheet of water, with its never-ending sarcastic hiss at their baffled attempts to make themselves one flesh. Returning to the house they would sit down together to tea, after which, and the confidential chat that accompanied it, he walked home by the declining light. This proceeding became as periodic as an astronomical recurrence. Twice a week he came – all through that winter, all through the spring following, through the summer, through the autumn, the next winter, the next year, and the next, till an appreciable span of human life had passed by. Bellston still tarried.

Years and years Nic walked that way, at this interval of three days, from his house in the neighbouring town; and in every instance the aforesaid order of things was customary; and still on his arrival the form of words went on –

'He has not come?'

'He has not.'

So they grew older. The dim shape of that third one stood continually between them; they could not displace it; neither, on the other hand, could it effectually part them. They were in close communion, yet not indissolubly united; lovers, yet never growing cured of love. By the time that the fifth year of Nic's visiting had arrived, on about the five-hundredth occasion of his presence at her tea-table, he noticed that the bleaching process which had begun upon his own locks was also spreading to hers. He told her so, and they laughed. Yet she was in good health: a condition of suspense, which would have half-killed a man, had been endured by her without complaint, and even with composure.

One day, when these years of abeyance had numbered seven, they had strolled as usual as far as the waterfall, whose faint roar formed a sort of calling voice sufficient in the circumstances to direct their listlessness. Pausing there, he looked up at her face and said, 'Why should we not try again, Christine? We are legally at liberty to do so now. Nothing venture, nothing have.'

But she would not. Perhaps a little primness of idea was by this time ousting the native daring of Christine. 'What he has done once he can do twice,' she said. 'He is not dead, and if we were to marry he would say we had "forced his hand", as he said before, and duly reappear.'

Some years after, when Christine was about fifty, and Nicholas fifty-three, a new trouble of a minor kind arrived. He found an inconvenience in traversing the distance between their two houses, particularly in damp weather, the years he had spent in trying climates abroad having sown the seeds of rheumatism, which made a journey undesirable on inclement days, even in a carriage. He told her of this new difficulty, as he did of everything.

'If you could live nearer,' suggested she.

Unluckily there was no house near. But Nicholas, though not a millionaire, was a man of means; he obtained a small piece of ground on lease at the nearest spot to her home that it could be so obtained, which was on the opposite brink of the Froom, this river forming the boundary of the Froom-Everard manor; and here he built a cottage large enough for his wants. This took time, and when he got into it he found its situation a great comfort to him. He was not more than five hundred yards from her now, and gained a new pleasure in feeling that all sounds which greeted his ears, in the day or in the night, also fell upon hers – the caw of a particular rook, the voice of a neighbouring nightingale, the whistle of a local breeze, or the purl of the fall in the meadows, whose rush was a material rendering of Time's ceaseless scour over themselves, wearing them away without uniting them.

Christine's missing husband was taking shape as a myth among the surrounding residents; but he was still believed in as corporeally imminent by Christine herself, and also, in a milder degree, by Nicholas. For a curious unconsciousness of the long lapse of time since his revelation of himself seemed to affect the pair. There had been no passing events to serve as chronological milestones, and the evening on which she had kept supper waiting for him still loomed out with startling nearness in their retrospects.

In the seventeenth pensive year of this their parallel march towards the common bourne, a labourer came in a hurry one day to Nicholas's house and brought strange tidings. The present owner of Froom-Everard – a non-resident – had been improving his property in sundry ways, and one of these was by dredging the stream which, in the course of years, had become choked with mud and weeds in its passage through the Sallows. The process necessitated a reconstruction of the waterfall. When the river had been pumped dry for this purpose, the skeleton of a man had been found jammed among the piles supporting the edge of the fall. Every particle of his flesh and clothing had been eaten by fishes or abraded to nothing by the water, but the relics of a gold watch remained, and on the inside of the case was engraved the name of the maker of her husband's watch, which she well remembered.

Nicholas, deeply agitated, hastened down to the place and examined the remains attentively, afterwards going across to Christine, and breaking the discovery to her. She would not come to view the skeleton, which lay extended on the grass, not a finger or toe-bone missing, so neatly had the aquatic operators done their work. Conjecture was directed to the question how Bellston had got there; and conjecture alone could give an explanation.

It was supposed that, on his way to call upon her, he had taken a short cut through the grounds, with which he was naturally very familiar, and coming to the fall under the trees had expected to find there the plank which, during his occupancy of the premises with Christine and her father, he had placed there for crossing into the meads on the other side instead of wading across as Nicholas had done. Before discovering its removal he had probably overbalanced himself, and was thus precipitated into the cascade, the piles beneath the descending current wedging him between them like the prongs of a pitchfork, and effectually preventing the rising of his body, over which the weeds grew. Such was the reasonable supposition concerning the discovery; but proof was never forthcoming.

'To think,' said Nicholas, when the remains had been decently interred, and he was again sitting with Christine – though not beside the waterfall – 'to think how we visited him! How we sat over him, hours and hours, gazing at him, bewailing our fate, when all the time he was ironically hissing at us from the spot, in an unknown tongue, that we could marry if we chose!'

She echoed the sentiment with a sigh.

'I have strange fancies,' she said. 'I suppose it *must* have been my husband who came back, and not some other man.'

Nicholas felt that there was little doubt. 'Besides – the skeleton,' he said.

'Yes. . . . If it could not have been another person's – but no, of course it was he.'

'You might have married me on the day we had fixed, and there would have been no impediment. You would now have been seventeen years my wife, and we might have had tall sons and daughters.'

'It might have been so,' she murmured.

'Well – is it still better late than never ?'

The question was one which had become complicated by the increasing years of each. Their wills were somewhat enfeebled now, their hearts sickened of tender enterprise by hope too long deferred. Having postponed the consideration of their course till a year after the interment of Bellston, each seemed less disposed than formerly to take it up again.

'Is it worth while, after so many years ?' she said to him. 'We are fairly happy as we are – perhaps happier than we should be in any other relation, seeing what old people we have grown. The weight is gone from our lives; the shadow no longer divides us; then let us be joyful together as we are, dearest Nic, in the days of our vanity; and

> With mirth and laughter let old wrinkles come.'

He fell in with these views of hers to some extent. But occasionally he ventured to urge her to reconsider the case, though he spoke not with the fervour of his earlier years.

Autumn 1887

Alicia's Diary

I. SHE MISSES HER SISTER

July 7. – I wander about the house in a mood of unutterable sadness, for my dear sister Caroline has left home to-day with my mother, and I shall not see them again for several weeks. They have accepted a long-standing invitation to visit some old friends of ours, the Marlets, who live at Versailles for cheapness – my mother thinking that it will be for the good of Caroline to see a little of France and Paris. But I don't quite like her going. I fear she may lose some of that childlike simplicity and gentleness which so characterize her, and have been nourished by the seclusion of our life here. Her solicitude about her pony before starting was quite touching, and she made me promise to visit it daily, and see that it came to no harm.

Caroline gone abroad, and I left here! It is the reverse of an ordinary situation, for good or ill-luck has mostly ordained that I should be the absent one. Mother will be quite tired out by the young enthusiasm of Caroline. She will demand to be taken everywhere – to Paris continually, of course; to all the stock shrines of history's devotees; to palaces and prisons; to kings' tombs and queens' tombs; to cemeteries and picture-galleries, and royal hunting-forests. My poor mother, having gone over most of this ground many times before, will perhaps not find the perambulation so exhilarating as will Caroline herself. I wish I could have gone with them. I would not have minded having my legs walked off to please Caroline. But this regret is absurd: I could not, of course, leave my father with not a soul in the house to attend to the calls of the parishioners or to pour out his tea.

July 15. – A letter from Caroline to-day. It is very strange that she tells me nothing which I expected her to tell – only trivial details. She seems dazzled by the brilliancy of Paris – which no doubt appears still more brilliant to her from the fact of her only being able to obtain occasional glimpses of it. She would see that Paris, too, has a seamy side if you live there. I was not aware that the Marlets knew so many people. If, as mother has said, they went to reside at Versailles for reasons of economy, they will not effect much in that direction while they make a practice of entertaining all the acquaintances who happen to be in their neighbourhood. They do not confine their hospitalities to English people, either. I wonder who this M. de la Feste is, in whom Caroline says my mother is so much interested.

July 18. – Another letter from Caroline. I have learnt from this epistle that M. Charles de la Feste is 'only one of the many friends of the Marlets'; that though a Frenchman by birth, and now again temporarily at Versailles, he has lived in England many many years; that he is a talented landscape and marine painter, and has exhibited at the *Salon*, and I think in London. His style and subjects are considered somewhat peculiar in Paris – rather English than Continental. I have not as yet learnt his age, or his condition, married or single. From the tone and nature of her remarks about him he sometimes seems to be a middle-aged family man, sometimes quite the reverse. From his nomadic habits I should say the latter is the most likely. He has travelled and seen a great deal, she tells me, and knows more about English literature than she knows herself.

July 21. – Letter from Caroline. Query: Is 'a friend of ours and the Marlets', of whom she now anonymously and mysteriously speaks, the same personage as the 'M. de la Feste' of her former letters? He must be the same, I think, from his pursuits. If so, whence this sudden change of tone? . . . I have been lost in thought for at least a quarter of an hour since writing the preceding sentence. Suppose my dear sister is falling in love with this young man – there is no longer any doubt about his age; what a very awkward, risky thing for her! I do hope that my mother has an eye on these proceedings. But, then, poor mother never sees the drift of anything: she is in truth less of a mother to Caroline than I am. If I were there, how jealously I would watch him, and ascertain his designs!

I am of a stronger nature than Caroline. How I have supported her in the past through her little troubles and great griefs! Is she agitated at the presence of this, to her, new and strange feeling? But I am assuming her to be desperately in love, when I have no proof of anything of the kind. He may be merely a casual friend, of whom I shall hear no more.

July 24. – Then he *is* a bachelor, as I suspected. 'If M. de la Feste ever marries he will', etc. So she writes. They are getting into close quarters, obviously. Also, 'Something to keep my hair smooth, which M. de la Feste told me he had found useful for the tips of his moustache.' Very naïvely related this; and with how much unconsciousness of the intimacy between them that the remark reveals! But my mother – what can she be doing? Does she know of this? And if so, why does she not allude to it in her letters to my father? ... I have been to look at Caroline's pony, in obedience to her reiterated request that I would not miss a day in seeing that she was well cared for. Anxious as Caroline was about this pony of hers before starting, she now never mentioned the poor animal once in her letters. The image of her pet suffers from displacement.

August 3. – Caroline's forgetfulness of her pony has naturally enough extended to me, her sister. It is ten days since she last wrote, and but for a note from my mother I should not know if she were dead or alive.

II. NEWS INTERESTING AND SERIOUS

August 5. – A cloud of letters. A letter from Caroline, another from mother; also one from each to my father.

The probability to which all the intelligence from my sister has pointed of late turns out to be a fact. There is an engagement, or almost an engagement, announced between my dear Caroline and M. de la Feste – to Caroline's sublime happiness, and my mother's entire satisfaction; as well as to that of the Marlets. They and my mother seem to know all about the young man – which is more than I do, though a little extended information about him, considering that I am Caroline's elder sister, would not have been amiss. I half feel with my father, who is much surprised, and, I am sure, not altogether satisfied, that he should not have been consulted at all before matters reached such a definite stage, though he is too amiable to say so openly. I don't quite say that a good thing should have been hindered for the sake of our opinion, if it is a good thing; but the announcement comes very suddenly. It must have been foreseen by my mother for some time that this upshot was probable, and Caroline might have told me more distinctly that M. de la Feste was her lover, instead of alluding so mysteriously to him as only a friend of the Marlets, and lately dropping his name altogether. My father, without exactly objecting to him as a Frenchman, 'wishes he were of English or some other reasonable nationality for one's son-in-law', but I tell him that the demarcations of races, kingdoms, and creeds, are wearing down every day, that patriotism is a sort of vice, and that the character of the individual is all we need think about in this case. I wonder if, in the event of their marriage, he will continue to live at Versailles, or if he will come to England.

August 7. – A supplemental letter from Caroline, answering, by anticipation, some of the aforesaid queries. She tells me that 'Charles', though he makes Versailles his present home, is by no means bound by his profession to continue there; that he will live just where she wishes, provided it be not too far from some centre of thought, art, and civilization. My mother and herself both think that the marriage should not take place till next year. He exhibits landscapes and canal scenery every year, she says; so I suppose he is popular, and that his income is sufficient to keep them in comfort. If not, I do not see why my father could not settle something more on them than he had intended, and diminish by a little what he had proposed for me, whilst it was imagined that I should be the first to stand in need of such.

'Of engaging manner, attractive appearance, and virtuous character,' is the reply I receive from her in answer to my request for a personal description. That is vague enough, and I would rather have had one definite fact of complexion, voice, deed, or opinion. But of course she has no eye now for material qualities; she cannot see him as he is. She sees him irradiated with glories such as never appertained and never will appertain to any man, foreign, English, or Colonial. To think that Caroline, two years my junior, and so childlike as to be five years my junior in nature, should be engaged to be married before me. But that is what happens in families more often than we are apt to remember.

August 16. – Interesting news to-day. Charles, she says, has pleaded that their marriage may just as well be this year as next; and he seems to have nearly converted my mother to the same way of thinking. I do not myself see any reason for delay, beyond the standing one of my father having as yet had no opportunity of forming an opinion upon the man, the time, or anything. However, he takes his lot very quietly, and they are coming home to talk the question over with us; Caroline having decided not to make any positive arrangements for this change of state till she has seen me. Subject to my own and my father's approval, she says, they are inclined to settle the date of the wedding for November, three months from the present time, that it shall take place here in the village, that I, of course, shall be bridesmaid, and many other particulars.

She draws an artless picture of the probable effect upon the minds of the villagers of this romantic performance in the chancel of our old church, in which she is to be chief actor – the foreign gentleman dropping down like a god from the skies, picking her up, and triumphantly carrying her off. Her only grief will be separation from me, but this is to be assuaged by my going and staying with her for long months at a time. This simple prattle is very sweet to me, my dear sister, but I cannot help feeling sad at the occasion of it. In the nature of things it is obvious that I shall never be to you again what I hitherto have been: your guide, counsellor, and most familiar friend.

M. de la Feste does certainly seem to be all that one could desire as protector to a sensitive fragile child like Caroline, and for that I am thankful. Still, I must remember that I see him as yet only through her eyes. For her sake I am intensely anxious to meet him, and scrutinize him through and through, and learn what the man is really made of who is to have such a treasure in his keeping. The engagement has certainly been formed a little precipitately; I quite agree with my father in that: still, good and happy marriages have been made in a hurry before now, and mother seems well satisfied.

August 20. – A terrible announcement came this morning; and we are in deep trouble. I have been quite unable to steady my thoughts on any-thing to-day till now – half-past eleven at night – and I only attempt writing these notes because I am too restless to remain idle, and there is nothing but waiting and waiting left for me to do. Mother has been taken dangerously ill at Versailles: they were within a day or two of starting; but all thought of leaving must now be postponed, for she cannot possibly be moved in her present state. I don't like the sound of hæmorrhage at all in a woman of her full habit, and Caroline and the Marlets have not exaggerated their accounts I am certain. On the receipt of the letter my father instantly decided to go to her, and I have been occupied all day in getting him off, for, as he calculates on being absent several days, there have been many matters for him to arrange before setting out – the chief being to find some one who will do duty for him next Sunday – a quest of no small difficulty at such short notice; but at last poor old feeble Mr Dugdale has agreed to attempt it, with Mr Higham, the Scripture reader, to assist him in the lessons.

I fain would have gone with my father to escape the irksome anxiety of awaiting her; but somebody had to stay, and I could best be spared. George has driven him to the station to meet the last train by which he will catch the midnight boat, and reach Havre some time in the morning. He hates the sea, and a night passage in particular. I hope he will get there without mishap of any kind; but I feel anxious for him, stay-at-home as he is, and unable to cope with any difficulty. Such an errand, too; the journey will be sad enough at best. I almost think I ought to have been the one to go to her.

August 21. – I nearly fell asleep of heaviness of spirit last night over my writing. My father must have reached Paris by this time; and now here comes a letter. . . .

Later. – The letter was to express an earnest hope that my father had set out. My poor mother is sinking, they fear. What will become of Caroline? O, how I wish I could see mother; why could not both have gone?

Later. – I get up from my chair, and walk from window to window, and then come and write a line. I cannot even divine how poor Caroline's marriage is to be carried out if mother dies. I pray that father may have got there in time to talk to her and receive some directions from her about Caroline and M. de la Feste – a man whom neither my father nor I have seen. I, who might be useful in this emergency, am doomed to stay here, waiting in suspense.

August 23. – A letter from my father containing the sad news that my mother's spirit has flown. Poor little Caroline is heart-broken – she was always more my mother's pet than I was. It is some comfort to know that my father arrived in time to hear from her own lips her strongly expressed wish that Caroline's marriage should be solemnized as soon as possible. M. de la Feste seems to have been a great favourite of my dear mother's; and I suppose it now becomes almost a sacred duty of my father to accept him as a son-in-law without criticism.

III. HER GLOOM LIGHTENS A LITTLE

September 10. – I have inserted nothing in my diary for more than a fortnight. Events have been altogether too sad for me to have the spirit to put them on paper. And yet there comes a time when the act of recording one's trouble is recognized as a welcome method of dwelling upon it. . . .

My dear mother has been brought home and buried here in the parish. It was not so much her own wish that this should be done as my father's, who particularly desired that she should lie in the family vault beside his first wife. I saw them side by side before the vault was closed – two women beloved by one man. As I stood, and Caroline by my side, I fell into a sort of dream, and had an odd fancy that Caroline and I might be also beloved of one, and lie like these together – an impossibility, of course, being sisters. When I awoke from my reverie Caroline took my hand and said it was time to leave.

September 14. – The wedding is indefinitely postponed. Caroline is like a girl awakening in the middle of a somnambulistic experience, and does not realize where she is, or how she stands. She walks about silently, and I cannot tell her thoughts, as I used to do. It was her own doing to write to M. de la Feste and tell him that the wedding could not possibly take place this autumn as originally planned. There is something depressing in this long postponement if she is to marry him at all; and yet I do not see how it could be avoided.

October 20. – I have had so much to occupy me in consoling Caroline that I have been continually overlooking my diary. Her life was much nearer to my mother's than mine was. She has never, as I, lived away from home long enough to become self-dependent, and hence in her first loss, and all that it involved, she drooped like a rain-beaten lily. But she is of a nature whose wounds soon heal, even though they may be deep, and the supreme poignancy of her sorrow has already passed.

My father is of opinion that the wedding should not be delayed too long. While at Versailles he made the acquaintance of M. de la Feste, and though they had but a short and hurried communion with each other, he was much impressed by M. de la Feste's disposition and conduct, and is strongly in favour of his suit. It is odd that Caroline's betrothed should influence in his favour all who come near him. His portrait, which dear Caroline has shown me, exhibits him to be of a physique that partly accounts for this; but there must be something more than mere appearance, and it is probably some sort of glamour or fascinating power – the quality which prevented Caroline from describing him to me with any accuracy of detail. At the same time, I see from the photograph that his face and head are remarkably well formed; and though the contours of his mouth are hidden by his moustache, his arched brows show well the romantic disposition of a true lover and painter of Nature. I think that the owner of such a face as this must be tender and sympathetic and true.

October 30. – As my sister's grief for her mother becomes more and

more calmed, her love for M. de la Feste begins to reassume its former
absorbing command of her. She thinks of him incessantly, and writes
whole treatises to him by way of letters. Her blank disappointment at his
announcement of his inability to pay us a visit quite so soon as he had
promised was quite tragic. I, too, am disappointed, for I wanted to see
and estimate him. But having arranged to go to Holland to seize some
aerial effects for his pictures, which are only to be obtained at this time
of the autumn, he is obliged to postpone his journey this way, which is
now to be made early in the new year. I think myself that he ought to
have come at all sacrifices, considering Caroline's recent loss, the sad
postponement of what she was looking forward to, and her single-
minded affection for him. Still, who knows; his professional success is
important. Moreover, she is cheerful, and hopeful, and the delay will
soon be overpast.

IV. SHE BEHOLDS THE ATTRACTIVE STRANGER

February 16. – We have had such a dull life here all the winter that I
have found nothing important enough to set down, and broke off my
journal accordingly. I resume it now to make an entry on the subject of
dear Caroline's future. It seems that she was too grieved, immediately
after the loss of our mother, to answer definitely the question of M. de la
Feste how long the postponement was to be; then, afterwards, it was
agreed that the matter should be discussed on his autumn visit; but as
he did not come, it has remained in abeyance till this week, when
Caroline, with the greatest simplicity and confidence, has written to
him without any further pressure on his part, and told him that she is
quite ready to fix the time, and will do so as soon as he arrives to see her.
She is a little frightened now, lest it should seem forward in her to have
revived the subject of her own accord; but she may assume that his
question has been waiting on for an answer ever since, and that she has,
therefore, acted only within her promise. In truth, the secret at the
bottom of it all is that she is somewhat saddened because he has not
latterly reminded her of the pause in their affairs – that, in short, his
original impatience to possess her is not now found to animate him so
obviously. I suppose that he loves her as much as ever; indeed, I am
sure he must do so, seeing how lovable she is. It is mostly thus with all
men when women are out of their sight; they grow negligent. Caroline

must have patience, and remember that a man of his genius has many and important calls upon his time. In justice to her I must add that she does remember it fairly well, and has as much patience as any girl ever had in the circumstances. He hopes to come at the beginning of April at latest. Well, when he comes we shall see him.

April 5. – I think that what M. de la Feste writes is reasonable enough, though Caroline looks heart-sick about it. It is hardly worth while for him to cross all the way to England and back just now, while the sea is so turbulent, seeing that he will be obliged, in any event, to come in May, when he has to be in London for professional purposes, at which time he can take us easily on his way both coming and going. When Caroline becomes his wife she will be more practical, no doubt; but she is such a child as yet that there is no contenting her with reasons. However, the time will pass quickly, there being so much to do in preparing a trousseau for her, which must now be put in hand in order that we may have plenty of leisure to get it ready. On no account must Caroline be married in half-mourning; I am sure that mother, could she know, would not wish it, and it is odd that Caroline should be so intractably persistent on this point, when she is usually so yielding.

April 30. – This month has flown on swallow's wings. We are in a great state of excitement – I as much as she – I cannot quite tell why. He is really coming in ten days, he says.

May 9. – Four p.m. – I am so agitated I can scarcely write, and yet am particularly impelled to do so before leaving my room. It is the un-expected shape of an expected event which has caused my absurd excitement, which proves me almost as much a school-girl as Caroline.

M. de la Feste was not, as we understood, to have come till to-morrow; but he is here – just arrived. All household directions have devolved upon me, for my father, not thinking M. de la Feste would appear before us for another four-and-twenty hours, left home before post time to attend a distant consecration; and hence Caroline and I were in no small excitement when Charles's letter was opened, and we read that he had been unexpectedly favoured in the dispatch of his studio work, and would follow his letter in a few hours. We sent the covered carriage to meet the train indicated, and waited like two newly strung harps for the first sound of the returning wheels. At last we heard them on the gravel; and the question arose who was to receive him. It was, strictly speaking, my duty; but I felt timid; I could not help shirking it, and insisted that Caroline should go down. She did not, however, go near the door as she usually does when anybody is expected, but waited palpitating in the drawing-room. He little thought when he saw the silent hall, and the apparently deserted house, how that house was at the very same moment alive and throbbing with interest under the surface. I stood at the back of the upper landing, where nobody could see me from downstairs, and heard him walk across the hall – a lighter step than my father's – and heard him then go into the drawing-room, and the servant shut the door behind him and go away.

What a pretty lovers' meeting they must have had in there all to themselves! Caroline's sweet face looking up from her black gown – how it must have touched him. I know she wept very much, for I heard her; and her eyes will be red afterwards, and no wonder, poor dear, though she is no doubt happy. I can imagine what she is telling him while I write this – her fears lest anything should have happened to prevent his coming after all – gentle, smiling reproaches for his long delay; and things of that sort. His two portmanteaus are at this moment crossing the landing on the way to his room. I wonder if I ought to go down.

A little later. – I have seen him! It was not at all in the way that I intended to encounter him, and I am vexed. Just after his portmanteaus were brought up I went out from my room to descend, when, at the moment of stepping towards the first stair, my eyes were caught by an object in the hall below, and I paused for an instant, till I saw that it was a bundle of canvas and sticks, composing a sketching tent and easel. At the same nick of time the drawing-room door opened and the affianced pair came out. They were saying they would go into the garden; and he waited a moment while she put on her hat. My idea was to let them pass on without seeing me, since they seemed not to want my company, but I had got too far on the landing to retreat; he looked up, and stood staring at me – engrossed to a dream-like fixity. Thereupon I, too, instead of advancing as I ought to have done, stood moonstruck and awkward, and before I could gather my weak senses sufficiently to descend, she had called him, and they went out by the garden door together. I then thought of following them, but have changed my mind, and come here to jot down these few lines. It is all I am fit for. . . .

He is even more handsome than I expected. I was right in feeling he must have an attraction beyond that of form: it appeared even in that momentary glance. How happy Caroline ought to be. But I must, of course, go down to be ready with tea in the drawing-room by the time they come indoors.

11 p.m. – I have made the acquaintance of M. de la Feste; and I seem to be another woman from the effect of it. I cannot describe why this should be so, but conversation with him seems to expand the view, and open the heart, and raise one as upon stilts to wider prospects. He has a good intellectual forehead, perfect eyebrows, dark hair and eyes, an animated manner, and a persuasive voice. His voice is soft in quality – too soft for a man, perhaps; and yet on second thoughts I would not have it less so. We have been talking of his art: I had no notion that art demanded such sacrifices or such tender devotion; or that there were two roads for choice within its precincts, the road of vulgar money-making, and the road of high aims and consequent inappreciation for many long years by the public. That he has adopted the latter need not be said to those who understand him. It is a blessing for Caroline that she has been chosen by such a man, and she ought not to lament at postponements and delays, since they have arisen unavoidably. Whether he finds hers a sufficiently rich nature, intellectually and emotionally, for his own, I know not, but he seems occasionally to be disappointed at her simple views of things. Does he really feel such love for her at this moment as he no doubt believes himself to be feeling, and as he no doubt hopes to feel for the remainder of his life towards her?

It was a curious thing he told me when we were left for a few minutes alone; that Caroline had alluded so slightly to me in her conversation and letters that he had not realized my presence in the house here at all. But, of course, it was only natural that she should write and talk most about herself. I suppose it was on account of the fact of his being taken in some measure unawares, that I caught him on two or three occasions regarding me fixedly in a way that disquieted me somewhat, having been lately in so little society; till my glance aroused him from his reverie, and he looked elsewhere in some confusion. It was fortunate that he did so, and thus failed to notice my own. It shows that he, too, is not particularly a society person.

May 10. – Have had another interesting conversation with M. de la Feste on schools of landscape painting in the drawing-room after dinner this evening – my father having fallen asleep, and left nobody but Caroline and myself for Charles to talk to. I did not mean to say so much to him, and had taken a volume of *Modern Painters* from the bookcase to occupy myself with, while leaving the two lovers to themselves; but he would include me in his audience, and I was obliged to lay the book aside. However, I insisted on keeping Caroline in the conversation, though her views on pictorial art were only too charmingly crude and primitive.

To-morrow, if fine, we are all three going to Wherryborne Wood, where Charles will give us practical illustrations of the principles of colouring that he has enumerated to-night. I am determined not to occupy his attention to the exclusion of Caroline, and my plan is that when we are in the dense part of the wood I will lag behind, and slip away, and leave them to return by themselves. I suppose the reason of his attentiveness to me lies in his simply wishing to win the good opinion of one who is so closely united to Caroline, and so likely to influence her good opinion of him.

May 11. *Late*. – I cannot sleep, and in desperation have lit my candle and taken up my pen. My restlessness is occasioned by what has occurred to-day, which at first I did not mean to write down, or trust to any heart but my own. We went to Wherryborne Wood – Caroline, Charles and I, as we had intended – and walked all three along the green track through the midst, Charles in the middle between Caroline and myself. Presently I found that, as usual, he and I were the only talkers, Caroline amusing herself by observing birds and squirrels as she walked docilely alongside her betrothed. Having noticed this I dropped behind at the first opportunity and slipped among the trees, in a direction in which I knew I should find another path that would take me home. Upon this track I by-and-by emerged, and walked along it in silent thought till, at a bend, I suddenly encountered M. de la Feste standing stock still and smiling thoughtfully at me.

'Where is Caroline?' said I.

'Only a little way off,' says he. 'When we missed you from behind us we thought you might have mistaken the direction we had followed, so she has gone one way to find you and I have come this way.'

We then went back to find Caroline, but could not discover her anywhere, and the upshot was that he and I were wandering about the woods alone for more than an hour. On reaching home we found she had given us up after searching a little while, and arrived there some time before. I should not be so disturbed by the incident if I had not perceived that, during her absence from us, he did not make any earnest effort to rediscover her; and in answer to my repeated expressions of wonder as to whither she could have wandered he only said, 'Oh, she's quite safe; she told me she knew the way home from any part of this wood. Let us go on with our talk. I assure you I value this privilege of being with one I so much admire more than you imagine'; and other things of that kind. I was so foolish as to show a little perturbation – I cannot tell why I did not control myself; and I think he noticed that I was not cool. Caroline has, with her simple good faith, thought nothing of the occurrence; yet altogether I am not satisfied.

V. HER SITUATION IS A TRYING ONE

May 15. – The more I think of it day after day, the more convinced I am that my suspicions are true. He is too interested in me – well, in plain words, loves me; or, not to degrade that phrase, has a wild passion for me; and his affection for Caroline is that towards a sister only. That is the distressing truth; how it has come about I cannot tell, and it wears upon me.

A hundred little circumstances have revealed this to me, and the longer I dwell upon it the more agitating does the consideration become. Heaven only can help me out of the terrible difficulty in which this places me. I have done nothing to encourage him to be faithless to her. I have studiously kept out of his way; have persistently refused to be a third in their interviews. Yet all to no purpose. Some fatality has seemed to rule, ever since he came to the house, that this disastrous inversion of things should arise. If I had only foreseen the possibility of it before he arrived, how gladly would I have departed on some visit or other to the meanest friend to hinder such an apparent treachery. But I blindly welcomed him – indeed, made myself particularly agreeable to him for her sake.

There is no possibility of my suspicions being wrong; not until they have reached absolute certainty have I dared even to admit the truth to myself. His conduct to-day would have proved them true had I entertained no previous apprehensions. Some photographs of myself came for me by post, and they were handed round at the breakfast-table and criticized. I put them temporarily on a side-table, and did not remember them until an hour afterwards when I was in my own room. On going to fetch them I discovered him standing at the table with his back towards the door bending over the photographs, one of which he raised to his lips.

The witnessing this act so frightened me that I crept away to escape observation. It was the climax to a series of slight and significant actions all tending to the same conclusion. The question for me now is, what am I to do? To go away is what first occurs to me, but what reason can I give Caroline and my father for such a step? Besides, it might precipitate some sort of catastrophe by driving Charles to desperation. For the present, therefore, I have decided that I can only wait, though his contiguity is strangely disturbing to me now, and I hardly retain strength of mind to encounter him. How will the distressing complication end?

May 19. – And so it has come! My mere avoidance of him has precipitated the worst issue – a declaration. I had occasion to go into the kitchen-garden to gather some of the double ragged-robins which grew in a corner there. Almost as soon as I had entered I heard footsteps without. The door opened and shut, and I turned to behold him just inside it. As the garden is closed by four walls and the gardener was absent, the spot ensured absolute privacy. He came along the path by the asparagus-bed, and overtook me.

'You know why I come, Alicia?' said he, in a tremulous voice.

I said nothing, and hung my head, for by his tone I did know.

'Yes,' he went on, 'it is you I love; my sentiment towards your sister is one of affection too, but protective, tutelary affection – no more. Say what you will I cannot help it. I mistook my feeling for her, and I know how much I am to blame for my want of self-knowledge. I have fought against this discovery night and day; but it cannot be concealed. Why did I ever see you, since I could not see you till I had committed myself? At the moment my eyes beheld you on that day of my arrival, I said, "This is the woman for whom my manhood has waited." Ever since an unaccountable fascination has riveted my heart to you. Answer one word!'

'O, M. de la Feste!' I burst out. What I said more I cannot remember, but I suppose that the misery I was in showed pretty plainly, for he said, 'Something must be done to let her know; perhaps I have mistaken her affection, too; but all depends upon what you feel.'

'I cannot tell what I feel,' said I, 'except that this seems terrible treachery; and every moment that I stay with you here makes it worse! ... Try to keep faith with her – her young heart is tender; believe me there is no mistake in the quality of her love for you. Would there were! This would kill her if she knew it!'

He sighed heavily. 'She ought never to be my wife,' he said. 'Leaving my own happiness out of the question, it would be a cruelty to her to unite her to me.'

I said I could not hear such words from him, and begged him in tears to go away; he obeyed, and I heard the garden door shut behind him. What is to be the end of the announcement, and the fate of Caroline?

May 20. – I put a good deal on paper yesterday, and yet not all. I was, in truth, hoping against hope, against conviction, against too conscious self-judgment. I scarcely dare own the truth now, yet it relieves my aching heart to set it down. Yes, I love him – that is the dreadful fact, and I can no longer parry, evade, or deny it to myself, though to the rest of the world it can never be owned. I love Caroline's betrothed, and he loves me. It is no yesterday's passion, cultivated by our converse; it came at first sight, independently of my will; and my talk with him yesterday made rather against it than for it, but, alas, did not quench it. God forgive us both for this terrible treachery.

May 25. – All is vague; our courses shapeless. He comes and goes, being occupied, ostensibly at least, with sketching in his tent in the wood. Whether he and she see each other privately I cannot tell, but I rather think they do not; that she sadly awaits him, and he does not appear. Not a sign from him that my repulse has done him any good, or that he will endeavour to keep faith with her. O, if I only had the compulsion of a god, and the self-sacrifice of a martyr!

May 31. – It has all ended – or rather this act of the sad drama has ended – in nothing. He has left us. No day for the fulfilment of the engagement with Caroline is named, my father not being the man to press anyone on such a matter, or, indeed, to interfere in any way. We two girls are, in fact, quite defenceless in a case of this kind; lovers may come when they choose, and desert when they choose; poor father is too urbane to utter a word of remonstrance or inquiry. Moreover, as the approved of my dead mother, M. de la Feste has a sort of autocratic power with my father, who holds it unkind to her memory to have an opinion about him. I, feeling it my duty, asked M. de la Feste at the last moment about the engagement, in a voice I could not keep firm.

'Since the death of your mother all has been indefinite – all!' he said gloomily. That was the whole. Possibly, Wherryborne Rectory may see him no more.

June 7. – M. de la Feste has written – one letter to her, one to me. Hers could not have been very warm, for she did not brighten on reading it. Mine was an ordinary note of friendship, filling an ordinary sheet of paper, which I handed over to Caroline when I had finished looking it through. But there was a scrap of paper in the bottom of the envelope, which I dared not show anyone. This scrap is his real letter: I scanned it alone in my room, trembling, hot and cold by turns. He tells me he is very wretched; that he deplores what has happened, but was helpless. Why did I let him see me, if only to make him faithless? Alas, alas!

June 21. – My dear Caroline has lost appetite, spirits, health. Hope deferred maketh the heart sick. His letters to her grow colder – if indeed he has written more than one. He has refrained from writing again to me – he knows it is no use. Altogether the situation that he and she and I are in is melancholy in the extreme. Why are human hearts so perverse?

VI. HER INGENUITY INSTIGATES HER

September 19. – Three months of anxious care – till at length I have taken the extreme step of writing to him. Our chief distress has been caused by the state of poor Caroline, who, after sinking by degrees into such extreme weakness as to make it doubtful if she can ever recover full vigour, has to-day been taken much worse. Her position is very critical. The doctor says plainly that she is dying of a broken heart – and that even the removal of the cause may not now restore her. Ought I to have written to Charles sooner? But how could I when she forbade me? It was her pride only which instigated her, and I should not have obeyed.

Sept. 26. – Charles has arrived and has seen her. He is shocked, conscience-stricken, remorseful. I have told him that he can do no good beyond cheering her by his presence. I do not know what he thinks of proposing to her if she gets better, but he says little to her at present: indeed he dares not: his words agitate her dangerously.

Sept. 28. – After a struggle between duty and selfishness, such as I pray to Heaven I may never have to undergo again, I have asked him for pity's sake to make her his wife, here and now, as she lies. I said to him that the poor child would not trouble him long; and such a solemnization would soothe her last hours as nothing else could do. He said that he would willingly do so, and had thought of it himself; but for one forbidding reason: in the event of her death as his wife he can never marry me, her sister, according to our laws. I started at his words. He went on: 'On the other hand, if I were sure that immediate marriage with me would save her life, I would not refuse, for possibly I might after a while, and out of sight of you, make myself fairly content with one of so sweet a disposition as hers; but if, as is probable, neither my marrying her nor any other act can avail to save her life, by so doing I lose both her and you.' I could not answer him.

Sept. 29. – He continued firm in his reasons for refusal till this morning, and then I became possessed with an idea, which I at once propounded to him. It was that he should at least consent to a *form* of marriage with Caroline, in consideration of her love; a form which need not be a legal union, but one which would satisfy her sick and enfeebled soul. Such things have been done, and the sentiment of feeling herself his would inexpressibly comfort her mind, I am sure. Then, if she is taken from us, I should not have lost the power of becoming his lawful wife at some future day, if it indeed should be deemed expedient; if, on the other hand, she lives, he can on her recovery inform her of the incompleteness of their marriage contract, the ceremony can be repeated, and I can, and I am sure willingly would, avoid troubling them with my presence till gray hairs and wrinkles make his unfortunate passion for me a thing of the past. I put all this before him; but he demurred.

Sept. 30. – I have urged him again. He says he will consider. It is no time to mince matters, and as a further inducement I have offered to enter into a solemn engagement to marry him myself a year after her death.

Sept. 30. Later. – An agitating interview. He says he will agree to whatever I propose, the three possibilities and our contingent acts being recorded as follows: First, in the event of dear Caroline being taken from us, I marry him on the expiration of a year: Second, in the forlorn chance of her recovery I take upon myself the responsibility of explaining to Caroline the true nature of the ceremony he has gone through with her, that it was done at my suggestion to make her happy at once, before a special licence could be obtained, and that a public ceremony at church is awaiting her: Third, in the unlikely event of her cooling, and refusing to repeat the ceremony with him, I leave England, join him abroad, and there wed him, agreeing not to live in England again till Caroline has either married another or regards her attachment to Charles as a bygone matter. I have thought over these conditions, and have agreed to them all as they stand.

11 p.m. – I do not much like this scheme, after all. For one thing, I have just sounded my father on it before parting with him for the night, my impression having been that he would see no objection. But he says he could on no account countenance any such unreal proceeding; how-

ever good our intentions, and even though the poor girl were dying, it
would not be right. So I sadly seek my pillow.

October 1. – I am sure my father is wrong in his view. Why is it not
right, if it would be balm to Caroline's wounded soul, and if a real
ceremony is absolutely refused by Charles – moreover is hardly practicable in the difficulty of getting a special licence, if he were agreed? My
father does not know, or will not believe, that Caroline's attachment has
been the cause of her hopeless condition. But that it is so, and that the
form of words would give her inexpressible happiness, I know well; for
I whispered tentatively in her ear on such marriages, and the effect was
great. Henceforth my father cannot be taken into confidence on the
subject of Caroline. He does not understand her.

12 o'clock noon. – I have taken advantage of my father's absence to-day
to confide my secret notion to a thoughtful young man, who called here
this morning to speak to my father. He is the Mr Theophilus Higham,
of whom I have already had occasion to speak – a Scripture reader in
the next town, and is soon going to be ordained. I told him the pitiable
case, and my remedy. He says ardently that he will assist me – would do
anything for me (he is, in truth, an admirer of mine); he sees no wrong
in such an act of charity. He is coming again to the house this afternoon
before my father returns, to carry out the idea. I have spoken to Charles,
who promises to be ready. I must now break the news to Caroline.

11 o'clock p.m. – I have been in too much excitement till now to set
down the result. We have accomplished our plan; and though I feel like
a guilty sinner, I am glad. My father, of course, is not to be informed as
yet. Caroline has had a seraphic expression upon her wasted, transparent
face ever since. I should hardly be surprised if it really saved her life
even now, and rendered a legitimate union necessary between them. In
that case my father can be informed of the whole proceeding, and in the
face of such wonderful success cannot disapprove. Meanwhile poor
Charles has not lost the possibility of taking unworthy me to fill her
place should she— But I cannot contemplate that alternative unmoved,
and will not write it. Charles left for the South of Europe immediately
after the ceremony. He was in a high-strung, throbbing, almost wild
state of mind at first, but grew calmer under my exhortations. I had to
pay the penalty of receiving a farewell kiss from him, which I much
regret, considering its meaning; but he took me so unexpectedly, and
in a moment was gone.

Oct. 6. – She certainly is better, and even when she found that Charles had been suddenly obliged to leave, she received the news quite cheerfully. The doctor says that her apparent improvement may be delusive; but I think our impressing upon her the necessity of keeping what has occurred a secret from papa, and everybody, helps to give her a zest for life.

Oct. 8. – She is still mending. I am glad to have saved her – my only sister – if I have done so; though I shall now never become Charles's wife.

VII. A SURPRISE AWAITS HER

Feb. 5. – Writing has been absolutely impossible for a long while; but I now reach a stage at which it seems possible to jot down a line. Caroline's recovery, extending over four months, has been very engrossing; at first slow, latterly rapid. But a fearful complication of affairs attends it!

> O what a tangled web we weave
> When first we practise to deceive!

Charles has written reproachfully to me from Venice, where he is. He says how can he fulfil in the real what he has enacted in the counterfeit, while he still loves me ? Yet how, on the other hand, can he leave it unfulfilled ? All this time I have not told her, and up to this minute she believes that he has indeed taken her for better, for worse, till death them do part. It is a harassing position for me, and all three. In the awful approach of death, one's judgment loses its balance, and we do anything to meet the exigencies of the moment, with a single eye to the one who excites our sympathy, and from whom we seem on the brink of being separated for ever.

Had he really married her at that time all would be settled now. But he took too much thought; she might have died, and then he had his reason. If indeed it had turned out so, I should now be perhaps a sad woman; but not a tempest-tossed one. . . . The possibility of his claiming me after all is what lies at the root of my agitation. Everything hangs by a thread. Suppose I tell her the marriage was a mockery; suppose she is indignant with me and with him for the deception – and then ? Otherwise, suppose she is not indignant but forgives all; he is bound to marry her; and honour constrains me to urge him thereto, in spite of what he protests, and to smooth the way to this issue by my method of informing her. I have meant to tell her the last month – ever since she has been strong enough to bear such tidings; but I have been without the power – the moral force. Surely I must write, and get him to come and assist me.

March 14. – She continually wonders why he does not come, the five months of his enforced absence having expired; and still more she wonders why he does not write oftener. His last letter was cold, she says, and she fears he regrets his marriage, which he may only have celebrated with her for pity's sake, thinking she was sure to die. It makes one's heart bleed to hear her hovering thus so near the truth, and yet never discerning its actual shape.

A minor trouble besets me, too, in the person of the young Scripture reader, whose conscience pricks him for the part he played. Surely I am punished, if ever woman were, for a too ingenious perversion of her better judgment!

April 2. – She is practically well. The faint pink revives in her cheek, though it is not quite so full as heretofore. But she still wonders what she can have done to offend 'her dear husband', and I have been obliged to tell the smallest part of the truth – an unimportant fragment of the whole, in fact, I said that I feared for the moment he might regret the precipitancy of the act, which her illness caused, his affairs not having been quite sufficiently advanced for marriage just then, though he will doubtless come to her as soon as he has a home ready. Meanwhile I have written to him, peremptorily, to come and relieve me in this awful dilemma. He will find no note of love in that.

April 10. – To my alarm the letter I lately addressed to him at Venice, where he is staying, as well as the last one she sent him, have received no reply. She thinks he is ill. I do not quite think that, but I wish we could hear from him. Perhaps the peremptoriness of my words had offended him; it grieves me to think it possible. *I* offend him! But too much of this. I *must* tell her the truth, or she may in her ignorance commit herself to some course or other that may be ruinously compromising. She said plaintively just now that if he could see her, and know how occupied with him and him alone is her every waking hour, she is sure he would forgive her the wicked presumption of becoming his wife. Very sweet all that, and touching. I could not conceal my tears.

April 15. – The house is in confusion; my father is angry and distressed, and I am distracted. Caroline has disappeared – gone away secretly. I cannot help thinking that I know where she is gone to. How guilty I seem, and how innocent she! O that I had told her before now!

1 o'clock. – No trace of her as yet. We find also that the little waiting-maid we have here in training has disappeared with Caroline, and there is not much doubt that Caroline, fearing to travel alone, has induced this girl to go with her as companion. I am almost sure she has started in desperation to find him, and that Venice is her goal. Why should she run away, if not to join her husband, as she thinks him? Now that I consider, there have been indications of this wish in her for days, as in birds of passage there lurk signs of their incipient intention; and yet I did not think she would have taken such an extreme step, unaided, and without consulting me. I can only jot down the bare facts – I have no time for reflections. But fancy Caroline travelling across the continent of Europe with a chit of a girl, who will be more of a charge than an assistance! They will be a mark for every marauder who encounters them.

Evening: 8 o'clock. – Yes, it is as I surmised. She has gone to join him. A note posted by her in Budmouth Regis at daybreak has reached me this afternoon – thanks to the fortunate chance of one of the servants calling for letters in town to-day, or I should not have got it until to-morrow. She merely asserts her determination of going to him, and has started privately, that nothing may hinder her; stating nothing about her route. That such a gentle thing should suddenly become so calmly resolute quite surprises me. Alas, he may have left Venice – she may not find him for weeks – may not at all.

My father, on learning the facts, bade me at once have everything ready by nine this evening, in time to drive to the train that meets the night steam-boat. This I have done, and there being an hour to spare before we start, I relieve the suspense of waiting by taking up my pen. He says overtake her we must, and calls Charles the hardest of names. He believes, of course, that she is merely an infatuated girl rushing off to meet her lover; and how can the wretched I tell him that she is more, and in a sense better than that – yet not sufficiently more and better to make this flight to Charles anything but a still greater danger to her than a mere lover's impulse? We shall go by way of Paris, and we think we may overtake her there. I hear my father walking restlessly up and down the hall, and can write no more.

VIII. SHE TRAVELS IN PURSUIT

April 16. Evening, Paris, Hôtel ——. – There is no overtaking her at this place; but she has been here, as I thought, no other hotel in Paris being known to her. We go on to-morrow morning.

April 18. Venice. – A morning of adventures and emotions which leave me sick and weary, and yet unable to sleep, though I have lain down on the sofa of my room for more than an hour in the attempt. I therefore make up my diary to date in a hurried fashion, for the sake of the riddance it affords to ideas which otherwise remain suspended hotly in the brain.

We arrived here this morning in broad sunlight, which lit up the sea-girt buildings as we approached so that they seemed like a city of cork floating raft-like on the smooth, blue deep. But I only glanced from the carriage window at the lovely scene, and we were soon across the intervening water and inside the railway station. When we got to the front steps the row of black gondolas and the shouts of the gondoliers so bewildered my father that he was understood to require two gondolas instead of one with two oars, and so I found him in one and myself in another. We got this righted after a while, and were rowed at once to the hotel on the Riva degli Schiavoni where M. de la Feste had been staying when we last heard from him, the way being down the Grand Canal for some distance, under the Rialto, and then by narrow canals which eventually brought us under the Bridge of Sighs – harmonious to our moods! – and out again into open water. The scene was purity itself as to colour, but it was cruel that I should behold it for the first time under such circumstances.

As soon as we entered the hotel, which is an old-fashioned place, like most places here, where people are taken *en pension* as well as the ordinary way, I rushed to the framed list of visitors hanging in the hall, and in a moment I saw Charles's name upon it among the rest. But she was our chief thought. I turned to the hall porter, and – knowing that she would have travelled as 'Madame de la Feste' – I asked for her under that name, without my father hearing. (He, poor soul, was making confused inquiries outside the door about 'an English lady', as if there were not a score of English ladies at hand.)

'She has just come,' said the porter. 'Madame came by the very early train this morning, when Monsieur was asleep, and she requested us not to disturb him. She is now in her room.'

Whether Caroline had seen us from the window, or overheard me, I do not know, but at that moment I heard footsteps on the bare marble stairs, and she appeared in person descending.

'Caroline!' I exclaimed, 'why have you done this?' and rushed up to her.

She did not answer; but looked down to hide her emotion, which she conquered after the lapse of a few seconds, putting on a practical tone that belied her.

'I am just going to my husband,' she said. 'I have not yet seen him. I have not been here long.' She condescended to give no further reason for her movements, and made as if to move on. I implored her to come into a private room where I could speak to her in confidence, but she objected. However, the dining-room, close at hand, was quite empty at this hour, and I got her inside and closed the door. I do not know how I began my explanation, or how I ended it, but I told her briefly and brokenly enough that the marriage was not real.

'Not real?' she said vacantly.

'It is not,' said I. 'You will find that it is all as I say.'

She could not believe my meaning even then. 'Not his wife?' she cried. 'It is impossible. What am I, then?'

I added more details, and reiterated the reason for my conduct as well as I could; but Heaven knows how very difficult I found it to feel a jot more justification for it in my own mind than she did in hers.

The revulsion of feeling, as soon as she really comprehended all, was most distressing. After her grief had in some measure spent itself she turned against both him and me.

'Why should I have been deceived like this?' she demanded, with a bitter haughtiness of which I had not deemed such a tractable creature capable. 'Do you suppose that *anything* could justify such an imposition? What, O what a snare you have spread for me!'

I murmured, 'Your life seemed to require it', but she did not hear me. She sank down in a chair, covered her face, and then my father came in. 'O, here you are!' he said. 'I could not find you. And Caroline!'

'And were *you*, papa, a party to this strange deed of kindness?'

'To what?' said he.

Then out it all came, and for the first time he was made acquainted with the fact that the scheme for soothing her illness, which I had sounded him upon, had been really carried out. In a moment he sided with Caroline. My repeated assurance that my motive was good availed less than nothing. In a minute or two Caroline arose and went abruptly out of the room, and my father followed her, leaving me alone to my reflections.

I was so bent upon finding Charles immediately that I did not notice whither they went. The servants told me that M. de la Feste was just outside smoking, and one of them went to look for him, I following; but before we had gone many steps he came out of the hotel behind me. I expected him to be amazed; but he showed no surprise at seeing me, though he showed another kind of feeling to an extent which dismayed me. I may have revealed something similar; but I struggled hard against all emotion, and as soon as I could I told him she had come. He simply said 'Yes' in a low voice.

'You know it, Charles?' said I.

'I have just learnt it,' he said.

'O, Charles,' I went on, 'having delayed completing your marriage with her till now, I fear – it has become a serious position for us. Why did you not reply to our letters?'

'I was purposing to reply in person: I did not know how to address her on the point – how to address you. But what has become of her?'

'She has gone off with my father,' said I; 'indignant with you, and scorning me.'

He was silent: and I suggested that we should follow them, pointing out the direction which I fancied their gondola had taken. As the one we got into was doubly manned we soon came in view of their two figures ahead of us, while they were not likely to observe us, our boat having the 'felze' on, while theirs was uncovered. They shot into a narrow canal just beyond the Giardino Reale, and by the time we were floating up between its slimy walls we saw them getting out of their gondola at the steps which lead up near the end of the Via 22 Marzo. When we reached the same spot they were walking up and down the Via in consultation. Getting out he stood on the lower steps watching them. I watched him. He seemed to fall into a reverie.

'Will you not go and speak to her?' said I at length.

He assented, and went forward. Still he did not hasten to join them, but, screened by a projecting window, observed their musing converse. At last he looked back at me; whereupon I pointed forward, and he in obedience stepped out, and met them face to face. Caroline flushed hot, bowed haughtily to him, turned away, and taking my father's arm violently, led him off before he had had time to use his own judgment. They disappeared into a narrow *calle*, or alley, leading to the back of the buildings on the Grand Canal.

M. de la Feste came slowly back; as he stepped in beside me I realized my position so vividly that my heart might almost have been heard to beat. The third condition had arisen – the least expected by either of us. She had refused him; he was free to claim me.

We returned in the boat together. He seemed quite absorbed till we had turned the angle into the Grand Canal, when he broke the silence. 'She spoke very bitterly to you in the *salle-à-manger*,' he said. 'I do not think she was quite warranted in speaking so to you, who had nursed her so tenderly.'

'O, but I think she was,' I answered. 'It was there I told her what had been done; she did not know till then.'

'She was very dignified – very striking,' he murmured. 'You were more.'

'But how do you know what passed between us ?' said I. He then told me that he had seen and heard all. The dining-room was divided by folding-doors from an inner portion, and he had been sitting in the latter part when we entered the outer, so that our words were distinctly audible.

'But, dear Alicia,' he went on, 'I was more impressed by the affection of your apology to her than by anything else. And do you know that now the conditions have arisen which give me liberty to consider you my affianced ?' I had been expecting this, but yet was not prepared. I stammered out that we would not discuss it then.

'Why not ?' said he. 'Do you know that we may marry here and now ? She has cast off both you and me.'

'It cannot be,' said I firmly. 'She has not been fairly asked to be your wife in fact – to repeat the service lawfully; and until that has been done it would be grievous sin in me to accept you.'

I had not noticed where the gondoliers were rowing us. I suppose he had given them some direction unheard by me, for as I resigned myself in despairing indolence to the motion of the gondola, I perceived that it was taking us up the Canal, and, turning into a side opening near the Palazzo Grimani, drew up at some steps near the end of a large church.

'Where are we ?' said I.

'It is the Church of the Frari,' he replied. 'We might be married there.

At any rate, let us go inside, and grow calm, and decide what to do.'

When we had entered I found that whether a place to marry in or not, it was one to depress. The word which Venice speaks most constantly – decay – was in a sense accentuated here. The whole large fabric itself seemed sinking into an earth which was not solid enough to bear it. Cobwebbed cracks zigzagged the walls, and similar webs clouded the window-panes. A sickly-sweet smell pervaded the aisles. After walking about with him a little while in embarrassing silences, divided only by his cursory explanations of the monuments and other objects, and almost fearing he might produce a marriage licence, I went to a door in the south transept which opened into the sacristy.

I glanced through it, towards the small altar at the upper end. The place was empty save of one figure; and she was kneeling here in front of the beautiful altarpiece by Bellini. Beautiful though it was she seemed not to see it. She was weeping and praying as though her heart was broken. She was my sister Caroline. I beckoned to Charles, and he came to my side, and looked through the door with me.

'Speak to her,' said I. 'She will forgive you.'

I gently pushed him through the doorway, and went back into the transept, down the nave, and onward to the west door. There I saw my father, to whom I spoke. He answered severely that, having first obtained comfortable quarters in a *pension* on the Grand Canal, he had gone back to the hotel on the Riva degli Schiavoni to find me; but that I was not there. He was now waiting for Caroline, to accompany her back to the *pension*, at which she had requested to be left to herself as much as possible till she could regain some composure.

I told him that it was useless to dwell on what was past, that I no doubt had erred, that the remedy lay in the future and their marriage. In this he quite agreed with me, and on my informing him that M. de la Feste was at that moment with Caroline in the sacristy, he assented to my proposal that we should leave them to themselves, and return together to await them at the *pension*, where he had also engaged a room for me. This we did, and going up to the chamber he had chosen for me, which overlooked the Canal, I leant from the window to watch for the gondola that should contain Charles and my sister.

They were not long in coming. I recognized them by the colour of her sunshade as soon as they turned the bend on my right hand. They were side by side of necessity, but there was no conversation between them, and I thought that she looked flushed and he pale. When they were

rowed in to the steps of our house he handed her up. I fancied she might
have refused his assistance, but she did not. Soon I heard her pass my
door, and wishing to know the result of their interview I went downstairs, seeing that the gondola had not put off with him. He was turning
from the door, but not towards the water, intending apparently to walk
home by way of the *calle* which led into the Via 22 Marzo.

'Has she forgiven you?' said I.

'I have not asked her,' he said.

'But you are bound to do so,' I told him.

He paused, and then said, 'Alicia, let us understand each other. Do
you mean to tell me, once for all, that if your sister is willing to become
my wife you absolutely make way for her, and will not entertain any
thought of what I suggested to you any more?'

'I do tell you so,' said I with dry lips. 'You belong to her – how can I
do otherwise?'

'Yes; it is so; it is purely a question of honour,' he returned. 'Very
well then, honour shall be my word, and not my love. I will put the
question to her frankly; if she says "Yes", the marriage shall be. But
not here. It shall be at your own house in England.'

'When?' said I.

'I will accompany her there,' he replied, 'and it shall be within a week
of her return. I have nothing to gain by delay. But I will not answer for
the consequences.'

'What do you mean?' said I. He made no reply, went away, and I
came back to my room.

IX. SHE WITNESSES THE END

April 20. Milan, 10.30 p.m. – We are thus far on our way homeward. I,
being decidedly *de trop*, travel apart from the rest as much as I can.
Having dined at the hotel here, I went out by myself, regardless of the
proprieties, for I could not stay in. I walked at a leisurely pace along
the Via Allesandro Manzoni till my eye was caught by the grand Galleria
Vittorio Emanuele, and I entered under the high glass arcades till I
reached the central octagon, where I sat down on one of a group of
chairs placed there. Becoming accustomed to the stream of promenaders,
I soon observed, seated on the chairs opposite, Caroline and Charles.

This was the first occasion on which I had seen them *en tête à tête* since my conversation with him. She soon caught sight of me; averted her eyes; then, apparently abandoning herself to an impulse, she jumped up from her seat and came across to me. We had not spoken to each other since the meeting in Venice.

'Alicia,' she said, sitting down by my side, 'Charles asks me to forgive you, and I do forgive you.'

I pressed her hand, with tears in my eyes, and said, 'And do you forgive him?'

'Yes,' said she shyly.

'And what's the result?' said I.

'We are to be married directly we reach home.'

This was almost the whole of our conversation; she walked home with me, Charles following a little way behind, though she kept turning her head, as if anxious that he should overtake us. 'Honour and not love' seemed to ring in my ears. So matters stand. Caroline is again happy.

April 25. – We have reached home, Charles with us. Events are now moving in silent speed, almost with velocity, indeed; and I sometimes feel oppressed by the strange and preternatural ease which seems to accompany their flow. Charles is staying at the neighbouring town; he is only waiting for the marriage licence; when obtained he is to come here, be quietly married to her, and carry her off. It is rather resignation than content which sits on his face; but he has not spoken a word more to me on the burning subject, or deviated one hair's breadth from the course he laid down. They may be happy in time to come: I hope so. But I cannot shake off depression.

May 6. – Eve of the wedding. Caroline is serenely happy, though not blithe. But there is nothing to excite anxiety about her. I wish I could say the same of him. He comes and goes like a ghost, and yet nobody seems to observe this strangeness in his mien. I could not help being here for the ceremony; but my absence would have resulted in less disquiet on his part, I believe. However, I may be wrong in attributing causes: my father simply says that Charles and Caroline have as good a chance of being happy as other people. Well, to-morrow settles all.

May 7. – They are married: we have just returned from church. Charles looked so pale this morning that my father asked him if he was ill. He said, 'No: only a slight headache'; and we started for the church. There was no hitch or hindrance; and the thing is done.

4 p.m. – They ought to have set out on their journey by this time; but there is an unaccountable delay. Charles went out half-an-hour ago, and has not yet returned. Caroline is waiting in the hall; but I am dreadfully afraid they will miss the train. I suppose the trifling hindrance is of no account; and yet I am full of misgivings. . . .

Sept. 14. – Four months have passed; *only* four months! It seems like years. Can it be that only seventeen weeks ago I set on this paper the fact of their marriage? I am now an aged woman by comparison!

On that never to be forgotten day we waited and waited, and Charles did not return. At six o'clock, when poor little Caroline had gone back to her room in a state of suspense impossible to describe, a man who worked in the water-meadows came to the house and asked for my father. He had an interview with him in the study. My father then rang his bell, and sent for me. I went down; and I then learnt the fatal news. Charles was no more. The waterman had been going to shut down the hatches of a weir in the meads when he saw a hat on the edge of the pool below, floating round and round in the eddy, and looking into the pool saw something strange at the bottom. He knew what it meant, and lowering the hatches so that the water was still, could distinctly see the body. It is needless to write particulars that were in the newspapers at the time. Charles was brought to the house, but he was dead.

We all feared for Caroline; and she suffered much; but strange to say, her suffering was purely of the nature of deep grief which found relief in sobbing and tears. It came out at the inquest that Charles had been accustomed to cross the meads to give an occasional half-crown to an old man who lived on the opposite hill, who had once been a landscape painter in an humble way till he lost his eyesight; and it was assumed that he had gone thither for the same purpose to-day, and to bid him farewell. On this information the coroner's jury found that his death had been caused by misadventure; and everybody believes to this hour that he was drowned while crossing the weir to relieve the old man. Except one: she believes in no accident. After the stunning effect of the first news, I thought it strange that he should have chosen to go on such an errand at the last moment, and to go personally, when there was so little time to spare, since any gift could have been so easily sent by another hand. Further reflection has convinced me that this step out of life was as much a part of the day's plan as was the wedding in the church hard by. They were the two halves of his complete intention when he gave me on the Grand Canal that assurance which I shall never forget: 'Very well, then; honour shall be my word, not love. If she says "Yes", the marriage shall be.'

I do not know why I should have made this entry at this particular time; but it has occurred to me to do it – to complete, in a measure, that part of my desultory chronicle which relates to the love-story of my sister and Charles. She lives on meekly in her grief, and will probably outlive it; while I – but never mind me.

X. SHE ADDS A NOTE LONG AFTER

Five years later. – I have lighted upon this old diary, which it has interested me to look over, containing, as it does, records of the time when life shone more warmly in my eye than it does now. I am impelled to add one sentence to round off its record of the past. About a year ago my sister Caroline, after a persistent wooing, accepted the hand and heart of Theophilus Higham, once the blushing young Scripture reader who assisted at the substitute for a marriage I planned, and now the fully-ordained curate of the next parish. His penitence for the part he played ended in love. We have all now made atonement for our sins against her: may she be deceived no more.

1887

The Grave by the Handpost

I NEVER pass through Chalk-Newton without turning to regard the neighbouring upland, at a point where a lane crosses the lone straight highway dividing this from the next parish; a sight which does not fail to recall the event that once happened there; and, though it may seem superfluous, at this date, to disinter more memories of village history, the whispers of that spot may claim to be preserved.

It was on a dark, yet mild and exceptionally dry evening at Christmas-time (according to the testimony of William Dewy of Mellstock, Michael Mail, and others), that the choir of Chalk-Newton – a large parish situate about half-way between the towns of Ivell and Casterbridge, and now a railway station – left their homes just before midnight to repeat their annual harmonies under the windows of the local population. The band of instrumentalists and singers was one of the largest in the county; and, unlike the smaller and finer Mellstock string-band, which eschewed all but the catgut, it included brass and reed performers at full Sunday services, and reached all across the west gallery.

On this night there were two or three violins, two 'cellos, a tenor viol, double bass, hautboy, clarionets, serpent, and seven singers. It was, however, not the choir's labours, but what its members chanced to witness, that particularly marked the occasion.

They had pursued their rounds for many years without meeting with any incident of an unusual kind, but to-night, according to the assertions of several, there prevailed, to begin with, an exceptionally solemn and thoughtful mood among two or three of the oldest in the band, as if they were thinking they might be joined by the phantoms of dead friends who had been of their number in earlier years, and now were mute in the churchyard under flattening mounds – friends who had shown greater zest for melody in their time than was shown in this; or that some past voice of a semi-transparent figure might quaver from some bedroom-window its acknowledgment of their nocturnal greeting, instead of a familiar living neighbour. Whether this were fact or fancy, the younger members of the choir met together with their customary thoughtlessness and buoyancy. When they had gathered by the stone stump of the cross in the middle of the village, near the White Horse Inn, which they made their starting-point, some one observed that they were full early, that it was not yet twelve o'clock. The local waits of those days mostly refrained from sounding a note before Christmas morning had astronomically arrived, and not caring to return to their beer, they decided to begin with some outlying cottages in Sidlinch Lane, where the people had no clocks, and would not know whether it were night or morning. In that direction they accordingly went; and as they ascended to higher ground their attention was attracted by a light beyond the houses, quite at the top of the lane.

The road from Chalk-Newton to Broad Sidlinch is about two miles long, and in the middle of its course, where it passes over the ridge dividing the two villages, it crosses at right angles, as has been stated, the lonely monotonous old highway known as Long Ash Lane, which runs, straight as a surveyor's line, many miles north and south of this spot, on the foundation of a Roman road, and has often been mentioned in these narratives. Though now quite deserted and grass-grown, at the beginning of the century it was well kept and frequented by traffic. The glimmering light appeared to come from the precise point where the roads intersected.

'I think I know what that mid mean!' one of the group remarked.

They stood a few moments, discussing the probability of the light having origin in an event of which rumours had reached them, and resolved to go up the hill.

Approaching the high land their conjectures were strengthened. Long Ash Lane cut athwart them, right and left; and they saw that at the junction of the four ways, under the handpost, a grave was dug, into which, as the choir drew nigh, a corpse had just been thrown by the four Sidlinch men employed for the purpose. The cart and horse which had brought the body thither stood silently by.

The singers and musicians from Chalk-Newton halted, and looked on while the gravediggers shovelled in and trod down the earth, till, the hole being filled, the latter threw their spades into the cart, and prepared to depart.

'Who mid ye be a-burying there?' asked Lot Swanhills in a raised voice. 'Not the sergeant?'

The Sidlinch men had been so deeply engrossed in their task that they had not noticed the lanterns of the Chalk-Newton choir till now.

'What – be you the Newton carol-singers?' returned the representatives of Sidlinch.

'Ay, sure. Can it be that it is old Sergeant Holway you've a-buried there?'

' 'Tis so. You've heard about it, then?'

The choir knew no particulars – only that he had shot himself in his apple-closet on the previous Sunday. 'Nobody seem'th to know what 'a did it for, 'a b'lieve? Leastwise, we don't know at Chalk-Newton,' continued Lot.

'O yes. It all came out at the inquest.'

The singers drew close, and the Sidlinch men, pausing to rest after their labours, told the story. 'It was all owing to that son of his, poor old man. It broke his heart.'

'But the son is a soldier, surely; now with his regiment in the East Indies?'

'Ay. And it have been rough with the army over there lately. 'Twas a pity his father persuaded him to go. But Luke shouldn't have twyted the sergeant o't, since 'a did it for the best.'

The circumstances, in brief, were these: The sergeant who had come to this lamentable end, father of the young soldier who had gone with his regiment to the East, had been singularly comfortable in his military experiences, these having ended long before the outbreak of the great war with France. On his discharge, after duly serving his time, he had returned to his native village, and married, and taken kindly to domestic life. But the war in which England next involved herself had cost him many frettings that age and infirmity prevented him from being ever again an active unit of the army. When his only son grew to young manhood, and the question arose of his going out in life, the lad expressed his wish to be a mechanic. But his father advised enthusiastically for the army.

'Trade is coming to nothing in these days,' he said. 'And if the war with the French lasts, as it will, trade will be still worse. The army, Luke – that's the thing for 'ee. 'Twas the making of me, and 'twill be the making of you. I hadn't half such a chance as you'll have in these splendid hotter times.'

Luke demurred, for he was a home-keeping, peace-loving youth. But, putting respectful trust in his father's judgment, he at length gave way, and enlisted in the —d Foot. In the course of a few weeks he was sent out to India to his regiment, which had distinguished itself in the East under General Wellesley.

But Luke was unlucky. News came home indirectly that he lay sick out there; and then on one recent day when his father was out walking, the old man had received tidings that a letter awaited him at Caster-bridge. The sergeant sent a special messenger the whole nine miles, and the letter was paid for and brought home; but though, as he had guessed, it came from Luke, its contents were of an unexpected tenor.

The letter had been written during a time of deep depression. Luke said that his life was a burden and a slavery, and bitterly reproached his father for advising him to embark on a career for which he felt unsuited. He found himself suffering fatigues and illnesses without gaining glory, and engaged in a cause which he did not understand or appreciate. If it had not been for his father's bad advice he, Luke, would now have been working comfortably at a trade in the village that he had never wished to leave.

After reading the letter the sergeant advanced a few steps till he was quite out of sight of everybody, and then sat down on the bank by the wayside.

When he arose half-an-hour later he looked withered and broken, and from that day his natural spirits left him. Wounded to the quick by his son's sarcastic stings, he indulged in liquor more and more frequently. His wife had died some years before this date, and the sergeant lived alone in the house which had been hers. One morning in the December under notice the report of a gun had been heard on his premises, and on entering the neighbours found him in a dying state. He had shot himself with an old firelock that he used for scaring birds; and from what he had said the day before, and the arrangements he had made for his decease, there was no doubt that his end had been deliberately planned, as a consequence of the despondency into which he had been thrown by his son's letter. The coroner's jury returned a verdict of *felo-de-se*.

'Here's his son's letter,' said one of the Sidlinch men. ' 'Twas found in his father's pocket. You can see by the state o't how many times he read it over. Howsomever, the Lord's will be done, since it must, whether or no.'

The grave was filled up and levelled, no mound being shaped over it. The Sidlinch men then bade the Chalk-Newton choir good-night, and departed with the cart in which they had brought the sergeant's body to the hill. When their tread had died away from the ear, and the wind swept over the isolated grave with its customary siffle of indifference, Lot Swanhills turned and spoke to old Richard Toller, the hautboy player.

' 'Tis hard upon a man, and he a wold sojer, to serve en so, Richard. Not that the sergeant was ever in a battle bigger than would go into a half-acre paddock, that's true. Still, his soul ought to hae as good a chance as another man's, all the same, hey?'

Richard replied that he was quite of the same opinion. 'What d'ye say to lifting up a carrel over his grave, as 'tis Christmas, and no hurry to begin down in parish, and 'twouldn't take up ten minutes, and not a soul up here to say us nay, or know anything about it?'

Lot nodded assent. 'The man ought to hae his chances,' he repeated.

'Ye may as well spet upon his grave, for all the good we shall do en by what we lift up, now he's got so far,' said Notton, the clarionet man and professed sceptic of the choir. 'But I'm agreed if the rest be.'

They thereupon placed themselves in a semicircle by the newly-stirred earth, and roused the dull air with the well-known Number Sixteen of their collection, which Lot gave out as being the one he thought best suited to the occasion and the mood: –

> He comes' the pri'-soners to' re-lease',
> In Sa'-tan's bon'-dage held'.

'Jown it – we've never played to a dead man afore,' said Ezra Catt-stock, when, having concluded the last verse, they stood reflecting for a breath or two. 'But it do seem more merciful than to go away and leave en, as they t'other fellers have done.'

'Now backalong to Newton, and by the time we get overright the pa'son's 'twill be half after twelve,' said the leader.

They had not, however, done more than gather up their instruments when the wind brought to their notice the noise of a vehicle rapidly driven up the same lane from Sidlinch which the gravediggers had lately retraced. To avoid being run over when moving on, they waited till the benighted traveller, whoever he might be, should pass them where they stood in the wider area of the Cross.

In half a minute the light of the lanterns fell upon a hired fly, drawn by a steaming and jaded horse. It reached the handpost, when a voice from the inside cried, 'Stop here!' The driver pulled rein. The carriage door was opened from within, and there leapt out a private soldier in the uniform of some line regiment. He looked around, and was apparently surprised to see the musicians standing there.

'Have you buried a man here?' he asked.

'No. We bain't Sidlinch folk, thank God; we be Newton choir. Though a man is just buried here, that's true; and we've raised a carrel over the poor mortal's natomy. What – do my eyes see before me young Luke Holway, that went wi' his regiment to the East Indies, or do I see his spirit straight from the battlefield? Be you the son that wrote the letter—'

'Don't – don't ask me. The funeral is over, then?'

'There wer no funeral, in a Christen manner of speaking. But's buried, sure enough. You must have met the men going back in the empty cart.'

'Like a dog in a ditch, and all through me!'

He remained silent, looking at the grave, and they could not help pitying him. 'My friends,' he said, 'I understand better now. You have, I suppose, in neighbourly charity, sung peace to his soul? I thank you, from my heart, for your kind pity. Yes; I am Sergeant Holway's miserable son – I'm the son who has brought about his father's death, as truly as if I had done it with my own hand!'

'No, no. Don't ye take on so, young man. He'd been naturally low for a good while, off and on, so we hear.'

'We were out in the East when I wrote to him. Everything had seemed to go wrong with me. Just after my letter had gone we were ordered home. That's how it is you see me here. As soon as we got into barracks at Casterbridge I heard o' this—. . . . Damn me! I'll dare to follow my father, and make away with myself, too. It is the only thing left to do!'

'Don't ye be rash, Luke Holway, I say again; but try to make amends by your future life. And maybe your father will smile a smile down from heaven upon 'ee for 't.

He shook his head. 'I don't know about that!' he answered bitterly.

'Try and be worthy of your father at his best. 'Tis not too late.'

'D' ye think not? I fancy it is! . . . Well, I'll turn it over. Thank you for your good counsel. I'll live for one thing, at any rate. I'll move father's body to a decent Christian churchyard, if I do it with my own hands. I can't save his life, but I can give him an honourable grave. He shan't lie in this accursed place!'

'Ay, as our pa'son says, 'tis a barbarous custom they keep up at

Sidlinch, and ought to be done away wi'. The man a' old soldier, too.
You see, our pa'son is not like yours at Sidlinch.'

'He says it is barbarous, does he? So it is!' cried the soldier. 'Now
hearken, my friends.' Then he proceeded to inquire if they would
increase his indebtedness to them by undertaking the removal, privately,
of the body of the suicide to the churchyard, not of Sidlinch, a parish he
now hated, but of Chalk-Newton. He would give them all he possessed
to do it.

Lot asked Ezra Cattstock what he thought of it.

Cattstock, the 'cello player, who was also the sexton, demurred, and
advised the young soldier to sound the rector about it first. 'Mid be he
would object, and yet 'a midn't. The pa'son o' Sidlinch is a hard man,
I own ye, and 'a said if folk will kill theirselves in hot blood they must
take the consequences. But ours don't think like that at all, and might
allow it.'

'What's his name?'

'The honourable and reverent Mr Oldham, brother to Lord Wessex.
But you needn't be afeared o' en on that account. He'll talk to 'ee like a
common man, if so be you haven't had enough drink to gie 'ee bad
breath.'

'O, the same as formerly. I'll ask him. Thank you. And that duty
done—'

'What then?'

'There's war in Spain. I hear our next move is there. I'll try to show
myself to be what my father wished me. I don't suppose I shall – but
I'll try in my feeble way. That much I swear – here over his body. So
help me God.'

Luke smacked his palm against the white handpost with such force
that it shook. 'Yes, there's war in Spain; and another chance for me to
be worthy of father.'

So the matter ended that night. That the private acted in one thing
as he had vowed to do soon became apparent, for during the Christmas
week the rector came into the churchyard when Cattstock was there,
and asked him to find a spot that would be suitable for the purpose of
such an interment, adding that he had slightly known the late sergeant,
and was not aware of any law which forbade him to assent to the removal,
the letter of the rule having been observed. But as he did not wish to
seem moved by opposition to his neighbour at Sidlinch, he had stipulated
that the act of charity should be carried out at night, and as privately as

possible, and that the grave should be in an obscure part of the enclosure. 'You had better see the young man about it at once,' added the rector.

But before Ezra had done anything Luke came down to his house. His furlough had been cut short, owing to new developments of the war in the Peninsula, and being obliged to go back to his regiment immediately, he was compelled to leave the exhumation and reinterment to his friends. Everything was paid for, and he implored them all to see it carried out forthwith.

With this the soldier left. The next day Ezra, on thinking the matter over, again went across to the rectory, struck with sudden misgiving. He had remembered that the sergeant had been buried without a coffin, and he was not sure that a stake had not been driven through him. The business would be more troublesome than they had at first supposed.

'Yes, indeed!' murmured the rector. 'I am afraid it is not feasible after all.'

The next event was the arrival of a headstone by carrier from the nearest town; to be left at Mr Ezra Cattstock's; all expenses paid. The sexton and the carrier deposited the stone in the former's outhouse; and Ezra, left alone, put on his spectacles and read the brief and simple inscription: –

HERE LYETH THE BODY OF SAMUEL HOLWAY, LATE SERGEANT IN HIS MAJESTY'S —D REGIMENT OF FOOT, WHO DEPARTED THIS LIFE DECEMBER THE 20TH, 180–. ERECTED BY L.H.
     'I AM NOT WORTHY TO BE CALLED THY SON.'

Ezra again called at the riverside rectory. 'The stone is come, sir. But I'm afeared we can't do it nohow.'

'I should like to oblige him,' said the gentlemanly old incumbent. 'And I would forgo all fees willingly. Still, if you and the others don't think you can carry it out, I am in doubt what to say.'

'Well, sir; I've made inquiry of a Sidlinch woman as to his burial, and what I thought seems true. They buried en wi' a new six-foot hurdle-saul drough's body, from the sheep-pen up in North Ewelease, though they won't own to it now. And the question is, Is the moving worth while, considering the awkwardness?'

'Have you heard anything more of the young man?'

Ezra had only heard that he had embarked that week for Spain with the rest of the regiment. 'And if he's as desperate as 'a seemed, we shall never see him here in England again.'

'It is an awkward case,' said the rector.

Ezra talked it over with the choir; one of whom suggested that the stone might be erected at the cross-roads. This was regarded as impracticable. Another said that it might be set up in the churchyard without removing the body; but this was seen to be dishonest. So nothing was done.

The headstone remained in Ezra's outhouse till, growing tired of seeing it there, he put it away among the bushes at the bottom of his garden. The subject was sometimes revived among them, but it always ended with: 'Considering how 'a was buried, we can hardly make a job o't.'

There was always the consciousness that Luke would never come back, an impression strengthened by the disasters which were rumoured to have befallen the army in Spain. This tended to make their inertness permanent. The headstone grew green as it lay on its back under Ezra's bushes; then a tree by the river was blown down, and, falling across the stone, cracked it in three pieces. Ultimately the pieces became buried in the leaves and mould.

Luke had not been born a Chalk-Newton man, and he had no relations left in Sidlinch, so that no tidings of him reached either village throughout the war. But after Waterloo and the fall of Napoleon there arrived at Sidlinch one day an English sergeant-major covered with stripes and, as it turned out, rich in glory. Foreign service had so totally changed Luke Holway that it was not until he told his name that the inhabitants recognized him as the sergeant's only son.

He had served with unswerving effectiveness through the Peninsular campaigns under Wellington; had fought at Busaco, Fuentes d'Onoro, Ciudad Rodrigo, Badajoz, Salamanca, Vittoria, Quatre Bras, and Waterloo; and had now returned to enjoy a more than earned pension and repose in his native district.

He hardly stayed in Sidlinch longer than to take a meal on his arrival. The same evening he started on foot over the hill to Chalk-Newton, passing the handpost, and saying as he glanced at the spot, 'Thank God: he's not there!' Nightfall was approaching when he reached the latter village; but he made straight for the churchyard. On his entering it there remained light enough to discern the headstones by, and these he narrowly scanned. But though he searched the front part by the road, and the back part by the river, what he sought he could not find – the grave of Sergeant Holway, and a memorial bearing the inscription: 'I AM NOT WORTHY TO BE CALLED THY SON.'

He left the churchyard and made inquiries. The honourable and reverend old rector was dead, and so were many of the choir; but by degrees the sergeant-major learnt that his father still lay at the cross-roads in Long Ash Lane.

Luke pursued his way moodily homewards, to do which, in the natural course, he would be compelled to repass the spot, there being no other road between the two villages. But he could not now go by that place, vociferous with reproaches in his father's tones; and he got over the hedge and wandered deviously through the ploughed fields to avoid the scene. Through many a fight and fatigue Luke had been sustained by the thought that he was restoring the family honour and making noble amends. Yet his father lay still in degradation. It was rather a sentiment than a fact that his father's body had been made to suffer for his own misdeeds; but to his super-sensitiveness it seemed that his efforts to retrieve his character and to propitiate the shade of the insulted one had ended in failure.

He endeavoured, however, to shake off his lethargy, and, not liking the associations of Sidlinch, hired a small cottage at Chalk-Newton which had long been empty. Here he lived alone, becoming quite a hermit, and allowing no woman to enter the house.

The Christmas after taking up his abode herein he was sitting in the chimney-corner by himself, when he heard faint notes in the distance, and soon a melody burst forth immediately outside his own window. It came from the carol-singers, as usual; and though many of the old hands, Ezra and Lot included, had gone to their rest, the same old carols were still played out of the same old books. There resounded through the sergeant-major's window-shutters the familiar lines that the deceased choir had rendered over his father's grave: –

> He comes' the pri'-soners to' re-lease',
> In Sa'-tan's bon'-dage held'.

When they had finished they went on to another house, leaving him to silence and loneliness as before.

The candle wanted snuffing, but he did not snuff it, and he sat on till it had burnt down into the socket and made waves of shadow on the ceiling.

The Christmas cheerfulness of next morning was broken at breakfast-time by tragic intelligence which went down the village like wind. Sergeant-Major Holway had been found shot through the head by his own hand at the cross-roads in Long Ash Lane where his father lay buried.

On the table in the cottage he had left a piece of paper, on which he had written his wish that he might be buried at the Cross beside his father. But the paper was accidentally swept to the floor, and overlooked till after his funeral, which took place in the ordinary way in the church-yard.

Christmas 1897

Enter a Dragoon

I LATELY had a melancholy experience (said the gentleman who is answerable for the truth of this story). It was that of going over a doomed house with whose outside aspect I had long been familiar – a house, that is, which by reason of age and dilapidation was to be pulled down during the following week. Some of the thatch, brown and rotten as the gills of old mushrooms, had, indeed, been removed before I walked over the building. Seeing that it was only a very small house – which is usually called a 'cottage-residence' – situated in a remote hamlet, and that it was not more than a hundred years old, if so much, I was led to think in my progress through the hollow rooms, with their cracked walls and sloping floors, what an exceptional number of abrupt family incidents had taken place therein – to reckon only those which had come to my own knowledge. And no doubt there were many more of which I had never heard.

It stood at the top of a garden stretching down to the lane or street that ran through a hermit-group of dwellings in Mellstock parish. From a green gate at the lower entrance, over which the thorn hedge had been shaped to an arch by constant clippings, a gravel path ascended between the box edges of once trim raspberry, strawberry, and vegetable plots, towards the front door. This was in colour an ancient and bleached green that could be rubbed off with the finger, and it bore a small long-featured brass knocker covered with verdigris in its crevices. For some years before this eve of demolition the homestead had degenerated, and been divided into two tenements to serve as cottages for farm labourers; but in its prime it had indisputable claim to be considered neat, pretty, and genteel.

The variety of incidents above alluded to was mainly owing to the nature of the tenure, whereby the place had been occupied by families not quite of the kind customary in such spots – people whose circumstances, position, or antecedents were more or less of a critical happy-go-lucky cast. And of these residents the family whose term comprised the story I wish to relate was that of Mr Jacob Paddock the market-gardener, who dwelt there for some years with his wife and grown-up daughter.

I

An evident commotion was agitating the premises, which jerked busy sounds across the front plot, resembling those of a disturbed hive. If a member of the household appeared at the door it was with a countenance of abstraction and concern.

Evening began to bend over the scene; and the other inhabitants of the hamlet came out to draw water, their common well being in the public road opposite the garden and house of the Paddocks. Having wound up their bucketsfull respectively they lingered, and spoke significantly together. From their words any casual listener might have gathered information of what had occurred.

The woodman who lived nearest the site of the story told most of the tale. Selina, the daughter of the Paddocks opposite, had been surprised that afternoon by receiving a letter from her once intended husband, then a corporal, but now a sergeant-major of dragoons, whom she had hitherto supposed to be one of the slain in the Battle of the Alma two or three years before.

'She picked up wi'en against her father's wish, as we know, and before he got his stripes,' their informant continued. 'Not but that the man was as hearty a feller as you'd meet this side o' London. But Jacob, you see, wished her to do better, and one can understand it. However, she was determined to stick to him at that time; and for what happened she was not much to blame, so near as they were to matrimony when the war broke out and spoiled all.'

'Even the very pig had been killed for the wedding,' said a woman, 'and the barrel o' beer ordered in. O, the man meant honourable enough. But to be off in two days to fight in a foreign country – 'twas natural of her father to say they should wait till he got back.'

'And he never came,' murmured one in the shade.

'The war ended but her man never turned up again. She was not sure he was killed, but was too proud, or too timid, to go and hunt for him.'

'One reason why her father forgave her when he found out how matters stood was, as he said plain at the time, that he liked the man, and could

see that he meant to act straight. So the old folks made the best of what
they couldn't mend, and kept her there with 'em, when some wouldn't.
Time has proved seemingly that he did mean to act straight, now that he
has writ to her that he's coming. She'd have stuck to him all through the
time, 'tis my belief, if t'other hadn't come along.'

'At the time of the courtship,' resumed the woodman, 'the regiment
was quartered in Casterbridge Barracks, and he and she got acquainted
by his calling to buy a penn'orth of rathe-ripes off that tree yonder in her
father's orchard – though 'twas said he seed *her* over hedge as well as the
apples. He declared 'twas a kind of apple he much fancied; and he called
for a penn'orth every day till the tree was cleared. It ended in his calling
for her.'

' 'Twas a thousand pities they didn't jine up at once and ha' done wi'
it.'

'Well; better late than never, if so be he'll have her now. But, Lord,
she'd that faith in en that she'd no more belief that he was alive, when a'
didn't come, than that the undermost man in our churchyard was alive.
She'd never have thought of another but for that – O no!'

' 'Tis awkward, altogether, for her now.'

'Still she hadn't married wi' the new man. Though to be sure she
would have committed it next week, even the licence being got, they say,
for she'd have no banns this time, the first being so unfortunate.'

'Perhaps the sergeant-major will think he's released, and go as he
came.'

'O, not as I reckon. Soldiers bain't particular, and she's a tidy piece o'
furniture still. What will happen is that she'll have her soldier, and break
off with the master-wheelwright, licence or no – daze me if she won't.'

In the progress of these desultory conjectures the form of another
neighbour arose in the gloom. She nodded to the people at the well, who
replied, 'G'd-night, Mrs Stone,' as she passed through Mr Paddock's
gate towards his door. She was an intimate friend of the latter's household, and the group followed her with their eyes up the path and past
the windows, which were now lighted up by candles inside.

II

Mrs Stone paused at the door, knocked, and was admitted by Selina's
mother, who took her visitor at once into the parlour on the left hand,

where a table was partly spread for supper. On the 'beaufet' against the wall stood probably the only object which would have attracted the eye of a local stranger in an otherwise ordinarily furnished room, a great plum-cake guarded as if it were a curiosity by a glass shade of the kind seen in museums – square, with a wooden back like those enclosing stuffed specimens of rare feather or fur. This was the mummy of the cake intended in earlier days for the wedding-feast of Selina and the soldier, which had been religiously and lovingly preserved by the former as a testimony to her intentional respectability in spite of an untoward subsequent circumstance, which will be mentioned. This relic was now as dry as a brick, and seemed to belong to a pre-existent civilization. Till quite recently, Selina had been in the habit of pausing before it daily, and recalling the accident whose consequences had thrown a shadow over her life ever since – that of which the water-drawers had spoken – the sudden news one morning that the Route had come for the —th Dragoons, two days only being the interval before departure; the hurried consultation as to what should be done, the second time of asking being past but not the third; and the decision that it would be unwise to solemnize matrimony in such haphazard circumstances, even if it were possible, which was doubtful.

Before the fire the young woman in question was now seated on a low stool, in the stillness of reverie, and a toddling boy played about the floor around her.

'Ah, Mrs Stone!' said Selina, rising slowly. 'How kind of you to come in. You'll bide to supper? Mother has told you the strange news, of course?'

'No. But I heard it outside, that is, that you'd had a letter from Mr Clark – Sergeant-Major Clark, as they say he is now – and that he's coming to make it up with 'ee.'

'Yes; coming to-night – all the way from the north of England where he's quartered. I don't know whether I'm happy or – frightened at it. Of course I always believed that if he was alive he'd come and keep his solemn vow to me. But when it is printed that a man is killed – what can you think?'

'It *was* printed?'

'Why, yes. After the Battle of the Alma the book of the names of the killed and wounded was nailed up against Casterbridge Town Hall door. 'Twas on a Saturday, and I walked there o' purpose to read and see for myself, for I'd heard that his name was down. There was a crowd of

people round the book, looking for the names of relations; and I can
mind that when they saw me they made way for me – knowing that we'd
been just going to be married – and that, as you may say, I belonged to
him. Well, I reached up my arm, and turned over the farrels of the book,
and under the "killed" I read his surname, but instead of "John" they'd
printed "James", and I thought 'twas a mistake, and that it must be he.
Who could have guessed there were two nearly of one name in one
regiment.'

'Well – he's coming to finish the wedding of 'ee as may be said; so
never mind, my dear. All's well that ends well.'

'That's what he seems to say. But then he has not heard yet about Mr
Miller; and that's what rather terrifies me. Luckily my marriage with
him next week was to have been by licence, and not banns, as in John's
case; and it was not so well known on that account. Still, I don't know
what to think.'

'Everything seems to come just 'twixt cup and lip with 'ee – don't it
now, Miss Paddock? Two weddings broke off – 'tis odd! How came you
to accept Mr Miller, my dear?'

'He's been so good and faithful! Not minding about the child at all;
for he knew the rights of the story. He's dearly fond o' Johnny, you
know – just as if 'twere his own – isn't he, my duck? Do Mr Miller love
you or don't he?'

'Iss! An' I love Mr Miller,' said the toddler.

'Well, you see, Mrs Stone, he said he'd make me a comfortable home;
and thinking 'twould be a good thing for Johnny, Mr Miller being so
much better off than me, I agreed at last, just as a widow might – which
is what I have always felt myself, ever since I saw what I thought was
John's name printed there. I hope John will forgive me!'

'So he will forgive 'ee, since 'twas no manner of wrong to him. He
ought to have sent 'ee a line, saying 'twas another man.'

Selina's mother entered. 'We've not known of this an hour, Mrs
Stone,' she said. 'The letter was brought up from Lower Mellstock
Post-office by one of the schoolchildren, only this afternoon. Mr Miller
was coming here this very night to settle about the wedding doings.
Hark! Is that your father? Or is it Mr Miller already come?'

The footsteps entered the porch; there was a brushing on the mat, and
the door of the room sprung back to disclose a rubicund man about
thirty years of age, of thriving master-mechanic appearance and obviously
comfortable temper. On seeing the child, and before taking any notice

whatever of the elders, the comer made a noise like the crowing of a cock and flapped his arms as if they were wings, a method of entry which had the unqualified admiration of Johnny.

'Yes – it is he,' said Selina constrainedly advancing.

'What – were you all talking about me, my dear?' said the genial young man when he had finished his crowing and resumed human manners. 'Why, what's the matter?' he went on. 'You look struck all of a heap.' Mr Miller spread an aspect of concern over his own face, and drew a chair up to the fire.

'O mother, would you tell Mr Miller, if he don't know?'

'*Mister* Miller! and going to be married in six days!' he interposed.

'Ah – he don't know it yet!' murmured Mrs Paddock.

'Know what?'

'Well – John Clark – now Sergeant-Major Clark – wasn't shot at Alma after all. 'Twas another of almost the same name.'

'Now that's interesting! There were several cases like that.'

'And he's home again; and he's coming here to-night to see her.'

'Whatever shall I say, that he may not be offended with what I've done?' interposed Selina.

'But why should it matter if he be?'

'O! I must agree to be his wife if he forgives me – of course I must.'

'Must! But why not say nay, Selina, even if he do forgive 'ee?'

'O no! How can I without being wicked? You were very very kind, Mr Miller, to ask me to have you; no other man would have done it after what had happened; and I agreed, even though I did not feel half so warm as I ought. Yet it was entirely owing to my believing him in the grave, as I knew that if he were not he would carry out his promise; and this shows that I was right in trusting him.'

'Yes. . . . He must be a goodish sort of fellow,' said Mr Miller, for a moment so impressed with the excellently faithful conduct of the sergeant-major of dragoons that he disregarded its effect upon his own position. He sighed slowly and added, 'Well, Selina, 'tis for you to say. I love you, and I love the boy; and there's my chimney-corner and sticks o' furniture ready for 'ee both.'

'Yes, I know! But I mustn't hear it any more now,' murmured Selina quickly. 'John will be here soon. I hope he'll see how it all was when I tell him. If so be I could have written it to him it would have been better.'

'You think he doesn't know a single word about our having been on the brink o't. But perhaps it's the other way – he's heard of it and that may have brought him.'

'Ah – perhaps he has!' she said brightening. 'And already forgives me.'

'If not, speak out straight and fair, and tell him exactly how it fell out. If he's a man he'll see it.'

'O he's a man true enough. But I really do think I shan't have to tell him at all, since you've put it to me that way!'

As it was now Johnny's bedtime he was carried upstairs, and when Selina came down again her mother observed with some anxiety, 'I fancy Mr Clark must be here soon if he's coming; and that being so, perhaps Mr Miller wouldn't mind – wishing us good-night! since you are so determined to stick to your sergeant-major.' A little bitterness bubbled amid the closing words. 'It would be less awkward, Mr Miller not being here – if he will allow me to say it.'

'To be sure; to be sure,' the master-wheelwright exclaimed with instant conviction, rising alertly from his chair. 'Lord bless my soul,' he said, taking up his hat and stick, 'and we to have been married in six days! But, Selina – you're right. You do belong to the child's father since he's alive. I'll try to make the best of it.'

Before the generous Miller had got further there came a knock to the door accompanied by the noise of wheels.

'I thought I heard something driving up!' said Mrs Paddock.

They heard Mr Paddock, who had been smoking in the room opposite, rise and go to the door, and in a moment a voice familiar enough to Selina was audibly saying, 'At last I am here again – not without many interruptions! How is it with 'ee, Mr Paddock? And how is she? Thought never to see me again, I suppose?' A step with a clink of spurs in it struck upon the entry floor.

'Danged if I bain't catched!' murmured Mr Miller, forgetting company-speech. 'Never mind – I may as well meet him here as elsewhere; and I should like to see the chap, and make friends with en, as he seems one o' the right sort.' He returned to the fireplace just as the sergeant-major was ushered in.

III

He was a good specimen of the long-service soldier of those days; a not unhandsome man, with a certain undemonstrative dignity, which some might have said to be partly owing to the stiffness of his uniform about his neck, the high stock being still worn. He was much stouter than when Selina had parted from him. Although she had not meant to be demonstrative she ran across to him directly she saw him, and he held her in his arms and kissed her.

Then in much agitation she whispered something to him, at which he seemed to be much surprised.

'He's just put to bed,' she continued. 'You can go up and see him. I knew you'd come if you were alive! But I had quite gi'd you up for dead. You've been home in England ever since the war ended?'

'Yes, dear.'

'Why didn't you come sooner?'

'That's just what I ask myself! Why was I such a sappy as not to hurry here the first day I set foot on shore! Well, who'd have thought it – you are as pretty as ever!'

He relinquished her to peep upstairs a little way, where, by looking through the balusters, he could see Johnny's cot just within an open door. On his stepping down again Mr Miller was preparing to depart.

'Now, what's this? I am sorry to see anybody going the moment I've come,' expostulated the sergeant-major. 'I thought we might make an evening of it. There's a nine-gallon cask o' "Phœnix" beer outside in the trap, and a ham, and half a rawmil' cheese; for I thought you might be short o' forage in a lonely place like this; and it struck me we might like to ask in a neighbour or two. But perhaps it would be taking a liberty?'

'O no, not at all,' said Mr Paddock, who was now in the room, in a judicial measured manner. 'Very thoughtful of 'ee, only 'twas not necessary, for we had just laid in an extry stock of eatables and drinkables in preparation for the coming event.'

' 'Twas very kind, upon my heart,' said the soldier, 'to think me worth such a jocund preparation, since you could only have got my letter this morning.'

Selina gazed at her father to stop him, and exchanged embarrassed glances with Miller. Contrary to her hopes Sergeant-Major Clark plainly did not know that the preparations referred to were for something quite other than his own visit.

The movement of the horse outside, and the impatient tapping of a whip-handle upon the vehicle reminded them that Clark's driver was still in waiting. The provisions were brought into the house, and the cart dismissed. Miller, with very little pressure indeed, accepted an invitation to supper, and a few neighbours were induced to come in to make up a cheerful party.

During the laying of the meal, and throughout its continuance, Selina, who sat beside her first intended husband, tried frequently to break the news to him of her engagement to the other – now terminated so suddenly, and so happily for her heart, and her sense of womanly virtue. But the talk ran entirely upon the late war; and though fortified by half a horn of the strong ale brought by the sergeant-major she decided that she might have a better opportunity when supper was over of revealing the situation to him in private.

Having supped, Clark leaned back at ease in his chair and looked around. 'We used sometimes to have a dance in that other room after supper, Selina dear, I recollect. We used to clear out all the furniture into this room before beginning. Have you kept up such goings on?'

'No, not at all!' said his sweetheart sadly.

'We were not unlikely to revive it in a few days,' said Mr Paddock. 'But, howsomever, there's seemingly many a slip, as the saying is.'

'Yes, I'll tell John all about that by-and-by!' interposed Selina; at which, perceiving that the secret which he did not like keeping was to be kept even yet, her father held his tongue with some show of testiness.

The subject of a dance having been broached, to put the thought in practice was the feeling of all. Soon after the tables and chairs were borne from the opposite room to this by zealous hands, and two of the villagers sent home for a fiddle and tambourine, when the majority began to tread a measure well known in that secluded vale. Selina naturally danced with the sergeant-major, not altogether to her father's satisfaction, and to the real uneasiness of her mother, both of whom would have preferred a postponement of festivities till the rashly anticipated relationship between their daughter and Clark in the past had been made fact by the Church's ordinances. They did not, however, express a positive objection, Mr Paddock remembering, with self-reproach, that it was owing to his original strongly expressed disapproval of Selina's being a soldier's wife that the wedding had been delayed, and finally hindered – with worse consequences than were expected; and ever since the misadventure brought about by his government he had allowed events to steer their own courses.

'My tails will surely catch in your spurs, John!' murmured the daughter of the house, as she whirled around upon his arm with the rapt soul and look of a somnambulist. 'I didn't know we should dance, or I would have put on my other frock.'

'I'll take care, my love. We've danced here before. Do you think your father objects to me now? I've risen in rank. I fancy he's still a little against me.'

'He has repented, times enough.'

'And so have I! If I had married you then 'twould have saved many a misfortune. I have sometimes thought it might have been possible to rush the ceremony through somehow before I left; though we were only in the second asking, were we? And even if I had come back straight here when we returned from the Crimea, and married you then, how much happier I should have been!'

'Dear John, to say that! Why didn't you?'

'O – dilatoriness and want of thought, and a fear of facing your father after so long. I was in hospital a great while, you know. But how familiar the place seems again! What's that I saw on the beaufet in the other room? It never used to be there. A sort of withered corpse of a cake – not an old bride-cake surely?'

'Yes, John, ours. 'Tis the very one that was made for our wedding three years ago.'

'Sakes alive! Why, time shuts up together, and all between then and now seems not to have been! What became of that wedding-gown that they were making in this room, I remember – a bluish, whitish, frothy thing?'

'I have that too.'

'Really!... Why, Selina—'

'Yes!'

'Why not put it on now?'

'Wouldn't it seem— And yet, O how I should like to! It would remind them all, if we told them what it was, how we really meant to be married on that bygone day!' Her eyes were again laden with wet.

'Yes.... The pity that we didn't – the pity!' Moody mournfulness seemed to hold silent awhile one not naturally taciturn. 'Well – will you?' he said.

'I will – the next dance, if mother don't mind.'

Accordingly, just before the next figure was formed, Selina disappeared, and speedily came downstairs in a creased and box-worn, but still airy and pretty, muslin gown, which was indeed the very one that had been meant to grace her as a bride three years before.

'It is dreadfully old-fashioned,' she apologized.

'Not at all. What a grand thought of mine! Now, let's to't again.'

She explained to some of them, as he led her to the second dance, what the frock had been meant for, and that she had put it on at his request. And again athwart and around the room they went.

'You seem the bride!' he said.

'But I couldn't wear this gown to be married in now!' she replied ecstatically, 'or I shouldn't have put it on and made it dusty. It is really too old-fashioned, and so folded and fretted out, you can't think. That was with my taking it out so many times to look at. I have never put it on – never – till now!'

'Selina, I am thinking of giving up the army. Will you emigrate with me to New Zealand? I've an uncle out there doing well, and he'd soon help me to making a larger income. The English army is glorious, but it ain't altogether enriching.'

'Of course, anywhere that you decide upon. Is it healthy there for Johnny?'

'A lovely climate. And I shall never be happy in England. . . . Aha!' he concluded again, with a bitterness of unexpected strength, 'would to Heaven I had come straight back here!'

As the dance brought round one neighbour after another the re-united pair were thrown into juxtaposition with Bob Heartall among the rest who had been called in; one whose chronic expression was that he carried inside him a joke on the point of bursting with its own vastness. He took occasion now to let out a little of its quality, shaking his head at Selina as he addressed her in an undertone –

'This is a bit of a topper to the bridegroom, ho! ho! 'Twill teach en the liberty you'll expect when you've married en!'

'What does he mean by a "topper"?' the sergeant-major asked, who, not being of local extraction, despised the venerable local language, and also seemed to suppose 'bridegroom' to be an anticipatory name for himself. 'I only hope I shall never be worse treated than you've treated me to-night!'

Selina looked frightened. 'He didn't mean you, dear,' she said as they moved on. 'We thought perhaps you knew what had happened, owing to your coming just at this time. Had you – heard anything about – what I intended?'

'Not a breath – how should I, away up in Yorkshire? It was by the merest accident that I came just at this date to make peace with you for my delay.'

'I was engaged to be married to Mr Bartholomew Miller. That's what it is! I would have let 'ee know by letter, but there was no time, only hearing from 'ee this afternoon. . . . You won't desert me for it, will you, John? Because, as you know, I quite supposed you dead, and – and—' Her eyes were full of tears of trepidation, and he might have felt a sob heaving within her.

IV

The soldier was silent during two or three double bars of the tune. 'When were you to have been married to the said Mr Bartholomew Miller?' he inquired.

'Quite soon.'

'How soon?'

'Next week – O yes – just the same as it was with you and me. There's a strange fate of interruption hanging over me, I sometimes think! He had bought the licence, which I preferred so that it mightn't be like – ours. But it made no difference to the fate of it.'

'Had bought the licence! The devil!'

'Don't be angry, dear John. I didn't know!'

'No, no, I'm not angry.'

'It was so kind of him, considering!'

'Yes. . . . I see, of course, how natural your action was – never thinking of seeing me any more! Is it the Mr Miller who is in this dance?'

'Yes.'

Clark glanced round upon Bartholomew and was silent again for some little while, and she stole a look at him, to find that he seemed changed. 'John, you look ill!' she almost sobbed. ' 'Tisn't me, is it?'

'O dear, no. Though I hadn't, somehow, expected it. I can't find fault with you for a moment – and I don't. . . . This is a deuce of a long dance, don't you think? We've been at it twenty minutes if a second, and the figure doesn't allow one much rest. I'm quite out of breath.

'They like them so dreadfully long here. Shall we drop out? Or I'll stop the fiddler?'

'O no, no, I think I can finish. But although I look healthy enough I have never been so strong as I formerly was, since that long illness I had in the hospital at Scutari.'

'And I knew nothing about it!'

'You couldn't, dear, as I didn't write. What a fool I have been altogether!' He gave a twitch, as of one in pain. 'I won't dance again when this one is over. The fact is I have travelled a long way to-day, and it seems to have knocked me up a bit.'

There could be no doubt that the sergeant-major was unwell, and Selina made herself miserable by still believing that her story was the cause of his ailment. Suddenly he said in a changed voice, and she perceived that he was paler than ever:

'I must sit down.'

Letting go her waist he went quickly to the other room. She followed, and found him in the nearest chair, his face bent down upon his hands and arms, which were resting on the table.

'What's the matter?' said her father, who sat there dozing by the fire.

'John isn't well. . . . We are going to New Zealand when we are married, father. A lovely country! . . . John, would you like something to drink?'

'A drop o' that Schiedam of old Owlett's that's under stairs, perhaps,' suggested her father. 'Not that nowadays 'tis much better than licensed liquor.'

'John,' she said, putting her face close to his and pressing his arm. 'Will you have a drop of spirits or something?'

He did not reply, and Selina observed that his ear and the side of his face were quite white. Convinced that his illness was serious, a growing dismay seized hold of her. The dance ended; her mother came in, and learning what had happened, looked narrowly at the sergeant-major.

'We must not let him lie like that, lift him up,' she said. 'Let him rest in the window-bench on some cushions.'

They unfolded his arms and hands as they lay clasped upon the table, and on lifting his head found his features to bear the very impress of death itself. Bartholomew Miller, who had now come in, assisted Mr Paddock to make a comfortable couch in the window-seat, where they stretched out Clark upon his back.

Still he seemed unconscious. 'We must get a doctor,' said Selina. 'O, my dear John, how is it you be taken like this?'

'My impression is that he's dead!' murmured Mr Paddock. 'He don't breathe enough to move a tomtit's feather.'

There were plenty to volunteer to go for a doctor, but as it would be at least an hour before he could get there the case seemed somewhat hopeless. The dancing-party ended as unceremoniously as it had begun; but the guests lingered round the premises till the doctor should arrive. When he did come the sergeant-major's extremities were already cold, and there was no doubt that death had overtaken him almost at the moment that he had sat down.

The medical practitioner quite refused to accept the unhappy Selina's theory that her revelation had in any way induced Clark's sudden collapse. Both he and the coroner afterwards, who found the immediate cause to be heart-failure, held that such a supposition was unwarranted by facts. They asserted that a long day's journey, a hurried drive, and then an exhausting dance, were sufficient for such a result upon a heart enfeebled by fatty degeneration after the privations of a Crimean winter and other trying experiences, the coincidence of the sad event with any disclosure of hers being a pure accident.

This conclusion, however, did not dislodge Selina's opinion that the shock of her statement had been the immediate stroke which had felled a constitution so undermined.

V

At this date the Casterbridge Barracks were cavalry quarters, their adaptation to artillery having been effected some years later. It had been owing to the fact that the —th Dragoons, in which John Clark had served, happened to be lying there that Selina made his acquaintance. At the time of his death the barracks were occupied by the Scots Greys, but when the pathetic circumstances of the sergeant-major's end became known in the town the officers of the Greys offered the services of their fine reed and brass band, that he might have a funeral marked by due military honours. His body was accordingly removed to the barracks, and carried thence to the churchyard in the Durnover quarter on the following afternoon, one of the Greys' most ancient and docile chargers being blacked up to represent Clark's horse on the occasion.

Everybody pitied Selina, whose story was well known. She followed the corpse as the only mourner, Clark having been without relations in this part of the country, and a communication with his regiment having brought none from a distance. She sat in a little shabby brown-black mourning carriage, squeezing herself up in a corner to be as much as possible out of sight during the slow and dramatic march through the town to the tune from *Saul*. When the interment had taken place, the volleys been fired, and the return journey begun, it was with something like a shock that she found the military escort to be moving at a quick march to the lively strains of 'Off she goes!' as if all care for the sergeant-major was expected to be ended with the late discharge of the carbines. It was, by chance, the very tune to which they had been footing when he died, and unable to bear its notes, she hastily told her driver to drop behind. The band and military party diminished up the High Street, and Selina turned over Swan bridge and homeward to Mellstock.

Then recommenced for her a life whose incidents were precisely of a suit with those which had preceded the soldier's return; but how different in her appreciation of them! Her narrow miss of the recovered respectability they had hoped for from that tardy event worked upon her parents as an irritant, and after the first week or two of her mourning her life with them grew almost insupportable. She had impulsively taken to herself the weeds of a widow, for such she seemed to herself to be, and clothed little Johnny in sables likewise. This assumption of a moral relationship to the deceased, which she asserted to be only not a legal one by two most unexpected accidents, led the old people to indulge in sarcasm at her expense whenever they beheld her attire, though all the while it cost them more pain to utter than it gave her to hear it. Having become accustomed by her residence at home to the business carried on by her father, she surprised them one day by going off with the child to Chalk-Newton, in the direction of the town of Ivell, and opening a miniature fruit and vegetable shop, attending Ivell market with her produce. Her business grew somewhat larger, and it was soon sufficient to enable her to support herself and the boy in comfort. She called herself 'Mrs John Clark' from the day of leaving home, and painted the name on her signboard – no man forbidding her.

By degrees the pain of her state was forgotten in her new circumstances, and getting to be generally accepted as the widow of a sergeant-major of dragoons – an assumption which her modest and mournful demeanour seemed to substantiate – her life became a placid one, her mind being nourished by the melancholy luxury of dreaming what might have been her future in New Zealand with John, if he had only lived to take her there. Her only travels now were a journey to Ivell on market-days, and once a fortnight to the churchyard in which Clark lay, there to tend, with Johnny's assistance, as widows are wont to do, the flowers she had planted upon his grave.

On a day about eighteen months after his unexpected decease, Selina was surprised in her lodging over her little shop by a visit from Bartholomew Miller. He had called on her once or twice before, on which occasions he had used without a word of comment the name by which she was known.

'I've come this time,' he said, 'less because I was in this direction than to ask you, Mrs Clark, what you mid well guess. I've come o' purpose, in short.'

She smiled.

' 'Tis to ask me again to marry you?'

'Yes, of course. You see, his coming back for 'ee proved what I always believed of 'ee, though others didn't. There's nobody but would be glad to welcome you to our parish again, now you've showed your independence and acted up to your trust in his promise. Well, my dear, will you come?'

'I'd rather bide as Mrs Clark, I think,' she answered. 'I am not ashamed of my position at all; for I am John's widow in the eyes of Heaven.'

'I quite agree – that's why I've come. Still, you won't like to be always straining at this shop-keeping and market-standing; and 'twould be better for Johnny if you had nothing to do but tend him.'

He here touched the only weak spot in Selina's resistance to his proposal – the good of the boy. To promote that there were other men she might have married off-hand without loving them if they had asked her to; but though she had known the worthy speaker from her youth, she could not for the moment fancy herself happy as Mrs Miller.

He paused a while. 'I ought to tell 'ee, Mrs Clark,' he said by-and-by, 'that marrying is getting to be a pressing question with me. Not on my own account at all. The truth is, that mother is growing old, and I am away from home a good deal, so that it is almost necessary there should be another person in the house with her besides me. That's the practical consideration which forces me to think of taking a wife, apart from my wish to take you; and you know there's nobody in the world I care for so much.'

She said something about there being far better women than she, and other natural commonplaces; but assured him she was most grateful to him for feeling what he felt, as indeed she sincerely was. However, Selina would not consent to be the useful third person in his comfortable home – at any rate just then. He went away, after taking tea with her, without discerning much hope for him in her good-bye.

VI

After that evening she saw and heard nothing of him for a great while. Her fortnightly journeys to the sergeant-major's grave were continued, whenever weather did not hinder them; and Mr Miller must have known, she thought, of this custom of hers. But though the churchyard was not nearly so far from his homestead as was her shop at Chalk-Newton, he never appeared in the accidental way that lovers use.

An explanation was forthcoming in the shape of a letter from her mother, who casually mentioned that Mr Bartholomew Miller had gone away to the other side of Shottsford-Forum to be married to a thriving dairyman's daughter that he knew there. His chief motive, it was reported, had been less one of love than a wish to provide a companion for his aged mother.

Selina was practical enough to know that she had lost a good and possibly the only opportunity of settling in life after what had happened, and for a moment she regretted her independence. But she became calm on reflection, and to fortify herself in her course started that afternoon to tend the sergeant-major's grave, in which she took the same sober pleasure as at first.

On reaching the churchyard and turning the corner towards the spot as usual, she was surprised to perceive another woman, also apparently a respectable widow, and with a tiny boy by her side, bending over Clark's turf, and spudding up with the point of her umbrella some ivy-roots that Selina had reverently planted there to form an evergreen mantle over the mound.

'What are you digging up my ivy for!' cried Selina, rushing forward so excitedly that Johnny tumbled over a grave with the force of the tug she gave his hand in her sudden start.

'Your ivy?' said the respectable woman.

'Why, yes! I planted it there – on my husband's grave.'

'*Your* husband's!'

'Yes. The late Sergeant-Major Clark. Anyhow, as good as my husband, for he was just going to be.'

'Indeed. But who may be my husband, if not he? I am the only Mrs John Clark, widow of the late Sergeant-Major of Dragoons, and this is, his only son and heir.'

'How can that be?' faltered Selina, her throat seeming to stick together as she just began to perceive its possibility. 'He had been – going to marry me twice – and we were going to New Zealand.'

'Ah! – I remember about you,' returned the legitimate widow calmly and not unkindly. 'You must be Selina; he spoke of you now and then, and said that his relations with you would always be a weight on his conscience. Well; the history of my life with him is soon told. When he came back from the Crimea he became acquainted with me at my home in the North, and we were married within a month of first knowing each other. Unfortunately, after living together a few months, we could not agree; and after a particularly sharp quarrel, in which, perhaps, I was most in the wrong – as I don't mind owning here by his grave-side – he went away from me, declaring he would buy his discharge and emigrate to New Zealand, and never come back to me any more. The next thing I heard was that he had died suddenly at Mellstock at some low carouse; and as he had left me in such anger to live no more with me, I wouldn't come down to his funeral, or do anything in relation to him. 'Twas temper, I know, but that was the fact. Even if we had parted friends it would have been a serious expense to travel three hundred miles to get there, for one who wasn't left so very well off. .... I am sorry I pulled up your ivy-roots; but that common sort of ivy is considered a weed in my part of the country.'

December 1899

A Tryst at an Ancient Earthwork

AT one's every step forward it rises higher against the south sky, with an obtrusive personality that compels the senses to regard it and consider. The eyes may bend in another direction, but never without the consciousness of its heavy, high-shouldered presence at its point of vantage. Across the intervening levels the gale races in a straight line from the fort, as if breathed out of it hitherward. With the shifting of the clouds the faces of the steeps vary in colour and in shade, broad lights appearing where mist and vagueness had prevailed, dissolving in their turn into melancholy gray, which spreads over and eclipses the luminous bluffs. In this so-thought immutable spectacle all is change.

Out of the invisible marine region on the other side birds soar suddenly into the air, and hang over the summits of the heights with the indifference of long familiarity. Their forms are white against the tawny concave of cloud, and the curves they exhibit in their floating signify that they are sea-gulls which have journeyed inland from expected stress of weather. As the birds rise behind the fort, so do the clouds rise behind the birds, almost, as it seems, stroking with their bagging bosoms the uppermost flyers.

The profile of the whole stupendous ruin, as seen at a distance of a mile eastward, is cleanly cut as that of a marble inlay. It is varied with protuberances, which from hereabouts have the animal aspect of warts, wens, knuckles, and hips. It may indeed be likened to an enormous many-limbed organism of an antediluvian time – partaking of the cephalopod in shape – lying lifeless, and covered with a thin green cloth, which hides its substance, while revealing its contour. This dull green mantle of herbage stretches down towards the levels, where the ploughs have essayed for centuries to creep up near and yet nearer to the base of the castle, but have always stopped short before reaching it. The furrows of these environing attempts show themselves distinctly, bending to the incline as they trench upon it; mounting in steeper curves, till the steepness baffles them, and their parallel threads show like the striæ of waves pausing on the curl. The peculiar place of which these are some of the features is 'Mai-Dun', 'The Castle of the Great Hill', said to be the Dunium of Ptolemy, the capital of the Durotriges, which eventually came into Roman occupation, and was finally deserted on their withdrawal from the island.

The evening is followed by a night on which an invisible moon bestows a subdued, yet pervasive light – without radiance, as without blackness. From the spot wherein I am ensconced in a cottage, a mile away, the fort has now ceased to be visible; yet, as by day, to anybody whose thoughts have been engaged with it and its barbarous grandeurs of past time the form asserts its existence behind the night gauzes as persistently as if it had a voice. Moreover, the south-west wind continues to feed the intervening arable flats with vapours brought directly from its sides.

The midnight hour for which there has been occasion to wait at length arrives, and I journey towards the stronghold in obedience to a request urged earlier in the day. It concerns an appointment, which I rather regret my decision to keep now that night is come. The route thither is hedgeless and treeless – I need not add deserted. The moonlight is sufficient to disclose the pale riband-like surface of the way as it trails along between the expanses of darker fallow. Though the road passes near the fortress it does not conduct directly to its fronts. As the place is without an inhabitant, so it is without a trackway. So presently leaving the macadamized road to pursue its course elsewhither, I step off upon the fallow, and plod stumblingly across it. The castle looms out of the shade by degrees, like a thing waking up and asking what I want there. It is now so enlarged by nearness that its whole shape cannot be taken in at one view. The ploughed ground ends as the rise sharpens, the sloping basement of grass begins, and I climb upward to invade Mai-Dun.

Impressive by day as this largest Ancient-British work in the kingdom undoubtedly is, its impressiveness is increased now. After standing still and spending a few minutes in adding its age to its size, and its size to its solitude, it becomes appallingly mournful in its growing closeness. A squally wind blows in the face with an impact which proclaims that the vapours of the air sail low to-night. The slope that I so laboriously clamber up the wind skips sportively down. Its track can be discerned even in this light by the undulations of the withered grass-bents – the only produce of this upland summit except moss. Four minutes of ascent, and a vantage-ground of some sort is gained. It is only the crest of the outer rampart. Immediately within this a chasm gapes; its bottom is imperceptible, but the counterscarp slopes not too steeply to admit of a sliding descent if cautiously performed. The shady bottom, dank and chilly, is thus gained, and reveals itself as a kind of winding lane, wide enough for a waggon to pass along, floored with rank herbage, and trending away, right and left, into obscurity, between the concentric walls of earth. The towering closeness of these on each hand, their impenetrability, and their ponderousness, are felt as a physical pressure. The way is now up the second of them, which stands steeper and higher than the first. To turn aside, as did Christian's companion, from such a Hill Difficulty, is the more natural tendency; but the way to the interior is upward. There is, of course, an entrance to the fortress; but that lies far off on the other side. It might possibly have been the wiser course to seek for easier ingress there.

However, being here, I ascend the second acclivity. The grass stems – the grey beard of the hill – sway in a mass close to my stooping face. The dead heads of these various grasses – fescues, fox-tails, and ryes – bob and twitch as if pulled by a string underground. From a few thistles a whistling proceeds; and even the moss speaks, in its humble way, under the stress of the blast.

That the summit of the second line of defence has been gained is suddenly made known by a contrasting wind from a new quarter, coming over with the curve of a cascade. These novel gusts raise a sound from the whole camp or castle, playing upon it bodily as upon a harp. It is with some difficulty that a foothold can be preserved under their sweep. Looking aloft for a moment I perceive that the sky is much more over-cast than it has been hitherto, and in a few instants a dead lull in what is now a gale ensues with almost preternatural abruptness. I take advantage of this to sidle down the second counterscarp, but by the time the ditch is reached the lull reveals itself to be but the precursor of a storm. It begins with a heave of the whole atmosphere, like the sigh of a weary strong man on turning to recommence unusual exertion, just as I stand here in the second fosse. That which now radiates from the sky upon the scene is not so much light as vaporous phosphorescence.

The wind, quickening, abandons the natural direction it has pursued on the open upland, and takes the course of the gorge's length, rushing along therein helter-skelter, and carrying thick rain upon its back. The rain is followed by hailstones which fly through the defile in battalions – rolling, hopping, ricochetting, snapping, clattering down the shelving banks in an undefinable haze of confusion. The earthen sides of the fosse seem to quiver under the drenching onset, though it is practically no more to them than the blows of Thor upon the giant of Jotun-land. It is impossible to proceed further till the storm somewhat abates, and I draw up behind a spur of the inner scarp, where possibly a barricade stood two thousand years ago; and thus await events.

The roar of the storm can be heard travelling the complete circuit of the castle – a measured mile – coming round at intervals like a circumambulating column of infantry. Doubtless such a column has passed this way in its time, but the only columns which enter in these latter days are the columns of sheep and oxen that are sometimes seen here now; while the only semblance of heroic voices heard are the utterances of such, and of the many winds which make their passage through the ravines.

The expected lightning radiates round, and a rumbling as from its subterranean vaults – if there are any – fills the castle. The lightning repeats itself, and, coming after the aforesaid thoughts of martial men, it bears a fanciful resemblance to swords moving in combat. It has the very brassy hue of the ancient weapons that here were used. The so sudden entry upon the scene of this metallic flame is as the entry of a presiding exhibitor who unrolls the maps, uncurtains the pictures, unlocks the cabinets, and effects a transformation by merely exposing the materials of his science, unintelligibly cloaked till then. The abrupt configuration of the bluffs and mounds is now for the first time clearly revealed – mounds whereon, doubtless, spears and shields have frequently lain while their owners loosened their sandals and yawned and stretched their arms in the sun. For the first time, too, a glimpse is obtainable of the true entrance used by its occupants of old, some way ahead.

There, where all passage has seemed to be inviolably barred by an almost vertical façade, the ramparts are found to overlap each other like loosely clasped fingers, between which a zigzag path may be followed – a cunning construction that puzzles the uninformed eye. But its cunning, even where not obscured by dilapidation, is now wasted on the solitary forms of a few wild badgers, rabbits, and hares. Men must have often gone out by those gates in the morning to battle with the Roman legions under Vespasian; some to return no more, others to come back at evening, bringing with them the noise of their heroic deeds. But not a page, not a stone, has preserved their fame.

Acoustic perceptions multiply to-night. We can almost hear the stream of years that have borne those deeds away from us. Strange articulations seem to float on the air from that point, the gateway, where the animation in past times must frequently have concentrated itself at hours of coming and going, and general excitement. There arises an ineradicable fancy that they are human voices; if so, they must be the lingering airborne vibrations of conversations uttered at least fifteen hundred years ago. The attention is attracted from mere nebulous imaginings about yonder spot by a real moving of something close at hand.

I recognize by the now moderate flashes of lightning, which are sheet-like and nearly continuous, that it is the gradual elevation of a small mound of earth. At first no larger than a man's fist it reaches the dimensions of a hat, then sinks a little and is still. It is but the heaving of a mole who chooses such weather as this to work in from some instinct that there will be nobody abroad to molest him. As the fine earth lifts and lifts and falls loosely aside fragments of burnt clay roll out of it – clay that once formed part of cups or other vessels used by the inhabitants of the fortress.

The violence of the storm has been counterbalanced by its transitoriness. From being immersed in wellnigh solid media of cloud and hail shot with lightning, I find myself uncovered of the humid investiture and left bare to the mild gaze of the moon, which sparkles now on every wet grass-blade and frond of moss.

But I am not yet inside the fort, and the delayed ascent of the third and last escarpment is now made. It is steeper than either. The first was a surface to walk up, the second to stagger up, the third can only be ascended on the hands and toes. On the summit obtrudes the first evidence which has been met with in these precincts that the time is really the nineteenth century; it is in the form of a white notice-board on a post, and the wording can just be discerned by the rays of the setting moon:

CAUTION – Any Person found removing Relics, Skeletons, Stones, Pottery, Tiles, or other Material from this Earthwork, or cutting up the Ground, will be Prosecuted as the Law directs.

Here one observes a difference underfoot from what has gone before:

scraps of Roman tile and stone chippings protrude through the grass in
meagre quantity, but sufficient to suggest that masonry stood on the
spot. Before the eye stretches under the moonlight the interior of the
fort. So open and so large is it as to be practically an upland plateau, and
yet its area lies wholly within the walls of what may be designated as
one building. It is a long-violated retreat; all its corner-stones, plinths,
and architraves were carried away to build neighbouring villages even
before mediæval or modern history began. Many a block which once
may have helped to form a bastion here rests now in broken and diminished shape as part of the chimney-corner of some shepherd's cottage
within the distant horizon, and the corner-stones of this heathen altar
may form the base-course of some adjoining village church.

Yet the very bareness of these inner courts and wards, their condition
of mere pasturage, protects what remains of them as no defences could
do. Nothing is left visible that the hands can seize on or the weather
overturn, and a permanence of general outline at least results, which no
other condition could ensure.

The position of the castle on this isolated hill bespeaks deliberate and
strategic choice exercised by some remote mind capable of prospective
reasoning to a far extent. The natural configuration of the surrounding
country and its bearing upon such a stronghold were obviously long
considered and viewed mentally before its extensive design was carried
into execution. Who was the man that said, 'Let it be built here!' – not
on that hill yonder, or on that ridge behind, but on this best spot of all?
Whether he were some great one of the Belgæ, or of the Durotriges, or
the travelling engineer of Britain's united tribes, must for ever remain
time's secret; his form cannot be realized, nor his countenance, nor the
tongue that he spoke, when he set down his foot with a thud and said,
'Let it be here!'

Within the innermost enclosure, though it is so wide that at a superficial glance the beholder has only a sense of standing on a breezy down,
the solitude is rendered yet more solitary by the knowledge that between
the benighted sojourner herein and all kindred humanity are those three
concentric walls of earth which no being would think of scaling on such
a night as this, even were he to hear the most pathetic cries issuing hence
that could be uttered by a spectre-chased soul. I reach a central mound
or platform – the crown and axis of the whole structure. The view from
here by day must be of almost limitless extent. On this raised floor, daïs,
or rostrum, harps have probably twanged more or less tuneful notes in

celebration of daring, strength, or cruelty; of worship, superstition, love, birth, and death; of simple loving-kindness perhaps never. Many a time must the king or leader have directed his keen eyes hence across the open lands towards the ancient road, the Icening Way, still visible in the distance, on the watch for armed companies approaching either to succour or to attack.

I am startled by a voice pronouncing my name. Past and present have become so confusedly mingled under the associations of the spot that for a time it has escaped my memory that this mound was the place agreed on for the aforesaid appointment. I turn and behold my friend. He stands with a dark lantern in his hand and a spade and light pickaxe over his shoulder. He expresses both delight and surprise that I have come. I tell him I had set out before the bad weather began.

He, to whom neither weather, darkness, nor difficulty seems to have any relation or significance, so entirely is his soul wrapt up in his own deep intentions, asks me to take the lantern and accompany him. I take it and walk by his side. He is a man about sixty, small in figure, with gray old-fashioned whiskers cut to the shape of a pair of crumb-brushes. He is entirely in black broadcloth – or rather, at present, black and brown, for he is bespattered with mud from his heels to the crown of his low hat. He has no consciousness of this – no sense of anything but his purpose, his ardour for which causes his eyes to shine like those of a lynx, and gives his motions all the elasticity of an athlete's.

'Nobody to interrupt us at this time of night!' he chuckles with fierce enjoyment.

We retreat a little way and find a sort of angle, an elevation in the sod, a suggested squareness amid the mass of irregularities around. Here, he tells me, if anywhere, the king's house stood. Three months of measurement and calculation have confirmed him in this conclusion.

He requests me now to open the lantern, which I do, and the light streams out upon the wet sod. At last divining his proceedings I say that I had no idea, in keeping the tryst, that he was going to do more at such an unusual time than meet me for a meditative ramble through the stronghold. I ask him why, having a practicable object, he should have minded interruptions and not have chosen the day? He informs me, quietly pointing to his spade, that it was because his purpose is to dig, then signifying with a grim nod the gaunt notice-post against the sky beyond. I inquire why, as a professed and well-known antiquary with capital letters at the tail of his name, he did not obtain the necessary authority, considering the stringent penalties for this sort of thing; and he chuckles fiercely again with suppressed delight, and says, 'Because they wouldn't have given it!'

He at once begins cutting up the sod, and, as he takes the pickaxe to follow on with, assures me that, penalty or no penalty, honest men or marauders, he is sure of one thing, that we shall not be disturbed at our work till after dawn.

I remember to have heard of men who, in their enthusiasm for some special science, art, or hobby, have quite lost the moral sense which would restrain them from indulging it illegitimately; and I conjecture that here, at last, is an instance of such an one. He probably guesses the way my thoughts travel, for he stands up and solemnly asserts that he has a distinctly justifiable intention in this matter; namely, to uncover, to search, to verify a theory or displace it, and to cover up again. He means to take away nothing – not a grain of sand. In this he says he sees no such monstrous sin. I inquire if this is really a promise to me? He repeats that it is a promise, and resumes digging. My contribution to the labour is that of directing the light constantly upon the hole. When he has reached something more than a foot deep he digs more cautiously, saying that, be it much or little there, it will not lie far below the surface; such things never are deep. A few minutes later the point of the pickaxe clicks upon a stony substance. He draws the implement out as feelingly as if it had entered a man's body. Taking up the spade he shovels with care, and a surface, level as an altar, is presently disclosed. His eyes flash anew; he pulls handfuls of grass and mops the surface clean, finally rubbing it with his handkerchief. Grasping the lantern from my hand he holds it close to the ground, when the rays reveal a complete mosaic – a pavement of minute tesseræ of many colours, of intricate pattern, a work of much art, of much time, and of much industry. He exclaims in a shout that he knew it always – that it is not a Celtic stronghold exclusively, but also a Roman; the former people having probably contributed little more than the original framework which the latter took and adapted till it became the present imposing structure.

I ask, What if it is Roman?

A great deal, according to him. That it proves all the world to be wrong in this great argument, and himself alone to be right! Can I wait while he digs further?

I agree – reluctantly; but he does not notice my reluctance. At an adjoining spot he begins flourishing the tools anew with the skill of a navvy, this venerable scholar with letters after his name. Sometimes he falls on his knees, burrowing with his hands in the manner of a hare, and where his old-fashioned broadcloth touches the sides of the hole it gets plastered with the damp earth. He continually murmurs to himself how important, how very important, this discovery is! He draws out an object; we wash it in the same primitive way by rubbing it with the wet grass, and it proves to be a semi-transparent bottle of iridescent beauty, the sight of which draws groans of luxurious sensibility from the digger. Further and further search brings out a piece of a weapon. It is strange indeed that by merely peeling off a wrapper of modern accumulations we have lowered ourselves into an ancient world. Finally a skeleton is uncovered, fairly perfect. He lays it out on the grass, bone to its bone.

My friend says the man must have fallen fighting here, as this is no place of burial. He turns again to the trench, scrapes, feels, till from a corner he draws out a heavy lump – a small image four or five inches high. We clean it as before. It is a statuette, apparently of gold, or, more probably, of bronze-gilt – a figure of Mercury, obviously, its head being surmounted with the petasus or winged hat, the usual accessory of that deity. Further inspection reveals the workmanship to be of good finish and detail, and, preserved by the limy earth, to be as fresh in every line as on the day it left the hands of its artificer.

We seem to be standing in the Roman Forum and not on a hill in Wessex. Intent upon this truly valuable relic of the old empire of which even this remote spot was a component part, we do not notice what is going on in the present world till reminded of it by the sudden renewal of the storm. Looking up I perceive that the wide extinguisher of cloud has again settled down upon the fortress-town, as if resting upon the edge of the inner rampart, and shutting out the moon. I turn my back to the tempest, still directing the light across the hole. My companion digs on unconcernedly; he is living two thousand years ago, and despises things of the moment as dreams. But at last he is fairly beaten, and standing up beside me looks round on what he has done. The rays of the lantern pass over the trench to the tall skeleton stretched upon the grass on the other side. The beating rain has washed the bones clean and smooth, and the forehead, cheek-bones, and two-and-thirty teeth of the skull glisten in the candle-shine as they lie.

This storm, like the first, is of the nature of a squall, and it ends as abruptly as the other. We dig no further. My friend says that it is enough – he has proved his point. He turns to replace the bones in the trench and covers them. But they fall to pieces under his touch: the air has disintegrated them, and he can only sweep in the fragments. The next act of his plan is more than difficult, but is carried out. The treasures are inhumed again in their respective holes: they are not ours. Each deposition seems to cost him a twinge; and at one moment I fancied I saw him slip his hand into his coat pocket.

'We must re-bury them *all*,' say I.

'O yes,' he answers with integrity. 'I was wiping my hand.'

The beauties of the tessellated floor of the governor's house are once again consigned to darkness; the trench is filled up; the sod laid smoothly down; he wipes the perspiration from his forehead with the same handkerchief he had used to mop the skeleton and tesseræ clean; and we make for the eastern gate of the fortress.

Dawn bursts upon us suddenly as we reach the opening. It comes by the lifting and thinning of the clouds that way till we are bathed in a pink light. The direction of his homeward journey is not the same as mine, and we part under the outer slope.

Walking along quickly to restore warmth I muse upon my eccentric friend, and cannot help asking myself this question: Did he really replace the gilded image of the god Mercurius with the rest of the treasures? He seemed to do so; and yet I could not testify to the fact. Probably, however, he was as good as his word.

It was thus I spoke to myself, and so the adventure ended. But one thing remains to be told, and that is concerned with seven years after. Among the effects of my friend, at that time just deceased, was found, carefully preserved, a gilt statuette representing Mercury, labelled 'Debased Roman'. No record was attached to explain how it came into his possession. The figure was bequeathed to the Casterbridge Museum.

'Detroit Post',
March 1885

What the Shepherd Saw

A Tale of Four Moonlight Nights

FIRST NIGHT

THE genial Justice of the Peace – now, alas, no more – who made himself responsible for the facts of this story, used to begin in the good old-fashioned way with a bright moonlight night and a mysterious figure, an excellent stroke for an opening, even to this day, if well followed up.

The Christmas moon (he would say) was showing her cold face to the upland, the upland reflecting the radiance in frost-sparkles so minute as only to be discernible by an eye near at hand. This eye, he said, was the eye of a shepherd lad, young for his occupation, who stood within a wheeled hut of the kind commonly in use among sheep-keepers during the early lambing season, and was abstractedly looking through the loophole at the scene without.

The spot was called Lambing Corner, and it was a sheltered portion of that wide expanse of rough pastureland known as the Marlbury Downs, which you directly traverse when following the turnpike-road across Mid-Wessex from London, through Aldbrickham, in the direction of Bath and Bristol. Here, where the hut stood, the land was high and dry, open, except to the north, and commanding an undulating view for miles. On the north side grew a tall belt of coarse furze, with enormous stalks, a clump of the same standing detached in front of the general mass. The clump was hollow, and the interior had been ingeniously taken advantage of as a position for the before-mentioned hut, which was thus completely screened from winds, and almost invisible, except through the narrow approach. But the furze twigs had been cut away from the two little windows of the hut, that the occupier might keep his eye on his sheep.

In the rear, the shelter afforded by the belt of furze bushes was artificially improved by an inclosure of upright stakes, interwoven with boughs of the same prickly vegetation, and within the inclosure lay a renowned Marlbury-Down breeding flock of eight hundred ewes.

To the south, in the direction of the young shepherd's idle gaze, there rose one conspicuous object above the uniform moonlit plateau, and only one. It was a Druidical trilithon, consisting of three oblong stones in the form of a doorway, two on end, and one across as a lintel. Each stone had been worn, scratched, washed, nibbled, split, and otherwise attacked by ten thousand different weathers; but now the blocks looked shapely and little the worse for wear, so beautifully were they silvered over by the light of the moon. The ruin was locally called the Devil's Door.

An old shepherd presently entered the hut from the direction of the ewes, and looked around in the gloom. 'Be ye sleepy?' he asked in cross accents of the boy.

The lad replied rather timidly in the negative.

'Then,' said the shepherd, 'I'll get me home-along, and rest for a few hours. There's nothing to be done here now as I can see. The ewes can want no more tending till daybreak – 'tis beyond the bounds of reason that they can. But as the order is that one of us must bide, I'll leave 'ee, d'ye hear? You can sleep by day, and I can't. And you can be down to my house in ten minutes if anything should happen. I can't afford 'ee candle; but, as 'tis Christmas week, and the time that folks have holler-days, you can enjoy yerself by falling asleep a bit in the chair instead of biding awake all the time. But mind, not longer at once than while the shade of the Devil's Door moves a couple of spans, for you must keep an eye upon the ewes.'

The boy made no definite reply, and the old man, stirring the fire in the stove with his crook-stem, closed the door upon his companion and vanished.

As this had been more or less the course of events every night since the season's lambing had set in, the boy was not at all surprised at the charge, and amused himself for some time by lighting straws at the stove. He then went out to the ewes and new-born lambs, re-entered, sat down, and finally fell asleep. This was his customary manner of performing his watch, for though special permission for naps had this week been accorded, he had, as a matter of fact, done the same thing on every preceding night, sleeping often till awakened by a smack on the shoulder at three or four in the morning from the crook-stem of the old man.

It might have been about eleven o'clock when he awoke. He was so surprised at awaking without, apparently, being called or struck, that on second thoughts he assumed that somebody must have called him in spite of appearances, and looked out of the hut window towards the sheep. They all lay as quiet as when he had visited them, very little bleating being audible, and no human soul disturbing the scene. He next looked from the opposite window, and here the case was different. The frost-facets glistened under the moon as before; an occasional furze bush showed as a dark spot on the same; and in the foreground stood the ghostly form of the trilithon. But in front of the trilithon stood a man.

That he was not the shepherd or anyone of the farm labourers was apparent in a moment's observation, his dress being a dark suit, and his figure of slender build and graceful carriage. He walked backwards and forwards in front of the trilithon.

The shepherd lad had hardly done speculating on the strangeness of the unknown's presence here at such an hour, when he saw a second figure crossing the open sward towards the locality of the trilithon and furze clump that screened the hut. This second personage was a woman; and immediately on sight of her the male stranger hastened forward, meeting her just in front of the hut window. Before she seemed to be aware of his intention he clasped her in his arms.

The lady released herself and drew back with some dignity.

'You have come, Harriet – bless you for it!' he exclaimed fervently.

'But not for this,' she answered, in offended accents. And then, more good-naturedly, 'I have come, Fred, because you entreated me so! What can have been the object of your writing such a letter? I feared I might be doing you grievous ill by staying away. How did you come here?'

'I walked all the way from my father's.'

'Well, what is it? How have you lived since we last met?'

'But roughly; you might have known that without asking. I have seen many lands and many faces since I last walked these downs, but I have only thought of you.'

'Is it only to tell me this that you have summoned me so strangely?'

A passing breeze blew away the murmur of the reply and several succeeding sentences, till the man's voice again became audible in the words, 'Harriet – truth between us two! I have heard that the Duke does not treat you too well.'

'He is warm-tempered, but he is a good husband.'

'He speaks roughly to you, and sometimes even threatens to lock you out of doors.'

'Only once, Fred! On my honour, only once. The Duke is a fairly good husband, I repeat. But you deserve punishment for this night's trick of drawing me out. What does it mean?'

'Harriet, dearest, is this fair or honest? Is it not notorious that your life with him is a sad one – that, in spite of the sweetness of your temper, the sourness of his embitters your days? I have come to know if I can help you. You are a Duchess, and I am Fred Ogbourne; but it is not impossible that I may be able to help you. . . . By God! the sweetness of that tongue ought to keep him civil, especially when there is added to it the sweetness of that face!'

'Captain Ogbourne!' she exclaimed, with an emphasis of playful fear. 'How can such a comrade of my youth behave to me as you do? Don't speak so, and stare at me so! Is this really all you have to say? I see I ought not to have come. 'Twas thoughtlessly done.'

Another breeze broke the thread of discourse for a time.

'Very well. I perceive you are dead and lost to me,' he could next be heard to say; ' "Captain Ogbourne" proves that. As I once loved you I love you now, Harriet, without one jot of abatement; but you are not the woman you were – you once were honest towards me; and now you conceal your heart in made-up speeches. Let it be; I can never see you again.'

'You need not say that in such a tragedy tone, you silly. You may see me in an ordinary way – why should you not? But, of course, not in such a way as this. I should not have come now, if it had not happened that the Duke is away from home, so that there is nobody to check my erratic impulses.'

'When does he return?'

'The day after to-morrow, or the day after that.'

'Then meet me again to-morrow night.'

'No, Fred, I cannot.'

'If you cannot to-morrow night, you can the night after; one of the two before he comes please bestow on me. Now, your hand upon it! To-morrow or next night you will see me to bid me farewell!' He seized the Duchess's hand.

'No, but, Fred – let go my hand! What do you mean by holding me so ? If it be love to forget all respect to a woman's present position in thinking of her past, then yours may be so, Frederick. It is not kind and gentle of you to induce me to come to this place for pity of you, and then to hold me tight here.'

'But see me once more! I have come two thousand miles to ask it.'

'O, I must not! There will be slanders – Heaven knows what! I cannot meet you. For the sake of old times don't ask it.'

'Then own two things to me; that you did love me once, and that your husband is unkind to you often enough now to make you think of the time when you cared for me.'

'Yes – I own them both,' she answered faintly. 'But owning such as that tells against me; and I swear the inference is not true.'

'Don't say that; for you have come – let me think the reason of your coming what I like to think it. It can do you no harm. Come once more!'

He still held her hand and waist. 'Very well, then,' she said. 'Thus far you shall persuade me. I will meet you to-morrow night or the night after. Now, let me go.'

He released her, and they parted. The Duchess ran rapidly down the hill towards the outlying mansion of Shakeforest Towers, and when he had watched her out of sight, he turned and strode off in the opposite direction. All then was silent and empty as before.

Yes it was only for a moment. When they had quite departed, another shape appeared upon the scene. He came from behind the trilithon. He was a man of stouter build than the first, and wore the boots and spurs of a horseman. Two things were at once obvious from this phenomenon: that he had watched the interview between the Captain and the Duchess; and that, though he probably had seen every movement of the couple, including the embrace, he had been too remote to hear the reluctant words of the lady's conversation – or, indeed, any words at all – so that the meeting must have exhibited itself to his eye as the assignation of a pair of well-agreed lovers. But it was necessary that several years should elapse before the shepherd-boy was old enough to reason out this.

The third individual stood still for a moment, as if deep in meditation. He crossed over to where the lady and gentleman had stood, and looked at the ground; then he too turned and went away in a third direction, as widely divergent as possible from those taken by the two interlocutors. His course was towards the highway; and a few minutes afterwards the trot of a horse might have been heard upon its frosty surface, lessening till it died away upon the ear.

The boy remained in the hut, confronting the trilithon as if he expected yet more actors on the scene, but nobody else appeared. How long he stood with his little face against the loophole he hardly knew; but he was rudely awakened from his reverie by a punch in his back, and in the feel of it he familiarly recognized the stem of the old shepherd's crook.

'Blame thy young eyes and limbs, Bill Mills – now you have let the fire out, and you know I want it kept in! I thought something would go wrong with 'ee up here, and I couldn't bide in bed no more than thistledown on the wind, that I could not! Well, what's happened, fie upon 'ee?'

'Nothing.'

'Ewes all as I left 'em?'

'Yes.'

'Any lambs want bringing in?'

'No.'

The shepherd relit the fire, and went out among the sheep with a lantern, for the moon was getting low. Soon he came in again.

'Blame it all – thou'st say that nothing have happened; when one ewe have twinned and is like to go off, and another is dying for want of half an eye of looking to! I told 'ee, Bill Mills, if anything went wrong to come down and call me; and this is how you have done it.'

'You said I could go to sleep for a hollerday, and I did.'

'Don't you speak to your betters like that, young man, or you'll come to the gallows-tree! You didn't sleep all the time, or you wouldn't have been peeping out of that there hole! Now you can go home, and be up here again by breakfast-time. I be an old man, and there's old men that deserve well of the world; but no – I must rest how I can!'

The elder shepherd then lay down inside the hut, and the boy went down the hill to the hamlet where he dwelt.

SECOND NIGHT

When the next night drew on the actions of the boy were almost enough to show that he was thinking of the meeting he had witnessed, and of the promise wrung from the lady that she would come there again. As far as the sheep-tending arrangements were concerned, to-night was but a repetition of the foregoing one. Between ten and eleven o'clock the old shepherd withdrew as usual for what sleep at home he might chance to get without interruption, making up the other necessary hours of rest at some time during the day; the boy was left alone.

The frost was the same as on the night before, except perhaps that it was a little more severe. The moon shone as usual, except that it was three-quarters of an hour later in its course; and the boy's condition was much the same, except that he felt no sleepiness whatever. He felt, too, rather afraid: but upon the whole he preferred witnessing an assignation of strangers to running the risk of being discovered absent by the old shepherd.

It was before the distant clock of Shakeforest Towers had struck eleven that he observed the opening of the second act of this midnight drama. It consisted in the appearance of neither lover nor Duchess, but of the third figure – the stout man, booted and spurred – who came up from the easterly direction in which he had retreated the night before. He walked once round the trilithon, and next advanced towards the clump concealing the hut, the moonlight shining full upon his face and revealing him to be the Duke. Fear seized upon the shepherd-boy: the Duke was Jove himself to the rural population, whom to offend was starvation, homelessness, and death, and whom to look at was to be mentally scathed and dumbfoundered. He closed the stove, so that not a spark of light appeared, and hastily buried himself in the straw that lay in a corner.

The Duke came close to the clump of furze and stood by the spot where his wife and the Captain had held their dialogue; he examined the furze as if searching for a hiding-place, and in doing so discovered the hut. The latter he walked round and then looked inside; finding it to all seeming empty, he entered, closing the door behind him and taking his place at the little circular window against which the boy's face had been pressed just before.

The Duke had not adopted his measures too rapidly, if his object were concealment. Almost as soon as he had stationed himself there eleven o'clock struck, and the slender young man who had previously graced the scene promptly reappeared from the north quarter of the down. The spot of assignation having, by the accident of his running forward on the foregoing night, removed itself from the Devil's Door to the clump of furze, he instinctively came thither, and waited for the Duchess where he had met her before.

But a fearful surprise was in store for him to-night, as well as for the trembling juvenile. At his appearance the Duke breathed more and more quickly, his breathings being distinctly audible to the crouching boy. The young man had hardly paused when the alert nobleman softly opened the door of the hut, and, stepping round the furze, came full upon Captain Fred.

'You have dishonoured her, and you shall die the death you deserve!' came to the shepherd's ears, in a harsh, hollow whisper through the boarding of the hut.

The apathetic and taciturn boy was excited enough to run the risk of rising and looking from the window, but he could see nothing for the intervening furze boughs, both the men having gone round to the side. What took place in the few following moments he never exactly knew. He discerned portion of a shadow in quick muscular movement; then there was the fall of something on the grass; then there was stillness.

Two or three minutes later the Duke became visible round the corner of the hut, dragging by the collar the now inert body of the second man. The Duke dragged him across the open space towards the trilithon. Behind this ruin was a hollow, irregular spot, overgrown with furze and stunted thorns, and riddled by the old holes of badgers, its former inhabitants, who had now died out or departed. The Duke vanished into this depression with his burden, reappearing after the lapse of a few seconds. When he came forth he dragged nothing behind him.

He returned to the side of the hut, cleansed something on the grass, and again put himself on the watch, though not as before, inside the hut, but without, on the shady side. 'Now for the second!' he said.

It was plain, even to the unsophisticated boy, that he now awaited the other person of the appointment – his wife, the Duchess – for what purpose it was terrible to think. He seemed to be a man of such determined temper that he would scarcely hesitate in carrying out a course of revenge to the bitter end. Moreover – though it was what the shepherd did not perceive – this was all the more probable, in that the moody Duke was labouring under the exaggerated impression which the sight of the meeting in dumb show had conveyed.

The jealous watcher waited long, but he waited in vain. From within

the hut the boy could hear his occasional exclamations of surprise, as if
he were almost disappointed at the failure of his assumption that his
guilty Duchess would surely keep the tryst. Sometimes he stepped from
the shade of the furze into the moonlight, and held up his watch to learn
the time.

About half-past eleven he seemed to give up expecting her. He then
went a second time to the hollow behind the trilithon, remaining there
nearly a quarter of an hour. From this place he proceeded quickly over
a shoulder of the declivity, a little to the left, presently returning on
horseback, which proved that his horse had been tethered in some secret
place down there. Crossing anew the down between the hut and the
trilithon, and scanning the precincts as if finally to assure himself that
she had not come, he rode slowly downwards in the direction of
Shakeforest Towers.

The juvenile shepherd thought of what lay in the hollow yonder; and
no fear of the crook-stem of his superior officer was potent enough to
detain him longer on that hill alone. Any live company, even the most
terrible, was better than the company of the dead; so, running with the
speed of a hare in the direction pursued by the horseman, he overtook
the revengeful Duke at the second descent (where the great western
road crossed before you came to the old park entrance on that side –
now closed up and the lodge cleared away, though at the time it
was wondered why, being considered the most convenient gate of
all).

Once within the sound of the horse's footsteps, Bill Mills felt comparatively comfortable; for, though in awe of the Duke because of his
position, he had no moral repugnance to his companionship on account
of the grisly deed he had committed, considering that powerful nobleman to have a right to do what he chose on his own lands. The Duke
rode steadily on beneath his ancestral trees, the hoofs of his horse sending
up a smart sound now that he had reached the hard road of the drive,
and soon drew near the front door of his house, surmounted by parapets
with square-cut battlements that cast a notched shade upon the gravelled
terrace. These outlines were quite familiar to little Bill Mills, though
nothing within their boundary had ever been seen by him.

When the rider approached the mansion a small turret door was
quickly opened and a woman came out. As soon as she saw the horseman's outlines she ran forward into the moonlight to meet him.

'Ah, dear – and are you come?' she said. 'I heard Hero's tread just

when you rode over the hill, and I knew it in a moment. I would have
come further if I had been aware—'

'Glad to see me, eh?'

'How can you ask that?'

'Well; it is a lovely night for meetings.'

'Yes, it is a lovely night.'

The Duke dismounted and stood by her side. 'Why should you have
been listening at this time of night, and yet not expecting me?' he
asked.

'Why, indeed! There is a strange story attached to that, which I must
tell you at once. But why did you come a night sooner than you said you
would come? I am rather sorry – I really am!' (shaking her head playfully), 'for as a surprise to you I had ordered a bonfire to be built, which
was to be lighted on your arrival to-morrow; and now it is wasted. You
can see the outline of it just out there.'

The Duke looked across to a spot of rising glade, and saw the faggots
in a heap. He then bent his eyes with a bland and puzzled air on the
ground. 'What is this strange story you have to tell me that kept you
awake?' he murmured.

'It is this – and it is really rather serious. My cousin Fred Ogbourne –
Captain Ogbourne as he is now – was in his boyhood a great admirer of
mine, as I think I have told you, though I was six years his senior. In
strict truth, he was absurdly fond of me.'

'You have never told me of that before.'

'Then it was your sister I told – yes, it was. Well, you know I have not
seen him for many years, and naturally I had quite forgotten his admiration of me in old times. But guess my surprise when the day before
yesterday, I received a mysterious note bearing no address, and found
on opening it that it came from him. The contents frightened me out of
my wits. He had returned from Canada to his father's house, and conjured me by all he could think of to meet him at once. But I think I can
repeat the exact words, though I will show it to you when we get indoors.

   ' "MY DEAR COUSIN HARRIET," the note said, "After this long
   absence you will be surprised at my sudden reappearance, and more
   by what I am going to ask. But if my life and future are of any
   concern to you at all, I beg that you will grant my request. What
   I require of you, is, dear Harriet, that you meet me about eleven
   to-night by the Druid stones on Marlbury Downs, about a mile or
   more from your house. I cannot say more, except to entreat you
   to come. I will explain all when you are there. The one thing is, I

want to see you. Come alone. Believe me, I would not ask this if my happiness did not hang upon it – God knows how entirely! I am too agitated to say more – Yours,

FRED"

'That was all of it. Now, of course, I ought not to have gone, as it turned out, but that I did not think of then. I remembered his impetuous temper, and feared that something grievous was impending over his head, while he had not a friend in the world to help him, or anyone except myself to whom he would care to make his trouble known. So I wrapped myself up and went to Marlbury Downs at the time he had named. Don't you think I was courageous?'

'Very.'

'When I got there – but shall we not walk on; it is getting cold?' The Duke, however, did not move. 'When I got there he came, of course, as a full-grown man and officer, and not as the lad that I had known him. When I saw him I was sorry I had come. I can hardly tell you how he behaved. What he wanted I don't know even now; it seemed to be no more than the mere meeting with me. He held me by the hand and waist – O so tight – and would not let me go till I had promised to meet him again. His manner was so strange and passionate that I was afraid of him in such a lonely place, and I promised to come. Then I escaped – then I ran home – and that's all. When the time drew on this evening for the appointment – which, of course, I never intended to keep – I felt uneasy, lest when he found I meant to disappoint him he would come on to the house; and that's why I could not sleep. But you are so silent!'

'I have had a long journey.'

'Then let us get into the house. Why did you come alone and unattended like this?'

'It was my humour.'

After a moment's silence, during which they moved on, she said, 'I have thought of something which I hardly like to suggest to you. He said that if I failed to come to-night he would wait again to-morrow night. Now, shall we to-morrow night go to the hill together – just to see if he is there; and if he is, read him a lesson on his foolishness in nourishing this old passion, and sending for me so oddly, instead of coming to the house?'

'Why should we see if he's there?' said her husband moodily.

'Because I think we ought to do something in it. Poor Fred! He would listen to you if you reasoned with him, and set our positions in their true light before him. It would be no more than Christian kindness to a man who unquestionably is very miserable from some cause or other. His head seems quite turned.'

By this time they had reached the door, rung the bell, and waited. All the house seemed to be asleep; but soon a man came to them, the horse was taken away, and the Duke and Duchess went in.

THIRD NIGHT

There was no help for it. Bill Mills was obliged to stay on duty, in the old shepherd's absence, this evening as before, or give up his post and living. He thought as bravely as he could of what lay behind the Devil's Door, but with no great success, and was therefore in a measure relieved, even if awe-stricken, when he saw the forms of the Duke and Duchess strolling across the frosted greensward. The Duchess was a few yards in front of her husband and tripped on lightly.

'I tell you he has not thought it worth while to come again!' the Duke insisted, as he stood still, reluctant to walk further.

'He is more likely to come and wait all night; and it would be harsh treatment to let him do it a second time.'

'He is not here; so turn and come home.'

'He seems not to be here, certainly; I wonder if anything has happened to him. If it has, I shall never forgive myself!'

The Duke, uneasily, 'O, no. He has some other engagement.'

'That is very unlikely.'

'Or perhaps he has found the distance too far.'

'Nor is that probable.'

'Then he may have thought better of it.'

'Yes, he may have thought better of it; if, indeed, he is not here all the time – somewhere in the hollow behind the Devil's Door. Let us go and see; it will serve him right to surprise him.'

'O, he's not there.'

'He may be lying very quiet because of you,' she said archly.

'O, no – not because of me!'

'Come, then. I declare, dearest, you lag like an unwilling schoolboy to-night, and there's no responsiveness in you! You are jealous of that poor lad, and it is quite absurd of you.'

'I'll come! I'll come! Say no more, Harriet!' And they crossed over the green.

Wondering what they would do, the young shepherd left the hut, and doubled behind the belt of furze, intending to stand near the trilithon unperceived. But, in crossing the few yards of open ground he was for a moment exposed to view.

'Ah, I see him at last!' said the Duchess.

'See him!' said the Duke. 'Where?'

'By the Devil's Door; don't you notice a figure there? Ah, my poor lover-cousin, won't you catch it now?' And she laughed half-pityingly. 'But what's the matter?' she asked, turning to her husband.

'It is not he!' said the Duke hoarsely. 'It can't be he!'

'No, it is not he. It is too small for him. It is a boy.'

'Ah, I thought so! Boy, come here.'

The youthful shepherd advanced with apprehension.

'What are you doing here?'

'Keeping sheep, your Grace.'

'Ah, you know me! Do you keep sheep here every night?'

'Off and on, my Lord Duke.'

'And what have you seen here to-night or last night?' inquired the Duchess. 'Any person waiting or walking about?'

The boy was silent.

'He has seen nothing,' interrupted her husband, his eyes so forbiddingly fixed on the boy that they seemed to shine like points of fire. 'Come, let us go. The air is too keen to stand in long.'

When they were gone the boy retreated to the hut and sheep, less fearful now than at first – familiarity with the situation having gradually overpowered his thoughts of the buried man. But he was not to be left alone long. When an interval had elapsed of about sufficient length for walking to and from Shakeforest Towers, there appeared from that direction the heavy form of the Duke. He now came alone.

The nobleman, on his part, seemed to have eyes no less sharp than the boy's, for he instantly recognized the latter among the ewes, and came straight towards him.

'Are you the shepherd lad I spoke to a short time ago?'

'I be, my Lord Duke.'

'Now listen to me. Her Grace asked you what you had seen this last night or two up here, and you made no reply. I now ask the same thing, and you need not be afraid to answer. Have you seen anything strange these nights you have been watching here?'

'My Lord Duke, I be a poor heedless boy, and what I see I don't bear in mind.'

'I ask you again,' said the Duke, coming nearer, 'have you see anything strange these nights you have been watching here?'

'O, my Lord Duke! I be but the under-shepherd boy, and my father he was but your humble Grace's hedger, and my mother only the cinder-woman in the back-yard! I fall asleep when left alone, and I see nothing at all!'

The Duke grasped the boy by the shoulder, and, directly impending over him, stared down into his face, 'Did you see anything strange done here last night, I say?'

'O, my Lord Duke, have mercy, and don't stab me!' cried the shepherd, falling on his knees. 'I have never seen you walking here, or riding here, or lying-in-wait for a man, or dragging a heavy load!'

'H'm!' said his interrogator, grimly, relaxing his hold. 'It is well to know that you have never seen those things. Now, which would you rather – *see me do those things now*, or keep a secret all your life?'

'Keep a secret, my Lord Duke!'

'Sure you are able?'

'O, your Grace, try me!'

'Very well. And now, how do you like sheep-keeping?'

'Not at all. 'Tis lonely work for them that think of spirits, and I'm badly used.'

'I believe you. You are too young for it. I must do something to make you more comfortable. You shall change this smock-frock for a real cloth jacket, and your thick boots for polished shoes. And you shall be taught what you have never yet heard of, and be put to school, and have bats and balls for the holidays, and be made a man of. But you must never say you have been a shepherd boy, and watched on the hills at night, for shepherd boys are not liked in good company.'

'Trust me, my Lord Duke.'

'The very moment you forget yourself, and speak of your shepherd days – this year, next year, in school, out of school, or riding in your carriage twenty years hence – at that moment my help will be withdrawn, and smash down you come to shepherding forthwith. You have parents, I think you say?'

'A widowed mother only, my Lord Duke.'

'I'll provide for her, and make a comfortable woman of her, until you speak of – what?'

'Of my shepherd days, and what I saw here.'

'Good. If you do speak of it?'

'Smash down she comes to widowing forthwith!'

'That's well – very well. But it's not enough. Come here.' He took the boy across to the trilithon, and made him kneel down.

'Now, this was once a holy place,' resumed the Duke. 'An altar stood here, erected to a venerable family of gods, who were known and talked of long before the God we know now. So that an oath sworn here is doubly an oath. Say this after me: "May all the host above – angels and archangels, and principalities and powers – punish me; may I be tormented wherever I am – in the house or in the garden, in the fields or in the roads, in church or in chapel, at home or abroad, on land or at sea; may I be afflicted in eating and in drinking, in growing up and in growing old, in living and dying, inwardly and outwardly, and for always, if I ever speak of my life as a shepherd boy, or of what I have seen done on this Marlbury Down. So be it, and so let it be. Amen and amen." Now kiss the stone.'

The trembling boy repeated the words, and kissed the stone, as desired.

The Duke led him off by the hand. That night the junior shepherd slept in Shakeforest Towers, and the next day he was sent away for tuition to a remote village. Thence he went to a preparatory establishment, and in due course to a public school.

FOURTH NIGHT

On a winter evening many years subsequent to the above-mentioned occurrences, the *ci-devant* shepherd sat in a well-furnished office in the north wing of Shakeforest Towers in the guise of an ordinary educated man of business. He appeared at this time as a person of thirty-eight or forty, though actually he was several years younger. A worn and restless glance of the eye now and then, when he lifted his head to search for some letter or paper which had been mislaid, seemed to denote that his was not a mind so thoroughly at ease as his surroundings might have led an observer to expect. His pallor, too, was remarkable for a country-man. He was professedly engaged in writing, but he shaped not a word.

He had sat there only a few minutes, when, laying down his pen and pushing back his chair, he rested a hand uneasily on each of the chair-arms and looked on the floor.

Soon he arose and left the room. His course was along a passage which ended in a central octagonal hall; crossing this he knocked at a door. A faint, though deep, voice told him to come in. The room he entered was the library, and it was tenanted by a single person only – his patron the Duke.

During this long interval of years the Duke had lost all his heaviness of build. He was, indeed, almost a skeleton; his white hair was thin, and his hands were nearly transparent. 'Oh – Mills?' he murmured. 'Sit down. What is it?'

'Nothing new, your Grace. Nobody to speak of has written, and nobody has called.'

'Ah – what then? You look concerned.'

'Old times have come to life, owing to something waking them.'

'Old times be cursed – which old times are they?'

'That Christmas week twenty-two years ago, when the late Duchess's cousin Frederick implored her to meet him on Marlbury Downs. I saw the meeting – it was just such a night as this – and I, as you know, saw more. She met him once, but not the second time.'

'Mills, shall I recall some words to you – the words of an oath taken on that hill by a shepherd boy?'

'It is unnecessary. He has strenuously kept that oath and promise. Since that night no sound of his shepherd life has crossed his lips – even to yourself. But do you wish to hear more, or do you not, your Grace?'

'I wish to hear no more,' said the Duke sullenly.

'Very well; let it be so. But a time seems coming – may be quite near at hand – when, in spite of my lips, that episode will allow itself to go undivulged no longer.'

'I wish to hear no more!' repeated the Duke.

'You need be under no fear of treachery from me,' said the steward, somewhat bitterly. 'I am a man to whom you have been kind – no patron could have been kinder. You have clothed and educated me; have installed me here; and I am not unmindful. But what of it – has your Grace gained much by my stanchness? I think not. There was great excitement about Captain Ogbourne's disappearance, but I spoke not a word. And his body has never been found. For twenty-two years I have wondered what you did with him. Now I know. A circumstance that occurred this afternoon recalled the time to me most forcibly. To make it certain to myself that all was not a dream, I went up there with a spade; I searched, and saw enough to know that something decays there in a closed badger's hole.'

'Mills, do you think the Duchess guessed?'

'She never did, I am sure, to the day of her death.'

'Did you leave all as you found it on the hill?'

'I did.'

'What made you think of going up there this particular afternoon?'

'What your Grace says you don't wish to be told.'

The Duke was silent; and the stillness of the evening was so marked that there reached their ears from the outer air the sound of a tolling bell.

'What is that bell tolling for?' asked the nobleman.

'For what I came to tell you of, your Grace.'

'You torment me – it is your way!' said the Duke querulously. 'Who's dead in the village?'

'The oldest man – the old shepherd.'

'Dead at last – how old is he?'

'Ninety-four.'

'And I am only seventy. I have four-and-twenty years to the good!'

'I served under that old man when I kept sheep on Marlbury Downs. And he was on the hill that second night, when I first exchanged words with your Grace. He was on the hill *all the time*; but I did not know he was there – nor did you.'

'Ah!' said the Duke, starting up. 'Go on – I yield the point – you may tell!'

'I heard this afternoon that he was at the point of death. It was that which set me thinking of that past time – and induced me to search on the hill for what I have told you. Coming back I heard that he wished to see the Vicar to confess to him a secret he had kept for more than twenty years – "out of respect to my Lord the Duke" – something that he had seen committed on Marlbury Downs when returning to the flock on a December night twenty-two years ago. I have thought it over. He had left me in charge that evening; but he was in the habit of coming back suddenly, lest I should have fallen asleep. That night I saw nothing of him, though he had promised to return. He must have returned, and – found reason to keep in hiding. It is all plain. The next thing is that the Vicar went to him two hours ago. Further than that I have not heard.'

'It is quite enough. I will see the Vicar at daybreak to-morrow.'

'What to do?'

'Stop his tongue for four-and-twenty years – till I am dead at ninety-four, like the shepherd.'

'Your Grace – while you impose silence on me, I will not speak, even though my neck should pay the penalty. I promised to be yours, and I am yours. But is this persistence of any avail?'

'I'll stop his tongue, I say!' cried the Duke with some of his old rugged force. 'Now, you go home to bed, Mills, and leave me to manage him.'

The interview ended, and the steward withdrew. The night, as he had said, was just such an one as the night of twenty-two years before, and the events of the evening destroyed in him all regard for the season as one of cheerfulness and goodwill. He went off to his own house on the further verge of the park, where he led a lonely life, scarcely calling any man friend. At eleven he prepared to retire to bed – but did not retire. He sat down and reflected. Twelve o'clock struck; he looked out at the colourless moon, and, prompted by he knew not what, put on his hat and emerged into the air. Here William Mills strolled on and on, till he reached the top of Marlbury Downs, a spot he had not visited at this hour of the night during the whole score-and-odd years.

He placed himself, as nearly as he could guess, on the spot where the shepherd's hut had stood. No lambing was in progress there now, and the old shepherd who had used him so roughly had ceased from his labours that very day. But the trilithon stood up white as ever; and, crossing the intervening sward, the steward fancifully placed his mouth against the stone. Restless and self-reproachful as he was, he could not resist a smile as he thought of the terrifying oath of compact, sealed by a kiss upon the stones of a Pagan temple. But he had kept his word, rather as a promise than as a formal vow, with much worldly advantage to himself, though not much happiness; till increase of years had bred reactionary feelings which led him to receive the news of to-night with emotions akin to relief.

While leaning against the Devil's Door and thinking on these things, he became conscious that he was not the only inhabitant of the down. A figure in white was moving across his front with long, noiseless strides. Mills stood motionless, and when the form drew quite near he perceived it to be that of the Duke himself in his nightshirt – apparently walking in his sleep. Not to alarm the old man, Mills clung close to the shadow of the stone. The Duke went straight on into the hollow. There he knelt down, and began scratching the earth with his hands like a badger. After a few minutes he arose, sighed heavily, and retraced his steps as he had come.

Fearing that he might harm himself, yet unwilling to arouse him, the steward followed noiselessly. The Duke kept on his path unerringly, entered the park, and made for the house, where he let himself in by a window that stood open – the one probably by which he had come out. Mills softly closed the window behind his patron, and then retired homeward to await the revelations of the morning, deeming it unnecessary to alarm the house.

However, he felt uneasy during the remainder of the night, no less on account of the Duke's personal condition than because of that which was imminent next day. Early in the morning he called at Shakeforest Towers. The blinds were down, and there was something singular upon the porter's face when he opened the door. The steward inquired for the Duke.

The man's voice was subdued as he replied: 'Sir, I am sorry to say that his Grace is dead! He left his room some time in the night, and wandered about nobody knows where. On returning to the upper floor he lost his balance and fell downstairs.'

The steward told the tale of the Down before the Vicar had spoken. Mills had always intended to do so after the death of the Duke. The consequences to himself he underwent cheerfully; but his life was not prolonged. He died, a farmer at the Cape, when still somewhat under forty-nine years of age.

The splendid Marlbury breeding flock is as renowned as ever, and, to the eye, seems the same in every particular that it was in earlier times; but the animals which composed it on the occasion of the events gathered from the Justice are divided by many ovine generations from its members now. Lambing Corner has long since ceased to be used for lambing purposes, though the name still lingers on as the appellation of the spot. This abandonment of site may be partly owing to the removal of the high furze bushes which lent such convenient shelter at that date. Partly, too, it may be due to another circumstance. For it is said by present shepherds in that district that during the nights of

Christmas week flitting shapes are seen in the open space around the trilithon, together with the gleam of a weapon, and the shadow of a man dragging a burden into the hollow. But of these things there is no certain testimony.

Christmas 1881

A Committee-Man of 'the Terror'

WE had been talking of the Georgian glories of our old-fashioned watering-place, which now, with its substantial russet-red and dun brick buildings in the style of the year eighteen hundred, looks like one side of a Soho or Bloomsbury Street transported to the shore, and draws a smile from the modern tourist who has no eye for solidity of build. The writer, quite a youth, was present merely as a listener. The conversation proceeded from general subjects to particular, until old Mrs H——, whose memory was as perfect at eighty as it had ever been in her life, interested us all by the obvious fidelity with which she repeated a story many times related to her by her mother when our aged friend was a girl – a domestic drama much affecting the life of an acquaintance of her said parent, one Mademoiselle V——, a teacher of French. The incidents occurred in the town during the heyday of its fortunes, at the time of our brief peace with France in 1802–3.

'I wrote it down in the shape of a story some years ago, just after my mother's death,' said Mrs H——. 'It is locked up in my desk there now.'

'Read it!' said we.

'No,' said she; 'the light is bad, and I can remember it well enough, word for word, flourishes and all.' We could not be choosers in the circumstances, and she began.

'There are two in it, of course, the man and the woman, and it was on an evening in September that she first got to know him. There had not been such a grand gathering on the Esplanade all the season. His Majesty King George the Third was present, with all the princesses and royal dukes, while upwards of three hundred of the general nobility and other persons of distinction were also in the town at the time. Carriages and other conveyances were arriving every minute from London and elsewhere; and when among the rest a shabby stage-coach came in by a by-route along the coast from Havenpool, and drew up at a second-rate tavern, it attracted comparatively little notice.

'From this dusty vehicle a man alighted, left his small quantity of luggage temporarily at the office, and walked along the street as if to look for lodgings.

'He was about forty-five – possibly fifty – and wore a long coat of faded superfine cloth, with a heavy collar, and a bunched-up neckcloth. He seemed to desire obscurity.

'But the display appeared presently to strike him, and he asked of a rustic he met in the street what was going on; his accent being that of one to whom English pronunciation was difficult.

'The countryman looked at him with a slight surprise, and said, "King Jarge is here and his royal Cwort."

'The stranger inquired if they were going to stay long.

' "Don't know, Sir. Same as they always do, I suppose."

' "How long is that?"

' "Till some time in October. They've come here every zummer since eighty-nine."

'The stranger moved onward down St Thomas Street, and approached the bridge over the harbour backwater, that then, as now, connected the old town with the more modern portion. The spot was swept with the rays of a low sun, which lit up the harbour lengthwise, and shone under the brim of the man's hat and into his eyes as he looked westward. Against the radiance figures were crossing in the opposite direction to his own; among them this lady of my mother's later acquaintance, Mademoiselle V——. She was the daughter of a good old French family, and at that date a pale woman, twenty-eight or thirty years of age, tall and elegant in figure, but plainly dressed and wearing that evening (she said) a small muslin shawl crossed over the bosom in the fashion of the time, and tied behind.

'At sight of his face, which, as she used to tell us, was unusually distinct in the peering sunlight, she could not help giving a little shriek of horror, for a terrible reason connected with her history, and after walking a few steps further, she sank down against the parapet of the bridge in a fainting fit.

'In his preoccupation the foreign gentleman had hardly noticed her, but her strange collapse immediately attracted his attention. He quickly crossed the carriage-way, picked her up, and carried her into the first shop adjoining the bridge, explaining that she was a lady who had been taken ill outside.

'She soon revived; but, clearly much puzzled, her helper perceived that she still had a dread of him which was sufficient to hinder her complete recovery of self-command. She spoke in a quick and nervous way to the shopkeeper, asking him to call a coach.

'This the shopkeeper did, Mademoiselle V—— and the stranger remaining in constrained silence while he was gone. The coach came up, and giving the man the address, she entered it and drove away.

' "Who is that lady?" said the newly arrived gentleman.

' "She's of your nation, as I should make bold to suppose," said the shopkeeper. And he told the other that she was Mademoiselle V——, governess at General Newbold's, in the same town.

' "You have many foreigners here?" the stranger inquired.

' "Yes, though mostly Hanoverians. But since the peace they are learning French a good deal in genteel society, and French instructors are rather in demand."

' "Yes, I teach it," said the visitor. "I am looking for a tutorship in an academy."

'The information given by the burgess to the Frenchman seemed to explain to the latter nothing of his countrywoman's conduct – which, indeed, was the case – and he left the shop, taking his course again over the bridge and along the south quay to the Old Rooms Inn, where he engaged a bedchamber.

'Thoughts of the woman who had betrayed such agitation at sight of him lingered naturally enough with the newcomer. Though, as I stated, not much less than thirty years of age, Mademoiselle V——, one of his own nation, and of highly refined and delicate appearance, had kindled a singular interest in the middle-aged gentleman's breast, and her large dark eyes, as they had opened and shrunk from him, exhibited a pathetic beauty to which hardly any man could have been insensible.

'The next day, having written some letters, he went out and made known at the office of the town "Guide" and of the newspaper, that a teacher of French and calligraphy had arrived, leaving a card at the bookseller's to the same effect. He then walked on aimlessly, but at length inquired the way to General Newbold's. At the door, without giving his name, he asked to see Mademoiselle V——, and was shown into a little back parlour, where she came to him with a gaze of surprise.

' "My God! Why do you intrude here, Monsieur?" she gasped in French as soon as she saw his face.

' "You were taken ill yesterday. I helped you. You might have been run over if I had not picked you up. It was an act of simple humanity certainly; but I thought I might come to ask if you had recovered?"

'She had turned aside, and had scarcely heard a word of his speech. "I hate you, infamous man!" she said. "I cannot bear your helping me. Go away!"

' "But you are a stranger to me."

' "I know you too well!"

' "You have the advantage then, Mademoiselle. I am a newcomer here. I never have seen you before to my knowledge; and I certainly do not, could not, hate you."

' "Are you not Monsieur B——?"

'He flinched. "I am – in Paris," he said. "But here I am Monsieur G——."

' "That is trivial. You are the man I say you are."

' "How did you know my real name, Mademoiselle?"

' "I saw you in years gone by, when you did not see me. You were formerly Member of the Committee of Public Safety, under the Convention."

' "I was."

' "You guillotined my father, my brother, my uncle – all my family, nearly, and broke my mother's heart. They had done nothing but keep silence. Their sentiments were only guessed. Their headless corpses were thrown indiscriminately into the ditch of the Mousseaux Cemetery, and destroyed with lime."

'He nodded.

' "You left me without a friend, and here I am now, alone in a foreign land."

' "I am sorry for you," said he. "Sorry for the consequence, not for the intent. What I did was a matter of conscience, and, from a point of view indiscernible by you, I did right. I profited not a farthing. But I shall not argue this. You have the satisfaction of seeing me here an exile also, in poverty, betrayed by comrades, as friendless as yourself."

' "It is no satisfaction to me, Monsieur."

' "Well, things done cannot be altered. Now to the question: are you quite recovered?"

' "Not from dislike and dread of you – otherwise, yes."

' "Good morning, Mademoiselle."

' "Good morning."

'They did not meet again till one evening at the theatre (which my mother's friend was with great difficulty induced to frequent, to perfect herself in English pronunciation, the idea she entertained at that time being to become a teacher of English in her own country later on). She found him sitting next to her, and it made her pale and restless.

' "You are still afraid of me?"

' "I am. O cannot you understand!"

'He signified the affirmative.

' "I follow the play with difficulty," he said presently.

' "So do I – *now*," said she.

'He regarded her long, and she was conscious of his look; and while she kept her eyes on the stage they filled with tears. Still she would not move, and the tears ran visibly down her cheek, though the play was a merry one, being no other than Mr Sheridan's comedy of "The Rivals", with Mr S. Kemble as Captain Absolute. He saw her distress, and that her mind was elsewhere; and abruptly rising from his seat at candle-snuffing time he left the theatre.

'Though he lived in the old town, and she in the new, they frequently saw each other at a distance. One of these occasions was when she was on the north side of the harbour, by the ferry, waiting for the boat to take her across. He was standing by Cove Row, on the quay opposite. Instead of entering the boat when it arrived she stepped back from the quay; but looking to see if he remained she beheld him pointing with his finger to the ferry-boat.

' "Enter!" he said, in a voice loud enough to reach her.

'Mademoiselle V—— stood still.

' "Enter!" he said, and, as she did not move, he repeated the word a third time.

'She had really been going to cross, and now approached and stepped down into the boat. Though she did not raise her eyes she knew that he was watching her over. At the landing-steps she saw from under the brim of her hat a hand stretched down. The steps were steep and slippery.

' "No, Monsieur," she said. "Unless, indeed, you believe in God, and repent of your evil past!"

' "I am sorry you were made to suffer. But I only believe in the god called Reason, and I do not repent. I was the instrument of a national principle. Your friends were not sacrificed for any ends of mine."

'She thereupon withheld her hand, and clambered up unassisted. He went on, ascending the Look-out Hill, and disappearing over the brow. Her way was in the same direction, her errand being to bring home the two young girls under her charge, who had gone to the cliff for an airing. When she joined them at the top she saw his solitary figure at the further edge, standing motionless against the sea. All the while that she remained with her pupils he stood without turning, as if looking at the frigates in the roadstead, but more probably in meditation, unconscious where he was. In leaving the spot one of the children threw away half a sponge-biscuit that she had been eating. Passing near it he stooped, picked it up carefully, and put it in his pocket.

'Mademoiselle V—— came homeward, asking herself, "Can he be starving?"

'From that day he was invisible for so long a time that she thought he had gone away altogether. But one evening a note came to her, and she opened it trembling.

' "I am here ill," it said, "and, as you know, alone. There are one or two little things I want done, in case my death should occur, and I should prefer not to ask the people here, if it could be avoided. Have you enough of the gift of charity to come and carry out my wishes before it is too late?"

'Now so it was that, since seeing him possess himself of the broken cake, she had insensibly begun to feel something that was more than curiosity, though perhaps less than anxiety, about this fellow-countryman of hers; and it was not in her nervous and sensitive heart to resist his appeal. She found his lodging (to which he had removed from the Old Rooms Inn for economy) to be a room over a shop, half-way up the steep and narrow street of the old town, to which the fashionable visitors seldom penetrated. With some misgiving she entered the house, and was admitted to the chamber where he lay.

' "You are too good, too good," he murmured. And presently, "You need not shut the door. You will feel safer, and they will not understand what we say."

' "Are you in want, Monsieur? Can I give you—"

' "No, no. I merely want you to do a trifling thing or two that I have not strength enough to do myself. Nobody in the town but you knows who I really am – unless you have told?"

' "I have not told . . . I thought you *might* have acted from principle in those sad days, even—"

' "You are kind to concede that much. However, to the present. I was able to destroy my few papers before I became so weak. . . . But in the drawer there you will find some pieces of linen clothing – only two or three – marked with initials that may be recognized. Will you rip them out with a penknife ?"

'She searched as bidden, found the garments, cut out the stitches of the lettering, and replaced the linen as before. A promise to post, in the event of his death, a letter he put in her hand, completed all that he required of her.

'He thanked her. "I think you seem sorry for me," he murmured. "And I am surprised. You are sorry ?"

'She evaded the question. "Do you repent and believe ?" she asked.

' "No."

'Contrary to her expectations and his own he recovered, though very slowly; and her manner grew more distant thenceforward, though his influence upon her was deeper than she knew. Weeks passed away, and the month of May arrived. One day at this time she met him walking slowly along the beach to the northward.

' "You know the news ?" he said.

' "You mean of the rupture between France and England again ?"

' "Yes; and the feeling of antagonism is stronger than it was in the last war, owing to Bonaparte's high-handed arrest of the innocent English who were travelling in our country for pleasure. I feel that the war will be long and bitter; and that my wish to live unknown in England will be frustrated. See here."

'He took from his pocket a piece of the single newspaper which circulated in the county in those days, and she read –

> "The magistrates acting under the Alien Act have been requested to direct a very scrutinizing eye to the Academies in our towns and other places, in which French tutors are employed, and to all of that nationality who profess to be teachers in this country. Many of them are known to be inveterate Enemies and Traitors to the nation among whose people they have found a livelihood and a home."

'He continued: "I have observed since the declaration of war a marked difference in the conduct of the rougher class of people here towards me. If a great battle were to occur – as it soon will, no doubt – feeling would grow to a pitch that would make it impossible for me, a disguised man of no known occupation, to stay here. With you, whose duties and ante-cedents are known, it may be less difficult, but still unpleasant. Now I propose this. You have probably seen how my deep sympathy with you has quickened to a warm feeling; and what I say is, will you agree to give me a title to protect you by honouring me with your hand? I am older than you, it is true; but as husband and wife we can leave England together, and make the whole world our country. Though I would propose Quebec, in Canada, as the place which offers the best promise of a home."

'"My God! You surprise me!" said she.

'"But you accept my proposal?"

'"No, no!"

'"And yet I think you will, Mademoiselle, some day!"

'"I think not."

'"I won't distress you further now."

'"Much thanks. . . . I am glad to see you looking better, Monsieur; I mean you are looking better."

'"Ah, yes. I am improving. I walk in the sun every day."

'And almost every day she saw him – sometimes nodding stiffly only, sometimes exchanging formal civilities. "You are not gone yet," she said on one of these occasions.

'"No. At present I don't think of going without you."

'"But you find it uncomfortable here?"

'"Somewhat. So when will you have pity on me?"

'She shook her head and went on her way. Yet she was a little moved. "He did it on principle," she would murmur. "He had no animosity towards them, and profited nothing!"

'She wondered how he lived. It was evident that he could not be so poor as she had thought; his pretended poverty might be to escape notice. She could not tell, but she knew that she was dangerously interested in him.

'And he still mended, till his thin, pale face became more full and firm. As he mended she had to meet that request of his, advanced with even stronger insistency.

'The arrival of the King and Court for the season as usual brought matters to a climax for these two lonely exiles and fellow country-people. The King's awkward preference for a part of the coast in such dangerous proximity to France made it necessary that a strict military vigilance should be exercised to guard the royal residents. Half-a-dozen frigates were every night posted in a line across the bay, and two lines of sentinels, one at the water's edge and another behind the Esplanade, occupied the whole sea-front after eight every night. The watering-place was growing an inconvenient residence even for Mademoiselle

V—— herself, her friendship for this strange French tutor and writing-master who never had any pupils having been observed by many who slightly knew her. The General's wife, whose dependent she was, repeatedly warned her against the acquaintance; while the Hanoverian and other soldiers of the Foreign Legion, who had discovered the nationality of her friend, were more aggressive than the English military gallants who made it their business to notice her.

'In this tense state of affairs her answers became more agitated. "O Heaven, how can I marry you!" she would say.

' "You will; surely you will!" he answered again. "I don't leave without you. And I shall soon be interrogated before the magistrates if I stay here; probably imprisoned. You will come?"

'She felt her defences breaking down. Contrary to all reason and sense of family honour she was, by some abnormal craving, inclining to a tenderness for him that was founded on its opposite. Sometimes her warm sentiments burnt lower than at others, and then the enormity of her conduct showed itself in more staring hues.

'Shortly after this he came with a resigned look on his face. "It is as I expected," he said. "I have received a hint to go. In good sooth, I am no Bonapartist – I am no enemy to England; but the presence of the King made it impossible for a foreigner with no visible occupation, and who may be a spy, to remain at large in the town. The authorities are civil, but firm. They are no more than reasonable. Good. I must go. You must come also."

'She did not speak. But she nodded assent, her eyes drooping.

'On her way back to the house on the Esplanade she said to herself, "I am glad, I am glad! I could not do otherwise. It is rendering good for evil!" But she knew how she mocked herself in this, and that the moral principle had not operated one jot in her acceptance of him. In truth she had not realized till now the full presence of the emotion which had unconsciously grown up in her for this lonely and severe man, who, in her tradition, was vengeance and irreligion personified. He seemed to absorb her whole nature, and, absorbing, to control it.

'A day or two before the one fixed for the wedding there chanced to come to her a letter from the only acquaintance of her own sex and country she possessed in England, one to whom she had sent intelligence of her approaching marriage, without mentioning with whom. This friend's misfortunes had been somewhat similar to her own, which fact had been one cause of their intimacy; her friend's sister, a nun of the

Abbey of Montmartre, having perished on the scaffold at the hands of the same Comité de Salut Public which had numbered Mademoiselle V——'s affianced among its members. The writer had felt her position much again of late, since the renewal of the war, she said; and the letter wound up with a fresh denunciation of the authors of their mutual bereavement and subsequent troubles.

'Coming just then, its contents produced upon Mademoiselle V—— the effect of a pail of water upon a somnambulist. What had she been doing in betrothing herself to this man! Was she not making herself a parricide after the event? At this crisis in her feelings her lover called. He beheld her trembling, and, in reply to his question, she told him of her scruples with impulsive candour.

'She had not intended to do this, but his attitude of tender command coerced her into frankness. Thereupon he exhibited an agitation never before apparent in him. He said, "But all that is past. You are the symbol of Charity, and we are pledged to let bygones be."

'His words soothed her for the moment, but she was sadly silent, and he went away.

'That night she saw (as she firmly believed to the end of her life) a divinely sent vision. A procession of her lost relatives – father, brother, uncle, cousin – seemed to cross her chamber between her bed and the window, and when she endeavoured to trace their features she perceived them to be headless, and that she had recognized them by their familiar clothes only. In the morning she could not shake off the effects of this appearance of her nerves. All that day she saw nothing of her wooer, he being occupied in making arrangements for their departure. It grew towards evening – the marriage eve; but, in spite of his reassuring visit, her sense of family duty waxed stronger now that she was left alone. Yet, she asked herself, how could she, alone and unprotected, go at this eleventh hour and reassert to an affianced husband that she could not and would not marry him while admitting at the same time that she loved him? The situation dismayed her. She had relinquished her post as governess, and was staying temporarily in a room near the coach-office, where she expected him to call in the morning to carry out the business of their union and departure.

'Wisely or foolishly, Mademoiselle V—— came to a resolution: that her only safety lay in flight. His contiguity influenced her too sensibly, she could not reason. So packing up her few possessions and placing on the table the small sum she owed, she went out privately, secured a last available seat in the London coach, and, almost before she had fully weighed her action, she was rolling out of the town in the dusk of the September evening.

'Having taken this startling step she began to reflect upon her reasons. He had been one of that tragic Committee the sound of whose name was a horror to the civilized world; yet he had been only *one* of several members, and, it seemed, not the most active. He had marked down names on principle, had felt no personal enmity against his victims, and had enriched himself not a sou out of the office he had held. Nothing could change the past. Meanwhile he loved her, and her heart inclined to as much of him as she could detach from that past. Why not, as he had suggested, bury memories, and inaugurate a new era by this union? In other words, why not indulge her tenderness, since its nullification could do no good.

'Thus she held self-communion in her seat in the coach, passing through Casterbridge, and Shottsford, and on to the White Hart at Melchester, at which place the whole fabric of her recent intentions crumbled down. Better be staunch having got so far; let things take their course, and marry boldly the man who had so impressed her. How great he was; how small was she! And she had presumed to judge him! Abandoning her place in the coach with the precipitancy that had characterized her taking it, she waited till the vehicle had driven off, something in the departing shapes of the outside passengers against the starlit sky giving her a start, as she afterwards remembered. Presently the down coach, "The Morning Herald", entered the city, and she hastily obtained a place on the top.

' "I'll be firm – I'll be his – if it cost me my immortal soul!" she said. And with troubled breathings she journeyed back over the road she had just traced.

'She reached our royal watering-place by the time the day broke, and her first aim was to get back to the hired room in which her last few days had been spent. When the landlady appeared at the door in response to Mademoiselle V——'s nervous summons, she explained her sudden departure and return as best she could; and no objection being offered to her re-engagement of the room for one day longer she ascended to the chamber and sat down panting. She was back once more, and her wild tergiversations were a secret from him whom alone they concerned.

'A sealed letter was on the mantelpiece. "Yes, it is directed to you,

Mademoiselle," said the woman who had followed her. "But we were wondering what to do with it. A town messenger brought it after you had gone last night."

'When the landlady had left, Mademoiselle V—— opened the letter and read –

"MY DEAR AND HONOURED FRIEND. – You have been throughout our acquaintance absolutely candid concerning your misgivings. But I have been reserved concerning mine. That is the difference between us. You probably have not guessed that every qualm you have felt on the subject of our marriage has been paralleled in my heart to the full. Thus it happened that your involuntary outburst of remorse yesterday, though mechanically deprecated by me in your presence, was a last item in my own doubts on the wisdom of our union, giving them a force that I could no longer withstand. I came home; and, on reflection, much as I honour and adore you, I decide to set you free.

"As one whose life has been devoted, and I may say sacrificed, to the cause of Liberty, I cannot allow your judgment (probably a permanent one) to be fettered beyond release by a feeling which may be transient only.

"It would be no less than excruciating to both that I should announce this decision to you by word of mouth. I have therefore taken the less painful course of writing. Before you receive this I shall have left the town by the evening coach for London, on reaching which city my movements will be revealed to none.

"Regard me, Mademoiselle, as dead, and accept my renewed assurances of respect, remembrance, and affection."

'When she had recovered from her shock of surprise and grief, she remembered that at the starting of the coach out of Melchester before dawn, the shape of a figure among the outside passengers against the starlit sky had caused her a momentary start, from its resemblance to that of her friend. Knowing nothing of each other's intentions, and screened from each other by the darkness, they had left the town by the same conveyance. "He, the greater, persevered; I, the smaller, returned!" she said.

'Recovering from her stupor, Mademoiselle V—— bethought herself again of her employer, Mrs Newbold, whom recent events had estranged. To that lady she went with a full heart, and explained everything. Mrs Newbold kept to herself her opinion of the episode, and reinstalled the deserted bride in her old position as governess to the family.

'A governess she remained to the end of her days. After the final peace with France she became acquainted with my mother, to whom by degrees she imparted these experiences of hers. As her hair grew white, and her features pinched, Mademoiselle V—— would wonder what nook of the world contained her lover, if he lived, and if by any chance she might see him again. But when, some time in the 'twenties, death came to her, at no great age, that outline against the stars of the morning remained as the last glimpse she ever obtained of her family's foe and her once affianced husband.'

1895

Master John Horseleigh, Knight

IN the earliest and mustiest volume of the Havenpool marriage registers (said the thin-faced gentleman) this entry may still be read by anyone curious enough to decipher the crabbed handwriting of the date. I took a copy of it when I was last there; and it runs thus (he had opened his pocket-book, and now read aloud the extract; afterwards handing round the book to us, wherein we saw transcribed the following) –

> Mast^r *John Horseleigh, Knyght, of the p'ysshe of Clyffton was maryd to Edith the wyffe late off John Stocker, m'chawnte of Havenpool the xiiij daie of December be p'vylegge gevyn by our sup'me hedd of the chyrche of Ingelonde Kynge Henry the viiith 1539.*

Now, if you turn to the long and elaborate pedigree of the ancient family of the Horseleighs of Clyfton Horseleigh, you will find no mention whatever of this alliance, notwithstanding the privilege given by the Sovereign and head of the Church; the said Sir John being therein chronicled as marrying, at a date apparently earlier than the above, the daughter and heiress of Richard Phelipson, of Montislope, in Nether Wessex, a lady who outlived him, of which marriage there were issue two daughters and a son, who succeeded him in his estates. How are we to account for these, as it would seem, contemporaneous wives? A strange local tradition only can help us, and this can be briefly told.

One evening in the autumn of the year 1540 or 1541, a young sailor, whose Christian name was Roger, but whose surname is not known, landed at his native place of Havenpool, on the South Wessex coast, after a voyage in the Newfoundland trade, then newly sprung into existence. He returned in the ship *Primrose* with a cargo of 'trayne oyle brought home from the New Founde Lande', to quote from the town records of the date. During his absence of two summers and a winter, which made up the term of a Newfoundland 'spell', many unlooked-for changes had occurred within the quiet little seaport, some of which

closely affected Roger the sailor. At the time of his departure his only
sister Edith had become the bride of one Stocker, a respectable townsman, and part owner of the brig in which Roger had sailed; and it was
to the house of this couple, his only relatives, that the young man
directed his steps. On trying the door in Quay Street he found it locked,
and then observed that the windows were boarded up. Inquiring of a
bystander, he learnt for the first time of the death of his brother-in-law,
though that event had taken place nearly eighteen months before.

'And my sister Edith?' asked Roger.

'She's married again – as they do say, and hath been so these twelve
months. I don't vouch for the truth o't, though if she isn't she ought to
be.'

Roger's face grew dark. He was a man with a considerable reserve of
strong passion, and he asked his informant what he meant by speaking
thus.

The man explained that shortly after the young woman's bereavement
a stranger had come to the port. He had seen her moping on the quay,
had been attracted by her youth and loneliness, and in an extraordinarily
brief wooing had completely fascinated her – had carried her off, and,
as was reported, had married her. Though he had come by water, he
was supposed to live no very great distance off by land. They were last
heard of at Oozewood, in Upper Wessex, at the house of one Wall, a
timber-merchant, where, he believed, she still had a lodging, though
her husband, if he were lawfully that much, was but an occasional
visitor to the place.

'The stranger?' asked Roger. 'Did you see him? What manner of
man was he?'

'I liked him not,' said the other. 'He seemed of that kind that hath
something to conceal, and as he walked with her he ever and anon turned
his head and gazed behind him, as if he much feared an unwelcome
pursuer. But, faith,' continued he, 'it may have been the man's anxiety
only. Yet did I not like him.'

'Was he older than my sister?' Roger asked.

'Ay – much older; from a dozen to a score of years older. A man of
some position, maybe, playing an amorous game for the pleasure of the
hour. Who knoweth but that he have a wife already? Many have done
the thing hereabouts of late.'

Having paid a visit to the graves of his relatives, the sailor next day
went along the straight road which, then a lane, now a highway,

conducted to the curious little inland town named by the Havenpool man. It is unnecessary to describe Oozewood on the South-Avon. It has a railway at the present day; but thirty years of steam traffic past its precincts have hardly modified its original features. Surrounded by a sort of fresh-water lagoon, dividing it from meadows and coppice, its ancient thatch and timber houses have barely made way even in the front street for the ubiquitous modern brick and slate. It neither increases nor diminishes in size; it is difficult to say what the inhabitants find to do, for though trades in woodware are still carried on, there cannot be enough of this class of work nowadays to maintain all the householders, the forests around having been so greatly thinned and curtailed. At the time of this tradition the forests were dense, artificers in wood abounded, and the timber trade was brisk. Every house in the town, without exception, was of oak framework, filled in with plaster, and covered with thatch, the chimney being the only brick portion of the structure. Inquiry soon brought Roger the sailor to the door of Wall, the timber-dealer referred to, but it was some time before he was able to gain admission to the lodging of his sister, the people having plainly received directions not to welcome strangers.

She was sitting in an upper room on one of the lath-backed, willow-bottomed 'shepherd's' chairs, made on the spot then as to this day, and as they were probably made there in the days of the Heptarchy. In her lap was an infant, which she had been suckling, though now it had fallen asleep; so had the young mother herself for a few minutes, under the drowsing effects of solitude. Hearing footsteps on the stairs, she awoke, started up with a glad cry, and ran to the door, opening which she met her brother on the threshold.

'O, this is merry; I didn't expect 'ee!' she said. 'Ah, Roger – I thought it was John.' Her tones fell to disappointment.

The sailor kissed her, looked at her sternly for a few moments, and pointing to the infant, said, 'You mean the father of this?'

'Yes, my husband,' said Edith.

'I hope so,' he answered.

'Why, Roger, I'm married – of a truth am I!' she cried.

'Shame upon 'ee, if true! If not true, worse. Master Stocker was an honest man, and ye should have respected his memory longer. Where is thy husband?'

'He comes often. I thought it was he now. Our marriage has to be kept secret for a while – it was done privily for certain reasons; but we

was married at church like honest folk – afore God we were, Roger, six
months after poor Stocker's death.'

' 'Twas too soon,' said Roger.

'I was living in a house alone; I had nowhere to go to. You were far
over sea in the New Found Land, and John took me and brought me
here.'

'How often doth he come?' says Roger again.

'Once or twice weekly,' says she.

'I wish th' 'dst waited till I returned, dear Edy,' he said. 'It mid be
you are a wife – I hope so. But, if so, why this mystery? Why this mean
and cramped lodging in this lonely copse-circled town? Of what standing
is your husband, and of where?'

'He is of gentle breeding – his name is John. I am not free to tell his
family-name. He is said to be of London, for safety' sake; but he really
lives in the county next adjoining this.'

'Where in the next county?'

'I do not know. He has preferred not to tell me, that I may not have
the secret forced from me, to his and my hurt, by bringing the marriage
to the ears of his kinsfolk and friends.'

Her brother's face flushed. 'Our people have been honest townsmen,
well-reputed for long; why should you readily take such humbling from
a sojourner of whom th' 'st know nothing?'

They remained in constrained converse till her quick ear caught a
sound, for which she might have been waiting – a horse's footfall. 'It is
John!' said she. 'This is his night – Saturday.'

'Don't be frightened lest he should find me here!' said Roger. 'I am
on the point of leaving. I wish not to be a third party. Say nothing at all
about my visit, if it will incommode you so to do. I will see thee before
I go afloat again.'

Speaking thus he left the room, and descending the staircase let
himself out by the front door, thinking he might obtain a glimpse of the
approaching horseman. But that traveller had in the meantime gone
stealthily round to the back of the homestead, and peering along the
pinion-end of the house Roger discerned him unbridling and haltering
his horse with his own hands in the shed there.

Roger retired to the neighbouring inn called the Black Lamb, and
meditated. This mysterious method of approach determined him, after
all, not to leave the place till he had ascertained more definite facts of his
sister's position – whether she were the deluded victim of the stranger or

the wife she obviously believed herself to be. Having eaten some supper, he left the inn, it being now about eleven o'clock. He first looked into the shed, and, finding the horse still standing there, waited irresolutely near the door of his sister's lodging. Half-an-hour elapsed, and, while thinking he would climb into a loft hard by for a night's rest, there seemed to be a movement within the shutters of the sitting-room that his sister occupied. Roger hid himself behind a faggot-stack near the back door, rightly divining that his sister's visitor would emerge by the way he had entered. The door opened, and the candle she held in her hand lighted for a moment the stranger's form, showing it to be that of a tall and handsome personage, about forty years of age, and apparently of a superior position in life. Edith was assisting him to cloak himself, which being done he took leave of her with a kiss and left the house. From the door she watched him bridle and saddle his horse, and having mounted and waved an adieu to her as she stood candle in hand, he turned out of the yard and rode away.

The horse which bore him was, or seemed to be, a little lame, and Roger fancied from this that the rider's journey was not likely to be a long one. Being light of foot he followed apace, having no great difficulty on such a still night in keeping within earshot some few miles, the horseman pausing more than once. In this pursuit Roger discovered the rider to choose bridle-tracks and open commons in preference to any high road. The distance soon began to prove a more trying one than he had bargained for; and when out of breath and in some despair of being able to ascertain the man's identity, he perceived an ass standing in the starlight under a hayrick, from which the animal was helping itself to periodic mouthfuls.

The story goes that Roger caught the ass, mounted, and again resumed the trail of the unconscious horseman, which feat may have been possible to a nautical young fellow, though one can hardly understand how a sailor would ride such an animal without bridle or saddle, and strange to his hands, unless the creature were extraordinarily docile. This question, however, is immaterial. Suffice it to say that at dawn the following morning Roger beheld his sister's lover or husband entering the gates of a large and well-timbered park on the south-western verge of the White Hart Forest (as it was then called), now known to everybody as the Vale of Blackmoor. Thereupon the sailor discarded his steed, and finding for himself an obscurer entrance to the same park a little further on, he crossed the grass to reconnoitre.

He presently perceived amid the trees before him a mansion which, new to himself, was one of the best-known in the county at that time. Of this fine manorial residence hardly a trace now remains; but a manuscript dated some years later than the events we are regarding describes it in terms from which the imagination may construct a singularly clear and vivid picture. This record presents it as consisting of 'a faire yellow freestone building, partly two and partly three storeys; a faire halle and parlour, both waynscotted; a faire dyning roome and withdrawing roome, and many good lodgings; a kitchen adjoyninge backwarde to one end of the dwelling-house, with a faire passage from it into the halle, parlour, and dyninge roome, and sellars adjoyninge.

'In the front of the house a square greene court, and a curious gate-house with lodgings in it, standing with the front of the house to the south; in a large outer court three stables, a coach-house, a large barne, and a stable for oxen and kyne, and all houses necessary.

'Without the gatehouse, paled in, a large square greene, in which standeth a faire chappell; of the south-east side of the greene court, towards the river, a large garden.

'Of the south-west side of the greene court is a large bowling greene, with fower mounted walks about it, all walled about with a batteled wall, and sett with all sorts of fruit; and out of it into the feildes there are large walks under many tall elmes orderly planted.'

Then follows a description of the orchards and gardens; the servants' offices, brewhouse, bakehouse, dairy, pigeon-houses, and corn-mill; the river and its abundance of fish; the warren, the coppices, the walks; ending thus –

'And all the country north of the house, open champaign, sandy feildes, very dry and pleasant for all kindes of recreation, huntinge, and hawkinge, and profitable for tillage. . . . The house hath a large prospect east, south, and west, over a very large and pleasant vale . . . is seated from the good markett towns of Sherton Abbas three miles, and Ivell a mile, that plentifully yield all manner of provision; and within twelve miles of the south sea.'

It was on the grass before this seductive and picturesque structure that the sailor stood at gaze under the elms in the dim dawn of Sunday morning, and saw to his surprise his sister's lover and horse vanish within the court of the building.

Perplexed and weary, Roger slowly retreated, more than ever

convinced that something was wrong in his sister's position. He crossed the bowling-green to the avenue of elms, and, bent on further research, was about to climb into one of these, when, looking below, he saw a heap of hay apparently for horses or deer. Into this he crept, and, having eaten a crust of bread which he had hastily thrust into his pocket at the inn, he curled up and fell asleep, the hay forming a comfortable bed, and quite covering him over.

He slept soundly and long, and was awakened by the sound of a bell. On peering from the hay he found the time had advanced to full day; the sun was shining brightly. The bell was that of the 'faire chappell' on the green outside the gatehouse, and it was calling to matins. Presently the priest crossed the green to a little side-door in the chancel, and then from the gateway of the mansion emerged the household, the tall man whom Roger had seen with his sister on the previous night, on his arm being a portly dame, and, running beside the pair, two little girls and a boy. These all entered the chapel, and the bell having ceased and the environs become clear, the sailor crept out from his hiding.

He sauntered towards the chapel, the opening words of the service being audible within. While standing by the porch he saw a belated servitor approaching from the kitchen-court to attend the service also. Roger carelessly accosted him, and asked, as an idle wanderer, the name of the family he had just seen cross over from the mansion.

'Od zounds! if ye modden be a stranger here in very truth, goodman. That wer Sir John and his dame, and his children Elizabeth, Mary, and John.'

'I be from foreign parts. Sir John what d'ye call'n?'

'Master John Horseleigh, Knight, who had a'most as much lond by inheritance of his mother as 'a had by his father, and likewise some by his wife. Why, bain't his arms dree goolden horses' heads, and idden his lady the daughter of Master Richard Phelipson, of Montislope, in Nether Wessex, known to us all?'

'It mid be so, and yet it mid not. However, th' 'lt miss thy prayers for such an honest knight's welfare, and I have to traipse seaward many miles.'

He went onward, and as he walked continued saying to himself, 'Now to that poor wronged fool Edy. The fond thing! I thought it; 'twas too quick – she was ever amorous. What's to become of her! God wot! How be I going to face her with the news, and how be I to hold it from her? To bring this disgrace on my father's honoured name, a double-tongued knave!' He turned and shook his fist at the chapel and all in it, and resumed his way.

Perhaps it was owing to the perplexity of his mind that, instead of returning by the direct road towards his sister's obscure lodging in the next county, he followed the highway to Casterbridge, some fifteen miles off, where he remained drinking hard all that afternoon and evening, and where he lay that and two or three succeeding nights, wandering thence along the Anglebury road to some village that way, and lying the Friday night after at his native place of Havenpool. The sight of the familiar objects there seems to have stirred him anew to action, and the next morning he was observed pursuing the way to Oozewood that he had followed on the Saturday previous, reckoning, no doubt, that Saturday night would, as before, be a time for finding Sir John with his sister again.

He delayed to reach the place till just before sunset. His sister was walking in the meadows at the foot of the garden, with a nursemaid who carried the baby, and she looked up pensively when he approached. Anxiety as to her position had already told upon her once rosy cheeks and lucid eyes. But concern for herself and child was displaced for the moment by her regard of Roger's worn and haggard face.

'Why – you are sick, Roger – you are tired! Where have you been these many days? Why not keep me company a bit – my husband is much away? And we have hardly spoke at all of dear father and of your voyage to the New Land. Why did you go away so suddenly? There is a spare chamber at my lodging.'

'Come indoors,' he said. 'We'll talk now – talk a good deal. As for him [nodding to the child], better heave him into the river; better for him and you!'

She forced a laugh, as if she tried to see a good joke in the remark, and they went silently indoors.

'A miserable hole!' said Roger, looking round the room.

'Nay, but 'tis very pretty!'

'Not after what I've seen. Did he marry 'ee at church in orderly fashion?'

'He did sure – at our church at Havenpool.'

'But in a privy way?'

'Ay – because of his friends – it was at night-time.'

'Ede, ye fond one – for all that he's not thy husband! Th' 'rt not his wife; and the child is a bastard. He hath a wife and children of his own

rank, and bearing his name; and that's Sir John Horseleigh, of Clyfton
Horseleigh, and not plain Jack, as you think him, and your lawful
husband. The sacrament of marriage is no safeguard nowadays. The
King's new-made headship of the Church hath led men to practise these
tricks lightly.'

She had turned white. 'That's not true, Roger!' she said. 'You are in
liquor, my brother, and you know not what you say! Your seafaring
years have taught 'ee bad things!'

'Edith – I've seen them; wife and family – all. How canst—'

They were sitting in the gathered darkness, and at that moment
steps were heard without. 'Go out this way,' she said. 'It is my husband.
He must not see thee in this mood. Get away till to-morrow, Roger, as
you care for me.'

She pushed her brother through a door leading to the back stairs, and
almost as soon as it was closed her visitor entered. Roger, however, did
not retreat down the stairs; he stood and looked through the bobbin-
hole. If the visitor turned out to be Sir John, he had determined to
confront him.

It was the knight. She had struck a light on his entry, and he kissed
the child, and took Edith tenderly by the shoulders, looking into her
face.

'Something's gone awry wi' my dear!' he said. 'What is it? What's
the matter?'

'O, Jack!' she cried. 'I have heard such a fearsome rumour – what
doth it mean? He who told me is my best friend. He must be deceived!
But who deceived him, and why? Jack, I was just told that you had a
wife living when you married me, and have her still!'

'A wife? – H'm.'

'Yes, and children. Say no, say no!'

'By God! I have no lawful wife but you; and as for children, many or
few, they are all bastards, save this one alone!'

'And that you be Sir John Horseleigh of Clyfton?'

'I mid be. I have never said so to 'ee.'

'But Sir John is known to have a lady, and issue of her!'

The knight looked down. 'How did thy mind get filled with such as
this?' he asked.

'One of my kindred came.'

'A traitor! Why should he mar our life? Ah! you said you had a
brother at sea – where is he now?'

'*Here!*' came from close behind him. And flinging open the door, Roger faced the intruder. 'Liar!' he said, 'to call thyself her husband!'

Sir John fired up, and made a rush at the sailor, who seized him by the collar, and in the wrestle they both fell, Roger under. But in a few seconds he contrived to extricate his right arm, and drawing from his belt a knife which he wore attached to a cord round his neck he opened it with his teeth, and struck it into the breast of Sir John stretched above him. Edith had during these moments run into the next room to place the child in safety, and when she came back the knight was relaxing his hold on Roger's throat. He rolled over upon his back and groaned.

The only witness of the scene save the three concerned was the nurse-maid, who had brought in the child on its father's arrival. She stated afterwards that nobody suspected Sir John had received his death-wound; yet it was so, though he did not die for a long while, meaning thereby an hour or two; that Mistress Edith continually endeavoured to staunch the blood, calling her brother Roger a wretch, and ordering him to get himself gone; on which order he acted, after a gloomy pause, by opening the window, and letting himself down by the sill to the ground.

It was then that Sir John, in difficult accents, made his dying declaration to the nurse and Edith, and, later, the apothecary; which was to this purport, that the Dame Horseleigh who passed as his wife at Clyfton, and who had borne him three children, was in truth and deed, though unconsciously, the wife of another man. Sir John had married her several years before, in the face of the whole county, as the widow of one Decimus Strong, who had disappeared shortly after her union with him, having adventured to the North to join the revolt of the Nobles, and on that revolt being quelled retreated across the sea. Two years ago, having discovered this man to be still living in France, and not wishing to disturb the mind and happiness of her who believed herself his wife, yet wishing for legitimate issue, Sir John had informed the King of the facts, who had encouraged him to wed honestly, though secretly, the young merchant's widow at Havenpool; she being, there-fore, his lawful wife, and she only. That to avoid all scandal and hubbub he had purposed to let things remain as they were till fair opportunity should arise of making the true case known with least pain to all parties concerned, but that, having been thus suspected and attacked by his own brother-in-law, his zest for such schemes and for all things had died out in him, and he only wished to commend his soul to God.

That night, while the owls were hooting from the forest that encircled the sleeping townlet, and the South-Avon was gurgling through the wooden piles of the bridge, Sir John died there in the arms of his wife. She concealed nothing of the cause of her husband's death save the subject of the quarrel, which she felt it would be premature to announce just then, and until proof of her status should be forthcoming. But before a month had passed, it happened, to her inexpressible sorrow, that the child of this clandestine union fell sick and died. From that hour all interest in the name and fame of the Horseleighs forsook the younger of the twain who called themselves wives of Sir John, and, being careless about her own fame, she took no steps to assert her claims, her legal position having, indeed, grown hateful to her in her horror at the tragedy. And Sir William Byrt, the curate who had married her to her husband, being an old man and feeble, was not disinclined to leave the embers unstirred of such a fiery matter as this, and to assist her in letting established things stand. Therefore, Edith retired with the nurse, her only companion and friend, to her native town, where she lived in absolute obscurity till her death in middle age. Her brother was never seen again in England.

A strangely corroborative sequel to the story remains to be told. Shortly after the death of Sir John Horseleigh, a soldier of fortune returned from the Continent, called on Dame Horseleigh the fictitious, living in widowed state at Clyfton Horseleigh, and, after a singularly brief courtship, married her. The tradition at Havenpool and elsewhere has ever been that this man was already her husband, Decimus Strong, who remarried her for appearance' sake only.

The illegitimate son of this lady by Sir John succeeded to the estates and honours, and his son after him, there being nobody on the alert to investigate their pretensions. Little difference would it have made to the present generation, however, had there been such a one, for the family in all its branches, lawful and unlawful, has been extinct these many score years, the last representative but one being killed at the siege of Sherton Castle, while attacking in the service of the Parliament, and the other being outlawed later in the same century for a debt of ten pounds, and dying in the county jail. The mansion-house and its appurtenances were, as I have previously stated, destroyed, excepting one small wing, which now forms part of a farmhouse, and is visible as you pass along the railway from Casterbridge to Ivell. The outline of the old bowling-green is also distinctly to be seen.

This, then, is the reason why the only lawful marriage of Sir John, as recorded in the obscure register at Havenpool, does not appear in the pedigree of the house of Horseleigh.

Spring 1893

The Duke's Reappearance

A Family Tradition

ACCORDING to the kinsman who told me the story, Christopher Swetman's house, on the outskirts of King's-Hintock village, was in those days larger and better kept than when, many years later, it was sold to the lord of the manor adjoining; after having been in the Swetman family, as one may say, since the Conquest.

Some people would have it to be that the thing happened at the house opposite, belonging to one Childs, with whose family the Swetmans afterwards intermarried. But that it was at the original homestead of the Swetmans can be shown in various ways; chiefly by the unbroken traditions of the family, and indirectly by the evidence of the walls themselves, which are the only ones thereabout with windows mullioned in the Elizabethan manner, and plainly of a date anterior to the event; while those of the other house might well have been erected fifty or eighty years later, and probably were; since the choice of Swetman's house by the fugitive was doubtless dictated by no other circumstance than its then suitable loneliness.

It was a cloudy July morning just before dawn, the hour of two having been struck by Swetman's one-handed clock on the stairs, that is still preserved in the family. Christopher heard the strokes from his chamber, immediately at the top of the staircase, and overlooking the front of the house. He did not wonder that he was sleepless. The rumours and excitements which had latterly stirred the neighbourhood, to the effect that the rightful King of England had landed from Holland, at a port only eighteen miles to the south-west of Swetman's house, were enough to make wakeful and anxious even a contented yeoman like him. Some of the villagers, intoxicated by the news, had thrown down their scythes, and rushed to the ranks of the invader. Christopher Swetman had weighed both sides of the question, and had remained at home.

Now as he lay thinking of these and other things he fancied that he could hear the footfall of a man on the road leading up to his house – a by-way, which led scarce anywhere else; and therefore a tread was at any time more apt to startle the inmates of the homestead than if it had stood in a thoroughfare. The footfall came opposite the gate, and stopped there. One minute, two minutes passed, and the pedestrian did not proceed. Christopher Swetman got out of bed, and opened the casement. 'Hoi! who's there?' cries he.

'A friend,' came from the darkness.

'And what mid ye want at this time o' night?' says Swetman.

'Shelter. I've lost my way.'

'What's thy name?'

There came no answer.

'Be ye one of King Monmouth's men?'

'He that asks no questions will hear no lies from me. I am a stranger; and I am spent, and hungered. Can you let me lie with you to-night?'

Swetman was generous to people in trouble, and his house was roomy. 'Wait a bit,' he said, 'and I'll come down and have a look at thee, anyhow.'

He struck a light, put on his clothes, and descended, taking his horn-lantern from a nail in the passage, and lighting it before opening the door. The rays fell on the form of a tall, dark man in cavalry accoutrements and wearing a sword. He was pale with fatigue and covered with mud, though the weather was dry.

'Prithee take no heed of my appearance,' said the stranger. 'But let me in.'

That his visitor was in sore distress admitted of no doubt, and the yeoman's natural humanity assisted the other's sad importunity and gentle voice. Swetman took him in, not without a suspicion that this man represented in some way Monmouth's cause, to which he was not unfriendly in his secret heart. At his earnest request the new-comer was given a suit of the yeoman's old clothes in exchange for his own, which, with his sword, were hidden in a closet in Swetman's chamber; food was then put before him and a lodging provided for him in a room at the back.

Here he slept till quite late in the morning, which was Sunday, the sixth of July, and when he came down in the garments that he had borrowed he met the household with a melancholy smile. Besides Swetman himself, there were only his two daughters, Grace and Leonard (the latter was, oddly enough, a woman's name here), and both had been enjoined to secrecy. They asked no questions and received no information; though the stranger regarded their fair countenances with an interest almost too deep. Having partaken of their usual breakfast of ham and cider he professed weariness and retired to the chamber whence he had come.

In a couple of hours or thereabout he came down again, the two young women having now gone off to morning service. Seeing Christopher bustling about the house without assistance, he asked if he could do anything to aid his host.

As he seemed anxious to hide all differences and appear as one of themselves, Swetman set him to get vegetables from the garden and fetch water from Buttock's Spring in the dip near the house (though the spring was not called by that name till years after, by the way).

'And what can I do next?' says the stranger when these services had been performed.

His meekness and docility struck Christopher much, and won upon him. 'Since you be minded to,' says the latter, 'you can take down the dishes and spread the table for dinner. Take a pewter plate for thyself, but the trenchers will do for we.'

But the other would not, and took a trencher likewise, in doing which he spoke of the two girls and remarked how comely they were.

This quietude was put an end to by a stir out of doors, which was sufficient to draw Swetman's attention to it, and he went out. Farm hands who had gone off and joined the Duke on his arrival had begun to come in with news that a midnight battle had been fought on the moors to the north, the Duke's men, who had attacked, being entirely worsted; the Duke himself, with one or two lords and other friends, had fled, no one knew whither.

'There has been a battle,' says Swetman, on coming indoors after these tidings, and looking earnestly at the stranger.

'May the victory be to the rightful in the end, whatever the issue now,' says the other, with a sorrowful sigh.

'Dost really know nothing about it?' said Christopher. 'I could have sworn you was one from that very battle!'

'I was here before three o' the clock this morning; and these men have only arrived now.'

'True,' said the yeoman. 'But still, I think—'

'Do not press your question,' the stranger urged. 'I am in a strait, and can refuse a helper nothing; such inquiry is, therefore, unfair.'

'True again,' said Swetman, and held his tongue.

The daughters of the house returned from church, where the service had been hurried by reason of the excitement. To their father's questioning if they had spoken of him who sojourned there they replied that they had said never a word; which, indeed, was true, as events proved.

He bade them serve the dinner; and, as the visitor had withdrawn since the news of the battle, prepared to take a platter to him upstairs. But he preferred to come down and dine with the family.

During the afternoon more fugitives passed through the village, but Christopher Swetman, his visitor, and his family kept indoors. In the evening, however, Swetman came out from his gate, and, harkening in silence to these tidings and more, wondered what might be in store for him for his last night's work.

He returned homeward by a path across the mead that skirted his own orchard. Passing here, he heard the voice of his daughter Leonard expostulating inside the hedge, her words being:

'Don't ye, sir; don't! I prithee let me go!'

'Why, sweetheart?'

'Because I've a-promised another!'

Peeping through, as he could not help doing, he saw the girl struggling in the arms of the stranger, who was attempting to kiss her; but finding her resistance to be genuine, and her distress unfeigned, he reluctantly let her go.

Swetman's face grew dark, for his girls were more to him than himself. He hastened on, meditating moodily all the way. He entered the gate, and made straight for the orchard. When he reached it his daughter had disappeared, but the stranger was still standing there.

'Sir!' said the yeoman, his anger having in no wise abated, 'I've seen what has happened! I have taken 'ee into my house, at some jeopardy to myself; and, whoever you be, the least I expected of 'ee was to treat the maidens with a seemly respect. You have not done it, and I no longer trust you. I am the more watchful over them in that they are motherless; and I must ask 'ee to go after dark this night!'

The stranger seemed dazed at discovering what his impulse had brought down upon his head, and his pale face grew paler. He did not reply for a time. When he did speak his soft voice was thick with feeling.

'Sir,' says he, 'I own that I am in the wrong, if you take the matter gravely. We do not what we would but what we must. Though I have not injured your daughter as a woman, I have been treacherous to her as a hostess and friend in need. I'll go, as you say; I can do no less. I shall doubtless find a refuge elsewhere.'

They walked towards the house in silence, where Swetman insisted that his guest should have supper before departing. By the time this was eaten it was dusk and the stranger announced that he was ready.

They went upstairs to where the garments and sword lay hidden, till the departing one said that on further thought he would ask another favour: that he should be allowed to retain the clothes he wore, and that his host would keep the others and the sword till he, the speaker, should come or send for them.

'As you will,' said Swetman. 'The gain is on my side; for those clouts were but kept to dress a scarecrow next fall.'

'They suit my case,' said the stranger sadly. 'However much they may misfit me, they do not misfit my sorry fortune now!'

'Nay, then,' said Christopher relenting, 'I was too hasty. Sh'lt bide!'

But the other would not, saying that it was better that things should take their course. Notwithstanding that Swetman importuned him, he only added, 'If I never come again, do with my belongings as you list. In the pocket you will find a gold snuff-box, and in the snuff-box fifty gold pieces.'

'But keep 'em for thy use, man!' said the yeoman.

'No,' says the parting guest; 'they are foreign pieces and would harm me if I were taken. Do as I bid thee. Put away these things again and take especial charge of the sword. It belonged to my father's father and I value it much. But something more common becomes me now.'

Saying which, he took, as he went downstairs, one of the ash sticks used by Swetman himself for walking with. The yeoman lighted him out to the garden hatch, where he disappeared through Clammers Gate by the road that crosses King's-Hintock Park to Evershead.

Christopher returned to the upstairs chamber, and sat down on his bed reflecting. Then he examined the things left behind, and surely enough in one of the pockets the gold snuff-box was revealed, containing the fifty gold pieces as stated by the fugitive. The yeoman next looked at the sword which its owner had stated to have belonged to his grandfather. It was two-edged, so that he almost feared to handle it. On the blade were inscribed the words 'ANDREA FERARA', and among the many fine chasings were a rose and crown, the plume of the Prince of Wales, and two portraits; portraits of a man and a woman, the man's having the face of the first King Charles, and the woman's, apparently, that of his Queen.

Swetman, much awed and surprised, returned the articles to the closet, and went downstairs pondering. Of his surmise he said nothing to his daughters, merely declaring to them that the gentleman was gone; and never revealing that he had been an eye-witness of the unpleasant scene in the orchard that was the immediate cause of the departure.

Nothing occurred in Hintock during the week that followed, beyond the fitful arrival of more decided tidings concerning the utter defeat of the Duke's army and his own disappearance at an early stage of the battle. Then it was told that Monmouth was taken, not in his own clothes but in the disguise of a countryman. He had been sent to London, and was confined in the Tower.

The possibility that his guest had been no other than the Duke made Swetman unspeakably sorry now; his heart smote him at the thought that, acting so harshly for such a small breach of good faith, he might have been the means of forwarding the unhappy fugitive's capture. On the girls coming up to him he said, 'Get away with ye, wenches: I fear you have been the ruin of an unfortunate man!'

On the Thursday night following, when the yeoman was sleeping as usual in his chamber, he was, he said, conscious of the entry of some one. Opening his eyes, he beheld by the light of the moon, which shone upon the front of his house, the figure of a man who seemed to be the stranger moving from the door towards the closet. He was dressed somewhat differently now, but the face was quite that of his late guest in its tragical pensiveness, as was also the tallness of his figure. He neared the closet; and, feeling his visitor to be within his rights, Christopher refrained from stirring. The personage turned his large haggard eyes upon the bed where Swetman lay, and then withdrew from their hiding the articles that belonged to him, again giving a hard gaze at Christopher as he went noiselessly out of the chamber with his properties on his arm. His retreat down the stairs was just audible, and also his departure by the side-door, through which entrance or exit was easy to those who knew the place.

Nothing further happened, and towards morning Swetman slept. To avoid all risk he said not a word to the girls of the visit of the night, and certainly not to anyone outside the house; for it was dangerous at that time to avow anything.

Among the killed in opposing the recent rising had been a younger brother of the lord of the manor, who lived at King's-Hintock Court hard by. Seeing the latter ride past in mourning clothes next day, Swetman ventured to condole with him.

'He'd no business there!' answered the other. His words and manner showed the bitterness that was mingled with his regret. 'But say no more of him. You know what has happened since, I suppose?'

'I know that they say Monmouth is taken, Sir Thomas, but I can't think it true,' answered Swetman.

'O zounds! 'tis true enough,' cried the knight, 'and that's not all. The Duke was executed on Tower Hill two days ago.'

'D'ye say it verily?' says Swetman.

'And a very hard death he had, worse luck for 'n,' said Sir Thomas. 'Well, 'tis over for him and over for my brother. But not for the rest. There'll be searchings and siftings down here anon; and happy is the man who has had nothing to do with this matter!'

Now Swetman had hardly heard the latter words, so much was he confounded by the strangeness of the tidings that the Duke had come to his death on the previous Tuesday. For it had been only the night before this present day of Friday that he had seen his former guest, whom he had ceased to doubt could be other than the Duke, come into his chamber and fetch away his accoutrements as he had promised.

'It couldn't have been a vision,' said Christopher to himself when the knight had ridden on. 'But I'll go straight and see if the things be in the closet still; and thus I shall surely learn if 'twere a vision or no.'

To the closet he went, which he had not looked into since the stranger's departure. And searching behind the articles placed to conceal the things hidden, he found that, as he had never doubted, they were gone.

When the rumour spread abroad in the West that the man beheaded in the Tower was not indeed the Duke, but one of his officers taken after the battle, and that the Duke had been assisted to escape out of the country, Swetman found in it an explanation of what so deeply mystified him. That his visitor might have been a friend of the Duke's, whom the Duke had asked to fetch the things in a last request, Swetman would never admit. His belief in the rumour that Monmouth lived, like that of thousands of others, continued to the end of his days.

Such, briefly, concluded my kinsman, is the tradition which has been handed down in Christopher Swetman's family for the last two hundred years.

A Mere Interlude

I

THE traveller in school-books, who vouched in dryest tones for the
fidelity to fact of the following narrative, used to add a ring of truth to it
by opening with a nicety of criticism on the heroine's personality.
People were wrong, he declared, when they surmised that Baptista
Trewthen was a young woman with scarcely emotions or character.
There was nothing in her to love, and nothing to hate – so ran the general
opinion. That she showed few positive qualities was true. The colours
and tones which changing events paint on the faces of active womankind
were looked for in vain upon hers. But still waters run deep; and no
crisis had come in the years of her early maidenhood to demonstrate
what lay hidden within her, like metal in a mine.

She was the daughter of a small farmer in St Maria's, one of the Isles
of Lyonesse beyond Off-Wessex, who had spent a large sum, as there
understood, on her education, by sending her to the mainland for two
years. At nineteen she was entered at the Training College for Teachers,
and at twenty-one nominated to a school in the country, near Tor-
upon-Sea, whither she proceeded after the Christmas examination and
holidays.

The months passed by from winter to spring and summer, and Baptista applied herself to her new duties as best she could, till an uneventful year had elapsed. Then an air of abstraction pervaded her bearing as
she walked to and fro, twice a day, and she showed the traits of a person
who had something on her mind. A widow, by name Mrs Wace, in
whose house Baptista Trewthen had been provided with a sitting-room
and bedroom till the schoolhouse should be built, noticed this change in
her youthful tenant's manner, and at last ventured to press her with a
few questions.

'It has nothing to do with the place, nor with you,' said Miss Trewthen.

'Then it is the salary?'

'No, nor the salary.'

'Then it is something you have heard from home, my dear.'

Baptista was silent for a few moments. 'It is Mr Heddegan,' she murmured. 'Him they used to call David Heddegan before he got his money.'

'And who is the Mr Heddegan they used to call David?'

'An old bachelor at Giant's Town, St Maria's, with no relations whatever, who lives about a stone's throw from father's. When I was a child he used to take me on his knee and say he'd marry me some day. Now I am a woman the jest has turned earnest, and he is anxious to do it. And father and mother say I can't do better than have him.'

'He's well off?'

'Yes – he's the richest man we know – as a friend and neighbour.'

'How much older did you say he was than yourself?'

'I didn't say. Twenty years at least.'

'And an unpleasant man in the bargain perhaps?'

'No – he's not unpleasant.'

'Well, child, all I can say is that I'd resist any such engagement if it's not palatable to 'ee. You are comfortable here, in my little house, I hope. All the parish like 'ee: and I've never been so cheerful, since my poor husband left me to wear his wings, as I've been with 'ee as my lodger.'

The schoolmistress assured her landlady that she could return the sentiment. 'But here comes my perplexity,' she said. 'I don't like keeping school. Ah, you are surprised – you didn't suspect it. That's because I've concealed my feeling. Well, I simply hate school. I don't care for children – they are unpleasant, troublesome little things, whom nothing would delight so much as to hear that you had fallen down dead. Yet I would even put up with them if it was not for the inspector. For three months before his visit I didn't sleep soundly. And the Committee of Council are always changing the Code, so that you don't know what to teach, and what to leave untaught. I think father and mother are right. They say I shall never excel as a schoolmistress if I dislike the work so, and that therefore I ought to get settled by marrying Mr Heddegan. Between us two, I like him better than school; but I don't like him quite so much as to wish to marry him.'

These conversations, once begun, were continued from day to day; till at length the young girl's elderly friend and landlady threw in her opinion on the side of Miss Trewthen's parents. All things considered, she declared, the uncertainty of the school, the labour, Baptista's natural dislike for teaching, it would be as well to take what fate offered, and make the best of matters by wedding her father's old neighbour and prosperous friend.

The Easter holidays came round, and Baptista went to spend them as usual in her native isle, going by train into Off-Wessex and crossing by packet from Pen-zephyr. When she returned in the middle of April her face wore a more settled aspect.

'Well?' said the expectant Mrs Wace.

'I have agreed to have him as my husband,' said Baptista, in an off-hand way. 'Heaven knows if it will be for the best or not. But I have agreed to do it, and so the matter is settled.'

Mrs Wace commended her; but Baptista did not care to dwell on the subject; so that allusion to it was very infrequent between them. Nevertheless, among other things, she repeated to the widow from time to time in monosyllabic remarks that the wedding was really impending; that it was arranged for the summer, and that she had given notice of leaving the school at the August holidays. Later on she announced more specifically that her marriage was to take place immediately after her return home at the beginning of the month aforesaid.

She now corresponded regularly with Mr Heddegan. Her letters from him were seen, at least on the outside, and in part within, by Mrs Wace. Had she read more of their interiors than the occasional sentences shown her by Baptista she would have perceived that the scratchy, rusty handwriting of Miss Trewthen's betrothed conveyed little more matter than details of their future housekeeping, and his preparations for the same, with innumerable 'my dears' sprinkled in disconnectedly, to show the depth of his affection without the inconveniences of syntax.

II

It was the end of July – dry, too dry, even for the season, the delicate green herbs and vegetables that grew in this favoured end of the kingdom tasting rather of the watering-pot than of the pure fresh moisture from the skies. Baptista's boxes were packed, and one Saturday morning she departed by a waggonette to the station, and thence by train to Pen-zephyr, from which port she was, as usual, to cross the water immediately to her home, and become Mr Heddegan's wife on the Wednesday of the week following.

She might have returned a week sooner. But though the wedding day had loomed so near, and the banns were out, she delayed her departure till this last moment, saying it was not necessary for her to be at home long beforehand. As Mr Heddegan was older than herself, she said, she was to be married in her ordinary summer bonnet and grey silk frock, and there were no preparations to make that had not been amply made by her parents and intended husband.

In due time, after a hot and tedious journey, she reached Pen-zephyr. She here obtained some refreshment, and then went towards the pier, where she learnt to her surprise that the little steamboat plying between the town and the islands had left at eleven o'clock; the usual hour of departure in the afternoon having been forestalled in consequence of the fogs which had for a few days prevailed towards evening, making twilight navigation dangerous.

This being Saturday, there was now no other boat till Tuesday, and it became obvious that here she would have to remain for the three days, unless her friends should think fit to rig out one of the island sailing-boats and come to fetch her – a not very likely contingency, the sea distance being nearly forty miles.

Baptista, however, had been detained in Pen-zephyr on more than one occasion before, either on account of bad weather or some such reason as the present, and she was therefore not in any personal alarm. But, as she was to be married on the following Wednesday, the delay was certainly inconvenient to a more than ordinary degree, since it would leave less than a day's interval between her arrival and the wedding ceremony.

Apart from this awkwardness she did not much mind the accident. It was indeed curious to see how little she minded. Perhaps it would not be too much to say that, although she was going to do the critical deed of her life quite willingly, she experienced an indefinable relief at the postponement of her meeting with Heddegan. But her manner after making discovery of the hindrance was quiet and subdued, even to passivity itself; as was instanced by her having, at the moment of receiving information that the steamer had sailed, replied 'Oh' so coolly to the porter with her luggage, that he was almost disappointed at her lack of disappointment.

The question now was, should she return again to Mrs Wace, in the village of Lower Wessex, or wait in the town at which she had arrived? She would have preferred to go back, but the distance was too great; moreover, having left the place for good, and somewhat dramatically, to become a bride, a return, even for so short a space, would have been a trifle humiliating.

Leaving, then, her boxes at the station, her next anxiety was to secure a respectable, or rather genteel, lodging in the popular seaside resort confronting her. To this end she looked about the town, in which, though she had passed through it half-a-dozen times, she was practically a stranger.

Baptista found a room to suit her over a fruiterer's shop; where she made herself at home, and set herself in order after her journey. An early cup of tea having revived her spirits she walked out to reconnoitre.

Being a schoolmistress she avoided looking at the schools, and having a sort of trade connection with books, she avoided looking at the book-sellers; but wearying of the other shops she inspected the churches; not that for her own part she cared much about ecclesiastical edifices; but tourists looked at them, and so would she – a proceeding for which no one would have credited her with any great originality, such, for instance, as that she subsequently showed herself to possess. The churches soon oppressed her. She tried the Museum, but came out because it seemed lonely and tedious.

Yet the town and the walks in this land of strawberries, these head-quarters of early English flowers and fruit, were then, as always, attractive. From the more picturesque streets she went to the town gardens, and the Pier, and the Harbour, and looked at the men at work there, loading and unloading as in the time of the Phœnicians.

'Not Baptista? Yes, Baptista it is!'

The words were uttered behind her. Turning round she gave a start, and became confused, even agitated, for a moment. Then she said in her usual undemonstrative manner, 'O – is it really you, Charles?'

Without speaking again at once, and with a half-smile, the new-comer glanced her over. There was much criticism, and some resent-ment – even temper – in his eye.

'I am going home,' continued she. 'But I have missed the boat.'

He scarcely seemed to take in the meaning of this explanation, in the intensity of his critical survey. 'Teaching still? What a fine school-mistress you make, Baptista, I warrant!' he said with a slight flavour of sarcasm, which was not lost upon her.

'I know I am nothing to brag of,' she replied. 'That's why I have given up.'

'O – given up? You astonish me.'

'I hate the profession.'

'Perhaps that's because I am in it.'

'O no, it isn't. But I am going to enter on another life altogether. I am going to be married next week to Mr David Heddegan.'

The young man – fortified as he was by a natural cynical pride and passionateness – winced at this unexpected reply, notwithstanding.

'Who is Mr David Heddegan?' he asked, as indifferently as lay in his power.

She informed him the bearer of the name was a general merchant of Giant's Town, St Maria's Island – her father's nearest neighbour and oldest friend.

'Then we shan't see anything more of you on the mainland?' inquired the schoolmaster.

'O, I don't know about that,' said Miss Trewthen.

'Here endeth the career of the belle of the boarding-school your father was foolish enough to send you to. A "general merchant's" wife in the Lyonesse Isles. Will you sell pounds of soap and pennyworths of tin tacks, or whole bars of saponaceous matter, and great tenpenny nails?'

'He's not in such a small way as that!' she almost pleaded. 'He owns ships, though they are rather little ones!'

'O, well, it is much the same. Come, let us walk on; it is tedious to stand still. I thought you would be a failure in education,' he continued, when she obeyed him and strolled ahead. 'You never showed power that way. You remind me much of some of those women who think they are sure to be great actresses if they go on the stage, because they have a pretty face, and forget that what we require is acting. But you found your mistake, didn't you?'

'Don't taunt me, Charles.' It was noticeable that the young schoolmaster's tone caused her no anger or retaliatory passion; far otherwise there was a tear in her eye. 'How is it you are at Pen-zephyr?' she inquired.

'I don't taunt you. I speak the truth, purely in a friendly way, as I should to anyone I wished well. Though for that matter I might have some excuse even for taunting you. Such a terrible hurry as you've been in. I hate a woman who is in such a hurry.'

'How do you mean that?'

'Why – to be somebody's wife or other – anything's wife rather than nobody's. You couldn't wait for me, O, no. Well, thank God, I'm cured of all that!'

'How merciless you are!' she said bitterly. 'Wait for you? What does that mean, Charley? You never showed – anything to wait for – anything special towards me.'

'O come, Baptista dear; come!'

'What I mean is, nothing definite,' she expostulated. 'I suppose you liked me a little; but it seemed to me to be only a pastime on your part, and that you never meant to make an honourable engagement of it.'

'There, that's just it! You girls expect a man to mean business at the first look. No man when he first becomes interested in a woman has any definite scheme of engagement to marry her in his mind, unless he is meaning a vulgar mercenary marriage. However, I *did* at last mean an honourable engagement, as you call it, come to that.'

'But you never said so, and an indefinite courtship soon injures a woman's position and credit, sooner than you think.'

'Baptista, I solemnly declare that in six months I should have asked you to marry me.'

She walked along in silence, looking on the ground, and appearing very uncomfortable. Presently he said, 'Would you have waited for me if you had known?' To this she whispered in a sorrowful whisper, 'Yes!'

They went still farther in silence – passing along one of the beautiful walks on the outskirts of the town, yet not observant of scene or situation. Her shoulder and his were close together, and he clasped his fingers round the small of her arm – quite lightly, and without any attempt at impetus; yet the act seemed to say, 'Now I hold you, and my will must be yours.'

Recurring to a previous question of hers he said, 'I have merely run down here for a day or two from school near Trufal, before going off to the North for the rest of my holiday. I have seen my relations at Red-rutin quite lately, so I am not going there this time. How little I thought of meeting you! How very different the circumstances would have been if, instead of parting again as we must in half-an-hour or so, possibly for ever, you had been now just going off with me, as my wife, on our honeymoon trip. Ha – ha – well – so humorous is life!'

She stopped suddenly. 'I must go back now – this is altogether too painful, Charley! It is not at all a kind mood you are in to-day.'

'I don't want to pain you – you know I do not,' he said more gently.

'Only it just exasperates me – this you are going to do. I wish you would not.'

'What ?'

'Marry him. There, now I have showed you my true sentiments.'

'I must do it now,' said she.

'Why ?' he asked, dropping the off-hand masterful tone he had hitherto spoken in, and becoming earnest; still holding her arm, however, as if she were his chattel to be taken up or put down at will. 'It is never too late to break off a marriage that's distasteful to you. Now I'll say one thing; and it is truth: I wish you would marry me instead of him, even now, at the last moment, though you have served me so badly.'

'O, it is not possible to think of that!' she answered hastily, shaking her head. 'When I get home all will be prepared – it is ready even now – the things for the party, the furniture, Mr Heddegan's new suit, and everything. I should require the courage of a tropical lion to go home there and say I wouldn't carry out my promise!'

'Then go, in Heaven's name! But there would be no necessity for you to go home and face them in that way. If we were to marry, it would have to be at once, instantly; or not at all. I should think your affection nor worth the having unless you agreed to come back with me to Trufal this evening, where we could be married by licence on Monday morning. And then no Mr David Heddegan or anybody else could get you away from me.'

'I must go home by the Tuesday boat,' she faltered. 'What would they think if I did not come ?'

'You could go home by that boat just the same. All the difference would be that I should go with you. You could leave me on the quay, where I'd have a smoke, while you went and saw your father and mother privately; you could then tell them what you had done, and that I was waiting not far off; that I was a schoolmaster in a fairly good position, and a young man you had known when you were at the Training College. Then I would come boldly forward; and they would see that it could not be altered, and so you wouldn't suffer a lifelong misery by being the wife of a wretched old gaffer you don't like at all. Now, honestly; you do like me best, don't you, Baptista ?'

'Yes.'

'Then we will do as I say.'

She did not pronounce a clear affirmative. But that she consented to the novel proposition at some moment or other of that walk was apparent by what occurred a little later.

III

An enterprise of such pith required, indeed, less talking than consideration. The first thing they did in carrying it out was to return to the railway station, where Baptista took from her luggage a small trunk of immediate necessaries which she would in any case have required after missing the boat. That same afternoon they travelled up the line to Trufal.

Charles Stow (as his name was), despite his disdainful indifference to things, was very careful of appearances, and made the journey independently of her though in the same train. He told her where she could get board and lodgings in the city; and with merely a distant nod to her of a provisional kind, went off to his own quarters, and to see about the licence.

On Sunday she saw him in the morning across the nave of the procathedral. In the afternoon they walked together in the fields, where he told her that the licence would be ready next day, and would be available the day after, when the ceremony could be performed as early after eight o'clock as they should choose.

His courtship, thus renewed after an interval of two years, was as impetuous, violent even, as it was short. The next day came and passed, and the final arrangements were made. Their agreement was to get the ceremony over as soon as they possibly could the next morning, so as to go on to Pen-zephyr at once, and reach that place in time for the boat's departure the same day. It was in obedience to Baptista's earnest request that Stow consented thus to make the whole journey to Lyonesse by land and water at one heat, and not break it at Pen-zephyr; she seemed to be oppressed with a dread of lingering anywhere, this great first act of disobedience to her parents once accomplished, with the weight on her mind that her home had to be convulsed by the disclosure of it. To face her difficulties over the water immediately she had created them was, however, a course more desired by Baptista than by her lover; though for once he gave way.

The next morning was bright and warm as those which had preceded it. By six o'clock it seemed nearly noon, as is often the case in that part of England in the summer season. By nine they were husband and wife. They packed up and departed by the earliest train after the service; and on the way discussed at length what she should say on meeting her parents, Charley dictating the turn of each phrase. In her anxiety they had travelled so early that when they reached Pen-zephyr they found there were nearly two hours on their hands before the steamer's time of sailing.

Baptista was extremely reluctant to be seen promenading the streets of the watering-place with her husband till, as above stated, the household at Giant's Town should know the unexpected course of events from her own lips; and it was just possible, if not likely, that some Lyonessian might be prowling about there, or even have come across the sea to look for her. To meet anyone to whom she was known, and to have to reply to awkward questions about the strange young man at her side before her well-framed announcement had been delivered at proper time and place, was a thing she could not contemplate with equanimity. So, instead of looking at the shops and harbour, they went along the coast a little way.

The heat of the morning was by this time intense. They clambered up on some cliffs, and while sitting there, looking around at St Michael's Mount and other objects, Charles said to her that he thought he would run down to the beach at their feet, and take just one plunge into the sea.

Baptista did not much like the idea of being left alone; it was gloomy, she said. But he assured her he would not be gone more than a quarter of an hour at the outside, and she passively assented.

Down he went, disappeared, appeared again, and looked back. Then he again proceeded, and vanished, till, as a small waxen object, she saw him emerge from the nook that had screened him, cross the white fringe of foam, and walk into the undulating mass of blue. Once in the water he seemed less inclined to hurry than before; he remained a long time; and, unable either to appreciate his skill or criticize his want of it at that distance, she withdrew her eyes from the spot, and gazed at the still outline of St Michael's – now beautifully toned in gray.

Her anxiety for the hour of departure, and to cope at once with the approaching incidents that she would have to manipulate as best she could, sent her into a reverie. It was now Tuesday; she would reach home in the evening – a very late time they would say; but, as the delay was a pure accident, they would deem her marriage to Mr Heddegan to-morrow still practicable. Then Charles would have to be produced from the background. It was a terrible undertaking to think of, and she almost regretted her temerity in wedding so hastily that morning. The rage of her father would be so crushing; the reproaches of her mother so bitter; and perhaps Charles would answer hotly, and perhaps cause estrangement till death. There had obviously been no alarm about her at St Maria's, or somebody would have sailed across to inquire for her. She had, in a letter written at the beginning of the week, spoken of the hour at which she intended to leave her country schoolhouse; and from this her friends had probably perceived that by such timing she would run a risk of losing the Saturday boat. She had missed it, and as a consequence sat here on the shore as Mrs Charles Stow.

This brought her to the present, and she turned from the outline of St Michael's Mount to look about for her husband's form. He was, as far as she could discover, no longer in the sea. Then he was dressing. By moving a few steps she could see where his clothes lay. But Charles was not beside them.

Baptista looked back again at the water in bewilderment, as if her senses were the victim of some sleight of hand. Not a speck or spot resembling a man's head or face showed anywhere. By this time she was alarmed, and her alarm intensified when she perceived a little beyond the scene of her husband's bathing a small area of water, the quality of whose surface differed from that of the surrounding expanse as the coarse vegetation of some foul patch in a mead differs from the fine green of the remainder. Elsewhere it looked flexuous, here it looked vermiculated and lumpy, and her marine experiences suggested to her in a moment that two currents met and caused a turmoil at this place.

She descended as hastily as her trembling limbs would allow. The way down was terribly long, and before reaching the heap of clothes it occurred to her that, after all, it would be best to run first for help. Hastening along in a lateral direction she proceeded inland till she met a man, and soon afterwards two others. To them she exclaimed, 'I think a gentleman who was bathing is in some danger. I cannot see him as I could. Will you please run and help him, at once, if you will be so kind?'

She did not think of turning to show them the exact spot, indicating it vaguely by the direction of her hand, and still going on her way with the idea of gaining more assistance. When she deemed, in her faintness, that she had carried the alarm far enough, she faced about and dragged herself back again. Before reaching the now dreaded spot she met one of the men.

'We can see nothing at all, Miss,' he declared.

Having gained the beach, she found the tide in, and no sign of Charley's clothes. The other men whom she had besought to come had disappeared, it must have been in some other direction, for she had not met them going away. They, finding nothing, had probably thought her alarm a mere conjecture, and given up the quest.

Baptista sank down upon the stones near at hand. Where Charley had undressed was now sea. There could not be the least doubt that he was drowned, and his body sucked under by the current; while his clothes, lying within high-water mark, had probably been carried away by the rising tide.

She remained in a stupor for some minutes, till a strange sensation succeeded the aforesaid perceptions, mystifying her intelligence, and leaving her physically almost inert. With his personal disappearance, the last three days of her life with him seemed to be swallowed up, also his image, in her mind's eye, waned curiously, receded far away, grew stranger and stranger, less and less real. Their meeting and marriage had been so sudden, unpremeditated, adventurous, that she could hardly believe that she had played her part in such a reckless drama. Of all the few hours of her life with Charles, the portion that most insisted in coming back to memory was their fortuitous encounter on the previous Saturday, and those bitter reprimands with which he had begun the attack, as it might be called, which had piqued her to an unexpected consummation.

A sort of cruelty, an imperiousness, even in his warmth, had characterized Charles Stow. As a lover he had ever been a bit of a tyrant; and it might pretty truly have been said that he had stung her into marriage with him at last. Still more alien from her life did these reflections operate to make him; and then they would be chased away by an interval of passionate weeping and mad regret. Finally, there returned upon the confused mind of the young wife the recollection that she was on her way homeward, and that the packet would sail in three-quarters of an hour.

Except the parasol in her hand, all she possessed was at the station awaiting her onward journey.

She looked in that direction; and, entering one of those undemonstrative phases so common with her, walked quietly on.

At first she made straight for the railway; but suddenly turning she went to a shop and wrote an anonymous line announcing his death by drowning to the only person she had ever heard Charles mention as a relative. Posting this stealthily, and with a fearful look around her, she seemed to acquire a terror of the late events, pursuing her way to the station as if followed by a spectre.

When she got to the office she asked for the luggage that she had left there on the Saturday as well as the trunk left on the morning just lapsed. All were put in the boat, and she herself followed. Quickly as these things had been done, the whole proceeding, nevertheless, had been almost automatic on Baptista's part, ere she had come to any definite conclusion on her course.

Just before the bell rang she heard a conversation on the pier, which removed the last shade of doubt from her mind, if any had existed, that she was Charles Stow's widow. The sentences were but fragmentary, but she could easily piece them out.

'A man drowned – swam out too far – was a stranger to the place – people in boat – saw him go down – couldn't get there in time.'

The news was little more definite than this as yet; though it may as well be stated once for all that the statement was true. Charley, with the over-confidence of his nature, had ventured out too far for his strength, and succumbed in the absence of assistance, his lifeless body being at that moment suspended in the transparent mid-depths of the bay. His clothes, however, had merely been gently lifted by the rising tide, and floated into a nook hard by, where they lay out of sight of the passers-by till a day or two after.

IV

In ten minutes they were steaming out of the harbour for their voyage of four or five hours, at whose ending she would have to tell her strange story.

As Pen-zephyr and all its environing scenes disappeared behind Mousehole and St Clement's Isle, Baptista's ephemeral, meteor-like husband impressed her yet more as a fantasy. She was still in such a trance-like state that she had been an hour on the little packet-boat before she became aware of the agitating fact that Mr Heddegan was on board with her. Involuntarily she slipped from her left hand the symbol of her wifehood.

'Hee-hee! Well, the truth is, I wouldn't interrupt 'ee. "I reckon she don't see me, or won't see me," I said, "and what's the hurry? She'll see enough o' me soon!" I hope ye be well, mee deer?'

He was a hale, well-conditioned man of about five-and-fifty, of the complexion common to those whose lives are passed on the bluffs and beaches of an ocean isle. He extended the four quarters of his face in a genial smile, and his hand for a grasp of the same magnitude. She gave her own in surprised docility, and he continued:

'I couldn't help coming across to meet 'ee. What an unfortunate thing you missing the boat and not coming Saturday! They meant to have warned 'ee that the time was changed, but forgot it at the last moment. The truth is that I should have informed 'ee myself, but I was that busy finishing up a job last week, so as to have this week free, that I trusted to your father for attending to these little things. However, so plain and quiet as it is all to be, it really do not matter so much as it might otherwise have done, and I hope ye haven't been greatly put out. Now, if you'd sooner that I should not be seen talking to 'ee – if 'ee feel shy at all before strangers – just say. I'll leave 'ee to yourself till we get home.'

'Thank you much. I am indeed a little tired, Mr Heddegan.'

He nodded urbane acquiescence, strolled away immediately, and minutely inspected the surface of the funnel, till some female passengers of Giant's Town tittered at what they must have thought a rebuff – for the approaching wedding was known to many on St Maria's Island, though to nobody elsewhere. Baptista coloured at their satire, and called him back, and forced herself to commune with him in at least a mechanically friendly manner.

The opening event had been thus different from her expectation, and she had adumbrated no act to meet it. Taken aback, she passively allowed circumstances to pilot her along; and so the voyage was made.

It was near dusk when they touched the pier of Giant's Town, where several friends and neighbours stood awaiting them. Her father had a lantern in his hand. Her mother, too, was there, reproachfully glad that the delay had at last ended so simply. Mrs Trewthen and her daughter went together along the Giant's Walk, or promenade, to the house, rather in advance of her husband and Mr Heddegan, who talked in loud tones which reached the women over their shoulders.

Some would have called Mrs Trewthen a good mother; but though well-meaning she was maladroit, and her intentions missed their mark.

This might have been partly attributable to the slight deafness from which she suffered. Now, as usual, the chief utterances came from her lips.

'Ah, yes, I'm so glad, my child, that you've got over safe. It is all ready, and everything so well arranged, that nothing but misfortune could hinder you settling as, with God's grace, becomes 'ee. Close to your mother's door a'most, 'twill be a great blessing, I'm sure; and I was very glad to find from your letters that you'd held your word sacred. That's right – make your word your bond always. Mrs Wace seems to be a sensible woman. I hope the Lord will do for her as he's doing for you no long time hence. And how did 'ee get over the terrible journey from Tor-upon-Sea to Pen-zephyr? Once you'd done with the railway, of course, you seemed quite at home. Well, Baptista, conduct yourself seemly, and all will be well.'

Thus admonished, Baptista entered the house, her father and Mr Heddegan immediately at her back. Her mother had been so didactic that she had felt herself absolutely unable to broach the subjects in the centre of her mind.

The familiar room, with the dark ceiling, the well-spread table, the old chairs, had never before spoken so eloquently of the times ere she knew or had heard of Charley Stow. She went upstairs to take off her things, her mother remaining below to complete the disposition of the supper, and attend to the preparation of to-morrow's meal, altogether composing such an array of pies, from pies of fish to pies of turnips, as was never heard of outside the Western Duchy. Baptista, once alone, sat down and did nothing; and was called before she had taken off her bonnet.

'I'm coming,' she cried, jumping up, and speedily disapparelling herself, brushed her hair with a few touches and went down.

Two or three of Mr Heddegan's and her father's friends had dropped in, and expressed their sympathy for the delay she had been subjected to. The meal was a most merry one except to Baptista. She had desired privacy, and there was none; and to break the news was already a greater difficulty than it had been at first. Everything around her, animate and inanimate, great and small, insisted that she had come home to be married; and she could not get a chance to say nay.

One or two people sang songs, as overtures to the melody of the morrow, till at length bedtime came, and they all withdrew, her mother having retired a little earlier. When Baptista found herself again alone in her bedroom the case stood as before: she had come home with much to say, and she had said nothing.

It was now growing clear even to herself that Charles being dead, she had not determination sufficient within her to break tidings which, had he been alive, would have imperatively announced themselves. And thus with the stroke of midnight came the turning of the scale; her story should remain untold. It was not that upon the whole she thought it best not to attempt to tell it; but that she could not undertake so explosive a matter. To stop the wedding now would cause a convulsion in Giant's Town little short of volcanic. Weakened, tired, and terrified as she had been by the day's adventures, she could not make herself the author of such a catastrophe. But how refuse Heddegan without telling? It really seemed to her as if her marriage with Mr Heddegan were about to take place as if nothing had intervened.

Morning came. The events of the previous days were cut off from her present existence by scene and sentiment more completely than ever. Charles Stow had grown to be a special being of whom, owing to his character, she entertained rather fearful than loving memory. Baptista could hear when she awoke that her parents were already moving about downstairs. But she did not rise till her mother's rather rough voice resounded up the staircase as it had done on the preceding evening.

'Baptista! Come, time to be stirring! The man will be here, by Heaven's blessing, in three-quarters of an hour. He has looked in already for a minute or two – and says he's going to the church to see if things be well forward.'

Baptista arose, looked out of the window, and took the easy course. When she emerged from the regions above she was arrayed in her new silk frock and best stockings, wearing a linen jacket over the former for breakfasting, and her common slippers over the latter, not to spoil the new ones on the rough precincts of the dwelling.

It is unnecessary to dwell at any great length on this part of the morning's proceedings. She revealed nothing; and married Heddegan, as she had given her word to do, on that appointed August day.

V

Mr Heddegan forgave the coldness of his bride's manner during and after the wedding ceremony, full well aware that there had been considerable reluctance on her part to acquiesce in this neighbourly arrangement, and, as a philosopher of long standing, holding that whatever Baptista's attitude now, the conditions would probably be much the same six months hence as those which ruled among other married couples.

An absolutely unexpected shock was given to Baptista's listless mind about an hour after the wedding service. They had nearly finished the midday dinner when the now husband said to her father, 'We think of starting about two. And the breeze being so fair we shall bring up inside Pen-zephyr new pier about six at least.'

'What – are we going to Pen-zephyr?' said Baptista. 'I don't know anything of it.'

'Didn't you tell her?' asked her father of Heddegan.

It transpired that, owing to the delay in her arrival, this proposal too, among other things, had in the hurry not been mentioned to her, except some time ago as a general suggestion that they would go somewhere. Heddegan had imagined that any trip would be pleasant, and one to the mainland the pleasantest of all.

She looked so distressed at the announcement that her husband willingly offered to give it up, though he had not had a holiday off the island for a whole year. Then she pondered on the inconvenience of staying at Giant's Town, where all the inhabitants were bonded, by the circumstances of their situation, into a sort of family party, which permitted and encouraged on such occasions as these oral criticism that was apt to disturb the equanimity of newly married girls, and would especially worry Baptista in her strange situation. Hence, unexpectedly, she agreed not to disorganize her husband's plans for the wedding jaunt, and it was settled that, as originally intended, they should proceed in a neighbour's sailing boat to the metropolis of the district.

In this way they arrived at Pen-zephyr without difficulty or mishap. Bidding adieu to Jenkin and his man, who had sailed them over, they strolled arm in arm off the pier, Baptista silent, cold, and obedient. Heddegan had arranged to take her as far as Plymouth before their return, but to go no further than where they had landed that day. Their first business was to find an inn; and in this they had unexpected difficulty, since for some reason or other – possibly the fine weather – many of the nearest at hand were full of tourists and commercial travellers. He led her on till he reached a tavern which, though comparatively unpretending, stood in as attractive a spot as any in the town; and this, somewhat to their surprise after their previous experience, they found apparently empty. The considerate old man, thinking that Baptista was educated to artistic notions, though he himself was deficient in them, had decided that it was most desirable to have, on such an occasion as the present, an apartment with 'a good view' (the expression being one he had often heard in use among tourists); and he therefore asked for a favourite room on the first floor, from which a bow-window protruded, for the express purpose of affording such an outlook.

The landlady, after some hesitation, said she was sorry that particular apartment was engaged; the next one, however, or any other in the house, was unoccupied.

'The gentleman who has the best one will give it up to-morrow, and then you can change into it,' she added, as Mr Heddegan hesitated about taking the adjoining and less commanding one.

'We shall be gone to-morrow, and shan't want it,' he said.

Wishing not to lose customers, the landlady earnestly continued that since he was bent on having the best room, perhaps the other gentleman would not object to move at once into the one they despised, since, though nothing could be seen from the window, the room was equally large.

'Well, if he doesn't care for a view,' said Mr Heddegan, with the air of a highly artistic man who did.

'O no – I am sure he doesn't,' she said. 'I can promise that you shall have the room you want. If you would not object to go for a walk for half-an-hour, I could have it ready, and your things in it, and a nice tea laid in the bow-window by the time you come back?'

This proposal was deemed satisfactory by the fussy old tradesman, and they went out. Baptista nervously conducted him in an opposite direction to her walk of the former day in other company, showing on her wan face, had he observed it, how much she was beginning to regret her sacrificial step for mending matters that morning.

She took advantage of a moment when her husband's back was turned to inquire casually in a shop if anything had been heard of the gentleman who was sucked down in the eddy while bathing.

The shopman said, 'Yes, his body has been washed ashore,' and had just handed Baptista a newspaper on which she discerned the heading, 'A Schoolmaster drowned while bathing', when her husband turned to join her. She might have pursued the subject without raising suspicion; but it was more than flesh and blood could do, and completing a small purchase she almost ran out of the shop.

'What is your terrible hurry, mee deer?' said Heddegan, hastening after.

'I don't know – I don't want to stay in shops,' she gasped.

'And we won't,' he said. 'They are suffocating this weather. Let's go back and have some tay!'

They found the much desired apartment awaiting their entry. It was a sort of combination bed- and sitting-room, and the table was prettily spread with high tea in the bow-window, a bunch of flowers in the midst, and a best-parlour chair on each side. Here they shared the meal by the ruddy light of the vanishing sun. But though the view had been engaged, regardless of expense, exclusively for Baptista's pleasure, she did not direct any keen attention out of the window. Her gaze as often fell on the floor and walls of the room as elsewhere, and on the table as much as on either, beholding nothing at all.

But there was a change. Opposite her seat was the door, upon which her eyes presently became riveted like those of a little bird upon a snake. For, on a peg at the back of the door, there hung a hat; such a hat – surely, from its peculiar make, the actual hat – that had been worn by Charles. Conviction grew to certainty when she saw a railway ticket sticking up from the band. Charles had put the ticket there – she had noticed the act.

Her teeth almost chattered; she murmured something incoherent. Her husband jumped up and said, 'You are not well! What is it? What shall I get 'ee?'

'Smelling salts!' she said, quickly and desperately; 'at that chemist's shop you were in just now.'

He jumped up like the anxious old man that he was, caught up his own hat from a back table, and without observing the other hastened out and downstairs.

Left alone she gazed and gazed at the back of the door, then spasmodically rang the bell. An honest-looking country maid-servant appeared in response.

'A hat!' murmured Baptista, pointing with her finger. 'It does not belong to us.'

'O yes, I'll take it away,' said the young woman with some hurry. 'It belongs to the other gentleman.'

She spoke with a certain awkwardness, and took the hat out of the room. Baptista had recovered her outward composure. 'The other gentleman?' she said. 'Where is the other gentleman?'

'He's in the next room, ma'am. He removed out of this to oblige 'ee.'

'How can you say so? I should hear him if he were there,' said Baptista, sufficiently recovered to argue down an apparent untruth.

'He's there,' said the girl, hardily.

'Then it is strange that he makes no noise,' said Mrs Heddegan, convicting the girl of falsity by a look.

'He makes no noise; but it is not strange,' said the servant.

All at once a dread took possession of the bride's heart, like a cold hand laid thereon; for it flashed upon her that there was a possibility of reconciling the girl's statement with her own knowledge of facts.

'Why does he make no noise?' she weakly said.

The waiting-maid was silent, and looked at her questioner. 'If I tell you, ma'am, you won't tell missis?' she whispered.

Baptista promised.

'Because he's a-lying dead!' said the girl. 'He's the schoolmaster that was drownded yesterday.'

'O!' said the bride, covering her eyes. 'Then he was in this room till just now?'

'Yes,' said the maid, thinking the young lady's agitation natural enough. 'And I told missis that I thought she oughtn't to have done it, because I don't hold it right to keep visitors so much in the dark where death's concerned; but she said the gentleman didn't die of anything infectious; she was a poor, honest, innkeeper's wife, she says, who had to get her living by making hay while the sun sheened. And owing to the drownded gentleman being brought here, she said, it kept so many people away that we were empty, though all the other houses were full. So when your good man set his mind upon the room, and she would have lost good paying folk if he'd not had it, it wasn't to be supposed, she said, that she'd let anything stand in the way. Ye won't say that I've told ye, please, m'm? All the linen has been changed, and as the inquest won't be till to-morrow, after you are gone, she thought you wouldn't know a word of it, being strangers here.'

The returning footsteps of her husband broke off further narration. Baptista waved her hand, for she could not speak. The waiting-maid quickly withdrew, and Mr Heddegan entered with the smelling salts and other nostrums.

'Any better?' he questioned.

'I don't like the hotel,' she exclaimed, almost simultaneously. 'I can't bear it – it doesn't suit me!'

'Is that all that's the matter?' he returned pettishly (this being the first time of his showing such a mood). 'Upon my heart and life such trifling is trying to any man's temper, Baptista! Sending me about from here to yond, and then when I come back saying 'ee don't like the place that I have sunk so much money and words to get for 'ee. 'Od dang it all, 'tis enough to— But I won't say any more at present, mee deer, though it is just too much to expect to turn out of the house now. We shan't get another quiet place at this time of the evening – every other inn in the town is bustling with rackety folk of one sort and t'other, while here 'tis as quiet as the grave – the country, I would say. So bide still, d'ye hear, and to-morrow we shall be out of the town altogether – as early as you like.'

The obstinacy of age had, in short, overmastered its complaisance, and the young woman said no more. The simple course of telling him that in the adjoining room lay a corpse which had lately occupied their own might, it would have seemed, have been an effectual one without further disclosure, but to allude to *that* subject, however it was disguised, was more than Heddegan's young wife had strength for. Horror broke her down. In the contingency one thing only presented itself to her paralyzed regard – that here she was doomed to abide, in a hideous contiguity to the dead husband and the living, and her conjecture did, in fact, bear itself out. That night she lay between the two men she had married – Heddegan on the one hand, and on the other through the partition against which the bed stood, Charles Stow.

VI

Kindly time had withdrawn the foregoing event three days from the present of Baptista Heddegan. It was ten o'clock in the morning; she had been ill, not in an ordinary or definite sense, but in a state of cold stupefaction, from which it was difficult to arouse her so much as to say a few sentences. When questioned she had replied that she was pretty well.

Their trip, as such, had been something of a failure. They had gone on as far as Falmouth, but here he had given way to her entreaties to return home. This they could not very well do without repassing through Pen-zephyr, at which place they had now again arrived.

In the train she had seen a weekly local paper, and read there a paragraph detailing the inquest on Charles. It was added that the funeral was to take place at his native town of Redrutin on Friday.

After reading this she had shown no reluctance to enter the fatal neighbourhood of the tragedy, only stipulating that they should take their rest at a different lodging from the first; and now comparatively braced up and calm – indeed a cooler creature altogether than when last in the town, she said to David that she wanted to walk out for a while, as they had plenty of time on their hands.

'To a shop as usual, I suppose, mee deer?'

'Partly for shopping,' she said. 'And it will be best for you, dear, to stay in after trotting about so much, and have a good rest while I am gone.'

He assented; and Baptista sallied forth. As she had stated, her first visit was made to a shop, a draper's. Without the exercise of much choice she purchased a black bonnet and veil, also a black stuff gown; a black mantle she already wore. These articles were made up into a parcel which, in spite of the saleswoman's offers, her customer said she would take with her. Bearing it on her arm she turned to the railway, and at the station got a ticket for Redrutin.

Thus it appeared that, on her recovery from the paralyzed mood of the former day, while she had resolved not to blast utterly the happiness of her present husband by revealing the history of the departed one, she had also determined to indulge a certain odd, inconsequent, feminine sentiment of decency, to the small extent to which it could do no harm to any person. At Redrutin she emerged from the railway carriage in the black attire purchased at the shop, having during the transit made the change in the empty compartment she had chosen. The other clothes were now in the bandbox and parcel. Leaving these at the cloak-room she proceeded onward, and after a wary survey reached the side of a hill whence a view of the burial ground could be obtained.

It was now a little before two o'clock. While Baptista waited a funeral procession ascended the road. Baptista hastened across, and by the time the procession entered the cemetery gates she had unobtrusively joined it.

In addition to the schoolmaster's own relatives (not a few), the paragraph in the newspapers of his death by drowning had drawn together many neighbours, acquaintances, and onlookers. Among them she passed unnoticed, and with a quiet step pursued the winding path to the chapel, and afterwards thence to the grave. When all was over, and the

A MERE INTERLUDE 401

relatives and idlers had withdrawn, she stepped to the edge of the chasm. From beneath her mantle she drew a little bunch of forget-me-nots, and dropped them in upon the coffin. In a few minutes she also turned and went away from the cemetery. By five o'clock she was again in Pen-zephyr.

'You have been a mortal long time!' said her husband, crossly. 'I allowed you an hour at most, mee deer.'

'It occupied me longer,' said she.

'Well – I reckon it is wasting words to complain. Hang it, ye look so tired and wisht that I can't find heart to say what I would!'

'I am – weary and wisht, David; I am. We can get home to-morrow for certain, I hope?'

'We can. And please God we will!' said Mr Heddegan heartily, as if he too were weary of his brief honeymoon. 'I must be into business again on Monday morning at latest.'

They left by the next morning steamer, and in the afternoon took up their residence in their own house at Giant's Town.

The hour that she reached the island it was as if a material weight had been removed from Baptista's shoulders. Her husband attributed the change to the influence of the local breezes after the hot-house atmo-sphere of the mainland. However that might be, settled here, a few doors from her mother's dwelling, she recovered in no very long time much of her customary bearing, which was never very demonstrative. She accepted her position calmly, and faintly smiled when her neighbours learned to call her Mrs Heddegan, and said she seemed likely to become the leader of fashion in Giant's Town.

Her husband was a man who had made considerably more money by trade than her father had done: and perhaps the greater profusion of surroundings at her command than she had heretofore been mistress of, was not without an effect upon her. One week, two weeks, three weeks passed; and, being pre-eminently a young woman who allowed things to drift, she did nothing whatever either to disclose or conceal traces of her first marriage; or to learn if there existed possibilities – which there undoubtedly did – by which that hasty contract might become revealed to those about her at any unexpected moment.

While yet within the first month of her marriage, and on an evening just before sunset, Baptista was standing within her garden adjoining the house, when she saw passing along the road a personage clad in a greasy black coat and battered tall hat, which, common enough in the slums of a city, had an odd appearance in St Maria's. The tramp, as he seemed to be, marked her at once – bonnetless and unwrapped as she was her features were plainly recognizable – and with an air of friendly surprise came and leant over the wall.

'What! don't you know me?' said he.

She had some dim recollection of his face, but said that she was not acquainted with him.

'Why, your witness to be sure, ma'am. Don't you mind the man that was mending the church-window when you and your intended husband walked up to be made one; and the clerk called me down from the ladder, and I came and did my part by writing my name and occupation?'

Baptista glanced quickly around; her husband was out of earshot. That would have been of less importance but for the fact that the wedding witnessed by this personage had not been the wedding with Mr Heddegan, but the one on the day previous.

'I've had a misfortune since then, that's pulled me under,' continued her friend. 'But don't let me damp yer wedded joy by naming the particulars. Yes, I've seen changes since; though 'tis but a short time ago – let me see, only a month next week, I think; for 'twere the first or second day in August.'

'Yes – that's when it was,' said another man, a sailor, who had come up with a pipe in his mouth, and felt it necessary to join in (Baptista having receded to escape further speech). 'For that was the first time I set foot in Giant's Town; and her husband took her to him the same day.'

A dialogue then proceeded between the two men outside the wall, which Baptista could not help hearing.

'Ay, I signed the book that made her one flesh,' repeated the decayed glazier. 'Where's her goodman?'

'About the premises somewhere; but you don't see 'em together much,' replied the sailor in an undertone. 'You see, he's older than she.'

'Older? I should never have thought it from my own observation,' said the glazier. 'He was a remarkably handsome man.'

'Handsome? Well, there he is – we can see for ourselves.'

David Heddegan had, indeed, just shown himself at the upper end of the garden; and the glazier, looking in bewilderment from the husband to the wife, saw the latter turn pale.

Now that decayed glazier was a far-seeing and cunning man – too far-seeing and cunning to allow himself to thrive by simple and straight-

forward means – and he held his peace, till he could read more plainly
the meaning of this riddle, merely adding carelessly, 'Well – marriage
do alter a man, 'tis true. I should never ha' knowed him!'

He then stared oddly at the disconcerted Baptista, and moving on to
where he could again address her, asked her to do him a good turn,
since he once had done the same for her. Understanding that he meant
money, she handed him some, at which he thanked her, and instantly
went away.

VII

She had escaped exposure on this occasion; but the incident had been
an awkward one, and should have suggested to Baptista that sooner or
later the secret must leak out. As it was, she suspected that at any rate
she had not heard the last of the glazier.

In a day or two, when her husband had gone to the old town on the
other side of the island, there came a gentle tap at the door, and the
worthy witness of her first marriage made his appearance a second time.

'It took me hours to get to the bottom of the mystery – hours!' he
said with a gaze of deep confederacy which offended her pride very
deeply. 'But thanks to a good intellect I've done it. Now, ma'am, I'm
not a man to tell tales, even when a tale would be so good as this. But
I'm going back to the mainland again, and a little assistance would be
as rain on thirsty ground.'

'I helped you two days ago,' began Baptista.

'Yes – but what was that, my good lady? Not enough to pay my
passage to Pen-zephyr. I came over on your account, for I thought there
was a mystery somewhere. Now I must go back on my own. Mind this –
'twould be very awkward for you if your old man were to know. He's
a queer temper, though he may be fond.'

She knew as well as her visitor how awkward it would be; and the
hush-money she paid was heavy that day. She had, however, the
satisfaction of watching the man to the steamer, and seeing him diminish
out of sight. But Baptista perceived that the system into which she had
been led of purchasing silence thus was one fatal to her peace of mind,
particularly if it had to be continued.

Hearing no more from the glazier she hoped the difficulty was past.
But another week only had gone by, when, as she was pacing the Giant's

Walk (the name given to the promenade), she met the same personage
in the company of a fat woman carrying a bundle.

'This is the lady, my dear,' he said to his companion. 'This, ma'am, is
my wife. We've come to settle in the town for a time, if so be we can find
room.'

'That you won't do,' said she. 'Nobody can live here who is not
privileged.'

'I am privileged,' said the glazier, 'by my trade.'

Baptista went on, but in the afternoon she received a visit from the
man's wife. This honest woman began to depict, in forcible colours, the
necessity for keeping up the concealment.

'I will intercede with my husband, ma'am,' she said. 'He's a true man
if rightly managed; and I'll beg him to consider your position. 'Tis a
very nice house you've got here,' she added, glancing round, 'and well
worth a little sacrifice to keep it.'

The unlucky Baptista staved off the danger on this third occasion as
she had done on the previous two. But she formed a resolve that, if the
attack were once more to be repeated, she would face a revelation –
worse though that must now be than before she had attempted to
purchase silence by bribes. Her tormentors, never believing her capable
of acting upon such an intention, came again; but she shut the door in
their faces. They retreated, muttering something; but she went to the
back of the house, where David Heddegan was.

She looked at him, unconscious of all. The case was serious; she knew
that well; and all the more serious in that she liked him better now than
she had done at first. Yet, as she herself began to see, the secret was one
that was sure to disclose itself. Her name and Charles's stood indelibly
written in the registers; and though a month only had passed as yet it
was a wonder that his clandestine union with her had not already been
discovered by his friends. Thus spurring herself to the inevitable, she
spoke to Heddegan.

'David, come indoors. I have something to tell you.'

He hardly regarded her at first. She had discerned that during the
last week or two he had seemed preoccupied, as if some private business
harassed him. She repeated her request. He replied with a sigh, 'Yes,
certainly, mee deer.'

When they had reached the sitting-room and shut the door she
repeated, faintly, 'David, I have something to tell you – a sort of tragedy
I have concealed. You will hate me for having so far deceived you; but

perhaps my telling you voluntarily will make you think a little better of me than you would do otherwise.'

'Tragedy ?' he said, awakening to interest. 'Much you can know about tragedies, mee deer, that have been in the world so short a time!'

She saw that he suspected nothing, and it made her task the harder. But on she went steadily. 'It is about something that happened before we were married,' she said.

'Indeed!'

'Not a very long time before – a short time. And it is about a lover,' she faltered.

'I don't much mind that,' he said mildly. 'In truth, I was in hopes 'twas more.'

'In hopes!'

'Well, yes.'

This screwed her up to the necessary effort. 'I met my old sweetheart. He scorned me, chid me, dared me, and I went and married him. We were coming straight here to tell you all what we had done; but he was drowned; and I thought I would say nothing about him: and I married you, David, for the sake of peace and quietness. I've tried to keep it from you, but have found I cannot. There – that's the substance of it, and you can never, never forgive me, I am sure!'

She spoke desperately. But the old man, instead of turning black or blue, or slaying her in his indignation, jumped up from his chair, and began to caper around the room in quite an ecstatic emotion.

'O, happy thing! How well it falls out!' he exclaimed, snapping his fingers over his head. 'Ha-ha – the knot is cut – I see a way out of my trouble – ha-ha!'

She looked at him without uttering a sound, till, as he still continued smiling joyfully, she said, 'O – what do you mean ? Is it done to torment me ?'

'No – no! O, mee deer, your story helps me out of the most heart-aching quandary a poor man ever found himself in! You see, it is this – *I've* got a tragedy, too; and unless you had had one to tell, I could never have seen my way to tell mine!'

'What is yours – what is it ?' she asked, with altogether a new view of things.

'Well – it is a bouncer; mine is a bouncer!' said he, looking on the ground and wiping his eyes.

'Not worse than mine ?'

'Well – that depends upon how you look at it. Yours had to do with the past alone; and I don't mind it. You see, we've been married a month, and it don't jar upon me as it would if we'd only been married a day or two. Now mine refers to past, present, and future; so that—'

'Past, present, and future!' she murmured. 'It never occurred to me that *you* had a tragedy too.'

'But I have!' he said, shaking his head. 'In fact, four.'

'Then tell 'em!' cried the young woman.

'I will – I will. But be considerate, I beg 'ee, mee deer. Well – I wasn't a bachelor when I married 'ee, any more than you were a spinster. Just as you was a widow-woman, I was a widow-man.'

'Ah!' said she, with some surprise. 'But is that all? – then we are nicely balanced,' she added, relieved.

'No – it is not all. There's the point. I am not only a widower.'

'O, David!'

'I am a widower with four tragedies – that is to say, four strapping girls – the eldest taller than you. Don't 'ee look so struck – dumb-like! It fell out in this way. I knew the poor woman, their mother, in Penzephyr for some years; and – to cut a long story short – I privately married her at last, just before she died. I kept the matter secret, but it is getting known among the people here by degrees. I've long felt for the children – that it is my duty to have them here, and do something for them. I have not had courage to break it to 'ee, but I've seen lately that it would soon come to your ears, and that hev worried me.'

'Are they educated?' said the ex-schoolmistress.

'No. I am sorry to say they have been much neglected; in truth, they can hardly read. And so I thought that by marrying a young schoolmistress I should get some one in the house who could teach 'em, and bring 'em into genteel condition, all for nothing. You see, they are growed up too tall to be sent to school.'

'O, mercy!' she almost moaned. 'Four great girls to teach the rudiments to, and have always in the house with me spelling over their books; and I hate teaching, it kills me. I am bitterly punished – I am, I am!'

'You'll get used to 'em, mee deer, and the balance of secrets – mine against yours – will comfort your heart with a sense of justice. I could send for 'em this week very well – and I will! In faith, I could send this very day. Baptista, you have relieved me of all my difficulty!'

Thus the interview ended, so far as this matter was concerned.

Baptista was too stupefied to say more, and when she went away to her room she wept from very mortification at Mr Heddegan's duplicity. Education, the one thing she abhorred; the shame of it to delude a young wife so!

The next meal came round. As they sat, Baptista would not suffer her eyes to turn towards him. He did not attempt to intrude upon her reserve, but every now and then looked under the table and chuckled with satisfaction at the aspect of affairs. 'How very well matched we be!' he said, comfortably.

Next day, when the steamer came in, Baptista saw her husband rush down to meet it; and soon after there appeared at her door four tall, hipless, shoulderless girls, dwindling in height and size from the eldest to the youngest, like a row of Pan pipes; at the head of them standing Heddegan. He smiled pleasantly through the gray fringe of his whiskers and beard, and turning to the girls said, 'Now come forrard, and shake hands properly with your stepmother.'

Thus she made their acquaintance, and he went out, leaving them together. On examination the poor girls turned out to be not only plain-looking, which she could have forgiven, but to have such a lamentably meagre intellectual equipment as to be hopelessly inadequate as companions. Even the eldest, almost her own age, could only read with difficulty words of two syllables; and taste in dress was beyond their comprehension. In the long vista of future years she saw nothing but dreary drudgery at her detested old trade without prospect of reward.

She went about quite despairing during the next few days – an un-promising, unfortunate mood for a woman who had not been married six weeks. From her parents she concealed everything. They had been amongst the few acquaintances of Heddegan who knew nothing of his secret, and were indignant enough when they saw such a ready-made household foisted upon their only child. But she would not support them in their remonstrances.

'No, you don't yet know all,' she said.

Thus Baptista had sense enough to see the retributive fairness of this issue. For some time, whenever conversation arose between her and Heddegan, which was not often, she always said, 'I am miserable, and you know it. Yet I don't wish things to be otherwise.'

But one day when he asked, 'How do you like 'em now?' her answer was unexpected. 'Much better than I did,' she said, quietly. 'I may like them very much some day.'

This was the beginning of a serener season for the chastened spirit of Baptista Heddegan. She had, in truth, discovered, underneath the crust of uncouthness and meagre articulation which was due to their Troglodytean existence, that her unwelcomed daughters had natures that were unselfish almost to sublimity. The harsh discipline accorded to their young lives before their mother's wrong had been righted, had operated less to crush them than to lift them above all personal ambition. They considered the world and its contents in a purely objective way, and their own lot seemed only to affect them as that of certain human beings among the rest, whose troubles they knew rather than suffered.

This was such an entirely new way of regarding life to a woman of Baptista's nature, that her attention, from being first arrested by it, became deeply interested. By imperceptible pulses her heart expanded in sympathy with theirs. The sentences of her tragi-comedy, her life, confused till now, became clearer daily. That in humanity, as exemplified by these girls, there was nothing to dislike, but infinitely much to pity, she learnt with the lapse of each week in their company. She grew to like the girls of unpromising exterior, and from liking she got to love them; till they formed an unexpected point of junction between her own and her husband's interests, generating a sterling friendship at least, between a pair in whose existence there had threatened to be neither friendship nor love.

October 1885

The Romantic Adventures
of a Milkmaid

I

It was half-past four o'clock (by the testimony of the land-surveyor, my authority for the particulars of this story, a gentleman with the faintest curve of humour on his lips); it was half-past four o'clock on a May morning in the eighteen-forties. A dense white fog hung over the Valley of the Exe, ending against the hills on either side.

But though nothing in the vale could be seen from higher ground, notes of differing kinds gave pretty clear indications that bustling life was going on there. This audible presence and visual absence of an active scene had a peculiar effect above the fog level. Nature had laid a white hand over the creatures ensconced within the vale, as a hand might be laid over a nest of chirping birds.

The noises that ascended through the pallid coverlid were perturbed lowings, mingled with human voices in sharps and flats, and the bark of a dog. These, followed by the slamming of a gate, explained as well as eyesight could have done, to any inhabitant of the district, that Dairyman Tucker's under-milker was driving the cows from the meads into the stalls. When a rougher accent joined in the vociferations of man and beast, it would have been realized that the dairy-farmer himself had come out to meet the cows, pail in hand, and white pinafore on; and when, moreover, some women's voices joined in the chorus, that the cows were stalled and proceedings about to commence.

A hush followed, the atmosphere being so stagnant that the milk could be heard buzzing into the pails, together with occasional words of the milkmaids and men.

'Don't ye bide about long upon the road, Margery. You can be back again by skimming-time.'

The rough voice of Dairyman Tucker was the vehicle of this remark.

The barton-gate slammed again, and in two or three minutes a something became visible, rising out of the fog in that quarter.

The shape revealed itself as that of a woman having a young and agile gait. The colours and other details of her dress were then disclosed – a bright pink cotton frock (because winter was over); a small woollen shawl of shepherd's plaid (because summer was not come); a white handkerchief tied over her head-gear, because it was so foggy, so damp, and so early; and a straw bonnet and ribbons peeping from under the handkerchief, because it was likely to be a sunny May day.

Her face was of the hereditary type among families down in these parts: sweet in expression, perfect in hue, and somewhat irregular in feature. Her eyes were of a liquid brown. On her arm she carried a withy basket, in which lay several butter-rolls in a nest of wet cabbage-leaves. She was the 'Margery' who had been told not to 'bide about long upon the road'.

She went on her way across the fields, sometimes above the fog, sometimes below it, not much perplexed by its presence except when the track was so indefinite that it ceased to be a guide to the next stile. The dampness was such that innumerable earthworms lay in couples across the path till, startled even by her light tread, they withdrew suddenly into their holes. She kept clear of all trees. Why was that? There was no danger of lightning on such a morning as this. But though the roads were dry the fog had gathered in the boughs, causing them to set up such a dripping as would go clean through the protecting handkerchief like bullets, and spoil the ribbons beneath. The beech and ash were particularly shunned, for they dripped more maliciously than any. It was an instance of woman's keen appreciativeness of Nature's moods and peculiarities: a man crossing those fields might hardly have perceived that the trees dripped at all.

In less than an hour she had traversed a distance of four miles, and arrived at a latticed cottage in a secluded spot. An elderly woman, scarce awake, answered her knocking. Margery delivered up the butter, and said, 'How is granny this morning? I can't stay to go up to her, but tell her I have returned what we owed her.'

Her grandmother was no worse than usual: and receiving back the empty basket the girl proceeded to carry out some intention which had not been included in her orders. Instead of returning to the light labours of skimming-time, she hastened on, her direction being towards a little neighbouring town. Before, however, Margery had proceeded far, she met the postman, laden to the neck with letter-bags, of which he had not yet deposited one.

'Are the shops open yet, Samuel?' she said.

'O no,' replied that stooping pedestrian, not waiting to stand upright. 'They won't be open yet this hour, except the saddler and ironmonger and little tacker-haired machine-man for the farm folk. They downs their shutters at half-past six, then the baker's at half-past seven, then the draper's at eight.'

'O, the draper's at eight.' It was plain that Margery had wanted the draper's.

The postman turned up a side-path, and the young girl, as though deciding within herself that if she could not go shopping at once she might as well get back for the skimming, retraced her steps.

The public road home from this point was easy but devious. By far the nearest way was by getting over a fence, and crossing the private grounds of a picturesque old country-house, whose chimneys were just visible through the trees. As the house had been shut up for many months, the girl decided to take the straight cut. She pushed her way through the laurel bushes, sheltering her bonnet with the shawl as an additional safeguard, scrambled over an inner boundary, went along through more shrubberies, and stood ready to emerge upon the open lawn. Before doing so she looked around in the wary manner of a poacher. It was not the first time that she had broken fence in her life; but somehow, and all of a sudden, she had felt herself too near womanhood to indulge in such practices with freedom. However, she moved forth, and the house-front stared her in the face, at this higher level unobscured by fog.

It was a building of the medium size, and unpretending, the façade being of stone; and of the Italian elevation made familiar by Inigo Jones and his school. There was a doorway to the lawn, standing at the head of a flight of steps. The shutters of the house were closed, and the blinds of the bedrooms drawn down. Her perception of the fact that no crusty caretaker could see her from the windows led her at once to slacken her pace, and stroll through the flower-beds coolly. A house unblinded is a possible spy, and must be treated accordingly; a house with the shutters together is an insensate heap of stone and mortar, to be faced with indifference.

On the other side of the house the greensward rose to an eminence, whereon stood one of those curious summer shelters sometimes erected on exposed points of view, called an all-the-year-round. In the present case it consisted of four walls radiating from a centre like the arms of a turnstile, with seats in each angle, so that whencesoever the wind came, it was always possible to find a screened corner from which to observe the landscape.

The milkmaid's trackless course led her up the hill and past this erection. At ease as to being watched and scolded as an intruder, her mind flew to other matters; till, at the moment when she was not a yard from the shelter, she heard a foot or feet scraping on the gravel behind it. Some one was in the all-the-year-round, apparently occupying the seat on the other side; as was proved when, on turning, she saw an elbow, a man's elbow, projecting over the edge.

Now the young woman did not much like the idea of going down the hill under the eyes of this person, which she would have to do if she went on, for as an intruder she was liable to be called back and questioned upon her business there. Accordingly she crept softly up and sat in the seat behind, intending to remain there until her companion should leave.

This he by no means seemed in a hurry to do. What could possibly have brought him there, what could detain him there, at six o'clock on a morning of mist when there was nothing to be seen or enjoyed of the vale beneath, puzzled her not a little. But he remained quite still, and Margery grew impatient. She discerned the track of his feet in the dewy grass, forming a line from the house steps, which announced that he was an inhabitant and not a chance passer-by. At last she peeped round.

II

A fine-framed dark-mustachioed gentleman, in dressing-gown and slippers, was sitting there in the damp without a hat on. With one hand he was tightly grasping his forehead, the other hung over his knee. The attitude bespoke with sufficient clearness a mental condition of anguish. He was quite a different being from any of the men to whom her eyes were accustomed. She had never seen mustachios before, for they were not worn by civilians in Lower Wessex at this date. His hands and his face were white – to her view deadly white – and he heeded nothing outside his own existence. There he remained as motionless as the bushes around him; indeed, he scarcely seemed to breathe.

Having imprudently advanced thus far, Margery's wish was to get back again in the same unseen manner; but in moving her foot for the purpose it grated on the gravel. He started up with an air of bewilderment, and slipped something into the pocket of his dressing-gown. She was almost certain that it was a pistol. The pair stood looking blankly at each other.

'My Gott, who are you?' he asked sternly, and with not altogether an English articulation. 'What do you do here?'

Margery had already begun to be frightened at her boldness in invading the lawn and pleasure-seat. The house had a master, and she had not known of it. 'My name is Margaret Tucker, sir,' she said meekly. 'My father is Dairyman Tucker. We live at Silverthorn Dairy-house.'

'What were you doing here at this hour of the morning?'

She told him, even to the fact that she had climbed over the fence.

'And what made you peep round at me?'

'I saw your elbow, sir; and I wondered what you were doing?'

'And what was I doing?'

'Nothing. You had one hand on your forehead and the other on your knee. I do hope you are not ill, sir, or in deep trouble?' Margery had sufficient tact to say nothing about the pistol.

'What difference would it make to you if I were ill or in trouble? You don't know me.'

She returned no answer, feeling that she might have taken a liberty in expressing sympathy. But, looking furtively up at him, she discerned to her surprise that he seemed affected by her humane wish, simply as it had been expressed. She had scarcely conceived that such a tall dark man could know what gentle feelings were.

'Well, I am much obliged to you for caring how I am,' said he with a faint smile and an affected lightness of manner, which, even to her, only rendered more apparent the gloom beneath. 'I have not slept this past night. I suffer from sleeplessness. Probably you do not.'

Margery laughed a little, and he glanced with interest at the comely picture she presented; her fresh face, brown hair, candid eyes, unpractised manner, country dress, pink hands, empty wicker-basket, and the handkerchief over her bonnet.

'Well,' he said, after his scrutiny, 'I need hardly have asked such a question of one who is Nature's own image. . . . Ah, but, my good little friend,' he added, recurring to his bitter tone and sitting wearily down, 'you don't know what great clouds can hang over some people's lives, and what cowards some men are in face of them. To escape themselves they travel, take picturesque houses, and engage in country sports. But here it is so dreary, and the fog was horrible this morning!'

'Why, this is only the pride of the morning!' said Margery. 'By-and-by it will be a beautiful day.'

She was going on her way forthwith; but he detained her – detained her with words, talking on every innocent little subject he could think of. He had an object in keeping her there more serious than his words would imply. It was as if he feared to be left alone.

While they still stood, the misty figure of the postman, whom Margery had left a quarter of an hour earlier to follow his sinuous course, crossed the grounds below them on his way to the house. Signifying to Margery by a wave of his hand that she was to step back out of sight, in the hinder angle of the shelter, the gentleman beckoned to the postman to bring the bag to where he stood. The man did so, and again resumed his journey.

The stranger unlocked the bag and threw it on the seat, having taken one letter from within. This he read attentively, and his countenance changed.

The change was almost phantasmagorial, as if the sun had burst through the fog upon that face: it became clear, bright, almost radiant. Yet it was but a change that may take place in the commonest human being, provided his countenance be not too wooden, or his artifice have not grown to second nature. He turned to Margery, who was again edging off, and, seizing her hand, appeared as though he were about to embrace her. Checking his impulse, he said, 'My guardian child – my good friend – you have saved me!'

'What from?' she ventured to ask.

'That you may never know.'

She thought of the weapon, and guessed that the letter he had just received had effected this change in his mood, but made no observation till he went on to say, 'What did you tell me was your name, dear girl?'

She repeated her name.

'Margaret Tucker.' He stooped, and pressed her hand. 'Sit down for a moment – one moment,' he said, pointing to the end of the seat, and taking the extremest further end for himself, not to discompose her. She sat down.

'It is to ask a question,' he went on, 'and there must be confidence between us. You have saved me from an act of madness! What can I do for you?'

'Nothing, sir.'

'Nothing?'

'Father is very well off, and we don't want anything.'

'But there must be some service I can render, some kindness, some votive offering which I could make, and so imprint on your memory as long as you live that I am not an ungrateful man?'

'Why should you be grateful to me, sir?'

He shook his head. 'Some things are best left unspoken. Now think. What would you like to have best in the world?'

Margery made a pretence of reflecting – then fell to reflecting seriously; but the negative was ultimately as undisturbed as ever: she could not decide on anything she would like best in the world; it was too difficult, too sudden.

'Very well – don't hurry yourself. Think it over all day. I ride this afternoon. You live – where?'

'Silverthorn Dairy-house.'

'I will ride that way homeward this evening. Do you consider by eight o'clock what little article, what little treat, you would most like of any.'

'I will, sir,' said Margery, now warming up to the idea. 'Where shall I meet you? Or will you call at the house, sir?'

'Ah – no. I should not wish the circumstances known out of which our acquaintance rose. It would be more proper – but no.'

Margery, too, seemed rather anxious that he should not call. 'I could come out, sir,' she said. 'My father is odd-tempered, and perhaps—'

It was agreed that she should look over a stile at the top of her father's garden, and that he should ride along a bridle-path outside, to receive her answer. 'Margery,' said the gentleman in conclusion, 'now that you have discovered me under ghastly conditions, are you going to reveal them, and make me an object for the gossip of the curious?'

'No, no, sir!' she replied earnestly. 'Why should I do that?'

'You will never tell?'

'Never, never will I tell what has happened here this morning.'

'Neither to your father, nor to your friends, nor to anyone?'

'To no one at all,' she said.

'It is sufficient,' he answered. 'You mean what you say, my dear maiden. Now you want to leave me. Good-bye!'

She descended the hill, walking with some awkwardness; for she felt the stranger's eyes were upon her till the fog had enveloped her from his gaze. She took no notice now of the dripping from the trees; she was lost in thought on other things. Had she saved this handsome, melancholy, sleepless, foreign gentleman who had had a trouble on his mind till the letter came? What had he been going to do? Margery could guess that he had meditated death at his own hand. Strange as the incident had been in itself, to her it had seemed stranger even than it was. Contrasting colours heighten each other by being juxtaposed; it is the same with contrasting lives.

Reaching the opposite side of the park there appeared before her for the third time that little old man, the foot-post. As the turnpike-road ran, the postman's beat was twelve miles a day; six miles out from the town, and six miles back at night. But what with zigzags, devious ways, offsets to country seats, curves to farms, looped courses, and triangles to outlying hamlets, the ground actually covered by him was nearer one-and-twenty miles. Hence it was that Margery, who had come straight, was still abreast of him, despite her long pause.

The weighty sense that she was mixed up in a tragical secret with an unknown and handsome stranger prevented her joining very readily in chat with the postman for some time. But a keen interest in her adventure caused her to respond at once when the bowed man of mails said, 'You hit athwart the grounds of Mount Lodge, Miss Margery, or you wouldn't ha' met me here. Well, somebody hev took the old place at last.'

In acknowledging her route Margery brought herself to ask who the new gentleman might be.

'Guide the girl's heart! What! don't she know? And yet how should ye – he's only just a-come. – Well, nominal, he's a fishing gentleman, come for the summer only. But, more to the subject, he's a foreign noble that's lived in England so long as to be without any true country: some of his letters call him Baron, some Squire, so that 'a must be born to something that can't be earned by elbow-grease and Christian conduct. He was out this morning a-watching the fog. "Postman," 'a said, "good-morning: give me the bag." O, yes, 'a's a civil genteel nobleman enough.'

'Took the house for fishing, did he?'

'That's what they say, and as it can be for nothing else I suppose it's true. But, in final, his health's not good, 'a b'lieve; he's been living too rithe. The London smoke got into his wyndpipe, till 'a couldn't eat. However, I shouldn't mind having the run of his kitchen.'

'And what is his name?'

'Ah – there you have me! 'Tis a name no man's tongue can tell, or even woman's, except by pen-and-ink and good scholarship. It begins with X, and who, without the machinery of a clock in's inside, can speak that? But here 'tis – from his letters.' The postman with his walking-stick wrote upon the ground:

'BARON VON XANTEN'

III

The day, as she had prognosticated, turned out fine; for weather-wisdom was imbibed with their milk-sops by the children of the Exe Vale. The impending meeting excited Margery, and she performed her duties in her father's house with mechanical unconsciousness.

Milking, skimming, cheesemaking were done. Her father was asleep in the settle, the milkmen and maids were gone home to their cottages, and the clock showed a quarter to eight. She dressed herself with care, went to the top of the garden, and looked over the stile. The view was eastward, and a great moon hung before her in a sky which had not a cloud. Nothing was moving except on the minutest scale, and she remained leaning over, the night-hawk sounding his croud from the bough of an isolated tree on the open hill-side.

Here Margery waited till the appointed time had passed by three-quarters of an hour; but no Baron came. She had been full of an idea, and her heart sank with disappointment. Then at last the pacing of a horse became audible on the soft path without, leading up from the water-meads, simultaneously with which she beheld the form of the stranger, riding home, as he had said.

The moonlight so flooded her face as to make her very conspicuous in the garden-gap. 'Ah, my maiden – what is your name – Margery!' he said. 'How came you here? But of course I remember – we were to meet. And it was to be at eight – *proh pudor!* – I have kept you waiting!'

'It doesn't matter, sir. I've thought of something.'

'Thought of something?'

'Yes, sir. You said this morning that I was to think what I would like best in the world, and I have made up my mind.'

'I did say so – to be sure I did,' he replied, collecting his thoughts. 'I remember to have had good reason for gratitude to you.' He placed his hand to his brow, and in a minute alighted, and came up to her with the bridle in his hand. 'I was to give you a treat or present, and you could not think of one. Now you have done so. Let me hear what it is, and I'll be as good as my word.'

'To go to the Yeomanry Ball that's to be given this month.'

'The Yeomanry Ball – Yeomanry Ball?' he murmured, as if, of all requests in the world, this was what he had least expected. 'Where is what you call the Yeomanry Ball?'

'At Exonbury.'

'Have you ever been to it before?'

'No, sir.'

'Or to any ball?'

'No.'

'But did I not say a gift – a present?'

'Or a treat?'

'Ah, yes, or a treat,' he echoed, with the air of one who finds himself in a slight fix. 'But with whom would you propose to go?'

'I don't know. I have not thought of that yet.'

'You have no friend who could take you, even if I got you an invitation?'

Margery looked at the moon. 'No one who can dance,' she said; adding, with hesitation, 'I was thinking that perhaps—'

'But, my dear Margery,' he said, stopping her, as if he half-divined what her simple dream of a cavalier had been; 'it is very odd that you can think of nothing else than going to a Yeomanry Ball. Think again. You are sure there is nothing else?'

'Quite sure, sir,' she decisively answered. At first nobody would have noticed in that pretty young face any sign of decision; yet it was discoverable. The mouth, though soft, was firm in line; the eyebrows were distinct, and extended near to each other. 'I have thought of it all day,' she continued, sadly. 'Still, sir, if you are sorry you offered me anything, I can let you off.'

'Sorry? – Certainly not, Margery,' he said, rather nettled. 'I'll show you that whatever hopes I have raised in your breast I am honourable enough to gratify. If it lies in my power,' he added with sudden firmness, 'you *shall* go to the Yeomanry Ball. In what building is it to be held?'

'In the Assembly Rooms.'

'And would you be likely to be recognized there? Do you know many people?'

'Not many, sir. None, I may say. I know nobody who goes to balls.'

'Ah, well; you must go, since you wish it; and if there is no other way of getting over the difficulty of having nobody to take you, I'll take you myself. Would you like me to do so? I can dance.'

'O yes, sir; I know that, and I thought you might offer to do it. But would you bring me back again?'

'Of course I'll bring you back. But, by-the-bye, can *you* dance?'

'Yes.'

'What?'

'Reels, and jigs, and country-dances like the New-Rigged-Ship, and Follow-my-Lover, and Haste-to-the-Wedding, and the College Hornpipe, and the Favourite Quickstep, and Captain White's dance.'

'A very good list – a very good! but unluckily I fear they don't dance any of those now. But if you have the instinct we may soon cure your ignorance. Let me see you dance a moment.'

She stood out into the garden-path, the stile being still between them, and seizing a side of her skirt with each hand, performed the movements which are even yet far from uncommon in the dances of the villagers of merry England. But her motions, though graceful, were not precisely those which appear in the figures of a modern ballroom.

'Well, my good friend, it is a very pretty sight,' he said, warming up to the proceedings. 'But you dance too well – you dance all over your person – and that's too thorough a way for the present day. I should say it was exactly how they danced in the time of your poet Chaucer; but as people don't dance like it now, we must consider. First I must inquire more about this ball, and then I must see you again.'

'If it is a great trouble to you, sir, I—'

'O no, no. I will think it over. So far so good.'

The Baron mentioned an evening and an hour when he would be passing that way again; then mounted his horse and rode away.

On the next occasion, which was just when the sun was changing places with the moon as an illuminator of Silverthorn Dairy, she found him at the spot before her, and unencumbered by a horse. The melancholy that had so weighed him down at their first interview, and had been perceptible at their second, had quite disappeared. He pressed her right hand between both his own across the stile.

'My good maiden, Gott bless you!' said he warmly. 'I cannot help

thinking of that morning! I was too much over-shadowed at first to take
in the whole force of it. You do not know all; but your presence was
a miraculous intervention. Now to more cheerful matters. I have a
great deal to tell – that is, if your wish about the ball be still the
same?'

'O yes, sir – if you don't object.'

'Never think of my objecting. What I have found out is something
which simplifies matters amazingly. In addition to your Yeomanry Ball
at Exonbury, there is also to be one in the next county about the same
time. This ball is not to be held at the Town Hall of the county-town
as usual, but at Lord Toneborough's, who is colonel of the regiment,
and who, I suppose, wishes to please the yeomen because his brother is
going to stand for the county. Now I find I could take you there very
well, and the great advantage of that ball over the Yeomanry Ball in this
county is, that there you would be absolutely unknown, and I also. But
do you prefer your own neighbourhood?'

'O no, sir. It is a ball I long to see – I don't know what it is like; it
does not matter where.'

'Good. Then I shall be able to make much more of you there, where
there is no possibility of recognition. That being settled, the next thing
is the dancing. Now reels and such things do not do. For think of this –
there is a new dance at Almack's and everywhere else, over which the
world has gone crazy.'

'How dreadful!'

'Ah – but that is a mere expression – gone mad. It is really an ancient
Scythian dance; but, such is the power of fashion, that, having once
been adopted by Society, this dance has made the tour of the Continent
in one season.'

'What is its name, sir?'

'The polka. Young people, who always dance, are ecstatic about it
and old people, who have not danced for years, have begun to dance
again on its account. All share the excitement. It arrived in London only
some few months ago – it is now all over the country. Now this is your
opportunity, my good Margery. To learn this one dance will be enough
They will dance scarce anything else at that ball. While, to crown all
it is the easiest dance in the world, and as I know it quite well I can
practise you in the step. Suppose we try?'

Margery showed some hesitation before crossing the stile: it was a
Rubicon in more ways than one. But the curious reverence which was

stealing over her for all that this stranger said and did was too much for prudence. She crossed the stile.

Withdrawing with her to a nook where two high hedges met, and where the grass was elastic and dry, he lightly rested his arm on her waist, and practised with her the new step of fascination. Instead of music he whispered numbers, and she, as may be supposed, showed no slight aptness in following his instructions. Thus they moved round together, the moon-shadows from the twigs racing over their forms as they turned.

The interview lasted about half-an-hour. Then he somewhat abruptly handed her over the stile and stood looking at her from the other side.

'Well,' he murmured, 'what has come to pass is strange! My whole business after this will be to recover my right mind!'

Margery always declared that there seemed to be some power in the stranger that was more than human, something magical and compulsory, when he seized her and gently trotted her round. But lingering emotions may have led her memory to play pranks with the scene, and her vivid imagination at that youthful age must be taken into account in believing her. However, there is no doubt that the stranger, whoever he might be, and whatever his powers, taught her the elements of modern dancing at a certain interview by moonlight at the top of her father's garden, as was proved by her possession of knowledge on the subject that could have been acquired in no other way.

His was of the first rank of commanding figures, she was one of the most agile of milkmaids, and to casual view it would have seemed all of a piece with Nature's doings that things should go on thus. But there was another side to the case; and whether the strange gentleman were a wild olive tree, or not, it was questionable if the acquaintance would lead to happiness. 'A fleeting romance and a possible calamity': thus it might have been summed up by the practical.

Margery was in Paradise; and yet she was not at this date distinctly in love with the stranger. What she felt was something more mysterious, more of the nature of veneration. As he looked at her across the stile she spoke timidly, on a subject which had apparently occupied her long.

'I ought to have a ball-dress, ought I not, sir?'

'Certainly. And you shall have a ball-dress.'

'Really?'

'No doubt of it. I won't do things by halves for my best friend. I have thought of the ball-dress, and of other things also.'

'And is my dancing good enough?'

'Quite – quite.' He paused, lapsed into thought, and looked at her. 'Margery,' he said, 'do you trust yourself unreservedly to me?'

'O yes, sir,' she replied brightly; 'if I am not too much trouble: if I am good enough to be seen in your society.'

The Baron laughed in a peculiar way. 'Really, I think you may assume as much as that. – However, to business. The ball is on the twenty-fifth, that is next Thursday week; and the only difficulty about the dress is the size. Suppose you lend me this?' And he touched her on the shoulder to signify a tight little jacket she wore.

Margery was all obedience. She took it off and handed it to him. The Baron rolled and compressed it with all his force till it was about as large as an apple-dumpling, and put it into his pocket.

'The next thing,' he said, 'is about getting the consent of your friends to your going. Have you thought of this?'

'There is only my father. I can tell him I am invited to a party, and I don't think he'll mind. Though I would rather not tell him.'

'But it strikes me that you must inform him something of what you intend. I would strongly advise you to do so.' He spoke as if rather perplexed as to the probable custom of the English peasantry in such matters, and added, 'However, it is for you to decide. I know nothing of the circumstances. As to getting to the ball, the plan I have arrranged is this. The direction to Lord Toneborough's being the other way from my house, you must meet me at Three-Walks-End in Chillington Wood, two miles or more from here. You know the place? Good. By meeting there we shall save five or six miles of journey – a consideration, as it is a long way. Now, for the last time: are you still firm in your wish for this particular treat and no other? It is not too late to give it up. Cannot you think of something else – something better – some useful household articles you require?'

Margery's countenance, which before had been beaming with expectation, lost its brightness: her lips became close, and her voice broken. 'You have offered to take me, and now—'

'No, no, no,' he said, patting her cheek. 'We will not think of anything else. You shall go.'

IV

But whether the Baron, in naming such a distant spot for the rendez-vous, was in hope she might fail him, and so relieve him after all of his undertaking, cannot be said; though it might have been strongly suspected from his manner that he had no great zest for the responsibility of escorting her.

But he little knew the firmness of the young woman he had to deal with. She was one of those soft natures whose power of adhesiveness to an acquired idea seems to be one of the special attributes of that softness. To go to a ball with this mysterious personage of romance was her ardent desire and aim; and none the less in that she trembled with fear and excitement at her position in so aiming. She felt the deepest awe, tenderness, and humility towards the Baron of the strange name; and yet she was prepared to stick to her point.

Thus it was that the afternoon of the eventful day found Margery trudging her way up the slopes from the vale to the place of appointment. She walked to the music of innumerable birds, which increased as she drew away from the open meads towards the groves. She had overcome all difficulties. After thinking out the question of telling or not telling her father, she had decided that to tell him was to be forbidden to go. Her contrivance therefore was this: to leave home this evening on a visit to her invalid grandmother, who lived not far from the Baron's house; but not to arrive at her grandmother's till breakfast-time next morning. Who would suspect an intercalated experience of twelve hours with the Baron at a ball? That this piece of deception was indefensible she afterwards owned readily enough; but she did not stop to think of it then.

It was sunset within Chillington Wood by the time she reached Three-Walks-End – the converging point of radiating trackways, now floored with a carpet of matted grass, which had never known other scythes than the teeth of rabbits and hares. The twitter overhead had ceased, except from a few braver and larger birds, including the cuckoo, who did not fear night at this pleasant time of year. Nobody seemed to be on the spot when she first drew near, but no sooner did Margery stand at the intersection of the roads than a slight crashing became audible, and her patron appeared. He was so transfigured in dress that she scarcely knew him. Under a light greatcoat, which was flung open, instead of his ordinary clothes he wore a suit of thin black cloth, an open waistcoat with a frill all down his shirt-front, a white tie, shining boots, no thicker than a glove, a coat that made him look like a bird, and a hat that seemed as if it would open and shut like an accordion.

'I am dressed for the ball – nothing worse,' he said, drily smiling. 'So will you be soon.'

'Why did you choose this place for our meeting, sir?' she asked, looking around and acquiring confidence.

'Why did I choose it? Well, because in riding past one day I observed a large hollow tree close by here, and it occurred to me when I was last with you that this would be useful for our purpose. Have you told your father?'

'I have not yet told him, sir.'

'That's very bad of you, Margery. How have you arranged it, then?'

She briefly related her plan, on which he made no comment, but, taking her by the hand as if she were a little child, he led her through the undergrowth to a spot where the trees were older, and standing at wider distances. Among them was the tree he had spoken of – an elm; huge, hollow, distorted, and headless, with a rift in its side.

'Now go inside,' he said, 'before it gets any darker. You will find there everything you want. At any rate, if you do not you must do without it. I'll keep watch; and don't be longer than you can help to be.'

'What am I to do, sir?' asked the puzzled maiden.

'Go inside, and you will see. When you are ready wave your handkerchief at that hole.'

She stooped into the opening. The cavity within the tree formed a lofty circular apartment, four or five feet in diameter, to which daylight entered at the top, and also through a round hole about six feet from the ground, marking the spot at which a limb had been amputated in the tree's prime. The decayed wood of cinnamon-brown, forming the inner surface of the tree, and the warm evening glow, reflected in at the top, suffused the cavity with a faint mellow radiance.

But Margery had hardly given herself time to heed these things. Her eye had been caught by objects of quite another quality. A large white oblong paper box lay against the inside of the tree; over it, on a splinter, hung a small oval looking-glass.

Margery seized the idea in a moment. She pressed through the rift into the tree, lifted the cover of the box, and, behold, there was disclosed within a lovely white apparition in a somewhat flattened state. It was the ball-dress.

This marvel of art was, briefly, a sort of heavenly cobweb. It was a gossamer texture of precious manufacture, artistically festooned in a dozen flounces or more.

Margery lifted it, and could hardly refrain from kissing it. Had anyone told her before this moment that such a dress could exist, she would have said, 'No; it's impossible!' She drew back, went forward, flushed, laughed, raised her hands. To say that the maker of that dress had been an individual of talent was simply understatement: he was a genius, and she sunned herself in the rays of his creation.

She then remembered that her friend without had told her to make haste, and she spasmodically proceeded to array herself. In removing the dress she found satin slippers, gloves, a handkerchief nearly all lace, a fan, and even flowers for the hair. 'O, how could he think of it!' she said, clasping her hands and almost crying with agitation. 'And the glass – how good of him!'

Everything was so well prepared, that to clothe herself in these garments was a matter of ease. In a quarter of an hour she was ready, even to shoes and gloves. But what led her more than anything else into admiration of the Baron's foresight was the discovery that there were half-a-dozen pairs each of shoes and gloves, of varying sizes, out of which she selected a fit.

Margery glanced at herself in the mirror, or at as much as she could see of herself: the image presented was superb. Then she hastily rolled up her old dress, put it in the box, and thrust the latter on a ledge as high as she could reach. Standing on tiptoe, she waved the handkerchief through the upper aperture, and bent to the rift to go out.

But what a trouble stared her in the face. The dress was so airy, so fantastical, and so extensive, that to get out in her new clothes by the rift which had admitted her in her old ones was an impossibility. She heard the Baron's steps crackling over the dead sticks and leaves.

'O, sir!' she began in despair.

'What – can't you dress yourself?' he inquired from the back of the trunk.

'Yes; but I can't get out of this dreadful tree!'

He came round to the opening, stooped, and looked in. 'It is obvious that you cannot,' he said, taking in her compass at a glance; and adding to himself, 'Charming! who would have thought that clothes could do so much! – Wait a minute, my little maid; I have it!' he said more loudly.

With all his might he kicked at the sides of the rift, and by that means broke away several pieces of the rotten touchwood. But, being thinly armed about the feet, he abandoned that process, and went for a fallen branch which lay near. By using the large end as a lever, he tore away pieces of the wooden shell which enshrouded Margery and all her loveliness, till the aperture was large enough for her to pass without tearing her dress. She breathed her relief: the silly girl had begun to fear that she would not get to the ball after all.

He carefully wrapped round her a cloak he had brought with him: it was hooded, and of a length which covered her to the heels.

'The carriage is waiting down the other path,' he said, and gave her his arm. A short trudge over the soft dry leaves brought them to the place indicated. There stood the brougham, the horses, the coachman, all as still as if they were growing on the spot, like the trees. Margery's eyes rose with some timidity to the coachman's figure.

'You need not mind him,' said the Baron. 'He is a foreigner, and heeds nothing.'

In the space of a short minute she was handed inside; the Baron buttoned up his overcoat, and surprised her by mounting with the coachman. The carriage moved off silently over the long grass of the vista, the shadows deepening to black as they proceeded. Darker and darker grew the night as they rolled on; the neighbourhood familiar to Margery was soon left behind, and she had not the remotest idea of the direction they were taking. The stars blinked out, the coachman lit his lamps, and they bowled on again.

In the course of an hour and a half they arrived at a small town, where they pulled up at the chief inn and changed horses; all being done so readily that their advent had plainly been expected. The journey was resumed immediately. Her companion never descended to speak to her; whenever she looked out there he sat upright on his perch, with the mien of a person who had a difficult duty to perform, and who meant to perform it properly at all costs. But Margery could not help feeling a certain dread at her situation – almost, indeed, a wish that she had not come. Once or twice she thought, 'Suppose he is a wicked man, who is taking me off to a foreign country, and will never bring me home again.'

But her characteristic persistence in an original idea sustained her against these misgivings except at odd moments. One incident in particular had given her confidence in her escort: she had seen a tear in his eye when she expressed her sorrow for his troubles. He may have divined that her thoughts would take an uneasy turn, for when they stopped for a moment in ascending a hill he came to the window. 'Are you tired, Margery?' he asked kindly.

'No, sir.'

'Are you afraid?'

'N-no, sir. But it is a long way.'

'We are almost there,' he answered. 'And now, Margery,' he said in a lower tone, 'I must tell you a secret. I have obtained this invitation in a peculiar way. I thought it best for your sake not to come in my own name, and this is how I have managed. A man in this county, for whom I have lately done a service, one whom I can trust, and who is personally as unknown here as you and I, has (privately) transferred his card of invitation to me. So that we go under his name. I explain this that you may not say anything imprudent by accident. Keep your ears open and be cautious.' Having said this the Baron retreated again to his place.

'Then he is a wicked man after all!' she said to herself; 'for he is going under a false name.' But she soon had the temerity not to mind it: wickedness of that sort was the one ingredient required just now to finish him off as a hero in her eyes.

They descended a hill, passed a lodge, then up an avenue; and presently there beamed upon them the light from other carriages, drawn up in a file, which moved on by degrees; and at last they halted before a large arched doorway, round which a group of people stood.

'We are among the latest arrivals, on account of the distance,' said the Baron, reappearing. 'But never mind; there are three hours at least for your enjoyment.'

The steps were promptly flung down, and they alighted. The steam from the flanks of their swarthy steeds, as they seemed to her, ascended to the parapet of the porch, and from their nostrils the hot breath jetted forth like smoke out of volcanoes, attracting the attention of all.

V

The bewildered Margery was led by the Baron up the steps to the interior of the house, whence the sounds of music and dancing were already proceeding. The tones were strange. At every fourth beat a deep and mighty note throbbed through the air, reaching Margery's soul with all the force of a blow.

'What is that powerful tune, sir – I have never heard anything like it?' she said.

'The Drum Polka,' answered the Baron. 'The strange dance I spoke of and that we practised – introduced from my country and other parts of the Continent.'

Her surprise was not lessened when, at the entrance to the ballroom, she heard the names of her conductor and herself announced as 'Mr and Miss Brown'.

However, nobody seemed to take any notice of the announcement, the room beyond being in a perfect turmoil of gaiety, and Margery's consternation at sailing under false colours subsided. At the same moment she observed awaiting them a handsome, dark-haired, rather *petite* lady in cream-coloured satin. 'Who is she?' asked Margery of the Baron.

'She is the lady of the mansion,' he whispered. 'She is the wife of a peer of the realm, the daughter of a marquis, has five Christian names; and hardly ever speaks to commoners, except for political purposes.'

'How divine – what joy to be here!' murmured Margery, as she contemplated the diamonds that flashed from the head of her ladyship, who was just inside the ballroom door, in front of a little gilded chair, upon which she sat in the intervals between one arrival and another. She had come down from London at great inconvenience to herself, openly to promote this entertainment.

As Mr and Miss Brown expressed absolutely no meaning to Lady Toneborough (for there were three Browns already present in this rather mixed assembly), and as there was possibly a slight awkwardness in poor Margery's manner, Lady Toneborough touched their hands lightly with the tips of her long gloves, said, 'How d'ye do ', and turned round for more comers.

'Ah, if she only knew we were a rich Baron and his friend, and not Mr and Miss Brown at all, she wouldn't receive us like that, would she?' whispered Margery confidentially.

'Indeed, she wouldn't!' drily said the Baron. 'Now let us drop into the dance at once; some of the people here, you see, dance much worse than you.'

Almost before she was aware she had obeyed his mysterious influence, by giving him one hand, placing the other upon his shoulder, and swinging with him round the room to the steps she had learnt on the sward.

At the first gaze the apartment had seemed to her to be floored with black ice; the figures of the dancers appearing upon it upside down. At last she realized that it was highly-polished oak, but she was none the less afraid to move.

'I am afraid of falling down,' she said.

'Lean on me; you will soon get used to it,' he replied. 'You have no nails in your shoes now, dear.'

His words, like all his words to her, were quite true. She found it amazingly easy in a brief space of time. The floor, far from hindering her, was a positive assistance to one of her natural agility and litheness. Moreover, her marvellous dress of twelve flounces inspired her as nothing else could have done. Externally a new creature, she was prompted to new deeds. To feel as well-dressed as the other women around her is to set any woman at her ease, whencesoever she may have come: to feel much better dressed is to add radiance to that ease.

Her prophet's statement on the popularity of the polka at this juncture was amply borne out. It was among the first seasons of its general adoption in country houses; the enthusiasm it excited to-night was beyond description, and scarcely credible to the youth of the present day. A new motive power had been introduced into the world of poesy – the polka, as a counterpoise to the new motive power that had been introduced into the world of prose – steam.

Twenty finished musicians sat in the music gallery at the end, with romantic mop-heads of raven hair, under which their faces and eyes shone like fire under coals.

The nature and object of the ball had led to its being very inclusive. Every rank was there, from the peer to the smallest yeoman, and Margery got on exceedingly well, particularly when the recuperative powers of supper had banished the fatigue of her long drive.

Sometimes she heard people saying, 'Who are they? – brother and sister – father and daughter? And never dancing except with each other – how odd!' But of this she took no notice.

When not dancing the watchful Baron took her through the drawing-rooms and picture-galleries adjoining, which to-night were thrown open like the rest of the house; and there, ensconcing her in some curtained nook, he drew her attention to scrap-books, prints, and albums, and left her to amuse herself with turning them over till the dance in which she was practised should again be called. Margery would much have preferred to roam about during these intervals; but the words of the

Baron were law, and as he commanded so she acted. In such alternations
the evening winged away; till at last came the gloomy words, 'Margery,
our time is up.'

'One more – only one!' she coaxed, for the longer they stayed the more
freely and gaily moved the dance. This entreaty he granted; but on her
asking for yet another, he was inexorable. 'No,' he said. 'We have a long
way to go.'

Then she bade adieu to the wondrous scene, looking over her shoulder
as they withdrew from the hall; and in a few minutes she was cloaked
and in the carriage. The Baron mounted to his seat on the box, where
she saw him light a cigar; they plunged under the trees, and she leant
back, and gave herself up to contemplate the images that filled her
brain. The natural result followed: she fell asleep.

She did not awake till they stopped to change horses, when she saw
against the stars the Baron sitting as erect as ever. 'He watches like the
Angel Gabriel, when all the world is asleep!' she thought.

With the resumption of motion she slept again, and knew no more
till he touched her hand and said, 'Our journey is done – we are in
Chillington Wood.'

It was almost daylight. Margery scarcely knew herself to be awake till
she was out of the carriage and standing beside the Baron, who, having
told the coachman to drive on to a certain point indicated, turned to her.

'Now,' he said, smiling, 'run across to the hollow tree; you know
where it is. I'll wait as before, while you perform the reverse operation
to that you did last night.' She took no heed of the path now, nor
regarded whether her pretty slippers became scratched by the brambles
or no. A walk of a few steps brought her to the particular tree which she
had left about nine hours earlier. It was still gloomy at this spot, the
morning not being clear.

She entered the trunk, dislodged the box containing her old clothing,
pulled off the satin shoes, and gloves, and dress, and in ten minutes
emerged in the cotton gown and shawl of shepherd's plaid.

The Baron was not far off. 'Now you look the milkmaid again,' he
said, coming towards her. 'Where is the finery?'

'Packed in the box, sir, as I found it.' She spoke with more humility
now. The difference between them was greater than it had been at the
ball.

'Good,' he said. 'I must just dispose of it; and then away we go.'

He went back to the tree, Margery following at a little distance.

Bringing forth the box, he pulled out the dress as carelessly as if it had been rags. But this was not all. He gathered a few dry sticks, crushed the lovely garment into a loose billowy heap, threw the gloves, fan, and shoes on the top, then struck a light and ruthlessly set fire to the whole.

Margery was agonized. She ran forward; she implored and entreated. 'Please, sir – do spare it – do! My lovely dress – my dear, dear slippers – my fan – it is cruel! Don't burn them, please!'

'Nonsense. We shall have no further use for them if we live a hundred years.'

'But spare a bit of it – one little piece, sir – a scrap of the lace – one bow of the ribbon – the lovely fan – just something!'

But he was as immovable as Rhadamanthus. 'No,' he said, with a stern gaze of his aristocratic eye. 'It is of no use for you to speak like that. The things are my property. I undertook to gratify you in what you might desire because you had saved my life. To go to a ball, you said. You might much more wisely have said anything else, but no; you said, to go to a ball. Very well – I have taken you to a ball. I have brought you back. The clothes were only the means, and I dispose of them my own way. Have I not a right to?'

'Yes, sir,' she said meekly.

He gave the fire a stir, and lace and ribbons, and the twelve flounces, and the embroidery, and all the rest crackled and disappeared. He then put in her hands the butter basket she had brought to take on to her grandmother's, and accompanied her to the edge of the wood, where it merged in the undulating open country in which her granddame dwelt.

'Now, Margery,' he said, 'here we part. I have performed my contract – at some awkwardness, if I was recognized. But never mind that. How do you feel – sleepy?'

'Not at all, sir,' she said.

'That long nap refreshed you, eh? Now you must make me a promise. That if I require your presence at any time, you will come to me. . . . I am a man of more than one mood,' he went on with sudden solemnity; 'and I may have desperate need of you again, to deliver me from that darkness as of Death which sometimes encompasses me. Promise it, Margery – promise it; that, no matter what stands in the way, you will come to me if I require you.'

'I would have if you had not burnt my pretty clothes!' she pouted.

'Ah – ungrateful!'

'Indeed, then, I will promise, sir,' she said from her heart. 'Wherever I am, if I have bodily strength I will come to you.'

He pressed her hand. 'It is a solemn promise,' he replied. 'Now I must go, for you know your way.'

'I shall hardly believe that it has not been all a dream!' she said, with a childish instinct to cry at his withdrawal. 'There will be nothing left of last night – nothing of my dress, nothing of my pleasure, nothing of the place!'

'You shall remember it in this way,' said he. 'We'll cut our initials on this tree as a memorial, so that whenever you walk this path you will see them.'

Then with a knife he inscribed on the smooth bark of a beech tree the letters M.T., and underneath a large X.

'What, have you no Christian name, sir?' she said.

'Yes, but I don't use it. Now, good-bye, my little friend. – What will you do with yourself to-day, when you are gone from me?' he lingered to ask.

'Oh – I shall go to my granny's,' she replied with some gloom; 'and have breakfast, and dinner, and tea with her, I suppose; and in the evening I shall go home to Silverthorn Dairy, and perhaps Jim will come to meet me, and all will be the same as usual.'

'Who is Jim?'

'O, he's nobody – only the young man I've got to marry some day.'

'What! – you engaged to be married? – Why didn't you tell me this before?'

'I – I don't know, sir.'

'What is the young man's name?'

'James Hayward.'

'What is he?'

'A master lime-burner.'

'Engaged to a master lime-burner, and not a word of this to me! Margery, Margery! when shall a straightforward one of your sex be found! Subtle even in your simplicity! What mischief have you caused me to do, through not telling me this? I wouldn't have so endangered anybody's happiness for a thousand pounds. Wicked girl that you were; why didn't you tell me?'

'I thought I'd better not!' said Margery, beginning to be frightened.

'But don't you see and understand that if you are already the property of a young man, and he were to find out this night's excursion, he may be angry with you and part from you for ever ? With him already in the field I had no right to take you at all; he undoubtedly ought to have taken you; which really might have been arranged, if you had not deceived me by saying you had nobody.'

Margery's face wore that aspect of woe which comes from the repentant consciousness of having been guilty of an enormity. 'But he wasn't good enough to take me, sir!' she said, almost crying; 'and he isn't absolutely my master until I have married him, is he ?'

'That's a subject I cannot go into. However, we must alter our tactics. Instead of advising you, as I did at first, to tell of this experience to your friends, I must now impress on you that it will be best to keep a silent tongue on the matter – perhaps for ever and ever. It may come right some day, and you may be able to say "All's well that ends well." Now, good morning, my friend. Think of Jim, and forget me.'

'Ah, perhaps I can't do that,' she said, with a tear in her eye, and a full throat.

'Well – do your best. I can say no more.'

He turned and retreated into the wood, and Margery, sighing, went on her way.

VI

Between six and seven o'clock in the evening of the same day a young man descended the hills into the valley of the Exe, at a point about midway between Silverthorn and the residence of Margery's grand-mother, four miles to the east.

He was a thoroughbred son of the country, as far removed from what is known as the provincial, as the latter is from the out-and-out gentle-man of culture. His trousers and waistcoat were of fustian, almost white, but he wore a jacket of old-fashioned blue West-of-England cloth, so well preserved that evidently the article was relegated to a box whenever its owner engaged in such active occupations as he usually pursued. His complexion was fair, almost florid, and he had scarcely any beard.

A novel attraction about this young man, which a glancing stranger would know nothing of, was a rare and curious freshness of atmosphere that appertained to him, to his clothes, to all his belongings, even to the room in which he had been sitting. It might almost have been said that by adding him and his implements to an over-crowded apartment you made it healthful. This resulted from his trade. He was a lime-burner; he handled lime daily; and in return the lime rendered him an incarnation of salubrity. His hair was dry, fair, and frizzled, the latter possibly by the operation of the same caustic agent. He carried as a walking-stick a green sapling, whose growth had been contorted to a corkscrew pattern by a twining honeysuckle.

As he descended to the level ground of the water-meadows he cast his glance westward, with a frequency that revealed him to be in search of some object in the distance. It was rather difficult to do this, the low sunlight dazzling his eyes by glancing from the river away there, and from the 'carriers' (as they were called) in his path – narrow artificial brooks for conducting the water over the grass. His course was something of a zigzag from the necessity of finding points in these carriers convenient for jumping. Thus peering and leaping and winding, he drew near the Exe, the central river of the miles-long mead.

A moving spot became visible to him in the direction of his scrutiny, mixed up with the rays of the same river. The spot got nearer, and revealed itself to be a slight thing of pink cotton and shepherd's plaid, which pursued a path on the brink of the stream. The young man so shaped his trackless course as to impinge on the path a little ahead of this coloured form, and when he drew near her he smiled and reddened. The girl smiled back to him; but her smile had not the life in it that the young man's had shown.

'My dear Margery – here I am!' he said gladly in an undertone, as with a last leap he crossed the last intervening carrier, and stood at her side.

'You've come all the way from the kiln, on purpose to meet me, and you shouldn't have done it,' she reproachfully returned.

'We finished there at four, so it was no trouble; and if it had been – why, I should ha' come.'

A small sigh was the response.

'What, you are not even so glad to see me as you would be to see your dog or cat?' he continued. 'Come, Mis'ess Margery, this is rather hard. But, by George, how tired you dew look! Why, if you'd been up all night your eyes couldn't be more like tea-saucers. You've walked tew far, that's what it is. The weather is getting warm now, and the air of these low-lying meads is not strengthening in summer. I wish you lived up on higher ground with me, beside the kiln. You'd get as strong as a hoss! Well, there; all that will come in time.'

Instead of saying yes, the fair maid repressed another sigh.

'What, won't it, then?' he said.

'I suppose so,' she answered. 'If it is to be, it is.'

'Well said – very well said, my dear.'

'And if it isn't to be, it isn't.'

'What? Who's been putting that into your head? Your grumpy granny, I suppose. However, how is she? Margery, I have been thinking to-day – in fact, I was thinking it yesterday and all the week – that really we might settle our little business this summer.'

'This summer?' she repeated, with some dismay. 'But the partnership? Remember it was not to be till after that was completed.'

'There I have you!' said he, taking the liberty to pat her shoulder, and the further liberty of advancing his hand behind it to the other. 'The partnership is settled. 'Tis "Vine and Hayward, lime-burners", now, and "Richard Vine" no longer. Yes, Cousin Richard has settled it so, for a time at least, and 'tis to be painted on the carts this week – blue letters – yaller ground. I'll hoss one of 'em, and drive en round to your door as soon as the paint is dry, to show 'ee how it looks?'

'Oh, I am sure you needn't take that trouble, Jim; I can see it quite well enough in my mind,' replied the young girl – not without a flitting accent of superiority.

'Hullo,' said Jim, taking her by the shoulders, and looking at her hard. 'What dew that bit of incivility mean? Now, Margery, let's sit down here, and have this cleared.' He rapped with his stick upon the rail of a little bridge they were crossing, and seated himself firmly, leaving a place for her.

'But I want to get home-along, dear Jim,' she coaxed.

'Fidgets. Sit down, there's a dear. I want a straightforward answer, if you please. In what month, and on what day of the month, will you marry me?'

'O, Jim,' she said, sitting gingerly on the edge, 'that's too plain-spoken for you yet. Before I look at it in that business light I should have to – to—'

'But your father has settled it long ago, and you said it should be as soon as I became a partner. So, dear, you must not mind a plain man wanting a plain answer. Come, name your time.'

She did not reply at once. What thoughts were passing through her brain during the interval? Not images raised by his words, but whirling figures of men and women in red and white and blue, reflected from a glassy floor, in movements timed by the thrilling beats of the Drum Polka. At last she said slowly, 'Jim, you don't know the world, and what a woman's wants can be.'

'But I can make you comfortable. I am in lodgings as yet, but I can have a house for the asking; and as to furniture, you shall choose of the best for yourself – the very best.'

'The best! Far are you from knowing what that is!' said the little woman. 'There be ornaments such as you never dream of; work-tables that would set you in amaze; silver candlesticks, tea and coffee pots that would dazzle your eyes; tea-cups, and saucers, gilded all over with guinea-gold; heavy velvet curtains, gold clocks, pictures, and looking-glasses beyond your very dreams. So don't say I shall have the best.'

'H'm!' said Jim gloomily; and fell into reflection. 'Where did you get those high notions from, Margery?' he presently inquired. 'I'll swear you hadn't got 'em a week ago.' She did not answer, and he added, '*Yew* don't expect to have such things, I hope; deserve them as you may?'

'I was not exactly speaking of what I wanted,' she said severely. 'I said, things a woman *could* want. And since you wish to know what I *can* want to quite satisfy me, I assure you I can want those!'

'You are a pink-and-white conundrum, Margery,' he said; 'and I give you up for to-night. Anybody would think the devil had showed you all the kingdoms of the world since I saw you last!'

She reddened. 'Perhaps he has!' she murmured; then arose, he following her; and they soon reached Margery's home, approaching it from the lower or meadow side – the opposite to that of the garden top, where she had met the Baron.

'You'll come in, won't you, Jim?' she said, with more ceremony than heartiness.

'No – I think not to-night,' he answered. 'I'll consider what you've said.'

'You are very good, Jim,' she returned lightly. 'Good-bye.'

VII

Jim thoughtfully retraced his steps. He was a village character, and he had a villager's simplicity: that is, the simplicity which comes from the lack of a complicated experience. But simple by nature he certainly was not. Among the rank and file of rustics he was quite a Talleyrand, or rather had been one, till he lost a good deal of his self-command by falling in love.

Now, however, that the charming object of his distraction was out of sight, he could deliberate, and measure, and weigh things with some approach of keenness. The substance of his queries was, What change had come over Margery – whence these new notions?

Ponder as he would he could evolve no answer save one, which, eminently unsatisfactory as it was, he felt it would be unreasonable not to accept: that she was simply skittish and ambitious by nature, and would not be hunted into matrimony till he had provided a well-adorned home.

Jim retrod the miles to the kiln, and looked to the fires. The kiln stood in a peculiar, interesting, even impressive spot. It was at the end of a short ravine in a limestone formation, and all around was an open hilly down. The nearest house was that of Jim's cousin and partner, which stood on the outskirts of the down beside the turnpike-road. From this house a little lane wound between the steep escarpments of the ravine till it reached the kiln, which faced down the miniature valley, commanding it as a fort might command a defile.

The idea of a fort in this association owed little to imagination. For on the nibbled green steep above the kiln stood a bygone worn-out specimen of such an erection, huge, impressive, and difficult to scale even now in its decay. It was a British castle or entrenchment, with triple rings of defence, rising roll behind roll, their outlines cutting sharply against the sky, and Jim's kiln nearly undermining their base. When the lime-kiln flared up in the night, which it often did, its fires lit up the front of these ramparts to a great majesty. They were old friends of his, and while keeping up the heat through the long darkness, as it was sometimes his duty to do, he would imagine the dancing lights and shades about the stupendous earthwork to be the forms of those giants who (he supposed) had heaped it up. Often he clambered upon it, and walked about the summit, thinking out the problems connected with his business, his partner, his future, his Margery.

It was what he did this evening, continuing the meditation on the young girl's manner that he had begun upon the road, and still, as then, finding no clue to the change.

While thus engaged he observed a man coming up the ravine to the kiln. Business messages were almost invariably left at the house below, and Jim watched the man with the interest excited by a belief that he had come on a personal matter. On nearer approach Jim recognized him as the gardener at Mount Lodge some miles away. If this meant business, the Baron (of whose arrival Jim had vaguely heard) was a new and unexpected customer.

It meant nothing else, apparently. The man's errand was simply to inform Jim that the Baron required a load of lime for the garden.

'You might have saved yourself trouble by leaving word at Mr Vine's,' said Jim.

'I was to see you personally,' said the gardener, 'and to say that the Baron would like to inquire of you about the different qualities of lime proper for such purposes.'

'Couldn't you tell him yourself?' said Jim.

'He said I was to tell you that,' replied the gardener; 'and it wasn't for me to interfere.'

No motive other than the ostensible one could possibly be conjectured by Jim Hayward at this time; and the next morning he started with great pleasure, in his best business suit of clothes. By eleven o'clock he and his horse and cart had arrived on the Baron's premises, and the lime was deposited where directed; an exceptional spot, just within view of the windows of the south front.

Baron von Xanten, pale and melancholy, was sauntering in the sun on the slope between the house and the all-the-year-round. He looked across to where Jim and the gardener were standing, and the identity of Hayward being established by what he brought, the Baron came down, and the gardener withdrew.

The Baron's first inquiries were, as Jim had been led to suppose they would be, on the exterminating effects of lime upon slugs and snails in its different conditions of slaked and unslaked, ground and in the lump. He appeared to be much interested by Jim's explanations, and eyed the young man closely whenever he had an opportunity.

'And I hope trade is prosperous with you this year,' said the Baron.

'Very, my noble lord,' replied Jim, who, in his uncertainty on the proper method of address, wisely concluded that it was better to err by giving too much honour than by giving too little. 'In short, trade is looking so well that I've become a partner in the firm.'

'Indeed; I am glad to hear it. So now you are settled in life.'

'Well, my lord, I am hardly settled, even now. For I've got to finish it – I mean, to get married.'

'That's an easy matter, compared with the partnership.'

'Now a man might think so, my baron,' said Jim, getting more confidential. 'But the real truth is, 'tis the hardest part of all for me.'

'Your suit prospers, I hope?'

'It don't,' said Jim. 'It don't at all just at present. In short, I can't for the life o' me think what's come over the young woman lately.' And he fell into deep reflection.

Though Jim did not observe it, the Baron's brow became shadowed with self-reproach as he heard those simple words, and his eyes had a look of pity. 'Indeed – since when?' he asked.

'Since yesterday, my noble lord.' Jim spoke meditatively. He was resolving upon a bold stroke. Why not make a confidant of this kind gentleman instead of the parson, as he had intended? The thought was no sooner conceived than acted on. 'My lord,' he resumed, 'I have heard that you are a nobleman of great scope and talent, who has seen more strange countries and characters than I have ever heard of, and know the insides of men well. Therefore I would fain put a question to your noble lordship, if I may so trouble you, and having nobody else in the world who could inform me so trewly.'

'Any advice I can give is at your service, Hayward. What do you wish to know?'

'It is this, my baron. What can I do to bring down a young woman's ambition that's got to such a towering height there's no reaching it or compassing it: how get her to be pleased with me and my station as she used to be when I first knew her?'

'Truly, that's a hard question, my man. What does she aspire to?'

'She's got a craze for fine furniture.'

'How long has she had it?'

'Only just now.'

The Baron seemed still more to experience regret. 'What furniture does she specially covet?' he asked.

'Silver candlesticks, work-tables, looking-glasses, gold tea-things, silver tea-pots, gold clocks, curtains, pictures, and I don't know what all – things I shall never get if I live to be a hundred – not so much that I couldn't raise the money to buy 'em, as that I ought to put it to other uses, or save it for a rainy day.'

'You think the possession of those articles would make her happy?'

'I really think they might, my lord.'

'Good. Open your pocket-book and write as I tell you.'

Jim in some astonishment did as commanded, and elevating his pocket-book against the garden-wall, thoroughly moistened his pencil, and wrote at the Baron's dictation:

'Pair of silver candlesticks: inlaid work-table and work-box: one large mirror: two small ditto: one gilt china tea and coffee service: one silver tea-pot, coffee-pot, sugar-basin, jug, and dozen spoons: French clock: pair of curtains: six large pictures.'

'Now,' said the Baron, 'tear out that leaf and give it to me. Keep a close tongue about this; go home, and don't be surprised at anything that may come to your door.'

'But, my noble lord, you don't mean that your lordship is going to give—'

'Never mind what I am going to do. Only keep your own counsel. I perceive that, though a plain countryman, you are by no means deficient in tact and understanding. If sending these things to you gives me pleasure, why should you object? The fact is, Hayward, I occasionally take an interest in people, and like to do a little for them. I take an interest in you. Now go home, and a week hence invite Marg – the young woman and her father to tea with you. The rest is in your own hands.'

A question often put to Jim in after times was why it had not occurred to him at once that the Baron's liberal conduct must have been dictated by something more personal than sudden spontaneous generosity to him, a stranger. To which Jim always answered that, admitting the existence of such generosity, there had appeared nothing remarkable in the Baron selecting himself as its object. The Baron had told him that he took an interest in him; and self-esteem, even with the most modest, is usually sufficient to over-ride any little difficulty that might occur to an outsider in accounting for a preference. He moreover considered that foreign noblemen, rich and eccentric, might have habits of acting which were quite at variance with those of their English compeers.

So he drove off homeward with a lighter heart than he had known for several days. To have a foreign gentleman take a fancy to him – what a triumph to a plain sort of fellow, who had scarcely expected the Baron to look in his face. It would be a fine story to tell Margery when the Baron gave him liberty to speak out.

Jim lodged at the house of his cousin and partner, Richard Vine, a widower of fifty-odd years. Having failed in the development of a household of direct descendants this tradesman had been glad to let his chambers to his much younger relative, when the latter entered on the business of lime manufacture; and their intimacy had led to a partnership. Jim lived upstairs; his partner lived down, and the furniture of all the rooms was so plain and old-fashioned as to excite the special dislike of Miss Margery Tucker, and even to prejudice her against Jim for tolerating it. Not only were the chairs and tables queer, but, with due regard to the principle that a man's surroundings should bear the impress of that man's life and occupation, the chief ornaments of the dwelling were a curious collection of calcinations, that had been discovered from time to time in the lime-kiln – misshapen ingots of strange substance, some of them like Pompeian remains.

The head of the firm was a quiet-living, narrow-minded, though friendly, man of fifty; and he took a serious interest in Jim's love-suit, frequently inquiring how it progressed, and assuring Jim that if he chose to marry he might have all the upper floor at a low rent, he, Mr Vine, contenting himself entirely with the ground level. It had been so convenient for discussing business matters to have Jim in the same house, that he did not wish any change to be made in consequence of a change in Jim's domestic estate. Margery knew of this wish, and of Jim's concurrent feeling, and did not like the idea at all.

About four days after the young man's interview with the Baron, there drew up in front of Jim's house at noon a waggon laden with cases and packages, large and small. They were all addressed to 'Mr Hayward', and they had come from the largest furnishing warehouses in that part of England.

Three-quarters of an hour were occupied in getting the cases to Jim's rooms. The wary Jim did not show the amazement he felt at his patron's munificence; and presently the senior partner came into the passage, and wondered what was lumbering upstairs.

'O – it's only some things of mine,' said Jim coolly.

'Bearing upon the coming event – eh ?' said his partner.

'Exactly,' replied Jim.

Mr Vine, with some astonishment at the number of cases, shortly after went away to the kiln; whereupon Jim shut himself into his rooms, and there he might have been heard ripping up and opening boxes with a cautious hand, afterwards appearing outside the door with them empty, and carrying them off to the outhouse.

A triumphant look lit up his face when, a little later in the afternoon, he sent into the vale to the dairy, and invited Margery and her father to his house to supper.

She was not unsociable that day, and, her father expressing a hard and fast acceptance of the invitation, she perforce agreed to go with him. Meanwhile at home Jim made himself as mysteriously busy as before in those rooms of his, and when his partner returned he too was asked to join in the supper.

At dusk Hayward went to the door, where he stood till he heard the voices of his guests from the direction of the low grounds, now covered with their frequent fleece of fog. The voices grew more distinct, and then on the white surface of the fog there appeared two trunkless heads, from which bodies and a horse and cart gradually extended as the approaching pair rose towards the house.

When they had entered Jim pressed Margery's hand and conducted her up to his rooms, her father waiting below to say a few words to the senior lime-burner.

'Bless me,' said Jim to her, on entering the sitting-room, 'I quite forgot to get a light beforehand; but I'll have one in a jiffy.'

Margery stood in the middle of the dark room, while Jim struck a match; and then the young girl's eyes were conscious of a burst of light, and the rise into being of a pair of handsome silver candlesticks containing two candles that Jim was in the act of lighting.

'Why – where – you have candlesticks like that?' said Margery. Her eyes flew round the room as the growing candle-flames showed other articles. 'Pictures too – and lovely china – why, I knew nothing of this, I declare.'

'Yes – a few things that came to me by accident,' said Jim in quiet tones.

'And a great gold clock under a glass, and a cupid swinging for a pendulum; and O what a lovely work-table – woods of every colour – and a work-box to match. May I look inside that work-box, Jim? – whose is it?'

'O yes; look at it, of course. It is a poor enough thing, but 'tis mine; and it will belong to the woman I marry, whoever she may be, as well as all the other things here.'

'And the curtains and the looking-glasses: why, I declare I can see myself in a hundred places.'

'That tea-set,' said Jim, placidly pointing to a gorgeous china service and a large silver tea-pot on the side-table, 'I don't use at present, being a bachelor-man; but, says I to myself, "whoever I marry will want some such things for giving her parties; or I can sell 'em" – but I haven't took steps for't yet—'

'Sell 'em – no, I should think not,' said Margery with earnest reproach. 'Why, I hope you wouldn't be so foolish! Why, this is exactly the kind of thing I was thinking of when I told you of the things women could want – of course not meaning myself particularly. I had no idea that you had such valuable—' Margery was unable to speak coherently, so much was she amazed at the wealth of Jim's possessions.

At this moment her father and the lime-burner came upstairs; and to appear womanly and proper to Mr Vine, Margery repressed the remainder of her surprise. As for the two elderly worthies, it was not till they entered the room and sat down that their slower eyes discerned anything brilliant in the appointments. Then one of them stole a glance at some article, and the other at another; but each being unwilling to express his wonder in the presence of his neighbours, they received the objects before them with quite an accustomed air; the lime-burner inwardly trying to conjecture what all this meant, and the dairyman musing that if Jim's business allowed him to accumulate at this rate, the sooner Margery became his wife the better. Margery retreated to the work-table, work-box, and tea-service, which she examined with hushed exclamations.

An entertainment thus surprisingly begun could not fail to progress well. Whenever Margery's crusty old father felt the need of a civil sentence, the flash of Jim's fancy articles inspired him to one; while the lime-burner, having reasoned away his first ominous thought that all this had come out of the firm, also felt proud and blithe.

Jim accompanied his dairy friends part of the way home before they mounted. Her father, finding that Jim wanted to speak to her privately, and that she exhibited some elusiveness, turned to Margery and said, 'Come, come, my lady; no more of this nonsense. You just step behind with that young man, and I and the cart will wait for you.'

Margery, a little scared at her father's peremptoriness, obeyed. It was plain that Jim had won the old man by that night's stroke, if he had not won her.

'I know what you are going to say, Jim,' she began, less ardently now, for she was no longer under the novel influence of the shining silver and glass. 'Well, as you desire it, and as my father desires it, and as I suppose it will be the best course for me, I will fix the day – not this evening, but as soon as I can think it over.'

VIII

Notwithstanding a press of business, Jim went and did his duty in thanking the Baron. The latter saw him in his fishing-tackle room, an apartment littered with every appliance that a votary of the rod could require.

'And when is the wedding-day to be, Hayward?' the Baron asked, after Jim had told him that matters were settled.

'It is not quite certain yet, my noble lord,' said Jim cheerfully. 'But I hope 'twill not be long after the time when God A'mighty christens the little apples.'

'And when is that?'

'St Swithin's – the middle of July. 'Tis to be some time in that month, she tells me.'

When Jim was gone the Baron seemed meditative. He went out, ascended the mount, and entered the weather-screen, where he looked at the seats, as though re-enacting in his fancy the scene of that memorable morning of fog. He turned his eyes to the angle of the shelter, round which Margery had suddenly appeared like a vision, and it was plain that he would not have minded her appearing there then. The juncture had indeed been such an impressive and critical one that she must have seemed rather a heavenly messenger than a passing milkmaid, more especially to a man like the Baron, who, despite the mystery of his origin and life, revealed himself to be a melancholy, emotional character – the Jaques of this forest and stream.

Behind the mount the ground rose yet higher, ascending to a plantation which sheltered the house. The Baron strolled up here, and bent his gaze over the distance. The valley of the Exe lay before him, with its shining river, the brooks that fed it, and the trickling springs that fed the brooks. The situation of Margery's house was visible, though not the house itself; and the Baron gazed that way for an infinitely long time, till, remembering himself, he moved on.

Instead of returning to the house he went along the ridge till he arrived at the verge of Chillington Wood, and in the same desultory manner roamed under the trees, not pausing till he had come to Three-

Walks-End, and the hollow elm hard by. He peeped in at the rift. In the soft dry layer of touchwood that floored the hollow Margery's tracks were still visible, as she had made them there when dressing for the ball.

'Little Margery!' murmured the Baron.

In a moment he thought better of this mood, and turned to go home. But behold, a form stood behind him – that of the girl whose name had been on his lips.

She was in utter confusion. 'I – I – did not know you were here, sir!' she began. 'I was out for a little walk.' She could get no further; her eyes filled with tears. That spice of wilfulness, even hardness, which characterized her in Jim's company, magically disappeared in the presence of the Baron.

'Never mind, never mind,' said he, masking under a severe manner whatever he felt. 'The meeting is awkward, and ought not to have occurred, especially if, as I suppose, you are shortly to be married to James Hayward. But it cannot be helped now. You had no idea I was here, of course. Neither had I of seeing you. Remember you cannot be too careful,' continued the Baron, in the same grave tone; 'and I strongly request you as a friend to do your utmost to avoid meetings like this. When you saw me before I turned, why did you not go away?'

'I did not see you, sir. I did not think of seeing you. I was walking this way, and I only looked in to see the tree.'

'That shows you have been thinking of things you should not think of,' returned the Baron. 'Good morning.'

Margery could answer nothing. A browbeaten glance, almost of misery, was all she gave him. He took a slow step away from her; then turned suddenly back and, stooping, impulsively kissed her cheek, taking her as much by surprise as ever a woman was taken in her life.

Immediately after he went off with a flushed face and rapid strides, which he did not check till he was within his own boundaries.

The haymaking season now set in vigorously, and the weir-hatches were all drawn in the meads to drain off the water. The streams ran themselves dry, and there was no longer any difficulty in walking about among them. The Baron could very well witness from the elevations about his house the activity which followed these preliminaries. The white shirt-sleeves of the mowers glistened in the sun, the scythes flashed, voices echoed, snatches of song floated about, and there were glimpses of red waggon-wheels, purple gowns, and many-coloured handkerchiefs.

The Baron had been told that the haymaking was to be followed by the wedding, and had he gone down the vale to the dairy he would have had evidence to that effect. Dairyman Tucker's house was in a whirlpool of bustle, and among other difficulties was that of turning the cheese-room into a genteel apartment for the time being, and hiding the awkwardness of having to pass through the milk-house to get to the parlour door. These household contrivances appeared to interest Margery much more than the great question of dressing for the ceremony and the ceremony itself. In all relating to that she showed an indescribable backwardness, which later on was well remembered.

'If it were only somebody else, and I was one of the bridesmaids, I really think I should like it better!' she murmured one afternoon.

'Away with thee – that's only your shyness!' said one of the milkmaids.

It is said that about this time the Baron seemed to feel the effects of solitude strongly. Solitude revives the simple instincts of primitive man, and lonely country nooks afford rich soil for wayward emotions. Moreover, idleness waters those unconsidered impulses which a short season of turmoil would stamp out. It is difficult to speak with any exactness of the bearing of such conditions on the mind of the Baron – a man of whom so little was ever truly known – but there is no doubt that his mind ran much on Margery as an individual, without reference to her rank or quality, or to the question whether she would marry Jim Hayward that summer. She was the single lovely human thing within his present horizon, for he lived in absolute seclusion; and her image unduly affected him.

But, leaving conjecture, let me state what happened. One Saturday evening, two or three weeks after his accidental meeting with her in the wood, he wrote the note following: –

DEAR MARGERY, –

You must not suppose that, because I spoke somewhat severely to you at our chance encounter by the hollow tree, I have any feeling against you. Far from it. Now, as ever, I have the most grateful sense of your considerate kindness to me on a momentous occasion which shall be nameless.

You solemnly promised to come and see me whenever I should send for you. Can you call for five minutes as soon as possible, and disperse those plaguy glooms from which I am so unfortunate as to

suffer ? If you refuse I will not answer for the consequences. I shall
be in the summer shelter of the mount to-morrow morning at half-
past ten. If you come I shall be grateful. I have also something for
you.

Yours,

X

In keeping with the tenor of this epistle the desponding, self-op-
pressed Baron ascended the mount on Sunday morning and sat down.
There was nothing here to signify exactly the hour, but before the
church bells had begun he heard somebody approaching at the back.
The light footstep moved timidly, first to one recess, and then to another;
then to the third, where he sat in the shade. Poor Margery stood before
him.

She looked worn and weary, and her little shoes and the skirts of her
dress were covered with dust. The weather was sultry, the sun being
already high and powerful, and rain had not fallen for weeks. The
Baron, who walked little, had thought nothing of the effects of this heat
and drought in inducing fatigue. A distance which had been but a
reasonable exercise on a foggy morning was a drag for Margery now.
She was out of breath; and anxiety, even unhappiness, was written on
her everywhere.

He rose to his feet and took her hand. He was vexed with himself at
sight of her. 'My dear little girl!' he said. 'You are tired – you should
not have come.'

'You sent for me, sir; and I was afraid you were ill; and my promise
to you was sacred.'

He bent over her, looking upon her downcast face, and still holding
her hand; then he dropped it, and took a pace or two backwards.

'It was a whim, nothing more,' he said sadly. 'I wanted to see my
little friend, to express good wishes – and to present her with this.' He
held forward a small morocco case, and showed her how to open it,
disclosing a pretty locket set with pearls. 'It is intended as a wedding
present,' he continued. 'To be returned to me again if you do not marry
Jim this summer – it is to be this summer, I think ?'

'It was, sir,' she said with agitation. 'But it is so no longer. And,
therefore, I cannot take this.'

'What do you say ?'

'It was to have been to-day; but now it cannot be.'

'The wedding to-day – Sunday ?' he cried.

'We fixed Sunday not to hinder much time at this busy season of the year,' replied she.

'And have you, then, put it off – surely not?'

'You sent for me, and I have come,' she answered humbly, like an obedient familiar in the employ of some great enchanter. Indeed, the Baron's power over this innocent girl was curiously like enchantment, or mesmeric influence. It was so masterful that the sexual element was almost eliminated. It was that of Prospero over the gentle Ariel. And yet it was probably only that of the cosmopolite over the recluse, of the experienced man over the simple maid.

'You have come – on your wedding day! – O Margery, this is a mistake. Of course, you should not have obeyed me, since, though I thought your wedding would be soon, I did not know it was to-day.'

'I promised you, sir; and I would rather keep my promise to you than be married to Jim.'

'That must not be – the feeling is wrong!' he murmured, looking at the distant hills. 'There seems to be a fate in all this; I get out of the frying-pan into the fire. What a recompense to you for your goodness! The fact is, I was out of health and out of spirits, so I – but no more of that. Now instantly to repair this tremendous blunder that we have made – that's the question.'

After a pause, he went on hurriedly, 'Walk down the hill; get into the road. By that time I shall be there with a phaeton. We may get back in time. What time is it now? If not, no doubt the wedding can be to-morrow; so all will come right again. Don't cry, my dear girl. Keep the locket, of course – you'll marry Jim.'

IX

He hastened down towards the stables, and she went on as directed. It seemed as if he must have put in the horse himself, so quickly did he reappear with the phaeton on the open road. Margery silently took her seat, and the Baron seemed cut to the quick with self-reproach as he noticed the listless indifference with which she acted. There was no doubt that in her heart she had preferred obeying the apparently important mandate that morning to becoming Jim's wife; but there was no less doubt that had the Baron left her alone she would quietly have gone to the altar.

He drove along furiously, in a cloud of dust. There was much to contemplate in that peaceful Sunday morning – the windless trees and fields, the shaking sunlight, the pause in human stir. Yet neither of them heeded, and thus they drew near to the dairy. His first expressed intention had been to go indoors with her, but this he abandoned as impolitic in the highest degree.

'You may be soon enough,' he said, springing down, and helping her to follow. 'Tell the truth: say you were sent for to receive a wedding present – that it was a mistake on my part – a mistake on yours; and I think they'll forgive. . . . And, Margery, my last request to you is this: that if I send for you again, you do not come. Promise solemnly, my dear girl, that any such request shall be unheeded.'

Her lips moved, but the promise was not articulated. 'O, sir, I cannot promise it!' she said at last.

'But you must; your salvation may depend on it!' he insisted almost sternly. 'You don't know what I am.'

'Then, sir, I promise,' she replied. 'Now leave me to myself, please, and I'll go indoors and manage matters.'

He turned the horse and drove away, but only for a little distance. Out of sight he pulled rein suddenly. 'Only to go back and propose it to her, and she'd come!' he murmured.

He stood up in the phaeton, and by this means he could see over the hedge. Margery still sat listlessly in the same place; there was not a lovelier flower in the field. 'No,' he said; 'no, no – never!' He reseated himself, and the wheels sped lightly back over the soft dust to Mount Lodge.

Meanwhile Margery had not moved. If the Baron could dissimulate on the side of severity she could dissimulate on the side of calm. He did not know what had been veiled by the quiet promise to manage matters indoors. Rising at length she first turned away from the house; and by-and-by, having apparently forgotten till then that she carried it in her hand, she opened the case and looked at the locket. This seemed to give her courage. She turned, set her face towards the dairy in good earnest, and though her heart faltered when the gates came in sight, she kept on and drew near the door.

On the threshold she stood listening. The house was silent. Decorations were visible in the passage, and also the carefully swept and sanded path to the gate, which she was to have trodden as a bride; but the sparrows hopped over it as if it were abandoned; and all appeared to have been checked at its climacteric, like a clock stopped on the strike. Till this moment of confronting the suspended animation of the scene she had not realized the full shock of the convulsion which her disappearance must have caused. It is quite certain – apart from her own repeated assurances to that effect in later years – that in hastening off that morning to her sudden engagement, Margery had not counted the cost of such an enterprise; while a dim notion that she might get back again in time for the ceremony, if the message meant nothing serious, should also be mentioned in her favour. But, upon the whole, she had obeyed the call with an unreasoning obedience worthy of a disciple in primitive times. A conviction that the Baron's life might depend upon her presence – for she had by this time divined the tragical event she had interrupted on the foggy morning – took from her all will to judge and consider calmly. The simple affairs of her and hers seemed nothing beside the possibility of harm to him.

A well-known step moved on the sanded floor within, and she went forward. That she saw her father's face before her, just within the door, can hardly be said: it was rather Reproach and Rage in a human mask.

'What! ye have dared to come back alive, hussy, to look upon the dupery you have practised on honest people! You've mortified us all; I don't want to see 'ee; I don't want to know anything!' He walked up and down the room, unable to command himself. 'Nothing but being dead could have excused 'ee for not meeting and marrying that man this morning; and yet you have the brazen impudence to stand there as well as ever! What be you here for?'

'I've come back to marry Jim, if he wants me to,' she said faintly. 'And if not – perhaps so much the better. I was sent for this morning early. I thought—' She halted. To say that she had thought a man's death might happen by his own hand, if she did not go to him, would never do. 'I was obliged to go,' she said. 'I had given my word.'

'Why didn't you tell us, then, so that the wedding could be put off, without making fools o' us?'

'Because I was afraid you wouldn't let me go, and I had made up my mind to go.'

'To go where?'

She was silent; till she said, 'I will tell Jim all, and why it was; and if he's any friend of mine he'll excuse me.'

'Not Jim – he's no such fool. Jim had put all ready for you, Jim had called at your house, a-dressed up in his new wedding clothes, and a-smiling like the sun; Jim had told the parson, had got the ringers in tow, and the clerk awaiting; and then – you was *gone*! Then Jim turned as pale as rendlewood, and busted out, "If she don't marry me to-day," 'a said, "she don't marry me at all! No; let her look elsewhere for a husband. For tew years I've put up with her haughty tricks and her takings," 'a said. "I've droudged and I've traipsed, I've bought and I've sold, all wi' an eye to her; I've suffered horse-flesh," he says – yes, them was his noble words – "but I'll suffer it no longer. She shall go!" "Jim," says I, "you be a man. If she's alive, I commend 'ee; if she's dead, pity my old age." "She isn't dead," says he; "for I've just heard she was seen walking off across the fields this morning, looking all of a scornful triumph." He turned round and went, and the rest o' the neighbours went; and here be I left to the reproach o't.'

'He was too hasty,' murmured Margery. 'For now he's said this I can't marry him to-morrow, as I might ha' done; and perhaps so much the better.'

'You can be so calm about it, can ye? Be my arrangements nothing, then, that you should break 'em up, and say off-hand what wasn't done to-day might ha' been done to-morrow, and such flick-flack? Out o' my sight! I won't hear any more. I won't speak to 'ee any more.'

'I'll go away, and then you'll be sorry!'

'Very well, go. Sorry – not I.'

He turned and stamped his way into the cheese-room. Margery went upstairs. She too was excited now, and instead of fortifying herself in her bedroom till her father's rage had blown over, as she had often done on lesser occasions, she packed up a bundle of articles, crept down again, and went out of the house. She had a place of refuge in these cases of necessity, and her father knew it, and was less alarmed at seeing her depart than he might otherwise have been. This place was Rook's Gate, the house of her grandmother, who always took Margery's part when that young woman was particularly in the wrong.

The devious way she pursued, to avoid the vicinity of Mount Lodge, was tedious, and she was already weary. But the cottage was a restful place to arrive at, for she was her own mistress there – her grandmother never coming downstairs – and Edy, the woman who lived with and attended her, being a cipher except in muscle and voice. The approach was by a straight open road, bordered by thin lank trees, all sloping away from the south-west wind-quarter, and the scene bore a strange resemblance to certain bits of Dutch landscape which have been imprinted on the world's eye by Hobbema and his school.

Having explained to her granny that the wedding was put off, and that she had come to stay, one of Margery's first acts was carefully to pack up the locket and case, her wedding present from the Baron. The conditions of the gift were unfulfilled, and she wished it to go back instantly. Perhaps, in the intricacies of her bosom, there lurked a greater satisfaction with the reason for returning the present than she would have felt just then with a reason for keeping it.

To send the article was difficult. In the evening she wrapped herself up, searched and found a gauze veil that had been used by her grandmother in past years for hiving swarms of bees, buried her face in it, and sallied forth with a palpitating heart till she drew near the tabernacle of her demi-god, the Baron. She ventured only to the back door, where she handed in the parcel addressed to him, and quickly came away.

Now it seems that during the day the Baron had been unable to learn the result of his attempt to return Margery in time for the event he had interrupted. Wishing, for obvious reasons, to avoid direct inquiry by messenger, and being too unwell to go far himself, he could learn no particulars. He was sitting in thought after a lonely dinner when the parcel intimating failure was brought in. The footman, whose curiosity had been excited by the mode of its arrival, peeped through the keyhole after closing the door to learn what the packet meant. Directly the Baron had opened it he thrust out his feet vehemently from his chair, and began cursing his ruinous conduct in bringing about such a disaster, for the return of the locket denoted not only no wedding that day, but none to-morrow, or at any time.

'I have done that innocent woman a great wrong!' he murmured. 'Deprived her of, perhaps, her only opportunity of becoming mistress of a happy home!'

X

A considerable period of inaction followed among all concerned.

Nothing tended to dissipate the obscurity which veiled the life of the Baron. The position he occupied in the minds of the country-folk around was one which combined the mysteriousness of a legendary character with the unobtrusive deeds of a modern gentleman. To this day whoever takes the trouble to go down to Silverthorn in Lower Wessex and make inquiries will find existing there almost a superstitious feeling for the moody, melancholy stranger who resided in the Lodge some forty years ago.

Whence he came, whither he was going were alike unknown. It was said that his mother had been an English lady of noble family who had married a foreigner not unheard of in circles where men pile up 'the cankered heaps of strange-achieved gold' – that he had been born and educated in England, taken abroad, and so on. But the facts of a life in such cases are of little account beside the aspect of a life; and hence, though doubtless the years of his existence contained their share of trite and homely circumstance, the curtain which masked all this was never lifted to gratify such a theatre of spectators, as those at Silverthorn. Therein lay his charm. His life was a vignette, of which the central strokes only were drawn with any distinctness, the environment shading away to a blank.

He might have been said to resemble that solitary bird, the heron. The still, lonely stream was his frequent haunt; on its banks he would stand for hours with his rod, looking into the water, beholding the tawny inhabitants with the eye of a philosopher, and seeming to say, 'Bite or don't bite – it's all the same to me.' He was often mistaken for a ghost by children; and for a pollard willow by men, when, on their way home in the dusk, they saw him motionless by some rushy bank, unobservant of the decline of day.

Why did he come to fish near Silverthorn ? That was never explained. As far as was known he had no relatives near; the fishing there was not exceptionally good; the society thereabout was decidedly meagre. That he had committed some folly or hasty act, that he had been wrongfully accused of some crime, thus rendering his seclusion from the world desirable for a while, squared very well with his frequent melancholy. But such as he was there he lived, well supplied with fishing-tackle, and tenant of a furnished house, just suited to the requirements of such an eccentric being as he.

Margery's father, having privately ascertained that she was living with her grandmother, and getting into no harm, refrained from communicating with her, in the hope of seeing her contrite at his door. It had, of course, become known about Silverthorn that at the last moment Margery refused to wed Hayward, by absenting herself from the house.

Jim was pitied, yet not pitied much, for it was said that he ought not to have been so eager for a woman who had shown no anxiety for him.

And where was Jim himself? It must not be supposed that that tactician had all this while withdrawn from mortal eye to tear his hair in silent indignation and despair. He had, in truth, merely retired up the lonesome defile between the downs to his smouldering kiln, and the ancient ramparts above it; and there, after his first hours of natural discomposure, he quietly waited for overtures from the possibly repentant Margery. But no overtures arrived, and then he meditated anew on the absorbing problem of her skittishness, and how to set about another campaign for her conquest, notwithstanding his late disastrous failure. Why had he failed? To what was her strange conduct owing? That was the thing which puzzled him.

He had made no advance in solving the riddle when, one morning, a stranger appeared on the down above him, looking as if he had lost his way. The man had a good deal of black hair below his felt hat, and carried under his arm a case containing a musical instrument. Descending to where Jim stood, he asked if there were not a short cut across that way to Tivworthy, where a fête was to be held.

'Well, yes, there is,' said Jim. 'But 'tis an enormous distance for 'ee.'

'O yes,' replied the musician. 'I wish to intercept the carrier on the highway.'

The nearest way was precisely in the direction of Rook's Gate, where Margery, as Jim knew, was staying. Having some time to spare, Jim was strongly impelled to make a kind act to the lost musician a pretext for taking observations in that neighbourhood; and telling his acquaintance that he was going the same way, he started without further ado.

They skirted the long length of meads, and in due time arrived at the back of Rook's Gate, where the path joined the high road. A hedge divided the public way from the cottage garden. Jim drew up at this point and said, 'Your road is straight on: I turn back here.'

But the musician was standing fixed, as if in great perplexity. Thrusting his hand into his forest of black hair, he murmured, 'Surely it is the same – surely!'

Jim, following the direction of his neighbour's eyes, found them to be fixed on a figure till that moment hidden from himself – Margery Tucker – who was crossing the garden to an opposite gate with a little cheese in her arms, her head thrown back, and her face quite exposed.

'What of her?' said Jim.

'Two months ago I formed one of the band at the Yeomanry Ball given by Lord Toneborough in the next county. I saw that young lady dancing the polka there in robes of gauze and lace. Now I see her carry a cheese!'

'Never!' said Jim incredulously.

'But I do not mistake. I say it is so!'

Jim ridiculed the idea; the bandsman protested, and was about to lose his temper, when Jim gave in with the good-nature of a person who can afford to despise opinions; and the musician went his way.

As he dwindled out of sight Jim began to think more carefully over what he had said. The young man's thoughts grew quite to an excitement, for there came into his mind the Baron's extraordinary kindness in regard to furniture, hitherto accounted for by the assumption that the nobleman had taken a fancy to him. Could it be, among all the amazing things of life, that the Baron was at the bottom of this mischief, and that he had amused himself by taking Margery to a ball?

Doubts and suspicions which distract some lovers to imbecility only served to bring out Jim's great qualities. Where he trusted he was the most trusting fellow in the world; where he doubted he could be guilty of the slyest strategy. Once suspicious, he became one of those subtle, watchful characters who, without integrity, make good thieves; with a little, good jobbers; with a little more, good diplomatists. Jim was honest, and he considered what to do.

Retracing his steps, he peeped again. She had gone in; but she would soon reappear, for it could be seen that she was carrying little new cheeses one by one to a spring-cart and horse tethered outside the gate – her grandmother, though not a regular dairywoman, still managing a few cows by means of a man and maid. With the lightness of a cat Jim crept round to the gate, took a piece of chalk from his pocket, and wrote upon the boarding '*The Baron*'. Then he retreated to the other side of the garden where he had just watched Margery.

In due time she emerged with another little cheese, came on to the garden door, and glanced upon the chalked words which confronted her. She started; the cheese rolled from her arms to the ground, and broke into pieces like a pudding.

She looked fearfully round, her face burning like sunset, and, seeing nobody, stooped to pick up the flaccid lumps. Jim, with a pale face, departed as invisibly as he had come. He had proved the bandsman's tale to be true. On his way back he formed a resolution. It was to beard the lion in his den – to call on the Baron.

Meanwhile Margery had recovered her equanimity, and gathered up the broken cheese. But she could by no means account for the handwriting. Jim was just the sort of fellow to play her such a trick at ordinary times, but she imagined him to be far too incensed against her to do it now; and she suddenly wondered if it were any sort of signal from the Baron himself.

Of him she had lately heard nothing. If ever monotony pervaded a life it pervaded hers at Rook's Gate; and she had begun to despair of any happy change. But it is precisely when the social atmosphere seems stagnant that great events are brewing. Margery's quiet was broken first, as we have seen, by a slight start, only sufficient to make her drop a cheese; and then by a more serious matter.

She was inside the same garden one day when she heard two watermen talking without. The conversation was to the effect that the strange gentleman who had taken Mount Lodge for the season was seriously ill.

'How ill?' cried Margery through the hedge, which screened her from recognition.

'Bad abed,' said one of the watermen.

'Inflammation of the lungs,' said the other.

'Got wet, fishing,' the first chimed in.

Margery could gather no more. An ideal admiration rather than any positive passion existed in her breast for the Baron: she had of late seen too little of him to allow any incipient views of him as a lover to grow to formidable dimensions. It was an extremely romantic feeling, delicate as an aroma, capable of quickening to an active principle, or dying to 'a painless sympathy', as the case might be.

This news of his illness, coupled with the mysterious chalking on the gate, troubled her, and revived his image much. She took to walking up and down the garden-paths, looking into the hearts of flowers, and not thinking what they were. His last request had been that she was not to go to him if he should send for her; and now she asked herself, was the name on the gate a hint to enable her to go without infringing the letter of her promise? Thus unexpectedly had Jim's manœuvre operated.

Ten days passed. All she could hear of the Baron were the same words, 'Bad abed', till one afternoon, after a gallop of the physician to the Lodge, the tidings spread like lightning that the Baron was dying.

Margery distressed herself with the question whether she might be permitted to visit him and say her prayers at his bedside; but she feared to venture; and thus eight-and-forty hours slipped away, and the Baron still lived. Despite her shyness and awe of him she had almost made up her mind to call when, just at dusk on that October evening, somebody came to the door and asked for her.

She could see the messenger's head against the low new moon. He was a man-servant. He said he had been all the way to her father's, and had been sent thence to her there. He simply brought a note, and, delivering it into her hands, went away.

'DEAR MARGERY TUCKER,' ran the note – 'They say I am not likely to live, so I want to see you. Be here at eight o'clock this evening. Come quite alone to the side-door, and tap four times softly. My trusty man will admit you. The occasion is an important one. Prepare yourself for a solemn ceremony, which I wish to have performed while it lies in my power.

VON XANTEN'

XI

Margery's face flushed up, and her neck and arms glowed in sympathy. The quickness of youthful imagination, and the assumptiveness of woman's reason, sent her straight as an arrow this thought: 'He wants to marry me!'

She had heard of similar strange proceedings, in which the orange-flower and the sad cypress were intertwined. People sometimes wished on their deathbeds, from motives of esteem, to form a legal tie which they had not cared to establish as a domestic one during their active life.

For a few minutes Margery could hardly be called excited; she was excitement itself. Between surprise and modesty she blushed and trembled by turns. She became grave, sat down in the solitary room, and looked into the fire. At seven o'clock she rose resolved, and went quite tranquilly upstairs, where she speedily began to dress.

In making this hasty toilet nine-tenths of her care were given to her hands. The summer had left them slightly brown, and she held them up and looked at them with some misgiving, the fourth finger of her left hand more especially. Hot washings and cold washings, certain products from bee and flower known only to country girls, everything she could think of, were used upon those little sunburnt hands, till she persuaded herself that they were really as white as could be wished by a husband with a hundred titles. Her dressing completed, she left word with Edy that she was going for a long walk, and set out in the direction of Mount Lodge.

She no longer tripped like a girl, but walked like a woman. While crossing the park she murmured 'Baroness von Xanten' in a pronunciation of her own. The sound of that title caused her such agitation that she was obliged to pause, with her hand upon her heart.

The house was so closely neighboured by shrubberies on three of its sides that it was not till she had gone nearly round it that she found the little door. The resolution she had been an hour in forming failed her when she stood at the portal. While pausing for courage to tap, a carriage drove up to the front entrance a little way off, and peeping round the corner she saw alight a clergyman, and a gentleman in whom Margery fancied that she recognized a well-known solicitor from the neighbouring town. She had no longer any doubt of the nature of the ceremony proposed. 'It is sudden – but I must obey him!' she murmured: and tapped four times.

The door was opened so quickly that the servant must have been standing immediately inside. She thought him the man who had driven them to the ball – the silent man who could be trusted. Without a word he conducted her up the back staircase, and through a door at the top, into a wide corridor. She was asked to wait in a little dressing-room, where there was a fire, and an old metal-framed looking-glass over the mantelpiece, in which she caught sight of herself. A red spot burnt in each of her cheeks; the rest of her face was pale; and her eyes were like diamonds of the first water.

Before she had been seated many minutes the man came back noiselessly, and she followed him to a door covered by a red and black curtain, which he lifted, and ushered her into a large chamber. A screened light stood on a table before her, and on her left the hangings of a tall, dark, four-post bedstead obstructed her view of the centre of the room. Everything here seemed of such a magnificent type to her eyes that she felt confused, diminished to half her height, half her strength, half her prettiness. The man who had conducted her retired at once, and some one came softly round the angle of the bed-curtains. He held out his hand kindly – rather patronisingly: it was the solicitor whom she knew by sight. This gentleman led her forward, as if she had been a lamb rather than a woman, till the occupant of the bed was revealed.

The Baron's eyes were closed, and her entry had been so noiseless that he did not open them. The pallor of his face nearly matched the white bed-linen, and his dark hair and heavy black moustache were like dashes of ink on a clean page. Near him sat the parson and another gentleman, whom she afterwards learnt to be a London physician; and on the parson whispering a few words the Baron opened his eyes. As soon as he saw her he smiled faintly, and held out his hand.

Margery would have wept for him, if she had not been too overawed and palpitating to do anything. She quite forgot what she had come for, shook hands with him mechanically, and could hardly return an answer to his weak 'Dear Margery, you see how I am – how are you?'

In preparing for marriage she had not calculated on such a scene as this. Her affection for the Baron had too much of the vague in it to afford her trustfulness now. She wished she had not come. On a sign from the Baron the lawyer brought her a chair, and the oppressive silence was broken by the Baron's words.

'I am pulled down to death's door, Margery,' he said; 'and I suppose I soon shall pass through. . . . My peace has been much disturbed in this illness, for just before it attacked me I received – that present you returned, from which, and in other ways, I learnt that you had lost your chance of marriage. . . . Now it was I who did the harm, and you can imagine how the news has affected me. It has worried me all the illness through, and I cannot dismiss my error from my mind. . . . I want to right the wrong I have done you before I die. Margery, you have always obeyed me, and, strange as the request may be, will you obey me now?'

She whispered 'Yes.'

'Well, then,' said the Baron, 'these three gentlemen are here for a special purpose: one helps the body – he's called a physician; another helps the soul – he's a parson; the other helps the understanding – he's a lawyer. They are here partly on my account, and partly on yours.'

The speaker then made a sign to the lawyer, who went out of the door. He came back almost instantly, but not alone. Behind him, dressed up in his best clothes, with a flower in his buttonhole and a bridegroom's air, walked – Jim.

XII

Margery could hardly repress a scream. As for flushing and blushing, she had turned hot and turned pale so many times already during the evening, that there was really now nothing of that sort left for her to do; and she remained in complexion much as before. O, the mockery of it! That secret dream – that sweet word 'Baroness!' – which had sustained her all the way along. Instead of a Baron there stood Jim, white-waistcoated, demure, every hair in place, and, if she mistook not, even a deedy spark in his eye.

Jim's surprising presence on the scene may be briefly accounted for. His resolve to seek an explanation with the Baron at all risks had proved unexpectedly easy: the interview had at once been granted, and then, seeing the crisis at which matters stood, the Baron had generously revealed to Jim the whole of his indebtedness to and knowledge of Margery. The truth of the Baron's statement, the innocent nature as yet of the acquaintanceship, his sorrow for the rupture he had produced, was so evident that, far from having any further doubts of his patron, Jim frankly asked his advice on the next step to be pursued. At this stage the Baron fell ill, and, desiring much to see the two young people united before his death, he had sent anew to Hayward, and proposed the plan which they were now about to attempt – a marriage at the bedside of the sick man by special licence. The influence at Lambeth of some friends of the Baron's, and the charitable bequests of his late mother to several deserving Church funds, were generally supposed to be among the reasons why the application for the licence was not refused.

This, however, is of small consequence. The Baron probably knew, in proposing this method of celebrating the marriage, that his enormous power over her would outweigh any sentimental obstacles which she might set up – inward objections that, without his presence and firmness, might prove too much for her acquiescence. Doubtless he foresaw, too, the advantage of getting her into the house before making the individuality of her husband clear to her mind.

Now, the Baron's conjectures were right as to the event, but wrong as to the motives. Margery was a perfect little dissembler on some occasions, and one of them was when she wished to hide any sudden mortification that might bring her into ridicule. She had no sooner recovered from her first fit of discomfiture than pride bade her suffer anything rather than reveal her absurd disappointment. Hence the scene progressed as follows:

'Come here, Hayward,' said the invalid. Hayward came near. The Baron, holding her hand in one of his own, and her lover's in the other, continued, 'Will you, in spite of your recent vexation with her, marry her now if she does not refuse?'

'I will, sir,' said Jim promptly.

'And Margery, what do you say? It is merely a setting of things right. You have already promised this young man to be his wife, and should, of course, perform your promise. You don't dislike Jim?'

'O no, sir,' she said, in a low, dry voice.

'I like him better than I can tell you,' said the Baron. 'He is an honourable man, and will make you a good husband. You must remember that marriage is a life contract, in which general compatibility of temper and worldly position is of more importance than fleeting passion, which never long survives. Now, will you, at my earnest request, and before I go to the South of Europe to die, agree to make this good man happy? I have expressed your views on the subject, haven't I, Hayward?'

'To a T, sir,' said Jim emphatically, with a motion of raising his hat to his influential ally, till he remembered he had no hat on. 'And, though I could hardly expect Margery to gie in for my asking, I feels she ought to gie in for yours.'

'And you accept him, my little friend?'

'Yes, sir,' she murmured, 'if he'll agree to a thing or two.'

'Doubtless he will – what are they?'

'That I shall not be made to live with him till I am in the mind for it; and that my having him shall be kept unknown for the present.'

'Well, what do you think of it, Hayward?'

'Anything that you or she may wish I'll do, my noble lord,' said Jim.

'Well, her request is not unreasonable, seeing that the proceedings are, on my account, a little hurried. So we'll proceed. You rather expected this, from my allusion to a ceremony in my note, did you not, Margery?'

'Yes, sir,' said she, with an effort.

'Good; I thought so; you looked so little surprised.'

We now leave the scene in the bedroom for a spot not many yards off.

When the carriage seen by Margery at the door was driving up to Mount Lodge it arrested the attention, not only of the young girl, but of a man who had for some time been moving slowly about the opposite lawn, engaged in some operation while he smoked a short pipe. A short observation of his doings would have shown that he was sheltering some delicate plants from an expected frost, and that he was the gardener. When the light at the door fell upon the entering forms of parson and lawyer – the former a stranger, the latter known to him – the gardener walked thoughtfully round the house. Reaching the small side-entrance he was further surprised to see it noiselessly open to a young woman, in whose momentarily illumined features he discerned those of Margery Tucker.

Altogether there was something curious in this. The man returned to the lawn front, and perfunctorily went on putting shelters over certain plants, though his thoughts were plainly otherwise engaged. On the grass his footsteps were noiseless, and the night moreover being still, he could presently hear a murmuring from the bedroom window over his head.

The gardener took from a tree a ladder that he had used in nailing that day, set it under the window, and ascended half-way, hoodwinking his conscience by seizing a nail or two with his hand and testing their twig-supporting powers. He soon heard enough to satisfy him. The words of a church-service in the strange parson's voice were audible in snatches through the blind: they were words he knew to be part of the solemnization of matrimony, such as 'wedded wife', 'richer for poorer', and so on; the less familiar parts being a more or less confused sound.

Satisfied that a wedding was in progress there, the gardener did not for a moment dream that one of the contracting parties could be other than the sick Baron. He descended the ladder and again walked round the house, waiting only till he saw Margery emerge from the same little door; when, fearing that he might be discovered, he withdrew in the direction of his own cottage.

This building stood at the lower corner of the garden, and as soon as the gardener entered he was accosted by a handsome woman in a widow's cap, who called him father, and said that supper had been ready for a long time. They sat down, but during the meal the gardener was so abstracted and silent that his daughter put her head winningly to one side and said, 'What is it, father dear?'

'Ah – what is it?' cried the gardener. 'Something that makes very little difference to me, but may be of great account to you, if you play your cards well. *There's been a wedding at the Lodge to-night!*' He related to her, with a caution to secrecy, all that he had heard and seen.

'We are folk that have got to get their living,' he said, 'and such ones mustn't tell tales about their betters – Lord forgive the mockery of the word! – but there's something to be made of it. She's a nice maid; so, Harriet, do you take the first chance you get for honouring her, before others know what has happened. Since this is done so privately it will be kept private for some time – till after his death, no question; when I expect she'll take this house for herself, and blaze out as a widow-lady ten thousand pound strong. You being a widow, she may make you her company-keeper; and so you'll have a home by a little contriving.'

While this conversation progressed at the gardener's Margery was on her way out of the Baron's house. She was, indeed, married. But, as we know, she was not married to the Baron. The ceremony over she seemed but little discomposed, and expressed a wish to return alone as she had come. To this, of course, no objection could be offered under the terms of the agreement, and wishing Jim a frigid good-bye, and the Baron a very quiet farewell, she went out by the door which had admitted her. Once safe and alone in the darkness of the park she burst into tears, which dropped upon the grass as she passed along. In the Baron's room she had seemed scared and helpless; now her reason and emotions returned. The farther she got away from the glamour of that room, and the influence of its occupant, the more she became of opinion that she had acted foolishly. She had disobediently left her father's house, to obey him here. She had pleased everybody but herself.

However, thinking was now too late. How she got into her grand-mother's house she hardly knew; but without a supper, and without confronting either her relative or Edy, she went to bed.

XIII

On going out into the garden next morning, with a strange sense of being another person than herself, she beheld Jim leaning mutely over the gate.

He nodded. 'Good morning, Margery,' he said civilly.

'Good morning,' said Margery in the same tone.

'I beg your pardon,' he continued. 'But which way was you going this morning?'

'I am not going anywhere just now, thank you. But I shall go to my father's by-and-by with Edy.' She went on with a sigh, 'I have done what he has all along wished, that is, married you; and there's no longer reason for enmity atween him and me.'

'Trew – trew. Well, as I am going the same way, I can give you a lift in the trap, for the distance is long.'

'No, thank you – I am used to walking,' she said.

They remained in silence, the gate between them, till Jim's convictions would apparently allow him to hold his peace no longer. 'This is a bad job!' he murmured.

'It is,' she said, as one whose thoughts have only too readily been identified. 'How I came to agree to it is more than I can tell!' And tears began rolling down her cheeks.

'The blame is more mine than yours, I suppose,' he returned. 'I ought to have said No, and not backed up the gentleman in carrying out this scheme. 'Twas his own notion entirely, as perhaps you know. I should never have thought of such a plan; but he said you'd be willing, and that it would be all right; and I was too ready to believe him.'

'The thing is, how to remedy it,' said she bitterly. 'I believe, of course, in your promise to keep this private, and not to trouble me by calling.'

'Certainly,' said Jim. 'I don't want to trouble you. As for that, why, my dear Mrs Hayward—'

'Don't Mrs Hayward me!' said Margery sharply. 'I won't be Mrs Hayward!'

Jim paused. 'Well, you are she by law, and that was all I meant,' he said mildly.

'I said I would acknowledge no such thing, and I won't. A thing can't be legal when it's against the wishes of the persons the laws are made to protect. So I beg you not to call me that any more.'

'Very well, Miss Tucker,' said Jim deferentially. 'We can live on exactly as before. We can't marry anybody else, that's true; but beyond that there's no difference, and no harm done. Your father ought to be told, I suppose, even if nobody else is? It will partly reconcile him to you, and make your life smoother.'

Instead of directly replying, Margery exclaimed in a low voice:

'O, it is a mistake – I didn't see it all, owing to not having time to reflect! I agreed, thinking that at least I should get reconciled to father by the step. But perhaps he would as soon have me not married at all as married and parted. I must ha' been enchanted – bewitched – when I gave my consent to this! I only did it to please that dear good dying nobleman – though why he should have wished it so much I can't tell!'

'Nor I neither,' said Jim. 'Yes, we've been fooled into it, Margery,' he said, with extraordinary gravity. 'He's had his way wi' us, and now we've got to suffer for it. Being a gentleman of patronage, and having bought several loads of lime o' me, and having given me all that splendid furniture, I could hardly refuse—'

'What, did he give you that?'

'Ay, sure – to help me win ye.'

Margery covered her face with her hands; whereupon Jim stood up from the gate and looked critically at her. ' 'Tis a footy plot between you two men to – snare me!' she exclaimed. 'Why should you have done it – why should he have done it – when I've not deserved to be treated so? He bought the furniture, did he! O, I've been taken in – I've been wronged!' The grief and vexation of finding that long ago, when fondly believing the Baron to have lover-like feelings himself for her, he was still conspiring to favour Jim's suit, was more than she could endure.

Jim with distant courtesy waited, nibbling a straw, till her paroxysm was over. 'One word, Miss Tuck – Mrs – Margery,' he then recommenced gravely. 'You'll find me man enough to respect your wish, and to leave you to yourself – for ever and ever, if that's all. But I've just one word of advice to render 'ee. That is, that before you go to Silverthorn Dairy yourself you let me drive ahead and call on your father. He's friends with me, and he's not friends with you. I can break the news, a little at a time, and I think I can gain his goodwill for you now, even though the wedding be no natural wedding at all. At any count, I can hear what he's got to say about 'ee, and come back here and tell 'ee.'

She nodded a cool assent to this, and he left her strolling about the garden in the sunlight while he went on to reconnoitre as agreed. It must not be supposed that Jim's dutiful echoes of Margery's regret at her precipitate marriage were all gospel; and there is no doubt that his private intention, after telling the dairy-farmer what had happened, was to ask his temporary assent to her caprice, till, in the course of time, she should be reasoned out of her whims and induced to settle down with Jim in a natural manner. He had, it is true, been somewhat nettled by her firm objection to him, and her keen sorrow for what she had done to please another; but he hoped for the best.

But, alas for the astute Jim's calculations! He drove on to the dairy, whose white walls now gleamed in the morning sun; made fast the horse to a ring in the wall, and entered the barton. Before knocking, he perceived the dairyman walking across from a gate in the other direction, as if he had just come in. Jim went over to him. Since the unfortunate incident on the morning of the intended wedding they had merely been on nodding terms, from a sense of awkwardness in their relations.

'What – is that thee?' said Dairyman Tucker, in a voice which unmistakably startled Jim by its abrupt fierceness. 'A pretty fellow thou be'st!'

It was a bad beginning for the young man's life as a son-in-law, and augured ill for the delicate consultation he desired.

'What's the matter?' said Jim.

'Matter! I wish some folks would burn their lime without burning other folks' property along wi' it. You ought to be ashamed of yourself. You call yourself a man, Jim Hayward, and an honest lime-burner, and a respectable, market-keeping Christen, and yet at six o'clock this morning, instead o' being where you ought to ha' been – at your work, there was neither vell or mark o' thee to be seen!'

'Faith, I don't know what you are raving at,' said Jim.

'Why – the sparks from thy couch-heap blew over upon my hay-rick, and the rick's burnt to ashes; and all to come out o' my well-squeezed pocket. I'll tell thee what it is, young man. There's no business in thee. I've known Silverthorn folk, quick and dead, for the last couple-o'-score year, and I've never knew one so three-cunning for harm as thee, my gentleman lime-burner; and I reckon it one o' the luckiest days o' my life when I 'scaped having thee in my family. That maid of mine was right; I was wrong. She seed thee to be a drawlacheting rogue, and 'twas her wisdom to go off that morning and get rid o' thee. I commend her for't, and I'm going to fetch her home to-morrow.'

'You needn't take the trouble. She's coming home-along to-night of her own accord. I have seen her this morning, and she told me so.'

'So much the better. I'll welcome her warm. Nation! I'd sooner see her married to the parish fool than thee. Not you – you don't care for my hay. Tarrying about where you shouldn't be – in bed, no doubt; that's what you was a-doing. Now, don't you darken my doors again, and the sooner you be off my bit o' ground the better I shall be pleased.'

Jim looked, as he felt, stultified. If the rick had been really destroyed, a little blame certainly attached to him, but he could not understand how it had happened. However, blame or none, it was clear he could not, with any self-respect, declare himself to be this peppery old gaffer's son-in-law in the face of such an attack as this.

For months – almost years – the one transaction that had seemed necessary to compose these two families satisfactorily was Jim's union with Margery. No sooner had it been completed than it appeared on all sides as the gravest mishap for both. Stating coldly that he would discover how much of the accident was to be attributed to his negligence, and pay the damage, he went out of the barton, and returned the way he had come.

Margery had been keeping a look-out for him, particularly wishing him not to enter the house, lest others should see the seriousness of their interview; and as soon as she heard wheels she went to the gate, which was out of view.

'Surely father has been speaking roughly to you!' she said, on seeing his face.

'Not the least doubt that he have,' said Jim.

'But is he still angry with me?'

'Not in the least. He's waiting to welcome 'ee.'

'Ah! because I've married you.'

'Because he thinks you have *not* married me! He's jawed me up hill and down. He hates me; and for your sake I have not explained a word.'

Margery looked towards home with a sad, severe gaze. 'Mr Hayward,' she said, 'we have made a great mistake, and we are in a strange position.'

'True, but I'll tell you what, mistress – I won't stand—' He stopped suddenly. 'Well, well; I've promised!' he quietly added.

'We must suffer for our mistake,' she went on. 'The way to suffer least is to keep our own counsel on what happened last evening, and not to meet. I must now return to my father.'

He inclined his head in indifferent assent, and she went indoors, leaving him there.

XIV

Margery returned home, as she had decided, and resumed her old life at Silverthorn. And seeing her father's animosity towards Jim, she told him not a word of the marriage.

Her inner life, however, was not what it once had been. She had suffered a mental and emotional displacement – a shock, which had set a shade of astonishment on her face as a permanent thing.

Her indignation with the Baron for collusion with Jim, at first bitter, lessened with the lapse of a few weeks, and at length vanished in the interest of some tidings she received one day.

The Baron was not dead, but he was no longer at the Lodge. To the surprise of the physicians, a sufficient improvement had taken place in his condition to permit of his removal before the cold weather came. His desire for removal had been such, indeed, that it was advisable to carry it out at almost any risk. The plan adopted had been to have him borne on men's shoulders in a sort of palanquin to the shore near Idmouth, a distance of several miles, where a yacht lay awaiting him. By this means the noise and jolting of a carriage, along irregular bye-roads, were avoided. The singular procession over the fields took place at night, and was witnessed by but few people, one being a labouring man, who described the scene to Margery. When the seaside was reached a long, narrow gangway was laid from the deck of the yacht to the shore, which was so steep as to allow the yacht to lie quite near. The men, with their burden, ascended by the light of lanterns, the sick man was laid in the cabin, and, as soon as his bearers had returned to the shore, the gangway was removed, a rope was heard skirring over wood in the darkness, the yacht quivered, spread her woven wings to the air, and moved away. Soon she was but a small shapeless phantom upon the wide breast of the sea.

It was said that the yacht was bound for Algiers.

When the inimical autumn and winter weather came on, Margery wondered if he were still alive. The house being shut up, and the servants gone, she had no means of knowing, till, on a particular Saturday, her father drove her to Exonbury market. Here, in attending to his business, he left her to herself for a while. Walking in a quiet street in the professional quarter of the town, she saw coming towards her the solicitor who had been present at the wedding, and who had acted for the Baron in various small local matters during his brief residence at the Lodge.

She reddened to peony hues, averted her eyes, and would have passed him. But he crossed over and barred the pavement, and when she met his glance he was looking with friendly severity at her. The street was quiet, and he said in a low voice, 'How's the husband?'

'I don't know, sir,' said she.

'What – and are your stipulations about secrecy and separate living still in force?'

'They will always be,' she replied decisively. 'Mr Hayward and I agreed on the point, and we have not the slightest wish to change the arrangement.'

'H'm. Then 'tis Miss Tucker to the world; Mrs Hayward to me and one or two others only?'

Margery nodded. Then she nerved herself by an effort, and, though blushing painfully, asked, 'May I put one question, sir? Is the Baron dead?'

'He is dead to you and to all of us. Why should you ask?'

'Because, if he's alive, I am sorry I married James Hayward. If he is dead I do not much mind my marriage.'

'I repeat, he is dead to you,' said the lawyer emphatically. 'I'll tell you all I know. My professional services for him ended with his departure from this country; but I think I should have heard from him if he had been alive still. I have not heard at all: and this, taken in connection with the nature of his illness, leaves no doubt in my mind that he is dead.'

Margery sighed, and thanking the lawyer she left him with a tear for the Baron in her eye. After this incident she became more restful; and the time drew on for her periodical visit to her grandmother.

A few days subsequent to her arrival her aged relative asked her to go with a message to the gardener at Mount Lodge (who still lived on there, keeping the grounds in order for the landlord). Margery hated that direction now, but she went. The Lodge, which she saw over the trees, was to her like a skull from which the warm and living flesh had vanished. It was twilight by the time she reached the cottage at the bottom of the Lodge garden, and, the room being illuminated within, she saw through the window a woman she had never seen before. She was dark, and rather handsome, and when Margery knocked she opened the door. It was the gardener's widowed daughter, who had been advised to make friends with Margery.

She now found her opportunity. Margery's errand was soon completed, the young widow, to her surprise, treating her with preternatural respect, and afterwards offering to accompany her home. Margery was not sorry to have a companion in the gloom, and they walked on together. The widow, Mrs Peach, was demonstrative and confidential, and told Margery all about herself. She had come quite recently to live with her father – during the Baron's illness, in fact – and her husband had been captain of a ketch.

'I saw you one morning, ma'am,' she said. 'But you didn't see me. It was when you were crossing the hill in sight of the Lodge. You looked at it, and sighed. 'Tis the lot of widows to sigh, ma'am, is it not?'

'Widows – yes, I suppose; but what do you mean?'

Mrs Peach lowered her voice. 'I can't say more, ma'am, with proper respect. But there seems to be no question of the poor Baron's death; and though these foreign princes can take (as my poor husband used to tell me) what they call left-handed wives, and leave them behind when they go abroad, widowhood is widowhood, left-handed or right. And really, to be the left-handed wife of a foreign baron is nobler than to be married all round to a common man. You'll excuse my freedom, ma'am; but being a widow myself, I have pitied you from my heart; so young as you are, and having to keep it a secret, and (excusing me) having no money out of his vast riches because 'tis swallowed up by Baroness Number One.'

Now Margery did not understand a word more of this than the bare fact that Mrs Peach suspected her to be the Baron's undowered widow, and such was the milkmaid's nature that she did not deny the widow's impeachment. The latter continued –

'But ah, ma'am, all your troubles are straight backward in your memory – while I have troubles before as well as grief behind.'

'What may they be, Mrs Peach?' inquired Margery, with an air of the Baroness.

The other dropped her voice to revelation tones: 'I have been forgetful enough of my first man to lose my heart to a second!'

'You shouldn't do that – it is wrong. You should control your feelings.'

'But how am I to control my feelings?'

'By going to your dead husband's grave, and things of that sort.'

'Do you go to your dead husband's grave?'

'How can I go to Algiers?'

'Ah – too true! Well, I've tried everything to cure myself – read the words against it, gone to the Table the first Sunday of every month, and all sorts. But, avast, my shipmate! – as my poor man used to say – there 'tis just the same. In short, I've made up my mind to encourage the new one. 'Tis flattering that I, a new-comer, should have been found out by a young man so soon.'

'Who is he?' said Margery listlessly.

'A master lime-burner.'

'A master lime-burner ?'

'That's his profession. He's a partner-in-co., doing very well indeed.'

'But what's his name ?'

'I don't like to tell you his name, for, though 'tis night, that covers all shame-facedness, my face is as hot as a 'Talian iron, I declare! Do you just feel it.'

Margery put her hand on Mrs Peach's face, and, sure enough, hot it was. 'Does he come courting ?' she asked quickly.

'Well – only in the way of business. He never comes unless lime is wanted in the neighbourhood. He's in the Yeomanry, too, and will look very fine when he comes out in regimentals for drill in May.'

'Oh – in the Yeomanry,' Margery said, with a slight relief. 'Then it can't – is he a young man ?'

'Yes, junior partner-in-co.'

The description had an odd resemblance to Jim, of whom Margery had not heard a word for months. He had promised silence and absence, and had fulfilled his promise literally, with a gratuitous addition that was rather amazing, if indeed it were Jim whom the widow loved. One point in the description puzzled Margery: Jim was not in the Yeomanry, unless, by a surprising development of enterprise, he had entered it recently.

At parting Margery said, with an interest quite tender, 'I should like to see you again, Mrs Peach, and hear of your attachment. When can you call ?'

'Oh – any time, dear Baroness, I'm sure – if you think I am good enough.'

'Indeed, I do, Mrs Peach. Come as soon as you've seen the lime-burner again.'

XV

Seeing that Jim lived several miles from the widow, Margery was rather surprised, and even felt a slight sinking of the heart, when her new acquaintance appeared at her door so soon as the evening of the following Monday. She asked Margery to walk out with her, which the young woman readily did.

'I am come at once,' said the widow breathlessly, as soon as they were in the lane, 'for it is so exciting that I can't keep it. I must tell it to somebody, if only a bird, or a cat, or a garden snail.'

'What is it?' asked her companion.

'I've pulled grass from my husband's grave to cure it – wove the blades into true lover's knots; took off my shoes upon the sod; but, avast, my shipmate!—'

'Upon the sod – why?'

'To feel the damp earth he's in, and make the sense of it enter my soul. But no. It has swelled to a head; he is going to meet me at the Yeomanry Review.'

'The master lime-burner?'

The widow nodded.

'When is it to be?'

'To-morrow. He looks so lovely in his accoutrements! He's such a splendid soldier; that was the last straw that kindled my soul to say yes. He's home from Exonbury for a night between the drills,' continued Mrs Peach. 'He goes back to-morrow morning for the Review, and when it's over he's going to meet me. . . . But, guide my heart, there he is!'

Her exclamation had rise in the sudden appearance of a brilliant red uniform through the trees, and the tramp of a horse carrying the wearer thereof. In another half-minute the military gentleman would have turned the corner, and faced them.

'He'd better not see me; he'll think I know too much,' said Margery precipitately. 'I'll go up here.'

The widow, whose thoughts had been of the same cast, seemed much relieved to see Margery disappear in the plantation, in the midst of a spring chorus of birds. Once among the trees, Margery turned her head, and, before she could see the rider's person, she recognized the horse as Tony, the lightest of three that Jim and his partner owned, for the purpose of carting out lime to their customers.

Jim, then, had joined the Yeomanry since his estrangement from Margery. A man who had worn the young Queen Victoria's uniform for seven days only could not be expected to look as if it were part of his person, in the manner of long-trained soldiers; but he was a well-formed young fellow, and of an age when few positions come amiss to one who has the capacity to adapt himself to circumstances.

Meeting the blushing Mrs Peach (to whom Margery in her mind sternly denied the right to blush at all), Jim alighted and moved on with her, probably at Mrs Peach's own suggestion; so that what they said, how long they remained together, and how they parted, Margery knew not. She might have known some of these things by waiting; but the presence of Jim had bred in her heart a sudden disgust for the widow, and a general sense of discomfiture. She went away in an opposite direction, turning her head and saying to the unconscious Jim, 'There's a fine rod in pickle for you, my gentleman, if you carry out that pretty scheme!'

Jim's military *coup* had decidedly astonished her. What he might do next she could not conjecture. The idea of his doing anything sufficiently brilliant to arrest her attention would have seemed ludicrous, had not Jim, by entering the Yeomanry, revealed a capacity for dazzling exploits which made it unsafe to predict any limitation to his powers.

Margery was now excited. The daring of the wretched Jim in bursting into scarlet amazed her as much as his doubtful acquaintanceship with the demonstrative Mrs Peach. To go to that Review, to watch the pair, to eclipse Mrs Peach in brilliancy, to meet and pass them in withering contempt – if she only could do it! But, alas! she was a forsaken woman. 'If the Baron were alive, or in England,' she said to herself (for sometimes she thought he might possibly be alive), 'and he were to take me to this Review, wouldn't I show that forward Mrs Peach what a lady is like, and keep among the select company, and not mix with the common people at all!'

It might at first sight be thought that the best course for Margery at this juncture would have been to go to Jim, and nip the intrigue in the bud without further scruple. But her own declaration in after days was that whoever could say that was far from realizing her situation. It was hard to break such ice as divided their two lives now, and to attempt it at that moment was a too humiliating proclamation of defeat. The only plan she could think of – perhaps not a wise one in the circumstances – was to go to the Review herself, and be the gayest there.

A method of doing this with some propriety soon occurred to her. She dared not ask her father, who scorned to waste time in sight-seeing, and whose animosity towards Jim knew no abatement; but she might call on her old acquaintance, Mr Vine, Jim's partner, who would probably be going with the rest of the holiday-folk, and ask if she might accompany him in his spring-trap. She had no sooner perceived the feasibility of this, through her being at her grandmother's, than she decided to meet with the old man early the next morning.

In the meantime Jim and Mrs Peach had walked slowly along the road together, Jim leading the horse, and Mrs Peach informing him that her father, the gardener, was at Jim's village farther on, and that she had come to meet him. Jim, for reasons of his own, was going to sleep at his partner's that night, and thus their route was the same. The shades of eve closed in upon them as they walked, and by the time they reached the lime-kiln, which it was necessary to pass to get to the village, it was quite dark. Jim stopped at the kiln, to see if matters had progressed rightly in his seven days' absence, and Mrs Peach, who stuck to him like a teazle, stopped also, saying she would wait for her father there.

She held the horse while he ascended to the top of the kiln. Then rejoining her, and not quite knowing what to do, he stood beside her looking at the flames, which to-night burnt up brightly, shining a long way into the dark air, even up to the ramparts of the earthwork above them, and overhead into the bosoms of the clouds.

It was during this proceeding that a carriage, drawn by a pair of dark horses, came along the turnpike-road. The light of the kiln caused the horses to swerve a little, and the occupant of the carriage looked out. He saw the bluish, lightning-like flames from the limestone, rising from the top of the furnace, and hard by the figures of Jim Hayward, the widow, and the horse, standing out with spectral distinctness against the mass of night behind. The scene wore the aspect of some unholy assignation in Pandæmonium, and it was all the more impressive from the fact that both Jim and the woman were quite unconscious of the striking spectacle they presented. The gentleman in the carriage watched them till he was borne out of sight.

Having seen to the kiln, Jim and the widow walked on again, and soon Mrs Peach's father met them, and relieved Jim of the lady. When they had parted, Jim, with an expiration not unlike a breath of relief, went on to Mr Vine's, and, having put the horse into the stable, entered the house. His partner was seated at the table, solacing himself after the labours of the day by luxurious alternations between a long clay pipe and a mug of perry.

'Well,' said Jim eagerly, 'what's the news – how do she take it?'

'Sit down – sit down,' said Vine. ' 'Tis working well; not but that I deserve something o' thee for the trouble I've had in watching her. The soldiering was a fine move; but the woman is a better! – who invented it?'

'I myself,' said Jim modestly.

'Well; jealousy is making her rise like a thunder-storm, and in a day or two you'll have her for the asking, my sonny. What's the next step?'

'The widow is getting rather a weight upon a feller, worse luck,' said

Jim. 'But I must keep it up until to-morrow, at any rate. I have promised to see her at the Review, and now the great thing is that Margery should see we a-smiling together – I in my full-dress uniform and clinking arms o' war. 'Twill be a good strong sting, and will end the business, I hope. Couldn't you manage to put the hoss in and drive her there? She'd go if you were to ask her.'

'With all my heart,' said Mr Vine, moistening the end of a new pipe in his perry. 'I can call at her grammer's for her – 'twill be all in my way.'

XVI

Margery duly followed up her intention by arraying herself the next morning in her loveliest guise, and keeping watch for Mr Vine's appearance upon the high road, feeling certain that his would form one in the procession of carts and carriages which set in towards Exonbury that day. Jim had gone by at a very early hour, and she did not see him pass. Her anticipation was verified by the advent of Mr Vine about eleven o'clock, dressed to his highest effort; but Margery was surprised to find that, instead of her having to stop him, he pulled in towards the gate of his own accord. The invitation planned between Jim and the old man on the previous night was now promptly given, and, as may be supposed, as promptly accepted. Such a strange coincidence she had never before known. She was quite ready, and they drove onward at once.

The Review was held on some high ground a little way out of the city, and her conductor suggested that they should put up the horse at the inn, and walk to the field – a plan which pleased her well, for it was more easy to take preliminary observations on foot without being seen herself than when sitting elevated in a vehicle.

They were just in time to secure a good place near the front, and in a few minutes after their arrival the reviewing officer came on the ground. Margery's eye had rapidly run over the troop in which Jim was enrolled, and she discerned him in one of the ranks, looking remarkably new and bright, both as to uniform and countenance. Indeed, if she had not worked herself into such a desperate state of mind she would have felt proud of him then and there. His shapely upright figure was quite note-worthy in the row of rotund yeomen on his right and left; while his charger Tony expressed by his bearing, even more than Jim, that he knew nothing about lime-carts whatever, and everything about trumpets and glory. How Jim could have scrubbed Tony to such shining blackness she could not tell, for the horse in his natural state was ingrained with lime-dust, that burnt the colour out of his coat as it did out of Jim's hair. Now he pranced martially, and was a war-horse every inch of him.

Having discovered Jim her next search was for Mrs Peach, and, by dint of some oblique glancing, Margery indignantly discovered the widow in the most forward place of all, her head and bright face conspicuously advanced; and, what was more shocking, she had abandoned her mourning for a violet drawn-bonnet and a gay spencer, together with a parasol luxuriously fringed in a way Margery had never before seen. 'Where did she get the money?' said Margery, under her breath. 'And to forget that poor sailor so soon!'

These general reflections were precipitately postponed by her discovering that Jim and the widow were perfectly alive to each other's whereabouts, and in the interchange of telegraphic signs of affection, which on the latter's part took the form of a playful fluttering of her handkerchief or waving of her parasol. Richard Vine had placed Margery in front of him, to protect her from the crowd, as he said, he himself surveying the scene over her bonnet. Margery would have been even more surprised than she was if she had known that Jim was not only aware of Mrs Peach's presence, but also of her own, the treacherous Mr Vine having drawn out his flame-coloured handkerchief and waved it to Jim over the young woman's head as soon as they had taken up their position.

'My partner makes a tidy soldier, eh – Miss Tucker?' said the senior lime-burner. 'It is my belief as a Christian that he's got a party here that he's making signs to – that handsome figure o' fun straight over-right him.'

'Perhaps so,' she said.

'And it's growing warm between 'em if I don't mistake,' continued the merciless Vine.

Margery was silent, biting her lip; and the troops being now set in motion, all signalling ceased for the present between soldier Hayward and his pretended sweetheart.

'Have you a piece of paper that I could make a memorandum on, Mr Vine?' asked Margery.

Vine took out his pocket-book and tore a leaf from it, which he handed her with a pencil.

'Don't move from here – I'll return in a minute,' she continued, with the innocence of a woman who means mischief. And, withdrawing herself to the back, where the grass was clear, she pencilled down the words –

'JIM'S MARRIED'

Armed with this document she crept into the throng behind the unsuspecting Mrs Peach, slipped the paper into her pocket on the top of her handkerchief, and withdrew unobserved, rejoining Mr Vine with a bearing of *nonchalance*.

By-and-by the troops were in different order, Jim taking a left-hand position almost close to Mrs Peach. He bent down and said a few words to her. From her manner of nodding assent it was surely some arrangement about a meeting by-and-by when Jim's drill was over, and Margery was more certain of the fact when, the Review having ended, and the people having strolled off to another part of the field where sports were to take place, Mrs Peach tripped away in the direction of the city.

'I'll just say a word to my partner afore he goes off the ground, if you'll spare me a minute,' said the old lime-burner. 'Please stay here till I'm back again.' He edged along the front till he reached Jim.

'How is she?' said the latter.

'In a trimming sweat,' said Mr Vine. 'And my counsel to 'ee is to carry this larry no further. 'Twill do no good. She's as ready to make friends with 'ee as any wife can be; and more showing off can only do harm.'

'But I must finish off with a spurt,' said Jim. 'And this is how I am going to do it. I have arranged with Mrs Peach that, as soon as we soldiers have entered the town and been dismissed, I'll meet her there. It is really to say good-bye, but she don't know that; and I wanted it to look like a 'lopement to Margery's eyes. When I'm clear of Mrs Peach I'll come back here and make it up with Margery on the spot. But don't say I'm coming, or she may be inclined to throw off again. Just hint to her that I may be meaning to be off to London with the widow.'

The old man still insisted that this was going too far.

'No, no, it isn't,' said Jim. 'I know how to manage her. 'Twill just mellow her heart nicely by the time I come back. I must bring her down real tender, or 'twill all fail.'

His senior reluctantly gave in and returned to Margery. A short time afterwards the Yeomanry band struck up, and Jim with the regiment followed towards Exonbury.

'Yes, yes; they are going to meet,' said Margery to herself, perceiving that Mrs Peach had so timed her departure as to be in the town at Jim's dismounting.

'Now we will go and see the games,' said Mr Vine; 'they are really worth seeing. There's greasy poles, and jumping in sacks, and other trials of the intellect, that nobody ought to miss who wants to be abreast of his generation.'

Margery felt so indignant at the apparent assignation, which seemed about to take place despite her anonymous writing, that she helplessly assented to go anywhere, dropping behind Vine, that he might not see her mood.

Jim followed out his programme with literal exactness. No sooner was the troop dismissed in the city than he sent Tony to stable and joined Mrs Peach, who stood on the edge of the pavement expecting him. But this acquaintance was to end: he meant to part from her for ever and in the quickest time, though civilly; for it was important to be with Margery as soon as possible. He had nearly completed the manœuvre to his satisfaction when, in drawing her handkerchief from her pocket to wipe the tears from her eyes, Mrs Peach's hand grasped the paper, which she read at once.

'What! is that true?' she said, holding it out to Jim.

Jim started and admitted that it was, beginning an elaborate explanation and apologies. But Mrs Peach was thoroughly roused, and then overcome. 'He's married, he's married!' she said, and swooned, or feigned to swoon, so that Jim was obliged to support her.

'He's married, he's married!' said a boy hard by who watched the scene with interest.

'He's married, he's married!' said a hilarious group of other boys near, with smiles several inches broad, and shining teeth; and so the exclamation echoed down the street.

Jim cursed his ill-luck; the loss of time that this dilemma entailed grew serious; for Mrs Peach was now in such a hysterical state that he could not leave her with any good grace or feeling. It was necessary to take her to a refreshment room, lavish restoratives upon her, and altogether to waste nearly half-an-hour. When she had kept him as long as she chose, she forgave him; and thus at last he got away, his heart

swelling with tenderness towards Margery. He at once hurried up the
street to effect the reconciliation with her.

'How shall I do it?' he said to himself. 'Why, I'll step round to her
side, fish for her hand, draw it through my arm as if I wasn't aware of it.
Then she'll look in my face, I shall look in hers, and we shall march off
the field triumphant, and the thing will be done without takings or tears.'

He entered the field and went straight as an arrow to the place appointed for the meeting. It was at the back of a refreshment tent outside
the mass of spectators, and divided from their view by the tent itself. He
turned the corner of the canvas, and there beheld Vine at the indicated
spot. But Margery was not with him.

Vine's hat was thrust back into his poll. His face was pale, and his
manner bewildered. 'Hullo? what's the matter?' said Jim. 'Where's my
Margery?'

'You've carried this footy game too far, my man!' exclaimed Vine,
with the air of a friend who has 'always told you so'. 'You ought to have
dropped it several days ago, when she would have come to 'ee like a
cooing dove. Now this is the end o't!'

'Hey! what, my Margery? Has anything happened, for God's sake?'

'She's gone.'

'Where to?'

'That's more than earthly man can tell! I never see such a thing!
'Twas a stroke o' the black art – as if she were sperrited away. When we
got to the games I said – mind, you told me to! – I said, "Jim Hayward
thinks o' going off to London with that widow woman" – mind, you
told me to! She showed no wonderment, though a' seemed very low.
Then she said to me, "I don't like standing here in this slummocky
crowd. I shall feel more at home among the gentlepeople." And then
she went to where the carriages were drawn up, and near her there was
a grand coach, a-blazing with lions and unicorns, and hauled by two
coal-black horses. I hardly thought much of it then, and by degrees lost
sight of her behind it. Presently the other carriages moved off, and I
thought still to see her standing there. But no, she had vanished; and
then I saw the grand coach rolling away, and glimpsed Margery in it,
beside a fine dark gentleman with black mustachios, and a very pale
prince-like face. As soon as the horses got into the hard road they
rattled on like hell-and-skimmer, and went out of sight in the dust,
and – that's all. If you'd come back a little sooner you'd ha' caught her.'

Jim had turned whiter than his pipeclay. 'O, this is too bad – too

bad!' he cried in anguish, striking his brow. 'That paper and that fainting woman kept me so long. Who could have done it? But 'tis my fault.
I've stung her too much. I shouldn't have carried it so far.'

'You shouldn't – just what I said,' replied his senior.

'She thinks I've gone off with that cust widow; and to spite me she's
gone off with the man! Do you know who that stranger wi' the lions
and unicorns is? Why, 'tis that foreigner who calls himself a Baron, and
took Mount Lodge for six months last year to make mischief – a villain!
O, my Margery – that it should come to this! She's lost, she's ruined! –
Which way did they go?'

Jim turned to follow in the direction indicated, when, behold, there
stood at his back her father, Dairyman Tucker.

'Now look here, young man,' said Dairyman Tucker. 'I've just heard
all that wailing – and straightway will ask 'ee to stop it sharp. 'Tis like
your brazen impudence to teave and wail when you be another woman's
husband; yes, faith, I seed her a-fainting in yer arms when you wanted
to get away from her, and honest folk a-standing round who knew you'd
married her, and said so. I heard it, though you didn't see me. "He's
married!" says they. Some sly register-office business, no doubt; but sly
doings will out. As for Margery – who's to be called higher titles in these
parts hencefor'ard – I'm her father, and I say it's all right what she's
done. Don't I know private news, hey? Haven't I just learnt that secret
weddings of high people can happen at expected deathbeds by special
licence, as well as low people at registrars' offices? And can't husbands
come back and claim their own when they choose? Begone, young man,
and leave noblemen's wives alone; and I thank God I shall be rid of a
numskull!'

Swift words of explanation rose to Jim's lips, but they paused there
and died. At that last moment he could not, as Margery's husband,
announce Margery's shame and his own, and transform her father's
triumph to wretchedness at a blow.

'I – I – must leave here,' he stammered. Going from the place in an
opposite course to that of the fugitives, he doubled when out of sight,
and in an incredibly short space had entered the town. Here he made
inquiries for the emblazoned carriage, and gained from one or two
persons a general idea of its route. They thought it had taken the highway to London. Saddling poor Tony before he had half eaten his corn,
Jim galloped along the same road.

XVII

Now Jim was quite mistaken in supposing that by leaving the field in a roundabout manner he had deceived Dairyman Tucker as to his object. That astute old man immediately divined that Jim was meaning to track the fugitives, in ignorance (as the dairyman supposed) of their lawful relation. He was soon assured of the fact, for, creeping to a remote angle of the field, he saw Jim hastening into the town. Vowing vengeance on the young lime-burner for his mischievous interference between a nobleman and his secretly-wedded wife, the dairy-farmer determined to balk him.

Tucker had ridden on to the Review ground, so that there was no necessity for him, as there had been for poor Jim, to re-enter the town before starting. The dairyman hastily untied his mare from the row of other horses, mounted, and descended to a bridle-path which would take him obliquely into the London road a mile or so ahead. The old man's route being along one side of an equilateral triangle, while Jim's was along two sides of the same, the former was at the point of intersection long before Hayward.

Arrived here, the dairyman pulled up and looked around. It was a spot at which the highway forked; the left arm, the more important, led on through Sherton Abbas and Melchester to London; the right to Idmouth and the coast. Nothing was visible on the white track to London; but on the other there appeared the back of a carriage which rapidly ascended a distant hill and vanished under the trees. It was the Baron's who, according to the sworn information of the gardener at Mount Lodge, had made Margery his wife.

The carriage having vanished, the dairyman gazed in the opposite direction, towards Exonbury. Here he beheld Jim in his regimentals, laboriously approaching on Tony's back.

Soon he reached the forking roads, and saw the dairyman by the wayside. But Jim did not halt. Then the dairyman practised the greatest duplicity of his life.

'Right along the London road, if you want to catch 'em!' he said.

'Thank 'ee, dairyman, thank 'ee!' cried Jim, his pale face lighting up with gratitude, for he believed that Tucker had learnt his mistake from Vine, and had come to his assistance. Without drawing rein he diminished along the road not taken by the flying pair. The dairyman rubbed his hands with delight, and returned to the city as the cathedral clock struck five.

Jim pursued his way through the dust, up hill and down hill; but never saw ahead of him the vehicle of his search. That vehicle was passing along a diverging way at a distance of many miles from where he rode. Still he sped onwards, till Tony showed signs of breaking down; and then Jim gathered from inquiries he made that he had come the wrong way. It burst upon his mind that the dairyman, still ignorant of the truth, had misinformed him. Heavier in his heart than words can describe he turned Tony's drooping head, and resolved to drag his way home.

But the horse was now so jaded that it was impossible to proceed far. Having gone about half a mile back he came again to a small roadside hamlet and inn, where he put up Tony for a rest and feed. As for himself, there was no quiet in him. He tried to sit and eat in the inn kitchen; but he could not stay there. He went out, and paced up and down the road.

Standing in sight of the white way by which he had come he beheld advancing towards him the horses and carriage he sought, now black and dæmonic against the slanting fires of the western sun.

The why and wherefore of this sudden appearance he did not pause to consider. His resolve to intercept the carriage was instantaneous. He ran forward, and doggedly waiting barred the way to the advancing equipage.

The Baron's coachman shouted, but Jim stood firm as a rock, and on the former attempting to push past him Jim drew his sword, resolving to cut the horses down rather than be displaced. The animals were thrown nearly back upon their haunches, and at this juncture a gentleman looked out of the window. It was the Baron himself.

'Who's there?' he inquired.

'James Hayward!' replied the young man fiercely, 'and he demands his wife.'

The Baron leapt out, and told the coachman to drive back out of sight and wait for him.

'I was hastening to find you,' he said to Jim. 'Your wife is where she ought to be, and where you ought to be also – by your own fireside. Where's the other woman?'

Jim, without replying, looked incredulously into the carriage as it turned. Margery was certainly not there. 'The other woman is nothing to me,' he said bitterly. 'I used her to warm up Margery: I have now done with her. The question I ask, my lord, is, what business had you with Margery to-day?'

'My business was to help her to regain the husband she had seemingly lost. I saw her; she told me you had eloped by the London road with another. I, who have – mostly – had her happiness at heart, told her I would help her to follow you if she wished. She gladly agreed; we drove after, but could hear no tidings of you in front of us. Then I took her – to your house – and there she awaits you. I promised to send you to her if human effort could do it, and was tracking you for that purpose.'

'Then you've been a-pursuing after me?'

'You and the widow.'

'And I've been pursuing after you and Margery!... My noble lord, your actions seem to show that I ought to believe you in this; and when you say you've her happiness at heart, I don't forget that you've formerly proved it to be so. Well, Heaven forbid that I should think wrongfully of you if you don't deserve it! A mystery to me you have always been, my noble lord, and in this business more than in any.'

'I am glad to hear you say no worse. In one hour you'll have proof of my conduct – good and bad. Can I do anything more? Say the word, and I'll try.'

Jim reflected. 'Baron,' he said, 'I am a plain man, and wish only to lead a quiet life with my wife, as a man should. You have great power over her – power to any extent, for good or otherwise. If you command her anything on earth, righteous or questionable, that she'll do. So that, since you ask me if you can do more for me, I'll answer this, you can promise never to see her again. I mean no harm, my lord; but your presence can do no good; you will trouble us. If I return to her, will you for ever stay away?'

'Hayward,' said the Baron, 'I swear to you that I will disturb you and your wife by my presence no more.' And he took Jim's hand, and pressed it within his own upon the hilt of Jim's sword.

In relating this incident to the present narrator Jim used to declare that, to his fancy, the ruddy light of the setting sun burned with more than earthly fire on the Baron's face as the words were spoken; and that the ruby flash of his eye in the same light was what he never witnessed before nor since in the eye of mortal man. After this there was nothing more to do or say in that place. Jim accompanied his never-to-be-forgotten acquaintance to the carriage, closed the door after him, waved his hat to him, and from that hour he and the Baron met not again on earth.

A few words will suffice to explain the fortunes of Margery while the foregoing events were in action elsewhere. On leaving her companion Vine she had gone distractedly among the carriages, the rather to escape his observation than of any set purpose. Standing here she thought she heard her name pronounced, and turning, saw her foreign friend, whom she had supposed to be, if not dead, a thousand miles off. He beckoned, and she went close. 'You are ill – you are wretched,' he said, looking keenly in her face. 'Where's your husband?'

She told him her sad suspicion that Jim had run away from her. The Baron reflected, and inquired a few other particulars of her late life. Then he said, 'You and I must find him. Come with me.' At this word of command from the Baron she had entered the carriage as docilely as a child, and there she sat beside him till he chose to speak, which was not till they were some way out of the town, at the forking ways, and the Baron had discovered that Jim was certainly not, as they had supposed, making off from Margery along that particular branch of the fork that led to London.

'To pursue him in this way is useless, I perceive,' he said. 'And the proper course now is that I should take you to his house. That done I will return, and bring him to you if mortal persuasion can do it.'

'I didn't want to go to his house without him, sir,' said she, tremblingly.

'Didn't want to!' he answered. 'Let me remind you, Margery Hayward, that your place is in your husband's house. Till you are there you have no right to criticize his conduct, however wild it may be. Why have you not been there before?'

'I don't know, sir,' she murmured, her tears falling silently upon her hand.

'Don't you think you ought to be there?'

She did not answer.

'Of course you ought.'

Still she did not speak.

The Baron sank into silence, and allowed his eye to rest on her. What thoughts were all at once engaging his mind after those moments of reproof? Margery had given herself into his hands without a remonstrance. Her husband had apparently deserted her. She was absolutely in his power, and they were on the high road.

That his first impulse in inviting her to accompany him had been the legitimate one denoted by his words cannot reasonably be doubted. That his second was otherwise soon became revealed, though not at first to her, for she was too bewildered to notice where they were going. Instead of turning and taking the road to Jim's, the Baron, as if influenced suddenly by her reluctance to return thither if Jim was playing truant, signalled to the coachman to take the branch road to the right, as her father had discerned.

They soon approached the coast near Idmouth. The carriage stopped. Margery awoke from her reverie.

'Where are we?' she said, looking out of the window, with a start. Before her was an inlet of the sea, and in the middle of the inlet rode a yacht, its masts repeating as if from memory the rocking they had practised in their native forest.

'At a little sea-side nook, where my yacht lies at anchor,' he said tentatively. 'Now, Margery, in five minutes we can be aboard, and in half-an-hour we can be sailing away all the world over. Will you come?'

'I cannot decide,' she said, in low tones.

'Why not?'

'Because—'

Then on a sudden Margery seemed to see all contingencies: she became white as a fleece, and a bewildered look came into her eyes. With clasped hands she leant on the Baron.

Baron von Xanten observed her distracted look, averted his face, and coming to a decision opened the carriage door, quickly mounted outside, and in a second or two the carriage left the shore behind, and ascended the road by which it had come.

In about an hour they reached Jim Hayward's home. The Baron alighted, and spoke to her through the window. 'Margery, can you forgive a lover's bad impulse, which I swear was unpremeditated?' he asked. 'If you can, shake my hand.'

She did not do it, but eventually allowed him to help her out of the carriage. He seemed to feel the awkwardness keenly; and seeing it, she said, 'Of course I forgive you, sir, for I felt for a moment as you did. Will you send my husband to me?'

'I will, if any man can,' said he. 'Such penance is milder than I deserve! God bless you and give you happiness! I shall never see you again!' He turned, entered the carriage, and was gone; and having found out Jim's course, came up with him upon the road as described.

In due time the latter reached his lodging at his partner's. The woman

who took care of the house in Vine's absence at once told Jim that a lady
who had come in a carriage was waiting for him in his sitting-room. Jim
proceeded thither with agitation, and beheld, shrinkingly ensconced in
the large slippery chair, and surrounded by the brilliant articles that
had so long awaited her, his long-estranged wife.

Margery's eyes were round and fear-stricken. She essayed to speak,
but Jim, strangely enough, found the readier tongue then. 'Why did I
do it, you would ask,' he said. 'I cannot tell. Do you forgive my deception? O Margery – you are my Margery still! But how could you trust
yourself in the Baron's hands this afternoon, without knowing him
better?'

'He said I was to come, and I went,' she said, as well as she could for
tearfulness.

'You obeyed him blindly.'

'I did. But perhaps I was not justified in doing it.'

'I don't know,' said Jim musingly. 'I think he's a good man.' Margery
did not explain. And then a sunnier mood succeeded her tremblings and
tears, till old Mr Vine came into the house below, and Jim went down to
declare that all was well, and sent off his partner to break the news to
Margery's father, who as yet remained unenlightened.

The dairyman bore the intelligence of his daughter's untitled state
as best he could, and punished her by not coming near her for several
weeks, though at last he grumbled his forgiveness, and made up matters
with Jim. The handsome Mrs Peach vanished to Plymouth, and found
another sailor, not without a reasonable complaint against Jim and
Margery both that she had been unfairly used.

As for the mysterious gentleman who had exercised such an influence
over their lives, he kept his word, and was a stranger to Lower Wessex
thenceforward. Baron or no Baron, Englishman or foreigner, he had
shown a genuine interest in Jim, and real sorrow for a certain reckless
phase of his acquaintance with Margery. That he had a more tender
feeling toward the young girl than he wished her or anyone else to
perceive there could be no doubt. That he was strongly tempted at
times to adopt other than conventional courses with regard to her is also
clear, particularly at that critical hour when she rolled along the high
road with him in the carriage, after turning from the fancied pursuit of
Jim. But at other times he schooled impassioned sentiments into fair
conduct, which even erred on the side of harshness. In after years there
was a report that another attempt on his life with a pistol, during one

of those fits of moodiness to which he seemed constitutionally liable, had been effectual; but nobody in Silverthorn was in a position to ascertain the truth.

There he is still regarded as one who had something about him magical and unearthly. In his mystery let him remain; for a man, no less than a landscape, who awakens an interest under uncertain lights and touches of unfathomable shade, may cut but a poor figure in a garish noontide shine.

When she heard of his mournful death Margery sat in her nursing-chair, gravely thinking for nearly ten minutes, to the total neglect of her infant in the cradle. Jim, from the other side of the fireplace, said, 'You are sorry enough for him, Margery. I am sure of that.'

'Yes, yes,' she murmured, 'I am sorry.' After a moment she added: 'Now that he's dead I'll make a confession, Jim, that I have never made to a soul. If he had pressed me – which he did not – to go with him when I was in the carriage that night beside his yacht, I would have gone. And I was disappointed that he did not press me.'

'Suppose he were to suddenly appear now, and say in a voice of command, "Margery, come with me!" '

'I believe I should have no power to disobey,' she returned, with a mischievous look. 'He was like a magician to me. I think he was one. He could move me as a loadstone moves a speck of steel. . . . Yet no,' she added, hearing the infant cry, 'he would not move me now. It would be so unfair to baby.'

'Well,' said Jim, with no great concern (for '*la jalousie rétrospective*', as George Sand calls it, had nearly died out of him), 'however he might move 'ee, my love, he'll never come. He swore it to me: and he was a man of his word.'

Midsummer 1883

Notes

Life's Little Ironies

The stories fall into two major groups: those which are more obviously 'Wessex' tales ('The Fiddler of the Reels' and 'A Few Crusted Characters'); and nearly all the remainder, which reflect a serious side of the mature Hardy, using fiction to convey by imaginative illustration criticisms of contemporary life, particularly of the appraisal of people not by intrinsic worth but by differences of class, wealth, and respectability. The reason given by Hardy in his preface for including 'An Imaginative Woman' in this volume does not relate to *Life's Little Ironies* as a whole. Resemblances depending on 'vivid imaginings' and tricks of Nature may be seen in some of the stories, but not in all, even when 'A Few Crusted Characters' is regarded as supplementary.

An Imaginative Woman. Hardy's first version of the story was inspired by contemporary psychological views on a possible transference of physical traits through 'vivid imaginings' when conception takes place. Such a 'trick of Nature' has not been substantiated (nor is it consistent with 'Squire Petrick's Lady'), and the story illustrates the dangers inherent in *avant-garde* fiction based on the latest 'scientific' theories. It was 'found and touched up' in December 1893,[1] but it would never have taken its present form had Hardy not fallen imaginatively in love with Mrs Henniker soon after meeting her the previous May. The setting is Southsea, where Hardy visited the Hennikers. She was a writer; her husband was an army officer who did not read poetry but spent most of his spare time in sporting activities. Hardy and Mrs Henniker were both admirers of Shelley's poetry. The story reverses the situation in which the author found himself: as the poet lived in the vivid imaginings of the heroine, so the idealised Mrs Henniker became for Hardy the original of those qualities in Sue Bridehead that made her 'the sweetest and most disinterested comrade that [Jude] had ever had, living largely in vivid imaginings'.[2]

The Son's Veto. Hardy told Rebekah Owen in 1896 that this was his best short story. Consistently the emphasis is on the heartlessness of the class

[1] F. E. Hardy, *The Life of Thomas Hardy, 1840–1928* (1962), p. 260.
[2] *One Rare Fair Woman: Thomas Hardy's Letters to Florence Henniker, 1893–1922*, ed. E. Hardy and F. B. Pinion (1972), second preface.

system and convention. For the description of the market carts on their way to Covent Garden, compare Hardy's note of 7 July 1888 (*Life*, p. 210). It is his map of Wessex which indicates Theale for 'Gaymead'; whether he knew the village or not is uncertain.

For Conscience' Sake. Again the story hinges on class distinction ('it would be beneath my position to marry her') and appearances. His daughter's prospects would have been better had Mr Millborne not made the *amende honorable*. For the facial effect of sea-sickness on which the story turns, see Hardy's note of 2 January 1886 (*Life*, p. 177), and compare the adverse use to which he puts the facial effect of sleep in *The Mayor of Casterbridge*, ch. 19.

A Tragedy of Two Ambitions. This earlier story has the same theme, though the emphasis is on ambition. For the third time the Church is implicated, and Hardy's satire on the priority of the qualifications for priesthood (p. 69) should be taken at its face value; it did not appear in the magazine version. The passage on the grown walking-stick was added when the story was revised for inclusion in *Life's Little Ironies*. Blanching as the wind turns its leaves, it seems to look before and after, a living reminder of death. Whether the priest of 'The Son's Veto' learned wisdom from error is not told. Here the lesson is made explicit: 'To have endured . . . despising the shame – there lay greatness!' Soon after its first appearance, Edmund Gosse wrote to tell Hardy that this was one of his 'most thrilling and most complete stories . . . "I walked under the moral burden of it for the remainder of the day" ' (*Life*, p. 215).

On the Western Circuit. Of the stories in *Life's Little Ironies*, this was Florence Hardy's favourite. The hero's ambition is baulked considerably as a result of his folly, but the main interest is psychological. He wins a beautiful girl 'soul and body', only to find after their marriage that through correspondence (with her, he thought) he was married 'in soul and spirit' to another. There is a clear parallel in 'An Imaginative Woman', but here the tragic ending results from the 'vivid imaginings' of two people. The magazine version was completely bowdlerised. 'On the Western Circuit' provided the plot for *The Day after the Fair*, a full-length play which enjoyed a very successful run in London in recent years. The names of Hardy's characters sometimes originate from places in or near the settings; Harnham Bridge is on the main road into Salisbury from Dorchester, not far from Harnham village.

To Please His Wife. This may be one of the most moving of Hardy's short stories. It is a tale of a mother's love, warped by envy and social ambition until it destroys her soul and family. Another version of the ending is to be found in Hardy's poem 'The Sailor's Mother'.

The Fiddler of the Reels. Very Wessex in character, it supplies a transition between stories charged with criticism of contemporary society and the older localised tales which are related in 'A Few Crusted Characters'. Its subject, the almost preternaturally seductive power of dance-music in the hands of a cunning fiddler, recurs in Hardy's poetry. The topographical detail relating to Bloom's-End and the Quiet Woman is exact, unlike that of *The Return of the Native.* The story was written for the Exhibition number of *Scribner's Magazine* published in May 1893 to mark the Chicago World Fair; hence the opening lines, links with the Great Exhibition of 1851, and, incidentally, Hardy's recollection of the earliest passenger-trains he saw.

A Few Crusted Characters. The narrative device for assembling these tales (originally entitled 'Wessex Folk') is an interesting variant of that employed by Chaucer in *The Canterbury Tales.* Both are contemporary; Hardy's is local and more related to his stories. The significance of the name 'John Lackland' (suggested perhaps by White Lackington in 'Longpuddle') is made plain at the end. The plight of agricultural labourers in Dorset was such that many emigrated; the experience of a 'Lackland' on his return may have come to Hardy's notice. It is significant that this minor work, almost certainly written when the modification of *Tess of the d'Urbervilles* for serial purposes was completed, contains some of Hardy's most amusing stories.

I. 'Tony Kytes, the Arch-Deceiver'. The song he sang in the magazine version was much more respectable than 'The Tailor's Breeches'. As will be seen later, the carrier must, after leaving Dorchester by the eastern road, have turned along a minor road north of the town, probably calling at Charminster before joining the old Bristol coach-road; soon afterwards he turned off to Piddlehinton. It was on the corner before the descent to the village that the waggon accident occurred.

II. 'The History of the Hardcomes'. Hardy found death by water a useful expedient in three short stories. For the amatory power of music and dance, compare *The Return of the Native.* bk IV, ch. 3, where Clym Yeobright's wife Eustacia meets her former lover Wildeve at a village 'picnic' or 'gipsying'.

III. 'The Superstitious Man's Story'. Like some of his poems, this is a testimony to Hardy's wish – in the words of the general preface to his novels and poems – 'to preserve for my own satisfaction a fairly true record of a vanishing life'. Some of the most important superstitions in his novels are connected with Midsummer Eve, as here. Hardy's poem 'Premonitions' relates to this story. In a letter of 20 May 1924 he stated that the miller-moth incident took place at Buttock's Spring in the parish of Melbury Osmond (the site is mentioned in 'The Duke's Reappearance'). 'The old lady who told it me said it happened in her childhood, and that would be about 1820.' From this and other evidence it will be seen that some of the stories in 'A Few Crusted Characters' did not originate in the 'Longpuddle' area.

IV. 'Andrey Satchel and the Parson and Clerk'. Had Hardy lived in a broader-minded age and enjoyed a happier marriage, he might have indulged his humour more freely in fiction, as he does here, and as he often did in his earlier work. The original of Parson Toogood was the Rev. William Butler, a friend of the Prince Regent. He became vicar of Frampton in 1800. In his first preface to *Life's Little Ironies* Hardy described him as 'that truly delightful personage as he entirely was. . . . He had several imitators in his composite calling of sportsman and divine, but no rival.' It is a pity that Hardy did not find time to write the story 'of the bishop's descent one day upon the parsonage to convict Toogood of absenteeism, the latter's breakneck ride across country from a cocking party in consequence, and his breathless entry by his back door just in time to open his front to his visitor, whom he meekly received with ˄ quill behind his ear, and a sermon outspread'. The 'turnpike-road' which the hunters crossed is the old Bristol coach-road (already referred to) running north from Dorchester. The story appeared in a slightly chastened form in *Harper's New Monthly Magazine*, with 'Climmerston' for 'Waterston'.

V. 'Old Andrey's Experience as a Musician'. Where this story originated is not known, but it is possibly from a story told by Hardy's father about the Stinsford choir's Christmas supper at Kingston Maurward ('the manor-house'; compare Hardy's preface to *Under the Greenwood Tree*).

VI. 'Absent-Mindedness in a Parish Choir'. There was a gallery at Piddletrenthide, but no trace of Hardy's interest in its choir has been found. The instruments suggest Puddletown (see *Life*, p. 125, and the last page or two of *Far from the Madding Crowd*), where Hardy's grandfather played the violoncello in the church choir before his marriage (*Life*, p. 8). There was much indignation in Puddletown when the wind and string players were discarded for a barrel-organ in 1845. Yet, however much happenings in a village may have contributed to it, the story seems to be largely the delightful result of an inspiring fancy.

VII. 'The Winters and the Palmleys'. For 'the lane that connects that end of the village with this turnpike-road', see the introductory note on the route taken by the carrier. The manuscript, however, shows that the story originated in the Melbury Osmond region; Hardy may have heard it from his mother. The noise of the waggon bearing the coffin was heard from the direction of Holway Lane; Harriet and her husband could not continue to live at 'King's Hintock' and removed to 'Lewgate'. The story of the youth who was so light that heavy fetters were necessary to hang him was told by Hardy's father; the circumstances of his arrest were those given in 'The Withered Arm'. A simplified version of the main story is told in *Jude the Obscure* (bk v, ch. 4) with reference to the tradition that one of the Fawley family was gibbeted on Brown House Hill.

VIII. 'Incident in the Life of Mr George Crookhill'. Bissett Hill is beyond Coombe Bissett on the road from Salisbury to Blandford Forum. Woodyates (now demolished) was a coach-inn where George III stayed when travelling to or from Weymouth. The 'Trantridge' of the story is not the same as the 'Trantridge' of *Tess of the d'Urbervilles*. The main features of the narrative were taken from events reported in the *Dorset County Chronicle* on 2 April 1829.

IX. 'Netty Sargent's Copyhold'. The view of Lackland's informants 'that the remarkable was better worth telling than the ordinary' coincided with Hardy's (see *Life*, p. 252). The story depends on the 'livier' or life-holder system of tenure, whereby a house (sometimes built by the occupier) was leased by the landholder for three lives or generations. The lease was renewable by agreement, but families were often evicted as a result of the landowners' refusal to extend such leases when householders of the third generation died. The 're-liveing' is the renewal of such a contract. (This explanation refers to normal practice only.)

With the conclusion of the framework narrative, compare Hardy's poem 'Welcome Home'.

BIBLIOGRAPHICAL NOTE

The first edition of *Life's Little Ironies* appeared in February 1894. The interchange of stories to which Hardy refers in his preface was made for the Wessex Edition of 1912.

Of the stories included, all but one were written after Hardy had completed most of his work on *Tess of the d'Urbervilles*. The dates appended usually indicate when the stories were first published; that for 'On the Western Circuit' may indicate when it was written, as does that for 'An Imaginative Woman'. Their composition dates and probable chronological order are as follows:

A Tragedy of Two Ambitions	July–August 1888
A Few Crusted Characters	1890–1
For Conscience' Sake	1891
To Please His Wife	1891
On the Western Circuit	1891
The Son's Veto	1891
The Fiddler of the Reels	December–January 1892–3
An Imaginative Woman	(Revised) December 1893

'A Few Crusted Characters' appeared as 'Wessex Folk' in *Harper's New Monthly Magazine*; 'The Fiddler of the Reels' was posted to Messrs Scribner, New York, on 13 January 1893; and 'An Imaginative Woman' was first published in the *Pall Mall Magazine* for April 1894.

Manuscripts of four of the stories were presented as follows in 1911: 'An Imaginative Woman', Aberdeen University Library; 'For Conscience' Sake', Manchester University Library; 'A Tragedy of Two Ambitions', the John Rylands Library, Manchester; and 'On the Western Circuit', Manchester Central Library. That of 'The Son's Veto' is in the Bodmer Collection, Switzerland; and a rough and incomplete draft of 'A Few Crusted Characters' (with the original title 'Wessex Folk') is part of the Berg Collection at the New York Public Library.

A Changed Man

A Changed Man. Hardy's view that this was the best story in the volume owes something no doubt to its local and personal associations. It is an indirect tribute to the splendid work done by his friend Horace Moule's father in his parish during the cholera outbreaks of 1849 and 1854 (see *Life*, p. 391).

The Waiting Supper. Without any trace of the sentimental, this earlier story combines sadness and sensationalism in a style peculiarly characteristic of Hardy. Both aspects may be felt in the 'sarcastic hiss' of the waterfall whose 'rush' becomes 'a material rendering of Time's ceaseless scour' over the hero and heroine, 'wearing them away without uniting them'. The theme shows the influence of Browning's 'The Statue and the Bust' (*Men and Women*, 1855). It is strange that Hardy never realised the anachronism of making his heroine quote from this poem fifty years before his story was published. According to an old superstition, the falling clock betokened death in the family.

At the revision stage, Hardy's most important change produced greater tension with the arrival of the portmanteau instead of the reappearance of the husband. Originally the 'Froom' had been the 'Swenn', and 'Athelhall' 'Eldhampton'. Hutchins[1] shows that the house had been known as 'Frome Everard': Hardy's interest in the original, Stafford House, began with the restoration work in which his father participated for the architect Benjamin Ferrey in 1848–50 (see *Life*, pp. 35–6). The situation at the end is the subject of Hardy's poem 'Long Plighted', which opens with the closing question of the story, 'Is it worth while. . .?'

Alicia's Diary. This is Hardy's only experiment with the diary form in fiction. The details for the Italian scenes were drawn from the Hardys' holiday in Italy earlier in the year (1887) when the story was written. They also had stayed at 'the hotel on the Riva degli Schiavoni'. The 'Wherryborne' meadows and hatches recall the Frome valley.

The Grave by the Handpost. Hardy has a number of Christmas stories in verse and prose (several associated with members of the Mellstock choir). They rarely provide the festive cheer we associate with Dickens. This story is not without its fascination, but it is probably the most depressing of them. Suicides link it with 'Alicia's Diary'. It is based on a story remembered by Hardy's mother from her childhood, of a girl who committed suicide. Her body was buried at crossroads on Hendford Hill (cf. 'A Tragedy of Two Ambitions', p. 77) and a stake driven through it.

[1] John Hutchins, *The History and Antiquities of the County of Dorset*, 3rd ed. (1861–73).

Enter a Dragoon. One must not expect the last prose story Hardy wrote to show any technical advance. It is an honest piece of work for a magazine, but done rather perfunctorily, in late fulfilment of a promise, at a time when he was dedicated to poetry. For the setting he returned to Higher Bockhampton. He remembered 'the house by the well' for its Christmas celebrations before it was divided into two cottages (see his poem 'The House of Hospitalities').

A Tryst at an Ancient Earthwork. The narrative is slight, but the description of Maiden Castle (two miles south-west of Dorchester) is impressive and indicative of one of Hardy's interests as a member of the Dorset Natural History and Antiquarian Field Club. The article first appeared in the *Detroit Post*. When it was published with photographs more than eight years later in the *Illustrated London News* (December 1893), he was anxious because 'a character who appears in the narrative may be said to be drawn from a local man, still living, though it is really meant for nobody in particular'.

What the Shepherd Saw. This, like 'The Honourable Laura' in *A Group of Noble Dames*, was written for a Christmas number in 1881. Following the Dickens tradition, it supplies a touch of the supernatural at the end. The trilithon may be seen a few miles west of Marlborough. To the north of the town are two 'Ogbourne' villages. In the Christmas number the trilithon scenes are on 'Verncombe Down' south-west of Salisbury. From the surname of the unfortunate Fred, it may be assumed to be not far distant from Pentridge; and Vernditch Chase will be found to the north of this parish.

A Committee-Man of 'the Terror'. On page 94 of *The Journal of Mary Frampton* (edited by her niece H. G. Mundy and published in London in 1885) Hardy read:

> One of the Directory was seen a few days ago in the Strand, and was recognized by a French lady whose father, mother, and brother he had murdered. She fainted away in the street, and before she recovered enough to speak he had escaped in the crowd.

This must have been the germ of the story, as R. L. Purdy suggested.

Master John Horseleigh, Knight. Sir John Horsey's home was Clifton Maybank, a fifteenth-century building (of which little remains) near Yeovil. Its description and the discrepancy in his marriage records were found in Hutchins, vol. I, p. 50, and vol. IV, pp. 426–9. The story seems to have been planned for *A Group of Noble Dames*, as is confirmed by the opening.

The Duke's Reappearance. The tradition that the Duke of Monmouth took refuge in the house of the Swetmans, ancestors of Hardy on his mother's side (*Life*, p. 6) seems rather dubious, irrespective of the supernatural ending. Whether the latter was 'traditional' or Hardy's invention is uncertain. In 1685, on the death of Charles II, the Duke claimed the throne but was defeated at Sedgemoor in Somerset. He fled in disguise but was captured at Horton in east Dorset and beheaded on Tower Hill, London. The local tradition of his betrayal forms the subject of Hardy's poem 'At Shag's Heath'.

A Mere Interlude. How a young woman spent her first bridal night between two husbands, one dead, the other living, seems to be the startling idea around which the story was created. As is Hardy's custom, everything is explained (even Baptista's inability to see when Charles is in danger) to show that what may seem improbable is made possible by chance. Tragedy turns to comedy, then to an unromantic ending, in a very different key from the main theme of the story.

The Romantic Adventures of a Milkmaid. Hardy described this strange blending of realism and fantasy as 'a short hastily written novel' (*Life*, p. 158). It suggests a fairy tale for adults. Margery Tucker may be regarded as a Cinderella whose wish to attend a magnificent ball is granted. The story, however, is a peculiar expression of the psychological, possibly influenced by some of Nathaniel Hawthorne's quaint allegories. The Baron is one of Hardy's 'Mephistophelian visitants', a symbol of temptation. The Mephistophelian (and Satanic) elements in Hardy's fiction are associated with fire and smoke, and particularly denoted by a glowing cigar.

Yet the Baron is a gentleman; he is sick and dying and at one point suggests Tennyson's King Arthur in Victorian dress. With prospects of the dance, he seems to revive; his horses and the musicians belong to a preternatural world. When the dance is over he remains as 'immovable as Rhadamanthus' in his determination not to give way again. When he hears that Margery is engaged, he wishes he had not endangered her happiness. He supplies her with splendid furniture and articles of silver and gold, in the hope that they will reconcile her to marriage with the lime-burner Jim Hayward. But the Baron represents the world of her dreams, and he finds her more 'a heavenly messenger than a milkmaid'. When he feels lovelorn in his depression, she sacrifices her wedding to be with him. Hearing this, he is appalled and employs subterfuge to ensure that Jim and she are married. Her worldly romanticism is not wholly dead, however.

The main weakness of the story is the over-elaboration employed to bring about a satisfactory conclusion for Victorian magazine-readers. 'The ending originally sketched was a different one, Margery, instead of returning to Jim, disappearing with the Baron in his yacht at Idmouth after his final proposal to her, and being no more heard of in England.'

This unpublished note by Hardy is not quite correct, for the original story was set in Dorset and transferred to Devon, probably to ensure that the world of the romantic milkmaid was not associated with that of the tragic dairymaid in *Tess of the d'Urbervilles*, an important part of which is set in the 'Froom' valley. This is identical with the 'Swenn' valley in which 'The Romantic Adventures of a Milkmaid' was set originally, its main event taking place in the neighbourhood of 'Stickleford' and, with the Yeomanry Ball and Review, just outside 'Casterbridge'.

BIBLIOGRAPHICAL NOTE

A Changed Man, consisting of twelve stories which had appeared in magazines or weekly newspapers from 1881 to 1900, was first published in October 1913. Hardy told his friend Sir George Douglas (with some exaggeration, no doubt) that he 'heartily' wished he could 'snuff out several of them', but his hand was forced by the import of pirated editions from America. Their collection was also encouraged by readers' requests. Dates of composition seem to be as follows:

What the Shepherd Saw	1881
The Romantic Adventures of a Milkmaid	1882–3
A Tryst at an Ancient Earthwork	1884–5
A Mere Interlude	1885
Alicia's Diary	1887
The Waiting Supper	1887
Master John Horseleigh, Knight	1893
A Committee-Man of 'the Terror'	1896
The Duke's Reappearance	1896
The Grave by the Handpost	1897
A Changed Man	1900
Enter a Dragoon	1900

The last five stories belong to a period when novel-writing for Hardy was over; but for the existence of outstanding contracts or agreements, they would never have been written.

The dates given by Hardy to his stories usually indicate when they were first published. 'Autumn 1887', 'Spring 1893' and '1895' may show when 'The Waiting Supper', 'Master John Horseleigh, Knight', and 'A Committee-Man of "the Terror"' were written. The date for 'Enter a Dragoon' should read 'December 1900'.

The manuscripts of 'A Changed Man' and 'A Committee-Man of "the Terror"' are in the Berg Collection. Those of 'A Tryst at an Ancient Earthwork', 'Master John Horseleigh, Knight', and 'The Duke's Reappearance' belong to the University of Texas, Austin. That of 'The

Romantic Adventures of a Milkmaid' is in the Pierpont Morgan Library, New York. The manuscript of 'What the Shepherd Saw' was sold in London in 1955 and remains untraced. That of 'The Grave by the Handpost', when last traced, was the property of Halsted B. Vander-Poel, Rome.

Glossary of Dialect Words

'a he, she
bain't are not
barton farmyard
bobbin cord and attachment fastened to the latch (for opening a door)
croud fiddle
cust cussed, damned
dang damn
daze damn
drawlacheting lazy, useless
dree three
drough through
'ee you
en him
fall autumn
farrel book cover or binding
flick-flack thoughtless talk
footy mean
gaffer old man
gi'd given
goodman husband
gwine going
heft weight
hev have
hit take a short cut
home-along on the way home
hurdle-saul stake for fixing a hurdle
idden isn't
jine up join up, marry
jown damn
larry lark, joke
leery hungry
list please
mid may, might
miff tiff, quarrel

modden mustn't
nunch lunch
nunnywatch predicament
over-right directly opposite
rackety noisy
raft upset
randy party
rathe-ripes early-ripening apples
rawmil' made from unskimmed ('raw') milk
rendlewood oak stripped of its bark
rithe fast
sappy simpleton
seed saw
shrammed frozen, stiff with cold
slummocky dirty, slovenly
stand-to stubborn
tacker-haired with black wiry hair
teave get worked up or agitated
three-cunning knowing, sly
tole entice
topper something hard to beat
totties feet
trimming great
twyte reproach
vell trace
vew few
volk folk
wambling unsteady
wisht sad
withy willow
withywind bindweed
wold old
wool will
wot knows
zummat something

Glossary of Place-Names

N.B. (1) Identifications which are provided in the Notes are not included below. (2) Locations of smaller places are given in mileage and direction with reference to well-known places or to Wessex places. The latter may require a second reference, e.g. *Elsenford* is Ilsington, a mile and a half south of *Weatherbury*, i.e. Puddletown (which is located).

ABBOT'S-CERNEL. Cerne Abbas, 7N Dorchester.
ALDBRICKHAM. Reading.
ANGLEBURY. Wareham.
ATHELHALL. Athelhampton, near *Weatherbury*.
BROAD SIDLINCH. Sydling St Nicholas, 3SW *Abbot's-Cernel*.
BUDMOUTH-REGIS. Weymouth.
CASTERBRIDGE. Dorchester.
CHALK-NEWTON. Maiden Newton, 7½NW Dorchester.
CLIMMERSTON. Higher Waterston, 4½NNE Dorchester.
CRESTON. Preston, 3NE Weymouth.
DURNOVER. Fordington, on the south-east side of Dorchester.
EGDON (HEATH). Puddletown Heath and eastward, north of the Frome valley.
ELSENFORD. Ilsington, 1½S *Weatherbury*.
EVERSHEAD. Evershot, 6WNW *Abbot's-Cernel*.
EXONBURY. Exeter.
FOUNTALL. Wells, Somerset.
FROOM-EVERARD. West Stafford, 4ESE Dorchester.
GIANT'S TOWN. Hugh Town, St Mary's, Scilly Isles.
GREAT PLAIN, THE. Salisbury Plain.
GREENHILL. ½E Bere Regis, 10ENE Dorchester.
HAVENPOOL. Poole.
HIGHER JIRTON. Higher Forston, 4N Dorchester.
IDMOUTH. Sidmouth.
IVELL. Yeovil.
KING'S HINTOCK. Melbury Osmond, 7NW *Abbot's-Cernel*.
KING'S HINTOCK COURT. Melbury House, 1S *King's Hintock*.
KNOLLSEA. Swanage.
LEWGATE. Higher Bockhampton, 2ENE Dorchester.
LONGPUDDLE. Piddlehinton, 3NW *Weatherbury*, and Piddletrenthide, 2NNW Piddlehinton.

LULWIND. Lulworth Cove.
LYONESSE, ISLES OF. Scilly Isles.
MARLBURY DOWNS. Marlborough Downs.
MELCHESTER. Salisbury.
MELCHESTER, OLD. Old Sarum, 2N Salisbury.
MELLSTOCK. Stinsford (1ENE Dorchester) and the Bockhamptons.
MELLSTOCK, LOWER. Lower Bockhampton, 1S *Lewgate*.
MONKSBURY. Probably Abbotsbury, 7NW Weymouth.
MONTISLOPE. Montacute, 4W Yeovil.
MOREFORD. Moreton, 7E Dorchester.
NARROBOURNE. East or West Coker, 2–3SW Yeovil.
OOZEWOOD. Ringwood, Hampshire.
PEN-ZEPHYR. Penzance.
PORT-BREDY. Bridport.
REDRUTIN. Redruth, Cornwall.
ROY-TOWN. Troy Town, 3½NE Dorchester.
SANDBOURNE. Bournemouth.
SCRIMPTON. Frampton, 5NW Dorchester.
SHERTON (ABBAS). Sherborne.
SHOTTSFORD-FORUM. Blandford Forum.
SILVERTHORN. Silverton, in the Exe valley, Devon.
SOLENTSEA. Southsea.
STICKLEFORD. Tincleton, 1½SSE *Weatherbury*.
TIVWORTHY. Tiverton, Devon.
TONEBOROUGH. Taunton.
TOR-UPON-SEA. Torquay.
TRUFAL. Truro.
WEATHERBURY. Puddletown, 4½NE Dorchester.
YALBURY WOOD. Yellowhampton Wood, 3NE Dorchester.

trodden, beheld a crouching object beside a newly-made grave. She heard him, and sprang up.

'Ell, how silly this is!' he said indignantly. 'Running away from home – I never heard such a thing! Of course I am not jealous of this unfortunate man; but it is too ridiculous that you, a married woman with three children and a fourth coming, should go losing your head like this over a dead lover! . . . Do you know you were locked in ? You might not have been able to get out all night.'

She did not answer.

'I hope it didn't go far between you and him, for your own sake.'

'Don't insult me, Will.'

'Mind, I won't have any more of this sort of thing; do you hear ?'

'Very well,' she said.

He drew her arm within his own, and conducted her out of the Cemetery. It was impossible to get back that night; and not wishing to be recognized in their present sorry condition he took her to a miserable little coffee-house close to the station, whence they departed early in the morning, travelling almost without speaking, under the sense that it was one of those dreary situations occurring in married life which words could not mend, and reaching their own door at noon.

The months passed, and neither of the twain ever ventured to start a conversation upon this episode. Ella seemed to be only too frequently in a sad and listless mood, which might almost have been called pining. The time was approaching when she would have to undergo the stress of childbirth for a fourth time, and that apparently did not tend to raise her spirits.

'I don't think I shall get over it this time!' she said one day.

'Pooh! what childish foreboding! Why shouldn't it be as well now as ever ?'

She shook her head. 'I feel almost sure I am going to die; and I should be glad, if it were not for Nelly, and Frank, and Tiny.'

'And me!'

'You'll soon find somebody to fill my place,' she murmured, with a sad smile. 'And you'll have a perfect right to; I assure you of that.'

'Ell, you are not thinking still about that – poetical friend of yours ?'

She neither admitted nor denied the charge. 'I am not going to get over my illness this time,' she reiterated. 'Something tells me I shan't.'

This view of things was rather a bad beginning, as it usually is; and, in fact, six weeks later, in the month of May, she was lying in her room, pulseless and bloodless, with hardly strength enough left to follow up one feeble breath with another, the infant for whose unnecessary life she was slowly parting with her own being fat and well. Just before her death she spoke to Marchmill softly: –

'Will, I want to confess to you the entire circumstances of that – about you know what – that time we visited Solentsea. I can't tell what possessed me – how I could forget you so, my husband! But I had got into a morbid state: I thought you had been unkind; that you had neglected me; that you weren't up to my intellectual level, while he was, and far above it. I wanted a fuller appreciator, perhaps, rather than another lover—'

She could get no further then for very exhaustion; and she went off in sudden collapse a few hours later, without having said anything more to her husband on the subject of her love for the poet. William Marchmill, in truth, like most husbands of several years' standing, was little disturbed by retrospective jealousies, and had not shown the least anxiety to press her for confessions concerning a man dead and gone beyond any power of inconveniencing him more.

But when she had been buried a couple of years it chanced one day that, in turning over some forgotten papers that he wished to destroy before his second wife entered the house, he lighted on a lock of hair in an envelope, with the photograph of the deceased poet, a date being written on the back in his late wife's hand. It was that of the time they spent at Solentsea.

Marchmill looked long and musingly at the hair and portrait, for something struck him. Fetching the little boy who had been the death of his mother, now a noisy toddler, he took him on his knee, held the lock of hair against the child's head, and set up the photograph on the table behind, so that he could closely compare the features each countenance presented. By a known but inexplicable trick of Nature there were undoubtedly strong traces of resemblance to the man Ella had never seen; the dreamy and peculiar expression of the poet's face sat, as the transmitted idea, upon the child's, and the hair was of the same hue.

'I'm damned if I didn't think so!' murmured Marchmill. 'Then she *did* play me false with that fellow at the lodgings! Let me see: the dates – the second week in August . . . the third week in May. . . . Yes . . . yes. . . . Get away, you poor little brat! You are nothing to me!'

1893

The Son's Veto

I

To the eyes of a man viewing it from behind the nut-brown hair was a
wonder and a mystery. Under the black beaver hat surmounted by its
tuft of black feathers, the long locks, braided and twisted and coiled
like the rushes of a basket, composed a rare, if somewhat barbaric,
example of ingenious art. One could understand such weavings and
coilings being wrought to last intact for a year, or even a calendar
month; but that they should be all demolished regularly at bedtime,
after a single day of permanence, seemed a reckless waste of successful
fabrication.

And she had done it all herself, poor thing. She had no maid, and it
was almost the only accomplishment she could boast of. Hence the
unstinted pains.

She was a young invalid lady – not so very much of an invalid –
sitting in a wheeled chair, which had been pulled up in the front part of
a green enclosure, close to a bandstand where a concert was going on,
during a warm June afternoon. It had place in one of the minor parks
or private gardens that are to be found in the suburbs of London, and
was the effort of a local association to raise money for some charity.
There are worlds within worlds in the great city, and though nobody
outside the immediate district had ever heard of the charity, or the
band, or the garden, the enclosure was filled with an interested audience
sufficiently informed on all these.

As the strains proceeded many of the listeners observed the chaired
lady, whose back hair, by reason of her prominent position, so challenged
inspection. Her face was not easily discernible, but the aforesaid cunning
tress-weavings, the white ear and poll, and the curve of a cheek which
was neither flaccid nor sallow, were signals that led to the expectation
of good beauty in front. Such expectations are not infrequently

disappointed as soon as the disclosure comes; and in the present case, when the lady, by a turn of the head, at length revealed herself, she was not so handsome as the people behind her had supposed, and even hoped – they did not know why.

For one thing (alas! the commonness of this complaint), she was less young than they had fancied her to be. Yet attractive her face unquestionably was, and not at all sickly. The revelation of its details came each time she turned to talk to a boy of twelve or thirteen who stood beside her, and the shape of whose hat and jacket implied that he belonged to a well-known public school. The immediate bystanders could hear that he called her 'Mother'.

When the end of the recital was reached, and the audience withdrew, many chose to find their way out by passing at her elbow. Almost all turned their heads to take a full and near look at the interesting woman, who remained stationary in the chair till the way should be clear enough for her to be wheeled out without obstruction. As if she expected their glances, and did not mind gratifying their curiosity, she met the eyes of several of her observers by lifting her own, showing these to be soft, brown, and affectionate orbs, a little plaintive in their regard.

She was conducted out of the gardens, and passed along the pavement till she disappeared from view, the schoolboy walking beside her. To inquiries made by some persons who watched her away, the answer came that she was the second wife of the incumbent of a neighbouring parish, and that she was lame. She was generally believed to be a woman with a story – an innocent one, but a story of some sort or other.

In conversing with her on their way home the boy who walked at her elbow said that he hoped his father had not missed them.

'He have been so comfortable these last few hours that I am sure he cannot have missed us,' she replied.

'*Has*, dear mother – not *have*!' exclaimed the public-school boy, with an impatient fastidiousness that was almost harsh. 'Surely you know that by this time!'

His mother hastily adopted the correction, and did not resent his making it, or retaliate, as she might well have done, by bidding him to wipe that crumby mouth of his, whose condition had been caused by surreptitious attempts to eat a piece of cake without taking it out of the pocket wherein it lay concealed. After this the pretty woman and the boy went onward in silence.

That question of grammar bore upon her history, and she fell into